E. V. Thompson was born in London. After spending nine years in the Royal Navy, he served as a Vice Squad policeman in Bristol, became an investigator for British Overseas Airways (during which time he was seconded to the Hong Kong Police Narcotics Bureau), then headed Rhodesia's Department of Civil Aviation Security Section. While in Rhodesia, he published over two hundred short stories before moving back to England to become a full-time award-winning writer.

His first novel, *Chase the Wind*, the opening book in the Retallick saga, won the Best Historical Novel Award, and since then more than thirty novels have won him thousands of admirers around the world.

Praise for E. V. Thompson

'With settings that stretch from China to Cornwall, these romantic sagas delight'
Independent

'From the pen of a first-class professional'
Sunday Telegraph

'This top writer of romantic adventure will hold you spellbound'
Peterborough Evening Telegraph

'An extremely good st___

D0589041

Also by E. V. Thompson

THE MUSIC MAKERS
THE DREAM TRADERS
CRY ONCE ALONE
BECKY
GOD'S HIGHLANDER
WYCHWOOD
BLUE DRESS GIRL
TOLPUDDLE WOMAN
LEWIN'S MEAD
MOONTIDE
CAST NO SHADOWS
SOMEWHERE A BIRD IS SINGING
WINDS OF FORTUNE
SEEK A NEW DAWN
PATHS OF DESTINY
TOMORROW IS FOR EVER
THE VAGRANT KING
THOUGH THE HEAVENS MAY FALL

The Retallick Saga

BEN RETALLICK
CHASE THE WIND
HARVEST OF THE SUN
SINGING SPEARS
THE STRICKEN LAND
LOTTIE TRAGO
RUDDLEMOOR
FIRES OF EVENING
BROTHERS IN WAR

The Jagos of Cornwall

THE RESTLESS SEA
POLRUDDEN
MISTRESS OF POLRUDDEN

As James Munro

HOMELAND

Cassie

E.V. Thompson

sphere

SPHERE

First published in Great Britain in 1991 by Macmillan London Ltd
Published in 1992 by Pan Books Ltd
This paperback edition published in 2007 by Sphere
Reprinted 2012

Copyright © 1988 E.V. Thompson 1991

The moral right of the author has been asserted.

*All characters and events in this publication, other than those
clearly in the public domain, are fictitious and any resemblance
to real persons, living or dead, is purely coincidental.*

All rights reserved.
No part of this publication may be reproduced, stored in
a retrieval system, or transmitted, in any form or by any means, without
the prior permission in writing of the publisher, nor be otherwise circulated
in any form of binding or cover other than that in which it is published
and without a similar condition including this condition
being imposed on the subsequent purchaser.

A CIP catalogue record for this book
is available from the British Library.

ISBN 978-0-7515-4587-6

Typeset in Palatino by Palimpsest Book Production Limited,
Grangemouth, Stirlingshire
Printed and bound by CPI Group (UK) Ltd, Croydon, CR0 4YY
Papers supplied by Hellefoss AS, Norway

Papers used by Sphere are from well-managed forests
and other responsible sources.

MIX
Paper from
responsible sources
FSC® C104740

Sphere
An imprint of
Little, Brown Book Group
100 Victoria Embankment
London EC4Y 0DY

An Hachette UK Company
www.hachette.co.uk

www.littlebrown.co.uk

Cassie

BAY OF BISCAY

San Sebastian

Santander

Corunna

Oviedo

Bilbao

Lugo

Medina
de Pomar

Vittoria

Santiago de
Compostela

GALICIA

Leon

Sahagun

Burgos

ATLANTIC OCEAN

Palencia

Bragança

Valladolid

Douro R.

TRÁS OS MONTES

Zamora

OLD CASTILE

Oporto

Douro R.

Salamanca

Segovia

Almeida

Freixedas

Pedrosillo

Ciudad Rodrigo

El Cabaco

Madrid

El Bodon

SPAIN

Figueira

PORTUGAL

Toledo

MONTES DE TOLEDO

Tagus R.

NEW CASTILE

Guadiana R.

LA MANCHA

Elves

Badajos

Lisbon

Evora

Almendralejo

Cordova

Seville

ANDALUSIA

Cape St Vincent

Faro

Granada

Malaga

Cadiz

Cape Trafalgar

Gibraltar

John Trend del. 1990

THE PENINSULA

at the time of
The Napoleonic Wars

MILES   50   100

Foreword

By the first decade of the nineteenth century Napoleon Bonaparte had reached the peak of his brilliant campaign of conquest. He had fought and won battles in Africa and Asia and in 1809 he drove the British from Spain – part of the 'Peninsula'. Only the might of the British navy saved the army from total annihilation.

That same year Arthur Wellesley, later to become the Duke of Wellington, returned to the Peninsula with another British army to help the Portuguese oust Napoleon's soldiers from their country. For five years his army alternately advanced and retreated through Portugal and Spain until, in 1814, Lord Wellington pushed the French across the Pyrenees and defeated them in battle on their own soil.

The Peninsular War was fought against a background of political intrigue, parsimonious military budgeting and national prejudice.

There were many in England who bitterly resented the success and growing popularity of Wellington, and their machinations meant he was forced to fight many of his battles desperately short of funds for his army.

His two principal allies, Spain and Portugal, hated each other with a bitterness that at times superseded their hatred for the common enemy. The Portuguese kept their unfortunate troops without pay or equipment for alarmingly long periods of time while they were fighting on Spanish soil. Meanwhile, the Spanish fought the war with a casualness that constantly infuriated the British commander-in-chief, and occasionally brought him to the brink of defeat.

There were times, too, when Wellington was contemptuous of his own soldiers. They fought, won battles, and even coined French currency for him. Many thousands also died for him. Yet the general they admired so much once referred to the British soldier as the 'scum of the earth'.

Following in the wake of the soldiers throughout the years of the Peninsular campaign were others who on occasion also incurred the wrath of the great general. These were the soldiers' women, who followed the army wherever it travelled and fought. The 'camp followers'.

Some were the legally wedded wives of the men they followed. Others were mistresses. A few were prostitutes. Their nationalities were equally varied: Scots, Irish, Welsh and English in plenty, but there were Portuguese, Spanish and French women, too.

These women shared with their men the hardships of the march, comfortless night camps, the many dangers of battle and the terror of sudden attack. Performing duties as cook, nurse, laundress, seamstress, mistress and mother, each was as proud of the regiment to which she 'belonged' as was the man she followed.

The women posed many problems for the provost marshals, the army's 'policemen', and Wellington was himself obliged to issue orders forbidding the women from buying the bread he needed to feed his army. He also found it necessary on occasion to forbid the women from crowding on his supply wagons or taking over billets, and he constantly attempted to limit their numbers. Sometimes it was deemed necessary to have them flogged, but disciplining such a motley assortment of women was never easy.

The number of wives permitted to travel with the army never exceeded six for every hundred men. It was not a vast number, but in an army of, say, 36,000 English soldiers this meant that there were more than 2000 wives, with possibly twice this number of unofficial camp followers – and their children. By the time the army reached the borders of France after five years of warfare it had close to 10,000 women and children following in its wake. It is small wonder they posed a major headache to the British commander-in-chief.

Cassie is the story of a young girl who leaves a Cornish fishing village to follow the 32nd (Cornwall) Regiment to the Peninsula. It is also the story of the thousands of women who left their homelands to follow their men to war.

1

❦

The day Cassie Whetter realised she was pregnant turned out to be one of the worst days of her young life. She had suspected it for some time, of course, but fear of the consequences was sufficient reason in itself for not facing up to the facts. Now she could evade the issue no longer.

Her family believed her sickness that morning had been caused by something she had eaten, and her mother was duly sympathetic. It was natural, too, that the smell in the fish cellar where Cassie worked should turn her stomach. However, such an excuse would produce a few raised eyebrows if she used it again tomorrow morning. And the day after ... ?

Cassie's concern for her condition was tempered by the confident belief that Harry Clymo would marry her as soon as he knew. They had been walking out together for more than a year and it was accepted by

Cassie's family and friends that she and he would one day marry.

Harry Clymo had no family. Orphaned in a cholera epidemic when he was six, the Poor Board authorities had put him out to work on a farm when he reached the age of eight. That had been ten years ago.

There were those who said Harry would never amount to anything more than a farm-hand. That he was not much of a catch for a girl, especially a bright and lively one like Cassie. Some even suggested Harry was simple. But Cassie knew he was shy. He was also kind, and Cassie had come to look forward to Sundays when he came to the village for the afternoon service and was able to spend a couple of hours with her. They would walk around the harbour, gaze at the fishing-boats that were never worked on Sunday, and talk about nothing in particular.

There was no doubting that Harry Clymo was the father of the child growing inside her. Cassie knew this, and Harry would too. It had happened on the last night of Mevagissey Feast when a week of celebrations ended in a grand finale.

It had been the finest Feast Week anyone could remember. When darkness fell, every house for miles around stood empty, the residents thronging the narrow streets of the small fishing village. There was dancing, singing, a travelling theatrical group – and drinking. A great deal of drinking.

Even when a light drizzle moved inshore from the sea it did not dampen the festive spirit. Nevertheless, Cassie had decided to return home for her cloak. She

2

was wearing a new dress made up from cheap patterned cotton. She feared the dye would run if it became wet and she did not want that to happen today.

Harry accompanied her to the small but comfortable terraced house perched on the hillside above the harbour. All was in darkness, but it did not seem worthwhile wasting tinder to light a candle, even when she discovered the cloak was not in its usual place behind the kitchen door. Then Cassie remembered she had been repairing the cloak's fastening only that morning. She must have left it in the bedroom she shared with her two sisters.

Groping in the darkness, Cassie found the cloak on the bed where she had left it and called the news to Harry. But he had followed her upstairs and Cassie collided heavily with him in the doorway as she hurried from the bedroom.

'You fill the space better than that old door.' There was laughter in Cassie's voice as she clung to him to maintain her balance, her mind on the music and dancing in the streets.

Harry laughed with her, a short, nervous laugh. Then they both fell silent and neither attempted to move apart. Cassie opened her mouth to suggest they should move, but she closed it again without uttering a word. Standing against him in the darkness Cassie could not see Harry's face, but there was a tension in his body that both frightened and excited her.

'What is it, Harry? What's the matter?'

The spurious questions came out as a whisper, yet they had to be asked. Cassie needed time to struggle

3

with an emotional decision she had known must be taken before long. The decision whether or not she would allow Harry to do what so many of their friends boasted of doing.

Harry reached out and pulled her to him clumsily and uncertainly. Cassie knew with instinctive certainty that this was the moment to stop him if she wanted to. She *should* stop him. A sharp, shocked word from her would be sufficient. He would drop his arms to his sides and mumble a foolish, embarrassed apology . . . She said nothing.

The cloak slipped to the ground and Harry stumbled over it as, arms about her, he guided Cassie to where he imagined her bed to be.

Cassie protested mildly when they fell upon the bed together, but only because it was the bed shared by her two younger sisters. Her bed was a few feet away across the room and they moved to it hurriedly and clumsily.

Harry's lovemaking was as hurried and clumsy as the preliminaries had been. It was all over in a few confused, uncomfortable minutes. As he rose from her the realisation of what she had just done overshadowed any other emotion she might have felt. She had given herself to Harry without so much as a single protest. Indeed, she had encouraged him by her silence. By so doing she had become one of the girls the minister preached about at most of his Sunday services. A 'hussy'. No better than the girls from the nearby town of St Austell, who flaunted themselves on the Mevagissey quayside whenever an Italian or Portuguese ship docked to load a cargo of salted pilchards.

'Are you all right?'

Harry's voice carried a conflicting blend of concern and proprietorial pride. He and Cassie had known each other for more than a year but had never gone beyond hand-holding and kissing. Tonight she had given herself to him.

'You'll not tell anyone?'

'Of course not – but we'd better go back to the others before they miss us and suspect what we've been up to.'

Cassie trusted Harry and she was grateful that when they returned to the others he made no attempt to drop boastful hints, as she had heard some of his friends doing . . .

All this had taken place three months before, in December. Now it was March. Harry had been very kind and considerate during the intervening weeks and they made love on two subsequent occasions. Both had been as unsatisfactory as the first. It was winter and the soft grass fields and cliff tops around the village were out of the question. They had made love once in the lean-to wash-house, with Cassie bent uncomfortably over the copper, and again in a derelict fish cellar. Any hope of romance on this latter occasion had swiftly disappeared when a rat scampered from a pile of rubble. It had brushed against Cassie's skin as she lay straddle-legged beneath Harry, with only his coat between her and the cold, stone-flagged floor.

During the weeks since December it had been evident from the sly, knowing glances cast in her direction by Harry's friends that they had guessed the extent of his new relationship with her. Cassie tried hard not to allow it to matter. However, the time was fast approaching when her condition would become obvious to every man, woman and child in Mevagissey.

'I think I'll go out for a walk.'

Cassie had spent a couple of hours lying on her bed, thinking. Now she walked through the kitchen where the family were gathered and took her cloak from the door.

Joan Whetter looked up from her sewing and smiled at her daughter. 'That's a good idea. The fresh air will do you good. Mind you wrap up warm, though. There's a cold wind blowing off the sea.'

'It'll get a sight worse after nightfall, so be back home before dark.'

There were at least five hours before it became dark, but Samuel Whetter spoke grumpily. The owner of a small fishing-boat, he had been unable to put to sea for days because of a strong onshore south-easterly wind.

Seated at the table, Cassie's two young sisters, Anne and Beth, hardly gave her a glance. Both were sulking because Samuel had insisted they spend the afternoon copying out a chapter of the Bible. It was a task that had been set for them by the teacher at the thrice-weekly Methodist-run school.

When the door closed behind his elder daughter, Samuel frowned. 'I'm concerned about that girl. She hasn't looked herself this past couple of weeks. If she's no better tomorrow I'll have old Polly look in on her.'

Polly Dunne was a Mevagissey woman who attended

births, laid out the dead, and administered herb potions to those who could not, or would not, call on the services of a physician. She 'specialised' in pregnancy and childbirth and had attended every birth in Mevagissey for the last twenty years. Polly had been an old woman for as long as Joan Whetter could remember.

'There'll be no need for any of Polly Dunne's mumbo-jumbo in this house. All sixteen-year-old girls have times when they're out of sorts. I've felt like it myself, many a time.'

'I can remember only three times when you've looked the way our Cassie does. The last time was when you were expecting our Beth. If Cassie's no better tomorrow she'll be seen by Polly Dunne. You might have blind faith in that young Clymo boy. I haven't.'

Standing just outside the thin wooden kitchen door, Cassie had heard every word her father said. It did nothing to help the way she felt – but being outside the house did. She realised she had felt trapped in a cocoon of guilt inside the cottage and no answer to her problem would be found there. She had to talk to Harry.

The place where Harry lived and worked was in a remote spot off the Pentewan valley. Halfway between Mevagissey and the market town of St Austell, it was about four miles away. She had never been to the farm before, but Harry had described it so well she had no difficulty finding her way there.

Cassie had hoped to find Harry working in one of the fields before she reached the farm, but there was no one to be seen. Only a few sheep and lambs in one field, and a herd of dejected, hollow-flanked cattle in another.

Neither could she see him in the farmyard that was flanked by house and outbuildings. In fact there was a puzzling air of neglect about the place. An appearance of tasks only half done.

Cassie stood uncertainly at the edge of a knee-deep morass of mud, manure and stagnant, stinking puddles for several minutes, wondering whether she dared go to the house and ask for Harry. Her dilemma was resolved when a stocky barrel-chested man emerged from one of the outbuildings. He wore a smock the colour of the farmyard and beneath one arm he held a wriggling piglet, which was squealing noisily.

When he saw Cassie the man stopped and glared. 'What do you want? We've no work here for milkmaids, or any other sort of maid – though if you was a young lad I'd soon find something for you to be doing.'

'I'm not looking for work. I've come to speak to Harry. He usually comes to chapel on Sunday. He wasn't there last week. I thought there might be something wrong . . .'

This much at least was true. Harry had not come to the Mevagissey chapel the previous Sunday but there was nothing unusual in this. He would often miss a Sunday service if there was work to be done on the farm.

'If you want Harry Clymo you've come to the wrong place.' With this the farmer's mouth clamped shut in a thin, disapproving line and he began to walk towards the house.

'You mean . . . Harry *doesn't* live and work here?'

Cassie was puzzled. This *was* the farm Harry had told her about. She was certain of it. Even the farmer himself was just as Harry had described him.

'This is the farm where Harry Clymo *used* to work, but he ain't here no more. He'll never dare show his face here again, neither. Not after the way he's behaved.'

Cassie felt as though the ground was opening up beneath her feet as the farmer turned his attention upon the noisy pig. 'Shut your row, or I'll slit your throat 'afore Sunday!'

'Where's Harry gone? Why did you send him away?'

'*Send* him off? I did no such thing to the ungrateful young wretch. After all I've done for him these past ten years he ups and goes without so much as a thought for how I'll manage without him. Treated that boy like a son, I did. A good straw bed in the barn, a fire in the kitchen for him to warm his hands before milking on a cold winter's morning. Even let him eat in the house with us once or twice. There's no gratitude in you young folk these days.'

Dismissing the picture of Harry's life conjured up by the farmer's words, Cassie asked anxiously, 'Do you know where he's gone?'

Her plea exposed the desperation she felt. The farmer peered at her with a new interest. 'You'll be that Cassie girl, from down Mevagissey. The one he'd talk about whenever I gave him half a chance.' The farmer grinned maliciously. 'What's the matter, girl? Harry left you in the lurch, too? Left you with more than he's left here, I'll be bound. That reminds me, there's a few bits and pieces of his up in the barn. When he left me in St Austell market he said I was to give his things to Cassie Whetter. That'll be you, I dare say?'

Cassie could only nod.

'There's a letter for you too. Not much more than a line or two. He scribbled it out and handed it to me, for you. Don't ask me what it says. I've never had no need to learn to read or write, nor the missus neither. She's got the letter up at the house.'

Suddenly losing interest in Cassie, the farmer turned away, but Cassie called after him.

'Where did Harry go? Where is he now?'

The farmer jerked the wriggling pig to a more secure position beneath his arm. 'Your guess as to where he is now will be as good as mine. He took the King's bounty and went off with a recruiting sergeant. Harry Clymo's joined the army. Gone to fight Napoleon.'

The farmer's information shook Cassie to the core, but she hoped the note Harry had left would explain his actions. Taking off her shoes she hitched up the skirt of her dress and made her way through the evil-smelling farmyard mud to the dark and gloomy outhouse pointed out to her by the farmer.

Harry's clothes and pitifully sparse belongings were strewn untidily about the heap of blanket-covered straw that had been his bed. Cassie suspected the farmer had already looked through his possessions. In spite of her own predicament, pity for Harry welled up inside her. This had been his home for ten years. This was where the Poor Board authorities had sent him as punishment for being an orphan in receipt of parish relief. There was nothing here Cassie wanted. She had a constant reminder of Harry Clymo inside her belly.

Leaving the cursing farmer to chase the lively piglet

which had finally wriggled free in the yard, Cassie made her way to the house to collect Harry's letter.

She had met few farmers' wives. They rarely came to Mevagissey, preferring to shop in St Austell on market days. Most of those she had met had been solid and comfortable, rather jolly women. The wife of Harry Clymo's employer was none of these things. At least a head taller than her husband, she was thin and gaunt-featured, with a nose that reminded Cassie of a chicken's beak.

'So you're the girl young Harry told me about.' The farmer's wife looked at Cassie equally critically. She saw a brown-eyed girl with dark hair pulled back and tied behind her head. Small, only a lingering hint of imma-turity concealed a figure such as the older woman had never possessed.

The beak sniffed noisily and lifted a little. 'I'm blessed if I can see why he was so smitten, I'm sure.'

'It seems he wasn't so smitten as everyone keeps telling me.' Cassie spoke sharply, stung by the woman's words. 'If he had been he wouldn't have run off and joined the army.'

'There's something in that . . .' Rummaging inside a huge earthenware pot, the farmer's wife suddenly lost patience and upended the contents on the kitchen table. Picking out a piece of folded and crumpled paper, she handed it to Cassie. 'Here. Perhaps this'll tell you why he upped and left.'

Suddenly the woman's face softened and she looked at Cassie wistfully for a moment. 'Mind you, there was nothing for Harry here. He was a hired hand, earning

11

barely enough to keep him in necessities. All he got from life was a beating when he did something wrong, and not a word of praise for working hard for months and years. I'd have had him in the house sometimes, but Bill would have none of it. Even when Harry first came and I could hear him crying with the cold out there in the barn, his little legs and hands fair raw with chilblains.'

Cassie was only half listening. The note – and it was no more – had been written hurriedly in pencil upon a page torn from the recruiting sergeant's notebook. In a few lines, Harry confirmed what the farmer's wife had just said.

> Can see no future on the farm. The serjant says a bright lad like me can be a serjant in the army in a year. An officer in two. He says I'm the sort the army has need of. He's given me three guineas for signing on. Wish I could have seen you before going but I'm off to Horsham, in Sussex, wherever that is. Wait for me Cassie. I'll be back to marry you as soon as I can.
>
> Harry

The letter was addressed to 'Cassie Whetter, Mevagissey'. She doubted whether it would ever have reached its destination had she not come looking for Harry.

'What does it say? Will he be coming back?'

Folding the note carefully and tucking it inside her purse, Cassie said, 'He'll be coming back to marry me, but you won't see him on the farm again.'

'He'd get no welcome from my Bill if he did come back – and I trust you've no reason to want him to marry you in a hurry? Gone off to fight a war, has he? I've got a sister who promised to wait when her man went off to fight in India, more'n twenty years ago. She's still waiting, and none the wiser whether he's dead or alive. You'll be the same if you wait for a soldier to come home and wed you. But I haven't all day to spend chattering . . .'

The farmer's wife had seen her husband walking towards the house. His scowl was as black as the mud-covered piglet he held up by its back legs.

'Be off with you, and wish that young man well for me . . . if you ever see hide or hair of him again.'

Pausing by the river which ran parallel to the valley road, Cassie washed off her legs before replacing her shoes. Her initial dismay had passed and she was beginning to marshal her thoughts.

She knew what she had to do, but her plans were far from clear yet. Two basic facts had to be faced. She was pregnant – and the father of the child she was expecting had gone off to join the army. Unlike the sister of the farmer's wife, Cassie could not await the return of her lover for ever.

Quite apart from the shock to her family and the anger of her father, there were the laws of the land to be considered. Bastardy laws were harsh in the extreme and if the Reverend Mr Tremayne happened to be on the bench she could look forward to a lengthy spell in gaol. The choleric old cleric was fond of saying there was nothing like a few months in a prison cell for teaching an unmarried girl the errors of sinful ways. The fact that a St Austell girl returned to prison after her sixth illegitimate child did nothing to shake his faith in this custodial panacea.

Lost in her thoughts, Cassie sat on the river bank for so long that darkness overtook her well before she reached Mevagissey. She entered the house and went straight to her room, accepting without complaint the cuff to the side of her head administered by her father because she was late home.

That night, when Joan Whetter took a mug of hot milk and a chunk of fish pie to her daughter, she thought the tears on Cassie's face were the result of her chastisement. Her hug, and a whispered, 'He didn't mean anything by it,' only made Cassie cry more.

When Cassie's tears ceased, Joan went downstairs to remonstrate with her husband for what had really been no more than a light tap. Samuel justified his actions indignantly. He had told Cassie to be home before dark and she had disobeyed him. He had been fully justified in chastising her. Indeed, if it happened again his punishment would be even more severe . . .

Later, after leaving the kitchen without a word, Samuel returned from Cassie's bedroom and reported that he had made peace with his daughter. As proof of her forgiveness, she had hugged him more warmly than he could ever remember since she was a young, totally dependent little girl.

All was well in the Whetter household.

*   *   *

14

Cassie left home the next morning as soon as the house had emptied of her family. The weather having improved overnight, Samuel had set off in his fishing-boat at dawn. Joan went to the fish cellar in place of Cassie and at 8.30 a.m. the two youngest girls set off for the Methodist school.

Before leaving, Cassie wrote an explanatory note to her parents, omitting only her destination. Then, making a bundle of all the clothes she thought she would need, she took her savings from the small tin box beneath her bed. Encouraged by her mother, she had saved something each week from the pay she earned at the fish cellar. Sometimes it had been no more than a penny, more often sixpence and, very rarely, as much as a shilling. Changing it into coins of a larger denomination whenever she had enough, Cassie had amassed the sum of seven pounds, four shillings and threepence.

It was a small fortune. Enough, surely, to take her to Horsham in unknown Sussex.

2

⚜

Cassie walked the seven miles to St Austell town, arriving to catch the coach to Plymouth with only minutes to spare. The timing was sheerest luck on her part. She had little knowledge of coach timetables – and none at all of the routes they followed. Before setting off from Mevagissey she had looked at a map of Britain kept in a drawer in her mother and father's bedroom. The map had once belonged to her grandfather, who was talked of with great respect as being 'a scholarly man', and it had become a treasured family possession.

Poring over the map, Cassie had eventually located Sussex. She had not found Horsham, but that did not matter too much. Cassie expected everyone to know where it was once she reached Sussex. Getting there would be the main problem. She knew it was in the general direction of London. So too was Plymouth and she decided this would be the place she must make for first of all.

The cost of the fare to Plymouth dismayed Cassie, even though she opted to travel outside, perched among the baggage of those passengers who were more comfortably accommodated. The fare had taken a frightening portion of the money she had with her. However, it would be a fast journey, only six hours to Plymouth – and speed was essential until Mevagissey and possible pursuit were far behind. For the next leg of her journey she would consider travelling on a stage-wagon. The wagon would take much longer, the heavy vehicle moving at no more than four miles an hour, but it was the cheapest form of transport.

Seven miles from St Austell the coach stopped at the ancient town of Lostwithiel to take on another passenger, a young dark-haired man with a great deal of baggage. When it was loaded he climbed up to the roof to check it was secure. While he made his check Cassie was obliged to move for him, accepting his apology.

Satisfied, the young man climbed down off the roof, nodding amiably in Cassie's direction before entering the coach. A number of well-dressed men and women had come to see the young man safely ensconced in the vehicle. When it moved off he hung from the window, acknowledging their waving kerchiefs until a curve in the road hid them from view.

A few miles further on they stopped again, this time at Liskeard. Here the passengers were allowed twenty minutes to stretch their legs and partake of tea, ale or stronger spirits, as their inclination took them.

It was cold travelling on the roof of the coach and Cassie would dearly have liked to buy a drink of tea, but the need to conserve her depleted funds was paramount. She warmed herself by walking briskly back and forth along the road outside the inn, ensuring she never let the coach out of her sight.

The coach was late setting off from Liskeard, delayed by a joining passenger. An elderly lady, she was boarding the coach when she discovered a vital piece of her baggage had been left behind at her house. Assuring the coachman it would take no more than three minutes to have it fetched, she despatched a hotel porter. Thirty-five minutes later, panting beneath the weight of a large trunk, the porter returned.

The fuming coachman drove his vehicle out of Liskeard as though he led a cavalry charge. Clinging tightly to the rail beside her, Cassie could hear the squeals of protest coming from inside. Loudest of all was the voice of the woman who was the cause of the coachman's anger.

There was good reason for haste. The coach needed to be ferried across the wide Tamar, the river that formed the border between Cornwall and the remainder of England. The ferryman was renowned for his irascibility and impatience. He would wait for the coach for no longer than five minutes beyond the appointed time – ten if he had few other passengers on board – but he would wait no longer.

Missing the ferry might delay the Plymouth-bound coach by as much as two hours – and the owners of the coach imposed a fine on the coachman that increased proportionately for every fifteen minutes it was delayed. Missing a ferry could cost him as much as a day's pay.

Unfortunately, the coachman's haste on this day would cost him far more than money. Whipping up the horses for a final two-mile dash to the ferry, he took his vehicle around a corner much too fast. Even so, he might have made it safely had not a householder been building a garden wall at the side of the road. A large boulder the size of a man's head had fallen from the wall to the road. One of the coach-wheels struck the boulder, bouncing in the air and coming down again with a bone-jarring crash. There was the sound of splintering wooden spokes and the coach lurched down on its axle. The momentum of the galloping horses swung the toppling coach in a calamitous, lopsided arc towards a muddy bank that plunged twelve feet to a fast-moving stream.

As the coach left the road, Cassie's screams mingled with those of the passengers travelling inside and as it toppled she was thrown over the back of the rolling vehicle. Two of the panic-stricken horses were pulled over with it. The traces of the others broke and they maintained a terrified gallop along the road.

Cassie landed in a tangle of long grass and low bushes growing beside the stream. Although scratched and shaken, she was otherwise unhurt and she had no time to worry about any effect the accident might have on her unborn baby. Sitting up she was just in time to watch the coach complete its final roll and come to rest on its side in the water, two wheels still spinning noisily.

The first passenger to climb from the overturned coach was the young man who had joined the ill-fated vehicle at Liskeard. His coat and shirt were ripped from shoulder to wrist and blood was running down his arm.

The young man looked both ways along the empty road and then, shaking his head in a dazed manner, he helped Cassie clear of the bushes.

'Your arm looks bad. Let me do something . . .'

'It will wait. There are passengers inside the coach. I fear they may be hurt badly . . .' As though to confirm his words the woman who had delayed the coach began calling for help from inside the overturned vehicle.

'We'll need to find help for them.'

At that moment, a figure splashed into view from the stream beyond the coach. It was the guard who had been travelling with the coach. Reaching the bank beside them, he sat down heavily clutching his shoulder, face contorted with pain.

Leaving Cassie, her rescuer called on the guard to give him assistance. 'Here, man. Come inside the coach with me. A number of passengers are trapped . . .'

The guard turned pain-filled eyes up towards the younger man. 'I can't – I think my collar-bone's broken. I needs help meself.'

'Pull yourself together! You have passengers to think of. Where's the driver?'

'Somewhere under there, I reckon.' The guard jerked a thumb in the direction of the coach, grimacing at the pain caused by the sudden movement.

'I'll help.'

When the young man looked doubtful, Cassie added, 'I'm stronger than I look. Besides, there's no one else.'

Inside the overturned coach a man began moaning and the woman renewed her cries for help.

Turning to the guard, the young man said, 'Get on

20

your feet and go and find help. There are houses no more than a mile along the road – and a farm closer still. We'll need men, and ropes – and a surgeon.'

'I can't. My shoulder!'

'Stop moaning.' The young man spoke sharply and scornfully. 'I've seen soldiers with worse injuries than yours helping wounded comrades to climb mountains. If you don't get on your feet immediately I'll drag you up to the road and use the toe of my boot to set you on your way.'

The young man moved forward menacingly as though to carry out his threat and the guard overcame his incapacity hastily. Still clutching his shoulder he scrambled up the bank and made off along the road, hunched over in pain.

Cassie felt sorry for the injured guard, but the young man had already dismissed him from his own thoughts.

'Come with me, young lady. We're needed inside the coach.'

Scrambling to the top of the overturned coach, he pulled Cassie up beside him. As he did so he asked her name, informing her that his was Gorran ... Gorran Fox. Wasting no time, he dropped inside the coach and lifted her down after him.

The scene was one of grim chaos. The coach had been carrying eight inside passengers, in addition to Cassie on the outside. Only six could be seen amid the debris of broken coach fittings and hand luggage flung from broken racks above the seats. Gorran Fox made the seventh. One was missing.

Three passengers were conscious and two of these

were nursing broken limbs. Of more immediate concern was the woman. Half flung from the coach during its final gyration, she was trapped with her legs outside the vehicle and there was foot-deep water flowing about her.

As Cassie crouched beside the woman to comfort her, Gorran examined the section of coach beneath which the woman was trapped.

'I can do nothing in here,' he muttered eventually. 'The coach needs to be levered up from outside – but someone must stay inside to pull her free.'

'Get outside and do what needs to be done. I'll stay here and try to pull her free when I feel the coach lift. It shouldn't be difficult, she's no weight at all.'

'Good girl!' Resting a hand briefly on her shoulder, Gorran climbed out of the coach once more.

Cassie succeeded in quietening the woman, assuring her she would be free before many more minutes had passed. Then she looked to the others in the coach. One of the conscious men had a badly broken leg, the other had suffered an injury to his ribs. Cassie made them both as comfortable as she could, using one man's kerchief to bind a cut on his head, before turning to the unconscious passengers.

She quickly ascertained that all three were alive and set about making them as safe as possible, keeping their heads above water. It was not easy. The coach was acting as a dam in the fast-running stream and as the water level rose she called for Gorran to hurry.

When Cassie had returned her attention to the woman, Gorran called to her from outside. A passing rider had stopped to give assistance. Between them they had loosed the fallen horses and detached the carriage-pole. They intended using it to lever the carriage up sufficiently for Cassie to pull the woman passenger free.

Their first attempt almost ended in disaster. The coach moved, but not quite in the manner they had planned. The movement caused it to slide into deeper water. Only by dragging the screaming woman along with the coach was Cassie able to prevent her from disappearing beneath it.

During the frantic few minutes that followed the abortive rescue attempt, Cassie clambered around lifting the heads of the unconscious male passengers clear of the water. At the same time she shouted an explanation to the anxious would-be rescuers, urging them to exercise more caution in moving the trapped coach.

As Cassie was binding the elderly woman's injured arm, she felt the coach rise a few inches above the bed of the stream and she was able to pull the woman's legs clear. Jubilantly she shouted news of her success to the two hard-working rescuers outside.

A few minutes later the first of many helpers from the nearby village reached the scene of the accident. The village was, in fact, much nearer than a mile and rescuers had been hurrying to the scene long before the guard from the coach arrived. They had been alerted to the accident by the sight of the two leading coach horses galloping through the village, frothing at the mouth and clearly in a state of terror.

With the arrival of the villagers, men began swarming over and inside the coach. When the passengers were

23

lifted clear, the vehicle was righted and manhandled back to the road. The body of the missing passenger was discovered underneath, with that of the coachman. He had paid a tragic price for his haste.

As the number of rescuers continued to increase, Cassie saw Gorran standing on the road, gazing down upon the busy scene. His torn and bloody sleeve reminded her of the injury he had sustained. He was probably the only passenger not to have received attention.

Gorran saw Cassie climbing towards him and reached down to help her up the last few feet of the steep bank. When she stood beside him, he said, 'You did a magnificent job, Cassie. You'll be pleased to know Mrs Elliott has no broken bones. Apart from a wetting and the cut you bound so efficiently she's quite unhurt.'

'Right now I'm more concerned with your injuries. Let me have a look at that arm.'

Without waiting for a reply, Cassie took hold of the bloody arm and pulled the remains of the sleeve back from the wound. There was a deep gash extending almost the full length of his forearm and it was extremely dirty.

'This needs a thorough washing. You'd better come down to the stream.'

'I don't trust water from streams and rivers. Use this.'

The baggage from the bent and broken coach had been gathered up and piled in a heap at the side of the roadway. From a trunk Gorran lifted a small wooden canteen. Pulling the stopper free, he handed the bottle to her.

'It's water from St Neot's holy well, and reputed to

have worked all sorts of miracles for the saint. It ought to do to clean up a small cut.'

'It's not such a small cut . . .'

One of the trunks from the coach had burst open leaving a number of women's garments hanging out. Cassie pulled a white linen petticoat free and tore it into strips. When Gorran protested that it was not necessary to ruin her clothes for him, Cassie replied curtly that the trunk did not belong to her. The reply brought an amused smile to his face. Pouring water from the container into the long gash she cleaned and dried it as best she could and then bound it tightly.

'You're a very resourceful young lady.' As Gorran spoke he stretched his arm painfully, flexing his fingers.

'And you're no stranger to such injuries.' While binding the arm, Cassie had seen a long scar on his upper arm, caused by a wound far more serious than the one she had just bound. 'You spoke a while ago of seeing wounded men helping their comrades. Are you a soldier? Is that how you got that scar?'

'Yes – and one or two more. I fell foul of a French heavy cavalry troop before Walcheren. It taught me a lesson I ought to have learned long before. An infantryman should have more sense than to dispute a cavalryman's right of way on a narrow path.'

Cassie shuddered involuntarily and Gorran smiled sympathetically. 'What of you? Where were you bound before your journey was so rudely interrupted?'

His words brought Cassie's thoughts back to her own problems. 'I'm on my way to Horsham – that's in Sussex. I'm to marry a soldier there.'

25

Gorran's interest quickened immediately. 'A soldier? What regiment is he with?'

Cassie's blank expression provided its own answer.

'You don't know his regiment? My dear girl, there are thousands of soldiers camped in and about Horsham, all preparing to join Wellington's army in the Peninsula.'

His words dismayed Cassie. She had not anticipated any problems once she reached her destination. She had not even given any detailed thought to what she would do when she reached the unknown town. In her mind it had all been quite straightforward. She would find Harry, tell him of her condition – and they would be married. It had all seemed so simple and logical.

'I'll find him.' Cassie spoke with a confidence she no longer felt.

'How long has this young man of yours been in the army?' Gorran continued his questioning. 'Was he involved in any of the fighting at Walcheren?'

'Harry's not much of a man for fighting. He only joined the army just over a week ago. Took the King's bounty when he went to St Austell market.'

'Ah! Then your young man will be with the Thirty-second Regiment, the Cornwalls. My regiment.'

Gorran gave the astonished Cassie a direct look and frowned. 'I've never been to Horsham, but I'm familiar with garrison towns and conditions within a barracks. I doubt if *you* are. Not only that, the army discourages its soldiers from marrying, especially recruits who haven't had time to get used to military ways. Why did this young man of yours join the army if you were to be married so soon?'

Cassie hesitated before replying and Gorran said hurriedly, 'It's none of my business, of course, and you're far too polite to tell me so. I'm sorry.'

'It's all right. It's just ... well, Harry's an orphan. He's been living on a farm – in an old barn, since he was eight. He spoke with the recruiting sergeant when he went to St Austell market. The sergeant promised him an exciting life and gave Harry more money than he's ever had before – and that was just for joining!'

'That would be Sergeant Jessop. He spent his child-hood in a workhouse. For him the army is all he claims it to be. How much was the bounty – three guineas?'

Cassie nodded and Gorran hoped his expression did not give away his thoughts. From his three guineas the new recruit would be called upon to pay the justice's fee for attestation, an examining surgeon's fee, and a drink for the recruiting sergeant with which to toast the King's health. When the recruit arrived at the depot he would be issued with his uniform and the sum of two guineas deducted for his knapsack. Having spent money at inns and taverns along the road, he would begin his service life owing money to his new regiment.

That night the survivors of the coaching accident, including those who nursed broken limbs, were accommodated at a Torpoint inn 'with the compliments of the coaching company'.

Fearful that her father might have already set off in pursuit of her, Cassie would have preferred to continue her journey. Declining an invitation to take dinner with Gorran, Mrs Elliott and one of the rescued men, she remained in her room for the whole evening. Every time she heard a footstep in the passageway outside the room she feared it might be her father.

Later still, when it was quite dark outside and the sounds of the inn were dying away, Cassie felt homesick. For a while she almost hoped the footsteps passing her door might belong to her father. It was the first night she had ever spent away from home. She suddenly felt all alone and not a little frightened at what she was doing.

When she thought of her mother and sisters, and of the unhappiness and consternation she would have caused in the Mevagissey household, the down pillow on which Cassie was lying became wet with her tears.

Had there been some way of returning home that night, her resolve might have weakened. She had never felt so unhappy before – but there could be no going home. Not until Harry Clymo had made her his wife.

3

❧

Cassie came down to breakfast late the following morning. She had suffered a brief but violent bout of sickness and did not feel much like eating. However, the meal was being paid for by the company who owned the coach, so she intended consuming as much as she was able and having nothing else for the remainder of the day. Coach travel was far more expensive than she had realised and there would be accommodation to be paid for along the way.

The other passengers were all seated together at a large table, all social barriers temporarily overcome by the shared experiences of the previous day. Cassie stood hesitantly in the doorway until Gorran Fox looked up and called for her to join them. The two injured men struggled awkwardly to their feet. The leg of one was bound tightly to a wooden splint, the other's arm was strapped to his side. They and Mrs

29

Elliott greeted Cassie as though they were all old friends.

It was an embarrassing meal for Cassie. Feeling over-awed by the company, she was dismayed by the array of cutlery lined on either side of her plate. At home in Mevagissey it was rarely deemed necessary to provide more than a knife with which to eat a meal. On the occasions when the meal was soup, or fish stew, a wooden spoon might be added, but that was all. Here, she was faced with metal spoons, assorted knives, and an unfamiliar two-pronged fork. Fortunately, Gorran appeared to have commenced his meal later than the others and Cassie was able to observe the order in which he used his utensils, and follow suit.

Of almost equal embarrassment was the way her companions talked as though she was a heroine. Numerous versions of her behaviour when the coach overturned were repeated. Even Mrs Elliott, who seemed less prone to exaggeration than the others, declared Cassie's calmness and presence of mind had saved her life.

As Cassie was finishing her meal a coach was heard clattering over the cobblestones of the inn yard, and moments later the landlord entered the dining room. In a loud voice he informed the survivors of the coach accident that they might resume their journey as soon as they were ready.

Before Cassie's fellow passengers rose from the table, the elderly man with the broken leg cleared his throat noisily and spoke somewhat pompously to her.

'Mr Fox tells us you are on your way to marry one of his soldiers?'

30

Casting an accusing glance at the young army officer for betraying her confidence, Cassie nodded.

'Your husband-to-be is a very lucky young man. However, it's well known that our gallant young soldiers are paid far less than they deserve. In order that your marriage might get off to a good start, and as a token of our gratitude – and I hasten to add I speak for all of us here – we would like you to accept this small appreciation.'

Reaching inside a pocket, the elderly man pulled out a heavy soft-leather purse. Clearing his throat noisily once more, he beamed at Cassie and said, 'God bless you, my dear. God bless you both.'

Stammering her thanks, Cassie acknowledged their generosity and, as they went off to prepare themselves for the resumed journey, she fled to the privacy of her room. A cascade of golden sovereigns fell on the bed when she tipped out the purse and to her amazement she counted out thirty-five. It was a fortune!

When the coach pulled away from the inn Cassie was seated inside, her fellow passengers refusing to allow her to resume her place on the outside. When she thanked them for their gift, declaring they had been over-generous, Mrs Elliott cut her protest short. 'Nonsense, young lady, you deserve far more. How can you set a value on a life? I will always be in your debt.'

Turning to Gorran, who had said little since the journey resumed, Mrs Elliott asked, 'Is your commanding officer still Colonel Hinde? Colonel Samuel Hinde?'

'He is indeed, ma'am, and there's no finer soldier in the service of His Majesty.'

'Samuel has always thought so. Be that as it may, I trust you intend escorting this young lady to Horsham. If Samuel is there I wish you to bring her to his attention. Tell him his Aunt Florence conveys her fondest regards – and requests that he do all he can to help this young lady.'

Mrs Elliott's imperious manner dropped away and she leaned forward to pat Gorran gently on the knee while he was still recovering from the surprise of learning he was travelling with the aunt of his commanding officer.

'I shall write to him and tell him all about you too, young man. He is fortunate to have such a resourceful officer in his regiment and I intend telling him so.'

In Plymouth the passengers who had shared the adventurous journey parted company. Mrs Elliott was travelling to Torquay, the two injured men to Barnstaple in North Devon. Half an hour later, Cassie and Gorran were settling back on the hard leather seat of a crowded coach that would take them on the next leg of their lengthy journey.

That night was spent at the New London Inn at Exeter. Soon after their arrival Gorran asked Cassie to dress his injured arm once more. The makeshift linen binding had worked loose and he had obtained a bandage from the inn landlord.

'It's healing well,' said Cassie when she exposed the long gash. 'Much better than I thought it would when I saw it yesterday.'

'Well enough to wield a sword and cut down the King's enemies?' Gorran spoke jocularly, but Cassie shuddered involuntarily. 'You don't like the thought of killing?'

'No.'

'Yet you'd marry a soldier whose duty is to kill his enemies?'

'I'm marrying Harry Clymo.' Cassie spoke the words in the manner of someone who had repeated them to herself many times. 'Perhaps he won't be called upon to kill anyone.'

'Is this young man of yours expecting you to arrive at Horsham?'

It was an unexpected and forthright question and Cassie found she could not lie to her companion. 'No.'

'I see. Yet you are quite certain he'll wed you?'

'Yes.'

It was almost true. When Cassie had set out from Mevagissey she had entertained no doubts. They had come, unwanted and uninvited, during the journey.

Gorran Fox was an astute young man and he felt Cassie was being less than honest with him – and also with herself. 'What do you intend doing after you're wed to your soldier?'

Cassie had thought little about married life with Harry Clymo. Her plans for the future did not go beyond ensuring her child would bear its father's name. 'I . . . I don't know. I'll stay with Harry, I suppose.'

'That might prove difficult, Cassie. The Thirty-second Regiment is on its way to the war in the Peninsula. Your husband-to-be and the remainder of his company will join the regiment as soon as their training is complete – within a month, in all probability. Each company is allowed to take no more than five or six wives. That's for every hundred men. If you are one of the few, you'll be marching with the men, sharing their privations and hardships and witnessing all the horrors of war. On the other hand, if you're one of the majority of wives who are left behind you'll be given a letter to present to every workhouse authority on the road back to Cornwall. They'll feed you and give you just enough money to enable you to reach the next district, but once you reach home you'll be expected to keep yourself until your husband's return.'

'I *can't* return home.' Cassie was binding Gorran's arm in a quiet corner of the inn lounge and her outcry turned the heads of the others in the room. 'I mean . . . I don't *want* to go home again. Not just yet, anyway.'

Cassie meant every word. Married or not, she would be ashamed to return home in an advanced state of pregnancy so soon after her marriage. Going back when she had been married for a year or two would be quite different.

'I think you were telling the truth the first time, Cassie. Have you run away from home?' Gorran spoke kindly. He was very taken with this young girl. He correctly guessed her age as being no more than fifteen or sixteen, but for a few moments the gap in their ages yawned far wider than the actual eight or nine years and Cassie made no reply.

'Are you in trouble? If not, the best thing you can do is catch the next coach back to Cornwall and forget all about marrying a soldier.'

'I don't remember asking for your advice, Mr Fox.' Cassie sat in her chair as rigid as a musket barrel, yet Gorran thought her frighteningly vulnerable.

34

'You're quite right, of course, Cassie, but I was only thinking of you. Women who marry soldiers have a hard time – wherever they are.'

'I'll take my chances.'

'That's what I feared. Very well, Cassie. You must do what you feel is best. All I ask is that you regard me as a friend, a good friend, and call on my assistance should you ever need help.'

Gorran said no more on the subject the next day, and the following evening at their next stop she thought he remained slightly aloof. Cassie wondered whether it had anything to do with her refusal to take the young officer's advice. She dismissed the thought as swiftly as it had come to mind. There was no reason why he should care whether or not a young village girl heeded him. He was more likely to be preoccupied with the thought of rejoining his regiment. She had heard that gentlemen like Gorran Fox who chose an army career put their duty to the regiment above all else.

The next night would be their last on the road before reaching Horsham and shortly before dusk the coach rumbled over cobblestones into the courtyard of the Red Lion Inn at Petersfield, a small but busy market town no more than thirty miles from their destination.

As the lathered horses were unhitched from the coach, a party of mounted, blue-coated cavalry officers clattered into the yard, scattering servants and passengers alike. Gorran paused in the act of handing Cassie from the coach to allow the officers to pass.

The newly arrived cavalrymen were in a jubilant and

arrogant mood. The senior of them was no older than Gorran and he called on the servants to 'jump to it' and see to their horses, suggesting they should put the needs of men who served the King before tending to a team of horses 'fit only for a glue pot'.

When the danger of being trampled by a high-spirited horse was over, Gorran helped Cassie to the ground.

'Do you know those soldiers?'

The question was asked in all innocence and Gorran smiled. 'There are tens of thousands of men in the army, Cassie, and I'm only a junior infantry officer. Those men are cavalry. Light Dragoons, at that. They go into battle as though they're riding to hounds – and give the enemy as much quarter as they would a fox.'

'You don't like them?' It was a statement of fact as much as a question.

'As I said, they are cavalry officers. I'm infantry. There's scant love lost between the two. But go on inside. I must make certain the trunk containing my uniform is brought in. I'll need to wear it tomorrow.'

Cassie tried to imagine Gorran in a soldier's uniform, but failed. The matter was still occupying her thoughts when she entered the inn. As she opened the door a wave of sound reached out and enveloped her. To her surprise she found herself in a room filled with noisy drinking men. Cassie realised she had come through the wrong entrance. She turned to retrace her steps, but before she reached the door one of the blue-uniformed dragoon officers was at her side.

'You're not thinking of leaving us so soon, surely? My companions and I would be devastated. Why not join us at our table? You'll find us good company – and not ungenerous.'

'I don't need entertaining – and I'll thank you to let go of my arm.'

Cassie tried to shake off the hand gripping her elbow, but the dragoon officer retained his grip of her. He had taken a good look at her while she was talking. She was good-looking. *Handsome*, even, though she was dressed in the manner of a country girl. Such young women did not enter the taproom of an inn unless they were in search of an evening's fun – and perhaps the opportunity of having a couple of shillings in her purse by morning.

'Come now, don't be put off by the crowd in here. I'll look after you.'

'I don't need looking after. *Let go of my arm!*'

Gorran was on the roof of the coach when he saw Cassie enter the inn. He realised from the noise that escaped from inside when she opened the door she had entered the taproom by mistake. He expected her to come out again immediately. When she did not reappear, he climbed from the coach and hurried after her.

The persistent dragoon officer was trying to lead Cassie towards the table from which his fellow officers shouted encouragement. It was evident to Gorran this was not the first inn the dragoon officers had visited that day and he intervened immediately.

'Are you having some trouble, Cassie?'

Before she could answer, the dragoon snapped, 'This is nothing to do with you, sir. Kindly go about your business.'

'I was talking to the lady – and I doubt if *she's* invited your attentions.'

The dragoon eyed Gorran Fox speculatively. Gorran's garb was that of a gentleman, but his speech carried a distinct West Country accent. The dragoon officer correctly judged him to belong to a family of 'lesser' country gentry. If he was acquainted with this young woman the relationship would be of no more lasting a nature than that which the dragoon officer had in mind.

'No doubt the lady has a patriotic nature. I'm sure she will be delighted to bring a little pleasure into the lives of soldiers who will soon be fighting His Majesty's enemies.'

As the dragoon officer was speaking, Cassie felt his tight grip on her arm ease slightly. Swiftly pulling the arm free, she rubbed the spot bruised by his finger and said, 'Mr Fox is a soldier too – *and* he's been wounded.'

The dragoon officer looked at Gorran with sudden respect. 'Indeed? You were wounded in the Peninsular War, Mr Fox?'

'I survived unscathed to salute Sir John Moore's grave at Corunna. My wound came at Walcheren, where my regiment fought to regain an advantage lost by cavalry impetuosity.'

'Ah! You're an infantryman, Mr Fox.' The statement contained the contempt felt by cavalrymen for those who fought a war on foot. 'Perhaps your, er, companion would prefer some impetuous company for the evening?'

'I'm escorting the young lady to Horsham where she is to marry one of my soldiers.'

'Marrying a soldier – an *infantryman*? My dear young

lady, why on earth should you contemplate such a foolish thing?' Raising his eyebrows in an expression of mock dismay, the dragoon officer proffered a shallow bow to Cassie. 'I trust your future husband fully appreciates his good fortune.'

Returning his attention to Gorran, the dragoon officer's bow was stiffer and deeper. 'Dalhousie, at your service, Mr Fox. Should we meet in the Peninsula, I trust you will have no cause to complain of the courage, or impetuosity, call it what you will, of the Sixteenth Light Dragoons. I bid you a good evening, sir.'

Lieutenant Dalhousie swaggered rather than walked across the room. His spurs made a musical sound on the stone floor until it was lost in the cheer that rose from the carousing dragoons.

As Gorran led Cassie from the taproom, she rubbed her bruised arm once more and asked, 'Do all soldiers behave like that towards women?'

Remembering some of the scenes he had witnessed in Spain, when soldiers fighting for the possession of a town came across stocks of wine, Gorran wondered how best to reply to Cassie's question. 'Mr Dalhousie and his companions are officers, Cassie. Gentlemen. If you marry a soldier you'll be thrown into the company of coarse, uncouth men – and their women. Some would have ended their lives dangling from a hangman's rope had they not joined the army. Most are held in check only from fear of the lash. Others carry the scars of a flogging on their backs. When they go into battle they're magnificent. In retreat they're as ready to kill friend as foe in order to survive.'

Cassie listened wide-eyed to Gorran's astonishing diatribe.

'Are you certain you wish to marry a soldier, Cassie? It's still not too late to go home. I'll be happy to pay your fare.'

'Harry wouldn't do all those things you say other soldiers do. He isn't like that.'

A sudden, uncomfortable spasm caught Cassie's stomach muscles, reminding her of her reason for pursuing Harry Clymo halfway across England.

'I've come all this way to marry Harry Clymo, and that's what I'm going to do. There's no going back for me.'

4

The coach reached Horsham in the late afternoon. The pleasant little market town's role as a garrison town in this year of 1811 was immediately apparent. Mounted cavalrymen, singly and in troops of varying size, clattered through the town's main street. Their uniforms of blue or red, heavily adorned with gold, brought a splash of welcome colour to a grey, sunless, lack-lustre day.

There were many infantrymen on the streets here too: blue-coated artillerymen, bandsmen resplendent in yellow, green-uniformed riflemen, tartan-kilted Highlanders and a plentiful sprinkling of red-coated infantrymen. Red was the colour of the uniform jacket worn by Gorran Fox with tight white breeches and shiny black boots on this the last day of the journey. He looked so smart that Cassie felt somewhat in awe of him.

When they alighted at the coaching-inn, Gorran suggested Cassie should remain there while he made inquiries for the 32nd Regiment. Upon his return he confirmed that only a single training company of the Cornish regiment was in the area. They would find it stationed in a barracks a few hundred yards from the edge of town, on the Worthing road.

Now Cassie had reached her destination and a reunion with Harry was imminent, she found her thoughts were in a turmoil. She had told Gorran, with great confidence, that Harry would be pleased to see her and anxious for them to be married. Now much of her confidence had deserted her. She had even begun to wonder what she would do if Harry refused to marry her. She dismissed the thought hurriedly. He would marry her. He *had* to . . .

'You won't change your mind, even at this late hour?' As though sensing her sudden uncertainty, Gorran put the question to Cassie as they approached a gated archway, beneath which was the entrance to the barracks. Cassie shook her head, not entirely trusting her voice.

Gorran sighed. 'Then so be it, Cassie – but I believe you are making a dreadful mistake.'

The guard on duty at the barracks' entrance sprang to attention as Gorran approached. Because Cassie was so obviously in his company the sentry did not bother to challenge her.

Walking inside they found themselves standing on a huge open square which formed the parade ground and around which the barrack buildings were situated. Here a large number of recruits and longer-serving soldiers were undergoing instruction in drill movements. Marching and counter-marching back and forth, changing direction, forming squares, and presenting and aiming muskets to which long bayonets were attached.

The drill movements were carried out at the shouted commands of the drill sergeants, one of whom was allocated to each company. The drill sergeants were trying hard to outshout each other and Cassie found the noise and movement totally confusing.

'Ah! There are the men of the Thirty-second.' Gorran pointed vaguely and set off to skirt the busy parade ground.

'How can you tell the men of your regiment?' Cassie did not understand how Gorran Fox could possibly know. With the exception of one group of soldiers dressed in dark green, and another wearing blue jackets, there seemed no way of identifying the companies.

'It will soon be your regiment, too, Cassie. Army wives have as much pride in their regiment as their husbands and you'll be able to pick them out even in the heat of battle. Each regiment has different-coloured facings and braid on their uniforms. You'll soon learn to distinguish them.'

Cassie tried to dismiss the thought of so many soldiers fighting and perhaps dying on a battlefield. For now it was enough to think of what she was going to say to Harry. Thoughts of what marriage would bring could wait.

Walking around the edge of the huge parade ground with Gorran, Cassie attracted a great many whistles and cat-calls from soldiers who looked out from barrack-room windows. Most were harmless bids to attract her attention, but one or two included crude suggestions that made her cheeks burn with embarrassment.

Gorran was aware of Cassie's discomfiture, but he said nothing. He had warned her what she could expect from her intended way of life. The cat-calling was a very mild taste of what she would have to endure as the wife of a serving soldier.

Gorran did not come to a halt until they reached the far side of the huge parade ground. His attention was focused upon a group of some hundred soldiers being drilled by a burly sergeant who sported a moustache waxed stiffly in the Continental style.

For some little while the sergeant was unaware of the presence of Gorran and Cassie, although they were creating an increasing interest in the ranks of the men being drilled by him. Among the many heads turned in her direction Cassie tried to identify Harry, but each soldier's face was shadowed by the peak of the tall black shako he wore and it was difficult to tell one from another.

Eventually the drill sergeant brought the company to a halt, demanding to know the reason for their inattention. One of the men said something that could not be heard by Cassie, at the same time nodding his head in the direction of the two onlookers.

The sergeant turned, a frown upon his face. Suddenly the frown changed to a smile. Marching swiftly and stiffly to where Cassie and Gorran stood, he halted in front of the officer and brought his hand up in a smart salute. 'Mr Fox, sir! It's good to see you've recovered so well from your wound. Are you here to rejoin the regiment, sir? We've a lot of men recovered from the Walcheren fever – a number of new recruits, too. Useless at the moment, quite useless. But we'll have them in shape by the time they need to tickle a Frenchman's belly with a bayonet.'

'It's good to see you again, too, Sergeant Tonks – and to know at least one good soldier survived Walcheren.'

'There's more than you'd think, sir. Some I'm pleased to see again. Others I'd have been happy to lose.' Sergeant Tonks glanced uncertainly at Cassie, then returned his attention to Gorran. 'Is there something I can do for you right now, sir?'

'Yes. I've travelled from Cornwall with this young lady, Miss Whetter. She's seeking one of your recruits, a Harry Clymo. In spite of all my warnings she's set on marrying him and becoming a soldier's wife.'

Sergeant Tonks's gaze dropped to Cassie's midriff and when it returned to her face she was blushing furiously.

'Following the army during a campaign's not the best place for a woman . . . any woman.'

Gorran smiled. 'I seem to remember your wife being present throughout the last campaign, Sergeant Tonks – and many men have cause to be grateful to her, myself included.'

Sergeant Tonks's smile was more rueful than that of his officer. 'I was merely telling you my thoughts, sir. I'm not saying as my wife agrees with me.' The burly sergeant glanced at Cassie once more. 'Shall I tell Harry Clymo to fall out and come across here?'

'If you please, Sergeant Tonks.'

Saluting smartly once more, Sergeant Tonks executed

45

a sharp about-turn. Before marching back to the company of soldiers lolling at-ease on the parade ground, he looked back over his shoulder at Gorran. 'Begging your pardon, sir, but the barracks is no place for a young girl. I've been able to rent a small cottage in the town. Miss Whetter had best stay there with Mrs Tonks until the wedding.'

Without waiting for a reply the burly sergeant headed back to the squad of waiting men, his loud voice castigating them for their slovenly deportment in front of one of their own officers. Then he ordered, 'Harry Clymo, fall out and go and speak to Mr Fox.'

A soldier in the rear rank of the company detached himself from the ranks, breaking into an awkward trot at a bellowed command from the sergeant. Coming to an ungainly halt before Gorran, Harry Clymo saluted awkwardly and uncertainly, trying unsuccessfully to keep his gaze from straying to Cassie.

Cassie was looking at Harry with an expression that bordered upon incredulity. He looked totally different in his soldier's uniform. Almost as though he was another person. One change, immediately discernible, was his hair. It had been worn very long at home in Cornwall. Too long, her father had always said. He would have had no cause for complaint now. The hair that could be seen beneath his black, shiny shako was cropped to within a finger's breadth of his head.

'I've had the pleasure of Cassie's company on a rather eventful coach journey from Cornwall, Clymo. You're a lucky man. I know few girls who'd travel so far to marry a man who'd run off to join the army.'

46

The expression of blank bewilderment in the glance Harry threw at Cassie confirmed what the Cornish lieutenant already suspected. Talk of an immediate marriage had come as a surprise to the young soldier.

'You'll both have much to say to each other – but Sergeant Tonks's patience will probably run short if you're longer than a quarter of an hour.' There was a clock in the tower above the barracks' entrance, its hands closing upon each other at a quarter past four. 'I'll find out where Rose Tonks is staying and meet you at the barracks' entrance at half past, Cassie.' With an expressionless nod in Harry Clymo's direction, Gorran retraced his steps.

'What did the lieutenant mean about you coming all this way to marry me, Cassie? I don't understand. What are you doing here?'

These were the first words spoken by Harry since he had first caught sight of Cassie standing at the edge of the parade ground with the officer. Seeing her had erased what little drill instruction he had acquired during the few days he had been in the barracks, and it earned him the curses of his fellow recruits.

'I don't understand why you've become a soldier either, Harry Clymo. You certainly never mentioned it when you were busy getting me pregnant.'

Harry gaped at her and his mouth opened and closed at least three times before he gasped, 'Pregnant? You? Are you sure . . . ?'

'I'm as sure as any girl who's being sick every morning can be.'

Suddenly Cassie felt sorry for the confused young

47

man standing before her. He was not a brave soldier serving King George III but an unworldly farm-hand from Cornwall in unfamiliar and bewildering surroundings. Now she had arrived and presented him with a situation for which he was totally unprepared. Harry was not a man with an ability to meet and solve life's problems head-on. She suspected that joining the army had not been a bold decision made on the spur of the moment. It probably owed far more to his inability to give the recruiting sergeant a firm 'no'.

For a moment her shoulders sagged with the realisation that Harry might not want to marry her after all. She wanted to be able to say it did not matter, but it did. She wanted to marry Harry and she needed him to want to marry her, but all she could say was, 'What are we going to do, Harry?'

'I . . . I don't know. I hadn't thought about getting married. Well . . . I *had*, but not just yet.'

Cassie looked at Harry for so long he began to feel uncomfortable. Suddenly she straightened her shoulders. To Gorran, watching the scene with the width of the parade ground between them, she seemed to have cast off the mantle of despondency that had descended upon her a few minutes before. 'Neither had I before I knew I was expecting your child. Now it's something we both have to face. I don't want you to think I've trapped you into marriage. I believed you loved me when you made me pregnant, same as I loved you. I thought you wanted to marry me when we were both back home in Mevagissey. Was I wrong, Harry?'

'No . . .'

His reply was not as reassuring as Cassie had hoped it would be. '*Do* you want to marry me?'

'Yes, Cassie . . . but I've no money for a wedding. All my bounty money's gone to buy bits and pieces of equipment.'

'Money's no problem. I've more than thirty guineas in my purse.'

Harry gasped. Thirty guineas was a fortune. His face expressed his amazement, but Cassie was still talking.

'It isn't the means I'm talking about, Harry. It's you and me. How you feel about marrying me. I've travelled all this way because I believed you'd want to marry me when you heard about the baby I'm having . . . *our* baby. If you don't, I'll find somewhere else to go. London, perhaps.'

For a moment the brisk and businesslike façade cracked to reveal the uncertain sixteen-year-old country girl hiding inside, but Cassie recovered quickly. 'It's for you to decide, Harry. No one else can make up your mind for you.'

Harry Clymo stood looking at her and momentarily he forgot the painful blisters raised upon toes and heels by ill-fitting boots. He saw Cassie as he had known her in Mevagissey. A warm, intelligent young girl who stirred his emotions as no other girl ever had.

'All right.'

'That isn't what I was hoping to hear, Harry. I was hoping you'd tell me you really *wanted* to marry me and that everything is going to be the way it should be.'

'I *do* want to marry you, Cassie. I always have.' Harry made a gallant attempt to bring a little romance into the

49

moment. 'I didn't run away from you, I was going to come back to marry you. I said so in my letter. It was just . . . the farm. There was nothing for us there. Nothing at all. I hated it. I've always hated it. If you only knew . . .'

'I do, Harry. I went to the farm looking for you. I saw where they made you sleep.' Cassie reached out her hand and gripped his arm in an affectionate gesture of sympathy. 'It was horrible.' Dropping the hand to her side once more, Cassie asked, 'Are you quite sure you want to marry me?'

Harry nodded, without speaking, but the look in his eyes gave Cassie hope once more.

'Then I'll tell Gorran Fox. He's said he'll make all the arrangements for us.' Suddenly Cassie moved forward and kissed Harry.

The action provoked a raucous reaction from the watchers at the barrack-room windows. It made Harry writhe self-consciously, but Cassie showed no sign she had heard. 'I'll be a good wife to you, Harry. You'll not regret marrying me.'

A shout from Sergeant Tonks rose above all the other parade-ground sounds and caused Harry to start nervously.

'I must go now. Where will I find you?'

'At Sergeant Tonks's house. Come there as soon as you can.'

5

❧

Sergeant Tonks was a large man, but he conceded at least three stone in weight and six inches in height to his wife. Rose Tonks was a big woman in every sense of the word.

When she opened the door and saw Gorran Fox standing on the step she opened her muscular arms wide and hugged him in an embrace that Cassie thought would not have disgraced a Cornish wrestler.

'Mr Fox! You're a sight to delight these eyes of mine, and no mistake.'

Releasing Gorran, she stepped back and beamed delightedly at him. 'Does Elijah know you've rejoined the regiment? He swears that if you hadn't been wounded you'd have been promoted captain and put in charge of the company – and no one deserves it more. But it's good to see you on your feet again. Last time I see'd you there was blood all over the place with not enough left in your body to keep you standing upright. I thought you was going to leave your bones on Walcheren, and no mistake.'

'And so I might, had it not been for you, Rose.'

Red-faced from the strength of Rose Tonks's bear-like hug, Gorran turned to Cassie. 'I was lying wounded with a battle going on all around when Rose walked through the fighting as though she was on a Sunday-evening stroll. She picked me up like a baby and carried me back behind the lines to a surgeon. She's a very special lady.'

Drawing Cassie forward, Gorran said, 'Rose, I'd like you to meet Cassie. We've travelled up from Cornwall together – and a very eventful journey it was too. She's here to marry one of the regiment, a recruit. Your husband said she could stay with you until the wedding.'

'Marrying a soldier! Why, she's hardly more than a child! Come on inside, girl. Come in. You'll be tired out after all that travelling. You'll stay and have a cup of tea with us, Mr Fox?'

'I must report my arrival to headquarters. I'll come visiting as soon as I'm able.' To Cassie, he said, 'I'm leaving you in good hands. The whole regiment would as soon go to war for Rose Tonks as for King George, if the need arose. I'm hoping she might succeed where I've failed in dissuading you from going ahead with this wedding.'

'Away with you, Mr Fox. You're like all other young bachelors – and some married men too. You think every pretty young girl should stay available for when you get your mind off war and take notice of other things.

52

Off you go now and leave me to take care of this young lady.'

Rose Tonks good-naturedly shooed Gorran from the house and returned to beam at Cassie. 'Come into the kitchen, dear. I've a brew of tea on the stove there.'

Leading the way, she said, 'Like a palace to me, this place is. It's the first home me and Elijah have ever had. Mind you, I told him, it was dangerous setting me up in such a nice house. If he's not careful I'll grow to enjoy it so much I won't want to go off on any more campaigns – and then where would he be? Every soldier needs a woman to look after him, specially when he's fighting a war. It doesn't matter whether he's a recruit, sergeant, lieutenant, colonel, or even a general.'

Rose waved Cassie to an ancient wooden chair that rocked alarmingly when Cassie sat on it. Lifting a heavy smoke-blackened kettle from the fire, she poured steaming water into a tea jug and replaced the kettle on the fire. Swirling the jug about vigorously, she poured the tea into two badly chipped cups. When sugar was added, she held out one and asked, 'When's the baby due, lovey?'

Cassie was thankful she had not taken the tea from Rose Tonks's hand. If she had she would certainly have dropped it to the floor. 'How . . . ? How do you know?'

'Bless me! The child's an innocent!'

Chuckling, Rose placed the tea on a table beside Cassie. 'If you'd seen as many pregnant women as I have you wouldn't need to ask such a question. With most of 'em I know before they do. Besides, unless there's a very good reason, no girl of your age and with your

53

looks is going to traipse halfway across England looking for a lad who's left her and joined the army. Not unless she's got a bellyful of baby, and don't want to shame her family.'

Cassie's eyes inexplicably filled with tears at mention of the family she had left behind in Mevagissey. She suddenly felt young, alone and very vulnerable. Rose had put her finger on Cassie's main reason for coming to find Harry Clymo. It was not because she loved him so much she could not bear to be parted from him – although she *did* love him. Neither was it because she wanted him to acknowledge his responsibility for the unborn baby. If she was ruthlessly honest with herself she would have to say it was because she had not wanted to bring shame upon her Methodist family. It was a truth she had not faced until that moment when the blunt-speaking Rose had put it into words.

'Here, drink this up, lovey. Things look better with a nice cup of tea inside you. You're tired out by your journey too, I dare say.'

Rose put the mug of tea in Cassie's hands and patted her shoulder in a gesture of comfort. 'I think we ought to have a word with this young man of yours before we decide about a wedding.'

'I didn't come all this way to *talk* about anything.' Cassie gained control of her emotions once more. 'I *am* going to marry Harry, and he'll not regret it. I'll be a good wife to him.'

'I don't doubt it, child, but there's more to marrying a soldier than being a good wife. You'll be wed not just to him, but to the regiment. You'll not only need to be able to cope with your husband's bad habits, but with those of hundreds of other soldiers. God knows, it's bad enough in barracks in *this* country. If you ever get to go abroad with your man on a campaign you'll find yourself acting as wife, washerwoman, forager, cook, clothes-mender, unpaid surgeon, house-builder . . . yes, mother too, and not just to the child you're carrying, either.'

'If it's so hard, why do you do it?'

'I've told you, Elijah needs me. Besides, I've never known anything else. My father was a soldier. I was born at Gibraltar at the height of a battle and I've followed the army in a dozen different countries ever since. Mind you, I've thought more than once of giving up the life, but I can't, not while Elijah's a soldier. When he's served his time I'll say goodbye and good riddance to the army and you won't see my heels for dust. What's more, I'd never let any daughter of mine marry a soldier, I'll tell you that straight.'

'Do you have any children?' Cassie was anxious to keep the talk on any subject except marriage to Harry.

'No, and a good thing too, as I'm often telling Elijah.' Rose's expression was at odds with her words. 'What would I know of being a mother? I can swab out a cannon with any man – and do it quicker and better – but clean up a baby's backside? That's something different.' Rose grimaced. 'I tell Elijah, if it's children he wants he'll need to find himself another woman, but God help him – and her – if he ever takes me at my word.'

Rose took a deep and noisy swig of tea before saying, 'Enough of such nonsense. When you've drunk up I'll

55

show you where you'll be sleeping. You'd better make the most of it. It's the last comfortable bed you'll sleep in for a while if you marry that soldier of yours. Come on, bring your tea with you and tell me something about yourself on the way upstairs.'

Sergeant Elijah Tonks brought Harry Clymo to the house when he came off duty that evening. Harry was even more shy and tongue-tied than usual and Cassie wondered what the army had done to him. Then she realised the reason. Harry was in unfamiliar surroundings. He had not lived in a house since he was a small child! He had gone from the poor-house to a barn at the Pentewan valley farm. He did not know how he should behave inside a house.

Cassie explained this to Rose when the two women were together in the kitchen and the big woman's heart went out immediately to Harry.

'Why, the poor young lad! Made him live in a barn like one of their animals, you say? He'd have been no more than eight years old when the poor-house put him out to work. They don't keep lads any longer than they have to. Poor little chap, he must have been frightened out of his life with all them rats and spiders roaming about him all night. Here, put a bit more meat on that plate for him, poor young soul.'

Cassie smiled, thinking of their earlier conversation. Rose would prove a doting mother if ever she had a child. This opinion was borne out during supper. Harry was unused to eating at a family table and while making him feel at ease Rose drew out a great deal of his life story.

By the end of the evening Rose had forgotten the opposition she had entertained towards a marriage between Cassie and Harry. Instead, she was scheming how best to ensure Cassie would accompany Harry when the new recruits were sent to join the regiment in the Peninsula.

It was this that Cassie spoke about when she was next in the kitchen with Rose. 'Do you really think Harry will be sent to the war in Spain?'

'He's a soldier, lovey. Soldiers are paid to fight when there's a war on – and no one who's ever fought against Napoleon's army has any doubts about being in a war. Every battle I've seen so far could have gone either way – and in eighteen hundred and nine they had the beating of us. The French didn't only wage war against soldiers then, either. I saw 'em cut down women and babes-in-arms, too. Once on the ground they were trampled in the mud by French horses. That was on the retreat to Corunna. I never want to see the like of that again.'

Cassie shuddered at the images conjured up by Rose. There were certain aspects of being a soldier's wife that she would prefer not to think about in any great detail.

'Who decides which wives will go with the regiment?'

'We draw lots. All those wanting to go assemble in the pay office, although those with too many children are usually persuaded to stay behind. The others are told how many will be allowed to go with the husbands. It's never more than six women for each company, and sometimes only four. We're lucky in the Thirty-second Regiment, the colonel allows six. Six wives for every hundred men. That means that "To go" is written on six pieces of paper and put in a hat. All the other pieces have "Not to go" written on 'em. Then we each draw a piece of paper out of the hat.'

'So you could always draw a "Not to go" from the hat, too?'

'I could – but I haven't yet, not since Elijah became a sergeant, and I don't intend drawing one if he has to go back to Spain with the recruits and this new company they've just formed.'

'When do you think they'll be leaving?' Cassie felt a strange feeling in the pit of her stomach. It could have been the baby, excitement – or fear!

'No one's supposed to know for certain, but it's an open secret. The rest of the regiment's in Guernsey right now, but orders have been sent for it to embark for the Peninsula. We'll be going as soon as the recruits and those recovered from wounds number a hundred.'

'When will that be?'

'Within the fortnight, Elijah says . . . so we'd better do something about this wedding of yours as quick as we can.'

Cassie and Harry Clymo were married only four days before the men of the 32nd Regiment's Training Company were ordered to leave the barracks and march to Portsmouth to embark for the war in the Peninsula.

It was necessary for Harry to obtain permission from his commanding officer for the wedding and this might have proved difficult. The army preferred that recruits to its army be unmarried. Fortunately for the young couple, Lieutenant Fox had been appointed temporary

58

commanding officer of the hundred men until they joined the main regiment which was already at sea *en route* for Lisbon.

Cassie and Harry were married in the barrack chapel, the service conducted by an army chaplain. It was a brief and simple ceremony, witnessed by Sergeant Elijah Tonks and his wife, a handful of recruits, and a large number of soldiers' wives. Gorran was not present. He had been called to the army's headquarters at Brighton to receive orders for the embarkation of the company.

The wedding was a quiet affair, but the celebrations that followed were not. In spite of Harry's quiet, almost shy manner, he was popular with the other soldiers and they were determined to make his wedding day an occasion he would always remember.

Cassie's few possessions had been moved to the barrack room to which the wedding party adjourned when the ceremony was over. A collection had been made among the soldiers, old and new, and the money used to purchase drink. Ale, porter, gin and even brandy had been acquired, while some of the more domesticated wives had collected a variety of ingredients with which they had baked cakes.

There was little privacy for a married couple in the barrack room, but for tonight a number of blankets had been donated and they were draped around the bottom half of a two-tier bunk. This would ensure they enjoyed at least a modicum of seclusion on their wedding night. It had not been easy to persuade the occupant of the top bunk to sleep elsewhere, but the promise of a liberal ration of ale and brandy succeeded where persuasion and the threat of physical violence failed.

Two bandsmen from one of the regimental bands in the barracks had also been procured to lead the dancing with fife and tin whistle. By popular demand, Harry and Cassie Clymo led the first dance. Harry had no idea of any dance steps but he soon discovered that nothing more was expected of him than a form of heavy-booted capering. Once others took to the floor he was able to retire with Cassie to a seat at the side of the barrack room.

The wedding celebrations lasted far into the night. As it became apparent to the occupants of adjacent barrack blocks that the revelry was not likely to subside quickly, they gave up all thought of sleep and joined in the festivities. Most brought drink with them, others contributed money to the kitty. All seemed intent on experiencing every degree of drunkenness until total oblivion was achieved.

By the early hours of the morning most of the revellers had forgotten what they were celebrating. A few late-comers never knew. This did not matter too much while Elijah Tonks and his fellow sergeants were present to maintain at least a semblance of order. However, soon after midnight the senior non-commissioned officers deemed it wise to take their leave. Drunken soldiers were beginning to air their grievances, real and imagined. It would be folly to risk argument with them.

Cupping her hands around Cassie's face, Rose Tonks kissed her, and there were tears in her eyes as she said, 'I wish you were spending your wedding night somewhere other than a barrack room, Cassie. There's no one kinder to his women than a British soldier, when he's sober, but after a few drinks there's a general inside every soldier's trousers giving him his orders. You just remember that, Cassie.'

With this piece of advice, Rose followed her husband from the barrack room, an affectionate slap from her muscular hand sending more than one soldier staggering from her path along the way.

There were a number of women in the room, not all of them soldiers' wives. Cassie was shocked when one of them paired off with a soldier, climbed into a top bunk with him and they began to make love beneath a blanket, encouraged by other soldiers and some of the women too.

'That sort of thing goes on all the time,' said Harry, apologetically. 'Especially on pay night. It embarrassed me at first, but if a man's in barracks and wants a woman there's nowhere he can take her. It's the same for married couples, Cassie. If you want each other you need to get used to everyone else knowing what you're doing.'

Harry's words dismayed Cassie. This was an aspect of army life to which she had given little thought.

'At least we've got some blankets around our bed for tonight.' Suddenly Harry did not seem able to look directly at Cassie. 'Shall we go to bed now?'

The din in the barrack room was deafening. A fiddler had been found from somewhere and singing now added to the noise of heavy-footed dancing. Soldiers and women were using beds as seats and there had already been three fights during the course of the evening. Cassie thought it would be like bedding down in the street during a street fair. Then she swallowed hard. Future nights might be quieter, but they would also be far more public.

'All right.'

No one noticed their departure from the immediate vicinity of the makeshift dance floor. As they left a fight broke out between a number of women whose men were from different regiments, none of which was quartered in this particular barrack block. Urged on by loudly cheering soldiers, the women screamed, bit, punched, kicked, clawed, and pulled out tufts of long, greasy hair as they rolled around the litter-strewn floor, locked in battle.

Cassie and Harry climbed into the blanket-hung bunk from opposite sides. They undressed clumsily in the cramped darkness, each trying to avoid touching the other.

Cassie still wore a petticoat when she slipped beneath the coarse blanket that was the only covering. She was immediately aware of Harry's naked body beside her in the narrow bed. She also realised that the blanket beneath her was every bit as coarse as the one covering them. It scratched at her exposed arms and shoulders.

When Harry slipped an arm clumsily beneath her body she turned to him, trying to ignore the cheers that marked the end of the fight. Then the fiddler began coaxing a tune from his out-of-tune instrument.

'You're not sorry you've married me, Harry?'

'Of course I'm not.'

'And you're not angry about the baby?'

'Not any more. It came as a bit of a surprise, but I know it's mine and, well . . . it'll be special to have something that really belongs to me . . . to us.'

Cassie suddenly hugged her new husband. 'Thank you for saying that, Harry. I was just as much to blame as you . . . but I'll make you a good wife, I promise.'

With both arms about Harry, Cassie pulled him to her. They were both rolling over together when the bunk suddenly lurched to one side. Cassie squealed with pain and surprise as the steel studs of a heavy boot came through the hanging blankets and scraped the skin of her thigh.

'What the . . . ? Ned! You're not supposed to be sleeping here tonight.'

Harry rolled away from Cassie and shouted to the man who was making hard work of climbing to the bunk above the newly married couple.

Ned's reply was inaudible, but it included an oath as he suddenly slipped and scraped his shin on the hard, wooden edge of the lower bunk.

His next attempt seemed doomed to failure, too, and Cassie cowered back in alarm as the heavy, studded boots swung to and fro only inches from her face. Then a desperate heave tipped the balance and the unseen soldier's legs followed the remainder of his body to the safety of the upper bunk.

'Damn! He promised . . .'

'Does he always go to bed wearing his boots?' Cassie's incredulous question cut across Harry's peevish complaint.

'He says it's a habit he picked up when the regiment

was last in the Peninsula. They retreated from Spain and right through Portugal until they reached the coast. Ned says they were surprised by the French army so often that if he'd taken his boots off he'd have lost 'em more than once.'

'He's not at war now. There are no French soldiers *here*.'

Cassie was not the only woman who disapproved of Ned Harrup wearing his boots to bed. While Cassie was still raised on one elbow, thinking about the strange habits of the soldier on the top bunk, another foot was set upon the mattress beside her. The double bunk complained beneath the weight of a fourth person, although this was no soldier. The foot was slim, unshod – and unwashed.

'Ned Harrup! You could have waited and let me get up there first!' There was anger in the low whisper as the unseen woman added, 'And you can take those boots off. I'll not share a bed with a man wearing boots.'

Harry drew in his breath sharply, then he whispered, 'That's Sarah Cottle, wife of one of our corporals. If he catches her with Ned he'll kill her – and Ned as well.'

The bare foot on the edge of the honeymoon bed was joined by another. There was muttered anger from Ned Harrup's would-be lover as she struggled to remove his offending footwear.

It was a long time before her success was indicated by a heavy thud as the first boot was thrown to the floor. Sarah Cottle cursed the second boot as much as the first while Cassie and Harry lay together in silence.

When the second boot had followed the first to the

floor, Sarah hoisted herself to the top bunk beside Ned. The whole structure swayed dangerously, creaking in complaint, and Cassie and Harry clung to each other until the woman was settled.

There was silence from the top bunk for a few moments until suddenly the pair of bunks began to move in an alarming fashion. Then Cassie and Harry heard Sarah say furiously, 'I'll teach you to bleedin' well fall asleep!'

Just as it seemed the two-tier bunk must disintegrate, something crashed to the ground in the narrow space between the bunks on Harry's side and they heard a loud groan.

Sarah clambered from the top bunk, her angry muttering lost in the sound of continuing revelry, but there was no further sound from Ned.

'What do you think we should do, Harry? Your friend might be badly hurt.'

'Ned Harrup's no friend of mine – and he was so drunk I doubt if he's suffered so much as a bruise.'

'But surely we should do something?'

'Yes, we should forget about Ned Harrup and remember it's our wedding night.'

'It's not easy, with so much going on around us.'

'It'll be worse tomorrow night. We'll have men in all the bunks and no blankets about us.'

The events of the past minutes had done nothing to arouse Cassie's romantic feelings, but it *was* their wedding night. Hers *and* Harry's.

'All right then . . .'

6

'I'm sorry it wasn't the sort of wedding night you'd hoped for, Cassie.'

It was the second apology Harry had made to Cassie in the space of three minutes. They were folding the blankets that had afforded them a scant privacy during the night that had just ended.

'It wasn't your fault. If anyone's to blame it's *him*.'

Cassie cast a scathing glance in the direction of Ned Harrup. Sitting on the barrack-room floor, hunched against the wall, Ned's knees were drawn up as though he was in pain.

'I don't think he's feeling too well this morning.'

'He deserves to feel ill,' Cassie said unsympathetically.

During the night, when Cassie and Harry had been about to make love, Ned had suddenly tried to rise to his feet, only to collapse, bringing down some of the blanket curtains and falling across their bunk, at the same time complaining loudly that he was going to be sick.

Swift action on Cassie's part ensured that he was facing in another direction when he fulfilled his promise. However, his intervention destroyed their moment of union. Although Harry tried desperately to recapture the lost moment it soon became apparent his physical ability trailed well behind hopeful ambition. It was for this he was apologising to Cassie.

In a bid to take Harry's mind off their wedding night, Cassie said, 'Look at the mess in this place! Who's going to have to clear it up?'

The barrack room looked much as Cassie imagined a battlefield would. Bodies lay in grotesque postures about the room. Many were on the floor, some on the bunks, others partly in both places. One woman, completely naked, lay snoring on a table. Another sprawled beneath it. Empty and broken bottles were strewn everywhere, and there was no shortage of blood. Fights and arguments had increased in frequency and ferocity as the drunken night stumbled towards dawn.

Harry looked sheepish. 'The wives usually clean up while we're on drill parade.'

'Where are the other wives?'

Harry nodded towards the women on and below the table. 'There's two of them. The rest will be here some-where.'

Cassie looked about her in despair. She, Harry, and two older soldiers were the only ones on their feet. The others looked as though they were unlikely to stir for at least twelve hours – and would be of little use to anyone when they did.

'It seems I'll be clearing up by myself.'

'No, the others'll be up and about by six o'clock, when we fall in for drill. They're drunk most nights, but they still seem to do all that needs doing.'

Harry was right. The women were on their feet before six o'clock, rousing their groaning husbands and getting them out of the barrack room in time for the first drill parade of the day. But the women did not set to work immediately. Praising Cassie's initiative in resuscitating the dying fire and boiling a pot of water, they made coffee and sat around the fire drinking.

There were a dozen different accents among the women, many strange to Cassie's ears. The 32nd was designated the Cornwall Regiment, but in wartime the regimental recruiting sergeants scoured the length and breadth of the country in search of men willing to enlist, and many men brought their women with them.

All agreed it had been a wedding party to remember. One or two repeated particularly lewd or amusing incidents, provoking raucous laughter. One woman who said little was Sarah Cottle. A tall, slim girl, she sat close to the fire, long, untidy blonde hair hiding much of her face, her hands wrapped about a metal mess-tin filled with weak, brown coffee, gazing thoughtfully into the glowing coals. Cassie wondered how much she recalled of the night's happenings – and whether she had succeeded in finding a more wide-awake soldier with whom to share the remaining night hours.

All the other women were older than Cassie. One,

closer to Cassie's own age than most, introduced herself as Polly Martin. Apologising for not attending Cassie's wedding, or the party that followed, she explained, 'I couldn't leave young Sam. He's not yet two and has had a fever these last few days. Sometimes he wakes up delirious and calls for me. I found a billet for the night in one of the other barrack rooms across the parade ground. Mind you, it must have been quite a wedding party, I could hear the music from there.'

'It can't be easy for you, looking after a two-year-old in these barracks.' Cassie expressed sympathy for the other woman, at the same time aware it was a problem she, too, would one day need to face.

'Oh, Sam doesn't mind. Not when he's well – neither does his sister. They're both thoroughly spoiled by everyone. Besides, he was born in a barrack room.'

Cassie looked about the filthy barrack room with the two-tier bunks in leaning lines, each no more than a foot away from its neighbour. She remembered the pandemonium of the night that had just passed – her wedding night. With difficulty she controlled a shudder. 'I don't think I'd care to have a baby in here.'

Polly Martin's snort contained more amusement than derision. 'After a month or two on campaign you'll ache to be back in the comfort of a barracks like this. My first-born, Jean, arrived when Wellington's army was retreating to Corunna. I had her at the height of a rainstorm and still don't know whether I was more frightened of losing her in the mud or both of us being trampled to death by the donkeys of the Portuguese carriers. I was about your age then, coming up sixteen.

Oh, yes, there'll be nights when you'll yearn for a nice warm barrack room, with a roof over your head and no danger of French soldiers launching an attack in the night.'

Suddenly Polly smiled. Reaching out, she gripped Cassie's arm reassuringly. 'Don't let me frighten you, Cassie – although you'll hear far worse stories from the other women. They do their best to scare new wives in the hope they won't want to go on campaign with the regiment. It's not *all* bad. I can remember some days when I wouldn't be anywhere else but with Enoch, my husband, and with the regiment. Days when there was no fighting, no shortage of food, and a hot sun giving a warm, lazy feeling. There's a smell about Spain, too, one you never forget.'

Polly drained the last of her coffee from the awkward-shaped mess-tin and banged it on the table noisily. 'Come on, let's make a start on this mess. The men will be back for breakfast at eight o'clock, and I'll need to pick up my two kids by then. The women in the other room will keep an eye on them while they're sleeping, but they have chores of their own to do.'

It quickly became evident that not all the soldiers' wives were as ready or as willing to work as Polly. One who continued to sit hunched over her coffee was Sarah Cottle. When it was suggested she too should start working, she declared unconvincingly that she would be with them, 'in a minute or two'.

When Cassie made some remark about Sarah's inactivity, Polly silenced her quickly. 'Don't let Sarah hear you say anything against her – and never show an interest in a man she's taken a fancy to. Sarah Cottle's a vindictive bitch and she'll tell her latest husband you've insulted her. He may be a corporal, but he's completely under her thumb. There's more than one man suffered the lash because of her. Hopefully she won't get a ticket to go to the Peninsula this time. The regiment would be better off without Mrs Corporal Cottle.'

After breakfast, when the soldiers had resumed drill, Cassie went into Horsham to buy provisions for herself, and a few extras to supplement Harry's meagre army rations. Horsham was a pleasant little town and seemed more so to Cassie after a day and a night spent in the gloomy, unpleasant-smelling barrack room. As a result she lingered for longer than she had intended. She was making her way leisurely towards the barracks when she was overtaken by Rose Tonks.

The sergeant's wife was breathing too heavily to explain her haste immediately. Seizing Cassie's arm in a powerful grip, she could only say 'Hurry!', matching the urgency of her words by pulling Cassie along with her.

'What is it? What's the matter?' Cassie tried unsuccessfully to free her arm and was forced to increase her pace to a near run in order to keep up with Rose.

'The men are being sent to the Peninsula . . . earlier than expected. Mr Fox returned from headquarters this morning . . . He has orders to take the company off to board a ship lying at Portsmouth. We leave barracks tomorrow.'

The news dismayed Cassie. She had hoped to remain a while longer to become accustomed to barracks life.

Alarmed by the tales other wives told of life on a campaign, she felt she would have liked to learn a great deal more about military ways – to sort out truth from gross exaggeration – before being thrust into a war in a strange country.

'Why are we hurrying now if we're not leaving until morning?'

'Lots are being drawn to decide which wives are to go, and who'll stay behind. Only the women there for the draw will have their names put in the hat.'

Further explanation was unnecessary. Apprehensive though Cassie was at the thought of going to war, the possibility of being left behind was unthinkable. The draw was taking place in the barracks administration office. Those wives chosen to go would be taken on the regimental strength for rations, receiving half the amount of food issued to a soldier. Children were also registered, those accompanying their parents being entitled to half a woman's ration.

The names of those unsuccessful in the draw would also be taken. Each would be given a letter from Gorran Fox. Presented to the supervisor of a workhouse it would entitle the woman to a night's lodging and a few pence with which to sustain herself until she reached the next workhouse along the route home.

There were fifteen women already in the small room, with as many children. The din was appalling. The nervous excitement of each wife seemed to manifest itself in loud talking, and the children had caught the mood. Gorran was in the room and he smiled a greeting to Cassie and Rose as they entered the noisy office.

'All right, let's have some quiet ... *silence!*' the pay sergeant bellowed irritably. When the noise died away, he scowled. 'A man can't hear himself think, let alone carry on serious business. Now, how many wives do we have here? Let's see now. One ... two ... three ...'

'There are seventeen.' Gorran broke in upon the pay sergeant's slow and laborious method of counting.

'I'm obliged to you, sir, but I need to count 'em for meself. It says so in orders – and I'll want to see wedding certificates from all you ladies before anyone's entered on the regimental roll. It's the army's money that will be spent on you. What goes to you can't be spent on soldiers who are out in Spain and Portugal, fighting a war. Now, where was I? One ... two ... Keep that child quiet, missus. Otherwise we're going to be here all day. One ... two ...'

Not until the pay sergeant succeeded in counting the women not once but twice did he declare his satisfaction. Then, tantalisingly slowly, he began tearing a piece of paper into seventeen parts. On six he wrote 'To go'. On the other eleven were the words every wife dreaded reading on her chosen slip of paper ... 'Not to go'.

After carefully folding each completed slip of paper and placing it on the desk in front of him with an irritating absence of any sense of urgency, the pay sergeant scooped them all up in his hands and dropped them into an upturned shako.

Shaking the hat with great gusto, the pay sergeant held it at shoulder height and looked about the room. 'All right, who's the wife of the senior non-commissioned officer?'

The women made way for Rose Tonks. Looking down at the pay sergeant, she plunged her hand inside the hat. As she rummaged among the folded slips, she glared down at the pay sergeant and said, 'Heaven help you if I draw a "Not to go", Sergeant Jarrett. I'll cut you into little pieces and feed you to Colonel Hinde's dog.'

'Now that's no way to talk to me, Rose. It's a fair draw. Everyone has the same chance.'

There were some women in the room who seemed not to be convinced of Pay Sergeant Jarrett's words. When Rose chose her piece of paper, read it, and held it in the air triumphantly, there were murmurs of disbelief. One woman close to Cassie grumbled, 'It'll be a miracle if she were ever to pick out a "Not to go". He has the nerve to tell us it's a "fair" draw.'

Such protests were low-voiced and passed unheeded. Next in seniority was Sarah Cottle, as wife of a corporal. Her success was greeted with a much more audible outcry that was not entirely due to her unpopularity. Two places had now been taken, leaving only four for the remaining fifteen women. The odds against them had lengthened considerably.

The next six women drew 'Not to go' slips and their anguish was echoed by the cries of their children, bewildered and frightened at their mothers' tears.

The next two women were successful. Now there were seven women left, Cassie among them, and only two places remaining. Cassie was the last to draw and as wife after wife drew a 'Not to go' ticket, her hopes soared. Then, with three wives to draw and two 'To go' slips left in the hat, another wife was successful.

Now the remaining place would go to either Cassie or Polly Martin. Neither dared look at the other as with a trembling hand Polly pulled a slip of paper from the hat. Opening it, she looked at the writing, and then thrust the paper towards Cassie.

'Tell me . . . please. I can't read.'

Cassie looked at the words on the small piece of paper. For a moment it seemed the whole room swung about her.

'It's a "To go" ticket. You're going with your husband, Polly. That means . . . I'm not.'

Polly hugged her youngest child to her, heedless of its squealing protest. Mouthing words of thanks to the God who had answered her prayers, she reached out and took the precious piece of paper from Cassie's hand.

'I'm sorry you didn't get a place, but I had to go. I just had to . . .'

Cassie could only nod speechlessly. She had never considered the possibility that she would not go to the Peninsula with Harry and the regiment. She did not know what she could do now. She would not go home to Mevagissey.

As the pay sergeant was calling for the women with the 'To go' tickets to come forward with their names and proof of marriage, Cassie turned away and walked disconsolately from the office.

Gorran caught up with her outside. 'Are you going to be all right, Cassie?'

When she nodded her head without speaking, Gorran said, 'It is very disappointing for you, but it's probably all for the best, you know. War is a ghastly thing for a woman to witness – and you're hardly even a woman yet.'

When Cassie still made no reply, he said gently, 'Go home to Mevagissey, Cassie. Wait for your husband there.'

'I'm *not* going home.'

Cassie would not return to face the scorn of her friends. She had no illusion about the interpretation they would put upon the facts. According to them, Harry had learned she was pregnant – and promptly ran away to join the army. Cassie had pursued him to force him to marry her and so enable her to escape the wrath of the law. She had succeeded – only to have him abandon her to her own resources when the ceremony was over. That was what they would say. Cassie's pride would not allow such stories to hurt her family. She would rather fend for herself.

'Are you coming to Portsmouth with us? Most of the wives will come to see their husbands embark.'

Cassie nodded. It would delay the decision on her fate for a few more days, at least.

'I'll speak to you again before embarkation. I'd like to give you a letter to take to my parents. They have quite a large house and will be able to find employment for you, Cassie. They also keep up to date with the latest news of what's happening to the regiment. You'll be independent of your family, yet close enough to turn to them if you change your mind about needing help from them. It will be far better than trying to make a life for yourself in a strange place, far from Cornwall. Think about it, Cassie, and we'll talk more about it later. Now I have to speak to the other unsuccessful wives.'

When Gorran returned to the office, Cassie walked slowly in the direction of the barrack room. Her first thought was to refuse his undoubtedly generous gesture. Yet she was sensible enough to realise this was a foolishly stubborn reaction. A return to Cornwall might seem an admission of defeat, even though she was not returning home, but in her heart she knew Gorran was right. Trying to make her way in the world among uncaring strangers would be very difficult indeed, especially with a baby in the offing.

If all the Fox family were as nice as Gorran she knew she would be able to trust them to help her. It was a most generous offer. She wondered why he should care what happened to her. Perhaps he took a similar interest in all the families of the soldiers under his command.

On the parade ground the soldiers were being put through their drill. Cassie saw the company of the 32nd Regiment soldiers forming a square in the centre of the parade ground. Soon their knowledge would be put to the test and Harry would be fighting a war without her support.

7

❧

The march from Horsham to Portsmouth took two days. Veterans of the regiment scornfully declared they had marched as many miles in a day while on a campaign. Cassie found it quite far enough and she was glad they had the supply wagons with them to slow the pace down.

The company of the 32nd Regiment were not the only soldiers on the move. Recruits and replacements for many other regiments were on the road to Portsmouth, including a whole regiment of dragoons. The infantrymen moved off the road and the cavalry passed through, mocking soldiers who went to war on their own two feet as they trotted past, saddles creaking and accoutrements of horse and rider jangling like a myriad of small bells. Cassie wondered whether Lieutenant Dalhousie was among them but there were far too many riders to pick out any individual, and the plumed helmets did much to hide their faces.

Cassie saw little of Harry on the march. The fever of Sam, Polly Martin's infant son, had worsened and more than once the young mother was forced to stop by the roadside to tend him before hurrying to catch up with the others. Cassie helped by taking care of young Jean Martin. The three-year-old girl was a seasoned campaigner and rarely complained. Only occasionally would her short legs tire. Whenever this happened Cassie was obliged to carry her for a while.

At noon on the first day the men halted for two hours at the edge of a strip of woodland. Those wives who had marched with their men before had hurried ahead and were waiting with fires burning and pots boiling by the time the soldiers arrived.

Rose Tonks had boiled water in a huge pot that looked as though it had survived a great many campaigns. She called Cassie to her when she reached the stopping place with Jean in her arms. 'Come on over here, there's plenty of water for you to make tea for that young husband of yours. Enough for Polly, too,' she added as the tired woman trudged into camp clutching her small son to her. 'How is the boy?'

'He's as hot as a blacksmith's furnace.' Polly looked pale and haggard. Young Sam had kept her awake for much of the night and his condition today worried her greatly.

Rose laid a large but gentle hand on the small boy's forehead. When she removed it she shook her head and made a clucking sound with her tongue. 'You're quite right. If he's no better when we stop for the night you'd better have a surgeon take a look at him. There's

79

one travelling with the men of the Irish regiment.'

Polly nodded miserably. The last thing she wanted right now was a sick child. Laying him on the grass, away from the heat of the fire, she prepared tea for her husband and Cassie did the same. Cassie had also brought along a loaf of newly baked bread and some cheese, which she and Harry shared with the worried Martin family.

Private Enoch Martin was a large, good-natured and slow-thinking countryman of infinite patience. He was greatly distressed by his son's condition, but declared stolidly, 'He'll be all right, don't you worry, Polly. We Martins are tough.'

There was some justification for his statement. In the closing stages of Lord Wellington's first Peninsular campaign he had suffered a serious wound that should have killed him. Not only did he survive, but six months later he was fighting with the regiment at Walcheren.

While they were seated around Rose's fire, Gorran rode up. After greeting the sergeant's wife he smiled down at Cassie. 'How are you enjoying marching with the Thirty-second?'

Rose answered for Cassie. 'She'll make a soldier's wife – but we have a very sick youngster travelling with us. Is there a chance of finding a space on one of the wagons for Sam Martin and his mother?'

'How sick is he?' Gorran looked concerned.

'Bad enough to need a surgeon to look at him when we stop for the night.'

Gorran knew Rose sufficiently well to accept she was not exaggerating. To Polly he said, 'Go and find the wagon that's carrying tents for the headquarters' staff.

It should be reasonably soft riding in the back. Tell the driver he's to make room for you and the boy.'

As Gorran turned his horse to ride away, Cassie asked, 'Will we have long at Portsmouth before it's time for the men to sail?'

'No time at all, I'm afraid. The Thirty-second is leaving before the others. We're to be at Portsmouth in time to board a seventy-four-gun warship late tomorrow afternoon. It will sail on the night tide. I'm sorry, Cassie.'

Not looking to see how Harry had taken the news, Cassie could only nod unhappily.

That night the main body of the army travelling to Portsmouth camped on the South Downs, close to the small village of Singleton. The sudden arrival of more than two thousand soldiers put a great strain on all local resources. Most villagers simply locked their doors, bolted the shutters and sat tight, waiting for the soldiers to move on. In spite of the lack of co-operation, Gorran Fox accommodated the hundred men of the 32nd Regiment and the fifteen wives travelling with them in a large barn on the outskirts of the village. The single men occupied the ground floor while families bedded down in the hay loft above them. The barn was also home for a flock of doves, numerous chickens and an unknown number of rats, yet Cassie thought its spaciousness was infinitely preferable to the cramped barrack room she had left that morning.

Cassie and Polly Martin shared Rose Tonks's huge cooking pot once more for the evening meal. Cassie contributed a chicken and an assortment of vegetables, purchased from the farmer's wife with some of the money given to her by the coach passengers.

It would have been a pleasant meal had the Irish surgeon not arrived accompanied by Gorran while they sat around eating.

The surgeon examined Sam, then stood back, his expression grave. 'I wouldn't like to say for certain, but it looks mighty like typhoid to me.'

'Can't you be more certain?' Gorran was alarmed. If typhoid broke out among his men it would cause havoc on board the ship they took passage in. It might even be passed on to the army in the Peninsula.

'I wish I could. I've heard of no cases at Horsham lately, but it's one of those diseases that seems to occur when you're least expecting it.'

'Surely there must be some way of telling?'

'In a child of this age ... ?' The surgeon shook his head. 'I'll bleed him a little for now, then come back and see him in the morning – if he survives that long.'

The families spent a sleepless night on what for many of them was to be their last time together. Sam Martin cried for most of it and he constantly called for water, complaining that his skin was burning.

In an attempt to spend the night with Harry without fear of interruption, Cassie managed to find a quiet corner of the hay loft, separated from the others by a wooden partition. Unfortunately, no sooner had they settled down than it began to rain. They quickly discovered that, although their spot might have been reasonably private, it was most certainly not weatherproof. A number of tiles were missing from the ancient roof and rain poured in upon them.

Eventually they were forced to move to a less secluded

but drier spot – and it was now that Polly Martin chose to bring Jean to them once more. Demanding attention and unable to receive it from her mother, the little girl was screaming in temper and it took Cassie more than an hour to quieten her.

Lying with the fretful child between them, Cassie and Harry could only express their frustration with a touch, a squeezed hand, and a whispered word.

The rain cleared before dawn, much to the relief of the men of the 32nd, who were on the road before the sun rose. They and a squadron of dragoons were the only troops embarking on the seventy-four-gun man-of-war. The remainder of the reinforcements would proceed at a more leisurely pace to take passage on transports during the course of the next week or so.

Before his company took to the road, Gorran Fox sent Sergeant Tonks to rouse the Irish surgeon. He wanted him to re-examine young Sam Martin before moving off. The surgeon arrived showing every indication of having dressed hurriedly in the dark and his temper matched his appearance. However, he gave the small boy a thorough examination and when he stood up from Sam's straw bed, the surgeon's expression was grim.

Taking him to one side, away from the women, Gorran asked, 'Well, sir? Have you been able to make a diagnosis? Is it typhoid?'

'I still can't tell – and won't be able to for at least another twenty-four hours. All I can say with certainty is that the lad is extremely sick. He has a high temperature – a *very* high temperature. But typhoid? I just don't know.'

83

'That isn't good enough, sir. The health of my company, perhaps the health of the whole army in Spain, depends upon your diagnosis. I must have your considered opinion. How likely is it that the boy is suffering from typhoid?' Gorran gave the surgeon no room to prevaricate. He wanted an answer to his question – and he wanted it now.

'There's a one-in-five chance that he has scarlet fever – a child's disease.'

'And the other four chances?'

'Typhoid.'

Thank you, surgeon. You've decided the course of action I must take.'

Still inside the barn, Gorran returned to the women gathered anxiously about the sick boy, and Polly Martin was the first to speak. 'What's he say, Mr Fox, sir? Sam's going to be all right, ain't he? By tonight his temperature will have dropped, I'm sure of it.'

'I'm sorry, Polly. The surgeon's almost certain the boy's suffering from typhoid fever. He says it should be evident within twenty-four hours whether it is typhoid, or whether it's scarlet fever. I can't give you twenty-four hours. We sail for the Peninsula in twelve and my first concern has to be for the health of my men. I have no option but to cancel your ticket to go with the regiment.'

The wail that rose from Polly's throat sent a chill through even the most battle-hardened of the men and women who heard it. It was followed by a bout of heart-rending sobbing that was muffled as Rose Tonks's great arms went about the young mother and drew her in close.

Above Polly's head the sergeant's wife nodded reassuringly at Gorran. 'She'll be all right in a minute or two, sir. Just leave her with me for a while and tell my Elijah I'll catch up with the regiment before you embark at Portsmouth.'

Gorran fumbled inside his waistband and pulled out a small money bag. Emptying a quantity of gold coins into his hand he passed them to Rose. 'Give her these. They should see her and the children safely home. I'll fall-out her husband and allow him to remain with her for an hour, but be certain he comes back with you.'

As Cassie moved towards the still sobbing woman to add her support, Gorran brought her to a halt with his next words. 'Cassie, the last "To go" ticket was decided between you and Polly Martin. Now she's been prevented from going the place is yours. I'll inform the pay sergeant. See him and complete all the necessary formalities before going on board the warship.'

Cassie was overcome with joy at his words. She felt she ought to rush off and find Harry, to share the wonderful news with him. The joy changed almost immediately to remorse. Her happiness had been brought about by little Sam's illness.

'I'll be ready to move off with the regiment – but I'd like to speak with Polly first.'

The men of the 32nd Regiment completed their embarkation on the warship *Terrible* in good order a full hour before the ship was due to sail, and before the squadron of dragoons had put in an appearance.

The cavalrymen arrived twenty minutes before the ship

was due to sail and their embarkation was accompanied by the utmost confusion. After an hour and a half the master of the vessel was pacing the quarter deck roaring that if they hadn't completed boarding in another half an hour he was setting sail, even if it meant leaving most of the cavalry stranded on the quayside.

There was no need to carry out his threat. By the time the deadline was reached the sailors of the heavily laden man-of-war were coiling the mooring ropes on deck and the ship was heeling over to catch the wind that would carry her into the open sea, and the war in the Peninsula.

Conditions in the army barracks at Horsham had been primitive, but those encountered on board the man-of-war were appalling. The hundred men and six women of the 32nd Regiment were lodged between decks together with the hundred men of the dragoons, who had no women with them.

While the ship had been in Portsmouth the dockyard carpenters had installed rough bunks to accommodate the soldiers but they had erected only one hundred, not the two hundred required. In a space where a tall man needed to stoop, the bunks had been put up in tiers of three and were occupied regardless of sex, or rank.

Hammocks had been slung between the bunks for the extra hundred men. Unfortunately, the soldiers lacked the sailors' skill in slinging hammocks. They hung so loosely that when a man was in one of them he was bent almost double, his backside close to the deck. Consequently, the only way to move around the mess deck at night was by crawling between, or over, the bunks.

One of the dragoon NCOs, angry that the infantrymen

had arrived earlier and claimed the bunks, complained to his commanding officer about conditions. The result was that soon after sailing a dragoon officer came below decks to inspect the accommodation.

As soon as he entered the mess deck a cry went up for the men present to 'Stand to attention, officer present.' The order provoked an outburst of derisive laughter. It would have been impossible to stand to attention in the crowded quarters had King George himself been present.

Cassie paid little attention to the order. She and Harry were sharing a middle bunk with all Harry's army equipment and her belongings, in a space that was no more than two feet wide. She was arranging their things around the bunk when she heard the sound of heavy boots along the narrow gangway. As she drew in her legs from the gangway she looked up and found herself staring into the face of Lieutenant Dalhousie, the cavalry officer she had encountered at the inn *en route* to Horsham.

He recognised her immediately. 'Well, well! If it isn't the little country girl. Where's your protector now? He was an infantry officer, as I remember?'

'Mr Fox is commanding officer of this company – and I'm here with my husband.' Cassie nodded towards Harry who stood pressed against the bulkhead behind her, listening to the conversation with a puzzled expression. She had not told him of the incident inside the inn.

Lieutenant Dalhousie did not trouble himself to look in Harry's direction. 'Such a pity. I might have been able to find you rather more comfortable quarters than this.' Inclining his head to her, the dragoon officer passed on his way, leaving Cassie to explain to Harry what the officer had been talking about.

'He's got a nerve!' said Harry angrily. 'And he spoke to you as though I wasn't here.'

'Take no notice of him, Harry.' Cassie folded the clothes that would also serve as a pillow. 'Mr Fox said that all cavalry officers think they're irresistible to women. Mr Dalhousie doesn't seem to be any different.'

Harry was still frowning when he went to answer an order to parade on the upper deck, but Cassie was not sure whether it was because of Lieutenant Dalhousie or her mention of Gorran. She wondered whether her husband cared to be reminded that she had travelled from Cornwall to Sussex in the company of the young lieutenant.

Conditions on board the crowded man-of-war deteriorated rapidly when the vessel drew clear of the shelter afforded by land and butted its way into the choppy waters of the English Channel.

At first the soldiers and wives found it hilarious to watch the antics of others as they tried to maintain their balance on the heaving decks of the warship, but the joke quickly wore thin. When Lieutenant Fox came to inspect the quarters allocated to his soldiers there was little merriment and the stomachs of the soldiers were beginning to rebel against the unceasing movement of the sea.

Gorran also stopped at Cassie's bunk but, unlike the cavalry officer, he acknowledged the presence of Harry Clymo before speaking to Cassie. 'I warned you you'd find little comfort in life as the wife of a serving soldier.'

'We'll make out all right,' declared Cassie. At least she did not feel sea-sick. She had made so many trips in her father's fishing-boat she was used to the motion of the sea.

'Do you know Mr Dalhousie is on board?' Cassie thought there was a warning in Gorran's voice.

'He came around here a while ago and stopped to speak to me.'

'Cassie told me of what happened at the inn when you was kindly helping her to find her way to Horsham. I'm grateful to you, sir.' It was quite a speech from Harry and the first time he had said more than 'yes, sir' or 'no, sir' to the lieutenant.

'Mr Dalhousie intended no offence, I'm sure. It was no more than high spirits. But it seems cavalrymen are more used to comfort than the infantry. His men have complained that the quarters here are cramped. Unfortunately, nothing can be done to make them any roomier. Everyone on board is having to make sacrifices, including the man-o'-war's crew. This mess deck has been taken from them. However, in order to ease the conditions down here the men and women will be divided into four groups. Each will spend four hours on the upper deck during daylight hours. Sergeant Tonks will detail you off into the groups. I wish I could tell you it was going to be a pleasant voyage, but the captain tells me the barometer is falling. It means the weather is likely to become worse before there's any improvement.'

Many of the soldiers in the crowded mess deck were

listening to Gorran Fox's words and they groaned. Some had been on troop decks before and had experienced the abominable conditions caused by bad weather. Others were already feeling ill. They tried not to think of what might happen if they encountered really bad weather.

When Gorran moved off to speak to his sergeant, Harry began carefully folding his uniform jacket and placing it on the bed. Without looking up at Cassie, he said, 'Mr Fox has a fondness for you.'

'We were both involved in the coach accident in Cornwall, that's all. I told you all about it.'

'Corporal Cottle says his wife travelled all the way from Scotland on a coach with a captain of the Thirty-second at one time, yet he wouldn't speak to *her* when they met up in barracks afterwards.'

'Knowing Sarah Cottle as I do there would have been a good reason for the captain not talking to her . . .' Rose Tonks had heard Harry's words as she approached. Brushing aside the neatly folded uniform jacket, she squeezed her bulk to a sitting position on the centre bunk and the wooden frame complained alarmingly. 'Besides, if anything turned over on Sarah Cottle and the captain you're talking about it would have been a bed, not a coach – and she didn't save anyone. Cassie did. She also bound up Mr Fox's arm so that the surgeon thought it must have been done by a medical man.'

Putting a big arm about Cassie's shoulders, the sergeant's wife said, 'That's why Mr Fox pays your Cassie special attention. He told my Elijah that she'll prove herself a credit to the regiment. You're a lucky man, young Harry. There's more than one NCO owes his promotion to a wife – and I don't mean in the same way Sarah Cottle got her husband made corporal, neither.'

Struggling to her feet in the cramped surroundings, Rose said, 'Come on, Cassie, it's time we went to fetch tea for the men, not that many of them will want it. If you've got a strong stomach you'll be able to gorge yourself like a pig for the next few days. The very smell of food will have this lot bowing to King Neptune over the ship's side.'

Rose was proved uncomfortably correct. The weather worsened during the night and it was blowing a full gale by morning. With only a tiny area of sail raised to keep the ship manoeuvrable, the man-of-war wallowed along with a stomach-churning motion.

Because no more than a quarter of the passengers were allowed on the upper deck at any one time, the living quarters became almost untenable. The movement of the sea did not trouble Cassie, but the stench of the mess deck did. She became as ill as everyone else and could only eat when she was on deck in the fresh air.

These conditions lasted until Cassie believed she could not survive for another twenty-four hours. Then, when the ship changed course to skirt the notoriously rough Bay of Biscay, the weather improved dramatically. Suddenly the wind was little more than a pleasant breeze, the sea ceased its assault on the wooden ship, and life became bearable once more.

After sea water had been pumped inboard and the mess decks thoroughly washed and cleaned, life took on a much more agreeable aspect. It became warmer too, and sitting lazing in the sun was an unaccustomed luxury for the soldiers and their wives.

During the first evening of good weather, the crew and passengers combined to put on an impromptu concert. Everyone was allowed on deck and the sailors clung to the rigging, or sat precariously on the yard-arms to watch the proceedings.

As the sun eased slowly into the sea on the western horizon the 'stage' was illuminated by an array of gently swaying lanterns. A sailors' choir was followed by solo singers, barefooted sailor dances, coarse but funny comedians, and performances of half-remembered sketches from the continents and oceans of the world.

One surprise was the singing of Sarah Cottle. The corporal's wife had a beautiful soprano voice and the audience was reluctant to have her leave the stage. When she declared she would sing an aria from one of Handel's operas, a man called from the audience, asking that he be permitted to sing a duet with her. It was Lieutenant Dalhousie. The dragoon officer had a fine baritone voice and he sang two duets before relinquishing the stage to Sarah once more.

It was an evening that left Cassie with a memory that would remain with her for ever – almost enough to compensate for the misery of the early days of the voyage. Cassie was sorry when it came to an end. It had been a magical few hours.

As everyone jostled to reach the hatchways leading

to the lower decks, she braced herself to face the crowded mess deck. There had been no cases of cholera yet on the overcrowded ship, but there had been an uncomfortable increase in the number of lice and bed-bugs in the sleeping quarters. Cassie had tried very hard to keep her bed space clear of the tormenting insects, but it was quite impossible in the prevailing overcrowded conditions.

There was one more surprise waiting for her tonight. As she and Harry were swept along with the crowd, Harry took her elbow, steering her clear of the others and heading for the deserted stern of the man-of-war.

'Where are you taking me?' Cassie was puzzled.

'Wait and see.'

It was all Harry would say as he battled against the tide of happily chattering soldiers, exhilarated by the concert, their days of miserable discomfort temporarily forgotten.

Eventually Harry brought Cassie to a halt before the outline of a canvas-covered ship's boat, raised on blocks on the deck. When Cassie turned her face up to his for an explanation, he said, 'The ship's master spoke to me today. He's a Cornishman and recognised my accent. We got to talking and I told him about you and me. How we was married only a couple of days before coming on board. He said a crowded mess deck was no place for a newly wed couple. He said we could sleep in the boat here, if we'd a mind. I brought our blankets up earlier, without you knowing. It's not much . . . but it's better than sharing a bunk down below.'

Harry spoke apologetically, but Cassie silenced him

with a kiss. 'It's a wonderful idea, Harry. You're very, very clever. With just the two of us and no one else around I'll feel we're really married.'

Cassie had been suffering pangs of guilt about the physical side of her marriage to Harry. Since Sarah Cottle and Ned Harrup had spoiled their wedding night they had spent no time alone and Cassie could not give herself wholeheartedly to lovemaking with so many others in close proximity. She knew other wives were not so inhibited. Indeed, their lovemaking was often the subject of ribald comments the following morning. But Cassie had not yet come to terms with the total lack of privacy afforded a married soldier and his wife, and the baby inside her belly did not help.

Harry had been very patient with her and now Cassie squeezed his arm affectionately. 'It'll be just like being at home in Mevagissey ... do you remember, Harry?'

They had never made love in comfortable circumstances before Harry ran off to join the army but compared with the army it had been idyllic.

Mevagissey seemed very far away in both distance and time. Almost as though it formed part of another life in another world. For the first time for many nights Cassie found herself wondering about her parents ... her sisters.

'Are you sure it's what you want?' Harry became concerned about her sudden silence.

'Of course. Come on, let's go to bed.'

For the second time in Harry and Cassie's brief married life Sarah Cottle came close to ruining their plans.

Cuddling close beneath their blankets, trying to pretend the boards of the boat were not uncomfortable beneath them, the young couple heard the sound of footsteps and hushed voices. Suddenly there was a bump against the side of the boat. Moments later they heard the sound of heavy breathing before Sarah's voice said quickly, 'No! Not here.'

Both Harry and Cassie held their breath and for a moment Cassie wondered whether the corporal's wife would also think of the ship's boat as a possible place to make love away from prying eyes. She thought that Ned Harrup was perhaps being given a chance to make up for his poor showing on the night of their wedding.

However, although Sarah might be prepared to bed down with anyone in a soldier's barracks, on board a crowded ship with only five other women, she could afford to be far more selective.

'I share a cabin but I'll have my companion move out for tonight.'

It was the voice of Lieutenant Dalhousie! It seemed he had plans to extend his duet with Sarah beyond a song.

'He'll need to be gone before I come to your cabin. I've my reputation to think of . . .'

'Of course.'

For a minute or so the voices were silenced and there was the sound of more heavy breathing. Then Lieutenant Dalhousie's voice, husky with anticipation, said, 'Wait for me by the hatchway that leads to the officers' quarters. It's on the far side of the ship, by the quarterdeck. I'll be gone no more than a minute or two.'

The sound of voices moved away from the boat and Cassie relaxed in Harry's arms once more. Another few minutes and the amoral corporal's wife and her latest lover were forgotten.

Later, as she lay beside her contented and gently snoring husband, Cassie's thoughts returned to the conversation she and Harry had overheard. She had a strong feeling the liaison with Sarah Cottle would bring trouble to the dashing young cavalry officer.

8

❦

Nine days after setting sail from Portsmouth, the man-of-war carrying the men and wives of the 32nd Regiment dropped anchor in Figueira Bay, at the mouth of the Mondego River. It was early morning and there had been a storm during the night hours.

The sea was still rough and the ship tugged at its anchor chain in the manner of a large and boisterous puppy introduced to a leash for the first time. The shore was no more than a quarter of a mile away and looking out from the ship Cassie could see the surf crashing against the shore with an ominous rumble and an eruption of foaming spray.

'Looks beautiful, don't it? All that sand and sun on the beach.' Sarah Cottle had come up unnoticed. The soldiers were below decks, checking and cleaning their muskets. 'And it is beautiful. I remember it all from the last time I was here. Sunshine, fruit and wine, and suntanned men. But there's a war going on too. With men killing each other.'

It was the first time Sarah had ever spoken directly to Cassie and her words came as a surprise.

'Why did you want to come on the campaign if you hate war so much?'

'Did I say I hated war? Oh, no, there's something exciting about a battle. Our bugles, the Frenchies' drums, gunfire and shouting, men and animals all over the place. It makes you want to shout yourself hoarse and you wish you could be fighting with 'em. Oh, yes, it's exciting right enough. Trouble is . . . it's such a waste of good men. Do you know I lost two men in battle before I married Walter Cottle? One was my husband, all proper. The other died before we could find a padre.'

'It must have been awful for you, Sarah. I'm sorry.' Cassie had a sudden feeling that she was in need of words of comfort.

The other woman shrugged. 'There's no reason why anyone should feel sorry for me. Neither of 'em amounted to very much. Walter's worth more than both of 'em put together – and he's nothing special.'

The reply bewildered Cassie. 'But . . . if you don't care very much for your husband, why have you come here on the campaign?'

'There's your answer, love.' Sarah inclined her head shorewards. 'New places . . . new men . . . excitement. I might even end the campaign married to someone else. You'll come across women who've been married four, five, six times . . . or even more. It's the only thing to do if your man gets killed, you take it from me. You

98

need a man to look after you out here. If you haven't got one you're taken off the strength of the regiment and get no rations, nor any consideration, neither. If your man gets killed the only thing to do is look around for someone else – and quick. Better still, pick one out before anything happens to the one you've got, and make sure you pick one with a bit of rank. A corporal – or sergeant even. I've even known girls manage to find an officer to look after 'em – though I've never heard of a battlefield widow marrying one.'

She gave Cassie a sidelong glance. 'But I don't think I need tell you what you should do. The way Mr Fox looks at you you'd only need crook your little finger to have him come running after you.'

'That isn't true!' Cassie flushed angrily. 'Mr Fox and me travelled to Horsham on the same coach from Cornwall, that's all.'

'That's not what I've heard.' Sarah shrugged. 'But it's none of my business. All I'm interested in is getting ashore, though by the look of that surf it's going to be days before we come any closer to the war.'

Sarah Cottle was wrong. A dispatch boat from England was waiting for the larger vessel in Figueira Bay. The warship was ordered to proceed to join a small British fleet cruising off the coast of Naples. There was a prospect of action – and action carried with it the twin rewards of promotion and prize-money. The captain of the man-of-war warned his military passengers to make ready for immediate disembarkation.

The deck of the warship soon resembled a summer

fair and horse market. As soldiers mustered on the heaving upper deck the horses were hoisted up from the lower decks. Here, according to grumbling sailors, the horses had been accommodated 'better than anyone except the captain himself'.

The horses might have enjoyed excellent accommodation but they had spent ten days shut up without exercise and each animal was thoroughly bad-tempered. More than one sailor was kicked as he tried to detach a sling, and many of the horses showed dangerous exuberation when they encountered sunshine and fresh air once more. On a number of occasions, seamen, soldiers and equipment were scattered in every direction.

Meanwhile the boat that had provided a private bedroom for Cassie and Harry had gone ashore with an officer whose orders were to hire local boats and boatmen to assist in carrying soldiers, horses and equipment to the shore. Watching the boat riding the breakers to crash heavily on the beach, Cassie realised that only the skill and hard work of the sailors prevented it from up-ending and spilling its occupants in the cold, green waters of the Atlantic Ocean.

Soon there was a motley collection of boats clustered around the bulbous wooden sides of the British man-of-war, but nothing had been found large enough to carry the horses. There was nothing for it but to swim them ashore, secured behind the boats. Now the slings were brought into use once again, causing more injuries to the long-suffering sailors. The horses were swung over the side and lowered into the water, each boat being expected to tow two horses to the shore.

The arrangement caused chaos! Once in the breakers horses were often swept past the boats to which they were attached. The instant a horse's hooves touched firm sand its sole object was to reach the safety of dry land as speedily as possible. If the boat was still riding the waves this had disastrous results. The boat would be pulled around, broadside on to the heavy swell. Carried in to the beach in this fashion it invariably spilled occupants and cargo into the water.

Fortunately there were many willing helpers on the beach to grab the floundering soldiers and drag them ashore. Most were large, laughing Portuguese women who were thoroughly enjoying this diversion from their daily chores.

There were others who were interested only in pilfering any item of value that they could snatch from the water. In the main these were small boys who would stuff the stolen item beneath a ragged shirt and run from the scene as though they had a devil after them.

Cassie went ashore in a small boat just large enough to carry the six army wives and a half-dozen soldiers. Harry was not among them. There were only two Portuguese men rowing the boat. Brown, muscled men, stripped to the waist, they had Sarah Cottle drooling over them. Nudging Cassie who was seated next to her on the boat's rough wooden seat, she whispered, 'There! Didn't I tell you about the Portuguese men? Have you ever seen such a glorious tan? And those muscles . . . !'

Unfortunately, the muscles of the two Portuguese sailors proved insufficient to prevent a disaster. They towed the obligatory two horses behind them, but the horses seemed intent on landing at a different spot from the one chosen by the sailors. True, the spot towards which the horses were heading was closer than the other but it was guarded by a great many rocks, which were alternately exposed and then covered by the breakers.

The captain of the man-of-war had chosen his time for disembarkation badly. The tide was rising and the breakers were increasing in both size and unpredictability, but it was the tide which ultimately decided the fate of the boat on which Cassie was a passenger.

As the small boat neared the shore the two Portuguese boatmen began speaking to each other in increasingly excited voices. It was evident to everyone they were well off course, the tide favouring the horses' chosen course rather than their own. Suddenly, when they were still many yards from the shore the swell lifted the boat, turned it sideways, and began carrying it shorewards at an alarming speed.

'We're heading for the rocks ...'

A scream went up from one of the women as the Portuguese boatmen strained fruitlessly at the oars. A cry went up for someone to cut the horses free, but it was too late. The bottom of the boat struck an unseen rock and the sound of splintering wood carried to the horrified watchers onshore.

Cassie saw the planking of the boat split wide open as a black, glistening, sharp-pointed rock penetrated the hull. Then the whole world turned topsy-turvy and she was thrown into the sea. It seemed to Cassie she was underwater for a frighteningly long time, although it was probably no more than twenty seconds. Then her head rose above water but even as she took a deep breath, gulping in both sea air and water, she was flung against a rock and pain surged through her whole body. Moments later the sea sucked her away from the rock, only to throw her back to it again as though she was a scrap of flotsam. This time she struck her head and remembered no more ...

It was more usual for troops and stores to be landed at Lisbon, a hundred miles to the south, but the war was being fought on more than one front against the French forces occupying Spain. The 32nd Regiment was part of the army's 6th Division, currently advancing upon the heavily fortified Spanish town of Ciudad Rodrigo, known to the troops simply as Rodrigo. By landing ammunition and reinforcements at the mouth of the Mondego River many days could be saved that would otherwise have been wasted at sea, and men and supplies were a hundred and fifty miles closer to their destination.

Gorran Fox had been in the first boat to land on the beach. It was his task to hire as many carts and wagons as were available, to carry his stores and equipment, together with a large amount of powder and ammunition being brought ashore for the whole regiment. His orders were to ensure the powder and shot reached its destination safely and the squadron of dragoons was to provide an additional escort. He watched in consternation as the small boat was carried off course on its way to shore. He was aware that Cassie and the other wives were on board and the knowledge added to his concern.

From the ship, waiting to board a boat, Harry also watched, helpless to take any part in the drama unfolding close inshore. It was soon apparent that the boat was being carried well away from the safe beach and would come ashore amid the rocks at the northern end of the beach. Calling for all the soldiers working nearby to stop what they were doing and come with him, Gorran ran towards the scene of the impending disaster.

He was still some distance away when the boat struck the rocks and its occupants were thrown into the sea. He sprinted faster, not pausing when he reached the water's edge. Floundering into the water, he narrowly escaped being struck by the wrecked boat. Now empty, it gyrated wildly in the surf, prevented from being driven ashore by the ropes attached to the two horses, both trapped among the rocks.

One of the soldiers from the boat, unable to swim, struggled feebly among the breakers. Grabbing the man's cross-belts, Gorran heaved him to the safety of shallow water before plunging back into the sea once more.

Sarah Cottle struggled to the shore and collapsed on the sand, choking and retching. Behind her Rose Tonks rose from the water like a surfacing walrus, towing an unconscious soldier behind her.

A woman floated face down in the water and Gorran struck out towards her. 'Cassie . . . ?'

It was not Cassie but another soldier's wife and she had an ugly wound spilling blood from the back of her head. He towed her back towards the shore where one of the strong Portuguese women took her from him.

Returning once more to deeper water, Gorran was no

longer alone: English soldiers, Portuguese women – and Rose – were also here.

It was the sergeant's wife who located Cassie. She had been thrown between two rocks and one more wave would have washed her out to sea. 'Here . . . help me!' Rose was herself being battered against the barnacle-encrusted rocks as she struggled to free Cassie. Gorran reached her at the same time as a Portuguese woman and between them they managed to drag Cassie to the shore.

She was badly scratched on one side of her face and was unconscious, but putting her ear to Cassie's breast, Rose listened intently for perhaps a minute before raising her head and saying with considerable relief, 'Her heart's beating as strong as a blacksmith's hammer. We'll save her.'

Cassie was more fortunate than some. The woman pulled from the water by Gorran died within an hour. Two soldiers and a Portuguese boatman also died. Nor was that the final total of fatalities that day. A number of boats capsized and although no more men of the 32nd Regiment were lost, five dragoons were drowned, together with two sailors and another Portuguese boatman. In addition, seven of the dragoons' horses were lost, or had to be destroyed.

The captain of the man-of-war succeeded in setting off that same day to rendezvous with the fleet off Naples, but the price paid for his promotion chances was paid for with the blood of British soldiers – and their women.

9

For a long time Cassie had been vaguely aware of strange sounds about her, but she was unable to focus her mind upon them. It was almost as though she was protected from reality by a thick layer of soft down, paring all sound to a bearable level. How long she remained in this state she did not know, but suddenly the memory of being in the water returned to her with cruel clarity. Crying out, she opened her eyes and started up, only to sink back again with a groan. There seemed to be pain in every muscle, in every bone – and the pain in her head was worst of all. It made her want to cry out.

'Don't try to move, lovey. You just lie still. The surgeon says you must have banged your head hard enough to split a rock.'

'That's what it feels like,' Cassie replied to Rose, then closed her eyes again, wincing with pain. She had seen enough to know she was lying beneath a canopy of

106

branches laid across a rough wooden frame. Beyond the canopy it was still day, the light strong enough to aggravate the pain in her head. She felt other pains too . . .

'I'll send someone to tell your Harry you've come round. He's going to be the happiest man in the regiment. My Elijah says he doubts if Harry's heard one in ten of the orders he's been given since your accident.'

'Harry's ashore then?' The pain was causing Cassie to drift away from consciousness once more but she tried desperately to hold on. There was so much she needed to know.

'Ashore . . . ? Of course – how would you know? You've been lying here unconscious since yesterday, lovey. The whole company's ashore, the dragoons, too, and the ship's long gone. By nightfall Mr Fox will have enough wagons to carry the stores and we'll be off at first light tomorrow. At least, some of us will.'

Even in her present confused state Cassie understood the implications of Rose's words. 'I'll be all right by morning. Well enough to travel . . .' Even as she spoke Cassie was forced to bite back a cry and for several moments her body tensed in pain.

'You'll be travelling nowhere in the morning, lovey, nor for a few mornings yet. It isn't only the bang on your head we're all worried about. You see . . . you've lost the baby, too.'

'Oh no!' Cassie's eyes opened wide and filled with tears.

'It's probably for the best, lovey. A campaign's no place for a baby – or a pregnant woman. Most seem to want to give birth in the middle of a battle. You're young enough to have lots more when the time's right.'

Cassie's throbbing head rolled from side to side, her agonised thoughts overriding pain. After all that had happened ... The break with home ... Her flight to Horsham ... The revolting conditions in the barracks ...

'But I *wanted* the baby. We both did. Where's Harry? I want Harry.'

'It's all right, Cassie. You're going to be fine.' Suddenly Harry was beside her, holding her hand tightly.

She opened her eyes and from the depths of her own misery recognised the honest anxiety in his expression. 'I've lost the baby.' She had an overwhelming urge to burst into tears.

'I know, but you're all right. That's all that really matters, Cassie. We can have lots more ... if that's what you'd like. The important thing is for you to get well quickly. I've been some worried about you, Cassie. Last night, after the surgeon came to see you I went down by the sea and prayed for you there, on my knees. I've never prayed for anyone before. Old Preacher Harris in Mevagissey would have been proud of me, Cassie ... and it's worked!'

Embarrassed by his disclosure, Harry looked to see if Rose had heard. The sergeant's wife was peering into her huge cooking pot, stirring the contents. She had apparently heard nothing.

'I know how you'll be feeling right now, Cassie. What with losing the baby an' all. But I don't care about nothing so long as you're going to be all right. I'm some pleased you're married to me.' Harry cast another shy glance in Rose's direction. She was still preoccupied with her cooking pot. 'Those last couple of days on the ship when we had the boat to sleep in have been the happiest of my whole life. I love you, Cassie. I really do.'

This time nothing would stop the tears and they coursed down Cassie's face as she squeezed Harry's hand, far too choked by emotion to speak. She had lost the baby and she was surprised to realise it meant so much to her, but it had brought her and Harry closer to each other.

Cassie drifted into a sleep that verged on unconsciousness. When she next opened her eyes the shelter was in semi-darkness and there was a great deal of noise going on about her. At first Cassie lay still, thinking the soldiers were preparing for bed. However, when she listened more attentively to the orders being shouted she realised it must be morning. The camp was on the move.

Her head felt better this morning – until she tried to sit up. The pain forced her to lie back again immediately. She lay on the blanket feeling foolishly helpless until the huge bulk of Rose Tonks came between Cassie and what little light there was outside the improvised tent.

'Hello, lovey. How you feeling this morning? I've brought you a cup of tea. Thought it might help to cheer you up a bit.'

Cassie protested she was unable to raise her head, but with Rose's muscular arm supporting her shoulders with surprising gentleness, she was able to sit up long enough to drink the tea. Lying back once more, she suggested she would now be fit enough to travel with the men of the 32nd.

Rose shattered her hopes immediately. 'You'll not be fit to go anywhere for at least another week – but here's Mr Fox. He'll tell you. When he's done you can thank him for saving your life. He's the one who went in the sea and pulled you out when we all thought you was drowned.'

Gorran reached the canvas shelter in time to hear Rose's words. Ducking low to come inside, he crouched beside Cassie and spoke to the sergeant's wife. 'This young lady knows all about saving people from drowning. She saved the passengers from an upturned coach in far more difficult circumstances.'

He smiled down at Cassie. 'How are you feeling this morning, young lady? You've given us all a very anxious time.'

'She thinks she's well enough to travel.' Rose spoke before Cassie could reply. 'I told her you'd have something to say about that.'

'I'm afraid Rose is right, Cassie. The surgeon and I have had a long chat about you. He's quite adamant that you shouldn't attempt to travel for at least a week.'

'But Rose says you're all setting off this morning – and I've heard the orders being given to the men. You're moving off. What will I do – and how will I find you again?' The thought of being left behind in this strange country dismayed Cassie.

'Don't worry, Cassie. You're part of the Thirty-second Regiment now and we look after our own, whether it be officer, man or woman. I've found quarters for you

110

in town, they were recommended by the local priest. You'll be in the house of a widow-woman. Unfortunately she speaks no English, but her husband was a Portuguese soldier who died fighting Napoleon's army. You can be certain of having her full sympathy and understanding.'

'How will I find you ... the regiment again, when I'm well?'

'Once again you're in luck. Mr Dalhousie and his dragoons are supposed to be providing an additional escort for the supplies we're taking to the Sixth Division. Unfortunately, his horses haven't recovered from the sea voyage. They won't be fit to travel for at least a week, or possibly ten days. It isn't serious from the army's point of view. The wagons will be travelling through friendly territory for at least a fortnight and we'll be moving so slowly he'll catch up with us in two days – and bring you with him.' Lieutenant Fox had his own opinion about the fitness of Lieutenant Dalhousie's horses. He carried with him a letter appointing him commanding officer of the wagon escort. It was his belief the cavalry officer resented being under the command of an infantryman and had used the condition of the horses to retain independent command of his squadron for as long as possible.

Cassie did not welcome the prospect of spending two days in the company of Lieutenant Dalhousie and his men and she made a last bid to be allowed to go with Harry and the 32nd Regiment.

'Couldn't I travel in one of the carts? I'll not be a nuisance.'

Gorran shook his head. He understood her reasons for wanting to travel with the regiment, but his duty was clear. The ammunition had to reach the 6th Division as soon as was possible. 'I'm sorry, Cassie. My orders are to make the best speed I can with the wagons – and I'd be concerned about you travelling in one of the Portuguese carts. They have solid wheels that I swear are more square than round.'

'I'll stay behind with her.'

The unexpected offer came from Sarah Cottle. In the early-morning gloom no one had seen her come to the camp fire for hot water to add to the half-drunk mug of tea she carried in her hand.

When the others looked in her direction, she shrugged. 'I saw enough battles when I was last in the Peninsula. I'm in no hurry to get to the next one. Besides, I twisted my ankle when I came ashore yesterday. A few days here will give it time to mend. You'll have no fear of Cassie not finding her way to the regiment with me here to help her. I've been following the army for long enough to know what's what. Ain't that so, Rose?'

Rose's sniff was clearer than any words, but she said, 'If anyone knows what's what it's certainly you, Sarah.'

'There you are then, sir. It's all settled. I'll stay with Cassie and bring her along with the cavalry when they're ready to catch you up.'

Cassie suspected Sarah's willingness to be left behind had less to do with her welfare than with the continued presence of Lieutenant Dalhousie in the village. She did not particularly mind. It would be reassuring to have another English woman around – and Sarah's presence

112

would divert Lieutenant Dalhousie's attention away from her.

'I'll leave rations for the two of you for ten days, and a little money. If you need more, borrow it from Mr Dalhousie. I . . . that is, the regiment, will ensure he's repaid.'

'I don't need any money. I still have some. But can I see Harry before you move off, so that he knows exactly what's happening?'

'Of course. I'll send him to you. He can remain behind for an hour or so after we're gone. He'll have no trouble catching up with us again.'

When Gorran had returned to his men and Rose had wandered off to find her husband, Sarah said to Cassie, 'One of the first things you'll learn in the army is never to turn down *anything* that's offered to you – especially when it comes from an officer. He must be really keen on you, that one. I think there's more to you than meets the eye, Cassie Clymo, but you need someone like me around for a while to put you right about a few things.'

Being called by her married name still came as something of a shock to Cassie, but she did not allow the pleasure she felt to cloud her judgement. There were things that needed to be said if Sarah Cottle was to remain with her for a week or two.

'I doubt if I'll see enough of you for you to put me right about anything, Sarah.'

'What do you mean? I'm staying with you. You heard Mr Fox give me permission.' Sarah gave Cassie a hard look.

'I also heard something else, when we were still on

the ship. You and Mr Dalhousie talking. I wasn't intending to spy on you, but the pair of you stopped by the ship's boat after the concert we had on board. Me and Harry were inside the boat.'

For a moment Sarah looked startled, but suddenly a grin crossed her face. 'If I'd known the pair of you were hiding in there we might have come and joined you. I've never done it in a boat. It would have been a lot more private than that cabin of his. We weren't in there above an hour. During that time everyone in the regiment must have come knocking at the door.'

Cassie was shaken by the other woman's brazen response to the disclosure that she had been overheard. Sarah had made no attempt to defend herself against Cassie's accusation. Indeed, she appeared to be proud of her behaviour. In that moment Cassie felt keenly aware of her own lack of years and experience of life. 'Don't you care what people think about you, Sarah? Or how your husband would feel if he knew what you were doing?'

'I certainly don't care what the other wives think of me, if that's who you mean by "people" – and if you've any sense in that pretty head of yours, neither will you. All this talk about pride, and of the regiment being one big family is fine, until things get tough. Then you look out for you and yours, because no one else will. In a retreat, with French cavalry horses breathing down your neck, you make absolutely sure you stay on your feet. If you fall, no one will stop and pull you out of the mud. On the contrary, they'll use you as a stepping-stone just to gain a pace. As for my husband ... Walter knew I

114

was no angel when he married me, and he's not fool enough to think he could change me. All the same, I'm more of a wife to him than most. What else I do is *my* business. No one owns Sarah Cottle. Not Walter Cottle, no, nor Mr John Dalhousie.'

Suddenly the grin returned to Sarah's face. 'There, you haven't been with the Thirty-second for more than a couple of weeks and you already know more about the way I think than do the wives who've followed the regiment for years. Don't worry, Cassie. I've said I'll look after you, and that's what I'll do. You'll lose neither the road, nor your honour while you're with me. You tell that nice-looking husband of yours to take care of his own skin and ignore what his so-called mates tell him. This isn't the countryside of Cornwall, or wherever it is you both come from. You're in the Peninsula now, and so is Napoleon's army. There's a war going on.'

Walking away from the shelter where Cassie lay, Sarah passed Harry Clymo. She gave him a smile that would have brightened the day of most of the men in the British army, but the young Cornish soldier was too concerned with the health of his wife even to notice. 'Mr Fox told me to come to you. He said I could only stay an hour. Are you all right? Has something happened?'

Cassie was touched by her husband's obvious concern. 'I'm on the mend, Harry, but the surgeon won't allow me to travel yet. I told Mr Fox I'd be all right on one of the wagons, but he won't let me come with you. He says the needs of the regiment come first.'

'I'll go and speak to him. He might listen to me.'

'You'll do no such thing! Sarah Cottle's going to stay behind with me. Mr Fox is leaving us money and rations and in no more than a week's time we'll be escorted by Mr Dalhousie and his dragoons to wherever you are.'

Harry was not reassured by Cassie's words. 'You haven't forgotten that night on the boat? What we heard going on between the lieutenant and Sarah Cottle?'

'I've forgotten nothing about that night, Harry. Neither what we heard ... nor what we did.'

Harry blushed as he remembered the first night of married privacy they had enjoyed together.

Cassie reached out and took his hand. 'You needn't worry about me, Harry. I've had a long chat to Sarah. I'm satisfied she'll do all she can for me. You just take care of yourself until we're together again. Now, see if there's another cup of tea going while I find some money I've got put by. Give some of it to Rose and she'll buy one or two extras for you along the road.'

10

❦

Cassie was moved to a house in the small town of Figueira later that morning. The move provided proof, if any was needed, that the surgeon's advice had been sound. The distance from the beach to the town was no more than two miles but Cassie was conveyed in a cart of the type used to carry the 32nd Regiment's stores. As a result she arrived at her destination with a head that felt as if it was about to burst. Gorran Fox had not exaggerated the shortcomings of the Portuguese peasant wagons. The wheels resembled misshapen barrel lids. Pursuing an elliptical orbit on ungreased wooden axles they shrieked in permanent protest behind the patient, plodding oxen.

The primitive cart eventually came to a halt in a narrow street lined for the whole of its length by irregular terraces of whitewashed houses. Without shifting from his perch on the shafts of the vehicle the driver of the cart, a greying, leather-skinned Portuguese, indicated an open doorway with a jerk of his thumb.

As Sarah Cottle helped Cassie from the back of the cart a small plump woman, dressed in drab, dark brown clothing, emerged from the house. Observing Cassie's face screwed up in an expression of pain, she hurried to Sarah's aid, at the same time directing a stream of shrill Portuguese invective at the unhelpful wagoner.

Her words had an immediate effect and the wagoner abandoned his seat on the shafts. Sullenly helpful, he made his way to the back of the cart and began gathering up the pots and pans and baggage belonging to the two Englishwomen. All the way to the house the Portuguese couple kept up a fast-talking exchange. Once inside, the woman showed her countryman where to place her guests' possessions and then shooed him unceremoniously from the house.

Returning to Cassie and Sarah, the woman offered them a smile. Jabbing a finger at herself she said, 'Teresa Fernandes, I.' Satisfied she had successfully identified herself to the guests, she extended her decidedly limited English vocabulary by saying, 'Come', and led the way to a narrow staircase set in a cool corner of the small house.

Halfway up the narrow, winding staircase, Cassie was obliged to pause and take a rest, having some difficulty for a while in breathing. Teresa returned down the stairs, saw her in this state and exhibited great concern. When Cassie felt fit enough to tackle the remainder of the stairs, the Portuguese widow led her by the hand and as they reached the top stair, slipped an arm about her body for support. She led Cassie to a small whitewashed bedroom. Low-ceilinged and sparsely furnished, the bed was tidily made up with clean linen and the room was light and airy. A gentle breeze blew through the window, from which there were views over the tiled rooftops of other houses to the river and the sea beyond.

A second bed was made up on the floor in a corner of the room for Sarah Cottle, but Cassie doubted whether the corporal's wife intended spending much time there.

Teresa lowered Cassie to the bed she would occupy during her stay, murmuring in unintelligible yet unmistakable sympathy. Moments later she was easing the shoes from Cassie's feet. Sinking back on the cool sheets, Cassie felt an absurd sense of well-being flood over her. This reminded her of home, and there was even a motherly Portuguese woman to look after her.

'We'll need food and stuff to take with us when we leave to rejoin the Thirty-second. I think I'll go out and find where we can buy it.'

'We've only just arrived here. We don't need to think about moving on for at least a week.'

'Perhaps not, but it's just as well to find the best places to buy from.'

Cassie knew Sarah was lying, but it did not matter. She would be perfectly safe on her own here. When Sarah left she lay back on the pillows and discovered she could see over the low sill of the window to the sea. There were boats on the water. Large ones with bare spars anchored offshore, smaller ones catching the wind in wine-red sails scudding through the water all about them.

119

Cassie heard Teresa mounting the steep stairs once more, muttering to herself in her own language. She entered the room carrying a tray on which was a huge wedge of cake and a large pottery mug. The Portuguese woman indicated the empty bed on the floor and her next words clearly contained a question, albeit in her own language.

Cassie shrugged apologetically and the woman clearly accepted the gesture as an answer. Shaking her head, she made disapproving noises as she placed the tray on a small table beside the bed. It seemed Teresa had already made an assessment of Sarah Cottle's character.

The mug contained wine, but it was warm and had been sweetened, most probably with honey. Although a little chary of trying it, Cassie did not want to offend and drank it first to help wash down the somewhat heavy cake. It was delicious and she wasted no time in drinking it all.

Whether as a result of the sweetened wine or the events of the past few days, Cassie fell asleep immediately after Teresa took the tray away. She did not hear the Portuguese woman come to the room and lay a light blanket over her. Neither did she witness Sarah's return to the room. The corporal's wife seemed relieved at finding her charge asleep and hastily departed once more.

It was night when Cassie woke and there was not a sound to be heard anywhere. She opened her eyes almost before she was awake and saw the path carved by moonlight across the surface of the sea. For a moment she

120

thought she was at home in Mevagissey and sat up in sudden excitement. The unfamiliar room and the empty bed in the far corner brought a return to reality and she sank back on the pillows.

Suddenly the moonlit sea was obscured by her own tears. Perhaps her mother was lying awake too, looking from the bedroom window of the Mevagissey cottage at the same sea, the same moonlight. She might even be wondering about her errant daughter. If it was a fine night Cassie's father would be at sea, fishing in a similar fashion to the small boats she could see now, each casting a small, yellow dot of light on the silver water offshore. Cassie thought of her sisters, in their bedroom – *her* bedroom. Both would be sleeping – Anne snoring gently with not a care in her young life, Beth restless, caught up in the dream-world of her overactive imagination.

Tears coursed down her cheeks as more and more memories returned to remind her of the life she had left behind for ever. Thoroughly miserable and suffering from a severe bout of what any soldier's wife would have diagnosed as homesickness, Cassie cried herself to sleep. She would have been even more homesick had she remembered that today was her sixteenth birthday.

When Cassie woke the next morning Sarah Cottle was up and about in the room. As though to convince Cassie she had been in the room all night, she commented that Cassie had slept wonderfully well and was looking better already.

Cassie thought she probably looked better than the other woman. Sarah appeared to have spent the night carousing and her next words confirmed Cassie's suspicion. Mumbling that she had been unable to sleep the previous night, she announced her intention of going to bed for another couple of hours.

By the time Teresa Fernandes climbed the stairs with a tray of breakfast for Cassie, Sarah was snoring gently, only the top of her head visible above the sheet. The Portuguese woman made no attempt to disguise her disapproval of the sleeping woman, expressing loud-voiced condemnation in a manner that required no translation.

Sarah slept for much of the day. When she woke in the late afternoon she remained in the house for no more than an hour. After bathing and washing her clothes, she went out again, establishing a pattern that would continue for the duration of her stay in Figueira.

On the third day of Cassie's convalescence in the small Portuguese town, Teresa came to the bedroom in the late afternoon. With a combination of gesticulation, mime and largely wasted explanation, she managed to make it understood she wished Cassie to come downstairs and spend a while in a small walled garden at the rear of the house.

After days spent in the tiny bedroom, Cassie was eager for a change. It would be a pleasure to put on her clothes. Washed and ironed by Teresa they were now neatly folded by her bedside. The loud voice of the Portuguese woman woke Sarah Cottle and she grumpily agreed to leave her bed and accompany Cassie.

It was beautifully warm in the small enclosed garden, the high, whitewashed walls effectively keeping the sea breeze at bay. Around the walls flowering bougainvil-laea, hibiscus, fig trees and grape vines provided colour, scent and sustenance. There was sound here, too. A noisy cicada provided a backing for the pleasant, soothing hum of the bees as they explored each flower.

Teresa led Cassie to a rough-wood seat, set back against the wall and shaded by a leafy vine, heavy with black grapes. When she was seated the Portuguese woman fussed about her with a number of cushions. At last she was satisfied and signalled for Cassie to remain where she was, hurrying inside the house once more.

'This is sheer bliss,' declared Cassie, closing her eyes and lying back against the cushions. 'I feel so much better today. Has Mr Dalhousie said anything about moving off?'

'Don't wish away an opportunity like this. You won't be getting feather beds and seats with cushions when we're back with the army. Short rations and a grass field is the best you can hope for – and that only on good days. Mr Dalhousie won't be leaving Figueira until he's good and ready – and that suits me.'

Cassie wondered, not for the first time, why Sarah chose to follow the army on its campaigns when she professed heartily to dislike its lack of comforts.

At that moment Teresa returned to the sunny garden. In her right hand she carried a jug of lemonade. Her other hand rested on the arm of a tall, smiling, power-fully built man who wore a long, black habit which reached to his sandalled feet.

'Oh, Jesus! She's putting us on show now. I wonder how much she's charging?'

The smile on the face of the Dominican friar never

123

faltered for a moment as he said, 'Hello to you. I'm Father Michael. Senhora Fernandes thought you would enjoy meeting someone who knows Figueira and who speaks English. She's not charging for the service – a fact of which I have no doubt Jesus is fully aware.'

The friar's voice carried a strong Irish accent and he seemed genuinely to be more amused than offended at Sarah's ungracious words and subsequent confusion. Turning his attention to Cassie, he said, 'You'll be the young lady who's been ill. Cassie, I believe you're called? I helped the young officer to find transport and wagon drivers. When he told me about you I made the arrangements for you to stay here with Senhora Fernandes. I trust you're comfortable?'

'Very. Mrs – Senhora Fernandes is very kind.'

'She is that. The young officer, now, he was most concerned about you. Would you be related to him, perhaps?'

'He's an officer in my husband's regiment. We all come from the same place – from Cornwall.'

Cassie would not have deemed the explanation necessary had not Sarah been smirking behind the friar's back, her own embarrassment temporarily forgotten.

Teresa began speaking rapidly to the Dominican friar, who interrupted her flow of words with an occasional gesture. As she talked his glance went more than once towards Sarah, who had poured lemonade for herself and for Cassie.

As Sarah passed the drink to Cassie, she said quietly, 'There seem to be more words in the Portuguese language than any other I've ever heard.'

Her voice was pitched low, but Father Michael heard. Interrupting Teresa with another gesture, he said, 'Portuguese is a very expressive language. It's a reflection of the people themselves. They're a very voluble people. Take the word *matrimónio*, for instance. The English word is marriage. I feel it loses something in translation, don't you? The Portuguese word now, it carries a certain dignity. There's a hint in it of maternity, and the blessed responsibility of motherhood. Their word *fidelidade* is another example. So much is contained in one word. You are married?'

When Sarah, somewhat puzzled, confirmed that she was, Father Michael inclined his head. 'Senhora Fernandes thought perhaps you were. She also suggested to me you might feel like attending confession before leaving Figueira to brave the hazards of war.'

Sarah flushed angrily. She could guess what Teresa Fernandes must have said to the Dominican friar about her need to 'confess her sins'. 'I'm *not* a Catholic – and I gave up "confessing" when I was ten. That was when I discovered the preacher who came to the workhouse would rather have me commit new sins with him than absolve me from those I'd confessed.'

To Cassie, she said, 'I'm going for a walk. This place has suddenly become stuffy – even out here in the garden.' Angrily, Sarah stalked off without another glance at either Father Michael or Teresa.

'I seem to have offended your friend.' Father Michael's words were an expression of fact, not an apology.

'Sarah's had a hard life and she's been a soldier's wife for a long time.'

125

'I doubt if she has ever gone far out of her way to make life any easier for herself. But enough of talking of other people. How are you feeling? I hear you're lucky to be alive. There are a number of new graves in the churchyard, those of two of our own villagers among them. It's very sad. Very sad indeed, but tragedy owes no allegiance to any one army. It travels hopefully with them all.'

'I'm feeling much better, thanks to Senhora Fernandes. Please give her my deepest thanks and tell her how grateful I am for her kindness. It's very difficult not being able to speak the language.'

Father Michael spoke to Teresa and she beamed at Cassie. Then, after making a lengthy reply, she hurried away.

'You've made Senhora Fernandes very happy, young lady. She's away now to fetch some food. She can't get used to having a lean friar in Figueira – and I am lean in her eyes. She'd like me to be as rotund as my Portuguese colleagues, not one of whom is less than twice my weight.'

'What's an Irish friar doing here, in a small Portuguese village?'

'Have you ever been to Ireland, Cassie?' the friar countered.

Cassie shook her head. 'I'd never been outside Cornwall until a few weeks ago.'

'Then you'll have no idea of the difficulties placed in the way of any man who tries to bring the teachings of the Catholic Church to his countrymen in my country. It was made doubly difficult when the British authori-

126

ties learned of the part I'd played in persuading France to invade Ireland – but you'd know nothing of such things, being no more than a child at the time.'

Cassie was shocked by the friar's revelation. 'But . . . if you're on the side of the French . . . what are you doing here, helping Mr Fox?'

'I didn't say I was a supporter of the French, my child. No, I rather naïvely believed *they* were anxious to support the Irish. As it happened they were totally ineffectual anyway, thanks to the vigilance of the English navy. Now I'm an older and wiser man I concede it was a happy escape for my country. The French would have added large-scale warfare to the misery of occupation – and I fear their troops are not so well disciplined as the English.'

'Does Gorran Fox know about this?'

'Mr Fox?' Father Michael showed none of the surprise he felt that a soldier's wife should refer to an officer by his first name. 'He knows only that when the French occupied Portugal I actively supported Portuguese patriots in their fight against them.'

Smiling at Cassie's confusion, Father Michael explained. 'When I fled from Ireland I made my way to Rome. There I met with priests, monks and friars from many lands. Fine men, many of them. I also met eminent churchmen with whom I had nothing in common. I learned it was not a particular race of people I disliked, but oppression. The arrogance of those who occupy a land against the will of its people. My views embarrassed many of my more senior colleagues in Rome and it was suggested I should come here to work with my brothers in Portugal. It was a happy move for me. The Portuguese are a fine people and my time among them has not been wasted. Indeed, it may be that my work here is only just beginning. I've come to say farewell to Senhora Fernandes. The Count of Resende, commander of the Portuguese Brigade, has asked me to accompany him to war as his padre. I believe he and your husband's regiment form part of the same army division. When you're fit to travel I'll accompany you to the battle-front. I understand we'll have an escort with us too – a squadron of dragoons? Ah! Here is the delightful Senhora Fernandes with some of her delicious cooking. It is without a shadow of doubt the finest in Figueira. I trust you're fully appreciative of her skills.'

When Father Michael left the small cottage some hours later dusk was beginning to settle over the town. Only a faint red glow linking sky and sea remained to mark the passing of the sun.

As the Dominican friar stepped from the doorway to the street he was forced to retreat hurriedly when a number of horsemen cantered noisily by. It was not necessary to hear their voices to know they were English cavalry officers. He could tell by the arrogance of their bearing. Leading the horsemen was an officer he had observed entering a *taverna* with Sarah Cottle the previous evening.

The relationship between the married woman and the officer disturbed Father Michael greatly, although he had seen far too much of human weakness for it to shock him. Similarly, the fact that an English soldier was being cuckolded by an English officer was not his concern. The friar was disturbed more because Sarah reminded him of his only sister whom he remembered with great affection. When he was twelve she had run off with a British army officer. The scandal in the small Irish community had brought lasting shame to the O'Rourke family. Kevin O'Rourke, now Father Michael, had never been clear whether it was his sister's moral lapse or that her lover was an English soldier, which had been the greater crime.

It was inevitable that Ena should be abandoned by the officer and she had died in childbirth in the poverty of an English workhouse. The community she had left behind were unanimous in agreeing that God had punished Ena for her immorality. Father Michael had always wished God's wrath might have been directed against the British officer and His undoubted mercy extended to Ena.

It was foolish to imagine that Sarah Cottle bore any resemblance to an artless Irish girl. Neither could Lieutenant Dalhousie be held responsible for a sin committed before he was born, yet Father Michael was honest enough with himself to accept that his view of the lieutenant's liaison with Sarah Cottle was coloured by childhood experience.

Teresa Fernandes was not a woman to keep gossip to herself and it was not long before every woman in Figueira knew of the carryings-on of the Englishwoman and the dragoon officer. They all agreed that something should be done about the situation, but no one knew quite what, or by whom, and so the illicit relationship continued.

The day before Father Michael was due to leave for the front with Cassie, he was walking in the grounds of the small village monastery when he heard sounds of laughter coming from the direction of the river. The laughter was in itself unusual. This part of the river passed through the monastery grounds and the inmates did not bathe in such a noisy fashion.

Making his way towards the sound, Father Michael paused in the shade of a vine-draped arbour. From here he could see three horses tied in a waterside orangery. Uniforms were strewn about the bank, as were a number of wine bottles, some empty, others full. Then he saw three men cavorting in the river. Each was stark naked. One of the men was Lieutenant Dalhousie and Father Michael recognised the others as cavalry officers too.

This should have been a time of quiet meditation for the occupants of the monastery. The sounds from the river could not fail to disturb them. In addition, the sight of the nude bathers would be offensive to women in the houses across the river.

Father Michael was about to go down to the river to remonstrate with the men when another sound impinged upon his angry thoughts. It was the gentle hum of thousands of industrious bees. The noise came from a line of white-painted beehives situated between the arbour and the river bank – and Father Michael had a sudden, most unchristian idea.

The beehives were shielded from the river by a low hedge of fragrant lavender and Father Michael was safe from the eyes of the revelling bathers as he crept along the line of hives. The one at the far end of the line was no more than thirty paces from the river bank, and the black-robed friar chose this as his target.

Untying the long cord that encircled his waist, Father Michael carefully looped it about the handle on the top of the hive. Then he just as cautiously backed off for the full extent of the cord. It needed only one powerful tug to dislodge the hive from its base and bring it crashing to the ground, exposing row upon row of glutinous honeycombs – and thousands of startled bees.

Back in the shelter of the vine-covered arbour, Father Michael watched in awed fascination as a cloud of bees rose in a dark, angry cloud above the upturned hive, seeking the cause of the sudden cruel destruction of their home. The only moving objects within striking range were the three horses and their naked, dismounted riders.

Lieutenant Dalhousie was standing on the river bank, head back and bottle to his lips, when the first wave of vengeful bees struck. It was as though he had backed on to the points of a hundred red-hot needles. The bottle dropped to the ground, its contents gurgling unnoticed in the mud. For a few desperate moments the dragoon officer flailed his arms in a wild and unsuccessful bid to beat off his winged attackers. Then he rushed to the river and plunged in, vaguely aware before he submerged of the cries of his fellow officers and the terror-stricken snorting of the horses.

Sarah Cottle slept in Cassie's room in Teresa Fernandes' little house that night and the period of unexpected

131

celibacy did nothing for her temper. Lieutenant Dalhousie, too, was in a foul mood the next morning, and there was certainly some justification for his ill humour. His face was a mass of ugly, angry-looking red lumps and he moved stiffly and painfully. When he mounted his horse he was forced to stand in the stirrups, keeping space between the seat of his trousers and the leather of the saddle.

Teresa and many of the inhabitants of Figueira turned out to bid farewell to her late guests and the departing friar. When she saw the cavalry lieutenant, she spoke to the padre. 'The Englishwoman slept in the house last night, now I can see why. What happened to the English cavalry officer?'

'The Lord works in mysterious ways, Senhora Fernandes – but rest assured, His will is always done in the end.'

11

⚜

The ammunition convoy escorted by the infantrymen of the 32nd Regiment made better time than had been expected. They were urged on by a message that reached Lieutenant Fox from Lord Wellington's headquarters. The ammunition was urgently required by the British forces currently investing the Spanish town of Rodrigo, a French stronghold on the road to Salamanca.

Riding in their wake, Lieutenant Dalhousie had almost fully recovered from his painful encounter with the bees, but he was angry not to have caught up with the convoy he was supposed to be guarding. The cavalrymen had already spent two nights on the road and should have been up with the convoy by now.

Riding through a wooded valley, high in the mountains, with no thought in mind but to catch up with Lieutenant Fox, the cavalry were still some twelve miles short of the Spanish border when they were surprised by a squadron of Napoleon's Polish lancers. The attack came at the widest section of the valley and took the dragoons entirely by surprise. Strung out in a long, loose formation with Dalhousie at their head and the two women, with Father Michael, bringing up the rear, the dragoons were travelling in a relaxed manner. The troopers did not share their commanding officer's irritability and were enjoying the hot Peninsular sun.

The horses of the Polish lancers were already galloping when they cleared a thinly wooded slope barely seventy yards to the right of the dragoons. Charging in a compact, well-disciplined formation, they carved a path through the centre of the dragoons, emptying twenty saddles. The momentum of the attack carried them well clear of the startled column before they could wheel and form for another charge. This time choosing the rear of the column for a target.

Given the sudden nature of the attack and Lieutenant Dalhousie's inexperience, the dragoons reacted remarkably fast. By the time the enemy lancers struck the column for the second time the dragoons had their sabres drawn to meet the charge and Lieutenant Dalhousie was riding back at the gallop with the front half of his squadron.

The next few minutes were filled with terror for Cassie. Her small donkey was buffeted first one way and then the other by the horses of dragoon and lancer. Braying in fear, the donkey turned a full circle on the spot. When she brought it under control, Cassie looked up to find herself confronted by a Polish cavalryman with his lance half-raised. He was a young man with a long, waxed moustache and on his face was an expression that combined exhilaration and fear.

The lancer and Cassie stared at each other for what seemed an age, yet could only have been a few seconds. Then, as the frightened donkey began backing away from the cavalry horse, which seemed as highly strung as its rider, the Polish cavalryman slowly and deliberately lowered his lance until the iron point was on a level with her throat. Cassie's horror was accentuated by the fresh blood glistening on the tip of the weapon and spattered on the red and white pennant fluttering in bizarre gaiety from the shaft. With a loud shout that startled Cassie's already frightened donkey even more, the Polish lancer kicked his horse into motion.

The horse was just finding its stride when a black-cloaked figure leaped between horse and donkey. Knocking the point of the lance downwards, Father Michael maintained a strong grip on the weapon. The bloody point of the lance was driven into the earth and the muscular power of the friar lifted the horseman clear of his saddle. He crashed to the ground, the lance still secured to his arm by a stout leather thong.

As the lancer struggled to regain his feet the three persons involved in the life-and-death drama were buffeted by Lieutenant Dalhousie and his men as they pursued the now retreating Polish horsemen. Without pausing in their headlong pursuit two of the dragoons sabred the fallen lancer in quick succession. As they rushed on he remained dangling like a bloody rag doll from his lance.

When Father Michael released his grip on the lance it

fell to the ground with the stricken soldier and Cassie suddenly realised she was shaking uncontrollably. Her condition was due as much to witnessing the violent death meted out to the lancer as to her own narrow escape.

'All they that take the sword, shall perish with the sword . . .' Kneeling beside the dead cavalryman, Father Michael disentangled the thong of the lance from the soldier's arm, then closed his eyes and murmured a brief prayer before making the sign of the cross above the dead man.

Rising to his feet, the friar put a comforting arm about Cassie's shaking shoulders. His glance followed the dragoons pursuing the fleeing lancers far along the valley. 'I just hope those damned fools don't get themselves lost or we'll all be in a sorry state.'

'You . . . saved my life.' As Cassie succeeded in bringing her shaking under control, she added, 'I think there are others who need your help more than I.'

A number of unhorsed dragoons sat on the ground nearby, nursing wounds. Others sprawled motionless about them.

'They'll have need of both of us . . . if you feel up to it?'

Cassie nodded. Sarah Cottle was already busy trying to staunch the bleeding of a badly wounded man and Cassie followed after the black-robed friar, trying not to look down at the bloody face of the Polish lancer as they passed by.

The dragoons had suffered twenty-three casualties in the surprise attack. Six were dead. Of the wounded, three more would die before they could be attended to by a surgeon. In addition to the dead and wounded, three dragoons failed to return from their pursuit of the Polish lancers.

The wounded men received the attentions of Cassie and Sarah for much of the night, aided by Father Michael.

Tending the wounded soldiers, Sarah Cottle revealed a side of her nature she had not shown before. She proved very efficient, even though some of the injuries were horrific. As the two women dressed a stomach wound sustained by a young and obviously dying trooper, Sarah said quietly, 'My first husband was killed by a lancer. Guns can cause terrible injuries, but somehow a lance wound is worst of all. It's easy to see why lancers are both feared and hated. They're usually chasing after men – and women too – who're running for their lives. Sometimes I've heard them screaming, like a rabbit with a dog at its tail. I could never learn to love a lancer.'

Cassie shuddered as she recalled the expression on the face of the Polish lancer when he was about to launch his attack on her. 'No, I don't think I could, either.'

On her knees, Sarah raised her eyes from a dressing she was laying out prior to applying it to the shattered chest of another dragoon. Suddenly grinning, she said, 'You strike me as being a girl who likes to have her feet planted firmly on the ground. A natural infantryman's woman. Me now, I've got ambitions. The cavalry, a guardsman, perhaps. I might even try for a man who's on the headquarters' staff one of these days.'

The grin faded for a moment. 'I wonder if things would have been different had Bill, my first husband, not been killed?' Shrugging with an indifference that failed to reach her face, she said, 'I doubt it. I've always been one to look for something I know I'll never find.'

The smile returned once more. 'Never mind, it's fun trying.' Looking down at the pale face of the dragoon whose wound she was about to dress, Sarah suddenly leaned down and kissed him on the lips. It was evident to Cassie that this man, too, was dying, but Sarah said to him, 'Hurry up and get well, my young hero. Who knows, you might be the next man in my life.'

Cassie found a grudging respect for her in that moment. She doubted whether there was another woman following the army who would have been able to raise a smile from the dying soldier. It was the last smile he would ever give anyone. Long before dawn broke he was dead.

Tending the wounded kept Sarah from Lieutenant Dalhousie that night. Not that the cavalry officer was in any mood for romance. His lax leadership had allowed his men to be surprised by the enemy. He had lost a fifth of his force as a result. In return the dragoons had managed to kill only two of the Polish lancers. It was a humiliating defeat on this his first temporary command.

Fuel was added to Lieutenant Dalhousie's chagrin the next morning when thirty infantrymen of the 32nd Regiment, led by Sergeant Elijah Tonks, arrived at the camp. Lieutenant Fox and the ammunition wagons were encamped in a small but comfortable village only two miles ahead. Portuguese peasants had brought news of the skirmish and Gorran had sent a third of his small force to investigate.

Harry was among the soldiers and his joy at seeing Cassie once more was plain for all to see. When he realised how serious the attack had been he was aghast. The 32nd Regiment had encountered no opposition during their march and all the soldiers were fit and well as a result of the leisurely pace set by the bullock carts, coupled with a plentiful supply of food and sun.

Rose Tonks followed the small party and she was pleased to see Cassie healthy again. She went among the wounded, inspecting their bandages, easing one here and tightening another there. She nevertheless expressed satisfaction with what had been done. 'I can see your hand in this, lovey,' she said to Cassie as the men of the infantry made litters on which to carry the wounded cavalrymen. 'You've done well. You'll be an asset to the regiment when they go into battle.'

'I helped out where I could,' admitted Cassie. 'It was Sarah who knew what needed to be done, Father Michael too. He saved my life when a lancer tried to kill me. I was lucky, it was the lancer who died . . .' Cassie had tried to put the image of the dead horseman's expression from her mind, but the bloody face kept returning to haunt her.

'You've had an adventurous time, lovey, and I don't doubt you did a sight more than Mrs Corporal Cottle.'

Seemingly determined not to give Sarah credit for anything she might have done well, Rose nodded to where the corporal's wife was talking earnestly to Lieutenant Dalhousie, both standing very close together.

Cassie was more interested in the expression upon

Corporal Cottle's face. He, too, was one of Sergeant Tonks's party and he was glowering in his wife's direction.

'That girl's head is turned as easily as any servant girl's at the sight of a soldier's uniform – then she's not happy until she's got him out of it. But if she starts getting ideas above her station in life there'll be trouble, take it from me. As for that poor husband of hers . . . When a soldier goes into battle he needs to be thinking of what he's doing. He won't last long if he's got half his mind on what his wife is likely up to while he's fighting. That's why she's had so many husbands, and there'll be more yet, you mark my words.'

So great was Harry's relief at seeing Cassie fit and well, he asked permission to fall out and walk beside the donkey as they made their way towards the place where the remainder of Gorran Fox's company was camped. However, aware that the 32nd would be marching under the watchful and resentful eye of the cavalry lieutenant, the request was refused. Sergeant Tonks would give the cavalryman no grounds for censure. Instead, and in view of the possible nearness of the enemy, Elijah Tonks requested that Lieutenant Dalhousie go on ahead with the women, leaving the infantrymen to follow with the wounded.

Scornful though he was of infantrymen, Lieutenant Dalhousie knew the sergeant's thinking was sound. They were close to the mountainous Spanish border now. On the other side was the French-held fortress of Rodrigo and French-occupied Spain. French soldiers roamed the countryside on both sides of the border in considerable strength. It would be foolhardy to leave the munition wagons with only a weak escort for too long.

As it happened, Lord Wellington had already arrived at the same conclusion. When Lieutenant Dalhousie reached the place where the wagons were in camp he discovered that half a regiment of cavalry, under the command of a lieutenant-colonel, were already there, having been sent from the force besieging Rodrigo to ensure the safety of the munitions for the last few miles of the long journey.

The lieutenant-colonel berated Dalhousie for remaining behind in Figueira and leaving the defence of the wagons to a single company of infantrymen. He told Dalhousie he should have walked his men and the horses until they were fit to ride. As for being taken unawares by a squadron of Polish lancers . . . ! The lieutenant-colonel left Lieutenant Dalhousie mortified by the suggestion that Lord Wellington might feel inclined to send a missive to England, requesting that officers of the calibre of Dalhousie be kept at home and stable boys be sent out in their place. He had no doubt, he added, 'They would be a damn sight more competent!'

The senior cavalry officer rubbed salt in Lieutenant Dalhousie's wounded pride by publicly praising Lieutenant Fox. He had completed his journey without losing either a single wagon or man. It was a feat so far unequalled and the lieutenant-colonel promised it would be brought to the personal attention of the commander-in-chief.

The final ignominy came when Sergeant Tonks returned to his company. With him he brought two of the missing dragoons, both minus their mounts. One was wounded and had fallen from his horse in a faint. The other had been swept from his horse by an over-hanging branch while galloping through woodland. Both had been hopelessly lost when found by men of the sergeant's patrol.

Three days later Cassie and the reinforcements for the 32nd Regiment arrived at the army's main encampment on the banks of the Aguala River, before the heavily fortified town of Rodrigo. As the column came down the winding road from the hill, Cassie marvelled at the number of soldiers in evidence.

Where possible the troops had been billeted in the towns and villages dotted around the plain, but there were not enough houses to accommodate troops numbered in tens of thousands. As far as the eye could see there were horses, wagons, guns and limbers – and the bright uniforms of the soldiers. Blues and greys, reds and green and tartan, all scattered in profusion on the dry, brown plain and on the green banks of the river.

At home in Cornwall Cassie had once looked across a valley and marvelled at a poppy-strewn field. Now, looking down at the regiments of English, German and Portuguese soldiers, it was as though the flowers of every season had been gathered in a vast, undulating field.

'Isn't that a stirring sight, Cassie?' Gorran Fox, mounted on the horse he had acquired at Figueira, put the question as he drew in beside Cassie's donkey. 'You're looking at the finest army in the world. A sight to give Napoleon pause, were he here.'

Gorran had been among the first to greet Cassie when she rejoined the other wives, and no one had been angrier at the danger she had been in from the Polish lancers. He blamed Lieutenant Dalhousie for having no outriders. He told the cavalry officer that had he accompanied the infantrymen of the 32nd Regiment he might have learned something of the art of soldiering.

'What will happen when we join up with the full regiment?' Cassie called back the question as the track narrowed and she urged her donkey ahead of Gorran's horse. She felt completely at ease with the Cornish lieutenant, although Rose had told her the other wives thought it wrong that she should be quite so friendly with an officer of the regiment.

'We'll be drafted into whatever company has need of us, I expect.'

'Does that mean you won't be with us any longer?' Cassie had not intended her question should sound quite so plaintive as it did, although she was dismayed that Gorran might no longer be Harry's company officer. She had come to rely upon his judgement and felt confident of Harry's safety while he was under Gorran's command.

Gorran was secretly pleased at Cassie's concern but he said, 'I'm neither the best nor the worst officer in the regiment, Cassie. You'll find every one of us is proud of the Thirty-second. When there's fighting to be done, we expect every soldier to fight harder than the soldiers of any other regiment but we'll never expose them to any unnecessary danger. You'll get along with whoever's in charge of your husband's company. But if you have any problems please don't hesitate to seek me out.'

He threw Cassie a smile and a salute before riding off to join the cavalry lieutenant-colonel who was impatiently waving the slow-moving wagons to the side of the track and calling for Lieutenant Fox to ride to the army headquarters with him.

He had decided to take Gorran personally to meet the commander-in-chief. The lieutenant-colonel had only been with the wagons and their Portuguese drivers for three days but that had been sufficient to increase his admiration of Lieutenant Fox for bringing the wagons safely from the coast without loss.

12

As Gorran had anticipated, the soldiers he had brought to the Peninsula were distributed among the five existing companies which together made up the 32nd Regiment. Sergeant Tonks, Corporal Cottle and Harry Clymo were all placed in Number 3 Company. The company had lost many men through sickness. Most had taken part in the disastrous campaign in the Low Countries the previous year and had never recovered their full health. So many of these veteran soldiers, in regiments throughout the army, had recurring illnesses that Lord Wellington had lodged a complaint with the army authorities in London. The high percentage of sick men was placing an unacceptable strain on his already inadequate medical resources.

As a reward for his success in bringing the reinforcements and heavily laden wagons safely from Figueira, Lieutenant Fox was appointed adjutant of the regiment.

It meant he would be personal assistant to Lieutenant-Colonel Hinde, commanding officer of the 32nd. The appointment was a double-edged sword. If he performed his duties well and met with the approval of Hinde he was assured of promotion. However, should he prove incompetent, or clash with the commanding officer, he would never receive further advancement within the regiment. Most lieutenants preferred to remain in a company where their shortcomings were less likely to come to the attention of the regiment's commanding officer.

Cassie soon settled down to the routine of regimental life in the field, although it was not at all what she had expected. For one thing, there were far more women accompanying the army than she had imagined. There were probably some two thousand wives, and possibly twice this number of Portuguese and Spanish camp followers. Most of the latter women were attached to a particular soldier, although a few, ostracised by the other women, shared their favours as it pleased them.

In the main the Portuguese and Spanish women had little to do with the wives and did nothing to help them. The camp followers knew that when the war was over only the official wives would return to England with their husbands. The local women would remain behind with their children, unsupported by the men they had followed through a long and gruelling campaign, and shunned by their own people. Only rarely, if a woman's exceptional bravery or devotion to her man was brought to the attention of a commanding officer, would she be allowed to marry the soldier.

Cassie discovered that two main problems beset the army wives. One was finding sufficient materials to build a home that would offer at least some privacy to husband and wife. The other was obtaining a little fresh food to supplement the meagre and often inedible army fare.

Home for Cassie and Harry was a flimsy, igloo-like structure of reeds, turf, grass and twigs. It looked as though it was likely to collapse at the first hint of a breeze, yet Cassie was to look back upon the time she spent in this strange dwelling with Harry as being among the happiest of the Peninsular campaign.

Although every effort was made to lead a domesticated existence, there were constant reminders that the British army was engaged in a campaign on foreign soil. The French army was only a few miles away, in the fortress of Rodrigo, and occasionally an armed force would sally forth to exchange shots with their besiegers. However, neither side appeared to take these minor incursions very seriously. Indeed, the British soldiers welcomed the skirmishes as a break in the monotony of the siege and a relief from the interminable drill parades that were the order of the day.

Most evenings the regimental pipes would put on a concert and, because of their closeness to Rodrigo, they were as popular with the besieged as with the besiegers. The French soldiers and many of the Spanish townspeople would crowd the high ramparts of the fortified town and applaud as loudly as the British soldiers at the end of an evening's performance.

Many men of the British army also found entertainment

of a more personal nature. Issued with rations of, at best, an indifferent nature by the commissariat, the soldiers were eager to buy anything that would supplement their monotonous diet. As a result, peasant girls from both sides of the Spanish–Portuguese border would walk miles to bring produce, livestock and wine to sell to the army. Not all the girls returned home.

The British soldier could be charming when it suited him, and he cut a fine figure with his uniform of red, blue or green. He had money to spend, albeit not too much, but to a peasant girl who had been brought up to accept poverty as the norm, a soldier was a wealthy man. The camps were lively places, too. Here were many musicians and sing-songs, and impromptu dances took place almost every evening. Suddenly, a poor and impressionable girl would realise there was more to life than drudgery and poverty.

It was the practice of many company officers to give their laundry to the soldiers' wives in rotation, in order that they might supplement their husbands' meagre pay. One week the task devolved upon Cassie and she set off for the river in the late morning, carrying a huge basket of washing.

A number of women from other regiments were already crowding the river banks with many children playing about them. Cassie knew none of the wives here, but there was a space alongside a Spanish girl Cassie knew as Josefa. Of about her own age, Josefa had turned the head of every man in the 32nd Regiment. Her isolation on the river bank was no accident. The wives, and even the other camp followers, were deeply jealous of her.

Dumping her basket of washing on the bank beside the Spanish girl, Cassie said, 'Good morning, Josefa. Do you mind if I do my washing here beside you?'

Cassie was not certain whether the girl understood English, but she had seen her about the camp of her own company only that morning. She could hardly work beside the girl without saying something.

Josefa shrugged. 'Is all right.' As she spoke she obligingly moved a basket containing wet washing closer to her.

'You speak English well.' Having once spoken it seemed stupid not to continue. Besides, Cassie was genuinely surprised. Josefa was dressed as a peasant girl; barefooted and bare-legged, with a bright blue scarf tied about her long, dark hair, there was something of the gipsy in her.

'And you speak Spanish not at all.' There was just a hint of resentment in Josefa's statement, but she smiled it away quickly. 'I learned to speak your language in Salamanca, from young men of the Irish College. I sold many things to them. So, too, did my mother, and we would often dance for them.'

Cassie was more convinced than ever of gipsy blood in this young girl. 'Why did you leave Salamanca?' As she spoke she began pounding a shirt against a flat rock that had been used many times for the same purpose.

'The French soldiers came and my mother went off with some of them. I came to the hills with my people.' Josefa shrugged once again. 'But the villages are too

149

quiet. There is no dancing and you need to go to church if you wish to sing together.' Josefa smiled, showing beautifully even, white teeth. 'I like it better here, among your soldiers. There is much singing and dancing, and Richard . . . He is nice. I like him much.'

For a moment Cassie was puzzled as she tried to think of a Richard in the company. Then she saw the clothes Josefa was washing. They were officer's clothes. There was only one Richard who held a commission – and only one who had not sent his clothes to be washed by Cassie. Josefa might have had a choice of any man irrespective of rank in the regiment, perhaps in the whole army, yet she had chosen Richard Kennelly, the young ensign of 3 Company. A painfully shy and unassuming young man, he was the most junior officer in the regiment and no more than two years older than Josefa.

Cassie was pleased for the young ensign. She had the impression he had known little joy in his life, but she had no doubt Josefa would change all that for him.

'Yes, Richard Kennelly *is* nice.' Cassie saw Josefa stiffen and she hurriedly added, 'He needs someone like you.'

'You think?'

Josefa was delighted that someone – an English-woman, a *wife* – actually approved of her. It was the first time she had encountered anything other than open hostility from the wives of soldiers. Even her own coun-trywomen resented her. She was a *gitana* – a gipsy-woman. Someone whom even the lowliest peasant might look down upon.

'Why you say this?' Josefa asked the question in order to delay this moment of rare approbation.

'Because Richard Kennelly is too quiet. Too serious. He has no fun. You'll be good for him.'

On her first night with 3 Company Cassie remembered hearing the soldiers telling Harry and the other newcomers of their officers. They told a story about Richard being sent back to Lisbon to bring thirty newly recovered men to the regiment from hospital and act as escort for a quantity of regimental baggage. He had arrived with half his men and much of the baggage missing. An ensign's most important duty was to carry the regimental colours in battle, to provide a rallying point for the officers and men. The gossiping soldiers had not been joking when they suggested that an ensign who was so careless with men and baggage could not be considered a responsible guardian of the regimental colours.

'How long you married to your man? Why you have no babies?'

'I've only been married a couple of months, and I lost the baby I was expecting. It happened when we were coming ashore at Figueira, in Portugal.' Cassie found the directness of the Spanish girl's questions somewhat disconcerting.

'Ah, the Portuguese! They are not like us.' Josefa spoke as though the loss of Cassie's baby had to be the fault of the people of Spain's neighbour. Cassie made no attempt to correct the assumption. Reaching out, Josefa took a number of items from Cassie's pile of washing. 'I help you. I have finished Richard's washing.' Without waiting for an answer, Josefa dipped the clothes in the river and as she thumped them against her own washing-rock she continued chatting.

151

Josefa was at times amusing, often inquisitive, but rarely revealed much about herself. Cassie was almost sorry when the washing had all been done. Josefa was a bright and intelligent companion. She was also to prove courageous and quick thinking.

The two women were walking away from the river when a sudden commotion broke out behind them. Turning, they saw a young child of no more than two or three years floundering in the deep water towards the middle of the river. The current was quite strong here and the child was being carried along, one moment above the water, the next disappearing beneath the surface.

A number of women were running along the river bank level with the child, gesticulating and screaming, but no attempt was made to rescue her. Dropping her basket to the ground, Josefa sprinted to the river bank. Pushing aside the shrieking women she dived head-first into the water. Caught by the current the Spanish girl was immediately swept downriver. However, she was a powerful swimmer. Battling across the current, Josefa reached the child as it disappeared beneath the dark water, leaving only two tiny hands showing above the surface.

Reaching down, Josefa grabbed a fistful of hair and hauled hard. The head of the small girl broke surface with water spewing from her mouth – but she exhibited no other sign of life. Using the current to edge closer to the river bank, Josefa was able to reach up and grasp Cassie's outstretched hand only yards from where the river passed between high, steep banks that would have made rescue impossible. Pushing the young child in front of her, Josefa scrambled up the bank to dry land.

At first glance the little girl appeared lifeless and a woman Cassie took to be the child's mother was already bewailing her death. Then, as the crowd of women struggled up the slippery river bank with the child – each eager to return to her regiment claiming it was she who had 'held the poor, dying mite in her last moments' – they fell over each other. The child was pitched to the ground and suddenly began retching and twitching convulsively.

The women immediately set up such a shout that a sentry on picket duty a half-mile away fired off his musket, convinced the French were launching a surprise attack. While the women kept up their excited din Cassie made her way to where Josefa sprawled on the grassy bank, breast heaving and scarcely able to speak after her exertions.

'Josefa, you were wonderful! You saved that little girl's life.'

'Someone . . . had to.' Josefa fought to regain control of her breathing. 'Why did . . . no one else try to . . . save her?'

'I doubt if any of them could swim.' It was probably the truth. Few girls learned to swim, even those whose homes were close to the sea. Cassie was also uncomfortably aware that she could swim but had failed to respond to the emergency with the speed shown by Josefa.

While Cassie spoke, Josefa was stripping off her flimsy white blouse and red skirt. Standing naked but quite

153

unselfconscious, Josefa first shook out her long black hair and then wrung as much water from her two garments as she could before slipping them on again. Watching the gipsy girl Cassie could see why she was resented by so many of the soldiers' wives. There were few women anywhere who could have matched the beauty of her body.

'Will you be all right like that? Your clothes are still wet.'

'They dry already.' Josefa raised her hands towards the hot sun. She was right. Steam was rising from her clothes in the heat of the Spanish summer day. 'Come, I must take Richard's washing to the camp.'

As the two women walked back along the river bank a number of women called out praise to Josefa, but she acknowledged them with only the slightest nod of her head. When they reached the spot where they had been washing, Josefa stopped and looked about her in puzzlement. Cassie's washing was where she had left it, but the smaller basket containing Richard Kennelly's clothing had disappeared.

In saving the drowning child Josefa had been clear-thinking and decisive, but losing Richard Kennelly's shirts threw her into panic. She ran first one way and then the other, seemingly incapable of coherent thought.

The women working on the river bank nearby could only offer their indignant sympathy. They had seen no one walking away with the ensign's clothes. Their attention had been focused on the drama being enacted in the river.

When Cassie was able to catch the young Spanish

girl by the arm and bring her to a halt, Josefa suddenly began to weep. 'What shall I do? It is first time I wash for him, and I lose his shirts. He will hate me. I am no good as his woman.'

'Stop it, Josefa!' Cassie spoke sharply in a bid to bring the other girl to her senses. 'Richard Kennelly is a nice young man who thinks you're the most wonderful thing that's ever happened to him, and you probably are. He'll tell you how brave you are for rescuing that little girl, and he'll understand about the loss of his shirts. It's a mean theft, but we all know there are thieves about.'

Richard Kennelly did understand and was fulsome in his praise of Josefa's courage and resourcefulness. He dismissed the loss of his shirts as being of no importance, although only he knew what a strain it would throw on his meagre resources.

Richard Kennelly was the seventh son of an impoverished Irish peer. It was a background he shared with the illustrious commander-in-chief of Britain's Peninsular army, but here the similarity ended. Worthy general though he had become, Lord Wellington had purchased his rapid progress up the promotion ladder, helped by members of his family who occupied important posts in government.

Richard Kennelly had none of these advantages. His ensigncy had been purchased by his father, who also granted him a tiny allowance to meet his basic needs, but this was as far as his father could afford to help him. Promotion for the young ensign would need to be earned in the field. Unfortunately, heroic deeds in Wellington's army were much more likely to bring death or serious injury than promotion.

Happily, on this occasion help was to come from an unexpected quarter. Gorran Fox came to the camp that evening accompanied by the divisional general and most of the divisional staff. With them was a woman who carried a parasol and wore clothes that would not have been out of place in a fashionable London salon.

Bringing up the rear of the impressive party was the woman Cassie had last seen caught in the throes of hysteria on the river bank that morning. In her arms was the small girl Josefa had rescued from the river.

Making his way to where she stood, Gorran asked, 'Cassie, have you heard anything of the rescue of a child from the river this morning? Someone said a woman from the Thirty-second was involved.'

'That's right, I was there and saw it happen. Josefa dived in and saved the little girl over there from drowning, and had her washing stolen as a result.'

'Josefa? I don't remember a wife called Josefa.'

'She isn't a wife. She's ... a Spanish friend of Mr Kennelly. It was his shirts that were stolen.'

'You know this ... Josefa?' The woman with the parasol had an accent as impeccable as her clothes, but her smile was disarming.

In spite of the smile Cassie was suspicious of the reason for this rather grand woman's interest, and she hesitated before making a reply.

'Cassie, this is Lady Fraser. Her husband is a general on Lord Wellington's staff. The rescued child is theirs.'

When Cassie's glance went to the young woman

holding the baby, Lady Fraser frowned. 'That is Emma's nursemaid, at least, she is until I find someone more reliable. Now, is this young Spanish girl – Josefa – in the camp?'

Cassie nodded to where Josefa walked towards them, a discreet distance behind Richard Kennelly. The visit by the divisional commander had taken the camp by surprise and the young ensign was the last of the officers to put in an appearance. 'That's Josefa, ma'am.'

'What a fascinating creature – and such looks! Does she speak English?'

Cassie nodded and Lady Fraser called to Josefa. The Spanish girl came towards Lady Fraser and the group of officers reluctantly. She believed her presence might have somehow caused trouble for Richard and she tried hard not to look towards him.

'My dear, I understand you dived in the river to save Emma, my daughter. I have been to the river and merely looking at it horrified me. It was very, very brave of you. You deserve a medal.'

Josefa shrugged. 'I could not see her die and do nothing.'

Lady Fraser shuddered. 'I would rather not think of what might have happened had you not been near. I would like to reward you.'

'For saving the life of a child?' Josefa was genuinely startled. Suddenly her expression changed. 'I want nothing, but Richard . . . Mr Kennelly . . . his shirts were stolen while I was in the river. It is not right he should suffer so for what I do. He is too nice.'

Lady Fraser cast an amused glance to where Richard

Kennelly stood, his face scarlet with embarrassment. 'I think you are quite right, Josefa. He is far too nice to stand such a loss. How many shirts were there?'

'Four – and of the finest silk.'

Josefa did not look at the ensign as she made her highly exaggerated statement and Cassie tried hard not to smile. There had been three shirts stolen, all of inferior quality.

'My husband is of much the same build as the ensign. I will have four of his new shirts sent to you, my dear. I regret they are not of silk, but they are of the finest linen – and perhaps this will help make up the difference.' Lady Fraser pressed a large bag of money in Josefa's hand. 'I will always be in your debt, my dear. Should you have any problems while you are following the army I trust you will bring them to me.'

Lady Fraser left the camp followed by the divisional commander and the rest of her entourage. As she went she was still talking of 'that charming girl'.

Gorran Fox was towards the end of the long line of officers and he gave Cassie a broad grin as he passed her. He, too, knew Richard Kennelly had never owned four silk shirts. When he reached the young ensign, Gorran leaned down from his saddle. 'Take care of that young lady, Richard. She'll make a wealthy man of you before this campaign comes to an end.'

13

❦

Two days after the rescue at the river a picket detail from the 32nd Regiment intercepted a large group of mounted Spanish guerrillas heading towards the British army lines.

More than a hundred strong, the guerrillas rode as though they had neither a care nor an enemy in the world. Yet these were men who had intercepted and slain hundreds of French soldiers along the long supply routes from France to the Peninsula. Fierce fighters who gave no quarter to those French patrols foolhardy enough to venture into the mountains in anything less than company strength.

It was a method of fighting at which the Spanish guerrillas excelled. There were some British officers who declared somewhat sourly that such hit-and-run warfare was the *only* fighting for which they were suited. Lord Wellington had tried incorporating Spanish fighting units into his army with a notable lack of success. The Spanish failed to understand the principles of British army discipline, insisting upon operating independently of the remainder of the army, often with disastrous results to themselves and those they were supporting.

The mounted guerrillas excited much interest as they passed through the various regimental encampment areas. They wore no uniform. Their leader, Don Xavier, was dressed in the gaudy style affected by Spanish gentlemen, but the appearance of the majority was decidedly ruffianly. Each man was heavily armed, a knife and pistol tucked in his waistband to supplement the musket slung over his shoulder.

When the picket first made contact with the Spanish irregulars a mounted messenger was despatched to Lord Wellington's headquarters with news of their arrival. He returned bearing a letter from a senior staff officer as the guerrillas were entering the 32nd Regiment's camp. It seemed Lord Wellington was unfortunately absent from his headquarters. The writer, who had himself commanded a Spanish regiment earlier in the campaign, requested that the guerrillas be entertained by the officers of the regiment which had brought them in.

After a hasty consultation with Gorran Fox and his fellow officers, the colonel of the 32nd Regiment decided to organise a feast for the guerrillas with entertainment provided by the regimental pipes. He also called on the services of a pipe band from one of the Scots regiments, always a huge success when playing for a foreign audience.

Having had the responsibility for the Spanish guer-

160

rillas thrust upon him, the 32nd Regiment's commanding officer responded by calling upon the services of chefs from headquarters and commandeering an outrageous amount of victuals from the commissariat. Two draft oxen were purchased from a Portuguese drover to be killed and roasted over a cooking fire. Soldiers' wives from the regiment were asked to wait upon the unexpected guests and much wine was donated by the local populace for 'Don Xavier and his brave partisans'.

The evening began well enough. As daylight gave way to the warmth of a star-sprinkled night the huge cooking fires spread a mouth-watering aroma over the surrounding countryside. The British rank and file, excluded from the feast, closed in around the fringes of the firelit area to share in the entertainment, at least.

The pipes, the wine and the food pleased the guerrillas and they began to relax. Some even went so far as to remove the guns from their waistbands. As the wine continued to flow Cassie learned it was wise to serve the Spaniards at arm's length. Those women who forgot this simple precaution were subjected to rough fumbling and an occasional none-too-gentle embrace from the regiment's uninvited 'guests'.

None of the guerrillas spoke English and communication proved difficult. Then it was remembered by someone that Father Michael spoke Spanish as fluently as Portuguese. His regiment, also part of the 6th Division, was camped nearby and the priest was called upon to act as an interpreter.

For a while, his services were little used. To the Spanish irregulars every English officer was an *amigo*, every refilled glass was greeted with a loud 'saludi' and the English women, including the muscular Rose Tonks, were 'atractivo'.

Shortly before midnight the Highland pipers decided to end their participation in the party. As they marched off they were given a rewarding round of applause from the guerrillas. Then, after a loud and argumentative discussion, the guerrillas decided they would repay their hosts with a performance of their own.

One of the guerrillas had entered the camp with a guitar slung from his saddle. Producing it now he began to play. It was wild, exciting music that belonged here with the warmth, the stars, the wine and the firelight. As their comrade played, the guerrillas sang and snapped their fingers in time to the music. Then a few stood up and began a stiff-backed and not-too-steady dance to the added accompaniment of hand-clapping from the others.

Josefa had deliberately stayed away from her countrymen during the feast, coming no closer than the shadows at the edge of the firelight, but now the guitar music drew her on like a moth to a flame. When Cassie first saw her she was edging closer to the space cleared by the guerrillas, behaving as though she was in a trance, almost oblivious of those about her.

Cassie felt instinctively that Josefa should not be here at this time. Setting down the heavy jug of wine she carried, she began to push her way through the crowd of men, heading towards Josefa – but she was already too late. The guitar-playing guerrilla had already seen her. He suddenly stopped playing. For a few moments the dancing continued and then it died away, uncertainly.

When he had silence the guitar player shouted, '*A gitana*' and struck a loud chord on his guitar. Others took up the shout as the chord continued in a frenzy of sound that ended with a flourish.

When the music resumed it had a new beat, one that set feet tapping all around the impromptu dance floor and brought shouts of approval from the Spanish guerrillas. Drawing back, they made the firelit dance floor larger and began clapping in a staccato, seemingly inharmonious accompaniment that added a new and exciting dimension to the rhythm.

When Josefa stepped into the firelight there were loud cries of '*A gitana!*' '*Flamenco!*'

'They're calling her a gipsy and wanting her to dance for them.'

Cassie turned to see Father Michael standing beside her. His expression might have been disapproval, or concern.

'Is Josefa a gipsy?'

'Probably. She certainly dances like one.'

Josefa had begun to move with the music. Arms held high above her head, hands close together and fingers clicking in time to the rhythm of the guitar. At the same time her feet were stamping almost petulantly, her hips swaying gently to the music.

'There'll be trouble from this, you mark my words. I should have seen it coming and put a stop to it earlier.'

Father Michael shook his head ruefully, but he offered no explanation for his words and Cassie's attention

163

returned to Josefa. The sheer excitement of the music was drawing a great many others to the scene. Officers from other regiments and soldiers with their women packed in behind the square of guerrillas, all there to watch Josefa dance.

It was soon clear that Josefa's performance was much more than a dance. It was skilful mime, set to music. She was at one moment passive, and then passionate; flirtatious and then powerfully arrogant. The soldiers and their wives who were watching would never forget Josefa's dance beneath the warm, star-spangled sky of Spain.

No one was aware of the passing of time. Josefa might have been dancing for half an hour, or it could have been an hour and a half. The tempo of the music changed, and changed again, the guitar accompanied by the hand-clapping of the guerrillas, and an occasional song to provide an abrasive, discordant, yet haunting sound.

By now perspiration darkened the back and sides of Josefa's blouse and glistened on her face, arms and legs. Suddenly the guerrilla leader, Don Xavier, lurched into the ring of men, and the mood underwent an immediate change.

Adopting an unsteady dancing stance in front of Josefa, Don Xavier bellowed information to his fellow guerrillas that he was about to show this Andalusian gipsy how Castilians danced. His words brought a mixture of applause and jeers from his own men, many of whom would have preferred watching only Josefa.

For the vast majority of watchers the magic of the evening had come to an end. The guerrilla leader capered about in a drunken parody of a dance, the guitar player loyally providing music for his chief while the other guerrillas clapped in ragged accompaniment.

For a while longer Josefa continued to dance, but after Don Xavier had twice pulled her to him, treading on her bare toes in the clumsy process, she shrugged her shoulders and began to walk away.

Grabbing her by the arm, Don Xavier pulled her back to him, his voice loud and angry. Cassie could not understand what he was saying, but it was clear that Josefa disagreed violently with his words. She tried to pull away as the guerrillas set up howls of encouragement and began to close about their chief and the struggling gipsy girl.

'This is what I feared would happen.' Father Michael pushed his way through the crowd towards the struggling couple.

Richard Kennelly understood no more of what was going on than did Cassie, but he could see Josefa was in trouble and he tried to go to her aid. Cassie saw him fighting his way through the crowd and intercepted him as he reached the outer ranks of the excited guerrillas. Placing herself in front of him she said, 'No, Richard. You'll only cause more trouble, for yourself and for Josefa. Leave it to Father Michael.'

'I can't leave her to deal with that drunken oaf alone.'

Peering anxiously over the heads of the guerrillas, Richard Kennelly tried to push past Cassie. She took hold of him but he would have broken free had not help been forthcoming from Rose Tonks. She, too, had seen what was happening and realised the danger the young ensign was in.

'You'll be doing yourself no good going among that

lot, young Richard me lad.' As she spoke to the concerned ensign Rose cast a look of approval in Cassie's direction. 'My Elijah fought alongside some o' them Spaniards the last time we was in the Peninsula. He says they'd as soon cut out the liver of an Englishman as slit the throat of a Frenchie. They'd put a knife in you and we'd never even see who did it.'

Trying to peer over the shoulder of the woman who was half a head taller than he and more than twice his weight, Richard became both angry and frustrated. 'Let me by, Rose. Josefa needs my help!'

'Leave it to Father Michael. He knows Don Xavier and is used to dealing with men like him.' Cassie spoke with more confidence than she felt. She prayed the tall Dominican friar would not let her down.

Josefa was struggling desperately in a vain bid to break the grip of the guerrilla leader when Father Michael reached her. 'Don Xavier! Is the hero of a thousand battles and liberator of his people reduced to forcing his attentions upon a young girl?'

Red-faced and perspiring as a result of his exertions, Don Xavier glared drunkenly at the friar. 'This is not church business, Padre. I will bring my men to pray with you tomorrow. Tonight? I do not force my attentions on this gipsy. She wants me but enjoys pretending she does not. Come, my beauty. I will show you there is more to life than dancing.'

Father Michael waited until the rowdy roar of approval from Don Xavier's men had died away. 'You disappoint me, my friend. I thought I saw in you a man with ambitions beyond his immediate needs. A man of

166

vision, whose first thoughts were not of his own desires, but the good of his people. A leader, not a man who wanted no more from life than a woman cast aside by the lowliest of British officers. A mere boy, at that.'

Don Xavier released his hold on Josefa and walked uncertainly to where the friar stood. Pushing his face up close to Father Michael's, he said, 'This one is not cast aside by an English officer. I take her from him.'

Father Michael shrugged. 'So you say. But although he is young he is an English officer. Who will his countrymen believe? Who will Lord Wellington believe? Are you to be written into the history of Spain as a great leader who threw off the yoke of Napoleon Bonaparte, or as the guerrilla who might have been great had he not been more interested in the cast-off woman of a junior English officer?'

Don Xavier did not have a quick brain and it had been slowed even more by the amount of drink he had consumed that evening.

At that moment Sarah Cottle came into the firelight. On her shoulder she balanced a huge earthenware jug overflowing with cheap but extremely potent brandy. Looking around the circle of guerrillas she caught the eye of Don Xavier.

'Bring me a drink!' The guerrilla wagged a finger and Sarah crossed the open space to him, smiling up in his face as she filled his pewter mug.

Draping an arm about Sarah's shoulders, Don Xavier beamed happily at Father Michael. 'You see? Don Xavier does not have to steal anyone's woman. I have only to crook my finger for an English woman to hurry to please me.' As he spoke Don Xavier drew Sarah to him, hugging her in a gesture of familiarity to which she seemed in no way averse.

'Tell the English officer he can have his *gitana* whore. I, Don Xavier, give her to him.'

Father Michael nodded, congratulating the guerrilla leader on his magnanimity. He had seen Josefa making good her escape, accompanied by the young English ensign. 'May you lead your people long and wisely, your praises sung wherever men gather to talk of brave Spanish patriots. God be with you, Don Xavier.'

As each Spanish guerrilla demarcated the four points of the cross on his breast, Father Michael led Cassie away from the firelight. 'Did I resolve the situation to your satisfaction, young lady?'

'I couldn't understand what you were saying, but it enabled Josefa to escape from that man, but I doubt if Sarah will be as fortunate.'

'That young lady is quite capable of taking care of herself, if she wants to.'

Cassie looked up at the tall man walking beside her, 'You're a strange man to be a friar, Father Michael.'

'Don't I know it, girl? I spend almost as much time on my knees asking the Lord's forgiveness for myself, as I do praying for the souls of those on whom I bestow His great mercy. I comfort myself with the certain knowledge that if I can forgive others their sins, then He surely can.'

'What about Josefa? You rescued her from Don Xavier, yet you made no attempt to stop her going off with Richard Kennelly. Isn't what they're doing supposed to be a sin too?'

'It is indeed, child, but a good priest must think like

168

a general on such occasions. He should never attempt the impossible, and needs to choose a course of action that will provide him with the greater victory. If I were to break up the relationship between your young ensign and Josefa, and it is by no means certain I could, I would gain two souls, albeit temporarily. Am I right?'

Cassie nodded, not quite certain what the tall black-cloaked friar was trying to say.

'Of course I am. However, if I were to have left Josefa with Don Xavier her night would not have ended when he had done with her. I have known him and his men for a long time. They live by the rule of the commune. When Don Xavier finished with Josefa she would have been passed on to his lieutenant, and so on, until all his men were satisfied. Perhaps Josefa will come to confession one day, perhaps she will not. Whatever she decides to do, it is one soul of which we are talking, and that may yet be saved. On the other hand, Don Xavier and his men will certainly not come to me with a catalogue of their sins. They would have ridden away tomorrow with who knows how many sins remaining unconfessed. Now, I ask you, Cassie, what would a good general do in such circumstances? What would the Good Lord want me to do? I like to think he'd pat me on the head and say, "You're a man after me own heart, Father Michael. I doubt if you'll ever be a saint, but I'm glad to have you on my side." At least, that's what I think I'd say if I were in His place.'

14

After the late-night celebrations, the soldiers of the 32nd Regiment hoped they might have a late call the next morning. They were sadly disappointed. Drummers were on the move among the sleeping men even earlier than usual and there was an urgency to the drum-beat of 'Assembly' that brought soldiers to the assembly point at the double.

Mustering in their companies, bleary-eyed and grumbling, the soldiers were given the news that the French had succeeded in bringing much needed supplies to the beleaguered fortified town of Rodrigo. The French army, estimated to be at least 60,000 strong, was expected to advance upon the smaller British force some time that day.

There was great excitement in every camp along the bank of the river. Cassie experienced for the first time the chaos of a British army breaking camp in the hours of darkness when an attack was believed to be imminent.

Most regiments were on the move before dawn, but the 32nd Regiment was ordered to act as the rearguard for the eight regiments comprising the army's 6th Division. It meant waiting until daylight. Although part of Cassie was apprehensive about being left behind, the practical Cornishwoman in her realised the delay would ensure she left nothing behind in the camp.

Others had been less fortunate. When daylight arrived it revealed hastily evacuated campsites strewn with belongings of every description. The camps had been occupied for many weeks during which time the occupants had accumulated an unaccustomed number of possessions. Some had simply been missed in the darkness, others had been dropped during the rush to move off.

The mislaid property would not remain for long. Already Spanish peasant women were picking their way through the vacated sites, pouncing upon anything that was likely to be valuable, or useful.

Other Spaniards were abroad too. Don Xavier and his guerrillas rode off without saying a goodbye to anyone. The British army was not striking eastwards into the heart of Spain, but heading west towards the Portuguese border. There was no glory to be gained by remaining with an army in retreat and Don Xavier had no wish to become embroiled in a battle between two armies. He and his men would disappear once more in the mountains to the south-west of Rodrigo, to continue their hit-and-run war with the French army of occupation.

Sarah Cottle returned to the camp of the 32nd

Regiment at about the same time. Bleary-eyed and gaunt-faced, she walked with the careful gait of a woman three times her age. No one actually saw her arrive, or could swear from which direction she had arrived, but her appearance was the subject of more than one nudge in the ribs and there were many knowing glances cast in her direction.

It was left to Rose Tonks to tell the corporal's wife she looked dreadful.

'I had too much to drink last night,' said Sarah, by way of explanation. 'It didn't agree with me.'

'Spanish wine, was it?' Rose asked, in apparent innocence. 'I can understand your problem. It's a bit too rough for most women's taste. Mind you, I never thought I'd hear you complain of having too much – of anything!'

Sarah's mouth clamped tight shut as someone sniggered and she began stuffing clothes in a saddle-bag with no attempt to fold them.

Half an hour after dawn the regiment was on the move, the tired women trailing behind with their heavily laden donkeys. They had not been travelling long before sporadic musket fire was heard from the hills towards which Don Xavier and his guerrillas had been heading.

'It sounds as though our Spanish allies might have run into trouble,' commented Rose, unemotionally.

'I wouldn't care if they were all killed,' said Sarah with sudden unexpected bitterness.

'All of 'em? Surely not?' Rose gave Sarah a look filled with exaggerated concern. 'You poor soul. 'Tis no wonder you don't want to sit on that there donkey.'

The women were still chuckling when Ensign Richard

172

Kennelly came back to direct the women to a position in the hills they were approaching. It was on the far side of the ridge where the 6th Division would take up a position in anticipation of a battle. From here there was a good view of a plain that stretched almost all the way to Rodrigo.

Josefa was travelling with the other women and Richard Kennelly stopped to exchange a few words with her before returning to the regiment.

'Look at them pair of young lovers,' Rose remarked, but there was none of the malice that was present in her voice when she spoke of Sarah Cottle.

'I think they make a lovely couple,' said Cassie. 'If Richard Kennelly had any sense he'd marry Josefa right away.'

'Perhaps you're right, lovey. But if men had that much sense they'd never fight wars, and we wouldn't be here a'saying what they ought to do. You and me had better pool what we've got to eat. It goes further that way. Josefa can bring her food along too, if she's a mind.'

It was a considerable concession on the part of the sergeant's wife. Josefa's situation was a difficult one. Had Richard Kennelly been a more senior officer he would have been able to flaunt her quite openly without risk of having her slighted by the promotion-conscious wives of more junior officers. However, as the mistress of the most junior officer in the regiment, as well as being a low-caste Spaniard, Josefa was socially unacceptable to the legitimate wives of officers. She was also resented by the wives of the soldiers and the other women classed loosely as camp followers.

In spite of a number of warnings and alarms, no battle was fought that day, and home for Cassie and Harry that night was a wood and grass shelter. It was no more than a flimsy canopy but it helped protect their bedding from the worst of the rain.

Cassie had little sleep during that seemingly long night, but it had nothing to do with the weather, or their primitive accommodation. Harry was nervous at the prospect of a battle and Cassie spent much of the night holding him in her arms, calming his fears as best she could.

The camp was astir early the next morning with more rumours of battle. The shivering of soldiers and their women owed as much to increasing excitement as to a chill wind blowing down from the mountains. Older soldiers grumbled that no other general would still be campaigning when winter was almost upon them. Some remembered the heat of India with more enthusiasm than they had ever shown while serving in that country.

There was to be no marching this morning. Instead, the army took up positions facing the direction from which the enemy was expected to arrive. As daylight advanced beyond the grey, indistinct mountain peaks situated in the heartland of Spain, an eerie, inexplicable silence fell upon the waiting army. Here and there an imaginative soldier thought he saw the shadow of an advancing French regiment – or heard the muffled jingle of cavalry harness.

Then, with a suddenness that was almost unreal, the waiting officers and men realised they were no longer looking into darkness. The whole plain stretched out before them – and it was empty. The advancing regiment was seen to be a drifting breath of fast disappearing mist and the sound of harness a waking bird. There was no French army arraigned for battle.

Feeling foolish, the soldiers heaved sighs of relief and voices were once more raised as bow-tight nerves relaxed. Moments later the order was passed along the lines that cooking fires might be lit and breakfast prepared.

Cassie had barely coaxed a flame from the damp grass and wood when a picket was called for from the 32nd to take up position on a low, loosely wooded slope in an area of ravines and broken ground more than half a mile ahead of the main position.

The 6th Division was on the extreme left of an alarmingly extended British front stretching sixteen miles from end to end. The divisions on either end occupied good positions in the hills, but those in between held dangerously exposed positions on the edge of a wide plain.

Unfortunately, there was no other way for Lord Wellington to deploy his army. Had the line been less extended the superior numbers of the enemy would have enabled the French general to surround the British force. Had the centre of the British line been pulled back to the hills the flanks would need to be brought back with them to form a line, thus enabling the French artillery to occupy positions dominating the whole British line.

The long front presented by the British army and their Portuguese allies was safe enough, if the French soldiers were not allowed to march around the divisions at either end and carry out a surprise attack from the rear.

The object of the picket sent out from the 32nd Regiment was to prevent such an attack being mounted. From their position they would use a spyglass to maintain observation of the road from Rodrigo. This responsible, though not especially dangerous task, was given to Ensign Kennelly. He took a party of twenty men with him, Harry Clymo among them. Meanwhile, a squadron of dragoons was also sent out from the line with orders to go as far as the gates of Rodrigo if necessary, in order to learn what they could of the enemy's intentions.

The picket left the regiment's position before breakfast was ready and when it was time for the remainder of the regiment to eat, Cassie suggested to Josefa that they should take food to their men.

Soon they were making their way over the rough ground, heading towards the picket's position. The rain clouds had drifted away in the early hours of the morning and the first warmth of the sun promised a fine, hot day.

'I hope there will be no fighting today,' Josefa said suddenly.

'So do I.' Cassie scrambled over a low, flat rock that was already warm to the touch. Safely on the far side she waited for the other girl. 'Do you have a special reason for wishing that?'

Josefa shrugged and avoided Cassie's gaze. 'I do not think Richard is happy to be a soldier.'

'Why? Because he lay awake all night worrying about the battle he thought he'd be fighting today?'

'You know?' In an instant suspicion had replaced surprise. 'How do you know?'

'Because Harry was awake for much of the night, too,

and Rose Tonks once told me her husband can never sleep the night before a battle. I doubt if any of the men can.'

Josefa gave Cassie a relieved smile. 'He is not frightened – well, not for himself. He fears he will not fight as well as others think he should.' Josefa walked in silence for a while before adding, 'Richard's mind is too full of thoughts for a soldier.'

'He's well liked by the men, Josefa.'

'I do not care about their like. I *love* him.'

The words came out with all the unreasonable passion of a sixteen-year-old and for the second time in only a few days Cassie had to remind herself that she, too, was only sixteen.

The two women found the majority of the picket relaxing among rocks and trees at the far end of a low ridge. Four of their number were peering out across the wide broken plains towards Rodrigo, the others lay sprawled on the ground, a few playing a game of cards, the remainder lazing or dozing.

The arrival of the two women was greeted with howls of good-natured envy, which changed to delight when Cassie revealed they had brought food for all the men. However, only Harry had bread purchased by Cassie from a Spanish baker the day before. The remainder had to make do with tough beef and stale biscuit.

Suddenly one of the men on watch called to Richard Kennelly, 'There's something happening over by Rodrigo. It looks as though the Frenchies might be coming out after all.'

All thought of food was forgotten for the moment as Cassie and Josefa joined the men scrambling up the rocks on the perimeter of the picket outpost. Richard extended the leather-bound brass telescope he carried and seemed to spend an interminable time focusing it. He remained perfectly still, peering out towards Rodrigo. When he eventually lowered the telescope, he said, with considerable awe, 'It must be the whole of the French cavalry out there. Thousands of them.'

The telescope was passed among the men and the two women. All agreed they were viewing a major force riding out from Rodrigo to do battle with the forces of Lord Wellington and Cassie felt her stomach contract in a breathless combination of fear and excitement.

After viewing the French cavalry force again and making a more precise estimate of their strength, Richard wrote a note and gave it to one of the soldiers with orders that he should run all the way to the 6th Division headquarters with the message.

'Is there going to be a battle?' Josefa asked the question querulously.

'No doubt about it.' The ensign gave his reply with the telescope to his eye. A few moments later he scribbled another note, giving another soldier the same instructions as the first. 'The infantry are moving out now, and they're dividing up. Some are heading this way, the remainder are marching across the plain.'

The messenger did not need to go all the way to the divisional headquarters. A small party of horsemen were already on their way from the British lines to the position occupied by the picket. After reading the note one of the horsemen spurred on his horse and the others followed suit.

Richard was engrossed in observing the French movements through the telescope and failed to hear the hoarse-voiced soldier who tried to attract his attention. When he did turn around he almost dropped his telescope in surprise. Recovering quickly he slipped to the ground from the rock on which he had been lying.

'My lord, I'm sorry, I didn't see you . . .'

'Of course you didn't. You were doing what you were sent here to do. Observing the enemy and reporting on their movements. They are good reports, ensign. Clear, concise, and not too wordy.' As he spoke he was polishing the lens of his own telescope. 'What's your name?'

'Kennelly, my lord. Ensign of the Thirty-second.'

Lord Wellington, commander-in-chief of the British army, nodded. 'Very good, sir. We'll both climb that rock and you can point out to me exactly what's happening.'

French soldiers, both infantry and cavalry, were still pouring along the road from Rodrigo, but Lord Wellington had grasped the situation long before the young ensign had finished giving his own nervous appraisal of the situation.

'Yes, I think I can see what their game is, but we'll give them a fight to remember. Yes indeed, a good fight, and we'll win the day.'

To his officers, Lord Wellington called, 'We have a busy day ahead of us, gentlemen.' Nodding his satisfaction to Richard Kennelly, he said, 'Remain here as long as you can, sir. I'll have reinforcements sent out to you. I have a feeling the dragoons I despatched may require assistance. But don't risk the lives of your own men unnecessarily. I'll have need of every good soldier in the army when the French army reaches us. You'd better have these two young ladies escorted back to the other women too. They are both far too attractive to risk having them taken by the French.'

With a nod to Cassie and Josefa, and another in the direction of the soldiers of the picket, Lord Wellington hurried to his horse followed by his staff officers. Moments later the high-ranking party was cantering back towards the British lines.

It was Josefa who broke the long silence that followed the departure of Lord Wellington. 'Was that really Lord Wellington? The great general?'

'It was – and you heard what he said. You'd better head back towards the other women.'

'I think it might be a bit late, sir. There are horsemen heading this way at the gallop. Our dragoons being chased by French lancers, I'd say.'

Richard scrambled to the top of the rock and he did not need a telescope to confirm the words of the look-out. The small squadron of British dragoons, sent out to the vicinity of Rodrigo, was riding pell-mell towards the British lines, pursued by at least two hundred lancers and a number of other French cavalrymen.

'Take up firing positions, but don't start shooting until I tell you. Josefa, Cassie, there isn't time for you to get back safely to our lines. Take cover among the rocks down here.'

This was a new Richard Kennelly. Gone were the nerves and the self-doubt. Decisions needed to be taken, and the ensign was taking them.

Cassie looked at Harry. His fears of the night had

also gone. On his face was the same expression of excited anticipation she could see on the faces of the other soldiers.

'There's a company on its way to help us, sir. Riflemen, by the looks of it.' One of the soldiers pointed to where about a hundred green-clad soldiers were running from the direction of the British lines, heading along the slope towards their position.

'The French will be here first, I fear.'

The British dragoons were only a few hundred yards away now, but their horses were tiring and the lancers of the French army were almost up with them.

'When I give the order, fire at the horses of the leading lancers. With any luck they'll fall and trip the others. Ready now ... !'

The dragoons were taking a curving course around the low ridge where the picket was posted, the hooves of the horses drumming on the ground and the creak of leather saddles mingling with the heavy blowing of the labouring animals.

'Now!'

The crack of twenty muskets was startling enough. More importantly, the musket balls produced the effect for which Richard had been hoping. Eight of the leading horses crashed to the ground, bringing a score more down behind them. For some moments all was chaos in the ranks of the lancers.

By the time the lancers had recovered from their surprise the first of the green-clad riflemen had reached the picket and their accurate fire, together with that of the reloaded infantrymen, quickly drove the lancers back towards their main force, leaving a number of dead and wounded men and horses lying on the ground behind them. Fighting against men hidden among rocks on a hillside was not a task for lancers. This would be left to the French infantrymen who were marching towards the British lines in a seemingly endless column.

Richard Kennelly sent four of his men to bring in two wounded French officers who were seated on the ground among the dead horses. When they returned, one of the Frenchmen was found to be the commanding officer of the regiment of lancers.

The French officer refused to hand his sword to anyone but the officer in command of the British picket. He was crestfallen to discover he had been captured by such a young and low-ranking officer. However, he handed over his sword and complimented the young ensign on his tactics. He also suggested Richard should take good care of the sword as he intended asking for its return when the French army beat the British in the forthcoming battle.

Richard was well pleased with his high-ranking prisoner, little knowing how much trouble his prize would bring in its wake. The brother of the Frenchman commanded a regiment of French *chasseurs*. He would make strenuous attempts to rescue his kinsman.

The French cavalry officer had been wounded in the knee by one of the shots which had downed his horse and he permitted Cassie to clean and dress the wound. Cassie would have called for Josefa to assist her, but the Spanish girl was finding it difficult to take her gaze off Richard. The young man's fear of his first battle had

182

gone for ever. His coolness in the face of danger and his natural authority in dealing with the situation had transformed him into a hero in her eyes.

However, Richard Kennelly's authority was about to be seriously undermined. The riflemen who had now all reached the picket's position were led by a lieutenant. He made it clear immediately that he had assumed command. When Richard suggested they should now try to return to the British lines, the lieutenant demurred. 'I've brought my men out here to support your position, not to escort you back to the army.'

'We'll serve no useful purpose by remaining here now,' insisted the young ensign.

'That's for me to decide,' snapped the lieutenant. 'I want you and your men to take up a position over there –' he pointed to a rocky outcrop overhanging the steepest spot along the ridge on which the picket had been positioned '– and you can send these women back to the lines.'

For the second time that morning the action of the enemy prevented such an order from being obeyed.

'More French cavalry coming this way. Looks like a whole regiment of them.'

This disturbing information came from a rifleman corporal squatting on a rock high above the outpost.

The lieutenant climbed up on the rock to see for himself. After only a few moments he slid down, saying, 'It's a full regiment of *chasseurs*. With any luck they'll pass close enough for us to get a shot or two at them.'

'Oh, you can be certain they will come close.' The senior French officer smiled. 'That will be my brother's

183

regiment. I think he has plans to return me to my own command.'

'If he does it will be to bury you,' declared the lieutenant. 'Should it look as though we're likely to be overrun I'll personally shoot you.'

'Not while he's *my* prisoner.' A shocked Richard Kennelly spoke heatedly. 'He gave his sword to me. That puts him under my protection.'

'We'll see about that if the occasion arises. For now you'd better get up there with your men. If you don't feel like fighting you can sit back with your Frenchman and see how riflemen fight a battle.'

The officer had been correct. The French cavalry rode directly towards the British outpost, apparently unaware that it was no longer occupied only by a small picket. However, these were not regular cavalrymen armed only with swords. The French horsemen also carried muskets and they were equipped and trained to fight either as cavalry or as infantry, and they must have been six or seven hundred strong.

When they were still out of range of the men manning the picket outpost, the French cavalrymen halted. About half their number dismounted, checked their guns and fixed bayonets. Then they began to advance. Meanwhile the remainder of the regiment formed a long double line, evidently preparing for a cavalry charge.

The lieutenant in charge of the riflemen, although arrogant, was no fool. He guessed the intention of the French. The dismounted men would storm the outpost, drawing fire from what they believed to be no more than a small picket. Then, when a volley had been fired at them, the mounted men would urge their horses up the slope and slaughter the English soldiers before they could reload.

The lieutenant had other ideas. At each order to fire no more than half his men would discharge their weapons. The others would be ready to obey his next command while their colleagues reloaded.

It worked as though it had been rehearsed. The dismounted French cavalrymen advanced ahead of their mounted colleagues, shooting and shouting as they came, convinced they would carry the picket's outpost with ease. The lieutenant waited until the Frenchmen were well within musket range before giving an order to fire. The effect was devastating. The riflemen were sharpshooters, equipped with the very latest Baker rifle. Not one musket ball was wasted. When the pall of black gunpowder smoke cleared, fifty French soldiers had been downed and their companions faltered.

It was now that Richard Kennelly ordered the men of the 32nd to fire upon the French soldiers. Their volley was less accurate than the shooting of the riflemen, but it was sufficient. Ten men fell and the remainder of the dismounted cavalrymen turned and fled, some of their less seriously wounded comrades limping after them.

When the French commander saw his dismounted men falter and retreat he gave the order for his horsemen to charge, leading the way himself. He was the first to fall, but he did not die alone. More than forty of the leading cavalrymen fell with him and the riderless and injured horses caused chaos. Some of the dismounted men, seeing their commander riding into battle, returned to the scene and their firing added to the increasing confusion.

To Cassie and Josefa crouched down among the rocks on the crest of the low ridge it sounded as though the whole French and British armies were fighting around the outpost. All about them they could hear the cries of the wounded, the screaming of injured horses, shooting, shouting and the singing of musket balls ricocheting from rocks.

Suddenly Richard slid from the dangerously exposed position he had been occupying on a large boulder and cried, 'The lieutenant's been hit.'

Two men were dragging the officer back to a cleared space in the centre of the besieged picket post. Abandoning her own scant shelter, Cassie ran to assist them – but it needed only a glance to see the lieutenant was beyond all help. A musket ball had struck him on the side of the head, above his right ear. Even as Cassie wiped blood from his face the lieutenant expelled his last breath in a great, juddering sigh.

Meanwhile the French cavalry was re-forming for another assault on the outpost and Richard ordered the riflemen to fight in the same manner as before, with only half the company firing at each order. There were a number of wounded and dead men inside the outpost by now and Cassie looked about her for Harry. She was relieved when she saw him, pale faced but unhurt and he even managed to give her an answering smile, albeit a somewhat sickly one.

Crawling among the wounded men, Cassie and Josefa did what they could to help. In most cases it meant no more than raising a water bottle to the lips of a dying man.

A volley crashed out from the riflemen, but not all the dismounted French soldiers fled this time. Some reached their objective and a number of desperate bayonet duels were fought inside the picket post – yet still the half-company of riflemen held their fire.

'Here they come,' Cassie heard one of the soldiers murmur. 'Now we're for it.'

At that moment there was a shout from one of the 32nd Regiment men, positioned higher on the ridge than the others. 'Here come the dragoons. Our dragoons!'

They were the same cavalrymen who had been chased back from Rodrigo. Observing the plight of the men who had drawn off their pursuers, the dragoons were determined to take revenge for their own ignominious flight – and now there were two full squadrons of them.

The French cavalry had seen the dragoons too. All thought of taking the outpost was temporarily forgotten as they turned to face the new and dangerous threat.

As the French cavalry tried to form in a confused line, sorely missing their fallen commander, Richard ordered the riflemen to fire a volley into their packed ranks. It was a long-range target, even for the excellent Baker rifles, but it achieved its purpose splendidly. The French cavalrymen had still not formed a line when the dragoons, led by Lieutenant Dalhousie, rode into and through them.

Throughout much of his Peninsular campaign Lord Wellington was to complain bitterly of the indiscipline of the cavalry units in his army but, watching the encounter through a telescope, he had no cause for complaint today. Having broken through the thinned ranks of the French force which, although suffering heavy casualties, still outnumbered them by three to one, Lieutenant Dalhousie's light dragoons turned, re-formed and rode through the milling French cavalry once more.

Loose horses were galloping in every direction as the fierce skirmish was fought. As well as felling French cavalrymen from their saddles, the British dragoons had cut down the soldiers holding the horses of their dismounted colleagues engaged in the assault on the picket outpost.

By now the Frenchmen on the hillside had abandoned their assault and were trying to catch their horses. Without them they would be stranded in easy artillery range of the British lines – and far from their own army. Running in as many directions as their freed horses, often pursued by vengeful dragoons, they added to the confusion.

As Lieutenant Dalhousie's dragoons turned for yet another charge, the surviving French cavalrymen decided they had taken enough punishment. Gathering up those wounded men who possessed strength enough to ride, they turned their backs on the British army and fled.

A great cheer went up from the British lines, but the fight was not over yet. The French commander-in-chief had also seen what was happening and had sent more cavalry forward. The skirmish was fast becoming a matter of honour for both sides.

Richard Kennelly ordered the riflemen and his men of the 32nd to retire along the ridge towards the British lines. The need for a picket was long gone and Lord Wellington himself had said lives should not be needlessly thrown away.

The soldiers gathered up their wounded together with the body of the lieutenant and began a slow retreat along the slope of the hill. They had not gone far when Lieutenant Dalhousie rode up with some of his dragoons. He gave a mock salute to Cassie before saying to Richard, 'You have the gratitude of my men, sir. We'll take the women and your wounded to the lines. You've a fight on your hands and you'll need to be free of encumbrances.'

'Will you take my prisoner too? He's the commander of the regiment that chased you back to the lines. Much of the fighting has been because the French want him back.'

'Delighted. Hurry, ladies, you and the wounded will have to share a horse with my men and I'll need them back here shortly.'

After the hastiest of farewells to Harry, Cassie mounted a horse behind a heavily perspiring trooper. Minutes later she slid from the horse's back in the safety of the British lines. Looking along the ridge she had just left she saw Richard organising the riflemen and his own men in an orderly, fighting retreat.

'I pray Richard gets back safely.' Josefa spoke in little more than a whisper, but it was heard by Gorran Fox who had come to take the French cavalry officer to the general commanding the 6th Division.

'They'll make it. This is Richard Kennelly's day. It sometimes happens in war. He's proved he's a first-class soldier and earned the respect of his men, the general – and of Lord Wellington too, I understand.'

Josefa could have burst with pride at Gorran's words, but all she said was, 'I will be very happy when he comes back to me.'

'You two young ladies must have had enough excitement for one day. You'll find the other women have been moved to a ridge behind the divisional headquarters. I'll show you the way.'

As Cassie and Josefa made their way up the steep hill with Gorran and the limping French officer they heard the sound of gunfire and a cheer rose from the British troops. Turning, they saw that Richard's small force had just beaten off another attack by French light cavalry and Lieutenant Dalhousie's squadron was making another charge.

They could also see that both British infantry and cavalry had suffered more casualties. Cassie prayed that Harry would not be among them and wished she had a telescope to train on the dwindling band of men. French infantry was advancing across the plain at a trot now and, although she knew nothing of military matters, common sense told her that Richard and his men could not survive unless they reached the British lines before the vastly superior French forces overtook them.

Others were aware of the danger and as they toiled up the hill in the direction of the divisional headquarters, a sergeant came half running, half sliding down the hill towards them. As he reached them the sergeant shouted, 'The general says the Thirty-second can go out and support their ensign.'

The NCO had taken only a few paces when Gorran called on him to stop. 'Escort this prisoner to divisional headquarters. I'll tell the Thirty-second.'

Before the sergeant could argue that the message had been given to him to pass on, Gorran had gone. He reached the place in the line held by the 32nd Regiment, shouting his news ahead of him. It brought a great cheer as men rose to their feet, eager to go to the aid of Ensign Kennelly and his party. And Gorran Fox led the way.

More dragoons had been thrown into the fight and the skirmish was beginning to take on the appearance of a full-scale battle as Richard fought his way towards the lines with an ever dwindling number of soldiers.

The low ridge was of sufficient size for a company of soldiers, but could not hold a full regiment. After making contact with the young ensign, the colonel of the 32nd brought the whole regiment down to level ground just as the French cavalry mounted an earth-pounding charge. The infantrymen had only just enough time to form into a tightly packed square before the French cavalry was upon them.

A volley fired from the square produced so much white smoke that for a few minutes the whole scene was hidden from the view of those watching anxiously from the British lines. Then a breeze parted the thick smoke and a cheer went up. The square was intact although French horses and riders were piled high about them.

For fifteen more minutes the French continued their costly charges while the men of the 32nd Regiment retreated slowly, maintaining their formation and enjoying an occasional respite when British dragoons made a charge in their support.

Suddenly the 32nd's square came within range of the British lines, and the French would venture no closer. The rescue of Ensign Richard Kennelly and his picket had been achieved and cheers rippled along the length of the British line.

Harry was safe, too, although his face was so blackened with dirt that Cassie began to panic before she recognised his relieved smile. There was no time to speak to each other until much later, when the French commander withdrew his forces and the wives were able to go down to the lines and take food to their men.

Richard Kennelly was the hero of the army that day. Messages praising his courageous and intelligent conduct poured in from the commanding officers of almost every regiment of the line. There was also a brief 'Well done, Mr Kennelly' written on a scrap of paper and signed by Lord Wellington. The final official seal on his bravery came from the captured French cavalry officer who made him a gift of the magnificent sword the young ensign had accepted from him on his capture.

Yet of all the praises heaped upon Richard that day, the one that gave him most pleasure was the look of pride on Josefa's face when she brought him his food, held his hand for a brief moment and called him her *'valiente guerrero'*.

15

That night Wellington ordered his army to retreat to new positions, farther back in the hills. After the successful defence of the day it came as a bewildering surprise to the men of his army, all of whom were eager to do battle and inflict a decisive defeat upon the French.

Only those very close to Wellington knew how carefully the brilliant British commander had weighed his chances of success against a French army which was numerically superior to his own, and which had an overwhelming number of cavalrymen.

The order was particularly hard on those who had fought during the day. Exhausted, they had been looking forward to a restful night's sleep, excused from further picket duties for a while. Instead the soldiers were ordered to pack their possessions and take up arms for a silent retreat, in order to leave the enemy unaware of their nocturnal movements.

The suddenness of the move proved disastrous for a number of non-combatants, including a regimental padre, many of whom were overlooked when the order for retreat was given. Falsely secure in the knowledge that the finest army in the world stood between themselves and the army of Napoleon, the padre and his companions had found quarters for the night in a nearby village. Not for them the discomfort of a damp and uncomfortable bed with only an army meal inside their bellies. The padre, in particular, enjoyed a vast amount of local food, washed down with a couple of bottles of fine local wine before retiring to bed, unaware that his security was quietly slipping away to the south and west of the village.

The padre had a rude awakening the next morning when French soldiers invaded his bedroom. Later that day he was returned to the British army, minus his clothes and with his dignity sorely ruffled.

It was a difficult move for Cassie. She was very tired and had trouble locating all her belongings in the darkness of the night. When she set off on her donkey, one of the provost marshals accompanying the departing army made her halt and repack the animal's saddlebags because the pots and pans were clattering together, making too much noise.

It did not help when the new line was reached and the 6th Division was ordered to take up a position on the right flank of the army. As they had been holding the left flank during the day it meant they had to march farther than any other division, not reaching their new position until long after daylight.

French skirmishers found the new British line shortly before noon but seemed uncertain of what to do. All day groups of French staff officers gathered on a small hill in front of the British army and perused the British defences. There was much gesticulation and argument clearly visible from the British lines but the French seemed to be as baffled by Wellington's fall-back as were the tired soldiers of the 32nd. Later in the day the main French army came into view but made no attempt to join battle with their tired adversaries.

This was Cassie's first experience of an army in retreat and she found it very disturbing. The men had merely withdrawn to new positions, not fled from an enemy, yet there was an air of dejection in marked contrast to the confidence and determination of the previous day.

As she and the other women prepared a meal for the men, who sat with their backs to a driving mountain drizzle, Rose Tonks was surprisingly philosophical about the mood of the army. 'It's always the same the day after a battle – not that yesterday was much of a battle. Mind you, it's even worse when they've been on the losing side. I never again want to see anything like the retreat to Corunna, when we were here before. Things got so bad then that if anyone fell, be it man, woman or child, they'd be trampled so deep in the mud they'd never be seen again.'

'But this is a retreat, surely?'

'It's nothing of the sort. If you was to read Lord Wellington's orders you'd see we'd merely "retired to new positions".'

'What's that if it's not a retreat?' retorted Sarah Cottle.

'It's exactly what it says.' Rose gave emphasis to her words by banging her ladle noisily on a mess-tin as she served up a stew concocted from salt beef and thickened with crumbled hard-tack biscuit. 'Take this to your husband – and remember, it's our job to keep our men happy, not to depress 'em even more than they are already.'

This pointed remark was aimed particularly at Sarah Cottle. The regiment was used to her indiscretions by now, but her association with Lieutenant Dalhousie was causing more raised eyebrows than any of her previous affairs. She had spent much of the day in the camp of the Light Dragoons. When Rose tackled her with her blatant 'carryings-on', Sarah claimed she had been asked to explain the duties of a camp follower to some Spanish girls who had attached themselves to the cavalrymen. The dragoons were not allowed to have wives with them on a campaign, but it was inevitable they should attract a number of local women.

'When Wellington lets us bed down for a night my husband will wake a sight happier than yours, Rose Tonks, so just you keep your accusations to yourself,' was Sarah's parting shot as the two wives parted company at the cooking fire.

It seemed Lord Wellington was not concerned with the sexual needs of his soldiers. As soon as darkness fell the order came for the army to move back once more, this time to positions centred on a village named Elboden.

By now the British soldiers were thoroughly dejected, as were many of the women who had followed the army for several years. There was talk of a retreat all the way to the coast, as had occurred in the harsh winter of 1808–9. Not willing to be loaded down with excess equipment as they were on that tragic occasion, a number of men abandoned anything they deemed non-essential.

The army did not retire as far on this night as on the previous two and most men were able to snatch a couple of hours' sleep, but not the 32nd Regiment. A strong picket was put out ahead of the main line. Ensign Kennelly, Corporal Cottle and Harry Clymo were all included in it once more, this time with orders to leave their women behind.

It was a cold night and Cassie and Josefa shared a small shelter they had built from the sparse under-growth. It served as no more than a windbreak, but it was better than nothing. The wind was strong with a hint of rain and the two women sat huddled in blankets, knees drawn up and talking in low voices so as not to disturb those who slept about them.

'I wish they send men from another regiment on picket duty tonight.' Josefa shivered and drew her blanket higher about her shoulders. 'After the last picket I have fear for Richard whenever he goes from my sight.'

'Most of us feel the same, Josefa,' Cassie replied sympathetically. 'That's the trouble with caring so much for someone, I suppose. You're always afraid you're going to lose him.'

As Cassie spoke there was movement among the sleeping soldiers. A figure picked its way carefully between the blanket-covered figures, heading towards a section of the line where cavalry horses could be heard

197

moving and blowing, seemingly troubled by the same uncertain restlessness that beset Wellington's soldiers.

As the figure crossed in front of a still-glowing fire, Cassie and Josefa both recognised Sarah Cottle.

'Not every woman is concerned about losing her man.' Josefa spoke contemptuously.

'Don't think too harshly of her, Josefa. Sarah Cottle has had a great many tragedies in her life, and much unhappiness. I think she's lost her man so many times she's frightened of caring too much for anyone any more.'

'She did not have to stay with the army when her first man was killed.'

'I don't suppose there's much for her at home. Besides, army life gets into your blood eventually, at least that's what Rose Tonks says.'

'Ah! There is a woman who cares for her man. She is the strength for him.' Josefa was silent for a few moments, then she said in a plaintive whisper, 'I do not know what I will do if anything happens to Richard.'

Cassie was sunk in thought for some time. When she spoke again she chose her words very carefully. 'The British army won't be in Spain for ever, Josefa. One day Richard will return to England. Will you try to go with him, or return to your own home?'

'I no longer have a home. They would not take me back. It is bad enough I run away with someone who is not of our people. For it to be a British soldier . . . It will not be forgiven.'

'These things often cause an upset at the time.' Cassie thought uncomfortably of her own abrupt departure from Mevagissey. 'I'm sure they'll forgive you, given time.'

'You do not know my people, Cassie. They are slow to forgive. No, if something happens to Richard it is better for me to die with him.'

'Shh! Don't talk of such things. Richard isn't going to die – and neither are you.'

Somewhere in the mountains behind them a wolf howled, the sound carrying on the wind and causing Cassie to shudder.

'Richard has asked me to marry him. I told him he was being foolish.'

'Why?'

Even as she asked the question, Cassie thought she knew the answer. Richard Kennelly and Josefa came from very different backgrounds. Josefa was a lovely girl and would be regarded as such wherever she happened to be, but much of her beauty was in her long black hair, dark skin, bare legs and colourful gipsy clothes. None of these would be considered an asset in the society to which Richard belonged. Cassie realised Josefa was intelligent enough to have reached the same conclusion for herself. Josefa's reply to her half-asked question confirmed this.

'Here we are good for each other. Richard is lonely. I am lonely. Together we can forget the war, forget he might be killed tomorrow. Nothing else matters. In England it would be different. I would not know his ways or what was expected of me. His mother would point to other girls he might have married. They would know what they must do and what they must not do.

I know nothing of his family. I do not ask him. Do you know anything?'

'Very little. His father is a lord, an earl, I believe.'

'An earl? *Uno conde?* There, you see! I am right. He cannot marry me.' Josefa struggled to contain the mixture of awe and unhappiness that filled her as a result of Cassie's revelation. 'Richard will be an earl too, one day?'

'No, he has too many older brothers. It isn't a very rich family. He'll have to make his own way in the world, and gain promotion by being a good soldier.'

'He will. He is very brave. Even Lord Wellington says so. I cannot marry Richard but I will help him while he is in my country. I think perhaps then he will remember and love me a little bit for always.'

Josefa became silent and Cassie did not disturb her thoughts. They would not be happy ones, but it was better than brooding on the possibility of Richard being killed in action. Soon the two young women fell asleep leaning against each other in the darkness.

The French army was on the move early the next morning and the 32nd Regiment's picket was recalled at dawn. Along the British line the men took up their positions to await the onslaught of the French army.

Lord Wellington had chosen his position well. Occupying a forward-facing slope on a small range of hills, the line stretched across a neck of land where the River Coa looped in a giant U-shape. The British army and their Portuguese allies were secure from a flank or rear attack and had only to repel the enemy in one direction.

However, should the numerically superior French army once breach the British line there was nowhere to which they might retreat. If the line failed to hold, Wellington's Peninsular army would cease to exist. Spain and Portugal would fall into Napoleon Bonaparte's hands once more and it was doubtful whether the British parliament would ever again risk sending another army against the 'Little Corporal'.

Set against this was the possibility of inflicting a decisive defeat upon the French army. This would guarantee the eventual fall of Rodrigo and open the way for Wellington to advance into the heart of Spain. Either eventuality would change the course of history – but fate in the form of the French general declined to put it to the test, although this was not immediately apparent.

From the hills behind the British line Cassie and the other women watched in awe as the French commander paraded regiment after regiment across the front of the British lines in an impressive show of strength.

First came the French cavalry, the lancers still capable of bringing a shudder to Cassie. Then the infantry, each regiment with its own band to provide a colourful display of its might. For most of the day the French army marched and counter-marched, trotted and galloped to the music of bugle and drum and fast-moving bands.

In the late afternoon the whole French army formed three columns, each twenty thousand strong. Then, to the total bewilderment of the watching British soldiers they marched away, as jauntily as though they had just won a resounding victory. The French commander had

201

quitted the field – without a shot being fired from either side!

The short Iberian winter had already begun and the French commander-in-chief was satisfied his show of strength would ensure the British made no move against him until the spring. By then much might have happened. The British king, George III, had been officially declared insane. His pleasure-loving son was acting as Regent, with limited powers that were to be greatly increased if the King had not recovered by February 1812. With a hedonistic monarch taking the place of austere insanity, the English might withdraw from a war they could not possibly win.

Warmed by this thought the French commander-in-chief went on his way feeling as jaunty as the troops marching at his back.

16

❧

With the departure eastwards of the French army, Lord Wellington retired to the west. Crossing the River Coa into Portugal, he put his army into cantonment for the winter.

The next three months were miserable ones for Cassie and the other women of the 32nd Regiment. Billeted in and about the village of Freixedas they shared houses with the Portuguese occupants.

Cassie had not been accustomed to luxury in her parents' terraced house in Mevagissey, but the conditions endured by the Portuguese peasants with whom she and Sarah Cottle were billeted were almost beyond belief. The house did not possess a fireplace and the roof leaked in a score of places. In addition, the house was infested with fleas. There were so many of the irritating insects that they could be found clustered together in their hundreds, looking for all the world like small heaps of onion seeds.

The elderly, wrinkled occupiers of the dingy and dirty hovel added to the general misery by spending most of the daylight hours sitting in corners, each with a shawl draped over head and shoulders as protection against the leaks. Rocking backwards and forwards in silent and abject misery they seemed, as Sarah said, 'to be waiting for a call from their Lord, to explain why he had not deigned to extend his bounty to the Catholic residents of Freixedas'.

Two nights of such primitive conditions were all the two British couples could take. Ushering the loudly protesting Portuguese couple out into the rain, Cassie and Sarah set to with brushes and water to rid the house of fleas and the army of spiders taking shelter from the rain. Meanwhile, ignoring the protests of the house owners, Harry and Corporal Cottle constructed a fireplace in a corner of the room, knocking a hole through the dried mud wall that would hopefully take out most of the smoke. It would not be entirely satisfactory, but, as Sarah cheerfully said, the smoke would rid the house of those fleas they had missed.

The leaking roof posed a greater problem, one that seemingly affected every country dwelling in Portugal. However, by forming work-teams the British soldiers were able to gather turf and grass to reduce the water entering each small cottage to an acceptable trickle.

The Portuguese residents failed to appreciate the improvements imposed upon them by their unasked-for tenants. They complained constantly to British army authorities about the troops who interfered with their way of life. The complaints would have received more serious attention had the officers to whom they were made not been billeted in similar houses.

The primitive conditions in the villages around Freixedas might have been satisfactory for the Portuguese inhabitants but they played havoc with the health of the British army. Within a month of going into cantonment a quarter of the army was sick with a fever that had men and women shivering one moment, perspiring the next. It left them weak and low-spirited for weeks after it had run its debilitating course.

Every one of the wives attached to the 32nd Regiment was taken ill. Cassie was affected particularly badly. For days she lay in near delirium and thoroughly alarmed Harry. Sarah Cottle was an excellent nurse, but she had no enthusiasm for nursing women when there were so many sick men around. Fortunately, Josefa took it upon herself to nurse Cassie through the day, remaining with her during the nights when the fever was at its climax.

One morning Cassie awoke feeling incredibly weak but with the heat of the fever gone. She felt hungry for the first time for days. When she asked Josefa for food the gipsy girl's face broke into a tired but relieved smile.

'At last you want to eat. It means you are now almost better. For three days I have had to beg you to take something. It is lucky for you I have a stew made from the chicken Mr Fox brought here for you.'

'Gorran Fox has been here?'

'Twice. The second time he brought the chicken and I have not dared to leave it for one minute or Sarah would have taken most of it for herself.'

Cassie moved her head. The small house was empty. Even the Portuguese woman was not in her usual place in the corner. 'Where's Sarah now?'

Josefa smiled scornfully. 'Ask her and she will say all day she spends trying to buy food. Most of the night too, I think.'

'Where is she spending her time?'

'With the dragoons and their young officer. You know the one. He travelled from the coast with you, and brought us in from the picket.'

'Mr Dalhousie? Is that still going on? I would have thought she'd have found someone else by now.'

'If she has any sense she'll find someone very quickly. Richard knows about it – and that means all the officers of the regiment know.'

Cassie lay back on her uncomfortable hay-filled mattress and closed her eyes as Josefa added, 'Walter Cottle knows, too, and it is making him very unhappy.'

As she ladled chicken stew into a mess-tin from the large pot dangling over the fire, Josefa added, 'I think every soldier in the regiment knows what Sarah Cottle is doing. Corporal Cottle knows Sarah's never been faithful to him, but I think this is different. She spends every moment she can with the dragoon officer. Sarah and her husband have argued about it a lot while I have been here.'

'Where's Harry?'

'On picket duty.' Josefa cast a sidelong glance at Cassie. 'I hope your Harry is not a jealous man. Mr Fox said he will call again this morning to see how you are.'

'Harry has no cause to be jealous. Gorran Fox spends

206

as much time talking to him as to me when we meet. We're all from Cornwall, that's why.'

'Perhaps ... but Mr Fox does not come here to see Harry.' Josefa smiled. 'I joke with you, Cassie. You and Sarah Cottle are very different. So, too, is the dragoon lieutenant and your Mr Fox. Gorran Fox is a nice man. If I did not have Richard, who knows, I might make him my man.'

It had not occurred to Cassie that Gorran might take a woman but he was an attractive man. What would he do if someone like Josefa came along? She thought she knew the answer. Josefa was an exceptionally attractive and vivacious girl. She would have no difficulty in winning the heart of any red-blooded young man on campaign, far from home.

'You would not like me to do with Mr Fox what Sarah does with her dragoon officer?'

'What you and Gorran Fox might get up to is none of my business but I doubt if Richard Kennelly would be very happy about it. Is that chicken broth ready yet? Now I've recovered from my fever I don't want to die of hunger.'

'Is coming.'

Josefa carefully carried a well-filled mess-tin to Cassie and set it on the floor beside her. Hoisting her to a sitting position and propping her against the wall behind the bed, Josefa began spooning soup into Cassie's mouth.

'You are right, Cassie. Richard would not like me to look at any other man. I would do nothing to hurt him. He is the most honest, handsome and kind man in the whole world. Is this how you think of your Harry?'

The question took Cassie by surprise and she choked on her soup. The bout of coughing gave her a few minutes to think of her answer. What were her feelings about her husband? She loved him, yes. He was the reason she was here in Spain, suffering conditions she had never known at home in Mevagissey. Yet it was not the passionate 'love or die' relationship that Josefa had with Richard Kennelly. She and Harry had something different. Theirs was a quiet, enduring love. Harry was a good, steady man. He needed her.

Josefa never received the reply Cassie was so carefully preparing. She was still choking when Gorran Fox came through the door, stamping rain from his coat. Hearing her coughing he said, 'That's the healthiest sound we've heard from you for almost a week. But, look, I have something to clear your throat and bring a little colour to your cheeks, too.'

From beneath his cloak the 32nd Regiment lieutenant produced a bottle. 'This is a fine port wine, sent up from Lisbon especially for the headquarters' staff. I thought it might be just what's needed to revive you a little. It's good to see you sitting up and taking notice of the world about you. I was quite concerned when I last paid you a visit. In fact I'm concerned both for you and for the men. If Napoleon attacked right now we'd be hard put to muster three-quarters of the troops fit for battle. I've suggested we move the army to a healthier cantonment, but I think Lord Wellington has something else in mind. However, there's no need for you to concern yourself with army matters right now. Josefa, can you find something from which to drink, while I open this bottle?'

The port wine was as superb as Gorran had promised. Cassie quickly felt its warmth spreading around her body.

'Do you take wine to the sick wives of all your soldiers, Mr Fox?' Josefa asked the question mischievously, after giving Cassie a quick smile.

'Only when there's wine available.' Gorran missed neither Josefa's smile, nor the innuendo contained in her words. 'But I've saved this bottle especially for Cassie. When I was hurt in a coaching accident in Cornwall she gave me the best of treatment. I'm returning the compliment.'

He went on to tell Josefa of the accident involving the coach on the journey to Horsham. He had not ended his story when there was a commotion outside and someone hammered on the door, shouting, 'Mr Fox! Mr Fox, sir!'

Gorran was at the door in a few quick strides and pulled it open. Outside was a young soldier, one of a party of recruits who had joined the 32nd Regiment from England only a few days before. He was on the same picket as Harry.

'Sergeant Tonks sent me to find you, sir. There's a French officer coming in under a flag of truce to speak to an officer of the Thirty-second. He has a woman and a child with him.'

Gorran knew the commanding officer had gone to the nearby fortified town of Almeida to inspect the work being carried out on the defences. Most of the regiment's officers had accompanied him. Gorran was probably the most senior regimental officer available.

'Very well, I'll receive him here and see what it is he wants.'

Gorran began straightening his uniform and he put on his hat, wishing the primitive cottage possessed a mirror. Despite the rain he did not doubt that the Frenchman had stopped before reaching the British cantonment and carefully attended to his own dress.

'Why would a Frenchman be coming here under a flag of truce?'

'There could be any number of reasons, Cassie.' Gorran was as satisfied as he could be that his shining leather hat was firmly in place. 'Last year they sent an officer to return the hound lost by one of our generals, but I can't imagine why he should bring a woman and child with him.'

The answer was not long in coming. There was another knock at the door and it was pushed open by the soldier who had brought news of the French officer's arrival.

'The French officer, sir. A Captain Furneaux, or something like that.'

The Frenchman paused in the doorway to remove his cloak. As Gorran had anticipated, he was as immaculately turned out as any officer could hope to be after a horse ride in the rain.

Both men exchanged salutes but before the French captain had time to express indignation at being received by an officer junior to himself, a woman pushed through the doorway. She was wet and bedraggled and Cassie did not immediately recognise her.

'Cassie! Surely you know me ... ? It's only been a few months ...'

It was Polly Martin, wife of Private Enoch Martin. The woman whose place Cassie had taken on the regiment's strength before leaving England. Behind her in the doorway stood the three-year-old Jean with her hair hanging wet about her face. She was clutching a small wooden-headed doll dressed in the uniform of a French general.

'Polly! What on earth are you doing here ... and where's little Sammy?'

The pleasure left Polly's face. 'Sammy's dead. He died a week after the regiment sailed. I buried him in my home village but there was no place there for me. I'd run off to marry a soldier – that's only half a step removed from being a fallen woman where I come from. I couldn't stay there. I belong here, with Enoch and the regiment.'

Behind the women, Gorran and the French officer were talking. Cassie suddenly felt very tired. She wondered whether Polly's unexpected arrival would affect her own position with the regiment. After all, the other girl had been the one chosen to accompany her husband.

'I can see you've been sick. There's always a lot of illness on a campaign. That's partly why I wanted to be with my Enoch. He needs someone to take care of him ... and I wanted to be the one to break the news of Sammy's death. He thought the world of that boy—'

Polly's voice broke with choked emotion and Cassie lay back with a groan. She closed her eyes. Her head suddenly ached fit to burst – and it was not entirely due to her recent illness and the possible predicament posed by the arrival of the other woman.

'Are you all right, Cassie?'

At Josefa's anxious inquiry Cassie's eyes opened. She nodded. She had not introduced the two women and immediately rectified the omission. Josefa's smile was warm enough but Polly was decidedly cool. Cassie realised with surprise that Polly regarded the Spanish girl with the contempt inherent in many of the soldiers' wives towards the Spanish and Portuguese camp followers. It made things even more difficult.

'Do you know where Enoch's billeted? No doubt he'll be drilling or working, or something, but I'd like to surprise him when he comes back.'

'I think he may be with the working party staying at Almeida.' Cassie's brain was battling against her headache and she tried desperately to think clearly. 'Josefa, would you go and find Rose Tonks? Tell her Enoch Martin's wife is here.'

Josefa was puzzled, but something in the look Cassie gave her stopped her from questioning the instruction.

'I'll go.' The offer came from Polly. 'Tell me where to find Rose and I'll give her a surprise.'

'No!' Cassie reached out a hand and kept Polly by her side. 'You've been out in the rain for far too long. Little Jean, too, she should have dry clothes on.'

At that moment Gorran came across the room, the French officer following in his wake. 'Your determination to rejoin your husband has impressed the French, Polly. They don't usually send a soldier's wife to her regiment under escort – and with a purse filled with Spanish dollars to accompany her.'

Polly looked embarrassed and Cassie took the oppor-

212

tunity to signal for Josefa to set off right away to find Rose. Pulling a shawl about her shoulders, the Spanish girl slipped unnoticed from the house.

'I . . . I got lost.' Polly felt a further explanation was called for. 'No one would guide me to the cantonments unless I paid them and I had no money.'

'Madame Martin strayed well away from your position, fortunately for our marshal. His personal baggage train and a lady of whom he is very fond were on the road to the north of Rodrigo and would have fallen into the hands of Don Xavier had we not been warned in time by the gallant Madame Martin.'

Her face scarlet with embarrassment, Polly explained, 'I thought the Spanish men were robbers. I saw them in hiding and they tried to capture me. When I fled they fired after me and warned the French soldiers who took me with them.'

'They treated you as a heroine, no doubt?'

'The marshal and his lady gave me clothes and money.'

'The marshal was deeply touched by her story,' said the French officer. 'She has suffered much to be with her husband. I trust he and his comrades will not prove so tenacious when we meet in battle after the winter.'

'Tenacity is a British trait common to both our men and women.'

'Then I fear your women will need to seek solace and not husbands.' The French officer bowed to Cassie, saluted Lieutenant Fox, and kissed Polly's hand. '*Au revoir*, Madame. I trust you and your husband will one day return safely to England.'

As Gorran was leaving to arrange for the French officer's return, Rose arrived at the house, red-faced and puffing heavily.

'Polly! It's good to see you – and little Jeannie too. But how did you get here ... and where's your youngest?'

As Polly found answers to Rose's rapid questions, Rose took the other woman in her huge arms and hugged her affectionately. Over Polly's head she looked at Cassie and closed one eye in a wink.

Cassie lay back in relief. Rose had assumed responsibility for dealing with the tricky situation created by Polly's sudden arrival.

Enoch Martin was not having to cope with the problems of campaigning on his own. He had another woman. A young, Portuguese camp follower.

Josefa returned to the hut as Rose went off with one arm about Polly's shoulders and young Jean holding her other hand. Cassie explained the problem to the Spanish girl.

'But this is terrible! What will happen?'

'I don't know, but I'm sure Rose will sort it out. It can't be the first time something like this has happened.'

Josefa shook her head unhappily. 'I don't know what I would do if an English woman arrived here and said she was Richard's wife. I think I might kill her – or kill myself.'

Cassie realised the other girl was looking at the problem from an entirely different point of view from the regimental wives.

214

'There's little likelihood of that happening. Richard is far too young to have a wife already.'

'Oh? Is he then so much younger than you or your Harry?'

'No, but ... Well ... it's different for him. He's an officer. From a good family ...'

Cassie was rescued from a difficult discussion by Gorran's return. Entering the small house he smiled at the two young women and said, 'Well, that was a most unexpected diversion. Full marks to young Polly Martin for making her own way here. It couldn't have been easy, especially as she had a young child with her. It's very sad about young Sammy, though. Many of the company knew him from the time he was born.'

Suddenly aware of the silence that had fallen upon the two young women, he asked, 'Is something wrong?'

Cassie shook her head. She felt she could speak freely to Gorran and she trusted him implicitly, but this was a matter between a soldier and his wife. It was preferable that officers did not become involved. Instead of enlightening him, she said, 'The company already has its full complement of wives. If one of us has to go, will it be Polly or me? She was the one who drew the "To go" ticket, remember?'

'So that's what's troubling you.' Gorran smiled. 'Neither of you will need to go. If necessary we could always transfer a soldier and his wife to another company but I doubt if that will be necessary. The colonel encourages initiative – and Polly Martin has certainly shown that. Now I'll go and leave you in peace. You're looking pale. I hope all this excitement hasn't exhausted you too much. Finish off the port wine, it will do you good. Goodbye, Cassie, Josefa.'

When he had left the house Cassie told Josefa she wished to sleep for a while. Her head ached with thinking of all that had happened that day.

Walking back towards the quarters she shared with Richard, Josefa was also thinking of the events of the day. Polly Martin had walked into a difficult situation – but her thoughts were of a look she had seen Gorran Fox give to Cassie when he thought neither woman was looking at him. She believed Gorran and Cassie had far more in common than their Cornish background.

If Josefa was right, then Polly's problems would be far easier to solve than those that might one day face Cassie Clymo.

17

⚜

Enoch Martin's Portuguese woman threw a fit of hysteria when she was told of Polly's arrival. When she recovered she declared she would never relinquish her hold on the big English soldier. It was her intention to remain in the camp and force Enoch to choose between her and his wife. Polly's claim on her husband backed by English law meant nothing here. This was not England.

His marriage to Polly had taken place in England, under the auspices of a church unrecognised by her own Catholic religion. Her claim on him was based on their relationship here. No, she would not give him up for any other woman.

Sergeant Tonks hastily organised a collection among the soldiers of the regiment. Not all gave their money readily, even when reminded that one day they, too, might find themselves in a similar situation to Enoch Martin. Nevertheless, the collection raised sufficient money for the Portuguese woman to set aside the arguments of true love and religious precedence. She promised to depart for Lisbon immediately.

A week later the men of the 32nd learned the Portuguese woman had not returned home as promised. Instead she had formed a liaison with a Scots soldier in another division. It was rumoured that the two of them were spending her money on a drunken spree that was the envy of her adopted regiment. Meanwhile, the touching reunion of husband, wife and young daughter brought tears to the eyes of those who witnessed it, even the men who were out of pocket as a result. Jean soon became the darling of the regiment and when she caught the fever so prevalent in the area, her progress aroused more concern than the lack of progress in the now stagnant war.

'Peninsular Fever' had claimed more casualties among the British soldiers than Napoleon's army. For a while, no fewer than 14,000 men were incapacitated from a total strength of 43,000. In a bid to shake his men free of its unremitting grip, the commander of the 6th Division took his men on a long and strenuous march southwards, through the mountains that formed a natural barrier between Portugal and Spain.

The British general chose his time badly. The Peninsular winter had begun. On the long march the men of the 6th Division encountered heavy rain, bitterly cold nights and even snow. They were still in the mountains on Christmas Day but had little cause for celebration. The 32nd Regiment spent the day camped in a narrow pass on the long road between Rodrigo and

Badajos. Father Michael and his Portuguese were with the division, but a stirring sermon on the Holy Birthday from the Irish friar failed to lift the day clear of the chilling rain that soaked men, women and animals alike.

Seven days and a hundred gruelling miles later they greeted the arrival of the New Year in the same rain-drenched pass. The only slight difference was that they were now heading northwards. Returning to the plains before Rodrigo.

Cassie grumbled as loudly as anyone else at the apparent futility of the regiment's aimless wanderings. The long marches had done nothing to cut down the numbers of soldiers falling ill and exhaustion had now been added to their many other problems.

However, while the 32nd Regiment stumbled through the rain-soaked mountains, a momentous decision had been reached. Lord Wellington decided that Rodrigo had impeded the progress of the British army for too long. He was gathering his forces for an assault that would clear the fortified town from his path.

Lord Wellington had been awaiting the right moment and it had finally arrived. Due to internal disputes and jealousies, the French forces in Spain were currently widely dispersed around the country. It was time to launch an attack on Rodrigo.

The 6th Division would not be taking part in the actual assault. Their task was to take up positions in the hills nearby and prevent any attempt by the French to send troops to the aid of the besieged garrison inside the town.

Two days after the 32nd Regiment moved into its

position overlooking a narrow pass, the cannons of Lord Wellington's artillery began the task of breaching the high, heavily defended walls of Rodrigo.

Huddled in a miserable shelter put together using rocks, twigs and turf, Cassie and Harry lay listening to the monotonous and relentless boom of the cannons. The sound had echoed among the hills for twelve hours. Word had reached the regiment that twenty-four guns were being used in the siege and the sound was likely to continue for many days – perhaps even weeks.

'Do you think many people are being killed inside the town, Harry?' Cassie whispered the question in the darkness, unable to sleep.

'I doubt it. The artillery's task is to reduce the wall, that's all. There's no reason for anyone to die. Not yet, anyway.'

Harry spoke with more confidence than he felt, expressing what he thought Cassie wanted to hear. In truth he knew no more of what was going on inside the walls of Rodrigo than she did.

'I'm glad you're not down there with them, Harry. Sarah says that when the walls are breached the first men sent in to try to take the breach are called the "Forlorn Hope". She says very few of them ever live to boast of what they've done.'

'You don't want to take any notice of what Sarah Cottle says. They're not all killed – and those who survive can expect to be given promotion straight away. That's how Sergeant Tonks won his promotion. He's twice been in a "Forlorn Hope".'

Cassie's shiver owed as much to what Harry had said

as to the weather. It was cold and frosty. She was glad she had Harry to cuddle up to and an extra blanket to help warm them both.

'Anyway, that isn't how the men in Sarah Cottle's life have got their promotion.' Harry shifted in order to place an arm about Cassie's shoulders. 'I'd rather earn promotion in a "Forlorn Hope" than have my wife sweat for it beneath an officer's blanket.'

Twenty yards from the flimsy shelter Josefa passed by and heard their low conversation. She had left Richard Kennelly sleeping in the pigsty of a tumbledown cottage that had been appropriated for the officers of 3 Company. Climbing the hill behind the temporary camp, she found a place among the rocks that sheltered her from the biting wind.

Josefa sat in the cold darkness with a shawl pulled about her shoulders and listened to the bombardment of the Spanish town with deep unhappiness. She stayed thinking deep thoughts until the increasing cold drove her back to the pigsty.

As she slipped beneath the blankets, Richard stirred and reached out for her. More asleep than awake he pulled her to him and complained, 'You're freezing! Let me cuddle you and get you warm.'

Most nights Josefa would have responded to such an invitation with an enthusiasm guaranteed to chase away all feelings of cold but tonight was different. The booming of the heavy siege guns upset her greatly. While Frenchmen were undoubtedly manning the walls of Rodrigo, the houses of the town were occupied by Spanish families. Her people. During all the talk she had heard of the siege and the effect the fall of Rodrigo would have on the outcome of the war, she had heard no mention of them.

For five days and nights the cannonade continued without respite, the shells and cannon balls pounding away at the walls of the fortified town. There were many guns directed against the town now, and more being brought into action as fast as firing positions could be made ready. By the sixth day two breaches had been made and Lord Wellington decided the time had come to launch his attack.

That night soldiers of the 'Forlorn Hope' supported by the Light Company and 3rd Divisions flung themselves against the breaches made in the walls of Rodrigo. In a desperately fought battle nine hundred British soldiers were killed and wounded, among them two well-liked major-generals.

Eventually, the garrison surrendered, but so savage had the fighting been, it was impossible to bring the assaulting army to an immediate halt. The soldiers who had fought their way into Rodrigo went on the rampage in a wild orgy of rape and looting. For the whole of one terrifying night the soldiers broke down doors, searching for drink, loot and women, their progress marked by the screams of the women they found.

Not until the light of day sought out the darkened recesses of the ravaged town and revealed the full extent of the carnage was a semblance of order restored.

News of the happenings in Rodrigo filtered back slowly to the divisions who had taken no part in the fighting, but who had heard the noise of battle many miles away, in the hills and valleys about the town. The reaction of the British soldiers was very mixed. Some, campaign-wise, shook their heads and said such happenings would not have occurred had their regiment taken part in the battle for the town. Others, less mindful of the reputations of their particular regiment, regretted they had not been permitted to enjoy the plundering of Rodrigo.

Josefa listened to all that was said, but kept her thoughts to herself. The next day when the 32nd marched past the fallen town and the soldiers marvelled at the two huge breaches in the walls, she turned her head away and said nothing. The war had suddenly assumed a more personal aspect for her.

For two more weeks the British army remained in the vicinity of Rodrigo, ready to defend the hard-won fortress against the French army should a bid be made to win it back from the victors.

When no such attack materialised, Lord Wellington decided to move against the one remaining fortress that barred his way to the heart of Spain. The army was given orders to march southward. To the town of Badajos.

It was an almost leisurely march of a hundred and fifty miles with no alarms and a welcome change in the weather. Almost overnight, it seemed, there was a marked improvement in the health of the British forces. The army left the shame of Rodrigo behind and spoke of the glories of battles to come. Josefa too seemed to have cast her doubts aside and she was as loving as ever towards Richard Kennelly.

Before Badajos was reached, the 32nd Regiment was rested for a week in a sizeable town where unaccustomed luxuries were available to the soldiers for the first time for many months. New uniforms arrived from England and did much to boost the morale of the men. Some soldiers had been reduced to wearing trousers so patched it had become impossible to tell at first glance their original colour or material.

Reinforcements also reached the army. For the first time in the long Peninsular campaign it was believed that Wellington's army was numerically equal to the forces available to the French commander. Newly created an earl in recognition of his victory at Rodrigo, Wellington seemed set to liberate Spain from the French yoke.

When the 32nd Regiment reached Badajos the men were disappointed to learn that, as at Rodrigo, they were excluded from the regiments chosen to take the town. Instead, they were ordered to by-pass Badajos and join up with other regiments to form a line between Badajos and the French army reported to be marching to the defence of the town.

Their disappointment was short-lived. The regiment had hardly taken up position when it was attacked by a strong French force and a brisk battle ensued. The French were beaten off but now, instead of holding their line, the British army set off in pursuit.

The French were driven through the Spanish town of Almendralejo and that night the men of the 32nd enjoyed the unaccustomed delight of being welcomed as heroes by the townspeople.

The regiment had seen little of the cavalry during the long march and the recent battle. As a result Sarah Cottle seemed to have settled down once more to life with her corporal, committing only an occasional indiscretion with her husband's fellow infantrymen. However, the fragility of such marital 'bliss' was soon to be exposed.

The women were in the town square with their men and many of the camp followers, enjoying the celebrations of the town, when a cry went up to make way for a cavalry division. A path was quickly cleared and the cavalry clattered by to the delighted cheers of the townsfolk. Among their ranks was a squadron of Light Dragoons headed by Lieutenant Dalhousie.

When Cassie saw Dalhousie her glance instinctively sought out Sarah Cottle. What she saw dispelled any thought that the affair between the two had ended. Sarah was looking towards the cavalry officer with an expression that would not have been out of place on the face of a starving man watching a beef steak being cooked before his eyes.

A quarter of an hour later, when Cassie looked for Sarah the corporal's wife was no longer in the square. Neither was Corporal Walter Cottle. Cassie hoped the two might have left together, but she thought it extremely unlikely.

Her fears were confirmed later that night by Harry. They were lying in bed in the attic of a small house, looking out through the open window at a plump yellow moon hanging in the dark night sky. Ordered to remain in the town in reserve, the 6th Division was enjoying more comfortable billets than Cassie had known for a very long time. 'Did you see Sarah's face when Mr Dalhousie and his men rode through the square tonight?' Cassie asked.

'No, but I was watching Walter Cottle. I can't ever remember seeing such hatred in a man's expression. If I was that cavalry lieutenant I'd be worried. Corporal Cottle is a vengeful man. He neither forgets nor forgives the slightest ill done to him. Despite the way Sarah behaves, Walter loves her.'

'I doubt if Mr Dalhousie would pay much heed to the feelings of a corporal, and there's not much Walter Cottle can do about what's going on. Rose says he knew what she was like when he married her. It didn't bother him too much then and she says if it wasn't for her he'd still be Private Cottle. He'll do nothing.'

18

❧

Cassie was wrong. Walter Cottle was waiting for a suitable opportunity to avenge himself on the cuckolding cavalry officer, and it was not long in coming.

After enjoying only two nights of the lavish hospitality offered by the inhabitants of the town of Almendralejo, orders came for the 6th Division, together with the 1st and 7th Divisions and the Cavalry Division, to go into battle. Lord Wellington had received reliable information that two French generals had joined forces at a rendezvous in the mountains not thirty miles from the Spanish town. The four divisions were given orders to find and destroy this potential danger to the British force investing Badajos.

The four divisions performed a remarkable march through rugged mountain country and by nightfall were within striking distance of the unsuspecting French armies. The next morning the British divisions were roused without the usual bugle calls and beating of drums.

After such a heroic march, the general in command had no wish to throw away the advantage he had gained.

All his precautions proved in vain. The long and rapid march proved to be a waste of energy. During their four years of occupation the French had made friends as well as enemies. One of these friends had witnessed the arrival of the British and hurried to warn the French commander of their presence, greatly exaggerating their strength in order to emphasise the importance of his information. During the night, while the British soldiers were sleeping off their exhaustion, the French army had slipped away, leaving behind only a strong cavalry rear-guard to hinder the advance of the British.

Daylight broke as the British army marched in silence towards the village where they believed the French army to be encamped, unaware of the danger they were in. Suddenly the silence was broken by the pounding of hooves and the charging French cavalry spilled from the cover of a large wood to one side of the line of march. Slashing about them with sharp-edged sabres the French horsemen cut a wide swathe through the ranks of the advancing soldiers, causing many casualties.

The British infantry immediately broke ranks, taking advantage of what little cover was available to them and firing in frustrated anger at the fast-moving French cavalry. Moments later a cry went up for the infantrymen to make way for the cavalry. As the soldiers of the 32nd Regiment scrambled out of the path of a new threat to their safety, a regiment of Light Dragoons swept past.

At the head of one of the squadrons was Lieutenant Dalhousie. As he passed through the infantry, the cavalry lieutenant called, 'That's right, stand aside and watch closely. We'll show you the way to win a battle.'

The Light Dragoons formed a line directly in front of the 32nd Regiment. As the French cavalry turned to receive them the colonel of the Light Dragoons shouted the order to advance. The order was relayed in a sharp bugle call that carried to every man in the line and the dragoons surged forward.

Suddenly a shot rang out from the British lines. No one had given an order to open fire and the enemy horsemen were well out of range, but such was the nervousness and tension on the battlefield that more than half of the British infantrymen followed suit in a futile volley.

Angry shouts went up from the infantry officers, but they were lost in the sound of battle as the two opposing cavalry forces met and engaged in a desperate duel of cut and thrust that was half hidden from view by a pall of gunpowder smoke drifting across the field from the infantrymen's volley.

The action lasted no more than ten minutes. It ended when the British infantry was ordered forward in support of their hard-pressed cavalry colleagues. Their advance swung the balance in favour of the British cause and the French were quick to break off the engagement.

Many casualties lay on the field of battle and one of the first to be carried to the rear of the British lines was Lieutenant Dalhousie. As he was borne through the lines of the 32nd Regiment, an unusually animated Walter Cottle called out to his bearers, 'Is he dead? Has he been killed?'

The two bearers wore the uniform of bandsmen and

one of them growled brusquely, 'What business is it of yours, soldier?'

The other bandsman was more communicative. 'He's bleeding a lot but I don't think it's too serious. Funny thing is it looks as though he's been wounded by a musket ball, not a sabre . . .'

Walter Cottle was placed under arrest that evening on the orders of the provost marshal. Lieutenant Dalhousie had been wounded by a musket ball. It had struck him in the back when he was lined up facing the enemy. The shot had knocked him from his saddle, but it was the fall that had rendered him unconscious. The surgeon had been able to find and remove the lead missile without too much difficulty and it was confirmed the ball was of a type used by British infantry.

Lieutenant Dalhousie was expected to be back in the saddle again in a few weeks and he scorned the sugges-tion that the shot had been deliberately fired at him from the ranks of the British infantry. Others thought differently.

The first unexpected shot had been fired from the section of line held by the 32nd Regiment and it seemed probable that this was the shot which had knocked the cavalry lieutenant from his saddle. There was no doubt the shot had startled others into firing and the volley might have had disastrous results for the cavalry forming up in front of the regiment's line.

It had not taken the provost marshal long to single out Walter Cottle as the soldier most likely to have fired the opening shot – with Lieutenant Dalhousie as his target. His arrest was ordered immediately. A court

230

martial was convened the following day with the general acting as presiding officer. The proceedings were briefer than anyone could have anticipated – and the verdict came as a surprise to all who were aware of Sarah Cottle's liaison with the cavalry lieutenant.

The provost marshal was unable to find an officer willing to give evidence of Dalhousie's association with Sarah Cottle. He could therefore only suggest that Walter Cottle believed his wife to be having an affair with the cavalry lieutenant. The prosecution had also been unable to produce anyone in the regiment to state that Walter Cottle had fired the opening shot before the battle.

The prosecution's case proved to be so unsatisfactory that the presiding officer was left with no alternative but to dismiss the charges against Walter Cottle without the corporal being required to say a single word in his own defence.

That evening Sarah Cottle left her husband and made her way back to the small town of Elves, just inside the Portuguese border. Here Lieutenant Dalhousie was recuperating in a comfortable billet only a few miles from the besieged town of Badajos.

Sarah said nothing of her intentions to her husband, or to the other wives. She simply packed her belongings, slung them over the back of her donkey and rode away. There was gossip among the wives, claiming she had received a message from Lieutenant Dalhousie urging her to come to him, but it seemed no one had actually witnessed such a message being delivered.

That night Corporal Walter Cottle sat alone eating his unappetising issue of biscuit and salt beef. No one spoke to him, even in passing, and he seemed disinclined to strike up a conversation with anyone.

Seated around a cheerful fire with the other wives and their husbands, Cassie frequently looked across at the solitary figure and finally she said, 'I can't help feeling sorry for Walter Cottle. Do you think we should invite him over here to eat with us?'

'No!' The reply was chorused by three soldiers, one of them being Harry.

'Why not? Sarah's gone off and left him and he's spent a day and a night under arrest for something he didn't do.'

'He's better off without her – and who says he didn't fire the shot that hit the cavalry lieutenant?'

'The court martial. He was found not guilty.'

'That don't mean he didn't do anything. Only that they couldn't prove it. If they'd been standing where I was he wouldn't have been let off.'

Cassie looked at Harry incredulously. 'You mean you saw him shoot Mr Dalhousie?'

She looked from Harry to those men about him. Not one would meet her eyes.

'Walter did shoot him. You all saw what happened. Why wouldn't you say something when the provost marshal asked you?'

'Would you say anything if you knew it would result in a man you know being put to death because of a woman like Sarah Cottle? We saw nothing, Cassie. It's better so. Besides, Walter Cottle has troubles enough.'

'I don't understand . . . If you're so sorry for him why not invite him to share our food – or at least have his food cooked enough to make it eatable?'

232

'If we've protected Walter Cottle it's because he belongs to the Thirty-second Regiment.' This time the reply came from Sergeant Tonks. 'It doesn't mean we approve of what he's done. No one has any time for a soldier who shoots one of his own officers in the back, whatever the reason. Corporal Cottle is fortunate to have loyal men about him who won't see him sentenced to die. He can expect nothing more. Now, enough's been said on the subject. It's best for everyone if no mention's ever made of it again. Harry . . . Enoch . . . There's a rum ration being dished out tonight. Take a clean bucket to the commissary and collect what's due to Three Company.'

While the two men were away from the fire Sergeant Tonks went on an errand of his own and the women began gathering their mess-tins in anticipation of their promised dose of 'comfort'.

As she worked, Cassie glanced again to where Corporal Cottle sat apart from the other soldiers, smoke rising in a faint spiral from the briar pipe clenched between his teeth.

'Will the others ever forgive him?' She put the question to Rose Tonks.

'That'll depend on Walter himself. If he covers himself in glory during the next battle he'll be the most popular man in the regiment. But I can't see him changing overnight. He never should have been made a corporal in the first place. It was her who got him his corporal's stripes – and it'll be her who'll lose them for him, you mark my words. Don't waste any time sympathising with Walter Cottle. He's no better than she is – and she at least looks as though she enjoys what she does.'

19

The four divisions continued to advance for five days with the French army reeling before them. Then, when they had driven the enemy a distance of seventy miles from Badajos, a messenger and escort galloped up to the headquarters carrying an urgent message from Lord Wellington.

The message acknowledged that the divisions had demonstrated their superiority to the French. However, Lord Wellington was not yet ready to advance so far inside Spain. First he needed to take the fortress of Badajos, and this was proving a more difficult task than had been anticipated. The advancing divisions were ordered to fall back and resume their defensive role in front of the invested town.

Wellington's reasons for recalling the divisions were not passed on to the soldiers who fought for him. They knew only that they had been ordered to retreat. The high morale that had driven them on now plunged them to the depths. Nevertheless, their withdrawal was orderly, even though French skirmishers constantly harried the flanks and rearguard, albeit with a marked lack of determination. But, casualties resulted and this increased the depression felt by the soldiers and the women who accompanied them.

On the third day of Lord Wellington's 'tactical withdrawal' the 32nd were acting as the rearguard regiment in heavily wooded country when they were surprised by a strong force of *chasseurs* which had succeeded in outflanking the rearguard and lay in wait for them. The French were not in sufficient strength to threaten annihilation to the Cornish regiment and were soon driven off, but it proved to be a sharp engagement while it lasted.

When the 32nd reached an area of open countryside the regiment was halted and a roll call taken. Seven men had been killed and twenty-two wounded, none of them seriously. There was also one man missing. Corporal Walter Cottle. Three Company had not been the direct target for the *chasseurs* and Walter Cottle was their only 'casualty'.

Sergeant Tonks immediately led a small party of soldiers back to the scene of the skirmish in an effort to locate the missing corporal. The French *chasseurs* were already on their way back to their own army, satisfied with the result of their surprise attack, and the 32nd Regiment soldiers were able to scour the area thoroughly. They did not find the missing corporal but Harry stumbled across his musket, apparently discarded in long grass beside a path leading from the road.

He carried the weapon back to Sergeant Tonks and handed it to him with a brief explanation of where it had been found. The sergeant examined the gun and said sharply, 'It hasn't been fired.'

'That's right. Neither was there any sign of blood or a struggle anywhere near where I found it.'

Sergeant Tonks handed the musket back to Harry, an expression of disgust on his face. 'Bring it back to the regiment with you. There's no sense in wasting any more time looking for Corporal Cottle. If we do ever see him again it'll be along the length of a musket barrel, I'll be bound.'

'Why, sergeant?' The puzzled question came from a young soldier who had joined the regiment straight from England only a few days before. 'What do you think has happened to him?'

'He's deserted his regiment, soldier. Thrown away his musket and gone across to the enemy. But he'll have a nasty shock when he reaches 'em. The French don't let our deserters live a life of ease. He'll be expected to fight alongside them against his own kind. Against you and me. His former mates.'

The walled town of Badajos fell to a determined British assault on the night of 16–17 April 1812 after a siege that had lasted for three weeks. It was a ferocious and bloody battle beside which the taking of Rodrigo paled. Five thousand British soldiers fell dead or wounded in the assault, among them no fewer than five generals. It was a price that was said to have brought Lord Wellington close to tears when he was told.

Inside the town the ferocity of the victorious army was turned yet again upon a populace which was believed to have given aid and comfort to the French garrison. The British soldiers wrought a terrible vengeance. In an orgy of drunkenness, looting and rape they left no house untouched and the officers were powerless to bring their men under control. The soldiers had suffered appalling losses in the capture of the town; now the suffering was being passed on to the Spanish residents.

Two days after the fall of Badajos Lieutenant Gorran Fox was ordered to take two companies of the 32nd Regiment into the captured town. His task was to restore order using soldiers from other regiments.

Gorran refused to allow wives to accompany their husbands inside the town until Rose Tonks argued that the presence of army wives might well help bring the rampaging soldiers to their senses. The lieutenant-colonel in overall command of the troops agreed with her and Cassie and the other wives of 3 Company marched behind their husbands. Josefa went with them, to act as interpreter for Gorran Fox.

The scene inside the walled town was one of utter chaos and the women looked about them in horror. The bodies of many of the fallen soldiers were still awaiting burial and scores of wounded required urgent attention – so, too, did many of the townspeople. Gangs of drunken soldiers still roamed the narrow streets shooting at everything that moved and at least five houses burned furiously, set ablaze by the looting soldiers.

Gorran set up his headquarters in a tall house that

had been ransacked time and time again. Cassie and the other women were billeted here, guarded by a platoon of 32nd Regiment soldiers.

The house was an utter shambles with broken furniture and household crockery strewn everywhere. As the wives set to and brought some order from the chaos they were joined by a Spanish mother and two daughters who worked in silence and when spoken to seemed ready to burst into tears.

Cassie would have liked to put a number of questions to the Spanish women but they did not appear to understand English and Josefa had gone off with Gorran Fox to translate the grievances of the many Spaniards clamouring to be heard by anyone in authority.

Josefa returned to the house that evening looking pale and shaken by what she had heard during the day. As she entered the kitchen where the other women were cooking a meal she murmured a greeting to the three Spanish women of the house. The older woman's immediate reaction was alarming. Screaming in her native tongue she rushed at Josefa with hands outstretched like talons.

Cassie leaped in the path of the apparently demented woman in order to protect Josefa, but Rose Tonks was quicker. Jumping at the Spanish woman she wrapped her arms about her and brought her to a pinioned halt – but she could not put a stop to her angry shouting. The two daughters also began hurling abuse at Josefa and order was not restored until the army wives succeeded in bundling all three women from the kitchen.

As the door was closed after the still shouting women, Cassie said to Josefa, 'What was all that about?'

Slumping in a chair, Josefa bowed her head for some moments before replying in a voice that contained despair.

'She was telling me I must be a *puta*, a whore, for having anything to do with British soldiers.'

'She has no right to say that,' said Cassie indignantly.

'She has *every* right.' Josefa spoke angrily, fighting to keep her voice under control. 'Do you know her story?'

Cassie shook her head. 'None of the women has said anything all day. Not even to each other.'

'I do not think they would enjoy talking of . . . what happened, but it will be difficult for them ever to forget . . .'

Josefa accepted the cup of tea handed to her by Polly Martin and nodded gratefully. 'When the soldiers took the town they broke in the door of this house and tried to rape her youngest daughter. The mother screamed and a British officer heard and came in the house. He threw the soldier out and called in another soldier to stand guard and keep others away.'

Josefa paused, unable to drink the tea she held because she was trembling with emotion. 'The soldier left to guard them called to all his friends. Eight . . . ten . . . or twelve, the mother is not certain. They raped both daughters and the mother too. The man who had been left to guard them was first, and then five or six more raped the youngest daughter. She was to have been married next month, to the son of the mayor. Fortunately, perhaps, he is dead. Shot by more of the drunken British soldiers.'

There was a long silence in the kitchen until Rose

said, 'It's regrettable. *Very* regrettable, but such things sometimes happen in a war.'

'Sometimes? *Sometimes?* Today I have been told such stories time after time after time. Why? We are your friends, not enemies. Why do you do this to us?'

Josefa looked at each of the women standing in the kitchen, but none had an answer for her.

'I think perhaps the owner of this house is right. I must be a *puta*. I feel dirty. How can I love a British soldier after all that has happened to my people, here in Badajos?'

While Josefa was talking Gorran Fox had entered the room. He was accompanied by Father Michael. Both men had been upstairs in the house when the commotion broke out and they came down in time to hear Josefa's words.

Stepping forward, Gorran said, 'Nothing can excuse what has happened here during the last days and nights, Josefa. Not even the horror of the battle for Badajos. But it isn't only British troops who are committing such atrocities. French troops are out at this very moment, scouring the countryside for food. I've received reports that they're shooting every man who protests – and ravishing every woman who falls into their hands.'

'The French seized Spain. We expect it of them. You say you are here to free us from the French. Do you also demand such a price for "freedom"?'

'There's always a price to be paid if a people are to live in freedom, Josefa – and it's demanded by your own fighters as well as ours. Lord Wellington has had to send a regiment to remove Don Xavier, your guerrilla chief,

240

from Rodrigo. Don Xavier rode into the town after it had been handed over to Spanish jurisdiction and presented a list of names to the mayor. He claimed they were citizens of Rodrigo who had co-operated with the French. I doubt whether it was coincidence that the list included every man who had ever slighted Don Xavier, or whose business interests clashed with those of his family and friends. His men scoured the town to gather those on the list. When they were found they were shot without trial.

'This was as inexcusable as what has happened here in Badajos. As regrettable as the loss of five thousand fine British soldiers who died taking the town from the French. Unfortunately such things happen during a war, Josefa. The sooner we can bring it to a close the better it will be – for everyone.'

For a moment Josefa hesitated, then she said, 'You would make excuses for your soldiers. You are English too.'

'Then perhaps you'll believe me, Josefa?' Father Michael spoke quietly. 'I've fought against both English and French with equal enthusiasm. Mr Fox is right. What has happened here is lamentable. It pains me to the very core of my being, but Mr Fox and his soldiers are working hard to restore order in Badajos. When they succeed we must look forward, not back.'

Josefa struggled with her feelings for some moments, then she turned and fled from the room. Behind her the others could hear her footsteps running up the stairs to the attic room she shared with Richard Kennelly.

'I'll go and speak to her.'

As Cassie made her way across the room, Gorran warned, 'Whatever you do, don't allow her to leave the house while she's in her present mood. There are still some three thousand men on the rampage out there. No woman is safe.'

'I'll make sure she stays in the house,' Cassie promised. 'But I agree with all she said. This should never have happened – whatever other armies have done elsewhere.'

Josefa had flung herself down on the bed in the attic. She lay with her face turned to the wall but Cassie believed she was crying. 'You've had a horrifying day, Josefa. Is there something I can get for you?'

Josefa shook her head without replying.

'Both Mr Fox and Father Michael were right, you know. By trying to blame all British soldiers for what's happened you'll make Richard very unhappy.'

'Tell that to the women of this house and see what they say to you.'

'Richard is here to help the women of this house and all the others who have suffered in the same way. It will do no one any good if you are angry with him.'

'I . . . I have to be angry with someone, Cassie. I see what happened at Ciudad Rodrigo. Now I see Badajos. Soon, perhaps, the army will be fighting in Salamanca. My mother is there. Must this happen to her too?'

Cassie reached out a hand and gripped Josefa's arm. 'I know how you must be feeling, Josefa, but it won't happen again. Lord Wellington won't allow it to happen.'

When Josefa did not reply, Cassie said, 'Is it really Badajos that's upsetting you so much, Josefa? Or is there something more? Have you stopped loving Richard?'

Josefa turned her head and the pain-filled look she gave Cassie was itself an answer to the blunt question.

'I love Richard more than anything else in the world, Cassie, but . . . I am so confused.'

Josefa's eyes filled with tears and Cassie took her in her arms and held her. She was still holding her when they both heard someone running up the stairs towards the attic. There was a knock on the door but before Cassie could respond the door opened and Rose Tonks crashed into the room, breathing heavily.

'You'd better come . . . A messenger has just arrived for Mr Fox. Mr Kennelly's been hurt. A crowd of drunken soldiers attacked a woman . . . He tried to stop them. Mr Fox and some of the regiment have gone to find him and take him to the hospital. I think he's hurt bad . . .'

20

❦

Cassie, Rose and Josefa hurried through the streets of Badajos with an escort of four soldiers. Their destination was a huge villa previously occupied by the French commandant of the garrison. It had been commandeered for use as a hospital to treat the soldiers wounded in the assault on the fortress.

Passing along the narrow streets, Cassie saw ample evidence of the violent excesses of the British soldiery. Doors and windows, smashed in by musket butts or booted feet, sagged drunkenly on broken hinges. Shattered furniture, thrown from the windows of upstairs rooms, littered the streets. Clothing of all description, mainly women's, was strewn everywhere and camp followers were still to be seen staggering away from the town, scarcely able to walk from the weight of the loot they carried.

There were soldiers here too. Drunken soldiers lying

in gutters and on roadways. Some had consumed so much wine they lay unconscious with wine oozing from open mouth and nostrils. Others reeled along cobbled streets cannoning from wall to wall. A few still prowled the alleyways and narrow lanes in search of loot or women. Three times the soldiers escorting Cassie and the others were obliged to step between the women they escorted and drunken men, and once it was necessary to emphasise their protective role with a brass-tipped musket butt.

The thick stone walls and marble floors of the villa suggested a welcome hint of coolness after the stifling heat of the narrow streets, but this was the only comfort the hospital was able to offer. Men lay everywhere in tight-packed rows, each with only a thin blanket separating him from the cold, hard floor.

The stench was overwhelming. It was the odour of death and dying, of putrefaction and amputation, of disease and incontinence, and the groans and moans of the wounded men might have been taken from a Dantesque melodrama.

The three women stopped inside the doors of the hospital villa, overwhelmed by what they could see and hear.

'Are you here to help?' The eager question came from a surgeon wrapped in an apron so bloody it might have been worn by a slaughterman.

'We're looking for Mr Kennelly of the Thirty-second Regiment.' Cassie spoke knowing full well that surrounded by such chaos the surgeon would not know where the young ensign could be found. She was right.

'Names or regiments mean little here. There are a thousand men – possibly one thousand five hundred, packed inside this villa. The garden and adjacent villas are also filled. There are as many more in the church off the square. Others are scattered all about the town, the Lord alone knows where. I have a mere handful of helpers – not enough to serve water to all those in need. Can't you hear the cries of the thirsty men?'

'Cassie, you and Josefa go and find Mr Kennelly. You!' Rose Tonks rounded on one of the soldiers who had escorted them to the makeshift hospital. 'Hurry back to the billet and fetch all the other women here. If you see Mr Fox ask him to send a message to any other regiment stationed nearby. There's urgent work here for as many women as can be found.'

'Bless you, ma'am.' The bloody surgeon wrung Rose's beefy hand. 'This ensign you seek. When did he fall?'

'Today. He was sent to Badajos to help restore order. We've just been told he's been hurt by some of the looters.'

'They should all be shot out of hand,' declared the surgeon savagely. 'Some were here yesterday demanding to be shown the entrance to the cellars. It's time something was done about them. But if this ensign of yours was hurt only today he'll be in the large white house across the street. That's the latest villa to be commandeered for casualties.'

A voice containing a note of urgency began calling for a surgeon. The man before them called in reply, 'All right, I'm coming . . .'

To Cassie and Josefa he said, 'I trust you'll find your ensign. If he's well enough to be moved I suggest you

246

take him elsewhere. Conditions are so bad in the hospital I swear I'm killing as many as I cure. We're losing almost all the amputees. Any man who survives this experience should lead a saintly existence for the remainder of his life. One glimpse of Hell is enough for anyone . . . All right! I've said I'm coming . . .'

The surgeon hurried away and, as Cassie and Josefa picked their way between the lines of close-packed men, Josefa whispered, 'Poor Richard! To be lying in such a place as this.'

The house to which they had been directed was less crowded than the larger villa they had just left, but conditions were no less chaotic. This was where the newly discovered wounded were being brought. Some were genuine casualties who had crawled into hiding places after being wounded during the heat of battle. Others had been shot or bayonetted by drunken comrades during the sacking of the town. Casualties were also beginning to trickle in from those regiments sent into Badajos to restore order.

To Josefa's great joy and relief, Richard was one of the first men the two women saw when they entered the villa. Seated on the floor in a passageway he had an ugly gash on his head, the side of his face and one shoulder stained red with his own blood. However, he was well enough to struggle to his feet and bear the full brunt of Josefa's exuberant embrace.

'Richard! Oh, Richard! They tell me you are badly hurt. I feared I would find you dying . . .'

Watching Josefa's joy at finding Richard, Cassie thought there was little evidence of the gipsy girl's earlier

247

doubts. She hugged and kissed the young ensign, oblivious to the envious glances and remarks of the other wounded soldiers.

Raising a hand to the gash on his head, Richard said, 'It looks a lot worse than it is. I was knocked unconscious for a while. I think the men thought I'd been killed.'

'And so you might have been.' There was great concern in Josefa's voice as she drew his head down to inspect the wound more closely. 'It is very nasty, but I will make it better more quickly than these people . . .' She waved a hand in the direction of a surgeon who had appeared at a doorway along the corridor. His apron was in a similar condition to that worn by the surgeon who had directed them here. 'They do not try to make people better. If a man has a wound in his arm they cut the arm off. In his leg . . . whoosh!' She made a cutting gesture as though her hand held a knife. 'You have a wound in your head . . . I think it best we return to the house where we stay. I will make you better.'

'There's still work for me to do. Mr Fox has taken men to clear the section of town where I was hurt . . .'

'I hope when he finds them he will send them all straight to gaol – but you will not be able to help him with such a wound in your head. You must go and rest.'

'That's what Mr Fox said,' Richard admitted. 'But I'm needed here . . .'

He was interrupted by the arrival of an assistant provost marshal. The army law enforcer brought with him a manacled soldier, who showed the effects of two nights of debauchery, and a small escort.

When his eyes had adjusted to the cool gloom of the

248

passageway, the assistant provost marshal made his way to where Richard stood with the two women.

'Mr Kennelly?'

When Richard nodded confirmation the manacled soldier was thrust forward. 'Mr Fox of your regiment picked up this man. He was told that this was the soldier who assaulted you. Can you confirm this?'

Richard nodded. 'Yes, this is the man.'

'You're quite certain?'

'I recognise the pendant hung around his neck. Stolen from some unfortunate woman, no doubt.'

'That's identification enough.'

The assistant provost marshal turned to the sergeant in charge of the prisoner. 'Take him to the square, gather up as many soldiers as you can, and have him shot.'

Cassie gasped and a startled Richard said, 'But . . . he hasn't been given a trial!'

'A trial isn't necessary. Lord Wellington's orders are that anyone found committing a capital offence in Badajos is to be executed immediately as an example to others. Thank you for your assistance, sir.'

Visibly shaken, Richard watched the condemned man and his escort march away along the corridor. 'I didn't realise . . . I wouldn't have been so positive with my identification had I known what was going to happen to him . . .'

'Do you think you could have been wrong? That he might not be the soldier who struck you?' Josefa was watching Richard closely.

'He was the one. There's no doubt at all. All the same . . .'

249

'He struck you and did not care that you were almost killed. He should die. Perhaps his death will save some of my people. It will certainly be seen to avenge some of them. Come, we must go back to the house now. You need something put on your wound before it turns bad.'

Order was restored in Badajos by nightfall, but an ugly and costly paragraph had been indelibly written into the history of the British army. Nevertheless, Lord Wellington's aim had been achieved. The strongholds of Rodrigo and Badajos had been secured and the French army elsewhere in Spain was in disarray. If the Spanish guerrillas could be persuaded to maintain pressure on the French and stop fighting each other, the doorway to Spain would open still further, leaving Lord Wellington to choose his own battlegrounds.

Placing strong garrisons at each of the two strongholds, Wellington withdrew his army into prepared cantonments inside Portugal and prepared them for the advance into Spain. Meanwhile, he applied himself to the near impossible task of reaching agreement with the governments of England, Portugal and free Spain for the campaign he planned.

While Lord Wellington went about his Herculean task, heavy rains swept the Peninsula and for two months Cassie looked after Harry in a billet that was as bad as any she had endured during the campaign. It seemed all the fleas in the mountainous border region were accompanying the 32nd Regiment on their journeys and sharing their primitive accommodation.

On 13 June in that eventful year of 1812, the rains

ceased and orders were issued for all the regiments of the British army to form divisions once more and turn their steps towards Spain.

This was the moment Josefa had been dreading. Haunted by what she had seen at Badajos, her fears had been the subject of numerous nightmares and Richard and Cassie were concerned for her.

On the first night of the advance, when the men had made camp and the women were busy preparing a meal for their menfolk, Gorran Fox put in an unexpected appearance at the camp fire. Exchanging greetings with the other women he singled out Cassie and, after asking her about her well-being, he said, 'I don't see Josefa here with you.'

'She's gone to the village to buy fresh vegetables for Three Company. She's always able to get them cheaper than the rest of us. The villagers are sure she intends charging us more than she pays them and they lower their prices accordingly.'

'How is she? Still having nightmares about an army attack on Salamanca?'

'Yes. She's worried because her mother's there, even though Richard has said there'll be no repeat of what happened at Rodrigo and Badajos. She trusts him so I think he'll win. I only hope he's proved right.'

'It won't be allowed to happen again.' Gorran spoke with conviction. 'Yet I can understand her concern. Will you ask her to come and see me when she returns from the village? I'll be at divisional headquarters.'

Cassie was puzzled. 'Why not ask Richard to send her to you?'

'I want him to know nothing of this conversation for a while. I'm sending him off on picket duty in a few minutes – and I'd rather neither you nor Josefa said anything to the other women about her coming to see me.'

Cassie's eyes opened wide as sudden enlightenment came to her. 'You're going to ask Josefa to spy for you! Is that fair to her? It's dangerous and if she's caught she'll be shot. You know this.'

'Josefa is concerned for her mother. She'll merely be given an opportunity to visit her in Salamanca and satisfy herself she's all right before returning to us – to Richard. All she'll be asked to do is observe what's happening about her while she's in Salamanca and report to us on her return.'

Cassie continued to look at him accusingly and Gorran felt obliged to defend his proposal. 'A great many men died at Badajos, Cassie. Good men, even though they weren't known personally to you and me. The army could ill afford to lose them. Lord Wellington has decided to use the Sixth Division to take Salamanca. It means the Thirty-second Regiment will be engaged. Men we do know. Josefa's information could make the difference between life and death for Richard, your Harry and a great many others – myself included.'

'That's cruel! If you put it that way to Josefa she couldn't possibly refuse to go, however great the danger to herself.'

'I never claimed I was being fair, Cassie. Only that I hoped to be able to reduce the number of casualties among the men of my regiment – our regiment. Yes, there's an element of risk for Josefa, but she's a bright girl and I'll make certain she takes no unnecessary risks. After all, we want her to come back and tell us what's happening, not get herself caught by the French. I can assure you, were it possible I would go in her place.'

Cassie became aware that the serious and low-voiced conversation she was having with Gorran was exciting a great deal of interest among the other women.

'I'll speak to Josefa when she comes back, but I wouldn't blame her if she refused to go.'

'Neither would I, but I believe we both know what she'll do.'

Josefa left camp early the next morning before Ensign Richard Kennelly and his picket had been recalled. Josefa and Cassie had talked far into the night after the Spanish girl's return from meeting not only Gorran Fox, but General Clinton, the 6th Division's commanding officer.

Theoretically Josefa's mission was perfectly straight-forward. She was to enter Salamanca quite openly. In the unlikely event of being challenged she would claim to be fleeing to the safety of Salamanca ahead of the British army to seek out her family. She would remain in Salamanca only long enough to learn what she could about the French defences and observe any significant troop movements. Then she would return to the division. During Josefa's absence, Cassie promised she would ensure Richard was properly fed and his clothes kept clean, as befitted an officer.

Cassie had food waiting for Richard when he rejoined 3 Company, but it was not easy to explain why Josefa was not there to provide him with his meal. It was not until Gorran rode up and took him aside later that morning that the young ensign was given the reason for Josefa's absence.

Gorran was quite frank about his reason for ensuring Richard was elsewhere when Josefa was briefed and sent on her way. He had feared the young ensign's unquestioned love for the Spanish gipsy girl might prove an obstacle to such an assignment. He stressed that both he and General Clinton considered the mission to be of the greatest importance. In addition to saving the lives of a great many soldiers it might also have a direct bearing on the success of the assault on the city by the 6th Division.

Richard was a professional soldier and he was forced to admit that Josefa's mission might prove of vital importance. He also knew more than anyone else that Josefa was extremely observant and had a quick and alert mind. Yet he wished desperately that someone else might have been sent in her place. He would worry about her until she returned safely to the regiment – and she would return safely. The young ensign repeated this bald statement of belief to himself many times that day, until he almost came to believe it was so.

21

❦

Josefa made good time during the day on her small donkey and she reached Salamanca soon after darkness had fallen. There were no sentries to challenge her as she entered the city and the streets were so busy it was difficult to believe an army was marching to do battle here. The only French soldiers she saw walked the streets peaceably, or sat outside the taverns, laughing and joking with each other and with the girls beside them. In the main square a troupe of gipsies were dancing, giving Salamanca an air of gaiety and a total absence of apprehension that Josefa found difficult to comprehend.

On the way to Salamanca Josefa had thought and rethought her plans a dozen times or more. She wanted first to see her mother again, to assure herself she was well and to persuade her to leave Salamanca before the English soldiers attacked.

Josefa observed a number of changes in the city. The

great bulk of the cathedral still dominated all else, but other buildings had been pulled down around French-built fortresses. Josefa's spirits sank when she saw that the great convent of San Vicente had been fortified by the French and was bristling with cannon. It meant the 6th Division – with Richard Kennelly – was likely to have a desperate fight on its hands.

Riding through the crowded streets, Josefa hoped she would not be recognised by any of her relatives. Some of her aunts were insatiably curious. They would demand to know all she had done during her absence from the city, and they would not be content to accept half-truths, or glossed-over explanations.

Josefa knew every back alleyway in the city and she rode her donkey to a small stable where the ostler was one of her own people and simple-minded. He recognised her immediately but his only comment was that he had not seen her about the city for a while.

'No, I've been away,' explained Josefa. 'I'm only home now because I'm worried about my mother. It's rumoured the English army is very near.'

'Bah! Why should you worry? Are the British soldiers any better than they were four years ago? They marched all the way to Sahagun then, but the French drove them back to the sea again. They will do the same now. You've seen the fortresses they have built here? Not even a Spanish army could take them.'

'Badajos was strong, but the British succeeded in taking the town.'

'Such talk is rumour, started by those sympathetic to the British, no more. Badajos can never be taken by force.

256

I was told so by a French colonel of cavalry. That's his horse over there, the Arab. There's not a finer stallion in the whole of Spain, and Colonel Clausel will trust it with no one else but me.'

Josefa made no attempt to convince the ostler that Badajos had fallen. It might call for awkward explanations.

'You're probably right but I've been away for a long time and am worried about my mother. I haven't heard from her recently. Do you know where she is – Estefanía, the dancer? You know her?'

The old ostler's face lit up immediately. 'Estefanía? Who in Salamanca does *not* know her? Well, well! So you're her daughter, eh?' He chuckled merrily. 'I trust she'll be as anxious to see you as you are to see her.' The chuckle deepened. 'Yes indeed, Estefanía is still in Salamanca, but she doesn't live in the back alleyways with her gipsy friends now. At this time of evening she'll be on the balcony of Colonel Clausel's house, on the square. The house which once belonged to the principal of the Irish College. She's almost as pampered as Colonel Clausel's horse. Yes, that's where you'll find her – and I'd pay money to see her face when you greet her.'

The old man's merriment began to choke him and Josefa turned away. The ostler's news had startled her. She knew the house of which he was talking. It was an impressive building in a part of Salamanca far removed from the dingy one-roomed shack Josefa had shared with her mother before running away.

It was not far to the square and the dancing was still going on, but Josefa had no eye for it now. She was straining to see if there was anyone on the balcony of the house where she had been told she would find her mother.

There was someone there. A woman, seemingly dressed in white. Not until a door opened from a lighted room off the balcony was Josefa able to make a positive identification. A servant girl came from the room with a drink for the woman and Josefa could see her face clearly. It was her mother, but there had been a dramatic transformation in appearance while Josefa had been away.

This woman did not display the bright clothes or wild, loose hair of a gipsy dancer. Dressed in a flowing white dress, her hair was drawn back, black, smooth and shining, with earrings that reflected fire in the lamplight. Josefa found such a dramatic change of circumstances astounding, but the woman on the balcony was certainly her mother.

Josefa's heart began beating faster with excitement and anticipation as she knocked on the door of the house. When there was no immediate reply Josefa knocked again, louder this time. There was the sound of movement on the balcony, and her mother's voice called, 'Yes? Who is it?'

Stepping back from the door, Josefa looked up to the balcony. 'It's me . . . Josefa!'

'Josefa? *Madre de Dios!* What are you doing here? What do you want?'

The light on the balcony was not good, but there was enough for Josefa to see the expression of dismay on her mother's face. Josefa was both hurt and bewildered.

Their relationship had never been as close as that of other mothers and daughters of her acquaintance, but she loved her mother.

'I'm your daughter. I've been away for a year and have come to visit you. Do I need to stand in the street and shout explanations for all the square to hear? What are you doing in such a house, anyway?'

'Hush! There's no need to shout. Stay there, I'll come down and let you in.'

Estefanía disappeared from view. Moments later Josefa heard the sound of hard-heeled shoes clip-clopping down stone stairs inside the house. Then a bolt was slid back, the door opened and, hiding in the shadows, her mother said, 'Come inside ... Quickly, before anyone sees you.'

Stepping in through the doorway, Josefa turned and said, 'Hello, Mama.'

The kiss she received in return was, at the most, perfunctory. Then, assured the door was secured, her mother lit a candle and looked at Josefa critically.

'You have changed little since you went away. More grown up, perhaps, but still as wild as ever, I've no doubt.'

'You've changed. The clothes, your hair ... and this house! What has happened?'

'I've found ... a friend. He's a French officer – a colonel, no less. He takes good care of me. Very good care of me. But ... he does not know I have a daughter of your age. Especially one as wild and as wilful. Why did you run away? I thought you must be dead. Where have you been?'

As she talked, Estefanía led the way upstairs. She did not return to the balcony. Instead, she took Josefa to a small room at the back of the house. It appeared to be Estefanía's private sitting room and Josefa marvelled once more at her mother's remarkable change of fortune. But her mother's words reminded her of the reason she had agreed to come to Salamanca.

'Your colonel . . . can he arrange for you to leave Salamanca? If he can, you must go as soon as possible. The British army is on its way here.'

Estefanía looked at her daughter as though she had taken leave of her senses. 'What nonsense is this? The British army has been beaten back to the Portuguese border. Soon they will be driven to the edge of the sea. My colonel has told me so.'

There was the sound of a door being closed on the ground floor and a man's voice called for Estefanía.

'It is him! My colonel . . .' Estefanía turned wide eyes upon Josefa. 'He knows nothing of you. He thinks . . . he thinks I am younger. Oh! Why did you have to come back? I have so much to lose . . .'

'I won't tell him.'

The words threatened to choke Josefa. She had been reunited with her mother, only to have to deny their relationship within minutes. Yet she could understand her mother's concern. Estefanía had never known such a way of life as this before. For as long as Josefa could remember she and her mother had been short of everything. Money . . . food. There had been times when she had woken for breakfast and found a strange man sharing the meagre food with them. On such days they would eat well. Things had improved for them once Josefa was old enough to dance, but then Josefa had left home.

The door was thrown open and a small, florid-complexioned man of middle age entered the room. He was dressed in the impressive uniform of a colonel of artillery.

'Estefanía, why were you not on the balcony to wave to me when I returned? For a moment I thought ...'

Seeing Josefa for the first time the colonel stopped talking and stared at her.

'Who is this?'

'I'm Estefanía's niece. The daughter of her sister.'

'Ah! I have so much to learn about Estefanía. Welcome, my dear.'

Stepping forward, the colonel took Josefa's hand and raised it to his lips, holding it there as he murmured, 'I am Colonel Clausel. You will have heard of me, I have no doubt. If there is anything I can do to be of assistance, in any way, you need only ask. Anything at all, you understand?'

Releasing her hand reluctantly, Colonel Clausel said, 'You will of course remain as a guest in my house while you are in Salamanca?'

'Josefa is unable to stay,' said Estefanía, hurriedly, a hint of desperation in her voice. 'She is passing through Salamanca only.'

'I called in only to warn ... Estefanía. The British army is coming. I thought she should leave before it arrived.'

'How do you know this?' Colonel Clausel spoke sharply. 'Who has said such a thing to you?'

'I told her it wasn't true. That the French army would never allow the British to cross the Portuguese border. Indeed, everyone in Spain knows you will soon drive them back to the sea.'

'I saw the British army at El Cabaco.' Josefa mentioned the name of a village little more than thirty miles away, and through which she knew the 6th Division to be marching.

'So close already!' Colonel Clausel showed consternation.

'You mean Josefa's news is true?'

'It is true, my dear. But you need not concern yourself. Our army will crush Lord Wellington as though he were no more than some irritating insect. A *puce*. A flea. Unfortunately, at this precise moment our army is scattered about Spain. The Lord Wellington has been astute enough to observe this and seized an opportunity to cross the border into Spain. It is a raid, no more. The last time he did this his country awarded him an earldom. He comes seeking higher honours. Yes, he will reach Salamanca, but there will be no battle. Our great Marshal Marmont has wisely decided to withdraw the French troops from Salamanca, leaving only a strong force of soldiers manning the fortress of San Vicente and two smaller fortresses with cannons trained upon the bridge. They will keep the British at bay until we return once more. It will be a matter of days only, no more, but have no fear, my dear. I do not intend to leave you behind to suffer any indignities. I have arranged for you to leave the town with our General Staff. A carriage will be here in the morning. There will also be a wagon to carry your most precious possessions. Have your maid pack everything during the night. Do not worry, you will return again very soon.'

Colonel Clausel smiled at Josefa. 'You see, child, you can remain with your aunt after all. You may stay the night and accompany us in the carriage tomorrow.'

'No!'

Estefanía and her daughter spoke simultaneously, but it was left to Josefa to provide an explanation. 'I came only to warn . . . Aunt Estefanía. I am happy to discover she enjoys your protection, Colonel Clausel. Now I must return . . . for the sake of my mother.'

Josefa had learned all that General Clinton wished to know. She also knew she need have no fears for the safety of her mother. Estefanía could not have chosen a more capable protector.

'I understand – but I insist you do not leave us tonight. I have some friends I would like you to meet. Young officers of my regiment. All from very good families. We will have a party and, who knows, tomorrow you might not be in such a hurry to leave. Estefanía, arrange for a drink to be brought for your beautiful niece while I fetch the young men. I will hurry back you can be certain.'

When Colonel Clausel had gone, Estefanía said, 'Now what are we to do? I said you should never have come here. It poses any number of problems – and I have to think of tomorrow. It is all very well to be told I need not worry. What shall I pack? How? I shall never be ready to leave, I just know it . . .'

'Don't concern yourself about me, Mama. I'll not stay

263

to complicate your life any more than it is already. I'll leave now. By the time your gallant colonel returns I'll be gone from Salamanca.'

'But where will you go – and what shall I tell him?'

Josefa looked at the woman standing before her, racked with uncertainty but concerned only for her own well-being. Suddenly she wanted to be with Richard. To feel the comfort of his arms. The warmth of his love and to love him in return. 'Tell him I left out of concern for my mother. Yes, tell him that, Mama. It's the truth, after all. Take care of yourself, I doubt we shall ever meet again.'

Kissing her mother's cheek quickly, Josefa hurried from the room. She had done her duty here. Now there was another duty to be performed.

Outside in the square, Josefa skirted the crowd watching the dancers. There had been a time in this very city when the sound of guitars, castanets and the tapping of dancing feet would have drawn her irresistibly. When she would have had to join in. Tonight the dance failed to stir her. There was so much to think about. Richard, General Clinton, her mother, Colonel Clausel, Salamanca itself.

Tonight French soldiers clapped in time to the music. Tomorrow night, or the night after, there would be British soldiers clapping in time to the music; British voices . . .

Josefa stopped. The British voices were not just a figment of her imagination. She had heard English being spoken. Turning, she saw three soldiers walking behind her. All were dressed in the uniform of French infantrymen, yet they spoke English! Suddenly the explanation came to her. They were deserters from the British army. At that very moment she recognised one of the three. It was Walter Cottle, husband of Sarah and lately corporal in the 32nd Regiment!

Unfortunately, Walter Cottle recognised Josefa at the same time. Momentarily startled, it did not take him long to find his voice.

'That girl – the gipsy! She's Mr Kennelly's woman, a camp follower with the Thirty-second. The last time I saw her she was all lovey-dovey with him. I'll wager she hasn't had an overnight change of heart. She's a spy, that's what she is! A spy! Nab her . . . *Quick!*'

Walter Cottle's companions had been drinking and their response to his words was far slower than Josefa's own. Diving into the crowd, she was ten paces clear of them before any of the three soldiers collected their thoughts.

Unfortunately, although the numbers in the square made pursuit difficult, it also hampered Josefa's escape and by now Walter Cottle's accusation had been taken up in three languages. Cries of 'Spy!' '*Espía!*' and '*Espionne!*' pursued her as she dodged this way and that among the crowd. Only her nimbleness prevented her capture, but she knew it was only a matter of time before she was taken.

Suddenly Josefa saw the entrance to a narrow alleyway in front of her and she darted into its shadows. She knew this area well from the days when she had lived in Salamanca. Praying that nothing had been built to obstruct the narrow footway, she never slackened her speed and quickly left her pursuers behind in the darkness.

She emerged at the far end of the alleyway into a street lit only by lights from the windows of surrounding houses. The stable where she had left her donkey was around a corner from here and Josefa fell inside the door gratefully. She was safe for the moment, but when Walter Cottle reported what he knew, the French authorities would scour the town until she was found. She needed to get away from Salamanca as quickly as she could. Her small donkey was here, but she knew it would not be able to outpace even the most mediocre of runners.

In a corner of the stable a horse, disturbed by her hurried and noisy entry, snorted disapproval, emphasising it with a backwards kick that rapped noisily against the wood partition of the stall. Suddenly Josefa remembered the Arab stallion that was the pride of Colonel Clausel.

An organised search had not yet got under way when soldiers spilled from the alleyway and someone remembered the stable. As the door was pulled open and an improvised torch raised in the air the stallion emerged from the stable like a cork from a shaken champagne bottle, scattering men on either side.

Josefa rode the stallion gipsy-style, with bridle but no saddle, and there was not a man nor animal in Salamanca with a hope of catching her. She galloped through the narrow streets, heading for the bridge that crossed the River Tormes, on the edge of the city. Josefa feared the bridge might be guarded by French soldiers, and her fears were confirmed. However, the soldiers were on guard against a force trying to enter the city, not to stop a reckless girl on an Arab stallion from galloping out to be lost in the night.

Josefa scattered them before they could gather their wits and was well on her way on the road before the first of them was able to fire his musket.

She heard the crackle of shots behind her but the musket balls fell far short of their rapidly moving target. A few minutes later the sounds ceased and Josefa knew she had made good her escape from Salamanca. The excitement of her encounter with Walter Cottle and the knowledge of how close she had been to capture, together with the feel of the powerful horse beneath her, bubbled up inside. It escaped with a wild yell that reached back to the men on the bridge.

By the time the conflicting stories got back to Colonel Clausel, it was clear that his horse had been stolen by a demented woman who had ridden off naked and screaming into the night.

267

22

Josefa reached the cautiously advancing 6th Division the following morning after riding all night along moonlit roads. Two days later, led by the 32nd Regiment, the division entered Salamanca with Lord Wellington riding at its head.

There were many senior officers in the procession, yet the finest horse was ridden by Ensign Richard Kennelly. He was also the proudest man. The story of how Josefa had obtained the animal had earned the admiration and respect of every man in the division. General Clinton had offered her a sum of money for the magnificent animal which would have made her a wealthy woman among her own people. Turning down the offer, she had presented the horse to Richard.

Yet Josefa's adventure had brought her monetary reward. As a result of the information supplied by her the 6th Division entered Salamanca via two fords, avoiding the bridge overlooked by the heavily armed fortresses and saving many hundreds of lives. It also meant Lord Wellington could release the remainder of his army to pursue the fleeing French forces. The British commander-in-chief was not noted for his generosity, but he authorised payment of fifty sovereigns to Josefa for her 'invaluable services'.

Josefa walked with Cassie and the store wagons behind the soldiers. She would retrieve her donkey from the stable later. She enjoyed seeing Richard riding into Salamanca on the stolen French stallion. More than one spectator in the crowd recognised the animal and it excited much comment.

When the parade entered the great square a deputation of civil dignitaries was waiting to greet Lord Wellington and hail his army as liberators. Josefa cast a glance towards the balcony where her mother had been enjoying such a comfortable way of life only a few evenings before. The balcony was empty, the house shuttered. She wondered where Estefania and her French lover were today.

Cassie saw Josefa's expression and followed her glance to the balcony. 'Is that where your mother was living?'

Josefa nodded. She had told her story only to Richard and Cassie. 'I wonder if I shall ever see her again.'

'Of course you will. Hopefully, it will be a much happier meeting and you'll both be able to say all the things you wished you'd said this time.'

'Perhaps.'

The welcoming ceremony was interrupted by a

defiant bombardment from the French garrison of Salamanca's largest fortress, sited in the San Vicente convent. The cannonade caused no casualties, but it was a sobering reminder to residents of Salamanca and to the British troops. There was a great deal of fighting to be done before the final victory could be celebrated.

That evening Cassie accompanied Richard and Josefa to the stable to retrieve the donkey and listen to a translation of the stableman's version of the theft of Colonel Clausel's horse. He assured them it had been taken by a woman as large as an imperial guardsman, armed with both sword and a hand-gun. The stableman had put up a heroic resistance but the woman struck him down and rode away, protected as though by a magical force from the shots that were fired after her.

As the trio walked away with Josefa's small donkey in tow, Richard suggested it might be a great joke to return the horse to the stable, to see if the story-telling old ostler recognised his lost charge.

However, there were more serious matters to be dealt with in Salamanca. Even as Richard, Josefa and Cassie were laughing at the lies of the stableman, soldiers of the 32nd Regiment were engaged in digging trenches and earthworks in front of the French-held fortresses.

It was a strenuous and dangerous task. The French had knocked down a great many buildings surrounding their strongholds to increase their field of power. The soldiers of the 32nd had to contend with heavy fire as they attempted to dig through the foundations of the demolished buildings. It was decided to carry out the work at night but the French garrisons were prepared

for this. They threw sacks of blazing hay from the fortifications and fired at everything that moved.

Harry was one of the working party on the first occasion and Cassie lay awake for much of the night listening
to the shooting and the cries of the wounded. She felt
a tremendous relief when dawn brought the return of
the working party with Harry among them, weary, but
unhurt.

The dangerous work went on for two more nights
against one of the two smaller fortresses. Cannon and
howitzers were brought up but made no impression on
the stout walls. Then a decision was made to storm the
fortress, under cover of darkness, using scaling ladders.
Three hundred men were chosen to take part in the
assault and so important was the attack that it was led
by a major-general.

Three Company was among the three hundred chosen
for the assault. As dusk approached a false gaiety
infected the men. There was much loud boasting about
the manner in which they intended chasing the French
soldiers from their seemingly impregnable fortress.

Harry did not join in the general merriment. He sat
near the cooking fire with Cassie, nursing the rum with
which the assaulting party had been issued, gazing
morosely into the fire. Cassie tried unsuccessfully to
draw him into quiet conversation and finally she slipped
her arm through his and leaned against him, assuming
a cheerfulness she was far from feeling. 'You're not
worried about tonight, are you, Harry? You mustn't.
You'll be all right, I'm sure of it.'

This was a lie. Cassie was more worried about the

forthcoming action than any other in which Harry had taken part.

'I'm not worried about being hurt, if that's what you mean.' Harry spoke slowly and deliberately, carefully choosing his words.

'What is it then?' Cassie raised her head from his shoulder to look at him questioningly.

'It's ... it's not easy to say. I'm not feared of being hurt, only of ... not behaving as well as I should.'

After thinking about his hesitant words, Cassie asked, 'Are you afraid, Harry?'

He nodded, mutely.

'Surely you don't think you're the only one? Why do you think everyone else is laughing and joking so much? It's because they don't want to think of what they have to do. Rose Tonks says she can remember her Elijah being sick more than once before a battle because he's so nervous – and I doubt if you'll find a braver soldier than Sergeant Tonks now, will you?'

Harry shook his head but Cassie could not tell whether her words had given him any comfort. She hugged his arm. 'I know you're a brave soldier, Harry, and I'm very proud of you. All the same, don't you get trying to prove how brave you are out there tonight. I want you back here safe and well in the morning because I've planned the best breakfast for you that any man could wish. You hear me, now?'

Harry managed a weak grin but there was no more time for talk. At that moment Sergeant Tonks strode into the firelight calling loudly and with a contagious confidence for 3 Company to muster and 'Get ready to winkle they Frenchies out like maggots from an apple.'

A quick kiss and Harry was gone, leaving Cassie holding the undrunk rum and murmuring a brief but fervent prayer for his safe return.

Cassie waited with the other wives in the houses nearest to the fortress as the assault party made its way cautiously across the open space before it. For a while she hoped they would make it to the fortress unseen but then she saw a flicker of light from one of the ramparts. The next moment a blazing sack of hay was tossed over the battlements, quickly followed by another . . . and another.

Suddenly it seemed that every gun from all the fortresses was firing and the result was bedlam. The men in the lee of the fortress were seen to fall by the score and the screams of the wounded men could be heard rising above the din of battle, yet still men attempted to raise their scaling ladders against the high walls.

Wounded men were being carried back now, the major-general among them. Many wives darted forward to aid the wounded, each fearing she would find her own man among the casualties.

Cassie was tending the major-general when Richard Kennelly scrambled over the heap of rubble that hid them from view of the fortress.

'Sir, I've been sent to tell you the attack is faltering. It's impossible to scale the walls.'

'Nonsense! The fortress must be taken.' Pulling a wounded arm free from Cassie, the general nodded. 'Thank you, girl. That will be all.'

'But I've only cleaned the wound. It needs bandaging.'

It was doubtful whether the wounded man heard her. He was already scrambling over the rubble, disappearing into the small patch of darkness that was the only cover before the battle area. He fell dead before reaching the walls and soon the survivors of the brief but bitter assault were scrambling back to safety and the French ceased sending their unorthodox 'torches' toppling from the battlements.

As the badly shaken survivors reached the shelter of the rubble in front of the houses the women of the regiment searched anxiously for a glimpse of their husbands. Many were disappointed.

Cassie was beginning to feel her own panic grow when the dim light of a lamp in the nearby command post fell upon Harry's face and she rushed to him and threw her arms about him crying, 'Thank God, Harry! Thank God.' She realised she was trembling violently.

'I'm all right, Cassie.' Harry released himself from Cassie's arms. 'But there are others out there who aren't. Wounded men. Why is nothing being done to help them?'

Gorran Fox, his face gaunt, was in the command post with the 32nd's commander. Both had taken part in the disastrous assault. He heard Harry's words and replied to them.

'A flag of truce has been sent out to enable us to bring in the wounded. We'll get them back.'

Polly Martin suddenly appeared in the light. Wide-eyed, she cried, 'I haven't seen Enoch. He's not returned. Have you seen him?'

'He was with me by the wall of the fort. I never saw him afterwards.' Harry's voice was hoarse, affected by the gunpowder smoke in the battle area.

'Don't worry, Polly.' Cassie sought to comfort the other woman. 'A flag of truce has been sent out. We'll soon have Enoch back.'

'The flag's been refused. The French won't accept it.' An unseen voice called the news and it was quickly taken up by the waiting women.

'Truce or no, someone has to go out and bring the wounded in. If it was me lying out there I'd expect someone to come and find me.'

Cassie was taken aback to hear Harry speak in such a manner. Rarely known to express a strong opinion, Harry preferred to remain in the middle of a crowd, unnoticed and unheard. The army was changing the quiet orphaned Mevagissey boy. Even more surprising, Gorran Fox accepted what Harry had to say, and was prepared to act upon it.

'You're quite right, Clymo.' Raising his voice, he called, 'I want volunteers to return to the fortress for the wounded. The French have refused to grant a truce so you'll be shot at.'

Almost every man who had escaped the slaughter around the fortress stepped forward, together with men from companies not taking part in the assault. There was also a response from an unexpected quarter. Pushing her way through the throng of soldiers, Polly said, 'If Enoch's lying close to the fortress he could be dead by the time you reach him. I'll go and find him myself. Here ... !'

Polly was holding Jean. Thrusting her into the arms of a startled woman standing nearby, she pushed her way back through the men and before anyone could restrain her she scrambled over the heap of rubble and was gone, heading through the darkness towards the fortress.

One of the officers from another company said, 'The woman's a fool. She'll not help a wounded husband by getting herself killed.'

Gorran disagreed. 'The soldiers inside the fortress are men, the same as us. Many will have wives and families of their own. It's not them who have refused to allow the wounded to be recovered – and I doubt if they'll shoot at a woman. Come on.'

As the soldiers left the shelter of the rubble, Cassie followed. She could hear Polly ahead of her in the darkness, calling her husband's name in a loud voice that could be heard above the sporadic musket fire that still came from the fortress.

'Enoch! Can you hear me?' Cassie also began calling as she advanced over the open ground with a number of wives whose husbands were also missing.

An answering cry came from nearby and Cassie headed towards the sound. It was not Enoch, but it *was* a wounded soldier. Cassie was trying to raise him to his feet when some soldiers came to her aid. Lifting the wounded man they carried him to safety.

As she rose to her feet, Cassie became aware that the shooting had ceased. The only sound now was the voices of the women who scoured the scene of the recent battle, calling the names of their missing men. Behind them the soldiers of the 6th Division carried away each wounded man as he was located.

The French commander had refused to grant a temporary truce, but he was powerless to prevent the soldiers under his command operating their own unofficial cease-fire by refusing to shoot while the women were roaming the battle-ground.

Enoch Martin eventually answered his wife's anxious calls and came back with her to safety looking extremely sheepish. He was not wounded. During the murderous fire that greeted the attack he had lost his musket. He succeeded in finding safety at the base of the fortress wall but every time he tried to venture forth to search for his gun he was driven back again by a hail of musket fire from above.

There were a great many wounded men who were brought back to the safety of the town, together with a number of bodies. The attack on the fortress had been a costly failure.

Later that evening, after another rum ration had been dispensed to the survivors of the attack, Cassie praised Polly for her courage in leading the search for wounded men.

'I couldn't leave Enoch out there believing him to be wounded,' replied Polly. 'No more than I would have left him in the clutches of that scheming Portuguese woman he was mixed up with when I came out here.'

'You know about her?' Cassie looked at the other woman in surprise. She had thought the soldiers and women of the regiment had kept it a close secret. 'How?'

'Sarah Cottle told me ... not that she needed to. I

know Enoch too well. He needs a woman to take care of him and he's far too soft-hearted. If I hadn't come out here he'd have felt responsible for that other woman. By the time the regiment was ready to return home she'd have had him twisted round her little finger. She'd have told him she was expecting, or some other such story, and he'd have likely deserted so he could stay and look after her. I wasn't having that happen.'

Cassie looked at Polly with a new respect. She wondered how she would have reacted in similar circumstances.

23

❦

For three more days the French fortresses held out against the 6th Division. Then, when a wall of the main fortress had been breached and men were being mustered for a renewed assault, the French commander surrendered.

The capitulation had been anticipated by many of the men in the French ranks. Deserting their posts they made their way to the cellars determined to enter captivity in as alcoholic a condition as time would allow. Most succeeded well. Among their number were found Walter Cottle and another deserter from the British army. Taken into custody by the provost marshal, the two men were lodged in another of the cellars until they sobered up. The next day, still wearing the French uniforms in which they had been arrested, they were arraigned before a court martial.

The findings of the court were never in doubt. Not

only had both men deserted from their own regiments in the heat of battle, they had also fought for the French against their countrymen, five hundred of whom had been killed and wounded in the attacks on the Salamanca fortresses. Their sacrifice demanded that such treachery should be suitably punished. Walter Cottle and his companion were sentenced to be shot. The sentence was to be carried out the following day by firing squads from the men's own regiments.

Talking about the court martial and its verdict that evening in the kitchen of the big house where the 32nd Regiment's married families were billeted, Rose Tonks expressed the opinion of the others when she said, 'There was no other verdict the court could reach and I've no complaint about it, neither. Walter Cottle knew what to expect when he went over to the French. All the same, he wasn't entirely to blame, I say. There's someone else should have been standing beside him at that trial.'

'Sarah, you mean?' asked Cassie.

'That's right, Sarah Cottle. Her who drove her husband to first shoot a British officer then desert from his regiment. It's a pity they can't charge wives along with their men. She was seen in Salamanca yesterday too. Buying vegetables in the market, she was, bold as brass.'

'Where is she now?'

'Where do you think? With the dragoons, camped along the river a mile or so. Women aren't allowed to go on campaign with cavalry – or so the wives were told before the regiments left England. Just look at 'em now! They've got twice as many camp followers as any infantry regiment. Mind you, there's only one or two English women among 'em, and they're of the very worst sort. The others are out-and-out riff-raff. Portuguese, Spanish and the like. Best sort of company for Sarah Cottle to keep, I'd say.'

'Don't you think Sarah ought to be told of what's happened to Walter? After all, he is still her husband.'

'So he might be, but it's never mattered much to Sarah Cottle whether a man was her husband, or someone else's. But you're right, Cassie. She should at least be told what's happening. Will you go and tell her? I don't trust myself to speak to her.'

Cassie nodded. It was not a task she relished but it had been her idea.

Harry was not on duty that evening and he walked over the bridge and along the river bank with Cassie, heading towards the camp of the Light Dragoons. It had been a long time since they had enjoyed each other's company without the noise of others all about them. As Cassie slipped her hand in his she pointed across the river to Salamanca, dominated by its magnificent great cathedral. 'Don't you think that's beautiful, Harry? It's difficult to believe so many men have fought and died there during the last week.'

'The dying isn't over yet,' said Harry, grimly. 'I've been detailed for the firing squad to execute Walter Cottle tomorrow morning.'

'But that's horrible! You've known Walter Cottle since you first joined the army. It'll be like murdering him. Can't you get someone else to take your place?'

'Who, for instance? We've all known him, some much

longer than me. No, it's all supposed to be part of his punishment. To be shot by the men who were once his friends. The men he betrayed.'

For a while they walked on in silence, until Harry said, 'In my heart I don't believe Walter betrayed anyone. It was the other way around, really. It was Walter who was betrayed ... by Sarah.'

'That's what everyone seems to think – but he didn't have to desert to the French and fight against the men who'd once been his friends. Against you.'

'I doubt if he ever shot at any of us, Cassie. If he ever did fire a gun against us I believe he'd have aimed to miss ... and that's what I intend doing tomorrow.'

'What would happen if everyone else did the same?'

'I don't know. Perhaps he'd be given a pardon, or something.'

Harry spoke without conviction, although he had heard somewhere that if a gallows failed to operate during a hanging the convicted man was granted a reprieve. There was just a possibility the same rule applied to an execution by shooting.

The dragoons had been called away to drive off a squadron of French cavalry reported to be harassing a British army company repairing a bridge across the Tormes River, some miles downstream, and Cassie and Harry found Sarah Cottle in the untidy and ill-organised camp occupied by the baggage wagons. There were no other English women with her, only a miscellany of Portuguese and Spanish women, and wagon drivers.

Most of the women were seated on the ground close to a cooking fire, passing a huge amphora of wine among themselves. They drank clumsily from the vessel, disregarding any wine that ran from the wide neck of the vessel and on to their clothes. It would be just one more stain to add to the many already there. Sarah Cottle was the only woman using a mug from which to drink her wine, but in every other respect she resembled the other women.

Cassie was shocked. Sarah possessed many faults but she had always taken a pride in her appearance. That she was aware of her unkempt appearance was apparent when she saw Cassie and Harry approaching and stood up unsteadily, her hand going first to her hair and then to her creased, untidy skirt.

'Well! Look who we have here. The Thirty-second's newlyweds, and still holding hands too. Come and sit down and have a drink. Maria! Stop guzzling wine and pass it over here. We've got guests – a legally married lady at that, not camp-following whores like the rest of us. That's right, isn't it, Cassie?'

'There's no call for such talk, Sarah. You're still a legally married woman too – and it's your husband we've come to talk to you about.'

'Oh? Well, if it's serious talk you're here for and not just paying a social call then I'll have some wine.'

Matching word with deed, Sarah slopped wine in her mug from the amphora, spilling a great deal on the ground and provoking noisy protests from her companions.

Ignoring the outcry, she half-emptied the mug before asking, 'What have you come to speak to me about? Is Walter missing his wifely comforts so much he's sent you to ask me to go back to him? Or is he being more masterful, seeing as how he's a corporal, and demanding I go back? Corporal indeed! He owes his corporal's stripes to me, and well he knows it. If it hadn't been for me he'd have spent a lifetime in the army without so much as being noticed – and you can tell him I said so. I must be the only one who believed him when he said he never shot John Dalhousie – and shall I tell you why? Because he hasn't the gumption to do it, that's why. You go back and tell him if he wants me back then he can come and tell me himself – not that it's likely to do him any good, but he can try.'

'He can't go anywhere, Sarah. He's been court-martialled again. For desertion, this time.' Cassie wondered whether Sarah could even hear her, she seemed so drunk. 'Walter was found in French uniform when the forts were taken in Salamanca. He's been sentenced to be shot.'

Sarah was not as drunk as she appeared and Cassie's bald statement sobered her as nothing else could. The mug of wine fell to the ground and her mouth dropped open. '*Shot!*' It came out as a horrified whisper. 'When?'

'Tomorrow morning.'

'Oh my God! Poor Walter. I never dreamed I'd drive him to this. If I'd known he cared that much I swear I'd have stuck to him through thick and thin. Why did he never tell me? Why didn't he say? How did he expect me to know if he never said?'

'I can't answer that, Sarah. We came here to tell you because we felt you ought to know. You should at least see him before . . . before tomorrow.'

'Where is he?'

'He and another deserter are in a cell in the Salamanca gaol.'

'I'll go and see him now. Will you wait for me? I haven't much to pack. A small bundle is all.'

Without waiting for a reply she hurried away, leaving Cassie and Harry in the midst of the heavily drinking Portuguese and Spanish women.

She returned carrying a small bundle wrapped in a colourful Spanish-style headscarf. Looking about her, she said, 'This is what I've come down to, living among women who are happy only when they're drunk. To them success is stealing something they wouldn't bother with if they were sober. Come, let's go to Salamanca. If John Dalhousie wants a woman tonight he can take his pick from these – and good luck to the one who gets him.'

When they were well clear of the camp, Sarah suddenly put down her bundle and said, 'I've a clean frock, here, but first I need a bath. I feel as though I haven't been clean in months.'

Without more ado she dropped her dress to the ground and stepped from it. Quite naked, she walked into the river.

Harry's face was scarlet with embarrassment as Sarah sank down in the water and moved her hands against the tide to maintain her balance. Smiling up at him, she said, 'It's no good you getting all excited at what you can see, young Harry. Cassie will make certain you do no more than look. Turn around now, will you? I've some ablutions to perform that shouldn't be seen by any young man who holds a woman's body in any esteem.'

The colour of Harry's cheeks shone through his Peninsular suntan as he turned away.

Cassie had been deeply affronted by Sarah's brazen conduct but suddenly she laughed. 'There are men who'd give a week's pay to see what you've just seen, Harry, yet I swear you'd as soon storm another fortress as look at it once more.'

Harry managed a weak smile. 'I don't know, and I don't suppose I'll ever be offered such a choice.'

A few minutes later Sarah stepped from the river with an equal lack of concern, slipped a clean dress over her head, then brushed out the many tangles in her hair.

Picking up her bundle once more, she said, 'There! Now I feel ready to face Walter – and the other wives of the Thirty-second. Let's go.'

In Salamanca, Harry returned to the house while Cassie accompanied Sarah as far as the city gaol. Here she stopped, refusing to go inside. The grim grey exterior sent shivers through her. She had no wish to sample what the interior had to offer.

Waiting while Sarah explained her mission with some difficulty to the Spanish turnkey, Cassie turned away as the great iron-studded gate crashed shut behind her. On the way back to the billet she wondered what Sarah would have to say to her condemned husband.

24

❧

Sarah Cottle arrived at the big house off the square where the wives of the 32nd Regiment were billeted after dark that night. When she walked into the kitchen where the women and their husbands were gathered, all conversation ceased.

The lack of a welcome reception seemed not to bother the wife of the condemned corporal.

'Is anyone going to offer me a cup of tea – or something stronger if it's going?'

The heady aroma of brandy hung on the air in the crowded kitchen, but no one replied, or made a move to offer her a drink, alcoholic or otherwise.

'Oh, well, I'll just have to help myself.'

Moving across the kitchen, she forced more than one man to draw back outstretched legs that barred her path. Taking a cup from the table she made some tea, pouring water from the heavy, smoke-blackened kettle which was steaming and rattling on the fire.

Adding sugar to the cup, she looked about the room for a place to sit. After a few moments Cassie moved along the rough wood bench on which she was seated to make room for the unexpected visitor.

'Have you seen Walter?'

'I have, and I left him a much happier man than when I first arrived. I can't save his life, but he'll die at peace with himself.'

Someone in the room snorted scornfully. Ignoring the interruption, she went on, 'Do you know where I can find that friar we travelled with from Figueira?'

'He's with the Portuguese brigade, on the other side of the city. A thanksgiving service is being held at the cathedral tonight. No doubt you'll find him there if you need to.'

'There's nothing I want with any priest, but Walter says he'd like to have one speak to him before the morning. Father Michael's the only one I know.'

'I'll go and see if I can find him.' Harry rose from his seat.

'You stay with Cassie. I'm the odd one out here. I'll go – but I'll be back. I'm as much a part of the Thirty-second as anyone in this room, with or without a man. Remember that.'

The events of the day of Walter Cottle's execution caused Cassie to have nightmares for many months to come.

Due to take place in the early morning, the execution was delayed by heavy rain which did not ease until mid-morning. The whole regiment had been paraded and the men were forced to find what shelter they could around the cleared area in front of the partly demolished fortresses. Meanwhile Walter Cottle chatted nonchalantly to his guards as he smoked a succession of pipes of tobacco.

After the delay had lasted for a couple of hours, Sarah was given permission to carry a jug of brandy to her husband, but the provost marshal, seemingly more agitated by the delay than his prisoner, would allow the condemned man no more than half a mugful. Neither would he permit Sarah to have more than the briefest of conversations with her husband.

When the rain began to ease, many of the Salamanca residents came from their houses and assembled to witness the execution. Soon it became necessary to muster a company of the Portuguese brigade to keep the onlookers clear of the execution area.

Eventually the rain stopped. As the 32nd Regiment was paraded to form three sides of a square, Walter Cottle knocked out his pipe and handed it to one of his escorts. It seemed the provost marshal was anxious to make up for the long delay. Walter was marched briskly to the shattered wall of the French-built fortress which formed the fourth side of the square. Here handcuffs secured his hands behind his back and he was offered, but refused, a blindfold.

He stood straight and stiff against the wall as the ten-strong firing squad was marched out from the ranks. It included Enoch Martin as well as Harry. As the execution squad lined up, Walter Cottle's head moved. His eyes sought and found his wife, standing among the wives no more than fifty paces from the condemned man.

When the firing squad was in position, each soldier was ordered to check his musket. The inspection completed, the men finally took up a firing position.

Father Michael had walked beside Walter to the place of execution. Now he made the sign of the Cross in the air, placed his hand briefly on Walter's bared head and walked away. Halfway between the condemned man and the watching wives, Father Michael halted and turned towards Walter. Bowing his head, he began praying for the soul of the condemned man.

'Take aim!'

The order rang out and a hush fell on the waiting onlookers, as though every man, woman and child had drawn in and held a breath.

'Fire!'

The end of the drawn-out command was lost in the noise of ten muskets firing in ragged unison. For perhaps two seconds the immediate scene of the execution was lost to view in a cloud of pungent smoke. When it cleared, the breath of the watchers was expelled in a gasp that combined astonishment and horror.

The decision to draw a firing squad from Walter Cottle's own company had been made with the intention of bringing home to the men the enormity of the condemned man's offence. The decision proved a ghastly mistake. All but two of the firing squad had served with him, through good times as well as through bad. Had shared with him triumph and disaster, celebration and sorrow.

The remaining two soldiers were recent recruits sent out from England – and only two musket balls had struck Walter Cottle, neither proving fatal. The condemned corporal had been knocked to his knees by the force of the two musket balls, blood now staining his uniform from wounds to his right side and groin.

As the firing squad stood uncertainly in line, a roar of excitement went up from the watching soldiers. Many believed, as did Harry Clymo, that the unsuccessful execution attempt would result in Walter being reprieved.

The provost marshal did not share their ignorance of military law. Stepping to the side of the kneeling man, he drew his pistol and held it to Walter Cottle's temple. He pulled the trigger ... and nothing happened. Hurriedly the provost marshal cocked the pistol and tried again – with the same result.

As Father Michael hurried towards the wounded man Walter Cottle made a painful attempt to rise to his feet but the provost marshal pushed him back to his knees.

'For God's sake, man! Hasn't he suffered enough?' Father Michael's words carried to the appalled onlookers.

It took the provost marshal perhaps half a minute to inspect and change the flint in his pistol, as the crowd murmured angrily and Father Michael protested at Walter Cottle's prolonged ordeal.

'This is inhuman! You wouldn't do this to an animal. Set him free. I'll speak to Lord Wellington myself.'

When the new flint was firmly in position, the provost marshal put the muzzle of the gun to the temple of the condemned man. Walter looked up at his would-be executioner, his face showing the strain and pain he was feeling.

The provost marshal squeezed the trigger of the pistol once more. There was a muffled report, a cloud of gunpowder smoke, and Walter pitched forward, his body jerking spasmodically as life ebbed away. Roughly brushing Walter's executioner to one side, Father Michael dropped to his knees beside the body and began to pray.

Among the crowd of watching wives, Cassie and Polly Martin stood with tears coursing down their faces. Others talked excitedly, most expressing anger at the scene they had just witnessed. Sarah Cottle said nothing and showed no emotion, but her face was as pale as that of her now dead husband.

That evening Sarah was married to Private Ned Harrup of the 32nd Regiment. Father Michael refused to conduct the ceremony and the couple were married by the 6th Division padre in a ceremony that was as brief as the law would allow.

Sarah, the new Mrs Harrup, informed the other wives of her marriage in the kitchen of the married women's billet that night. As she had anticipated, the other regimental wives were scandalised that she should have married so soon after the savage and public execution of her late husband, but Sarah was unrepentant.

'I told you I'd always been a Thirty-second Regiment wife – and I still am. All right, so Walter's hardly cold in his grave but many a woman's done the same thing when her man's been killed in battle. Walter would understand. I married him the same day my previous husband had died and for the same reason. If I wasn't properly married I could be packed off to England any time some officer took the notion to get rid of me. Now I'm safe. I'm married into the Thirty-second again.'

Rose Tonks sniffed contemptuously. 'I gather from that little speech that her fine cavalry gentleman's fed up with her and would like her packed off to England. He'll find it harder than prising a limpet from a rock. Sarah Cottle, or Harrup, as I suppose we'll have to get used to calling her, is in the Peninsula and here she'll stay. If it was anyone else but Mr Dalhousie I'd feel sorry for him. As it is, I'll save my sympathy for Ned Harrup. He doesn't deserve any either, but he'll certainly have need of it.'

Ignoring the loud whispering of the sergeant's wife, Sarah Harrup continued, 'I'll be moving in here with Ned tonight. The quartermaster's given us a room in the attic. There'll be a barrel of wine moving in with us. Anyone who wishes us well is welcome to help drink it.'

After a lengthy silence, Cassie crossed the room to where the newly married woman stood staring defiantly about her. 'I wish you well, Sarah. I hope you and Ned will be very happy together.' Cassie gave her a quick hug.

'There's nothing in the wedding service says we've got to be happy,' said Sarah. 'But I know you mean what you say. I thank you for that. Now, if you've all done

293

congratulating me I'll go and get the room ready for Ned and me. It's nice to be part of the regiment again.'

When the 6th Division rejoined his main army, Lord Wellington gave the order to advance. With their Portuguese allies the army now pushed deeper into the Spanish heartland, driving the French back until they chose to make a stand on the Douro River, more than fifty miles from Salamanca. Meanwhile, reinforcements for the French army had been rushed from every part of Spain.

By the time Lord Wellington reached the Douro he realised his own army was considerably outnumbered. Deciding the time had not yet arrived for the French to be pushed back to the borders of their homeland, he turned his army about and began a slow, tactical retreat, drawing the French army after him.

For more than a week the two armies marched and countermarched, each trying to out manoeuvre the other and entice them into committing a strategic blunder.

On 21 July both armies reached the Tormes River, not many miles distant from Salamanca, and camped on the same bank within hearing of one another. That night a storm, the like of which had been seen by no living man, broke upon French and British alike. Rain descended in a torrent and thunder and lightning vied with each other for domination of the skies. Soldiers were temporarily blinded by the lightning and, such was the noise of the thunder, terrified cavalry horses broke free from their pickets. Galloping this way and that in utter panic, the maddened animals trampled men and stores into the mud.

Huddled together in the lee of a rock, Cassie and Harry had been washed from their twig shelter by a torrent of water that cascaded from the hill behind them, bringing with it tons of mud and debris. Fleeing to the scant sanctuary offered by a low wall they narrowly escaped being run down by a number of cavalry horses. Heading towards the French lines, the horses were likely to be in French hands in the morning.

The wall offered the only shelter from the fury of the storm for some distance around and it was not long before more than a hundred soldiers and women huddled together hoping for an end to the deluge.

Dawn was showing in the grey sky before the rain ceased but even as Cassie and Harry emerged from beneath their sodden blankets, the drums of the French army could be heard, signalling their soldiers to arms. Minutes later British bugles followed suit.

The storm of the night might have been sent by the Prince of Darkness as an omen of the events of the day to come. It began, as had many others, with a duel between the cannons of the opposing artillery, accompanied by minor skirmishing as the two armies set off on a parallel course. Then Marshal Auguste Marmont, brilliant commander of the French army, committed the first error made by either side during the week-long game of cat-and-mouse.

Thinking he might contain the British army and bring them to bay in an unfavourable defensive position, Marmont sent the main body of his troops to cut off the British retreat. In so doing he extended his army too far, splitting it, unintentionally, into three separate parts.

Wellington spotted the error immediately and struck with a speed that took the French marshal completely by surprise. Throwing four British divisions into the attack, ably supported by a Portuguese brigade, he fell upon one of the detached segments of Marmont's army.

The French army reeled under the impact of the onslaught, held, and then broke, as the British troops substituted bayonet for bullet and charged the French ranks. Marmont, seeing the fatal results of his mistake from a nearby hill, himself led reinforcements to the rescue of his reeling army and fell wounded with a badly shattered arm. Carried to safety, his arm was immediately amputated. Behind him, lacking firm leadership, his troops were badly mauled.

That night both armies dropped in exhaustion on the field of battle. At dawn they rose from the hard ground and battle was joined once more. The fighting was so fierce that every soldier, cook, bandsman and general was thrown into the battle. The 6th Division bore the brunt of the conflict and the 32nd Regiment was wherever the battle was fiercest. The regiment's headquarters' staff was swept into the fight when the French launched a counter-attack and from the shelter she had sought on a nearby hillside, Cassie saw Gorran Fox and his colonel laying about them with their swords, fighting for their very lives.

As Cassie watched in horror, she saw Gorran stagger and drop to his knees as the 32nd fought its way back and drove the French off once more. The battlefield was strewn with fallen men and the wives deserted the safety of the hillside and ran to help the wounded. Soon, all over the battlefield, women were picking their way among the fallen. Some had seen their husbands fall, others had lost sight of theirs in the smoke and confusion of battle. Many of the wives found their men on the battlefield but cries of relief were coupled with those of anguish. It had been a costly battle.

Cassie saw Harry and another private of the 32nd carrying a wounded French general to the surgeon and she ran to where she had seen Gorran struck down. Much to her relief the Cornish lieutenant was sitting on the ground nursing a bloody arm. He even managed a wan smile when she dropped to her knees beside him.

'Hello, Cassie. You must be getting used to binding my arm by now. It's the same one. A musket ball this time. I think it's passed right through, just below the shoulder. It's a damned silly little wound, but I find I can't stay on my feet. I think I must have lost a lot of blood.'

Cassie stripped off his jacket and saw that the whole of the sleeve and the side of his shirt were soaked with blood, which dripped from his finger as he moved his arm.

'When did you do this? Not just now, surely?'

'No, this morning, during the first attack . . . Ouch!' His cry of pain came as Cassie ripped the sleeve of his shirt from cuff to shoulder and accidentally jarred the arm.

'You've had this all morning?' Cassie asked, incredulously. 'I think your brains must have leaked out with the blood. You could have died!'

'Not me, Cassie. The colonel couldn't spare me . . .'

Suddenly, Gorran slipped sideways to the ground. He lay there and looked up at Cassie with a surprised expression. 'That was a damned silly thing to do ... Help me back up again.'

'If I do you'll only slip down again. You stay where you are while I do something with this arm. You've lost more blood than you can afford to lose.'

Most soldiers' wives had acquired bandages for just such an occasion as this, and Cassie was no exception. After washing out the wound with water from Gorran's own canteen, she bound the wound tightly.

'There! That's clean – and a sight healthier than it'll be if you let a surgeon poke about in there but we'll need to get you somewhere to rest.' Suddenly Cassie discovered she was talking to herself. Gorran had drifted off into unconsciousness.

There was no more Cassie could do to help him and as she waited for someone to come and collect him, she dressed the wounds of other casualties. There was no need to stray far. At least forty men had fallen wounded within fifty paces of the headquarters' position.

Eventually she saw the commanding officer riding back through the field with a number of other officers. He was looking about him with an expression of great sadness. When Cassie drew his attention to the wounded Gorran Fox the colonel immediately had two of the more junior officers take care of him.

'Well done, young lady.' The colonel spoke to Cassie as Gorran was being carried away. 'It's Mrs Clymo, is it not? Do you have news of your husband?'

'He's taken a French general to the surgeon.'

'Of course! I remember. I'm glad to know he's safe. It's been a glorious day for the regiment – but at such a dreadful cost! There must be at least a hundred and fifty men dead or wounded, and we're one of the fortunate regiments. The Twenty-eighth have been almost annihilated.'

The colonel looked about him sadly before speaking again. 'If any of the wives are unable to find their husbands tell them to go to Salamanca. The wounded are being taken there. The Irish College has been turned into a hospital. Good day to you, Mrs Clymo. My thanks again for tending Mr Fox.'

Cassie met up with Harry after dark that night when the regiment mustered in a small village nearby. There was a pride among the men, but it was coupled with sadness. They had decisively defeated the French but the price had been appallingly high. More than 6000 British and Portuguese soldiers were dead or wounded.

The French losses were even higher. It was estimated that 14,000 of their men had been killed, wounded, or taken prisoner.

For days the more disreputable of the camp followers reaped a rich harvest among the fallen of both sides whose bodies lay thick upon the Spanish countryside. They shared the battlefield with a scurrying army of bloated vultures that quarrelled noisily over victor and vanquished alike.

25

❧

As the British army fought its way back and forth across the Spanish countryside, sickness continued to pose a serious problem. It continually foiled Lord Wellington's plans for attacking the enemy and hit hard at the women and children accompanying the army. Although sharing the same privations as the men, the families of the soldiers were on considerably reduced rations and so had less strength to ward off recurrent fevers.

Now aged four, little Jean Martin had been plagued with a feverish chill for some weeks. Each day she was thinner and more listless than before. The regimental surgeon saw her frequently and expressed grave concern at the child's condition but admitted he was at a loss to provide a remedy.

After consulting his divisional colleagues, the surgeon suggested Polly should take the child to the military hospital in Salamanca. Six thousand British soldiers were currently being treated in the Spanish city. Because of the vast numbers an appeal had gone to England for volunteer civilian surgeons to serve in the Peninsula on a temporary basis to relieve their hard-pressed military colleagues.

Many eminent physicians and surgeons had already answered the call and it was hoped one of these might have the experience to help Jean. Polly Martin had also been ill and, concerned lest she prove unable to cope with her sick child, she asked Cassie to accompany her to Salamanca.

As it happened, Harry was currently serving with the 32nd Regiment's Light Company, which had been particularly seriously hit by casualties and illness. Skirmishing well ahead of the remainder of the division, the success of the Light Company depended upon its speed of movement and absence of all encumbrances. Wives of Light Company soldiers were not allowed to accompany their husbands in the field.

Rose Tonks promised to cook for Harry, should he return unexpectedly. Sending a message to him explaining what she was doing, Cassie set off for Salamanca with Polly and her sick daughter.

The question of an escort for the journey had been solved in a most satisfactory way. Richard Kennelly had been detailed to escort a convoy of sick and wounded to Salamanca. Once there, his orders were to round up all the able-bodied men of the 32nd Regiment who had been discharged from the hospitals. They were urgently needed to fill the sorely depleted ranks of the regiment, which was operating at less than half strength.

Josefa travelled with Richard and the three women looked forward to spending a little time away from the alarms and tragedies of battle.

The storms that had swept over the countryside in recent weeks had moved away. The land was bathed in hot sunshine, luscious grapes were ripening everywhere and fresh produce was plentiful. As the women rode their donkeys through the peaceful countryside it was difficult to realise that war had rolled over this land and fierce battles were still being fought only a few miles away.

Had it not been for the pale-faced and listless child being nursed by each of the women in turn, they might have been three friends out to enjoy the pleasures of a sun-blessed land.

The residents of Salamanca were celebrating a saint's day and a carnival air was abroad when the convoy of sick and wounded reached the city. Pretty young girls wearing bright-coloured clothes threw flowers into the open, solid-wheeled carts occupied by the soldiers, making even the most gravely ill among them feel a little better.

Richard Kennelly carried a letter from the colonel of the 32nd to the quartermaster general stationed in Salamanca explaining about Jean Martin. As a result they were given an excellent billet in a house just off the square. Richard was accommodated in the same house, the quartermaster explaining that locating the men from his regiment would take some days.

Josefa was not entitled to a billet at the army's expense. However, when the landlady's young son excitedly informed her that Richard was riding the horse stolen from Colonel Clausel, she and the ensign were given the finest room in the house. For the whole of their stay, friends of the family called in every day to hear the story of how the horse had been stolen.

It gave Josefa a strange feeling when she walked past the house where she had met her mother, but the feeling did nothing to spoil the enjoyment of being able to spend time with Richard in an atmosphere far removed from battle, and free of the restrictions of regimental life.

Meanwhile, Polly Martin and Cassie were shuttled from one hospital to another as they sought a doctor able to do something for the sick child. On the third day, Jean was examined by a physician newly arrived from London where he taught medicine to others. The most experienced physician ever to come to the Peninsula, he examined the little girl thoroughly before declaring solemnly that the air in Spain did not suit her. He was able to offer nothing to ease her condition immediately but suggested a move to the clean air of rural England might be what was needed.

Returning to the house near the square after seeing the eminent London physician, Polly was overcome with a terrible despair. For the remainder of that day Cassie had to work hard to convince the young mother her daughter was not going to die.

It might have been that the London physician had powers far beyond his own comprehension. Or it could have been that all Jean needed was the comfort of a town house, far away from the chills, alarms and terrors of campaign life. Whatever the cause, Jean's health began to improve with dramatic suddenness.

The next morning, the little girl awoke and said she felt hungry. Given food, she ate as though she intended making up for all she had forgone in recent weeks. Fruit especially appealed to her and the delighted landlady of the house supplied more varieties than either of the English women had known existed.

While Polly rejoiced in the newly restored appetite of her young daughter, Cassie set off to visit Gorran Fox. She had learned he was in a villa on the edge of town that was being used as a convalescent hospital for officers.

Cassie had lain awake for a while during the night wondering whether it was proper for her, as a soldier's wife, to pay a call alone on an officer in her husband's regiment. Of course, she could have asked Josefa to come with her but Cassie told herself it would be unfair to deprive the young Spanish girl of Richard's company, even for such a short while. The two had been able to spend so little time with only each other for company.

Cassie also convinced herself that Gorran had always been so concerned for the welfare of the soldiers and their families under his command it would be churlish not to pay him a visit when she was in the same city. Besides, there might be a message he would like her to relay to the commanding officer of the 32nd.

At the door of the villa, Cassie almost changed her mind when she was forced to stand aside to allow a well-dressed and obviously well-bred woman to pass. The woman was talking to a diminutive colonel and not until she glanced casually in her direction did Cassie recognise her. It was Lady Fraser, whose child had been rescued by Josefa from the river during the previous year's campaign.

Much to Cassie's surprise the woman stopped and said to her, 'Don't I know you, my dear?'

Feeling awkward and ill-dressed beside the elegant Lady Fraser, Cassie dropped a brief curtsy. 'We met when my husband's regiment was camped near Rodrigo, ma'am. I was with Josefa, the Spanish girl who saved your little girl from the river.'

'Of course! I remember you now. You're the young Cornish girl, married to a soldier with the Thirty-second, I believe. The Spanish girl was a friend of one of your young ensigns. I've often wondered what happened to her.'

Marvelling at this woman's memory, Cassie stammered that Lady Fraser's belief was correct, and that Josefa was in Salamanca at this very moment.

'Really? Such a beautiful girl.' Turning to her companion, Lady Fraser gave him an outline of the incident involving her child at the river. Somehow she managed to do this without excluding Cassie from the conversation.

'How extraordinary! She sounds a quite remarkable girl!' The colonel appeared to show great interest but Cassie gained the impression his thoughts were probably on other things. She also doubted whether he fooled Lady Fraser.

'Are you visiting someone here?' Lady Fraser put the question to Cassie.

'Yes, Mr Fox. He was wounded outside Salamanca . . . I treated his wound then. I wanted to see how he is now.'

'Ah yes, I remember him. He's on the staff of General Clinton. He's Cornish too, I believe? Tell him I'll call on him when next I'm here. Perhaps you'll be good enough to ask this Spanish girl to call on me. I hope she may be interested in something I have in mind. Tell her she'll find me at the governor's house.'

Lady Fraser went on her way, the small colonel hurrying in order to keep up with her. Cassie thought it looked almost as though she had him on a lead and she entered the hospital smiling at the thought.

Cassie was taken to the villa's large walled garden by a Spanish servant and here she found Gorran. Seated alone on a garden seat, he was reading a book. He looked thinner than she remembered, almost frail, and he had lost much of the tan he had acquired during the summer campaign. Cassie felt a twinge of concern for him.

His smile when he looked up and saw Cassie standing before him dispelled all the doubts she had entertained about visiting him. Rising to his feet, he kissed her on the cheek and hugged her to him, but his sudden wince of pain dispelled all her momentary embarrassment.

'Is your arm still troubling you? It should be almost healed by now.' The battle in which he had been wounded had occurred almost three weeks before.

'It's my own silly fault, Cassie. When I was taken back to the surgeon he discovered the musket ball had passed through my arm and grazed one of my ribs. It wasn't serious, but I made the mistake of allowing him to probe my arm with the result that it became infected. I am lucky not to have lost the arm altogether. But enough of me. What are you doing in Salamanca? I trust there's nothing wrong with Harry?'

Cassie told Gorran of Harry's duty with the Light

Company and of the reason she was in Salamanca. She also told him of her meeting outside the villa with Lady Fraser.

'A visit from you *and* Lady Fraser! I'm indeed a fortunate man.'

Gorran saw the uncertain expression on Cassie's face and hastened to reassure her she was not being mocked.

'Lady Harriet Fraser is the most influential woman travelling with the army, Cassie. Not only is her husband a well-respected major-general, but her family hold positions of considerable power in all walks of English life, not least in the government. Many an ambitious officer would willingly give a year's pay for an introduction to her, and now she's to visit me as a result of speaking to you! This must be my lucky day. But where are my manners? You'll have something to drink, Cassie?'

Gorran led Cassie to a table in the shade of a large free-flowering bougainvillaea bush, at the same time calling to one of the many servants waiting to take care of the needs of the convalescing officers.

As they drank a sweet refreshing wine, Cassie asked him how long he thought it might be before he returned to the regiment.

All of a sudden, Gorran looked unhappy. 'I'm afraid I'll be away for quite some time, Cassie. You see . . . I've received a letter from home. My mother is rather ill and there are certain family matters that need attention due to the recent death of my grandfather. I've been granted leave to return to England for a while.'

Cassie felt absurdly dismayed to learn that Gorran was likely to be absent from the Peninsula for a long time, possibly for ever. His presence had always given her a great deal of confidence. Even during recent months while he had been absent from 3 Company, she had always somehow felt he was not far away, close enough for her to seek his advice in any emergency.

'When will you be going?'

'I leave for Lisbon in three days' time. I hope to be able to take passage, possibly in a warship, soon after my arrival there.'

Cassie felt suddenly terribly vulnerable and alone.

'I won't be gone from the regiment for ever, Cassie.' It was almost as though he was able to read her mind. The thought made Cassie feel uncomfortable.

'The men will miss you. Harry says ... they all say, you're the best officer in the Thirty-second. They believe you care what happens to them.'

'I do care, and I'm very flattered by their concern, but I'm convinced young Richard Kennelly will soon be promoted and he cares for them too. I'll miss the men, of course, but let's not get too depressed. I'll be back as soon as I'm able to return.'

Reaching across the table, Gorran gripped her hand tightly, then released it again almost immediately. 'I'll miss you, too, Cassie. When we were on the coach travelling to Horsham I doubted your ability to adapt to the hardships of a campaign. My doubts were misplaced. You're very much part of the regiment now. As much a part of it as Rose Tonks, or any other woman. Your Harry is a very fortunate soldier.'

*　　*　　*

Cassie met Gorran twice more before he left Salamanca. On the first occasion she and Josefa accompanied Richard to the villa where he was convalescing. Their last meeting was at the governor's house where Cassie had accompanied Josefa, although it had never been her intention to go any further than the gate.

They were approaching the villa when an open carriage pulled up beside them. Seated inside were Lady Fraser – and Gorran.

'Hello! How wonderful to see you both once more. Are you on your way to pay me a visit?' Lady Fraser beamed at each of them in turn.

'Josefa is. I'm just walking with her as far as the gate.' Cassie tried hard not to look at Gorran as she spoke to Lady Fraser.

'Nonsense! You'll both come in. I'm just bringing Mr Fox from the hospital for some tea. I'm quite certain he would rather talk to a young girl like yourself than to me. Besides, I wish to have a talk with Josefa. If you're on hand to talk to Mr Fox I won't need to feel quite so guilty.'

Tea was taken in the garden and Cassie said very little, but no one seemed to notice. Lady Fraser chattered on quite happily. Josefa too seemed not at all overawed by the grandeur and title of their hostess.

After almost an hour, Lady Fraser said to Cassie and Gorran, 'Will you both excuse Josefa and me? It's time Emma, my daughter, was awakened from her afternoon sleep. I would very much like Josefa to be there when she wakes and to renew their acquaintanceship. If you need anything please ring for the maid.'

When Josefa and Lady Fraser had gone inside the house, happily chatting to each other, Gorran smiled at Cassie. 'This is a most unexpected and delightful pleasure. I feared we might not meet again before I left for England.'

'Why is Lady Fraser taking such an interest in Josefa?' Cassie felt she did not want to discuss Gorran's return to England.

'Lady Fraser is fascinated by her story, the type of girl she is and her background. She would dearly like Josefa to become nursemaid to little Emma. I thought you knew?'

'Josefa would never work for anyone if it meant leaving Richard.'

'Ah! That's where Lady Fraser's influence comes to the fore.' Gorran leaned forward in his chair. 'We discussed this when she came to see me yesterday evening, and also in the carriage on the way here. As you know, Richard is the younger son of a somewhat impoverished earl. So, too, is Lord Wellington. What's more, Richard has already come to Lord Wellington's attention as a result of his courage and skill when under attack. Both are qualities our commander-in-chief admires above all others. Lady Fraser is confident she can arrange for Richard to be appointed to Lord Wellington's staff. He and Josefa will still be able to see each other, although it perhaps won't be quite the close relationship they have now. Lady Fraser is a remarkably broad-minded woman. She says if Josefa cares for Emma to her satisfaction she'll do nothing to discourage their liaison. On the contrary, she finds the situation highly romantic. The impoverished earl's son and the Spanish gipsy girl . . .'

'It's more than a liaison for Josefa – and for Richard, too, I believe. They're very much in love with each other.'

'I don't doubt it, Cassie, but the two have met in somewhat exceptional circumstances. Richard is a young officer on active service, his life constantly in danger. Josefa is an exciting young gipsy girl and attractive enough to turn the head of any man. There you have all the ingredients for a campaign romance. One to provide them both with life-long memories.'

'I think you're underestimating Josefa's feelings. Richard's too.'

'Possibly. If so, Josefa should be eager to accept Lady Fraser's offer. Richard Kennelly will never be offered a more certain path to promotion. I wish someone would offer me such an opportunity.'

'Perhaps you should find someone like Josefa, someone who'll make a good nursemaid for Lady Fraser's daughter, yet be available when you have the time for her.' Cassie was angry with Gorran without knowing why she should be.

'It's an interesting idea.' Gorran grinned at her. 'But let's talk about you, Cassie. Is there anything I can do for you while I'm in England? A message I might deliver? A letter?'

'No!' It came out suddenly, before Cassie had time to think. She had contemplated writing to her parents, to tell them where she was and what she was doing. She would write to them, but the time was not yet right.

'Are you quite certain? I'll have plenty of time on my hands while I'm at home.'

An unexpected wave of homesickness swept over Cassie as she thought of Gorran at home, amid the green fields of Cornwall.

'Thank you, but I'll write when I have more time to think of what I want to say.'

Their conversation was interrupted by the return of Lady Fraser and Josefa, the latter holding the hand of Emma.

Lady Fraser seemed very pleased with herself. Beaming at Gorran, she said, 'Didn't I tell you Josefa would make an excellent nursemaid for Emma? They get on splendidly with each other. I've spoken to her about my ideas and the advantages they would bring to both herself and her young ensign. Sensible girl that she is, she has promised to discuss what I've said with him. Don't you think she would make an absolutely wonderful nursemaid, Cassie?'

'I think anyone would enjoy looking after a little girl like Emma.' Cassie held out her arms and Emma came to her with a happy smile. 'I know I would.'

26

❦

Two days after being asked to become Emma Fraser's nursemaid, Josefa was taking an evening walk with Cassie in the town square. Jean Martin was making astonishing progress but Polly would not risk exposing her to the cooler night air just yet and she remained with her daughter in the house. Richard Kennelly had intended joining them on their walk, but at the last minute he was called to the office of the quartermaster general. There was a need to agree the final arrangements for returning the recovered soldiers of the 32nd to their regiment and the ensign's advice was being sought.

It appeared that an evening walk was mandatory for the residents of the city. Young girls were particularly in evidence and Josefa explained they would have taken an evening walk no matter whether the city was occupied by French, British or Moor. It was their way of bringing themselves to the attention of the eligible young men of Salamanca.

In the centre of the square a troupe of dancers and musicians was expending a great deal more energy than the leisurely evening walkers and Cassie and Josefa were drawn to this area by the sheer raw vitality of the exciting music.

The two young women watched happily for some minutes, both clapping in time to the clatter of castanets, when suddenly a tall black-haired woman danced her way to the centre of the ring of onlookers. The woman wore a tight-fitting red dress that burgeoned out below the knee in a series of frilled hoops.

The entry of the woman brought a shout of approval from the crowd, but Josefa caught her breath in a gasp of disbelief as she clutched Cassie's arm in a painful grip.

'That's my mother!'

'Are you sure?' It was a stupid reply, but the light provided by the flickering torches cast uncertain and distorting shadows across the faces of both dancers and their audience.

'I know it is, look . . .' Josefa pointed to where the woman in the red dress was dancing. Her feet were tapping out a staccato rhythm on the flagstones of the square while her body moved slowly, with the sinuous fluidity of a snake. 'No one else dances like that.'

The woman's dancing possessed a quality that held her audience spellbound, involving those who watched in a whole variety of emotions, one moment flirting, the next scorning them, a single movement of her body enough to convince a man she was dancing only for him while another took him to the brink of despair. Cassie had never before witnessed such sheer artistry in a dance.

When the music came to an end it was as though the audience had been released from a dream. It erupted in a storm of applause that startled the night-roosting pigeons on the cathedral ledges, sending them scattering in sudden alarm.

There were cries of '*Olé!*' and concerted shouts for a repeat of the performance but Estefanía did not even acknowledge their calls. She stood with bowed head, perspiration glistening on her face and neck. After remaining motionless for a full minute she turned and walked away without so much as a sidelong glance at the men and women who applauded her.

'Quick!'

Josefa took Cassie's hand and broke through the line of spectators at the front of the crowd. Pushing past protesting dancers, forming up for another performance, they caught up with Estefanía as she was about to enter an alleyway leading off the square.

'Mama!'

Josefa's cry brought Estefanía to an abrupt halt. She turned around to face her daughter, but there was no affection or even enthusiasm in her greeting.

'Oh, it's you again. Have you returned to gloat over my change of circumstances? Or have you learned that life with the British is no more certain than life with the French?'

'I suppose that means you've been deserted by your gallant colonel?'

315

'Deserted? I was lucky not to be arrested and shot after your escapade.' Estefanía glared accusingly at her daughter. 'When the description of the British spy was circulated he knew instantly it was you. Why did you do such a thing to me? If you want to spy for the British that's all right, but to have me introduce you to a colonel in the French army! It put me in an impossible situation.'

'I had no idea when I arrived in Salamanca that you were being kept by a French officer. I wanted only to warn you that the British army was coming. I didn't want you to suffer the fate of the women of Badajos, or Rodrigo.'

Estefanía continued as though she had not heard her daughter, 'Even so, all might still have been well had you not stolen his horse. That animal was the pride of his life. When Jacques Clausel sat on his horse he was noticed. Men and women looked at him. He actually felt like a colonel. When you stole his horse you took away his pride. His importance. He blamed me for everything – not that there's anything French in that. A Spaniard would have done the same.'

'I'm sorry, Mama, truly I am. I didn't know the horse belonged to your colonel. I was being chased by a British army deserter who knew I was with the British army. Had he and his friends caught me I would have been shot. I had to escape somehow.'

Suddenly and unexpectedly, Estefanía laughed. 'Who would believe I should be cast aside because of a horse? Another woman, yes, or some dark secret, but a *horse*! Ah, Josefa, that such a thing should happen to me! But what of yourself? Why do you travel with the army of the British? A spy for *them*? It cannot be patriotism, so it must be for the love of a man. Tell me about him.'

The conversation between mother and daughter had been in rapid Spanish and Cassie had not understood a word. Now Josefa introduced her to Estefanía, at the same time explaining their conversation, adding that they should now speak in English. Estefanía, too, had learned the language from students of the Irish College.

'What will you do now? Do you want to go home with your mother? If you do I'll tell Richard where you are.'

'That will not be necessary.' The firm reply came from Estefanía. 'I wish to meet this Irishman of yours, Josefa, but we'll meet at one of the cafés around the square. If you think of me at all I would rather you remembered me as living in the house over there, on the far side of the square. Not where I am now.'

'What you really mean is that you've found yourself another man. One not as grand as your French colonel, but one who, like Colonel Clausel, does not know about me?'

Josefa had lapsed into Spanish once more and, after a quick glance at Cassie, Estefanía nodded. 'He's a good man, Josefa. A strong man. I think this time it will last.'

'You've been saying that since I was old enough to understand what was going on about me. I always hoped one day it would be so. I still do, but I would like you to meet Richard before we leave Salamanca. Shall we make it tomorrow?'

*   *   *

317

Ensign Richard Kennelly left Salamanca without meeting Estefanía. He and Josefa waited at the café table for two hours before accepting she was not going to appear. In a bid to hide her disappointment from Richard, Josefa shrugged off the broken appointment. Her mother had rarely kept a promise to her in the past. It would have been too much to hope she had changed her ways.

Richard understood Josefa better than she knew. He was especially kind to her that night and pretended to be asleep when her tears came.

The 32nd Regiment ensign set off from Salamanca with two hundred infantrymen who had been declared fit to return to active service. A commissary convoy on its way to the front also took advantage of his protection. It was a considerable responsibility for the young ensign and his task was made no easier by the weather encountered along the way.

Rain began to fall on the night the large convoy set off. By the time Salamanca was two hours behind the last unwieldy, solid-wheeled, axle-screeching wagon, the road had become a quagmire of knee-deep, glutinous mud. Moving at no more than half their usual speed, the wagons frequently needed to be man-handled free of the mud. Broken wheels and axles were a constant source of irritation.

The soldiers grumbled incessantly, and with good cause. Never dry, day or night, hot food and drink and a snug billet became faintly remembered luxuries. After eight days of laboured progress, the rains ceased for a while. Richard immediately called a twenty-four-hour halt at a small roadside village, to give men and animals an opportunity to dry off.

The women and little Jean were as wet as the soldiers and Richard billeted them in a good-sized barn on the edge of the village. Soon the wet uniforms of the men were draped over bushes while the women strung up lines inside the barn to dry clothing and blankets.

They were many miles from the battle-front, but Richard Kennelly sent out pickets to guard the approaches to the village. The men detailed for this duty complained bitterly at having to perform such an unnecessary task when the enemy was many miles away.

The belief that they were performing a needless duty was to blame for them being taken completely by surprise by a small squadron of French hussars at dusk that evening. The British infantrymen failed to loose a single shot to give warning to their comrades in the village and were overrun and cut down in less than a minute. Then the cavalrymen galloped on to where other unsuspecting infantrymen were enjoying a well-deserved rest.

Had the Frenchmen struck from the other end of the village they could have inflicted heavy casualties among the unsuspecting soldiery. Instead, the first building they encountered was the barn occupied by the women. Because they were drying their clothes the women had barred the doors against unexpected visitors and the Frenchmen needed to uproot a fencing post and use it as a battering-ram in order to smash down the door.

The defences put up by the women had never been intended to keep out a determined attacker but it gave them time to put on still damp clothes, while the quick-thinking Josefa seized the opportunity to make her escape.

Josefa was in the barn's loft making up a bed for herself and Richard when the French cavalry struck. Out of sight in the shadows, she stayed only long enough to see the blue and white uniforms of the men who burst down the door.

Looking through a small opening from which the Spanish farmer threw down his hay, Josefa could see there were no cavalrymen at the rear of the building. Jumping to the soft ground she ran as fast as she could to warn Richard and the others of the French attack. Her cries brought soldiers tumbling from their billets in the village. Few wore full uniform, but every man carried his musket.

By the time the French cavalrymen left the barn to direct their attentions towards targets of a more military nature they had lost the essential element of surprise. Ensign Kennelly had wasted no time in acting upon Josefa's information. The leading French horsemen were met with a volley of musket fire that caused them to wheel about and leave the village in the direction from whence they had come. With them they took Cassie, Polly and Jean.

Richard organised a party to set off in pursuit of the French cavalrymen and their prisoners, but an hour after dark it began to rain heavily once more. Any faint hope of locating the raiding party swiftly vanished in the mud.

Riding their own donkeys, Cassie and Polly were led away by the French soldiers. Once away from the village they left the road. Circling the town in a wide arc they struck out across country, heading for the mountainous region to the north.

The Frenchmen knew the country well for this was a far-ranging squadron of veteran hussars. Living off the land through which they passed, their only orders were to harass Lord Wellington's supply lines and communications, wreaking all the mischief they could. Finding them was beyond the capabilities of infantrymen.

The Frenchmen did not ride furiously through the night but nevertheless they wasted no time. When one of the small donkeys ridden by the two Englishwomen showed signs of flagging, a French hussar dropped back and beat it with the flat of his sword until the animal increased its gait to the cavalryman's satisfaction.

So far the men had spoken only in French but when Cassie protested at the beating of her donkey, a corporal who appeared to be in charge of the party growled in English, 'If you don't want it to be beaten you must make it keep up with us. Otherwise I will cut its throat and you will have to walk.'

At that moment Jean let out a howl of protest. She was tired and protested that she wanted to be put to bed. The corporal was unsympathetic. 'The same goes for the child. Keep her quiet or her throat will be cut too.'

Neither Polly nor Cassie believed the Frenchman was serious but when next Jean began to protest her mother clamped a hand over her mouth and urged her to silence.

27

❧

The ride assumed nightmare proportions when the party reached the mountains with the storm increasing in ferocity about them. For a while the rain became hail that stung the faces of the women. It brought a wail of pain from Jean that her mother could not have prevented, no matter how hard she tried. However, the child's shrill voice was lost in the booming of thunder and the white-bright lightning that sizzled to earth all about them.

The French cavalrymen seemed to know the area well and continued to ride through the storm until suddenly a high wall loomed ahead of them, effectively cutting off much of the driving rain. As the tired horses came to a halt with heads drooping and water running from them, the cavalrymen dismounted and led the horses through a narrow archway set in the wall. When only a few horses remained outside, the English-speaking cavalryman nodded to Cassie and Polly. 'Now you.'

Both women were far too wet and miserable to argue and neither had the remotest idea of where they were. For the moment escape was out of the question.

The building was a one-time monastery. Its tenants had been evicted when Napoleon overran the country, four years before, and the buildings partly demolished. However, enough remained for the horses to be stabled in cells previously occupied by the men of God, while soldiers took over the spacious refectory, once used to feed travelling pilgrims.

Polly and Cassie were ordered to take Jean to the huge room. Here the French proved they had brought more than the two women with them as prizes. They produced stores taken from the commissary wagons and two piglets foraged from the cottage of an unfortunate Spanish peasant.

There were fresh vegetables to go with the meal, gathered from nearer at hand. The soldiers built a roaring fire in the huge grate and the two British women were ordered to produce a meal for the fifty or so French cavalrymen.

By now it was about three o'clock in the morning, but when Cassie protested that she and Polly were tired, the English-speaking corporal became angry. 'You will cook for the men. If not . . .' the Frenchman shrugged in an exaggerated manner, 'we will have to find another way for you to please us.'

There was no need for the corporal to explain his words. The French cavalrymen had stripped off their wet grey capes. Some had gone further, making remarks in French to the women accompanied by crude and unmistakable gestures that needed no translation.

Cassie looked in vain for an officer accompanying the cavalrymen. There was none. The corporal, or *brigadier*, appeared to be the senior-ranking soldier in the company.

'If you wish take off your own clothes and dry them, I do not think the men will mind.'

'They'll dry just as well on as they will anywhere else,' Cassie said firmly. Unlike the troopers, she and Polly had worn no protective clothing against the storm. Both dripped water wherever they walked, but she had no intention of removing any of her clothing in a room filled with French soldiers, even though steam rose from her dress because of her proximity to the roaring fire.

'Why have you taken us prisoner?' Polly asked as she and Cassie toiled over a huge cauldron, carried into the room and hung over the fire by two French soldiers.

'You were all we were able to find,' replied the soldier, ungraciously. 'Given time we would have preferred to have set fire to some of the wagons and killed a few Englishmen. As it is . . .' he shrugged, 'no doubt your loss will cause some alarm. After all, we are many miles behind the area of battle.'

'No doubt the capture of two women and a child is easier than doing battle with British soldiers able to fight back,' Cassie retorted.

The French corporal puffed up with anger. 'You are in no position to say such things to me. Men of the Twenty-fifth Cavalry Regiment are afraid of nothing. We kill British soldiers wherever we find them, their women too, if there is a need. Remember this!'

'Did he say they were soldiers of the Twenty-fifth Regiment?' Polly whispered as she turned the piglets on a spit at the side of the fire, her clothing already dry from the waist up.

'Why? It's going to make little difference to us, whatever regiment they're from.'

'It was officers of the Twenty-fifth who were so kind to me when I was captured. One of them brought me back when you were ill, remember?'

Cassie's mind began working quickly. 'Tell me all you remember about your time with them,' she whispered urgently. 'Names – everything.'

'All right, but don't anger the corporal, Cassie. French officers are proud of their reputation for gallantry – but there are no officers here and the ordinary French soldier is no better than ours. We're lucky they have no wine.'

Cassie was about to ask how Polly could possibly know so much about enemy soldiers, when Jean stirred in her sleep and Cassie moved her away from the roaring fire.

Dawn was already showing through the narrow windows by the time the meal was ready for the Frenchmen. Some of the soldiers had fallen asleep, but they awoke to receive their share of the food.

When they had been served, the French corporal told Cassie and Polly they could help themselves to what was left. Polly woke her daughter and although Jean complained at being awakened, she wolfed down everything placed in front of her.

The food was good, better than that enjoyed by British soldiers. The reason was the different catering systems used by the two armies. The British were supplied through their commissaries, the rations supplemented by whatever they could afford to purchase from the local populace. With 60,000 troops competing for a limited amount of spare produce, the price quickly soared far higher than the average soldier could afford.

The French system was entirely different. When they were on a campaign their soldiers foraged far and wide, taking whatever was needed. This system gave the French army far greater mobility, at least during the summer months. In winter the British army had the advantage of an assured source of supply.

The French cavalrymen remained at the monastery all the next day. The two women and Jean were kept locked in a monk's cell until evening, with stabled horses in the cells about them. Then they were brought out to prepare another meal for their captors.

Tonight the meat was goat, to which was added half a dozen ducks. The Frenchmen had also brought in far more vegetables than could possibly be used for one meal. It had been another successful day's foraging for them. A large quantity of wine had also been acquired and Cassie and Polly became increasingly nervous as the evening wore on.

When it was time for the women to partake of their food the Frenchmen noisily vied with each other in trying to persuade Cassie or Polly to sit down with them. When the two women refused the cavalrymen became angry. Neither of them understood French, but they realised the soldiers looked upon their aloofness as highly insulting.

One of the cavalrymen, his courage boosted by wine, lurched across the room to where the women and Jean huddled in a small group by the fireside. He stood swaying above them for a minute or two, saying nothing. When he did speak, his words were so slurred they were as unintelligible to his comrades as they were to the women.

Receiving no reply, he became angry. Reaching down he leaned heavily on Polly's shoulder and looked into her upturned face. Breathing wine fumes he uttered the first word either woman had understood.

'Come!'

Polly shook her head and the French soldier's English vocabulary immediately doubled. 'You come.'

This time he reached out and tangled his fingers in her long fair hair. In an effort to maintain his balance he pulled on it painfully. As Polly winced, her daughter, frightened by the drunken man looming over them, began to cry. Without releasing his hold on Polly's hair the Frenchman bellowed for Jean to be silent. The sound of his voice raised in anger only made her cry louder. Encouraged by some of his companions the drunken soldier raised his hand to strike the crying child.

It was doubtful whether the drunken cavalryman would have succeeded in hitting Jean without toppling over, but Cassie chose a far more positive deterrent. The monks who had occupied the building for centuries had made a special tool to push embers back inside the great fireplace. A long iron poker, it had a flat piece welded to the end, the whole resembling a long, toothless rake – or a branding iron. The poker had been left half in the ashes and the end glowed a fiery red.

Snatching it up, Cassie thrust the red-hot end so close to the Frenchman's face it scorched his bushy moustache and he suddenly lost interest in everything except the need to escape the heat of the poker. Staggering backwards as though someone had pushed him, the amorous cavalryman tripped over the deliberately positioned foot of one of his companions and he fell backwards.

The cavalrymen's reactions to his fate were as varied as they had been to his crude romantic advances. Most hooted with mirth, others were angry at the action of the British soldiers' woman.

The English-speaking corporal was among the latter and he ordered Cassie to put down the still-glowing iron. For what seemed long minutes Cassie defied him, until she said, 'I'll put it down as soon as you agree to take us straight to Major Rousselot.'

In the hushed room, where all waited to witness the outcome of the confrontation between Cassie and their corporal, the name of the regiment's second-in-command was recognised and there was an immediate surge of interest.

'You know Major Rousselot? How do you know him?'

'That's none of your business, but I know Colonel Montigny too.'

Cassie casually threw in the name of the commanding officer of the 25th Regiment of hussars, for good measure, in a bid to get Polly and herself out of an ugly situation. When Polly had been captured by the French the previous year Colonel Montigny and Major Rousselot had only one company of hussars with them. The remainder had been in the hills, hunting down Spanish guerrillas. Cassie sincerely hoped all the men in the room had been with the absent companies.

'Come, tell me. How do you, an English woman, know the Colonel and Major Rousselot?'

'I suggest you put your questions to them, when we meet up with them. Now, if you don't mind, my friend would like to put her daughter to bed. She's still tired after last night's ride and the noise of your men is upsetting her.'

Barracked on all sides by cavalrymen demanding to know what the English woman was saying about their officers, the corporal was undecided what to do. A little fun with the two English women would keep his men happy. On the other hand, if this one did know the two most senior officers in the regiment things would go badly with him if they were molested.

This was a decision that should be taken by an officer, not a low-ranking corporal. Unfortunately, both the captain and lieutenant who had set out with the company had been wounded in an early encounter with some British riflemen. Rather than abort the whole mission, the wounded French officers had sent the company on, under the command of the experienced corporal. Under battle conditions the corporal was capable of making quick and intelligent decisions – but these circumstances were very different.

'Do we have the same quarters as before?' Cassie was aware of the corporal's indecision. She also realised he held the fate of herself, Polly and Jean in his hands.

'Yes, the same place. I will take you there.'

As the corporal led the two women from the room they were followed by howls of disappointment and a torrent of abuse.

Outside the room, in the darkness of the corridor, Polly found Cassie's hand and squeezed it gratefully. Cassie's quick-thinking resourcefulness had rescued them both from a night of terror.

In spite of her own relief, Cassie realised it would be an all-too-brief respite. There would be other nights, and increasing pressure would be put upon the corporal by his companions . . .

28

❧

The precariousness of their situation was brought home to Cassie and Polly with horrifying clarity the very next day.

Awakened before dawn, they were told to prepare to move off immediately. Before fifteen minutes had elapsed they were ordered to lead their donkeys out to the courtyard. After an unsuccessful plea from Cassie that they be set free and allowed to return to their husbands, the two women were made to mount their donkeys and ride off with the French soldiers.

The English-speaking corporal's manner towards them stopped only just short of rudeness. Cassie believed his fellow soldiers had convinced him there was no substance in her claim to know the regiment's two most senior officers. She and Polly would certainly know that night whether her suspicions were correct but Cassie said nothing of her thoughts to her companion.

331

The weather had improved so much that it was difficult to believe they were now travelling under the same sky as when they were captured. From peak to peak in the mountainous country not a cloud was to be seen. Had circumstances been different, Cassie thought it would have been difficult to choose more idyllic surroundings.

They rode until early afternoon when two cavalrymen who had been well ahead of the main troop returned and sought out the corporal. For many minutes there was a lengthy discussion between them, in which a number of the cavalrymen joined. The dissertation ended with a nod from the corporal and Cassie suddenly sensed a new excitement in the ranks of the French cavalry troop.

Urging their horses on and driving the two donkeys with them, they rode for about a mile to where there was a slight dip in the ridge forming a barrier across their path. In the dip was a shallow and fertile valley. Grape vines spread along the slope immediately below the mounted Frenchmen and beyond this was a sprinkling of cottages. The whole was surrounded by fields of ripening corn, orchards of citrus trees and small dark green squares where vegetables grew.

Outside one of the cottages Cassie counted ten peasant carts in a line. With them was a British assistant commissary and six red-coated infantrymen. All were seated on the ground, their hats removed as they enjoyed wine and food with the peasants.

The French hussars had stumbled upon a commissary with a small escort party, buying food for the British

332

army. Well to the rear of the warring armies they would not expect to encounter any French troops here. The escort was with the carts to deter would-be thieves, not to defend them against attack.

Cassie's first thought was to call out and warn the unsuspecting soldiers. Her expression must have reflected her thinking because suddenly Polly leaned across and gripped her arm. 'Don't, Cassie. Don't do anything foolish or they'll kill us all.'

'That could be Harry down there – or Enoch.'

'Cassie, be sensible . . .'

'Quiet!' The French corporal rounded on the women furiously and two troopers closed in to drive the donkeys of the women well back from the edge of the slope.

While this was happening the corporal was dividing his troop. Half were sent off to attack the unsuspecting commissary party from the far end of the shallow valley. Meanwhile the corporal and the remaining hussars prepared to charge down the slope at them from this end.

The two women and Jean were kept back until the corporal drew his sabre and ordered his half-troop into action. As the cavalrymen disappeared over the rim of the downward slope, the two soldiers detailed to guard the English women urged them forward none too gently. They were not pleased to be missing the action and were determined they would at least see something of what was going on below them.

As the commissary party came into Cassie's view once more the British infantrymen had just spotted the French cavalrymen bearing down upon them at full gallop.

Their reactions were instinctive rather than ordered. Two of the soldiers snatched up their muskets and dropped to one knee, facing the enemy as they primed the ready-loaded weapons.

One actually managed to bring his gun up to his shoulder before being overrun by the hard-riding French soldiers. His companion was cut down as he stooped over his musket, his shaking hands scattering gunpowder everywhere but into the pan of the weapon.

The remaining four soldiers had begun to run at first sight of the enemy horsemen, two not stopping to snatch up their muskets. Both succeeded only in meeting the other half-troop of French hussars galloping in from the far end of the valley and they were promptly chopped down by a group of milling cavalrymen who hacked at them as though they were dangerous reptiles about to strike.

The unarmed men's remaining companions were cut down as they ran by the corporal's men and left to spill their red life-blood on the fertile earth of the valley.

Only the young assistant commissary put up any determined resistance, but it lasted only as long as it took him to snap off two quick pistol shots. Both were effective. The first took a French soldier in the face, blinding him. The second shattered the elbow of a hussar when he was in the act of bringing his sabre down upon the young assistant commissary's head. Finally, in a last futile gesture of defiance, the now-defenceless commissary hurled both empty pistols at his attackers before he, too, was cut down.

The one-sided action had been far too brief to satisfy

the aroused bloodlust of the cavalrymen. One of the wagoners was seen running away from the carts and, with a shout of exhilaration, one of the French soldiers set off in pursuit. Meanwhile, the other soldiers found the remaining wagoners and killed them too.

When the last wagoner had been hunted down it was the turn of the peasants. They were pursued like rabbits and, like rabbits, some of them ran squealing in their fright until they were cut down among the vines, amid the corn, or sent tumbling among the neat rows of vegetables. Some cavalrymen even drove their horses inside the small houses in pursuit of their quarry. When not a man was left alive it was the turn of the women – but only the very old and the very young were put to the sword immediately.

Polly had turned Jean's head to her so she should not see the slaughter going on about them. Now she tried to muffle her ears against the screams of the young women. Some were raped within the four walls of their own houses, with only their attackers bearing witness to the violation of their bodies. Others were knocked down by the horses of their pursuers and raped where they lay. Some, if they were particularly attractive, were violated by a succession of French soldiers.

As Polly sat on her donkey, hunched over her child, hot tears burned Cassie's eyes but did nothing to extinguish the hatred that had welled up inside her for their captors. It made things no easier to realise that what was happening to the Spanish peasant women might so easily have happened to her and Polly – and still could.

Not all the French hussars joined in the orgy of rape

335

and killing. About a dozen came to where Cassie and Polly sat with the child. Two of the soldiers murmured what might have been apologies to the two women. Others averted their eyes, at the same time trying to position their horses to shield the women from the ugly scenes going on around the houses of the peasants.

When the corporal rode up to the group, an animated discussion ensued between the non-commissioned officer and the women's self-appointed bodyguard. It ended when the corporal shrugged and kneed his horse alongside Cassie. 'You will tend our wounded then go on with my soldiers. I will follow with the others later.'

'When you've put all the surviving women to death, no doubt.'

Cassie knew it would have been more sensible to remain quiet but she could not. This man might have prevented all that had occurred here had he chosen to exert his leadership.

'Be grateful it is not happening to you.'

'Why don't you let us go? We are of no value to you and will only slow you down.'

'You are too modest, Madame. My men are convinced you would provide them with far more pleasure than some docile peasant girl. Go and tend the wounded men before they find wine and crave more excitement.'

There was nothing Cassie could do for the cavalryman who had been blinded by the assistant commissary's desperate shot. The pistol ball that had taken his sight seemed also to have robbed him of his sanity. He burbled like a child, sometimes laughing, sometimes crying. Cassie put a pad over his wound to soak up the blood and circled a bandage around his head, hiding the sightless eyes from view, before turning to his companion.

The second wounded man was in great pain from his shattered elbow. He needed the attentions of a surgeon but none would be available to him until the roving cavalrymen returned to the main French army. By that time the arm, and probably the man's life, would be in jeopardy. When there was nothing more Cassie could do, she and Polly set off with half the cavalry troop.

It was almost two hours before the corporal and the remainder of the troop caught up with their companions. They had located a store of wine. Now, drinking as they rode along, they became ever more boastful of the feats of masculine prowess they had performed that day.

The French cavalrymen rode to a narrow, steep-sided valley, high in the mountains. There had once been a stone-cutters' camp here. The sagging remains of their huts gave scant shelter now, but the rotting timbers provided good, fast-burning fuel for the cooking fires of the French soldiers.

There was ample meat to eat tonight. A number of oxen had been driven up from the village with the horsemen. One was slaughtered now and preparations made to grill the meat.

Darkness fell while the meal was being cooked and the French corporal sent out pickets to guard each end of the narrow valley. The men detailed for this duty grumbled that it was unnecessary to post pickets in such a remote spot. When the corporal insisted, the men went off to perform their duties still grumbling, and Cassie observed they carried off a large quantity of wine with them. The cavalrymen might be obeying the instructions of their corporal, but they intended interpreting them in their own way.

Due to the absence of cooking pots there was no central cooking fire. Small groups of men each had their own fire, over which they grilled a generous ration of beef. Some also had bread, pilfered from the houses of peasants they had murdered. Others made do with biscuits. All had large quantities of wine.

As darkness fell upon the camp there were frequent outbursts of drunken singing. Once a red-faced Frenchman made his way to the fire Cassie shared with Polly and her daughter. Standing over them and swaying alarmingly close to the fire, he spoke at some length in French. His effort was wasted upon the two women. They did not understand French and neither wished to have an interpretation of his words. They felt it wiser to keep their heads averted and not look at their uninvited camp-fire guest.

The Frenchman's attempts to socialise with the women meeting with no success, the cavalryman aimed a petulant kick at the fire, raising an ascending shower of sparks, before treading an erratic path back to his companions.

The cheers and jeers that greeted the return of the would-be suitor provided Cassie and Polly with ample proof that the others had followed his advances with great interest.

This was confirmed when the corporal strolled across to their fire a short time afterwards. Squatting beside

Cassie and gazing into the flames as he sucked on a pipe of tobacco, he said, 'You were not impressed by Barbet? You have struck a serious blow to his pride. He is fond of boasting that he has great success with women.'

'I saw the successes you and your soldiers had with women at the Spanish village. What is it your Trooper Barbet enjoys doing most, raping his women, or using a sabre to cut them to death afterwards?'

The corporal shrugged. 'We are fighting a war. I doubt if what happened today was any worse than the things your soldiers did in Rodrigo or Badajos. But perhaps such behaviour is acceptable when they are British soldiers and not Frenchmen who attack Spanish women?'

'It's unacceptable whichever side commits such deeds. Lord Wellington ordered the execution of his soldiers for what they did. You're in charge here, yet you did nothing. For all I know you might have done the same as your men.'

'I am one man, and only a *brigadier*. Had I tried to stop them they would have killed me too.'

Beside one of the fires a French soldier shouted something and it was immediately taken up by others. The cavalry corporal rose to his feet slowly, almost wearily. 'You hear them? They are saying you must join them in celebration of today's victory.'

'Victory? Killing unarmed peasants and their women? Is this how Napoleon measures his victories?'

The hussar corporal looked down at Cassie angrily. 'The army of the Republic of France does not go to war against women, but they sometimes need to be reminded of their place, especially when they have been taken in war. My comrades are becoming angry because you refuse their offers of wine. You would be foolish to anger them too much, Madame.'

'I have no wish to drink wine with any man, French or English, who maltreats women as your men did today. Besides, I am sure Major Rousselot will reward you for taking care of us.'

'Ah yes, Major Rousselot, your friend. Some of the men are resentful that you should be so friendly with an officer, yet refuse to share wine with them. They are constantly reminding me that it is against the spirit of the glorious Revolution. I would also like to remind you that Major Rousselot does not know you are our prisoners. He will not know until we return to the army. It may be many months away – or it may be never.'

The corporal knocked out his pipe against the heel of his high, well-worn boot before addressing Cassie again. 'Think of what I have said, Madame. Think carefully.' Suddenly he smiled at her. 'However, should you seek my protection I think my comrades will be understanding.'

'And what will happen to Polly?'

The corporal glanced briefly at Polly and shrugged. 'I can try to find a protector. Trooper Barbet, perhaps. We will speak of this again later.'

As the corporal walked away, Polly shuddered. 'I couldn't go with that man . . . or any of the others. We both saw what they did to those Spanish women today. But what can we do?'

'Our only hope is that they all get so drunk we can run away some time during the night.'

'We'd never get away, Cassie. They've got pickets at both ends of the valley. You saw them go out.'

'Yes, and I saw the amount of wine they took with them. The pickets will be as drunk as those who are left here. Anyway, I don't think we have any choice. If we stay we'll suffer the same fate as the Spanish women. I'd rather be cut down and killed.'

'But what of Jean?'

Cassie put out a hand. 'Shhh! Someone's coming. Say nothing more for now.'

Footsteps could be heard approaching the fire. When they came into the firelight Cassie saw it was the corporal and Trooper Barbet. The corporal was carrying a large gourd of wine which he placed on the ground and both men sat down.

Polly looked at Cassie, unable to hide her dismay. The French corporal saw the look.

'I brought Trooper Barbet to you because the other men were talking of sending someone here to bring you to them. I thought you might prefer to have a small party.'

Trooper Barbet did not understand a word that was said by his corporal, but he smiled warmly at Polly. Moving closer he slurped wine into a grubby mess-tin and passed it to her, talking indistinctly and smiling ingratiatingly.

Polly resembled a trapped animal as she looked desperately to Cassie for help.

'Take a sip, Polly, but not too much. Let him drink as much as he wants.'

The corporal chuckled. 'You are a cunning young

woman, Madame. Trooper Barbet will awake tomorrow morning convinced he is the greatest lover in the regiment. I regret you will not be able to trick me as easily. I drink very little.'

Cassie said nothing. Meanwhile Polly took a sip of the wine, but such cautious consumption did not please her companion. After saying something to her in French he put a hand to the mess-tin and tried to pour the contents down her throat.

Unprepared for such a direct method of persuasion, Polly choked on the first mouthful, causing most of the wine to spill from her mouth and cascade down the front of her dress.

Trooper Barbet filled and emptied the mess-tin himself before he noticed the red stain on her dress. He needed to peer at it closely before enlightenment came. Pulling out a filthy handkerchief he clumsily attempted to clean the mess he had made.

Halfway through his efforts he forgot his intentions. Distracted by the feel of Polly's body through her thin dress he began to fondle her clumsily.

By the time a trooper from one of the pickets galloped into the camp Barbet had pulled three buttons from Polly's dress and had his hand deep inside her bodice.

'*Brigadier!* We have been given a warning that Spanish irregulars are on their way to seek us out.' The trooper spoke rapidly and excitedly and the corporal rose to his feet, frowning deeply.

'A warning? Who delivered this warning?'

'A Spanish girl. She said the irregulars are at this very

342

moment in her village, no more than a half-hour ride away. There are three hundred or more, she said.'

'Why should a Spanish girl risk her life to warn us?'

'She told us she had a French lover who has promised he will one day return to her.'

'Where is she now? Bring her to me.'

'She would not stay. She said she feared for her life.'

Other soldiers had gathered around the mounted man. Some stared at him stupidly. Others were sober enough to realise the import of his news.

'Do you believe she spoke the truth?' One of the more sober soldiers put the question to the corporal.

'No. She and her people want us out of the area. If the picket had been alert they would have brought the woman here for me to learn the truth – but if she has been able to find us others will also know we are here. We must leave.'

'Shall we ride through her village, to teach her and her people a lesson?'

'We will put as many miles between us and her village as we can. We will go through the hills. You . . .' The corporal jabbed a finger at the newly arrived picket. 'Go back and tell the others to return here – and *hurry*! I have a bad feeling about this.'

As the picket galloped off into the night, the men in the camp ran around gathering up their belongings. Polly, trying to secure the front of her dress, asked, 'What's happening, Cassie? What's happening?'

'I don't know – but this could be our chance to escape.'

Polly drew in her breath sharply. 'All right . . . but where's Jean gone? Jean . . . !'

343

The little girl was nowhere to be seen, but as Polly began to run aimlessly, first in one direction and then in another, the French corporal entered the shifting circle of light thrown off by the fire.

'You are looking for the child?'

'Where is she?' Cassie asked the question.

'She is quite safe. With one of my troopers. I would not want anyone to become lost in such confusion. After all, we have unfinished business, Madame. The child will be returned to your friend when we are ready to go.'

The French cavalry troop was ready to move off in less than fifteen minutes. Only when Cassie and Polly were mounted on their donkeys and leads attached to the animals was Jean returned to her mother. Then they were forced to wait for the pickets to return from the far end of the valley.

After another ten minutes had elapsed the angry corporal despatched a trooper to hurry them along. The messenger should have returned in ten or fifteen minutes, even had he needed to ride the full distance and not met the picket along the way. When no one had returned to the camp after twenty minutes, the corporal said, 'I do not like this. Nothing feels right. We will leave and collect our other picket along the way.'

'What if the others come and find us gone?'

'They will know they have taken too long. We leave now and travel silently. Not a sound from horse or man. You understand?'

Few of the men did understand, but they had been under the corporal's command for long enough to know

344

that when he used such a tone of voice it was as well to obey him without question.

They had been travelling in silence for some time when Polly's donkey stumbled on a rock that turned beneath its hoof and Jean cried out in protest.

'Keep that child quiet!' The corporal hissed the order angrily.

'Shouldn't we have found the other picket by now?' asked the soldier nearest to the corporal. 'I can't even see their fire.'

'No, but I can smell its smoke. Someone has put it out in a hurry. Let's get out of here . . . At the gallop!'

The corporal's instinct told him his troop was riding into a trap – but he was already too late. Even as his own horse responded to a jab from blunted steel spurs, there was the flat crack of a musket shot and suddenly bundles of blazing grass and undergrowth floated down from the steep heights above the narrow valley.

In their light the mounted soldiers were clearly visible. So, too, were lines of waiting Spanish guerrillas on either side and in front of the French soldiers.

In an instant all was bedlam in the valley as almost five hundred muskets were discharged at the French hussars. In their midst Cassie slid from her donkey. Grabbing Jean she pulled her to the ground, at the same time shrieking at Polly, 'Get down and lie on the ground!'

Polly lay beside Cassie on the rock-strewn floor of the valley as horses and men fell all about them. For many minutes they were in very real danger of being trampled upon by cavalry horses. Riderless, they galloped back and forth in the narrow valley in a vain bid to escape from the Spanish guerrillas who had formed a tight, death-dealing noose about the French cavalrymen.

When the shooting finally stopped, the shouts of excited guerrillas and the groans of wounded men broke the sudden silence. As the guerrillas began the grisly task of locating and despatching the wounded, Cassie heard a familiar voice calling her name and she started up.

'Josefa! I'm here . . . with Polly and Jean.'

The Spanish girl found Cassie in the darkness and the two young women hugged each other, each overjoyed to find the other was safe. Polly soon became part of the joyful reunion too, while Jean could not make up her mind whether to laugh or to cry.

'This is all your doing! I should have known. How did you know where we were – and where did you find the guerrillas?'

'This is Spain, Cassie. My country. Finding Don Xavier and his men was easy. Every Spanish patriot knew where they were camped. Finding you and the Frenchmen was harder until we followed the flight of the vultures and came to the village attacked by the soldiers. Then our men would have followed the tracks of the Frenchmen to the ends of the earth. But you . . . ? Are you all right?'

'Yes, but I doubt if we would have survived another night had you and the guerrillas not found us. Have your people taken many prisoners?'

'They have taken no prisoners. Neither have any Frenchmen escaped, but it is over. Come, we will leave now.'

'I'd like to speak to Don Xavier first. To thank him for saving us.'

'That will not be necessary. Come.'

Torches were being lit in the valley as Don Xavier's guerrillas went about the ghoulish task of counting the extent of their victory and stripping the French cavalrymen of weapons and everything of value. One of the bodies Cassie passed had been stripped naked except for a bloody bandage about his head, covering his eyes. Turning her head away, Cassie mounted her donkey and urged the animal forward.

The three women were ready to ride away when the ebullient guerrilla leader rode up to them. His glance fixed on Josefa, he spoke to her in rapid Spanish.

Josefa's reply was curt and given without a glance in his direction. Cassie knew only a few Spanish words, all connected with bartering, yet she realised their talk had nothing to do with the battle that had just been fought and won.

Cassie began to thank Don Xavier for saving them, but she quickly realised he understood no more English than she did Spanish. Breaking off, she said lamely, '*Gracias, señor. Muchas gracias.*'

The words were totally inadequate to thank the guerrilla leader, but they seemed to please him. Smiling broadly, he spread out both his arms towards Josefa and said something in Spanish.

Cassie turned to ask Josefa what the words meant, but the Spanish girl had turned her back on the guerrilla leader. Saying only, 'Come,' to Cassie she rode away. The two Englishwomen followed after, with Jean already asleep on Polly's donkey.

*   *   *

On their way from the mountains Cassie learned of Richard Kennelly's reaction to the capture of the two women by the French cavalrymen. Although he had taken all possible precautions against a surprise attack, he blamed himself for the loss of Cassie and the two Martins. Searching until the weather and darkness rendered further pursuit impossible, he had resumed the search at first light the following morning.

Heavy rain had obliterated all tracks made by the departing horsemen and the young ensign had been forced to resume his march, the loss of the child and the two women weighing heavily upon his conscience.

When Josefa suggested enlisting Don Xavier's aid if he was in the area, Richard had at first refused to allow her to go. Not until she convinced him it was the only slim hope they had of recovering Cassie and Polly alive did he reluctantly consent to the scheme.

Josefa told the two women the details, playing down her own part in the rescue. It had been no problem to find Don Xavier's camp and the idea of destroying a French cavalry troop appealed to him. The massacre of the peasant men and women served to spur on the guerrillas. This was all there was to the matter.

Cassie felt there was much Josefa was leaving unsaid, but the Spanish girl refused to be drawn on the matter, changing the subject so abruptly that Cassie was left more convinced than ever that Josefa was keeping something from her.

The women rode hard to put as many miles as possible between themselves and the scene of the battle and not until the next morning did they stop to rest for a couple of hours, beside a cool river in the shade of a grove of overhanging trees.

Resuming their journey in the late afternoon they had been travelling for only an hour when they met with a squadron of Portuguese cavalry. Riding with the soldiers was Father Michael. He disclosed that the squadron had been despatched by the commander of the 6th Division as soon as Ensign Kennelly reached 6th divisional head-quarters and made his report. The orders given to the rescue party were to find and destroy the free-ranging French cavalrymen and rescue the two women if such a feat was possible.

'So Richard reached the army safely.' Josefa sounded relieved.

'He did – and I believe he made his men and the wagoners move faster than they ever thought possible. If he'd had his way the lad would have turned right around and come back to look for you himself. But the general said he had need of him. All he would spare were two hundred Portuguese cavalrymen and an Irish padre. No matter, you're safe. That's the main thing. Will you tell me what happened now?'

It was left to Cassie to tell Father Michael the story of their rescue. While she was talking, Jean and her mother disappeared to answer an urgent call of nature and Josefa wandered aimlessly to the edge of a nearby stream and began moodily lobbing pebbles in the water.

When Cassie came to the end of her story she suddenly remembered the words the guerrilla leader had spoken when she thanked him for his part in their

349

rescue. She repeated the words to Father Michael and asked him to translate them for her.

'Well now, you might not have repeated the words to me exactly as Don Xavier said them, but it sounds to me as though he was saying that Josefa kept her part of our bargain well, and he could do no less. Would that make any sense, do you think?'

Looking to where Josefa now sat on the river bank, arms wrapped around her drawn-up knees, Cassie said, 'Yes, it makes sense. Too much sense.'

'I'm inclined to agree with you.' Father Michael was also gazing at Josefa. 'When your friend returns with her little girl I want the two of you to go to the village, about a mile down the road. We'll put up there for the night. Right now I'd like to have a little chat with Josefa.'

Richard Kennelly's relief was almost overwhelming when Josefa returned to the regiment with Cassie and the two Martins. Alternately apologising to Cassie and Polly and hugging Josefa, it was as though he had not expected to see any of them alive again.

Harry returned to the regiment with the Light Company a week later having no knowledge of Cassie's adventures. For two days he wanted only to talk of his own exploits. The Light Company had ranged far and wide, seeking out and destroying the enemy many miles ahead of Lord Wellington's army. Harry had proved he could meet the additional demands of a Light Company and had rejoined his own company with a recommendation to the commanding officer that he be promoted to the rank of corporal as soon as the opportunity presented itself.

Eventually, Enoch Martin tired of hearing Harry's exploits and suggested that Cassie's and Polly's adventures might have been equally as exciting as Harry's own. When Harry learned what had befallen the two women he displayed a most satisfying concern, demanding to know every detail of Cassie's own three-day ordeal. He expressed his horror, but once Cassie satisfied him that nothing untoward had happened to her and she really was unhurt, Harry's thoughts swung back once more to his chances of promotion.

Cassie realised at that moment that Harry Clymo was no longer an awkward, uncertain farm labourer dressed in a soldier's uniform. His apprenticeship was over. He had become a professional soldier. Nothing in life would ever mean quite as much to him as the army.

29

❧

For the whole of the summer of 1812 Lord Wellington rolled the French army back over the towering hills and across the great plains of Spain. Legendary cities fell to his soldiers. Names that had painted the great canvases of history: Valladolid, Segovia, Salamanca – and then Madrid.

Entering the Spanish capital at the head of his conquering army, Wellington was the hero of Spain. Bells rang in his honour, dancers performed for him and wine and gifts were showered upon his soldiers. During a break in the festivities, Goya, one of the greatest artists of the day, painted a noble portrait of the great British general. Spain threw itself at Wellington's feet. His was the honour and the glory.

Yet Wellington had met with glory before. He recognised it as a fleeting will-o'-the-wisp. Privately, he told his generals he would gladly have exchanged all the celebrations for a division of well-trained and well-equipped Spanish troops, with generals prepared to put the task of winning the war before petty jealousies and ambitions.

It was a wish that would never be fulfilled and, such are the fickle fortunes of war, only a few weeks later Wellington was in Madrid once more. This time he was retreating before a numerically superior French force.

Lord Wellington's advance had ground to a halt before the heavily fortified walls of Burgos, ancient capital of the kings of Castile. The stubborn resistance made by the Burgos garrison threw all his plans into disarray. Without the fortified town he was left with a weakened defensive line to hold against an army that would soon outnumber his own by two to one, and with three times as many cavalrymen.

More importantly perhaps, Wellington's supply lines were dangerously extended. With his supply ships at the mercy of the uncertain weather, he was not prepared to take a chance on having his men starved into submission.

There had been many times when Wellington was prepared to take a calculated gamble on his army's fighting capability. Such occasions would inevitably occur again. For now, the odds were too great against him, the price of defeat too high. Painfully aware of what his eager critics in England would say about him, Wellington ordered his troops to retreat.

They stole away from Burgos silently in the night, hoping by such subterfuge to escape immediate pursuit.

*   *   *

Twenty-two days after retreating from Burgos, Cassie and the other wives struggled into Salamanca in the wake of what remained of the 32nd Regiment. Fewer than fifty men were recorded as casualties of war. The remainder were either sick, lost, or still trudging the increasingly muddy roads of Spain.

Few officers seemed to care what happened to the men. It had been raining hard for days, soldiers were just surviving on desperately low rations and the retreat was fast becoming a distressing débâcle.

When the retreating column reached Salamanca Josefa's mother was still there, although in the present mood of defeat no one felt inclined to pay for the services of a gipsy dancer. Those citizens of Salamanca who had been loudest in their welcome of the British a few weeks before now scowled in their direction. All were fearful of the price the French would exact from the town when they returned.

'Do you think you will see your Colonel Clausel?' Josefa put the question to her mother on the eve of the British departure. Cassie was with her and they were awaiting the arrival of Richard Kennelly. He had insisted that Josefa seek out her mother and arrange for him to be introduced to her.

The meeting was to take place outside the town. Estefanía was as reluctant to meet a British officer at such a time as Josefa was for Richard to meet her mother, but Richard had been insistent.

'I would doubtless bring back too many memories of Colonel Clausel's beloved horse should we meet again. No, it will not matter to me whether the soldiers walking about Salamanca are Englishmen or Frenchmen. I will dance for my living, as it was always intended.'

Josefa still felt guilty about her mother's reduced circumstances. It was she who had been responsible for breaking up the 'romance' between her mother and the French colonel. Josefa consoled herself with the thought that Colonel Clausel would one day have returned to a wife in France, abandoning Estefanía wherever she happened to be at the time. At least she had friends about her in Salamanca and many people who would pay to see her dance.

'Here's Richard now.' Cassie waved in the direction of the young ensign. She understood nothing of the conversation between mother and daughter, but she witnessed Josefa's unhappiness and was relieved to be able to bring the exchange to an end.

The meeting was taking place beside the road, along which many empty commissariat wagons, some artillery and a miscellany of refugees were heading, all leaving Salamanca ahead of the French advance.

'This is your man? Why, he is no more than a fresh-faced child!' Estefanía's glance shifted from the ensign hurrying towards them to her daughter. 'You stole Colonel Clausel's horse for *him*?'

'Lord Wellington has himself praised Richard for his bravery in fighting the French.' Josefa sprang to the defence of her lover. 'He will one day be a great general in the British army.'

'For your sake I hope it will not be too soon. Generals do not keep gipsy girls as mistresses – not even *boy* generals.'

355

Richard's smile went first to Josefa before it was expanded to include Estefanía and Cassie. When he reached the three women the young ensign saluted Estefanía before taking her hand and carrying it to his lips.

'I'm delighted to meet you, señora. I feel I would have known you had we met without an introduction. It is from you Josefa has inherited her beauty.'

'*Caramba!* The child has the tongue of a courtier! It is the French who claim a reputation for charm, yet my colonel never paid me such a compliment – or treated me as though I were a lady.'

Estefanía spoke in Spanish, but Richard smiled. 'I thank you, señora. Josefa is teaching me Spanish. My speech is not yet perfect, but I understand most of what is said to me. I can assure you that a British officer has little to learn from his French counterpart, whether it be in the art of warfare or the social graces.'

Estefanía viewed Richard with a new respect. 'You have the tongue of a gentleman. I thought my daughter foolish to give her heart to a soldier – any soldier. Now? I think perhaps she is wiser than I. You will hurt her, it cannot be otherwise, but it will not be a cruel hurt, I think.'

'I have no intention of hurting her, señora, cruelly, or in any other way. I wanted to meet you to ask your permission to marry Josefa.'

'Richard! This is foolish talk.' The outburst came from Josefa.

'No, it isn't. I've told you I will marry you, no matter how many times you say no. If I have your mother's permission it removes one more barrier.'

356

'Marriage?' Estefanía looked at Richard for a long time before giving him a sad smile. 'You are a young man. A very good-looking young man, and Josefa is my daughter. Both of you are trying to change the rules of the world to which each of you belongs. Very different worlds. You have my blessing in whatever you do, but for a future together you will need more than a mother's blessing. You must look for a miracle, and this I cannot give to you.'

'Your blessing will do. Thank you – but won't you allow me to buy you dinner in one of the coffee-houses about the square? I would dearly love to learn more about Josefa and yourself.'

Estefanía shook her head. 'You and your army are about to leave Salamanca. I must remain. There are many women who would be happy to tell the French how friendly I have been with British soldiers. I will return to the town alone. You will go with my blessing, both of you. Perhaps we will meet again, some day. Probably not.'

She hugged her daughter and after only a moment's hesitation, she kissed Richard. Then she was gone, hurrying towards Salamanca without a backward glance.

Josefa watched her mother until she was lost to sight among the refugees moving slowly along the road away from Salamanca. Then she turned fiercely upon Richard. 'That was a stupid thing to say. We can never marry, you know this. Now I must return and face being mocked by my own mother when you have left Spain and returned to England.'

'I am not going to return to England without you. If

357

you come back one day to visit your mother I want to be with you.'

Josefa looked at Richard for a long time, then a strange expression crossed her face and she turned and ran in the direction taken by her mother.

'What did I say?' Deeply hurt by Josefa's actions and words, Richard appealed to Cassie for enlightenment.

'I don't know – but I think you should go after her and try to sort it out.'

As he hurried after Josefa, Cassie began to walk slowly towards the camp of the 32nd, and her thoughts were greatly troubled.

Conditions on the retreat from Burgos had been bad before reaching Salamanca. When the British army left the beautiful cathedral city behind, they became infinitely worse. Rain fell more or less continually and the roads were churned up by the feet of tens of thousands of trudging men and women, by the narrow wheels of carts, the wider wheels of guns and the hooves of some six thousand horses. For a hundred paces on both sides of the road the ground was reduced to knee-deep morass. Men, women, children and animals who fell from exhaustion were trampled into the ground and never seen again. As if this nightmare was not enough, an inexperienced quartermaster general sent the army's supplies on a different route from that travelled by the men they were intended to feed.

For five days and five nights the soldiers and their women and children marched without food. It was too long for a great many, already weakened by illness and tribulation. They continued to fall beside the road. Those with the strength to talk pleaded with others who came behind to pick them up. To help them.

Many more said nothing at all. They simply lay down in the mud and died. It was all the same to those who trudged along behind. Lifting one foot clear of the mud and placing it in front of the other used up all the strength they possessed. They had none left to help others. Most had long ago lost shoes and boots in the mud, pulled from tired, numbed feet by the clinging, sucking, quagmire of the Spanish road. Day and night it rained. A cold, mind-dulling continuous downpour that sapped the strength and the will-power of the strongest men.

One day as Cassie plodded through the mud, leading her exhausted and hungry donkey, she thought she heard a faint, pathetic cry from somewhere beside the road. Her body told her to ignore the sound, as she had ignored so much else. But on this occasion her mind rebelled. Pulling the donkey off the road, she heard the cry once again before she saw the body of a woman lying in a posture of stiff repose, half-submerged in the mud.

Cassie had seen so many bodies along the route of the army's retreat they no longer called up either shock or sympathy. Each was simply the remains of 'a weaker being'. A man or woman who had lost the will or the ability to survive.

The sound came again and Cassie thought perhaps there was a small puppy nearby. She was about to turn away when the sound occurred yet again. This time it was accompanied by a sudden movement that caused

359

the sodden shawl about the dead woman's body to stir.

Bending over the other woman, Cassie saw she was probably Portuguese – and then she noticed the arm of a baby protruding from the shawl. As she watched, the tiny arm jerked weakly.

Dropping the rein of her tired donkey, Cassie reached inside the shawl and pulled out a tiny baby with red, chapped skin, black curly hair and eyes that blinked open with difficulty, unable to focus. 'You poor little soul!' Every scrap of Cassie's maternal instinct came to the fore as she picked up the child. 'How long have you been lying here?'

Unwinding the muddy shawl from about the shoulders of the child's dead mother, Cassie used it to cover the baby's nakedness. It was little more than a sodden mass, but she had nothing better. As she wrapped the child, Cassie saw it was a boy and probably no more than two days old.

Cassie took another look at the baby's mother and unexpected tears of pity sprang to her eyes. The mother was younger than Cassie, probably not yet sixteen, yet she had experienced the full cycle of life. Birth, motherhood and death. There was nothing more that could be done for her, but Cassie determined to do what she could for the baby.

Somehow, finding the child gave Cassie renewed strength, a new purpose to the struggle for survival. By the time the straggling army made a wet camp that night Cassie had acquired a dry piece of blanket to wrap around the baby, and a cavalryman's cape to keep it dry.

She even secured a space in a small hut, where a fire

of green wood provided a degree of warmth, although it also threatened to suffocate all those crammed within the four walls.

Feeding the foundling posed the biggest problem. Cassie had hoped they might find a village where there was a goat or two to provide a little milk, but all the villages they passed through had been in the path of a retreating army before. The goats had been taken by the young girls to secret valleys, high in the mountains. With them the girls also took everything of value that remained to the village families.

Eventually, among the followers of a Scots regiment, Cassie found a nursing mother whose own child was too ill to take what little milk her hungry body could provide. The mother put the baby to her breast and as it sucked with much noise and inexperience, she wept for her own sick child.

Harry regarded the baby with nervous awe, but he lay beside Cassie with the baby between them and when Cassie woke from a fitful sleep he had the baby pulled in close to him, passing on the warmth of his own body.

All the women attached to the 32nd Regiment had advice to give Cassie on how best to look after the baby, provisionally named Pedro after the village of Pedrosillo, near where he had been found. Even Sarah donated a dress to be torn up for the baby's use and the practical Polly Martin cut and stitched it to an approximate size.

Only Rose Tonks sounded a cautionary note. As she helped Cassie wrap the baby for the next day's march, she advised, 'Don't get too fond of him, lovey. If you hadn't found him he'd have been dead by now, like his mother. He's living on borrowed time and God don't give extra time on his dues. Not on campaign, he don't. Best thing you can do is to save your love for one of your own.'

All through that long day's march in conditions that showed no improvement on earlier days, Cassie hugged baby Pedro to her, disregarding all that Rose had said. She could only think that this was what it would have been like had she not lost her own baby upon her arrival in Portugal.

Although she would never have followed Harry to Horsham and ultimately to the Peninsula had she not been expecting his baby, she had come to believe that what had happened at Figueira had probably been for the best. Travelling in the wake of an army was no place to bring up a small child.

The appalling conditions on the retreat from Burgos had served to confirm Cassie's views – until the moment she found Pedro wrapped in his dead mother's shawl, lying in the mud of a Spanish road. During that long wet day Cassie began to recall other memories of the Peninsular campaign. The fuss the soldiers made of Jean and of their very real concern when she was ill. Of the way Cassie felt when she held baby Pedro in her arms and of her feelings when she woke and saw the baby being cuddled by Harry while both slept.

That evening, as dusk fell and the long, straggling column ground to a weary halt, Cassie prepared for yet another wet and foodless night. Despite her earlier gloomy prognosis, Rose was the first of the wives to seek out Cassie and ask after the baby's health. The sergeant's wife brought with her something that was of far more practical use than any amount of sympathy. Somehow during the horrors of the day's march, when most of the men and women in the four-mile-long column held no other thought than that of survival, Rose had managed to acquire a leather water bottle half-filled with fresh goat's milk.

When Cassie asked Rose where the amazing gift had come from, the big woman winked exaggeratedly. 'When I first began following the regiment I was told by a sergeant's wife never to question the source of a gift. A sergeant's wife "provides", a private's wife "accepts". One day when you're a sergeant's wife and you pass on that piece of advice you'll be as wise as me. For now, try and get some of the milk down Pedro's throat and then we'll wrap him in a piece of dry shirt I've kept warm half the day for the poor little mite.'

Rose had long ago acquired a cavalry cape to keep the rain from her. Unfastening the neck now, she plunged a hand inside her dress and pulled out a bright red piece of a good-quality shirt. It was most certainly not a service issue.

Pedro drank all the milk and although he brought some of it up again, Cassie felt satisfied he had kept enough down to sustain him for another day. Nevertheless, she went off in search of the woman who had fed him the previous night.

None of the wives of the regiment to which the woman's husband belonged had seen the woman or her ailing baby. Indeed, her husband had been given permission to return along the last few miles of the line of

363

march. In the darkness and in such atrocious weather, his search was doomed to failure. The other wives had already given her up as lost.

The missing woman would join the ranks of the five thousand soldiers and an unknown number of women and children who had been lost during a thirty-day retreat of almost three hundred miles from Burgos to the town of Rodrigo, so savagely taken by the British army when the campaign of 1812 opened, three hundred days before.

30

❧

Rose Tonks, genial wife of Sergeant Elijah Tonks of the 32nd Regiment, was killed soon after dawn on 12 November 1812. It was the last engagement of that year's campaign and occurred when the most disastrous retreat ever experienced by Lord Wellington's Peninsular army had almost reached its end.

During the previous night the French pursuers, now little more than a token force, had somehow managed to position a light cannon on a hill overlooking the road the British army would take when it resumed its retreat at dawn. The first indication of its presence was a cannon ball thudding into the ranks of the 32nd as they formed into line to take up their position for marching, in the centre of the long column.

The shot bowled over seven or eight soldiers and Sergeant Tonks was one of those who ran to the scene to render aid. He was hauling an injured soldier from the mud when a second shot fell in almost exactly the same spot and Rose saw her husband go down with a number of other soldiers.

The sergeant's burly wife had been tying pots and pans to her donkey, but when she saw her husband go down she let them drop to the ground. Lifting her skirts clear of the mud, she ran to where her husband had fallen. When she was still fifty yards from the spot Sergeant Tonks picked himself up, roundly cursing the soldier who had knocked him to the ground in his fright.

Rose stopped running and, as a huge smile broke across her face, she rested her knuckles on well-padded hips and called, 'Elijah Tonks, you're an old fraud! You almost gave me a heart attack . . .'

The third cannon ball struck only Rose. It was a small four-pounder, but the shot took her in the shoulder, shattering her upper arm and a number of ribs, and knocking her to the ground.

It seemed that every man and woman in the regiment rushed to her aid, but Sergeant Tonks reached her first. Dropping to his knees, he carefully lifted her head clear of the mud, trying to keep his eyes from wandering to the mangled mess where the cannon ball had struck.

The look Rose gave her husband contained more sorrow than pain as she said, 'I'm sorry, Elijah. I should have known they couldn't kill you.' Suddenly her eyes filled with tears and she cried, 'Oh, Elijah! Who'll take care of you now, my love?'

They were the last words Rose ever spoke and for a few moments of stunned silence the men of the 32nd Regiment watched as their sergeant, the toughest and most fearless man in the regiment, bowed his head over his wife's body and wept.

Another cannon ball buried itself harmlessly in the mud nearby and it galvanised the regiment into action. Led by the colonel himself, the avenging horde fanned out across the plain, heading towards the French gunners.

The French artillery officer in charge of the cannon risked two more shots before ordering his men to hitch the horses to the gun and run for safety. Meanwhile, Richard Kennelly had observed there was only one track the French gunners could take to escape from the hillside and he led a number of men to cut them off.

It was a close-run race. The French artillerymen galloped clear of the bulk of the 32nd's soldiers and outran their musket balls. They almost did the same to Richard but he stopped and steadied his men, ensuring they held their fire until exactly the right moment when the hard-riding French artillerymen passed closest to them.

The volley emptied half the saddles immediately and brought down one of the horses pulling the gun. The cannon bounced on its side and careered across the rocky ground for some yards before the other horses were brought to a halt. The surviving artillerymen tried to right their gun and cut free the dead horse, but the second volley from Ensign Kennelly's men brought them to the ground and the soldiers of the 32nd moved in with bayonet and musket butt to finish off the wounded survivors.

It was all over in a few minutes. The death of Rose

Tonks had been avenged but nothing would bring her back to life. She was buried beside the road, with the bare-headed colonel and every officer in the regiment in attendance, while Wellington's dejected army tramped past.

Two days later the army reached Rodrigo and set up camp around its war-scarred walls. The retreat was over. The army would go into cantonment and lick its wounds for the winter months. The more philosophical among the ranks of the army pointed out that Lord Wellington had not taken them all the way back to the coast. It must mean that he intended resuming the offensive when winter was over.

Those soldiers with a more pessimistic outlook on life grumbled that it meant they would need to fight yet again for the ground they had won and lost that year – and the year before. Some had met with similar fortunes when they fought under the command of Sir John Moore in 1809.

For Cassie, the respite meant she could ensure baby Pedro received a regular diet of milk and was kept warm and dry. Harry was happy to help in any way he could. He realised that taking care of the baby took Cassie's mind off Rose's death. Cassie had been very fond of the sergeant's wife and she grieved for her.

One other thing was upsetting Cassie. She and Josefa had always been close friends, but Cassie had seen very little of the Spanish girl during recent days. She had put it down to the extreme difficulties of the retreat, but now they were at Rodrigo Josefa had still not come near her.

On the regiment's fourth day there, orders came

through promoting Richard Kennelly to the rank of lieutenant. It was in recognition of the 'courage and leadership' he had displayed in capturing the French gun
that had caused Rose's death. Delighted for him, Cassie
took Pedro and went in search of the newly promoted
lieutenant, to offer him her congratulations. She found
him in the tent he shared with Josefa. The tents had been
sent out from England in an attempt to make the lot of
the soldier more comfortable. So far they had only been
issued to the officers of a few selected regiments.

Richard thanked Cassie for her good wishes and after
making as much fuss of Pedro as though the baby was
Cassie's own, he invited her inside the tent. Here, Josefa
was stitching the symbols of his new status to his
uniform coat.

Josefa greeted Cassie warmly enough but something
was missing from her greeting. There had always been
an easy companionship between the two young women,
but for some reason it was no longer there. Cassie was
both baffled and hurt. She was very fond of the Spanish
girl and when Richard was called from the tent by one
of the soldiers, Cassie took the opportunity to ask her
what was wrong.

'How do you mean, wrong?'

'I don't know . . . I wish I did. It's just that you seem
unhappy. I've been worrying that it might be something
I've done, or is there something wrong between you and
Richard?'

'Nothing is wrong between me and Richard, and I
am delighted his bravery has been rewarded . . .' For a
moment Josefa's fierce pride in Richard was evident.

'He still wants to marry me, even though he is now a lieutenant. I tell him it is foolish, that he is the son of a great lord, but it is good to know he loves me so much.'

Cassie did not correct Josefa about Richard's father being a 'great' lord. Instead, she said, 'Then, if you are happy with Richard, it must be something I've done. I wish you would tell me what it is, Josefa.'

'You have done nothing.' Josefa suddenly put out a hand and grasped Cassie's arm. 'I expect it is because I am worried about my mother.'

At that moment Pedro began to whimper and Josefa removed her hand as Richard came back inside the tent. Pedro was wrapped in the shawl Cassie had taken from the body of his mother and the newly promoted lieutenant pulled back the shawl to peer at the baby's face once more.

'He certainly is a handsome young fellow!' Beaming down at the baby, he added, 'Look at those dark eyes, and the colour of his skin. There is no doubting he belongs to this part of the world, even though we know nothing of his father. It's plain to see there's not a drop of English blood in his veins. What on earth are you going to do with him, Cassie?'

Neither Cassie nor Richard had been watching Josefa as they discussed the nationality of the baby. They were unaware of the strange expression that crossed her face. It contained the ingredients of distress and momentary panic. Rising to her feet, Josefa dropped the uniform jacket to the stool on which she had been seated. Pushing past Richard and Cassie without a word, she ran from the tent.

'Josefa ...' Richard called after her, but Josefa continued her flight through the camp.

He turned back to Cassie, thoroughly bewildered. 'I'm sorry, Cassie. I don't know what's the matter with her lately. She's been like this ever since we left Salamanca.'

Cassie feared Josefa's disturbed state originated far earlier than their last visit to Salamanca, but she said, 'She's very worried about her mother. Go and find her, Richard. She needs you.'

A few days later Cassie was at the river's edge, washing for Harry and Sergeant Tonks. Baby Pedro was nearby, wrapped in his shawl and lying inside a soft raffia basket. He had hiccups and the occasional tiny explosion of sound caused Cassie to smile happily. Pedro was a remarkably contented baby and Cassie had come to love him very much. He attracted a great deal of attention from the other women who came to the river to wash clothes. British, Portuguese and Spanish all stopped beside the basket to praise the baby.

Eventually the persistent hiccuping provoked a squall of protest from the baby and Cassie picked him up for a couple of minutes before settling him down again. Then she began humming a tune, as much to express her own happiness as to soothe Pedro to sleep.

She was still humming the same tune, although the baby was asleep, when she heard the sound of a horse blowing nearby. When she looked up she saw Father Michael riding along the river bank towards her. With him were a couple of Portuguese infantrymen, and a number of Portuguese women.

371

Cassie's face lit up with pleasure at seeing the Dominican friar. Unlike many of the padres attached to the army, Father Michael spent more time with the men than with their officers and he was never too busy to talk with anyone who brought a problem to him.

The Dominican friar nodded his head in acknowledgement of Cassie's greeting, but much to her surprise there was no answering smile from him. As he dismounted and handed his reins to one of the two soldiers, Cassie felt a sudden chill of fear. 'Is something wrong? Is it Harry?'

Harry had gone off that morning with the remainder of 3 Company to escort an incoming munitions convoy on its last few miles to the fortress of Rodrigo. They would be away overnight, but it had not been anticipated that they would encounter any trouble.

'My being here has nothing to do with Harry, Cassie. If he was all right when you last saw him he'll be the same now, for sure. No, I'm here about another matter. Something entirely different . . .'

While he was talking, one of the Portuguese women had walked to where Pedro lay and pulled back the shawl to look at him. Now she began talking loudly and excitedly to the Portuguese soldiers and another woman joined in the conversation.

'Shhh! You'll wake the baby. He's only just gone to sleep,' Cassie admonished the women.

'Cassie, it's the baby we've come to speak to you about. I've heard you found it back along the road during the retreat. Its poor mother lying dead, so it was said.'

'That's right. He would have died, too, had he not

372

made a noise as I passed by. I've had him ever since. He's a lovely child.'

'A baby has a remarkable talent for capturing the hearts of all those about him,' agreed Father Michael, gently. 'I'm sure you can well imagine the heartbreak of any man who loses not only such a child, but his wife too.'

One of the soldiers was now kneeling beside the basket containing Pedro, and suddenly Cassie realised what Father Michael was trying to tell her.

'No! It can't be . . . You can't be certain!'

'Cassie, it's plain to see the baby you have is not English, and the soldier who's kneeling beside the basket lost his wife and child during the retreat. She dropped behind with the baby, unnoticed. He and some of his friends searched all night without finding either of them. Then someone told him an English woman had found a baby. I knew his wife, Cassie. She was a pretty young thing, no more than sixteen, I'd say. He still doesn't know if she's alive, or dead.'

Cassie remembered the body of the young woman from whom she had taken Pedro. No more than sixteen . . .

'The baby's mother was a young woman. She was dead . . . but how can you be certain Pedro is his child? Lots of women and children were lost during the retreat.'

'That's true – far too many – but the shawl wrapped about the baby . . . One of the women is a sister of the child's mother. She says the shawl is one she made herself for her poor sister. Would you know anything about it?'

373

Cassie nodded, feeling numbed. 'I took it from the body of the baby's mother, to wrap the baby in.'

Father Michael passed on the information to the soldier and those about him. It brought a loud mixture of anguish and joy. Tears ran down the face of the soldier as he lifted the baby clear of the basket, holding him as gingerly as though the child was an explosive charge. Suddenly Cassie was surrounded by tearful women who insisted on kissing her cheeks and hugging her.

'It is the soldier's baby, Cassie. In your heart you know this, I'm sure.'

Cassie nodded, not trusting herself to speak for the moment.

Looking across at Cassie, with the baby cradled safely in his arms, the Portuguese soldier spoke rapidly and at some length to Father Michael. When the soldier ceased talking, Father Michael said to Cassie, 'He's asked me to bless you and to say you'll be in his prayers until he takes his dying breath. The baby will be in good hands, Cassie. The family will take him home with them and give him all the love and attention he needs, far from the dangers of war.'

The soldier spoke again and the Portuguese group fell silent until Father Michael smiled and gave the soldier a brief reply. Explaining the conversation to Cassie, he said, 'You had a proposal of marriage from the child's father. He has a house and a piece of good land. I told him you were already married but you would be pleased to know Pedro's father was a man of some substance.'

The pain at the thought of losing the tiny foundling

was growing but Cassie nodded and another volatile conversation erupted among the Portuguese, occasionally involving Father Michael.

When it subsided, the Irish friar turned to Cassie once more. 'The father says he would consider it a great honour if you and your husband would agree to become the baby's godparents. He regrets its first name cannot be Pedro, because his wife's choice was Afonso, but he promises the name will be Afonso Pedro. If you agree to become godparents I'll let you know the date of the christening – I've been invited to conduct the service.'

Cassie nodded and, after mumbling something about it being an honour, she gathered up her clothes, some still unwashed, and fled back to the camp occupied by the 32nd Regiment.

Cassie shared a small and grossly overcrowded hut with an aged Portuguese widow and a number of other army wives but she was relieved to find the hut empty when she returned to it. Most wives were at the river, the others had accompanied the widow to a market in a nearby town. Cassie immediately set to and cleaned the room as it had never been cleaned before. When it was done she started all over again.

When Josefa found Cassie she was seated on the blanket that marked out the bedspace allocated to her and Harry in a corner of the single-roomed hut. There were no windows and it was some moments before Josefa made out the half-hidden figure in the gloomy interior.

'Cassie? Is that you?'

'What do you want?' Cassie had seen nothing of Josefa

since the day she had taken the baby to the tent occupied by the Spanish girl and Richard.

'I've just heard about the baby from Father Michael. He's worried about you. I ... I'm sorry, Cassie, truly sorry. I know how much the baby meant to you.'

'How would you know? You've hardly been near me since I found him.'

'I know. I can't explain it to you now ... I wish I could.'

Josefa sounded so unhappy that Cassie was shaken out of her own state of abject misery. 'Does it have anything to do with what I heard Don Xavier saying to you?'

'What did you hear?' There was a note of alarm in Josefa's voice.

'I can't remember the Spanish words, but translated it was something like, "You've kept your bargain well. I could do no less." What did it mean, Josefa?'

'So it was you who mentioned it to Father Michael! You must have misheard. Don Xavier was pointing out to me that he is a man of his word.'

'Yes, I probably misheard. After all, he *was* speaking in Spanish.'

Cassie knew she had heard correctly, but she did not want to pursue the matter. Josefa had her own reasons for denying what had been said. Cassie hoped her own intuition about the incident was wrong. If not, she and Polly Martin owed Josefa a debt they could never repay.

31

By the time Harry returned from his escort duties Cassie had recovered sufficiently from the loss of Pedro to be able to discuss the baby's future reasonably dispassionately. She even argued with a very disappointed Harry that it was far better for the baby to grow up with his own family in his homeland. He would be better cared for in settled surroundings and it was reassuring to know he would not need to suffer the discomforts and hazards of life with an army on campaign, the din and dangers of battle never far away.

But when Harry awoke in the night to feel Cassie's body racked by silent sobs he knew the reason. Holding her tight in the darkness of the overcrowded room he did his best to comfort her but it was not easy to impart tenderness and solace in a room filled with snoring men and women, the nearest no more than a few inches away.

The next day the British regiments began moving to

permanent winter quarters, deep inside Portugal. Some had a long way to go and not until early December did the soldiers of the 32nd Regiment reach their allotted billets in the village of St Jago in Beira Province.

Cassie and Harry were put into a hut that had once been occupied by woodcutters, high on a mountainside. They shared the small hut with Enoch, Polly and Jean Martin, Sarah and Ned Harrup, and a young woman named Lily Bond who had a permanent cold and whose husband would disappear for days and nights at a time, on 'regimental business'.

The view from the woodcutter's hut was spectacular. All around were mountain peaks as far as the eye could see, with forests of pine, chestnut and cork trees covering the lower slopes. Below, in the rich soil of the valley, were fruit trees and gardens capable of providing produce for every month of the year.

Recruits began reaching the regiment now. Straight from England, they were fresh-faced young men with new uniforms and an eagerness to get to grips with the French. All were sadly lacking in the skills and discipline needed to win battles.

Non-commissioned officers were needed to carry out the training of the new arrivals and Harry was given his long-promised promotion to corporal. The promotion brought two cloth stripes and Cassie stitched them to the sleeve of his uniform jacket with great pride. There was also a pay rise of a full twopence-farthing a day. Harry Clymo had taken his first firm step on the promotion ladder. The promotion also brought about a change of billet. Cassie and Harry moved to another woodcutter's hut, but this one had two rooms and it was shared only with Sergeant Elijah Tonks.

Cassie welcomed the opportunity to cook for the sergeant. He and Rose had been extremely kind to her when she first joined the regiment, and the widowed sergeant looked as though he needed the care of a woman.

Elijah Tonks had aged alarmingly in the few weeks since his wife's death and seemed to have lost much of his zest for life. The only thing he now felt passionately about was killing Frenchmen. It had become an obsession with him and he complained long and bitterly about the army's inactivity, quartered miles from the enemy during the winter months.

Sergeant Tonks accepted that Lord Wellington had to cope with the problems of weather and obtaining sufficient supplies. However, the French faced similar problems – and they had not returned to France! Soldiers were paid to fight, not to skulk in cantonments far from the men they should be killing.

Because of his beliefs, Sergeant Tonks worked his men hard. When the 32nd went into battle once more he was determined it would be the finest fighting force in the British army, fully trained to kill more French soldiers than any other regiment.

The winter months passed pleasantly for the soldiers and their families and the woodcutter's hut became a home for Cassie and Harry. In a nearby village market Cassie bought a gay-coloured cloth to cover the rough-wood table and she always managed to find flowers to brighten the cabin. Outside, she planted a small vegetable garden and it gave her enormous pleasure to watch a shirt-sleeved Harry at work in the small plot. The cabin became a snug and happy place.

Although the soldiers trained hard, they enjoyed many diversions. Band and regimental concerts were popular with the men, and the officers had a pack of hounds shipped out from England. As a result the local populace was treated to the sight of 'the mad English', chasing dogs all over the countryside and attempting to leap every obstacle that loomed up in their paths. Shooting parties were organised to hunt the hungry wolves that came down from the mountains to raid livestock – although many believed the wolves were blamed for a great many crimes that had been committed by opportunist soldiers.

Soon after his promotion, Richard Kennelly was summoned to Wellington's headquarters for a most unsatisfactory interview that should have led to a posting on the staff of the commander-in-chief. But Wellington was not at his headquarters. He was in Cadiz, seeking improvements in the state of the Spanish army. As a result Richard was interviewed by a choleric old general who felt aggrieved because he had been left out of the commander-in-chief's entourage, currently being entertained on a lavish scale in the great Spanish city. Insufficiently briefed on the reason why Richard had been recommended for a posting to Lord Wellington's headquarters, the general pointed out that a great many other officers – cavalry officers – had quite as much battle experience as the very junior lieutenant before him.

When Richard hinted that perhaps Lady Fraser might be able to throw some light on the matter, the general became even more irascible. He was opposed to having women accompany the army on a campaign – especially if they travelled with the headquarters. They were, declared the general, 'always scheming and plotting for the advancement of a husband, or a relative. Nepotism' – declared the general finally – 'is the bane of the British army.' It had brought about a lowering of standards that would have been totally unacceptable when he joined the army more than fifty years before. He had actually heard of a young officer who tried to have his Spanish mistress introduced to the wife of his general!

On the ride back to St Jago, Richard consoled himself with the thought that if the general who had just interviewed him was representative of the other officers on the staff of the commander-in-chief, he would rather not serve with them. It was a great pity, though. He had hoped that working for Lady Fraser would give Josefa some idea of the comforts she would enjoy as the wife of a British army officer. They would not live on such a grand scale as the Frasers, of course, but she would have learned there was more to army life than dirt, discomfort and the rigours of campaigning.

Richard had also hoped that such a change might shake Josefa free of the doldrums that had affected her since learning of her mother's return to Salamanca. Most of all, he had hoped the move might persuade her to change her mind about marriage to him – and he was determined that one day she would become his wife.

* * *

In February 1813, the first of an increasing spate of rumours began to circulate that Lord Wellington was ready to resume his campaign against the French army. This time, it was said, he intended driving them out of Spain and across the Pyrenees into France.

After suffering many frustrations at home and abroad, it seemed Lord Wellington might at last have all the men and equipment needed for such a daunting task. His tried and proven regiments had been brought up to strength with eager recruits from home, giving him 70,000 fighting men in his Anglo-Portuguese army plus an indeterminate number of Spanish soldiers.

The state of the army's equipment had improved greatly too. Tents were being issued to the long-suffering troops who had spent too many miserable nights with only a blanket between them and a deluge. The cavalry had good, well-fed horses, and arrangements to supply the vast army were satisfactorily in hand. Now Wellington could choose where and when he would advance. Yet to an apprehensive enemy he seemed to lack any sense of urgency.

The rumours of an impending campaign were still rife when Gorran Fox returned to his regiment in March. Cassie had been shopping in the nearby village and was returning to the cantonment with Sarah Harrup and Polly Martin when she suddenly saw him. He was walking along the path towards them in company with the colonel of the regiment, apparently heading towards the officers' mess which was situated in an abandoned villa on the hillside.

Cassie's first emotion was one of great pleasure. She

would have liked to have run to him to welcome him back from England. Suddenly she felt like smiling at everyone. In that moment she realised just how much she had missed the 32nd's officer and his strength in times of trouble.

After a few moments Gorran saw Cassie, too, and his face broke into such an expression of delight that the colonel followed his gaze sharply.

'Cassie! I'm happy to see you safe and well. You ladies too – Sarah, Polly. I trust young Jean is keeping well?'

Gorran included the other women in his greeting quickly enough to take the frown from the commanding officer's face. It was replaced with a benevolent smile as the colonel nodded and said, 'Good afternoon, ladies,' adding, in recognition of their laden baskets, 'I'm glad to see you're feeding up the regiment's warriors. It won't be long before they're showing Napoleon's army what the Thirty-second is made of.'

Sarah and Polly smiled at the colonel's geniality but Cassie was still looking at Gorran. He looked pale but otherwise fit and well.

The colonel spoke to his young officer and Gorran replied, but he had not taken many paces before he turned and called, 'Cassie ... I'd like to see you and your husband some time – perhaps later this evening?'

Sarah nudged Polly, giving her a knowing wink. 'Did you hear that? Our Cassie's hob-nobbing with the officers again. I always did think Mr Fox was struck on her.'

'If I heard right he wants to see Harry as well,' retorted Cassie. 'I wonder what it's about?'

'Perhaps he wants to congratulate Harry on his promotion,' said Polly innocently. 'And I think you'll need to return the compliment. Unless I'm mistaken, Mr Fox is now a captain.'

Gorran confirmed his new rank when he came to the small cabin that evening. He first expressed his heart-felt sympathy with Sergeant Elijah Tonks on the loss of his wife. It was genuine sympathy. Rose Tonks had taken it upon herself to take care of Gorran when he first joined the regiment as a young ensign. She had nursed him through sickness, encouraged him when he doubted himself and shared his happiness during the good times. He would miss her greatly.

Gorran had not finished talking when Sergeant Tonks rose from his chair and walked from the hut without saying a word to anyone. His action took Gorran by surprise. 'What is that all about? I had to offer my sympathy, but if I had known how he would react . . .'

He made as though he would go after the sergeant, but, putting a hand on his arm, Cassie restrained him. 'He's best left alone. You'll only upset yourself if you try to reason with him. Elijah Tonks hasn't been the same man since Rose died. He's apt to get up and walk out in the middle of a conversation, no matter what it is you're talking about. All the wives have tried to help him, out of respect for Rose's memory, but nothing seems to work. Poor Rose, she was like a mother to all of us.'

'Ah! Talking of mothers . . . I have a letter for you, Cassie.'

Gorran delved deep inside a pocket and came out

with a flat pouch of waxed cloth. Opening it carefully, he took out a couple of neatly folded sheets of paper. Handing them to Cassie, he said, 'Here you are, all the way from Mevagissey.'

Taking the letter, Cassie spoke with something akin to awe in her voice. 'From my mother? You saw her? Why?'

'I lost my own mother while I was home, Cassie. When she died I thought of all the things I should have done for her. The opportunities I missed. If anything happened to your mother I know you'd feel the same way. I didn't think you'd want to bear such a burden.'

'I didn't even think to ask about your mother. That's very selfish of me . . . I'm sorry to hear she died.'

'I was fortunate enough to reach home while she still lived, Cassie – and it also made me happy to be able to visit your parents. I spent a very pleasant day with your mother and father and also met your sisters. They all send you their deepest love – and asked me to extend their affection to Harry. I told them he was a fine soldier and I don't doubt they will be very proud to hear of his promotion.'

Cassie was so choked with emotion she was unable to say anything for some minutes but when Gorran rose to go, she said, 'Please don't leave yet. It's just . . . I suddenly remembered so many things I've tried hard to forget. Stay and tell me all you did in Mevagissey. I'm all right now. Harry, bring Mr . . . Captain Fox some of the port wine we had to celebrate your promotion.'

As Harry moved away to fetch the port, Cassie smiled at Gorran. 'You'll enjoy the wine. Father Michael brought it for us.'

'You still see him?' Gorran sounded surprised.

'I found a Portuguese baby lying in the mud with its dead mother during the retreat from Burgos. Father Michael discovered the remainder of the child's family. He's been a regular visitor since then.' Cassie could talk about the baby now, but not for too long. 'Tell me about Mevagissey and my family.'

'It's a simple story, really. The family business I returned home to attend to took me to the port of Fowey. While I was there a fishing-boat put in from Mevagissey and I remembered your home was no more than a couple of miles across the bay. When my companion told the fishermen I was a wounded soldier, home from the Peninsular war, they happily agreed to take me as a passenger to Mevagissey. Indeed, when I mentioned I carried news of Cassie to her family I believe they'd have as happily carried me to the ends of the earth.'

Tasting the port wine Harry had brought to him, Gorran exclaimed, 'This is good. I must cultivate the friendship of Father Michael and learn where such port can be purchased.'

'Did you see my father?' Cassie asked eagerly.

'He was the first man we saw as we entered Mevagissey's delightful little harbour. The men who carried me in their boat called out my news long before we reached the harbour wall and it was your father who helped me from the boat. It seemed every man and woman in the village was eager to have news of you, but your father took me home and along the way I told him where you were.

'We were no more than fifty paces from the harbour

386

when we met your mother running to meet us. Someone had wasted no time in carrying the news to her. Then, of course, I had to repeat my news of you all over again. I told the story many times before I left, late that evening. I told it to sisters, aunts, uncles – and the preacher. I was even obliged to take off my coat, roll up my sleeve and show them the wounds you bound for me.'

'Are they all well?' Cassie's eyes glistened, but the emotion she felt was not unhappiness. Gorran was providing her with the first news of her family she had received in almost two years. It was a gap she herself should have bridged, but it had become increasingly difficult with the passing of time. Now Gorran had performed the task for her.

'Your father has enjoyed two very successful pilchard seasons, so he told me. The family are all well – and much better for learning of your whereabouts. When I told your mother about your work with the sick and wounded, she told me to tell you how proud she is of you – of both of you. She looks forward to the day when you are both safely beneath the roof of your home in Mevagissey. She asked me to stress that it is to be considered home for both of you – but I don't doubt she tells you all this in her letter. Your parents are nice people, Cassie. Very nice people. You will never again be able to say you have no home or family, Corporal Harry Clymo.'

Harry was so choked with emotion he could only say, 'Thank you, Captain Fox. Thank you very much, sir.' He would need to get used to the idea of being a member of a family.

'I'm obliged to you for the port, but I really must go now. We'll talk again after you've read your letter and I'll try to answer any questions you might have about your family, or about Mevagissey.'

He was walking away from the cabin in the darkness when the door opened behind him and Cassie called, 'Wait!' Running after him, Cassie thrust the half-empty bottle of port into his hands. 'I . . . We'd like you to have this. I wish it was more, much more. It's a very kind thing you've done, Gorran – for me and for Harry.'

It was the first time Gorran could remember Cassie calling him by his first name and it gave him a glow of pleasure. Even more unexpected was the quick kiss Cassie planted on his cheek. 'Thank you again. I think you're probably the kindest man I've ever met.'

As Cassie made her way back to the cabin Gorran was not quite certain he enjoyed being remembered by Cassie for his 'kindness'. He wanted to call her back, but he did not. Then she stopped and her voice came back to him in the darkness. 'If I want to speak to you, about the letter, will I find you at divisional headquarters?'

'No, Cassie, I forgot to tell you. I've been posted back to the regiment as the officer commanding Three Company. We'll all be seeing more of each other from now on.'

Gorran had been in command of the company for only a week when the long-awaited order for the regiment to move was received. They were to march north-eastwards, to meet up with other regiments in preparation for the offensive which every man in the opposing armies knew to be imminent.

The evening before the 32nd set off, Josefa left Richard Kennelly to make her way to Salamanca. She made her decision known to him shortly before he went to attend a meeting of the regiment's officers and she was gone by the time he returned.

The young officer asked Cassie if she knew for how long Josefa had been contemplating returning home? Cassie was able to say with complete honesty that Josefa had never given her a hint that she intended leaving. Neither had she come to say goodbye.

Cassie was almost as distressed as Richard at Josefa's sudden departure, but she could not share her thoughts with him. He was already worried to the point of distraction.

Josefa had become increasingly withdrawn during recent weeks as though something was worrying her but she had always responded to Richard's efforts to cheer her and he thought he had been able to convince her that all would be well with her mother. Her disappearance was all the more bewildering because only the previous night she had declared passionately that she loved him more than anyone or anything in the world. Now she had gone off and left him.

After leaving Cassie, Richard went to Gorran with a request that he be allowed to go after Josefa and reason with her. Gorran refused the request, pointing out that it would be impossible to find her in the darkness. She might have taken any one of a dozen paths through the mountains. Besides, the regiment was moving off at dawn, and Lieutenant Kennelly's first duty was to his men.

When the distraught young officer threatened to resign from the army and take off after Josefa, Gorran said he would refuse to accept such a resignation. Richard was needed by the regiment – and by Gorran in particular. He had been away from the country and the regiment for some months and needed a good officer to help him. All Gorran could promise was that when Salamanca was retaken he would consider sending his lieutenant on leave to find Josefa. It was an unsatisfactory solution, but it would have to suffice for now.

Preparing the company for its first march under his command was a formidable task, yet Gorran found time to seek out Cassie and ask if she could throw any light on Josefa's unexpected and rapid departure. At first Cassie repeated the same story Josefa had told to Richard, but Gorran was watching her closely.

When Cassie ended rather lamely without meeting his gaze, he said quietly, 'We've known each other a while now, Cassie. Long enough to trust each other – especially when friends are in trouble. I think we both look upon Richard as a friend, and I regard Josefa as a very exceptional girl. She would be so whatever her nationality and I am extremely fond of her. I hope you are keeping nothing back from me, Cassie. I believe Josefa is as much in need of help as Richard, but without all the facts I must remain baffled and unable to help either of them. Are you quite sure you can tell me *nothing* to throw light on Josefa's sudden departure?'

'I'm not sure, Gorran, and I wouldn't want you to repeat anything I tell you to Richard, especially as I might be quite wrong . . .'

'I'll say nothing to anyone, I promise. Now, what is it?'

Hesitantly at first, but gathering confidence as she went along, Cassie told Gorran of her capture by the French and of the part played by Josefa in her rescue by Don Xavier. Finally, Cassie told him of Father Michael's translation of the parting words spoken by Don Xavier to Josefa.

'Are you saying the price exacted by Don Xavier for rescuing you and Polly was . . . Josefa herself?'

'Yes.'

Gorran began pacing the small room of the cabin. 'I don't doubt but you're right. Don Xavier is a man devoid of all the principles a gentleman is supposed to possess. But this happened months ago. Why should Josefa decide to go off and leave Richard now?'

Gorran's mouth suddenly dropped open and Cassie knew he had arrived at the same conclusion as herself, 'That's right. I believe Josefa's pregnant. If she is, she won't know whether the father is Richard or Don Xavier. She must have been suffering torture about this for months!'

32

❦

Instead of marching eastwards towards Salamanca, the 32nd Regiment moved northwards accompanied by many other regiments. Lord Wellington had devised a daring plan to take the French army by surprise. He would accompany a single division and much of the cavalry along the road towards Salamanca and the long French line of defences, hoping the French would view this as his main offensive. Meanwhile, the bulk of the army would be toiling through a remote and mountainous area to emerge behind the enemy's line.

With increased guerrilla activity all over Spain and another British attack developing from the Mediterranean, Lord Wellington hoped to draw troops away from the French defences and so be faced with a weaker force than at any time before. By striking a sudden surprise blow, he expected to sow enough confusion to enable him to drive Napoleon's reeling army all the way across Spain to the French border. However, such a daring plan required fine timing and careful planning and, while the commander-in-chief made his final preparations, much of the army waited in the foothills of the mountains for a full month before receiving their final instructions.

The march through the mountains was extremely gruelling and was not made any easier by heavy rain which seemed always to dog the movements of the British army. Old hands used to the rigours of the campaign tucked in their chins and trudged forward, wasting little breath on complaint. Others, newly arrived from England, were less conditioned to the hardships they suffered and they complained bitterly each time they were called upon to help haul artillery pieces up mountain faces or take the strain on wet and heavy ropes as the same guns were eased down a steep and rocky slope.

It was on this march that Cassie saw a new Harry emerge. He revelled in the authority invested in him by the two stripes sewn on his arm. With Sergeant Tonks sunk into ever-deeper gloom, Harry assumed many of the sergeant's duties too. He bullied, cajoled and encouraged the men under his command, drawing more from them than they knew they had to give.

Watching her husband, Cassie knew that Harry Clymo, workhouse waif and butt for a bullying farmer, had gone for ever. In his place was Corporal Harry Clymo, seasoned soldier and leader of men. Harry had found his rightful place in life and Cassie was both happy and proud for him.

For two weeks the army toiled through the mountains. At night they huddled around spluttering camp fires, with wet blankets about their shoulders, camping on land too steep to pitch their newly issued tents. When they talked it was to grumble incessantly about the man who had thought of sending a whole army through such country as this. Yet, for all their grumbling, very few men dropped out or reported sick. The men were part of an advancing army, on its way to prove its superiority in battle with soldiers who were worthy adversaries for a British army.

On the last day of May the army emerged from the high mountains, the Trás os Montes. Now they were back in Spain, but still it rained. On and on they marched, always expecting that tomorrow they would top a rise and see the army of France drawn up in front of them in battle array, but the new dawn brought only more marching, more rumours – and even more rain.

The army zigzagged across Spain, putting mountains, hills and plains behind them: Zamora, Valladolid and Palencia – and it was here they saw the enemy. From the hills they looked down on the plains where Napoleon's brother, 'King' Joseph of Spain, was reviewing his troops. They even had a brief taste of battle, when the French drove the British advance guard from its hilltop vantage point before dusk fell.

The following morning the British army rose early and stood to arms – but the French had gone and the long march was on once more as they headed towards Burgos, the rock upon which Lord Wellington's hopes had foundered the previous year.

It would create no problems this time. The wives and soldiers of the 32nd heard the explosion from many miles away. The French had blown up the fortress, despite having worked all winter to improve its defences. It would claim the lives of no more British soldiers. And still the French army continued its frustrating retreat.

Now Lord Wellington swung north, to the coast, where he took the port of Santander. With the town safely in his hands he no longer had to rely upon supplies being hauled all the way from Portugal. They could be landed here.

The British commander-in-chief had kept the government in London apprised of his intentions and stores began arriving in vast quantities immediately. It was necessary to create a huge supply depot some miles inland. The supplies were vital to Lord Wellington's continuing success and he needed to guard it well. Much to the disgust of the 6th Division, they were ordered to leave the advancing army and mount guard on the stores.

For Cassie and the other wives the new duties came as a welcome relief from the long and arduous marches of recent weeks. The supply depot had been set up in a fertile valley with mountains and forests all around. Fresh food and fuel were plentiful.

Cassie found herself taking care of three men now. In addition to Harry and Sergeant Tonks, she was looking after Richard Kennelly. Convinced that Josefa had sacrificed her own happiness and Richard's for her sake, Cassie felt a responsibility for the young officer.

Her two additional charges were not easy men to care

for. Sergeant Tonks became more and more morose with each passing day, while Richard was a changed man. The men complained that since Josefa had gone, the lieutenant carried out his duties far *too* well. A natural leader in battle, Richard had been inclined to turn a blind eye to minor breaches of army regulations. Now he missed nothing that went on about him, however trivial it might be.

When Gorran Fox spoke to him about the increasing number of punishments he was meting out for minor offences, he received a terse reply. 'If you think it has anything to do with my private life, you're mistaken, sir. It's because of what I witnessed at Rodrigo and Badajos. There was a total breakdown of discipline at both places. I'm sure neither of us wishes to see such a thing happen in our regiment. It won't if the men become used to obeying regulations and orders – to the letter.'

'I appreciate your reasoning, lieutenant, but we're dealing with simple men. Most aren't even aware of the regulations they're breaking. They joined the army to fight the French and they're as frustrated as we are at being kept here, miles from any action.'

'I am aware of that, sir. That's why I'm treating the offences as trivial and not bringing the offenders before you and the colonel.'

For a moment Gorran hoped the unhappy young lieutenant might relax and talk to him as they would once talk when they were ensign and lieutenant. Instead, Richard suddenly stiffened and said, 'Is it your express order that I should overlook certain breaches of discipline committed by the men?'

Gorran shook his head. 'I'll not undermine your authority. You're my lieutenant and I'll support you in your dealings with private or general. All I ask is that you remember one day you'll be calling upon these same soldiers to die for you. They'll do it willingly if they like and respect you – and more often than not they'll need to break a few regulations along the way.'

Later that evening Gorran carried out the rounds to check out the men of his company, stopping at each cooking fire for a brief chat. He ended his rounds tonight at the fire shared by Cassie, Polly Martin and Sarah Harrup.

As they were talking the skirl of bagpipes wailed discordantly from a camp farther along the valley, before breaking into a rendering of a lively reel known as 'Gillespie's Hornpipe'.

'It's the Argylls. They're putting on a concert.' Sarah was on her feet in an instant. 'I'm going to watch. Anyone coming with me?'

All along the valley soldiers and their women were making their way to the camp of the Scots soldiers. A concert put on by the pipers of the 91st Regiment – the Argyll and Sutherland Highlanders – was a popular event. The music they played was capable of reducing their spellbound audience to tears, dreaming of home, wherever it might be. The next moment it would bring them to their feet, toes tapping, eager to join in a lively, whooping reel.

'Come along, Sergeant Tonks. You won't want to miss such a concert. You've always enjoyed them in the past.' Gorran paused in front of the only man still seated.

'I don't feel like any concert.' The sergeant sat blanketed in his misery.

'All the more reason why you should come with the rest of us.' Over the sergeant's head Gorran caught the eye of Harry Clymo.

'Come on, Elijah.' Harry confronted the sergeant. 'I'll need someone to help me keep order.'

Harry helped the sergeant to his feet and they followed on the heels of the others, walking along a darkened valley that was illuminated by a thousand camp fires below and a million stars above.

Gorran and Cassie walked together just behind Harry and Elijah Tonks.

'You've heard nothing from Josefa?' Gorran asked suddenly.

'Nothing. Why do you ask?'

'The effort of trying to shake Elijah Tonks out of his apathy reminded me of Richard Kennelly. He's behaving in a similar fashion, and for much the same reasons. Richard is a good officer, and I'd hoped we might have seen some action by now. It would have given him something else to think about.'

'Where is he now?'

'I don't know. Probably walking alone somewhere along the valley.'

'He's still very much in love with Josefa. The sad fact is that Josefa loves him too. I feel desperately guilty about the whole sad business.'

'You're not to blame, Cassie. The only person to have behaved with abject ignominy is Don Xavier – and we're not absolutely certain of that.'

'Richard asked me yesterday whether I thought Josefa would ever come back to him. I told him if they both loved each other enough everything would come right in the end for them.'

'Do you really believe that?'

'Yes.'

Cassie had an impression that Gorran would have liked to carry the conversation further, but at that moment Jean Martin looked back and saw Cassie as she passed through the light cast by a fire. Slipping free of her mother's hand, the little girl ran back to Cassie. Running in pursuit, Polly remained to chat to Cassie.

The performance of the Highland pipes lasted longer for some than for others. Cassie returned to the 32nd's camp with Polly when Jean fell asleep in her arms and Harry and Enoch accompanied them. Most of the regiment remained in the camp of the Highlanders until the revelry ended in the early hours of the morning. One, at least, was still there in the morning.

Soon after dawn Private Ned Harrup emerged bleary-eyed from his tent and wandered from cooking fire to cooking fire, enquiring whether anyone had seen Sarah that morning. Nobody had. Everyone could remember her dancing with enthusiastic abandon to the music of the pipes, partnering any soldier with the stamina to keep up with her. But no one knew where she had gone after the music had ceased – although everyone thought they could have made a fairly accurate guess.

Sarah Harrup did not return to the camp until the

men had fallen in for drill later that morning. Her appearance provoked much mirth among the men – with the notable exception of her husband. It seemed Sarah had somehow lost her clothes during the night and had been unable to borrow any from the women accompanying the Highland regiment. All she had been able to obtain were a patched and faded uniform jacket and a ragged and threadbare kilt that fell to only just below her knees. Quite unrepentant for her overnight absence, Sarah's first concern was not for her husband, but to obtain an alcoholic drink in an attempt to numb the aches and pains brought about by the excesses of the night.

That evening she and her husband had a violent argument that left Sarah with a bruised and swollen eye – and Ned without a wife. Gathering up her few belongings, Sarah left the camp of the 32nd and took herself off to the tents of the Highlanders.

Two weeks later, by which time Sarah was back with her husband, Gorran Fox's company of the 32nd and a regiment of Portuguese *caçadores* were detailed to escort a convoy of supplies and ammunition to the garrison at Salamanca. The news was welcomed by the soldiers. Thoroughly bored with maintaining a watch over the stores depot, they had hoped to be sent into battle, but returning to the remembered pleasures of Salamanca would make an acceptable alternative.

For one man the journey was to be far more than a diversion. Josefa was in Salamanca and Richard Kennelly determined he would find her. He would make whatever arrangements proved necessary for her mother and Josefa would come back to him. He never doubted that all would be well once he found her and for the first time in months Richard was seen to smile.

To the delight of Cassie, Father Michael was riding with the Portuguese *caçadores*. He had been a regular visitor to the camp fires of the 32nd and Cassie now regarded the cheerful and resourceful friar as a firm friend.

The *caçadores* were returning to Portugal to be disbanded because their term of engagement had expired. Due to gross mismanagement by the Portuguese government the Portuguese troops serving with the British army had not been paid for a year. The situation had recently been eased by the personal intervention of Lord Wellington, who had managed to obtain some money for them. This, coupled with an appeal to their national pride, succeeded in persuading most Portuguese regiments to remain with the army. However, this particular regiment were resentful because they were guarding stores and not fighting the French. They had opted to return home and disband.

The Portuguese soldiers proved troublesome from the outset. The convoy of stores did not move at sufficient speed to suit the Portuguese light infantrymen. The journey from the stores depot to Salamanca would take three weeks. It was far too long for disgruntled men, eager to be home.

Desertions became commonplace after the first few days. The *caçadores* were some of Portugal's finest fighting men, used to marching a greater distance in two hours than the slow-moving ox-carts would achieve in a full day. By the time the convoy was halfway to

Salamanca a man could be home with his wife and family, helping to harvest his crops.

Another major problem was preventing the *caçadores* from stealing and looting. They were issued with the same rations as the men of the 32nd but, unlike their English counterparts, they had no money to buy extra food and wine along the road, with the result that they turned increasingly to theft. The Portuguese and Spanish disliked each other intensely and the thefts were often accompanied by violence. Even in cases where they were not, the Spanish peasants would claim violence had been used.

As the officer commanding the convoy escort, the problem was a constant headache for Captain Fox. By the time the convoy reached the mountains four days from Salamanca, more than a quarter of the *caçadores* had gone their own way, some departing with their weapons, others leaving them behind.

Gorran was riding at the head of the long column with Father Michael and Richard Kennelly when a peasant woman came hobbling down the wooded slope beside the road, one hand lifting her skirt, the other waving for the soldiers to halt. As the woman drew closer she began shouting in a cracked breathless voice and Father Michael translated rapidly.

'She says deserters – Portuguese – are at her house just over the hill. They've beaten her husband into unconsciousness, cleared the house of everything valuable and are now attacking her two daughters!'

'Richard, take half a dozen men with you and find out what's happening.'

'I'll come too,' declared Father Michael.

Calling on Harry Clymo to gather a few men and follow on 'At the double!', Richard spurred his horse up the hill in the direction from which the peasant woman had come and Father Michael rode close behind, his black habit flapping as he rode.

On the ridge Richard pulled his horse to a halt and looked for the peasant woman's home. At first he could see nothing. Then, as Father Michael reined in beside him and as Harry and the men of the 32nd laboured up the slope behind them, he saw a movement in a copse of trees, no more than two hundred paces down the hill.

'There!'

The figure was indistinct among the vegetation beneath the trees – until the undergrowth suddenly parted and a naked woman stumbled into view. Behind her were two uniformed Portuguese soldiers. As Richard and Father Michael watched, one of the soldiers caught up with the fleeing woman and flung her to the ground.

There was a sudden loud report from behind Richard. Turning his head, acrid smoke drifted into his face from the pistol held in the friar's hand.

'Totally useless at this range, of course,' commented the friar as he tucked the pistol inside the cord about his waist. 'But I think it's served our purpose well enough.'

When Richard looked back to the scene below him the naked girl was lying where she had fallen, staring up the hill in the direction of the two horsemen. Behind her the Portuguese soldiers were running back to the shelter of the trees.

Richard drove his horse on down the hill, heading for the small house among the trees. By now Harry and his small party had reached the ridge and they too began running headlong down the slope after their lieutenant and Father Michael.

Richard had passed the naked Spanish woman, still sprawled on the ground, and a few more strides would have brought his horse to the shelter of the trees about the house when two shots rang out within a split second of each other. Fired at point-blank range, they could not miss. Richard felt an agonising pain in his leg and the next minute his horse, the magnificent stallion that had been the pride and joy of Colonel Clausel of the French army, collapsed beneath him.

The 32nd's lieutenant tried to kick his feet clear of the stirrups, but his left leg would not respond. When the horse went down, Richard Kennelly went with it.

Running down the hill behind the two mounted men, Harry saw Richard and his horse brought to the ground. He also saw the men who had fired the shots break from the undergrowth and run along the valley.

'Shoot them!' Harry called to his men as he continued to run towards Richard, still lying trapped beneath the horse which was now writhing in its death throes.

The men called upon by Harry to accompany him were all recent additions to the regiment, straight out from England. None had ever fired his gun at a man and they hesitated uncertainly.

Cursing their inexperience, Harry dropped to one knee, took a quick but careful aim and fired.

One of the fleeing Portuguese soldiers pitched to the

ground and lay still, as though felled by an axe. The other immediately stopped and threw his weapon to the ground.

He left his surrender a moment too long. Harry's shot had sufficed to overcome the soldiers' reluctance to shoot. Three of them fired at the same time and the unarmed Portuguese soldier dropped to the ground.

'Help me raise the horse off the lieutenant, then reload your guns. There are probably more deserters inside the house.'

Richard was gasping with pain, but he tried hard not to cry out loud. A musket ball had shattered his shin bone and the wounded leg was trapped beneath the now dead horse.

As some of the men tried to lift the horse, Harry tried clumsily to pull the young lieutenant clear. It was too soon, and now Richard did cry out in pain, but when he spoke it was not of his wound. 'My horse ... It's the one Josefa gave me ... The one she stole from the French colonel. Will it live?'

'Steady now!' Father Michael was off his own mount and he took a grip of the girth of Richard's horse. 'Lift together – and don't try to pull him out until you're sure the weight's off him. Now ... *heave!*'

The Irish friar's great strength made all the difference that was needed. The body of the horse was raised clear of the ground and Richard was pulled clear, whimpering with pain, in spite of his attempts to stifle the sound.

'Take your soldiers inside the house and leave me to cope with the lieutenant's leg.' Father Michael spoke to

Harry. 'Quickly now. There's another young woman inside and two deserters unaccounted for . . .'

When Harry and the soldiers left them, Father Michael eased Richard's boot off as gently as he could. There was no way it could be achieved without causing pain and by the time it was done each of the wounded lieutenant's breaths expressed his agony.

Father Michael tore the trouser leg up beyond the knee and winced at what he saw.

'Is it bad?' Lying back and perspiring with pain, Richard had seen the friar's fleeting expression.

'I'm afraid so, my son.'

It was worse than bad. Fired from close range, the musket ball had shattered Richard's shin bone and driven leather and cloth inside the wound. The horse's fall had compounded the fracture, leaving splintered bone exposed.

'I'll do what I can for you, but this is a task for a surgeon.'

'Do what you can, Father, then ask Cassie to have a look at it. She's clever with wounds. Will you see if there's anything can be done for the horse?'

'I will,' Father Michael reassured his patient. He knew of Cassie's reputation with wounds, but it would require more than skill to heal Richard's badly injured leg and the horse was beyond all help. Great though Father Michael's faith assuredly was, he had yet to witness his first miracle.

The Dominican friar padded the wound with one of the dressings he carried in his saddle bag, then cutting a sapling to the length of Richard's leg, he tied it so that the leg was immobilised. This would at least save the young lieutenant from too much pain when he was moved.

While Father Michael was carrying out his unhappy task he glanced towards the house and saw Harry and his men dragging two Portuguese soldiers out through the doorway and laying them alongside one another on the pathway.

When Harry came to see how his lieutenant was faring, the friar asked, 'Are they dead? Did you kill them?'

'They're drunk, not dead, and more's the pity. They showed no mercy to the other girl. She's as naked as her sister – and pinned to the dirt floor with a bayonet. Where's the other girl?'

'She went through the pockets of the dead Portuguese, then ran off down the valley wearing his coat. I'd say she didn't trust any of us – and who can blame the poor child? If this is how she's treated by Spain's allies, who knows what she's suffered at the hands of the French?'

'How's Mr Kennelly?' Harry looked to where Richard lay and saw his face contorted with pain. 'I've brought him a bottle of wine I found in the house.'

'Give it to him. Give it all to him. Anything that's likely to numb the pain will be a blessing. What he really needs is to see a surgeon – and quickly.'

'Is there nothing Cassie might do? She's very fond of him.'

Father Michael shook his head. 'I think we must get him back to the wagons and send someone on to Salamanca to find a surgeon.'

Harry nodded. 'I'll leave two men to guard the Portuguese. They can bring them on when they're sober enough to walk. I'm not carrying them. It will do them good to suffer a little.'

At Richard's insistence Cassie examined his leg, but she could only confirm Father Michael's gloomy prognosis. She could do nothing. His wounded leg required the services of a surgeon. When she said as much to him, the wounded man let out a moan of despair. 'Oh no, Cassie! I don't want to lose my leg. I couldn't ask Josefa to tie herself to a one-legged man.'

'Hush now. You haven't lost the leg yet. It might not have to happen, I'm not a surgeon.'

'You know the truth, Cassie, and so do I. I'm trying hard not to believe it, but in our hearts we both know. Well, they say things happen for the best, don't they? It's a good thing Josefa went away and didn't need to see me like this. I'll be no use to anyone now. No use to anyone at all.'

'I don't want to hear such talk, Mr Kennelly. You were promoted because of the courage you showed fighting the French. Now you've got another battle on your hands and you'll win this one too. Now you get that bottle of wine down you. When it's gone I'll make certain there's another for you. That deserter's shot might have killed you but it didn't. Be thankful for that. I've got to go now but I'll be back. When I return I want to hear you sounding more like your old self, do you hear me?'

Pausing before she walked away, Cassie reached down and grasped Richard's hand. Speaking more gently, she said, 'I mean it, Richard. You're going to recover because I'll make sure you do. Now, drink that wine and I'll come back to see you soon.'

Gorran Fox had been standing nearby and as he walked away with Cassie from the wagon where Richard lay, he said, 'You were certainly positive back there, Cassie, but I doubt if any of us here can give him the will to stay alive – and that's what he'll need as much as anything else if he's to survive an amputation.'

'I know. Where will we find the nearest surgeon?'

'Salamanca.'

'That's what I thought. Have you sent a rider to fetch him?'

'Mr Davey's getting ready now.'

Ensign Davey had arrived fresh from England to join the company a few weeks before.

'If you don't mind, I'd like to ask Father Michael to go – and to take me with him. While he finds the surgeon I'll go looking for Josefa. She's his reason for wanting to stay alive.'

33

❦

The two riders reached Salamanca after dark that same night, guided for the last hour by the lights of the town. Cassie wanted to begin her search immediately but Father Michael argued against it, suggesting she should wait until the morning, when she had rested after the long hard ride.

Cassie's argument was that their best lead to Josefa was through Estefanía, her mother, and night-time was when she was usually to be found dancing in the square. Reluctantly accepting the logic of her argument, Father Michael arranged for Cassie to be accommodated at the convent in the heart of the city and for her to be given a meal. While she ate he went off and found a military surgeon willing to ride out to the slow-moving convoy early the next morning.

Cassie thought the meal at the convent would choke her, so anxious was she to begin the search for Josefa.

For the same reason she knew she was a disappointment to the nun who sat with her during the meal and was anxious to air her limited English vocabulary.

It was a great relief when Father Michael came to fetch her. He had spoken to an army surgeon: 'The best in Salamanca – perhaps the best in the whole army.' Surgeon Callaghan was certainly the most highly qualified. He had been sent to Salamanca by Lord Wellington to advise the authorities on the setting up of an operating theatre in the new hospital being built in the city. He had promised to ride out to treat Richard Kennelly at first light.

Once outside the convent, Father Michael said, 'All right, young lady, and where are you going to take me first?'

'To the square where Estefanía dances. She should know where to find her daughter.'

The gipsies were dancing in the square, but Estefanía was nowhere to be seen. After watching the dancing with increasing impatience, Cassie asked her companion to make some inquiries among the dancers.

'Holy Mother!' Father Michael threw up his hands as though scandalised. 'If the news ever gets out that I've been wandering the streets of Salamanca at night in search of a gipsy dancer I'll be spending my remaining years translating musty documents in some remote ecclesiastical library for my sins.'

The first two gipsies to whom Father Michael spoke knew Estefanía but neither knew where she was, although one volunteered the information that she had not danced since the last liberation of the city. Another

411

dancer confirmed this. She was also able to tell them that Estefanía had taken another French lover, a captain this time. She added the information that Estefanía had not allowed this one to escape from her. When he left Salamanca shortly before the British troops arrived, she had gone with him.

'Ask her if Josefa was with her,' pleaded Cassie when Father Michael relayed the dancer's news to her.

Cassie saw the woman's exaggerated shrug and knew they were out of luck before the Spanish-speaking friar translated the woman's words. 'She asks what woman in her right senses would introduce her lover to a grown-up daughter – especially if the daughter is attractive.'

Cassie and Father Michael were walking away from the woman when she called out to them. After another brief conversation, Father Michael turned back to Cassie. 'She's told me where Estefanía was living with the French officer. The owner looked after them. She may know something.'

Cassie's hopes were raised for a while during Father Michael's conversation with the house owner. As the woman spoke her hands clearly described the distended stomach of a pregnant woman, but these hopes were dashed when Father Michael related all that had been said. A young, pregnant girl had visited the house on more than one occasion when the French officer was absent, but Estefanía had never introduced her to the house owner. She had no idea whence the girl had come or where she was now.

However, the woman knew where they might find another woman whose lover had also been a French

officer. It was just possible she might know something . . .

For two hours Cassie and Father Michael followed
one tenuous lead after another, but not one woman knew
any more than had the first. Eventually, Father Michael
called a halt to their fruitless inquiries, protesting that
if they continued any longer they would soon be the
only people left awake in the city. The dancers and musicians had long since ceased their entertainment; cafés
and taverns were closing, and very few house lights
were still burning.

'We've not given up, Cassie,' declared the tired friar
when Cassie expressed her reluctance to discontinue the
search. 'We'll begin again tomorrow with our bodies
and minds refreshed, and God's good light to guide our
footsteps. If we try to carry on for any longer tonight
every lamp in the town will be out and we'll end up
with broken limbs. Go to bed, girl, and say a prayer.
You'll find the Lord's a good listener, and He has all the
answers.'

As Cassie prepared for bed in the convent's tiny guest
cell, her mood was close to despair. She did not know
where to begin her search for Josefa the next morning.
Nevertheless, somewhat self-consciously she went down
on her knees and followed the advice given to her by
Father Michael.

Cassie was woken some time before dawn by a bell
calling the nuns to their early-morning devotions. As
she lay awake a horse galloped out of the town. It was
probably carrying an army messenger with despatches
for Lord Wellington at the front. A horse . . .

413

Suddenly, Cassie sat up in the narrow bed. She believed she knew where she would find Josefa. She should have thought of it before. Almost penniless, her mother gone, cast out by her own people and very close to her time – if the baby had not already been born – Josefa would have sought somewhere dry and warm. A place where little would be expected of her.

Throwing back the blanket, Cassie dressed hurriedly in the dark. Outside, in the dimly lit corridor she literally bumped into the English-speaking nun, apparently late for prayers.

'You are leaving so soon?'

The nun stopped to talk, realising that here she had an excuse for being late that even the strict Mother Superior would accept. 'You go and not say goodbye?'

'I'll be back . . . but I think I know where to find the girl Father Michael and I have been looking for.'

'Father Michael? *Si*. He not go?'

Cassie tried to curb her impatience. 'When he comes . . . When Father Michael comes, tell him I've gone to the stable behind the square. Ask him to come there. To come to the stable, you understand?'

The English-speaking nun concentrated on what had been said. When enlightenment came to her a beatific smile crossed her face. 'Stable . . . horses! Behind square. I tell him. Stable . . . horses . . . behind square. I tell.'

Outside the convent the sky was beginning to lighten. Across the square the dark grey bulk of the cathedral proclaimed its shape against the paler grey of the sky. Early though it was, others were already abroad.

The night-soil collectors called to each other as they

completed their unwholesome task; another army messenger, his despatch less urgent than that carried by his earlier colleague, the gait of his mount less hurried; a watchman, yawning farewell to the night; a young gallant returning home from a *burdel*, whistling softly.

The ostler was awake, too, smelling more like a horse than any of the animals in his care. In the yellow light cast by an oil lamp he was brushing down a horse required soon after dawn.

Cassie's unexpected arrival startled the simple old man and he said something to her in an accent she would have been hard put to understand had she been Spanish. When Cassie made no response the stable man turned his back and resumed his grooming. She asked if he knew anything of Josefa, but the ostler seemed not to understand and did not bother to reply. Frustrated, Cassie believed she would need to wait for Father Michael to arrive, but decided to have one last attempt to communicate with this man.

Tugging at the sleeve of the ostler's shirt, Cassie said, 'Josefa? Do you know where I can find her? *Josefa?*'

The stableman hesitated a little too long before shaking his head.

'Listen to me. I'm Josefa's friend . . . Josefa . . . *amigo!*' It was one of the few Spanish words Cassie knew, and once again the stableman hesitated.

'She's here somewhere, isn't she? Where?'

Cassie put a foot on the ladder leading up to the darkness of the hayloft. 'Up here? Is Josefa up here?'

To Cassie's great joy the simple old man nodded and

immediately poured out a torrent of unintelligible Spanish.

'Give me the lamp.'

Reminded yet again that he did not understand her, Cassie walked across the stable and lifted the lamp. The stableman protested and moved to take it back again, but Cassie swung it out of his reach. 'I'm sure you know where another is kept. Go and find it, I need this one.' Cassie's words conveyed nothing to the old man, but her meaning was quite clear and he shuffled away, grumbling incoherently.

She climbed the ladder to the hay-filled loft and held the lantern high to look about her. There was hay up here, strewn all about, but in insufficient quantity to conceal anyone. Then she saw a part of the loft was partitioned off, with a flimsy door giving access to the unseen section.

Opening the door and stepping inside, Cassie found herself in a junk room, with saddles lying in untidy piles on the floor and bridles, harness and the tack of generations gathering dust on wooden pegs around the room. There were blankets here too and suddenly Cassie detected a faint movement from a mixed pile of hay and ragged blankets in the shadows of a far corner. Moving cautiously forward, she held the lantern above the blankets. It was evident someone lay beneath them.

'Josefa, is that you?' Cassie put the question quietly and apprehensively. She had no wish to find herself alone in the loft room with one of the ostler's friends.

The blankets moved feebly, then a face emerged. *It was Josefa!*

But this was not the bright, clean and vivacious young gipsy girl who had won the hearts of all who saw her. Josefa's face was gaunt, with great dark rings about her eyes and her face was streaked with dirt and blood.

'Josefa, it's me. Cassie. You look dreadful. What's wrong with you?'

Cassie dropped to her knees beside the other girl. Putting the lamp on the dusty floor she would have hugged her friend, but Josefa somehow found the strength to raise an arm to ward her off.

'Careful . . . I am not alone.'

Cassie froze, momentarily taken aback by Josefa's words. Then, as understanding came, her shock changed to awe. 'You mean . . . the baby?'

'Yes. You know?'

'I guessed . . . but let me see it.'

Pulling back the blanket, Cassie saw a tiny, wrinkled baby lying beside Josefa. It was naked and covered with blood, as was the blanket around it.

'When was it born?' Cassie asked the question sharply, shocked by what she saw.

'Last night . . . I think.'

'And you were alone here? Oh my God, Josefa! What's happened to you? Why have you allowed yourself to come to this? No, don't try to answer. Let's try and sort you out first.'

Pulling the filthy blanket from mother and child, Cassie grimaced. 'We'll need to clean you both up – and get rid of some of these blankets.'

For a moment Cassie came close to panic. Someone

should have attended to Josefa at the time of the birth. A doctor should be called ...

Cassie pulled herself together. Mother and child had survived the birth. The worst part of their ordeal was over. Behind Cassie the door opened and the ostler stood in the doorway, a second lantern in his hand. As he stared at the scene in the corner of the room where Josefa lay, his mouth dropped open foolishly.

'Don't stand there like an idiot. Go and fetch some water ... *Agua*.' Cassie dredged up another word from her very limited Spanish vocabulary. 'You hear me? *Agua*. Go and fetch some.'

Josefa murmured something in a tired voice from the makeshift bed and the stableman wandered away, shaking his head and talking to himself.

'Couldn't you have sent him to get help when the baby started, Josefa? You might have died – you and your baby.'

'Carlos gets so drunk every night an earthquake wouldn't rouse him. Besides, I do not care whether I live or die. As for the baby ... I meant to kill it ... but I could not do it. Tell me, is it a boy or a girl?'

Cassie realised that during all the time she had been in the stable loft Josefa had not once turned her head to look at her new-born child.

'You don't know?' Cassie leaned over the baby, which was beginning to stir weakly. 'It's a boy ...' Suddenly a feeling of great joy swept over her.

'Josefa, I think I know why you ran away. You knew you were having a baby and feared its father might be Don Xavier. Am I right?'

'How do you know? Richard?'

'Richard knows nothing.' As she remembered her reason for coming to Salamanca, much of Cassie's joy ebbed away, but now was not the moment to talk of Richard Kennelly's injury. 'I've felt guilty ever since I realised what you did in order to rescue me and Polly.'

'No one need have known had it not been for the baby. It would have been my secret alone. Because of it I would have loved Richard all the more. But I did not know who was the baby's father. I will never know.'

'That isn't true. It's definitely Richard's baby. There can be no doubt about it. Look at him, Josefa. *Look at Richard's baby!*'

Cassie held up the lantern and Josefa turned her head slowly, as though frightened of what she would see. Then she gasped and looked up at Cassie, her whole being suddenly alive once more.

'His hair! It's red . . . like Richard's. It is his son. It is . . .'

By the time Father Michael arrived at the stables Josefa and her baby were fit to greet the world together. Both had been cleaned up and Josefa had dressed and was seated on the cleanest of the blankets, feeding her baby.

'Well now, isn't this a beautiful sight for a man of God to be seeing!' exclaimed the black-robed friar. 'A mother and baby in a stable and me visiting like one of the three wise men. Unfortunately I come bearing no gifts – only the news that the surgeon was on his way before the sun was awake. He'll be up with the convoy by late morning and will have young Richard sorted out in no time at all, I'm sure.'

Cassie had still not told Josefa of Richard's injury and as the Spanish girl looked aghast from Cassie to the friar the blood drained from her cheeks and Father Michael realised he had said too much.

'What's wrong with Richard? What's happened?'

'I seem to have let my tongue run ahead of my common sense. I'm sorry ... but don't you worry, my dear. Richard is going to be all right once his leg has been tended.'

'His leg?' Josefa's body sagged with relief. 'I feared it might be something serious. How did it happen? Where is he?'

'He'll be little more than a day's ride away now ... but the injury is serious.' Cassie tried to think of some way to soften the blow but Josefa needed to be told. 'He was shot by a Portuguese deserter. His horse was killed at the same time. It rolled onto him. Richard is probably going to lose a leg.'

'*No!* It mustn't happen to Richard. What will he do?' Josefa could not control her tears as she turned to Cassie. 'Do you think he'd want to see me after what I've done? I want to go to him, Cassie. I want to be with him.'

'Father Michael and I came to Salamanca to find you, Josefa. To take you back to Richard. We're afraid that without you he doesn't have the will to live. If you go to him and show him his son he'll realise he has everything to live for. With any luck the convoy will reach Salamanca in a couple of days' time. You'll be almost your old self by then, once you're out of this place.'

'I'll go to him today. I won't be able to ride, but I can walk. Richard will have his son in his arms before the sun sets today.'

Josefa kept her word. With the baby in her arms she walked doggedly all day, resting only when it was necessary to feed her young son. Some time during the middle of the morning a messenger came past, heading for the supply convoy, and Cassie sent word to Richard that Josefa was on her way.

The messenger arrived only minutes before the army surgeon amputated the young lieutenant's leg below the knee, but the thought that he was to see Josefa once more pulled Richard through the red haze of pain that accompanied the operation. It sustained him until he passed the point in the operation where so many men would have succumbed and died.

When Josefa placed his son in his arms, some of the pain and exhaustion left his face and wonder took their place. In that moment, those who watched knew Richard was going to recover.

Josefa travelled to Salamanca in the wagon carrying Richard and as the young couple shared the first days of their young son's life they worked out their future together. Richard accepted without question the story that Josefa had been frightened to tell him about the baby. She, in her turn, was able to convince him that the loss of his leg did not signal the end of life for him – or for them. Less certain was how Richard would earn a living for the three of them with only one leg, but he was determined that Josefa would not escape from him again.

Gorran Fox's company remained in Salamanca for a full week. The day before they left, Richard Kennelly and Josefa were married in the great cathedral with Father Michael officiating. The bride was given away by Harry Clymo with Cassie as her attendant. Gorran performed the duty of best man to the groom, who stood at the altar balancing on a crutch and occasionally resting on Josefa for support.

The wedding of the young gipsy girl and the British soldier, wounded while rescuing a Spanish girl, captured the hearts of the town and the mayor organised a reception in the square. The dancing and the celebrations continued in the streets of Salamanca all night and money and presents were showered on the young couple.

When the regiment marched off the next day they left Father Michael behind with Richard, his bride and their son. Father Michael intended continuing his journey to Lisbon with the remnants of the *caçadore* regiment, but he promised he would rejoin Wellington's army at a later date.

Richard remained in the military hospital with Josefa and their son to keep him company. The crippled lieutenant's service with his regiment was over, but the generosity of the people of Salamanca ensured he would not go hungry while he awaited repatriation.

34

❦

When Gorran Fox's company rejoined the regiment the men learned that their brief period of inactivity was over. The main British army had fought and won a major battle on the plains of Vittoria. It was a great victory for the British and their allies, but casualties had once again been very heavy. Lord Wellington urgently required more men if he was to press home his advantage.

The 32nd set off for Vittoria eager to do battle, but one of the wives of the regiment had more than war on her mind. On the first night stop, as Cassie was dishing out the evening meal for Harry and Sergeant Tonks, Sarah Harrup, sporting a black eye acquired only that day, intercepted the sergeant's plate.

'I'll give it to him, Cassie. I've a little something special for him, poor soul. New-baked bread, fresh today.'

'You have bread enough for Ned *and* Elijah?' Newly baked bread was a luxury rarely seen by men on the march.

'Ned's off playing cards with some of his friends. He can find his own bread – his own meals too if he's not careful.' Pointing to her bruised eye, she added, 'I got this because I wouldn't hand over money for his last night's losses. I'll take a beating as my due when I've been off with another man, but I'll not suffer because a man can't play cards.'

Setting down Sergeant Tonks's plate, Sarah reached inside her shawl and pulled out a large hunk of bread. Breaking it in two she handed a portion to Cassie. 'Here, give this to Harry. He'll need to have his strength built up before the regiment goes into battle again. There are so many new soldiers in the regiment all the fighting will be left to the sergeants and corporals.'

There would be plenty of time to build up Harry Clymo for battle and the newest of the recruits would be able to familiarise themselves with the ways of the regiment before becoming embroiled in warfare. Lord Wellington had driven the French forces the full length of Spain, from the Portuguese borders to the portals of France. He was blockading San Sebastian and investing Pamplona. It was time to draw breath before plunging into France.

The 32nd reached Vittoria in the third week of June, but not until mid-July did they move forward to San Esteva, twenty miles from the French border. Here the recruits saw their first hostile Frenchmen and came under musket fire. Half afraid and greatly excited, they returned the fire.

Watching the untried soldiers set off for picket duty led by a fresh-faced, excited young ensign, Cassie remembered the time when she was a new wife, Harry a young untried recruit, and Richard Kennelly the eager yet unsure ensign. It all seemed a lifetime ago. Now Harry was a battle-hardened corporal and poor Richard Kennelly, minus a leg, had been invalided from the regiment. Gorran Fox too had progressed from a young lieutenant to the captain in charge of the company. So much had happened – and yet Cassie was still only eighteen years old!

Sarah Harrup had not changed during this time. Recently she had taken on the task of preparing Sergeant Tonks's meals, usually managing to find something more for his plate than she served up to her husband. The regiment's wives were laying wagers on when Sarah would get the widower-sergeant beneath a blanket. Some were convinced she already had.

Cassie believed they would all be proved wrong. She had seen signs that Elijah Tonks was beginning to recover from the deep shock caused by the tragic death of his wife. Not that she thought this would make any difference to his course of action. She believed that with only half his wits about him Sergeant Tonks would have the sense to decline all that Sarah was offering him so blatantly. Cassie also realised Sarah was using Elijah Tonks as an unwitting protector. If Ned Harrup believed the sergeant was taking an interest in Sarah he might think twice about giving her a beating.

Gorran Fox was of the same opinion when he stopped to speak to Cassie and Harry one evening during his rounds of the company's camp. This was a routine that Cassie had come to look forward to each evening.

'All I hope is that Elijah Tonks will have the sense

not to take Sarah too seriously,' said the company commander. 'The loss of Rose has hit him very hard. From the days when I was a young ensign – even younger than poor Richard Kennelly – Rose and Elijah were a team. A great team. The regiment is certainly poorer for her death and I'm concerned that the loss might have affected Elijah Tonks's judgement.'

'You don't need to worry yourself about Sergeant Tonks, sir. He's going to be all right.'

Gorran looked at Harry in some surprise. Harry was regarded by the officers as a steady and deep-thinking young man who preferred to keep his thoughts and opinions to himself. He was rarely inclined to express an opinion to an officer.

'I'm very pleased to hear it, Harry, but do you have any particular reason for such a belief?'

'I'm probably as close to Sergeant Tonks as any man in the regiment and it hurt me to see how low he sunk after Rose was killed. He's always been such a good sergeant I don't think he could be anything else, not even if he tried. Although after Rose was killed he didn't seem to care about soldiering. He didn't even care about himself very much. But just lately he's been taking an interest in things again. Almost as though he's waking up from a deep sleep.'

'I'm pleased to hear you say that, Harry. It sets my mind at rest. Do you also think I needn't worry about Sarah whatever-her-name-is-now, getting her hooks into him?'

'I do, although I believe there's a lot more to her scheming than you think. Sarah Harrup sees Sergeant

Tonks as far more than a protector. You see, if he takes a fancy to her then she's got someone to turn to if anything happens to Ned Harrup – and Sarah seems to have some sixth sense about such matters, or so the men think. On the other hand, if nothing happens to Ned then she hopes Sergeant Tonks might recommend him for a corporal's stripes when promotion comes round again. She's a scheming woman, sir, but I don't think she'll fool Sergeant Tonks. He's known Sarah for far too long.'

'I'm relieved to have your views, Harry, and Sarah certainly hasn't fooled you! However, if she wants her husband to be considered for promotion she's going to have to make him work a lot harder than he does at the moment.'

As Cassie handed around the tea she had just made, Gorran asked, 'How about you, Cassie, do you agree with Harry?'

Pleased at the manner in which Harry had expressed his opinion to Gorran, Cassie said, 'I do. Sarah's nothing if not devious. It's such a pity really because she's big-hearted, in spite of all her faults.'

'I agree she seems to have no difficulty finding a new husband when the occasion arises,' conceded Gorran. 'She's been married more times than any other woman with the regiment – possibly more than any woman with the whole army. But I'll not have her stirring up trouble between the men and the non-commissioned officers. Keep me informed of anything you think I ought to know, Harry.'

The talk around the camp fire turned to Cornwall and Cassie's family. Gorran was pleased when Cassie told him she had written to them. He left after expressing the view that the war would probably not last too long and then Cassie would be able to return to Cornwall with Harry and set her parents' minds at ease once and for all.

Later that night Cassie lay awake long after the snores about her indicated that the other occupants of the shared tent slept. She thought Harry was asleep too, until he whispered, 'What's the matter, Cassie? Why aren't you sleeping?'

'I'm thinking of what Captain Fox was saying to us tonight.'

'About Sarah?'

'I wouldn't lose any sleep about her. No, I'm thinking about the war ending and the regiment going home. What are we going to do then?'

'I'll stay in the army. Make it to sergeant, or even sergeant major if I'm lucky. There's nothing for me outside the army, Cassie. I couldn't go back to working on a farm again.'

Thinking of the life Harry had led before becoming a soldier, Cassie hugged him sympathetically. 'Of course you couldn't. I wouldn't expect you to. You've done well in the army, Harry, and you're a well-respected man. Even Gorran Fox listened to what you had to say this evening. I was proud of you.'

'What about you, Cassie? How would you fancy being the wife of a sergeant major? Do you think you could follow the regiment for most of your life?'

'That's partly what's been keeping me awake, Harry. I know I could follow *you*, for as long as you're in the army, but I'd like to do more than just plod along in the mud behind the regiment, waiting for nightfall to come so I can rush up and cook a meal for you. I want to do more.'

'What sort of "more"?' There was the faintest hint of wariness in Harry's question. Cassie could be very strong-minded when she decided to do something. He did not want to find he had agreed to anything he might regret later.

'I don't know . . .' Cassie did know, but she was uncertain what to do about it, or where to begin. 'I . . . I wish there was something that could be done to help the men who are wounded in battle. Those so badly hurt they can't take themselves off to find a surgeon who's not too busy to deal with them.'

'You should have a word with Lady Fraser. I heard some of the officers saying that she's trying to do the same. It seems she was with her husband, Major-General Sir William Fraser, at the battle of Vittoria. There were a lot of wounded there on both sides, and more than the usual number of camp followers robbing the dead – ours as well as the French. Many of those who were still alive were killed by the wagon-drivers and their women.'

'That's the sort of thing I mean. We should be able to stop it, Harry. If there were men specially detailed to find the wounded and take them to a hospital so they could have help quickly, such things wouldn't happen. It would mean a lot more wounded men than now would survive.'

'Possibly, but what sort of men would carry out such duties?'

'I don't know, but I've thought for a long time that

429

something ought to be done. I'd hate to think of you lying wounded after a battle if I wasn't able to find you right away.'

Harry felt her shudder beside him and he said quickly, 'Don't think of such things, Cassie. I don't.'

For a few minutes they both clung to each other until Harry said softly, 'There's one thing I *do* know, Cassie. I don't have to worry what will happen to you if I get killed. I reckon Captain Fox would take good care of you.'

'What do you mean?' Cassie spoke far more loudly than she had intended and a nearby soldier stirred and grumbled sleepily. 'What do you mean?' she repeated, much more quietly this time.

'I mean that Captain Fox is especially fond of you, Cassie. I don't mean that in any nasty way. I know you far too well, and Captain Fox is too much of a gentleman to have ideas about another man's wife. I just mean . . . well, you travelled up from Cornwall to Horsham with him – and fixed his arm when he was hurt – and again when he was wounded. It makes you . . . just a bit *special* for him. I'm pleased about it, Cassie, truly I am. Captain Fox is a good officer and a man to rely on. I'm happy to know he'd take good care of you.'

Cassie was deeply moved by Harry's words and she pulled him in closer to her. 'You're a good man too, Harry – and nothing's going to happen to you, so you go to sleep now. There'll be a lot more marching to do tomorrow, and it might just turn out to be the day the French decide to do battle with us.'

430

35

❦

Cassie's late-night words to Harry proved prophetic. The French commander, smarting under the ignominy of being driven the whole length of Spain by Lord Wellington, decided, more in desperation than hope, to strike back. Mustering his army on the French side of the Pyrenees, he launched a counter-attack through the mountain passes in such strength that the British troops were taken by surprise.

Lord Wellington had many of his troops investing San Sebastian, others surrounded Pamplona. His lines were over-extended. Fearing the French would cut through them and swing around to annihilate whichever half they considered to be the weaker, he ordered a hasty retreat while he gauged the enemy's strength.

The British army fought a bitter rearguard action through the mountain passes, and was forced to leave its wounded men to the uncertain mercy of French soldiers, Spanish peasants, and the more predictable ferocity of Pyrenean wolves. When word reached Cassie of the fate of the wounded soldiers it added emphasis to her declared views on the need for a reliable system to tackle the problem of men wounded in battle.

The 32nd and the other regiments attached to the 6th Division were rushed to the front in a bid to head off the French army's advance along the road to Pamplona. By the time they reached the battle area the French advance had already been checked by the tenacious actions of the 4th Division and the arrival of the 6th put the outcome beyond doubt.

Nevertheless, the French army was not prepared to accept that its advance was over and its soldiers fought hard. The 32nd had just forced back a company of French skirmishers, the much vaunted *voltigeurs*, when suddenly a squadron of French cavalry bore down upon them.

The horsemen drove right through Captain Fox's company, cutting down many men in their path. Sergeant Tonks and Harry were quick to react and by the time the French *cuirassiers* turned and regrouped for a second charge, the 32nd were forming a square with muskets primed and aimed at the enemy.

A number of men had fallen wounded and could not reach the square. One was Enoch Martin. Behind the men the women watched in horror as he climbed to his feet unsteadily. With a hand clutched to his stomach and half doubled over he stumbled towards the safety of the square, only to be charged down and trampled on by the horse of a straggling *cuirassier*.

Beside Cassie, Polly Martin let out a scream. Abandoning her young daughter she began to run towards her fallen husband. She had covered only half the distance to him when the French cavalry began its return charge.

When Polly reached her husband and crouched over him the *cuirassiers* were no more than twenty horse-lengths away. One cavalry man clearly had either Enoch or Polly singled out as his target and he leaned low in the saddle, the point of his sword aimed at them.

Before he reached them a single shot rang out from the square. Fired by Harry, it was barely audible above the terrifying pounding of heavy hooves. The French *cuirassier* sagged in the saddle, the sword slipped from his grasp and he crashed to the ground no more than the length of a horse's stride beyond his intended victims.

Crouched protectively over Enoch, Polly looked up as a second line of horsemen bore down upon her. She watched in horror as yet another cavalryman selected her as his target and lowered his sword to strike her as he passed by. There was nothing she could do to avoid the sword thrust now. The soldiers of the 32nd Regiment were firing again, but their targets were all in the leading line of charging cavalry.

When the horseman was no more than a horse's length from Polly the point of the sword was raised abruptly. The terrified woman saw the grin on the *cuirassier*'s face, above the scarred and dented breast-plate he was wearing.

It was the *cuirassiers'* last charge that day. No match

for a square of well-disciplined infantrymen, they swept on towards a pass that would take them back through the Pyrenees, pursued by round shot from a battery of artillery, eager to have a part in the action.

Cassie ran across the battlefield to where Polly knelt beside her badly wounded husband. The hand Enoch clutched to his stomach was stained red with his own blood. Polly gently moved her husband's hand and eased up his jacket. As the clothing cleared his waistband both women gasped in horror. Enoch had received a sword slash across his stomach which laid his entrails bare. Only his hand prevented them from spilling out on the ground.

'We must get a surgeon, Cassie . . . Where can we find a surgeon?' The usually calm Polly was close to panic.

'There'll be one at the rear of the division, but we can't move Enoch while he's like this. It will kill him.' Cassie thought Enoch would probably die anyway, but she would not say so to Polly.

'Wait with him – and try to keep him from moving.'

Lifting her skirts high, Cassie ran back to where she had left her donkey. When she reached the animal she began rummaging through one of the saddle-bags.

'How is he?' The question was put to Cassie by the woman who held Jean Martin in her arms. One of the newly-arrived wives, this was her first experience of action and her face was as white as a flag of truce.

'Bad. Can you keep Jean with you for an hour or two? Polly will want to be with Enoch.'

The young wife nodded. 'I'll keep her for as long as need be.'

434

Cassie found what she was looking for and hurried with it to the scene of the skirmish.

The 32nd's defensive square had broken up now the French cavalry had ridden out of sight. Soldiers and wives were searching among the dead and wounded, and those still living were being carried from the field towards a temporary hospital being set up by the regimental surgeons in a barn, a half-mile away.

A group of soldiers had gathered about Polly and Enoch. They wanted to move the wounded man and take him to the hospital too, but Polly would not allow them to touch him.

'Out of the way! Let me through.' Cassie wasted no time on niceties. If a man did not move fast enough she pushed him aside. When she reached the wounded man she said, 'If you want to be helpful perhaps someone will find me some water.'

As she spoke Cassie was unrolling a canvas bundle and laying it out upon the ground. Inside were needles, threads and buttons, together with other items that went to make up a 'soldier's friend', the sewing kit with which Cassie did her best to repair the uniforms of Harry and his colleagues. The regiment was long overdue for an issue of new uniforms and Cassie was never short of work – but she had a very different task in mind today.

'You're not going to try to stitch Enoch up with that?' Polly looked at Cassie in wide-eyed disbelief.

'Can you think of any other way to get him and his stomach to a surgeon? If we move him as he is we'll lose half of him on the ground at the first jolting – then if a surgeon can't see him for an hour or two he'll bleed to death, same as he will if he's left here. Look at the sky over the mountains. There's a huge storm building up. Would you fancy moving him as he is in that? If I stitch him up he'll at least have *some* chance. Why, I saw one of the Highland officers stitching himself up after Badajos.'

Cassie thought it best not to add that the Highland officer had died soon after his painful attempt at self-surgery.

Enoch's wound was ugly and dangerous, but it was a clean, straight cut and stitching it posed no particular difficulty once Cassie overcame her initial revulsion for the task. As she plunged the needle into Enoch's flesh for the first stitch there was a gasp of sympathy for Enoch from the surrounding soldiers. Many turned away, unable to watch any more. Others remained to watch the whole operation, filled with either a morbid curiosity, or admiration for Cassie.

Enoch remained conscious during the whole, unorthodox operation. Apart from an initial murmur of pain, he made no sound.

When she had done, the wounded soldier closed his eyes with relief and whispered, 'Bless you, Cassie. If I live I'll owe it to you.'

'What do you mean, *if* you live? You're one of the toughest men I know, Enoch Martin. You'll live to see your daughter wed – and your grandchildren too, I don't doubt.'

Turning away, Cassie felt drained of all energy, but she said to the watching men, 'If you can find something on which to carry Enoch carefully you can take

436

him off to the surgeon now. Go with him, Polly – and make sure Enoch's not jolted. I'll make certain Jean's taken care of until you come back.'

Harry was one of those who had been watching Cassie at work and he put an arm about her shoulders and led her away just as the first spots of rain from the approaching storm were felt.

'That was a wonderful thing you did there, Cassie. Brave, too. I'd no more have dared try to stitch someone together like that than try to fly.'

'Something had to be done or Enoch would have died before our eyes. It's what I said to you only last night, Harry. It ought to be someone's *duty* to go and find wounded men after a battle and do what they can for them straight away. Not to cart a man off and hope he'll still be alive by the time an overworked surgeon can spare a moment to look at him.'

'I've always thought it foolishness to talk of such things, Cassie, but after seeing what you did today I admit I've been wrong. If the men had carried Enoch off as they wanted to he'd have been dead by now. I'll have a word with Captain Fox and see if he'll mention your ideas to Lady Fraser.'

Cassie leaned against Harry gratefully. 'You're a good man, Harry Clymo – but I hope the sutler has some brandy left. If I don't have something soon I'll begin thinking of what I just did and I won't stop shaking for a week. Now we'd better begin running or we're going to get soaked.'

The storm was one of the worst Cassie had witnessed in the mountains. Streams became rivers, rivers flooded

437

the surrounding countryside and at the storm's height angry lightning ripped the pall of dark cloud to shreds. The storm took the retreating French cavalrymen by surprise and a quarter of their number was lost attempting to ford a once-shallow river.

Three hours after it began, it was as though the storm had never happened. A hot sun blazed from a clear blue sky, birds sang, peasants worked happily in the fields, and the soldiers of the 32nd Regiment of infantry buried their dead.

The following day the regiment moved off to take up a position close to the French border. Before it set off, a very tired Polly came to retrieve her young daughter from Cassie. Enoch was still alive, but the surgeon was not optimistic about his chances of survival. However, he had not undone Cassie's handiwork, admitting he could probably do no better.

Cassie felt very depressed after Polly's departure. The two young women had been friends for a long time – ever since Cassie's first day with the regiment. Now she had lost three friends within the space of a few months. The mood was hard to shake off, even when the regiment moved to an attractive village high in the Pyrenees and she and Harry were given a snug billet in a cottage occupied by a woman who was convinced they both needed feeding up.

When Father Michael rejoined the 6th Division he brought news that left Cassie feeling happier than she had for many months. The Dominican friar had called in at the military hospital at Pamplona. Here he had found Enoch Martin. The big soldier was now well enough to sit up in bed and chat to Father Michael about his wound and of Cassie's part in saving his life. In another couple of weeks the family would be travelling to Santander to take passage to England in a transport ship. Enoch would recover from his wound but would never be fit enough to return to the rigours of campaigning. His army days were over. It was sad news for the wounded soldier, but Polly had confessed to Father Michael that she was secretly relieved. When she had first seen Enoch's wound she believed her husband to be a dying man. She could not face such anguish again.

Through Father Michael, Polly sent her heartfelt thanks to Cassie, together with an address where she could be found when Cassie returned to England. It was a very happy end to Cassie's first serious attempt at the surgeon's art.

But Father Michael was the bearer of even more good news. A man of considerable charm and personality, he had made many friends during his years in Portugal. One was Senhor Vicente Ferreira, possibly Portugal's most influential wine exporter. During dinner at his friend's house in Oporto, Father Michael had told his host the story of Richard Kennelly and his young wife, Josefa. When the friar mentioned Richard's noble background, the wine exporter took a great interest.

'This young man – an earl's son, you say? Does he speak any Portuguese, or Spanish?'

Father Michael confirmed that Richard had a good command of Spanish, and it was improving every day under his young wife's tuition.

'There is perhaps an important place for this young aristocrat on his father's estates in Ireland?'

Father Michael explained that as a younger son in a very large family, Richard Kennelly could have no expectation of the family lands providing a living for him and Josefa.

'Excellent! Tell this young man to come and see me. I need someone with a good British background to work in my export department and eventually take much of the responsibility from me. As you know, Father, my only son was killed by the French. A young man, a gallant young man of breeding, who has lost a leg fighting my son's killers can be assured of my help and support. I look forward to meeting his wife, too. Stole the horse of a French colonel in order to make her escape while on a spying mission for Lord Wellington, you say? Yes, she too can be assured of a welcome in my house!'

Father Michael related the story to Cassie, adding that he had stopped at Salamanca on his way to the front. He had been in time to speak to Richard and the young lieutenant was already on his way to Oporto with Josefa and their young child.

'The situation is as good as Richard's already,' added the Dominican friar. 'I called in to Lord Wellington's headquarters too, and caught the great man in a benevolent mood. At my request he wrote a letter to Senhor Ferreira, recommending Richard as one of the most promising young officers in the British army. One who would have become an aide had he not been wounded so tragically.'

'I'm very happy for both Richard and Josefa,' declared

Cassie joyfully. 'They both deserve all the happiness they can find.'

'Talking of the pursuit of happiness, on my way in here I saw the woman who was supposed to be taking care of you when you were lying ill at Figueira – Sarah, was that her name? She was plying one of your sergeants with drink. Is she widowed yet again?'

Cassie shook her head. 'No, but Sarah doesn't allow a husband to stand in her way when she takes a fancy to a man. She's set her bonnet at Sergeant Tonks. I'm sure he has more sense than to carry on with her, but it worries me sometimes when I see the way she plays up to him. He lost his wife not long ago and hasn't been the same man since.'

'I see.' Father Michael hid a smile as he remembered how a hive of bees had successfully put a stop to Sarah's amorous activities once before, at Figueira. 'If you think I can be of help in some way, just let me know.'

Father Michael's intervention between Sergeant Elijah Tonks and Sarah was not required. A week after the friar's return, the regiment was once more on the move, passing through mountainous country in the Pyrenees, heading towards the north-east corner of Spain, where the French retained their last tiny, fingertip hold on the country. The terrain through which the regiment marched was so rugged that tents were impracticable. They had been sent on by a more circuitous route, avoiding the most difficult sections of the march.

Gorran Fox had been placed in temporary command of the 32nd's Light Company and had taken Harry with

441

him. Ranging far ahead of the regiment the Light Company's task was to sweep any small pockets of French resistance from the 6th Division's path and ensure the division was not surprised by any larger units of the French army.

The nature of such duties meant that wives could not travel with their husbands. As a result, Cassie had very little to do. Feeling tired this particular evening she made up her blanket-bed close to the cooking fire and turned in much earlier than usual.

All the other women and men who shared the same cooking fire had gone off to help the sergeant of another company and his wife celebrate the birth of a son, born that morning on a rain-swept mountainside during a half-hour halt in the march. The celebrating father had persuaded a piper from the Argyll and Sutherland Highlanders to play for them and the music and rowdy singing echoed around the slopes of the high mountains.

Lying in a pleasantly drowsy state beneath her blanket, Cassie was glad she was not at the party and she felt sympathy for the sergeant's wife. Having a child on a campaign was a primitive, degrading affair: a public spectacle witnessed by all who could obtain a view of the proceedings. Wives, camp followers and pipe-smoking soldiers, all treating the event as a social occasion.

It remained a mystery to Cassie why she had not fallen pregnant again and she sometimes felt the loss of her unborn child keenly. She longed to have a child of her own, but whenever she witnessed a birth during the campaign she realised how lucky she was.

When low voices penetrated Cassie's drowsiness she thought she must have been asleep and had been wakened by the return of the soldiers and wives of the 32nd to their own bivouac area. Then she realised that there were only two voices and they belonged to Sarah Harrup and Sergeant Elijah Tonks.

Sarah was saying something, but Cassie could not catch the words. Then Elijah Tonks replied, 'You didn't have to leave the party. I'm quite capable of finding my own way back to a camp fire.'

'Don't I know that as well as anyone, Elijah? I dread to think what would have happened to this regiment sometimes without you to guide it. I just came along to keep you company. I don't like to see you on your own while others are having fun. A man like you deserves far more from life.'

'I'm not complaining.'

'Of course you're not. You've never been a man to complain, Elijah. Not even when life's treated you ill. I've always admired you for it. There's a man I'd willingly do anything for, I've said to myself. Of course, I wouldn't want to embarrass you by repeating it to anyone else, but it's the truth, Elijah. There's nothing at all I wouldn't do for you.'

'What you're really saying is you're quite ready to share a bed with me.'

Beneath her own blanket Cassie held her breath for fear she might miss Sarah's reply.

'If that's what you want, Elijah. We can do it now, if you like, while there's no one else around. I doubt if there'll be too many opportunities like this.'

'What about your husband? What would Ned say?'

'Ned Harrup? He wouldn't say a word. Not to you, he wouldn't. No, nor knock me about, neither, for fear of what you might do to him. Ned's not much of a man in any sense of the word when you really get down to it. But what are we talking about him for? Where do you want me, Elijah? Under your blanket? As it's the first time between us perhaps you'd rather we went a little way off, away from the firelight.'

'I don't want you *anywhere*, Sarah Harrup. Not tonight, nor any other night. My Rose was right when she said you were the "kiss of death" to any soldier you got your claws into. This regiment would be better off without you.'

'Your Rose didn't like me because she was jealous of the way men run after me – but she's gone and I'm still here, Elijah. You can't live feeding off a memory – I should know.'

'My memories of Rose are more precious than ten women like you, Sarah, and they'll keep me warmer of a night than you ever could.'

'I doubt it, Elijah Tonks. I doubt it *very* much.'

'Doubt all you wish. I don't expect you to understand – and you have my pity because you never will understand. You'll go on giving your body to any man who wants it because it means nothing to you. Sooner or later every man who takes it realises the truth. Then he discovers you have nothing else to offer him. Go back to your husband, Sarah. Go back to Ned Harrup and try to convince him you're not a whore. It shouldn't be too hard, the damn fool almost believes it already.'

'Please yourself!' Sarah shrugged indifferently to hide her disappointment. 'I'll not stay here to be insulted by a bitter old has-been – and I need no man's pity. I felt sorry for you, that's all it was. It won't happen again. You can die of loneliness for all I care.'

As Sarah flounced off into the darkness Cassie could hear Elijah Tonks sucking his pipe into life, using a flaming twig pulled from the fire. She thought Rose would have been proud of the way her husband had dealt with Sarah.

Cassie went to sleep feeling more contented than she had for many nights. Enoch Martin was recovering from his wound, the future of Richard and Josefa seemed assured – and now she no longer needed to worry about Elijah Tonks's relationship with Sarah. If only Harry and Gorran were safely back with the regiment all would be well with her world.

36

❦

On 31 August 1813, the town of San Sebastian fell after a siege lasting thirty-seven days and one of the cruellest battles ever to take place in the Peninsular War.

At the same time that French and allied soldiers were being slaughtered in their thousands, the 32nd Regiment was involved in an incident so minor it was worth no more than four lines in the regimental diary for that day. The entry read:

> Sighted a small enemy battery positioned on a hill two miles to the east of the line of march. Sent a small party to investigate. French battery fired one shot before withdrawing. Two casualties, both killed.

It was a brief, cold but accurate entry and was followed by the names of the dead men. Sergeant Elijah Tonks and Private Ned Harrup.

The death of the one man left Sarah in the familiar state of widowhood. The other death left hundreds stunned. The 32nd's most senior sergeant, Elijah Tonks, was known to every soldier in the regiment. His long service and participation in innumerable battles and combats were quoted to recruits as an illustration of a soldier's ability to survive years of warfare. Officers and men looked upon him as being indestructible. His loss caused every man in the regiment to make a sombre reassessment of his own mortality.

For many, and Harry was among their number, the death of Elijah Tonks was a more personal loss. He had been a friend, a never-failing source of military expertise and a non-commissioned officer of vast experience. At the funeral of the two men, the colonel spoke for both officers and men when he said Sergeant Tonks was irreplaceable, the regiment far poorer for his loss.

Of Ned Harrup, the colonel could only suggest he was 'a soldier sadly cut off before his true potential had been realised. A man who would undoubtedly be mourned by his own family.'

The colonel's words produced a flood of tears from Sarah Harrup, who needed to be comforted by the soldier standing next to her. A slow-thinking countryman, Damian Coombe had joined the army at the suggestion of his local squire and landlord, who could no longer overlook Coombe's bungling attempts to poach game from his lands.

The two men were buried on the hillside where they had fallen and as the regiment left the graves and made their way to the nearby camp, Gorran Fox caught up with Cassie and Harry. Falling in beside them, he said, 'I feel I've lost a life-long friend. Elijah Tonks was already a sergeant when I joined the Thirty-second as an ensign. He taught me more about soldiering than I could have learned from any other man. The Thirty-second is not going to be the same without him.'

'That's the way it is with me, too. I can't imagine life in the company without Sergeant Tonks. No one will be able to take his place.'

'Someone has to, Harry, and it will need to be a man I can trust in battle. I'm asking the colonel to promote *you* to take Elijah Tonks's place.'

Harry's expression was a confused mixture of delight at his advancement coloured with the distress he felt at the reason for his unexpected promotion. Eventually he managed to stammer that it would be a great honour to take the place of such a sergeant.

Harry's promotion was announced to the regiment the next morning when the men paraded in readiness to march off. It met with general approval among the men, many of whom had joined the regiment after Harry.

The only murmurings of discontent came from those wives jealous of their own husbands' promotion prospects. The wives of corporals in other companies, in particular, felt their husbands were more deserving of a sergeant's stripes than Corporal Harry Clymo. One or two murmured that the promotion was 'hardly surprising', hinting that Cassie and Captain Fox had a lot more to do with each other than was decent for a soldier's wife and the company commander.

Sarah Harrup told Cassie of the talk later that day

when they were nearing the end of another hard day's march and Cassie was leading her donkey, at the rear of the regiment.

There was a degree of malicious glee in Sarah's voice when she added, unnecessarily, 'Of course, we both know there's no truth in what they're saying, but you know soldiers' wives. If they've got no honest gossip to pass on they'll make it up. If poor Elijah Tonks hadn't been killed along with my Ned I might have been a sergeant's wife now – and they'd have had a lot more to say about *me*.'

Cassie opened her mouth to tell Sarah she knew different but closed it again without saying anything. Sarah was the last of the wives with whom she had left England and she had known more than her share of unhappiness. If she wanted others to believe Sergeant Tonks would have married her, it would do no harm.

'If they're talking about me they're giving you a rest, Sarah. What will you do now? You'll be taken off the regiment's strength as soon as the pay sergeant gets around to it.'

Sarah grinned wickedly. 'John Truscott's the pay sergeant now. I know him *very* well – and knew him better when the regiment was stationed in Ireland. That was before he married that tight-lipped wife of his. He'll be in no hurry to take me off the regiment's strength. By the time he does I expect to be Mrs Damian Coombe.'

Cassie remembered the fresh-faced young soldier who had comforted Sarah at Ned's funeral. 'How many husbands will that make, Sarah?'

'I don't know. Four or five, perhaps. I never was much good at counting.'

'Do you ever see anything of Mr Dalhousie?'

Sarah stiffened slightly. 'Sometimes, if his dragoons are in camp near ours. But no women are allowed to follow the cavalry. Besides, he's a user, that one. Takes what he wants and gives nothing in return, if he can help it.'

Sarah grinned, but this time it was less convincing than before. 'Strange you should mention him, though. I was thinking of him only this morning. He's one of those men you know is no good for you, yet you can't forget him.' With a sudden outburst of honesty, Sarah added, 'I probably fell harder for him than I ever have for any other man ... but I know he doesn't feel the same about me. Serves me right, I suppose. No good can come of women like us falling for officers. You remember that piece of advice, Cassie Clymo. And talking of our particular officers, here comes one of them now. I'll be off before he remembers I shouldn't be on the strength.' Without stopping to offer Gorran Fox a greeting, Sarah hurried away along the line of stationary baggage wagons.

Gorran raised his eyebrows at Sarah's rapid departure. 'Sarah seems anxious to avoid meeting me. What have I done?'

'She's worried you'll send her packing before she can remarry into the regiment.'

'Sarah should know me better than that by now. Anyway, Damian Coombe has already asked me for permission to marry her.'

'Have you given him your blessing?'

'He has my permission because I can think of no

reasonable grounds for withholding it. I can hardly tell a man that marrying Sarah is likely to reduce his chance of survival. It would be both cruel and unfair – but she does seem to cut short the life of a man in exchange for his name.'

Hearing the company commander express such an opinion to the wife of one of his sergeants would have shocked some people, but there was no one else within hearing and Cassie had long ago realised that Gorran felt able to speak more freely with her than he would with most other people.

'Poor Sarah. I'd like to think Coombe is going to make her happy, but he's much the same type of man as Ned Harrup was. I hope he turns out to be kinder to her, though.'

'Sarah will get by . . . but I haven't ridden back here to discuss Sarah Harrup. I came to speak to you. A messenger reached the division today with despatches from Lord Wellington. There was also a verbal message for you, from Lady Fraser. We'll be camping within a mile of Lord Wellington's headquarters tomorrow evening and she'd like you to call on her there.'

'Me? Why?'

Gorran grinned. 'You echo the words of our colonel, Cassie. "What the devil does a general's wife want with the wife of one of my sergeants?" were his exact words. I told him you and Lady Fraser were old friends and were in the habit of taking tea together. It left him speechless. His wife has been trying for years to have herself included on Lady Fraser's guest list.'

'But why does she want to see me?'

'I suspect it has something to do with your concern for wounded soldiers on the battlefield. If you'd like Harry to escort you to headquarters tell him it's all right with me.'

When Cassie spoke to Harry that night he said he would rather not be the one to take her to Wellington's headquarters and he gave her his reasons.

'Lady Fraser's an officer's wife, Cassie. A major-general's wife. It's all right for you to go and talk to her – to her husband too, if he's there. I'm not an officer and never could be. If I came with you I'd need to leave you among the officers while I went off to wait with the sergeants. I don't think I'd like that very much.'

'Lady Fraser isn't like that, Harry. It doesn't seem to matter to her whether she's talking to a sergeant's wife or to the wife of a field marshal. She'd treat us both the same. I'm sure you're exaggerating the difference between officers and the men. Why, Gorran Fox even calls you "Harry".'

'Lady Fraser's a very special woman, Cassie, everyone who's met her says so. She cares for people, really cares. Besides, you've had better schooling than me, you can talk to her about things I know nothing of. The only thing I've ever managed to learn well is how to be a soldier and I'll talk to anyone about soldiering – but I don't feel comfortable talking about anything else . . . except to you. As for Captain Fox . . . well, he's Cornish and so are we. It's well known that Cornish soldiers and their officers are much closer to each other than any other soldiers and their officers, but I wouldn't dare call Captain Fox by his first name, for all that.'

'Would you rather I didn't go to see Lady Fraser, Harry?'

'Of course not! I'm very proud that she wants to speak to my wife. I'm proud of you, too, Cassie, and what you're going to speak to Lady Fraser about. Every soldier who goes into a big battle is scared of being badly wounded and left to the mercy of the Spanish peasants. We'd all rather die cleanly.'

'Don't talk like that, Harry.' Cassie shuddered. 'You'll give me nightmares, and you'll have them too, you know you will.'

They both knew what Cassie was talking about. For a few nights after a particularly fierce battle Harry would wake in a cold sweat, calling out to someone only he could see.

'It's all right, Cassie. A few more battles and this war is going to be over. Then we'll return to England and you'll be able to entertain all the other sergeants' wives to tea, while I drill new recruits and bore everyone with my war experiences. But that's all in the future. It's the sergeant major's birthday and he's having a party. Let's hurry up and get across there before all the drink's gone.'

Cassie did not enjoy parties and that evening she was quieter than usual. It was Harry's words to her that had given her pause for thought. His picture of their life together when the war ended, as it surely would before too long. She wondered how she would adapt to army life when the war was over. She was concerned too that Harry might find that the peacetime army presented him with problems very different to those encountered on the battlefield.

*   *   *

Cassie rode her donkey to Lord Wellington's headquarters and she was amazed at the sheer size of the tented 'town'. Here were to be seen the heavily gold-braided uniforms of senior Spanish and Portuguese officers and representatives of guards, cavalry, infantry, artillery and engineers. There were quartermaster generals, assistant quartermasters and even deputy assistant quartermasters; adjutant generals, officers of the staff corps cavalry, a provost marshal, judge advocate, inspector of hospitals, paymaster general, commissary general, storekeeper general ... and many, many more, each with his own assistants and clerks, messengers and servants, all coming and going in every possible direction.

So many men were of senior rank that Cassie felt reluctant to ask directions of them. Eventually she seized upon a young and harassed-looking ensign and asked him where she might find Lady Fraser. The ensign was not yet of an age to have learned the skills of artifice. Taking in the faded ribbon holding back Cassie's hair, her homemade frock and cheap shoes, he blinked his surprise.

'Lady Fraser? You mean Major-General Sir William Fraser's wife?'

'Are there two Lady Frasers travelling with Lord Wellington's headquarters?' Cassie had correctly interpreted the reason for the young ensign's surprise.

'No, ma'am. I'm sorry, I'll take you to her tent.'

The ensign led the way, threading his way between tents and stopping frequently to give precedence to officers more senior than himself when they crossed his path. Soon after passing a tent outside which were posted armed guardsmen, the ensign indicated a large tent.

454

Outside stood a table, two armchairs and a number of everyday household items, all the more unusual in such surroundings on account of their very ordinariness.

Seated in one of the chairs, shielded from the sun by a parasol tied to the chair, Lady Fraser was reading from a book. Nearby, Emma played with a small toy donkey, made from straw.

Looking up from her book as Cassie dismounted, Lady Harriet Fraser greeted her with a smile that left the still dubious ensign open-mouthed. He had decided that Cassie must have been looking for employment with Major-General Sir William Fraser's household.

'Cassie, my dear. How kind of you to come to see me so quickly after such an exhausting few days. I've heard all about the marches performed by the Sixth Division. Do you know that the Sixth Division is known in the army as the "Marching Division" for its prodigious feats? I don't know how you manage to keep up with them. I'm quite certain I never could. Tea? Of course you will. Lucia! We'll take tea, please. Yes, *tea*, dear, there's a good girl.'

Shaking her head in despair, Lady Fraser explained, 'Lucia's only been with me for a few days and her English isn't terribly good, I'm afraid. I've only just managed to get her familiar with her own name. It isn't really "Lucia" of course, her real name is something quite unpronounceable. I have told her she will have to be "Lucia" for as long as she works for me. Every one of my maids has been "Lucia" since I've been here, I really don't see any sense in changing now. Oh, good girl, you did understand. I can see we're going to get along famously.'

Lady Fraser beamed as the servant nervously produced tea, milk and two cups on a tray. 'That's right, dear, put it all on the table – and bring some sugar, too. Yes, *sugar*, dear. Why, there's Lord Wellington.' She waved at a thin-faced man dressed in a sober grey cloak who rode past, inclining his head first to Lady Fraser – and then to an open-mouthed Cassie.

'That was Lord Wellington!'

'That's right, dear. Rumour has it he'll soon be made a duke. He deserves it, of course. He's a brilliant commander-in-chief. Quite brilliant. I only wish he would unbend and allow those of us around him to like him more. He seems to reserve his affections for those barefooted little urchins who sell food in the market-place . . . but I'm being dreadfully uncharitable. He and Emma are the warmest of friends. I think perhaps he prefers children to adults. Their attentions are not tempered by ambition and their demands are simple. No, dear, don't pull your donkey apart, it's really a rather splendid toy. Isabella! Do take Emma for a walk somewhere. I think she's a little bored with her donkey.'

A heavily built, slow-moving Spanish girl came from inside the tent where she had been folding Emma's clothes. Talking quietly to the little girl, she led her away. Cassie thought that Lady Fraser had no shortage of servants, even though her home was a tent – albeit a very large tent.

'I believe congratulations are in order, my dear? Hasn't your husband recently been made a sergeant?'

'Yes.'

Cassie was surprised that Lady Fraser should know anything about Harry.

'He's still a very young man, so I'm told. That's wonderful for him – for you both. You must persuade him to apply for a commission. The army's a very good career for a courageous young man with plenty of initiative.'

Cassie thought of Harry's 'home' before he had joined the army. A rat-ridden space in a barn was hardly the background for a successful officer in the British army, serving alongside young men accustomed to a lifestyle similar to that of Lady Fraser with servants . . . her own tent.

'I think Harry is quite happy to be a sergeant, for now. One day perhaps he might become a regimental sergeant major, if all goes well.'

'Well, we'll see. It isn't only women who are known to change their minds . . . But it's you I wish to talk about today. I believe there are a number of matters about which we both feel strongly. Matters concerning the lack of medical attention for wounded men immediately after a battle. Were you at Vittoria?'

'No, the Sixth Division was detached and sent to Medina de Pomar.'

'Ah yes, I remember. Lord Wellington placed his stores there. Perhaps it's as well, Vittoria would have broken your heart – as it almost broke mine. So many fine young men, good soldiers all, lying wounded for hours on the battlefield. By the time the ghouls, both Portuguese and Spaniards, had finished their evil work there were far more dead than there should have been – and their victims were not all *French* soldiers. Perhaps an even greater tragedy was that no one seemed to care. There have been similar incidents after far too many other battles. At Rodrigo and Badajos the wounded were left unattended for days while their companions went on the rampage.

'It's high time the army provided succour for its wounded on the battlefield. Specially trained men to tend their wounds on the spot and arrange for them to be taken to the rear. They should be conveyed in decent vehicles – and our army could take a lesson from the French here. The Portuguese carts we are using would bounce the life from the hale and hearty. God only knows what they do to a badly wounded man.'

Lady Fraser paused to pour a second cup of tea for herself and for Cassie. 'I know you care, Cassie, and Captain Fox is fulsome in his praise for your skill in tending wounded men. Unfortunately, it seems that women like you provide the only comfort our poor wounded men can expect. I suggested to Lord Wellington that he should form a special corps to find and collect the wounded after a battle, or even during prolonged fighting. Lord Wellington declared it would not be possible to find non-combatants willing to risk their lives on the battlefield. He went further, saying that even if it were possible, such men would get in the way of our troops and be cut down by the enemy in the fury of battle. He believes that soldiers' wives are the most suitable people to care for the wounded. I disagreed with him, but I would like to hear your views.'

When Cassie replied, she chose her words carefully.

'I think Lord Wellington is wrong. While a battle is going on a wife is trying to follow her husband's progress, to satisfy herself he's still on his feet. When the fighting moves on she's too busy searching for him, or tending him to care for others. Not until she's satisfied her own man is safe is she able to think of any one else.'

Cassie paused. 'There are some who could help without forming a special unit. Officers' servants, bandsmen, and others not involved in the actual fighting. Their duties could include caring for the wounded. One thing I would particularly like to see is the use of provost marshal's men to keep local peasants and the camp followers well clear of a battlefield. Such people are like vultures. Our men see them waiting on the edge of every battlefield and know they are hoping there will be many casualties. They're omens of evil who strike fear into the strongest men.'

Lady Fraser was nodding her head in agreement. 'I like your idea of using the provost marshal's department to keep camp followers from the field. I'll put the idea to Lord Wellington. It would be a beginning, at least, but I doubt if Lord Wellington will act without the sanction of the British government. In the meantime, do you think you might persuade the wives of the Thirty-second to involve themselves a little more? Taking on responsibility for dressing wounds, perhaps?'

'I'm certain I could. I think most wives regard the hospitals as I do. Some of them are so bad I wouldn't send a pig there for slaughtering.'

'My dear, we do think alike. Some of the hospitals I've seen have been appalling. Did you hear of the army surgeon captured by the French? He was sent back under a flag of truce after the French commander was heard to say that the surgeon would kill more British soldiers than his own men could! Having wives tend all the wounded could be a beginning. I shall obtain medical kits for each of you and leave you to organise the wives – and any other reliable women among the soldiers' "friends". Ah! If only more of the Spanish women were like Josefa.'

'I'll do my best, but I can't make any promises on behalf of the other women.'

'Of course not, my dear, but if you encounter any serious problems you must come back to me. I may not succeed in influencing Lord Wellington, or even my own husband, but they listen to me. Sometimes my better ideas have actually found their way into army orders – but as Lord Wellington's own, of course.'

Cassie returned to the 32nd Regiment convinced that Lady Fraser's suggestions would provide a good basis for caring for wounded soldiers, but she found a marked lack of enthusiasm for the plan. Most of the wives had come out to the regiment during the previous twelve months and their husbands had yet to be involved in a major battle. They had not witnessed the harrowing scenes of local peasants and the more unscrupulous of the camp followers picking their way over a battlefield, stealing from the dead and dying and not hesitating to hasten the end of a man who wore a ring, or even a good pair of boots. Cassie had even witnessed young children using heavy stones to batter the remaining life from a badly wounded man, with scant regard for the colour of his uniform.

460

When Cassie went around the camp discussing the ideas put forward by Lady Fraser, few of the wives showed any interest. After outlining the plans to help the wounded after a battle, Cassie would ask how many of the wives were prepared to take a medical pack and participate in the scheme. At the end of the day only two women had made a firm commitment. Somewhat surprisingly, one of the two was Sarah – now Sarah Coombe.

Later that night, when Cassie had returned to her own camp fire, Sarah asked, 'Are you surprised at the response to your ideas?'

'Not really. Disappointed, perhaps, but I told Lady Fraser that during and after a battle a wife's only thought is for her own husband. Besides, many wives are new to the regiment. They're hardly used to being part of the army yet.'

'That's true, but you've sowed the seed. When the regiment's involved in its first major battle you'll see what the wives are made of. My guess is that the wife of every unwounded man will be out there with us. We were all new once, Cassie. I must admit that when I first met you I despaired of you ever becoming a regimental wife – and now look at you!'

Cassie remembered her first awareness of Sarah, and how close the much married woman had come to ruining her wedding night. It all seemed a very long time ago.

37

❧

The army suffered great privation in the Pyrenees during the winter of 1813–14, although the tents issued to each regiment gave the soldiers some protection against the wind and snow. Meanwhile, the French commander had formed his defence lines some miles back from the mountains and, as soon as it was practicable, Lord Wellington brought his army down from the mountains – on the French side of the border.

With the army were Spanish regiments which had been conspicuous by their absence when the armies of Britain and France were locked in battle to free the Spanish homeland. Now the Spaniards poured down the mountain slopes intent on seeking revenge from the French who dwelled in the border towns and villages.

Their depredations proved a serious embarrassment to Lord Wellington. His plans for the defeat of Napoleon on French soil depended upon gaining the co-operation and goodwill of the inhabitants of the countryside. A shrewd general, Lord Wellington knew he had neither the men nor the time to fight two wars – one against a regular army, the other against a populace aroused to guerrilla action. He ordered the offending Spanish regiments back to their own land – enforcing his order with soldiers of his own regiments, many of whom would as soon have fought against their Spanish 'allies' as against the French army.

The British commander-in-chief's next move was also calculated to keep the civilian population of France on his side. He needed to buy provisions for his troops, but the French producers were, not unnaturally, wary of accepting payment in the currency of an enemy. After due deliberation, Lord Wellington issued instructions for his divisional commanders secretly to gather together any men in their divisions who possessed expert knowledge of coining. The commander-in-chief was well aware that the only reason many of his soldiers had joined the army was to put distance between themselves and the hangman. He felt certain there were counterfeiters included in their ranks.

Wellington was not disappointed. He quickly assembled a sufficient number of coiners to rival the Royal Mint. Soon they were melting down Spanish and Portuguese currency and minting five-franc Napoleonic coins which were fully acceptable to the French traders. Keeping the French populace happy was only a means to Lord Wellington's main aim – that of defeating the French army and toppling Napoleon from his Emperor's throne.

*   *   *

Cassie found the country on the borders between Spain and France breathtakingly beautiful and the road coming down from the mountains provided a panoramic view of the French countryside. Near at hand a great river unwound to the Bay of Biscay and beyond lay the fertile plains of France, a vast patchwork of fields and well-ordered châteaux.

It was like a vision of heaven after the mountain fogs, where hailstones the size of huge pebbles dropped from the sky and snow fell so heavily it was capable of burying a bivouacked army in the course of a single night. There had been times when Cassie awoke in the morning to find her blankets frozen fast to the ground.

After a short sharp engagement at the foot of the mountains it seemed for a while that the French might throw the British army back into Spain. But Lord Wellington rallied his men personally and they won the day.

Both commanders now settled down to complete their plans, one for an offensive, the other to prepare defences. There were still a couple of months of winter left and the British tents really came into their own. Encampments became ordered communities, and tents, snug against wind and rain, places where private belongings could be brought into use once more.

It was not long before the soldiers added another dimension to life in their well-ordered cantonments on French soil. One evening Harry came into the tent where Cassie was preparing their bed for the night and told her to leave what she was doing and get dressed up in her best clothes. He was taking her to a party. His manner was distinctly mysterious and when Cassie asked him where they were going, she was told to wait and see.

Putting on her best clothes did not take Cassie long. All she needed was to substitute a clean dress for the not-so-clean one she had been wearing all day and she was ready.

Even when they left the tent and went out into the night Harry would not enlighten her as to their destination. At the edge of the camp they joined a party of sergeants of the other companies whose wives were equally mystified. There were Spanish and Portuguese mistresses too, most of whom were thrilled to be going to a party with the women whose official status they greatly envied. Now Cassie's curiosity was well and truly aroused, but in answer to her repeated questions Harry urged her to remain quiet and not get lost in the darkness.

The direction taken by the sergeants of the 32nd Regiment was as mysterious as their ultimate destination. Instead of heading for the camp of one of the other regiments attached to the division, as Cassie had been expecting, the party left the British cantonments behind and made their way towards the unofficial demarcation line, where British and French pickets occupied positions within shouting distance of each other.

Eventually the sergeant in the lead opened a gate, its rusty hinges shrieking a protest to the night skies that set some of the Spanish girls into paroxysms of giggling, and then the dark bulk of a farmhouse loomed up ahead.

The sergeants and their women filed inside, most being forced to stoop in order to pass through the low doorway. Once inside they found themselves in a stone-flagged passageway. When the last man was in, the door was

465

closed behind him and an inner door opened. As Cassie followed Harry into the room it erupted with sound. Well lit, with a number of lamps about the room, there was also a blazing fire in the hearth and a blanket covering the window to prevent light escaping. A table was laden with an astonishing quantity and variety of food – but it was the other occupants of the room who provided the greatest surprise of all. They were *French* sergeants and they, too, had brought their women with them.

The sight of so many light-blue uniforms brought a great many unpleasant memories flooding back to Cassie and she turned to Harry for an explanation. Grinning sheepishly, he said, 'We've met so often on picket duty, everyone thought it would be a good idea to have a "get-together".'

'A good idea? Harry, these are our *enemies*. What do you think would happen if the officers learned of what you are doing?'

'There would be trouble for all of us, Madame.' The reply to Cassie's question came not from Harry, but from a heavily moustached French sergeant who bowed over the glass of wine he handed to her. 'But I do not think either regiment would wish to lose all its sergeants and we are only enemies on the field of battle. At other times we are soldiers. Men who understand each other's problems. The officers, yours *and* mine, understand such matters. Our captain has developed a taste for whisky and if you were to dine at your commanding officer's table you would be offered a cognac that is usually served only at the table of a French army officer. Please, come and meet my wife and enjoy the party.'

It was one of the strangest parties Cassie had ever attended. Yet, once she had surmounted her initial revulsion each time she looked at a French uniform, she had to admit to herself it was also one of the most enjoyable. The French sergeants proved to be excellent hosts, lavishing food and drinks upon their guests, all served in fine porcelain and glassware 'borrowed' for the occasion from the baggage train of the French commander.

A great deal of flirting went on between the men and women of both sides and Cassie thought there might be trouble from this source as the men drank more. Her fears were almost realised when one of the French women returned to the room with a young English sergeant after a lengthy absence. However, the Frenchmen headed off their countryman, who had drunk far too much to know how long his wife had been out of the room with the English sergeant.

The English sergeant's wife had no such problem. She harangued her husband in a manner that drew heavily upon the adjectives currently in vogue among the Irish-Liverpool community whence she came. Finally satisfied she had left her husband in no doubt of her displeasure, she proceeded to pay him back in kind with the enthusiastic help of a white-uniformed French sergeant from his regiment's *élite* company. Meanwhile, the French woman who had been the cause of the trouble was practising her wiles on another English sergeant. Cassie thought Sarah would have felt very much at home in such company.

The party eventually broke up in the early hours of the morning with much kissing and back-slapping, and expressions of *bonhomie* from every side. All the way

467

back to the British lines the sergeants of the 32nd whispered of the charms of the French women, while the English women spoke of the liberties taken with them by the moustached French sergeants. Cassie was in agreement with them about the liberties taken, but did not agree with the source of the problem. As she left the farmhouse a hand had twice traced the contours of her bottom in the darkness of the corridor. However, when she used her elbow to good effect, the resulting curse had been Anglo-Saxon, not Gallic.

The 32nd remained in cantonment for two months and for the first time during the Peninsular campaign the army was able to celebrate Christmas in traditional fashion. The wives did the cooking and every officer and man contributed something to the feast. Wine, vegetables, fruit, flour or money. A number of sheep were bought and slaughtered and the women baked mince pies and a variety of puddings.

Fraternisations occurred more openly during the Christmas celebrations and a barrel of brandy was sent across the lines as a present to the sergeants of the 32nd Regiment from the sergeants facing them across the lines. It was a pleasant two days of peaceful festivities, but the soldiers of both armies knew such amity could not last for ever.

As January 1814 drew to a freezing close, the British army was warned to prepare itself for a new offensive. It began for the 32nd Regiment with an attack on the French picket occupying the farmhouse, beyond which was a wide stream and the enemy lines. It was a dawn attack that was as brisk as it was brief.

Afterwards the regiment filed past the farmhouse on its way to a narrow crossing. The stream was fed with freezing waters pouring from the Pyrenees and the crossing place was cold and narrow. Cassie was waiting with the other women to go over the stream in the wake of the army when she remembered the water bottles she carried, both of which were almost empty. There was a well in the garden of the house and Cassie rode her donkey into the garden, avoiding a number of French-uniformed bodies on the way.

By the time the bottles were full there were still soldiers waiting to cross the narrow ford. Not until they were all on the far bank would it be the turn of the baggage carts and the women. Remembering the pleasant and unusual evening she had spent in this house, Cassie thought she would go inside and see how it looked in daylight.

Most of the fighting had apparently taken place outside, in the garden and its surrounds, but successive pickets had not treated the contents of the house with the same degree of care as had the sergeants. The place had been ransacked frequently. What furniture remained was broken and useless.

Cassie found it rather depressing and was on her way out again when she thought she heard a movement in a room above her. Thinking it possible that a wounded man might be lying forgotten somewhere, Cassie made her way cautiously upstairs. She heard the sound again. It came from behind a closed door. Approaching very quietly she gently opened the door and found herself gazing down into the face of the French sergeant who had been the first to bring her a drink at the party two months before. Behind him in the room were other French soldiers, all seated or lying.

When Cassie pushed the door open wider the sergeant said breathlessly, 'Madame! This is an unexpected pleasure.'

The Frenchman's face was contorted in a painful semblance of a smile and for the first time Cassie noticed the blood staining the side of his tunic. A quick glance was enough to tell her all the other French soldiers were wounded too.

'You need help.'

'Please, Madame, leave us and say nothing – as one of your sergeants has already done.'

'Those wounds should be cleaned and dressed.'

'An untreated wound is preferable to life as a prisoner-of-war – or being killed. Go, we are no danger to your soldiers. Our own people will take care of us when you have gone. My wife will find a way to come to me.'

From the window Cassie could see the queue at the crossing. The first of the baggage wagons was about to enter the water and she reached a quick decision.

'Take your jacket off and let me look at that wound.'

The sergeant had a shattered rib, but the musket ball that caused the wound appeared to have passed out through his body without causing any serious internal damage. She could not be certain, of course, but a surgeon probing inside the sergeant's chest would probably only cause more damage.

In the panniers of her donkey Cassie carried some of the medical packs sent to her by Lady Fraser and she

470

put them to good use in the next twenty minutes. Two were wasted, the recipients would die anyway, but the attention gave them some brief comfort. The remainder of the men would recover, but would take no further part in the war. When she had bound up the last wound, Cassie saw from the window that the women were now beginning to cross the stream.

'I'll leave you with a little food. It's not much, but it should suffice until help comes.'

'Madame, you are an angel of mercy. May you and your husband live to see the end of the war and enjoy many years together.'

That evening Cassie told Harry of the wounded French soldiers and was immediately suspicious when he evinced no surprise.

'Harry, did you know those French soldiers were in the house?'

Harry nodded. 'We all did. Word was passed back to the men that they weren't to go upstairs. No one did.'

Looking slightly sheepish, Harry added, 'We'd all got to know each other too well, Cassie. Killing them would have been like turning on friends. Some died in the fighting, of course, but that couldn't be helped.'

Cassie looked at Harry in silence for some minutes, then suddenly and unexpectedly she kissed him.

'Harry Clymo, you're a good man – but don't get to thinking that everyone else is the same as you. I want you to survive this war. I've got plans for you.'

38

❦

Lord Wellington's army marched in strength and with supreme confidence in its ability to defeat the French whenever and wherever they met in battle. The weather, too, favoured an advance. Heavy frost had put a solid surface on the mud of the roads and the guns and wagons bounced excruciatingly on the rough surface. However, there was no danger of any equipment being trapped in glutinous mud, as had happened so frequently after long periods of rain.

At first the 6th Division travelled in the rear of the army, untroubled by French skirmishers who were trying to delay the British advance while their commander put the final touches to the defensive position he had taken up with some 40,000 men on a ridge of hills close to the French town of Orthez.

The other divisions had already crossed the River Pau, close to the town, when the 6th Division crossed by means of a cleverly constructed pontoon bridge. They immediately took up a position with the 3rd and Light Divisions on high ground facing the centre of the French defences.

Fierce battles were being fought along the whole length of the enemy's line and especially in a small village to one side of the French positions. As often as the village was taken by a British force, the French counter-attacked and took it back again.

At the other end of the French line a British division tried in vain to force a small bridge. All depended upon the efforts of the British troops in the centre and the 6th Division came under such a heavy cannonade that the women were sent to the shelter of the reverse slope of a hill until a cry came back to them that a number of men had been wounded by exploding shells. Cassie went forward to the battle area accompanied by the wife of another 32nd sergeant and Sarah.

As they made their way to where the wounded men were lying, Sarah said, 'I prefer to be out here where I can see what's going on. If I had to listen to those young wives for very much longer I'd go out of my mind. Every one of them is convinced the whole of the French artillery is firing at *her* husband.'

The French artillery might not have been laying its sights on any particular soldier, but they were causing a great many casualties. With shells still falling about them the three women were hard put to bandage all the wounded, even when they were joined by two more of the wives.

While the women were still working the order came

for the 6th Division to advance against the enemy. They went off down the slope of their hill at a run, anxious to escape from the heavy shell fire.

As Gorran Fox's company passed Cassie, Harry gave her a wave and she returned the greeting, murmuring a brief but heartfelt prayer for his safety. Gorran also turned in her direction and gave Cassie a quick, pale-faced smile that made her aware of the tension that was in him.

A few minutes later, leaving the other women still treating the casualties caused by the artillery fire, Cassie and Sarah gathered up their medical packs and set off after the 32nd Regiment. The British soldiers were advancing up a difficult hillside and forced to use a path bordered by huge boulders. It was so narrow in one part that they could move only six or seven abreast. Casualties were heaviest in this spot and as the soldiers were checked they were subjected to the renewed attentions of French artillery-men.

When it seemed the sheer ferocity of the French barrage might force the 32nd to retreat, the artillery fire ceased abruptly. A strong British force had fought its way around the flank of the French line, threatening their communications and cutting off an escape route. No intelligent commander would run the risk of having his position surrounded by a strong enemy. The order to retreat was given to the French soldiers. With a rousing cheer the British soldiers swarmed over the ridge in close pursuit and the French retreat quickly became a rout.

Cassie wanted to stay close to the 32nd, but there

were so many wounded men on the slope of the hill it was impossible to ignore their pleas and the two women were kept busy for some hours.

Their task ended when a party of men arrived, sent back by the divisional commander to carry the wounded to a regimental hospital, set up in the municipal building in Orthez, the town having been abandoned in haste by the French. There had been a series of fierce battles in front of Orthez. The truckloads of wounded would rumble into the town all through the night and far into the next day, but when night fell Cassie and Sarah set off to find their regiment.

The 32nd had been put in billets in a nearby village and Harry had managed to obtain lodgings in a small house where the owner treated them as though they were victors in their own country. When Cassie expressed her surprise, the woman informed them she was tired of war and troops who requisitioned all the available food. She no longer cared who won the war, declaring that the British could be no worse than 'that upstart Bonaparte'. All he had succeeded in doing was to bring tragedy and despair to the ordinary people of the land, the very people to whom the Revolution was to have brought a richer and happier life.

The house owner's views were translated by her young grandson, a boy of no more than ten years of age. Dressed in army uniform, he was a pupil at the military school of nearby St Sever. His scornful expression when passing on his grandmother's words indicated that her views were not necessarily those of a younger generation.

475

The woman was still castigating Napoleon Bonaparte when Gorran Fox came to the house. Upon being informed he was the commander of Harry's company the house owner welcomed him as an honoured guest, insisting he be seated in the most comfortable chair. Producing a vintage cognac from a hiding place that would have remained a secret from Harry and Cassie, she poured Gorran a carefully measured drink.

The young grandson, too, seemed suitably impressed to have an officer in the house and when Gorran said yes, he had met and spoken to Lord Wellington, he became a hero. The small boy ran from the house to inform his friends that a guest in his grandmother's house was a personal friend of Lord Wellington.

Gorran had come to the house to tell Harry they were both needed for the Light Company the following day. The Light Company had been very heavily engaged during the day and suffered many casualties, among them its commanding officer. Gorran was to take his place and he wanted Harry as his sergeant.

'You don't need to worry about him,' Gorran assured Cassie. 'The French are on the run. My guess is that they won't stop until they reach Toulouse. Our task is to behave like terriers, snapping at their heels to keep them running.'

Gorran looked very tired, but he passed it off, saying, 'This war is almost ended, Cassie. The news from the other fronts is that Napoleon is being pushed back on Paris by every army opposing him. We're likely to wake up one morning soon and learn it's all over. Then we'll all be able to rest, or celebrate, as we please.'

'The celebrations will come too late for some,' suggested Cassie. 'We suffered a great many casualties today.'

'It was a hard-fought battle,' agreed the Cornish captain, soberly. 'I've been to visit our own casualties in the hospital and many of the men spoke of your attentions – yours and Sarah's. Lady Fraser has the right idea, but it needed more women to take care of the wounded after today's battle.'

'Women can't move wounded men from a battlefield by themselves. It needs a special unit to seek and care for them. Something similar to the commissary, perhaps, who take no part in the actual fighting.'

'We won't see it come to pass in this campaign, Cassie. All Lord Wellington's energies are directed towards winning the war as quickly as possible.'

'That's always been his only concern, and it's scant comfort to those thousands still to fall wounded. Not that the commander-in-chief can be expected to understand. If he fell he'd be immediately surrounded by officers and surgeons.'

'As a matter of fact Lord Wellington was wounded today, Cassie. A musket ball struck him in the thigh. Fortunately, the force of the ball was almost spent, but I believe he's in some pain. It's not known for certain how bad it is because he says he hasn't time to let a doctor examine it. However, I do understand your concern for the men and have nothing but admiration for what you're doing. I'll see you in the morning, Harry.'

Cassie felt vaguely foolish at having made such a sweeping statement about Lord Wellington, but when

477

she saw Gorran from the house she said, 'I trust you're off to get some sleep now. You look very tired.'

'Unfortunately, I have more rounds to carry out, casualty reports to write – and my company to hand over to a temporary commanding officer. Then I need to attend a meeting with the divisional general to discuss tomorrow's advance – but we don't all need to be awake for half the night. Give Harry a large brandy and make sure, at least, he has a good night's sleep. I, and the company, rely very heavily on him.'

When Cassie told Harry what Gorran had said, he replied, 'Captain Fox does far too much. He works twice as hard as any other officer and marches twice as far as the men, going back and forward, urging on stragglers and keeping the company together. It's the same in action. You don't need to go looking for him to find out what to do, he's always there, in front of the men. How it is he's not been killed I'll never know.'

The thought that Gorran was in constant danger of being killed made Cassie go suddenly cold. There had been very many sad losses since the campaign, but Gorran Fox? He was the tower of strength they all relied upon.

Keeping such thoughts to herself, Cassie said, 'I think you ought to follow his advice, Harry. While you're getting ready for bed I'll go and find the old lady. I doubt if she'll give us any more of that special cognac she produced for Gorran, but I've no doubt she has something she could sell us in its place.'

Later that night Cassie lay awake for a long time in the upstairs room she and Harry occupied. It was a clear and frosty night and through the open curtains Cassie looked out at a sky filled with stars. The house backed on to open fields and in a nearby copse an owl hooted a melancholy proclamation of its territorial rights. Beside her, Harry turned over restlessly.

'Aren't you asleep yet?'

It was an unnecessary question, but Cassie asked it just the same.

'No.'

'What are you thinking about?'

'Tomorrow . . . The Light Company . . . Captain Fox.'

Cassie turned towards him, 'Tell me about your thoughts, Harry.'

'I'm not sure I can. I mean . . . they don't make very much sense, even to me.'

'They don't need to make sense. Just tell me about them.'

'I was wondering what we'd be doing tomorrow. Captain Fox said we'd just be snapping at the heels of the French to make them run faster but I doubt it. The French are like us, they don't like running. They're good soldiers, with good officers. They'll try to hit back at us.'

Harry stopped talking, but Cassie remained silent, knowing there was more to come.

'It's an honour to serve in the Light Company. I'm proud Captain Fox has chosen me to go with him, but I don't feel comfortable with a Light Company, Cassie. Not the way I do with our own men. I wish I wasn't going out with them tomorrow.'

'Tell Gorran Fox how you feel. He'll understand.'

Cassie felt alarmed, this was the way Harry had been during the early uncertain days of the campaign. He would lie awake at night worrying over battles that might never be fought. Uncertain of himself. Afraid . . .

'I can't say anything to him, Cassie. You heard what he said tonight. He relies on me. I can't let him down.'

'You'll not be letting him down. You'd be serving in the place where you do best. He'll understand.'

'No, I can't do it. You know I can't.'

Cassie understood. To admit he did not enjoy the manner in which the Light Company fought its battles would invite taunts from the other men that Harry was scared. The essence of the light infantry was speed. Quick thinking and quick action. Harry was not a fast thinker. He was slow, steady and thoroughly reliable. At his best in situations that called for such qualities.

Cassie decided that although Harry might not want to tell Gorran about his dislike of the Light Company, she would find some way to ensure Harry remained with 3 Company in the future.

'Go to sleep now, Harry. You need to be up early.' Cassie cuddled him to her, feeling an overwhelming need to protect him. 'Try not to worry about tomorrow. You heard what Gorran Fox said. We might wake up to find the war is over.'

'That would be nice. I feel I've had enough fighting to last me a while.'

39

❧

The Light Companies from each regiment of the 6th Division formed the spearhead for the army when it moved off and they were first to reach the River Adour, where the bridge had been blown up by the retreating enemy. Here, too, were a great many wounded French soldiers, abandoned by their countrymen in the knowledge that they would be cared for by the advancing British army.

Many of the wounded men lacked even a rudimentary dressing. Cassie and some of the other women set about tending the French soldiers while ropes were thrown across the river, which was almost five foot deep at this point. Some of the Light Companies began to cross, the soldiers clinging to the ropes, and Cassie paused to watch Harry who was among the first to reach the other side. He saw her watching and waved cheerily, his gloom of the previous night seemingly dispelled.

As others began to cross one man was washed away, taking with him another who tried to save him. The fast-moving current carried both men off swiftly. Within a matter of seconds both bobbing heads disappeared beneath the surface of the water and neither man was seen again.

The soldiers were reluctant to risk the crossing for a while but some dragoons were brought up to provide assistance. One dragoon swam his horse across the river and, taking up station below the crossing, secured a rope to his horse. The other end was secured to a second horse on the near bank. It provided a safety line for any man whose numbed fingers lost their grip and caused him to drop into the icy waters of the deep ford.

Additional dragoons joined their companions, ready to go to the aid of any infantryman who failed to secure a hold on the safety rope. Soon afterwards Lieutenant Dalhousie rode up to speak to one of the dragoons and Cassie realised the cavalrymen were from his troop. His squadron of dragoons must be attached to the 6th Division once more. Cassie wondered whether Sarah had seen him.

The Light Companies crossed quickly and formed up on the far bank before setting off at a fast pace through a wide, undulating and well wooded valley.

Cassie paused as she bound the leg of a French *grenadier* and watched the Light Companies setting off, but Harry was busy keeping his cold, wet men in close order. He did not look back and she doubted if he had seen her wave.

'Your man . . . he is with them?' The *grenadier* spoke

English with difficulty and his voice was that of a man in pain.

'My husband is a sergeant with one of the companies, yes.'

For a moment it seemed the *grenadier* would say something more. Instead he lapsed into silence.

'Lie back while I cut off your trouser leg. This wound should have been treated last night. It's a mess.'

The French *grenadier* was a victim of one of Henry Shrapnel's exploding shells. There were fragments of metal embedded in his leg. Cassie was able to remove two small, protruding particles, but it would need a surgeon's skill to locate and take out others.

When she had done all she could for the *grenadier*, Cassie moved on to help another prisoner. The regular regiments of the 6th Division were crossing the river now, but Cassie was in no hurry to join them. The 32nd would not be among the first to cross and it would be a couple of hours before the last soldier reached the far bank.

As she worked, Cassie thought she heard the sound of musketry somewhere in the distance. It came from the direction taken by the Light Companies and she paused to listen, but a soldier had just slipped from the ropes and was being rescued by the dragoons. The mixture of jeers and shouted encouragement drowned all other sounds.

When the shouting died down, Cassie resumed her work. Her patient on this occasion was a young drummer who would undoubtedly need to have his right arm amputated close to the shoulder. He seemed so young that Cassie would not have been surprised had he burst into tears while she dressed his wound. He did not shed a tear and when Cassie had finished her hopeless task she gave the surprised drummer boy a quick hug.

Cassie was giving a drink to a Frenchman who was beyond all help when she heard her name being called. Looking up, she saw one of the 32nd Light Company soldiers on the far bank of the river, waving to attract attention.

'Mrs Clymo! Mrs Clymo! I've a message for Mrs Clymo. Will someone go and find her?'

'I'm here.' Cassie stood up, feeling as though her heart was beating at twice its normal rate. 'What do you want of me?' Cassie asked the question although she dreaded the reply.

'It's your husband, Mrs Clymo. He's been wounded. A French brigade was hiding in the woods waiting for us. Captain Fox told me to come back and fetch you as quick as I could. I've run all the way.'

On the way to the river Cassie passed the French *grenadier*. Suddenly she stopped and looked down at him, 'You knew, didn't you? You knew they were lying in wait?'

The French *grenadier* averted his eyes from her tortured face and Cassie knew his information could have prevented the Light Companies from walking into a trap.

At the river bank Cassie called, anxiously, 'Is Harry badly hurt?'

'I . . . I don't know.' Cassie knew the man was being

evasive and she became more frightened than before.

The men at the water's edge had heard the exchange and they made way for her, some murmuring their sympathy. She had almost reached the bank when a voice called, 'Get up behind me,' and Lieutenant Dalhousie rode his horse up to her, extending his hand.

'Hold tight to me and don't let go. You'll get a soaking, but it will be a quicker crossing.'

The dragoon lieutenant's horse was a large animal. It crossed the river in a series of powerful bounds and soldiers on the far side helped to haul horse and riders to the bank.

When Cassie released her hands in order to slide to the ground, Lieutenant Dalhousie said, 'Sit tight, you'll be there far more quickly if we ride.'

The cavalry lieutenant dug in his spurs and with Cassie clinging tightly to him they took off along the valley at a ground-consuming gallop.

The Light Companies had fallen foul of the French brigade about two miles from the river crossing. The French soldiers had fired a single volley from their concealed position before retiring through the forest. The Light Companies were at this moment in close pursuit, but about sixty casualties and a dozen soldiers who had been left to protect them formed a small group at the edge of the roadway.

Cassie did not remember sliding from the horse, but as she reached the ground the soldiers made way for her – and she saw Harry.

Cassie knew even before she dropped to her knees beside her husband that she could do nothing to help him. As a sergeant he would have been singled out as a special target and three musket balls had struck him. Two were high in the chest, the third lower down on his body. It was little short of a miracle that he was still alive.

Harry's mouth was wide open in a desperate fight for breath. His eyes were open too and he saw her arrive. When she took his hand he tried to smile at her but the muscles of his face would not obey the command.

'I ... I'm sorry, Cassie.' The words were barely audible.

'You have nothing to be sorry about, Harry. Nothing at all. We've had over two wonderful years together. Years I wouldn't have missed for anything.'

Cassie felt his hand tighten in hers. It might have been recognition of her words, or no more than his response to a spasm of pain.

'I wish ... I wish I wasn't leaving you alone.'

'Don't worry about me, Harry. You just try to rest now.'

As Cassie leaned over him she could do nothing to stop the tears that ran from her cheeks to drop on his face.

'Ask Captain Fox to take you home. Captain Fox ...'

These were the last words Harry Clymo ever uttered. There was no great spasm to mark the passing of his life. He merely closed his eyes, as though to blink, and died. It was such a gentle passing that it was a moment or two before Cassie realised the end had come – and gone.

She bowed her head and cried until she was lifted to her feet by a surprisingly gentle Lieutenant Dalhousie.

'Come, I'll take you back to your regiment.'

As he spoke the words, Cassie realised the 32nd was no longer *her* regiment. All her ties with it had died along with Harry. She had nothing . . . No one . . .

'I can't go away and leave him lying here, like this . . .'

'I'll send out some Pioneers to bury him. He won't be alone, you know. A great many of his friends have died with him.'

Cassie nodded, still numbed by the swiftness and the finality of it all.

'We have to go now. I need to rejoin my own regiment.'

Cassie used the sleeve of her dress to wipe tears from her face and, trying hard to keep her voice from breaking, she said, 'I'm grateful to you. Very grateful. If it hadn't been for you I wouldn't have got here in time.'

They rode back to the river at a slower gait than before and Cassie was able to shed a few more tears against the back of Lieutenant Dalhousie's cloak without fear of anyone seeing her.

At the river, the 32nd had crossed together with their women and much of the baggage. The dragoon officer rode to where Sarah Coombe was seated on the ground. Ignoring the frostiness of her look, he said, 'Your friend has need of your help, Sarah. Her husband has just been killed.'

Sarah's wail of grief was far more genuine than the

487

tears she had shed at the loss of her most recent husband. Holding out her arms she caught Cassie as she slid from the horse and pulled her close. 'Oh, you poor thing! Your Harry! You poor, poor girl.'

The 32nd were assembling nearby and word that Sergeant Clymo had been killed rippled through their ranks with a sense of deep shock and dismay. After surviving two and a half years on campaign, earning promotion from raw recruit to a reliable and experienced sergeant, he had been the perfect example of what progress could be made in the King's army. His loss in a minor and fruitless skirmish would affect the morale of the whole regiment.

The colonel, his officers and many of the soldiers came to Cassie to express their sympathy, but she said little in return. She sat with Sarah, numbed and in a state of shock, sipping tea laced heavily with brandy.

The colonel informed Cassie that she need be in no hurry to leave the regiment. She would remain on their strength for as long as she wished. He also promised that a burial party of his own regiment would attend to the funeral of Sergeant Harry Clymo.

For two days Cassie said hardly a word to anyone. If she was aware that Lieutenant Dalhousie visited her on more than one occasion she gave no indication of it. Neither did she appear to notice that Sarah went missing moments after each of his visits.

Then Cassie finally came to terms with her loss and began to take on her share of the camp chores. She was helping to cook a midday meal for the soldiers when

488

the colonel sent an orderly to find her and bring her to him. Fearing the worst, Cassie made her way to where the regiment's commanding officer was dining with some of his company commanders. Much to Cassie's surprise, the officers stood up as she approached, as though she were a lady of some social standing. One of the captains even offered her a chair.

'Please sit down, Mrs Clymo,' said the colonel. 'I have two messages for you. The first is in the form of a letter from Captain Fox.'

'He's all right?' Cassie had hoped Gorran would come to see her before this. Receiving a letter instead, she feared the worst.

'Quite all right. He and the Light Company have had some notable successes. I'm proud to say that Lord Wellington has included them in his despatches – and his lordship doesn't do that without good reason. But no doubt Captain Fox explains this in his letter, which brings me to the second message. It's from Lady Fraser – I understand you and her ladyship have met before?'

When Cassie nodded, the colonel continued, 'Lady Fraser asks me to express her very deepest sympathy to you on the loss of your husband. She also requests that I persuade you to join her at Lord Wellington's headquarters. Her ladyship says there's urgent work to be done and she has desperate need of your help.'

Now Cassie understood why she had received such deferential treatment from the officers of the regiment. If she agreed to help Lady Fraser Cassie would have access to the headquarters of the British army in the Peninsula. A chance remark might be overheard by the commander-in-chief himself. On such trivia were reputations – and promotions – often based.

Cassie felt no rancour towards the colonel and his officers. There were many fine regimental commanders in the Peninsula, each fully deserving of promotion. Yet only a few would ever command a brigade or a division. Competition for the most senior ranks was fierce. Ability needed all the help it could muster to put one officer a shade ahead of his fellows.

'You'll go, of course?'

After only a moment's hesitation, Cassie nodded. It would be a relief to leave the 32nd for a while, at least. If Cassie stayed she would find herself often caught off-guard, looking for Harry when the women caught up with the regiment at the end of the day.

'Splendid! I'll arrange an escort to take you to head-quarters first thing in the morning. In the meantime, if you think of anything you may need please let me know.'

40

Cassie read Gorran's letter for the fourth time that night by the light of the fire outside the hut she shared with the other regimental wives. The letter warmed her more than the fire.

Gorran expressed his very real sorrow at the death of Harry and apologised that he had not been able to deliver a few words of comfort in person. The Light Companies were ranging far ahead of the main body of the army and had successfully carried out the task Lord Wellington had set out for them. Insufficient in numbers to inflict a severe defeat upon the French army, they had nevertheless kept it moving until it eventually reached Toulouse. Gorran predicted that the French army would make a determined stand before the city but, should it be defeated here, he believed the French commander would have no alternative but to surrender his army to the British, so bringing the war to a close.

Lord Wellington and his headquarters' staff had already visited the Light Companies' positions to take a preliminary look at the Toulouse defences and Gorran had taken the opportunity to acquaint Lady Harriet Fraser with the death of Harry. He wrote that she had shed a tear on Cassie's behalf before asking whether he thought Cassie would feel able to come to help the wounded in what might turn out to be one of the fiercest battles of the whole campaign.

If Cassie agreed, Gorran promised to make his way to Lord Wellington's headquarters at the earliest possible opportunity to visit her there. He ended his letter by urging Cassie, whatever decision she made, not to think of returning to England until he had an opportunity to speak to her.

Gorran's concern for her showed in every line of his letter and helped dull the raw sense of loss as nothing else had been able to do. It was part of Gorran's strength that things seemed much better after his intervention. Cassie had always been aware of this. So too had Harry . . .

Lady Harriet Fraser could not have been more kind to Cassie. When the young widow arrived at army head-quarters after a long ride she was immediately taken into Lady Fraser's household, not as a servant or employee but as a companion. Rose Tonks had once told Cassie that a hard campaign lowered social barriers between women who followed all ranks of the army, but this was the first occasion Cassie had experienced it to the extent she did now.

Lord Wellington's headquarters were in a village not too far from Toulouse. Lady Fraser had obtained a villa at least twice the size of that allocated to the commander-in-chief – and seemed to accept it as no more than her due. She was, in fact, entertaining Lord Wellington to dinner that evening and tried to persuade Cassie to join the party, but Cassie declined. Quite apart from feeling totally out of place in such company, Cassie doubted her ability to cope with the frivolity of such an occasion. It was too soon.

Lady Fraser accepted Cassie's reasons for not wanting to socialise just yet. That evening, after dinner, while the men smoked and told stories, she came to Cassie's room and stayed for half an hour, determined that Cassie should not feel too lonely.

During this time Lady Fraser spoke of her plans for all available women to help with the wounded. She had obtained the support of James MacGrigor, the inspector of hospitals on Lord Wellington's staff. He, too, would like to see a special unit present at the scene of every battle to bring in the wounded as they fell. However, it seemed that Lord Wellington, although occasionally known to agonise over the numbers of British casualties, was not yet ready to provide the means to bring them speedily to hospital. His favourite saying was that his duty was to fight and *win* battles. Nothing else mattered.

Finally, Lady Fraser mentioned the visit of Gorran Fox on Cassie's behalf. 'He's a fine young man,' she declared. 'He is everything that Lord Wellington looks for in an officer – and he is very fond of you.'

'He's a very special man,' agreed Cassie. Taking a deep breath, she added, 'Harry was very fond of him, too. He trusted him and his last words were of Captain Fox.'

It was the first time since Harry's death that she had actually mentioned his name. She realised she had been afraid to speak of him, fearing it would reduce her to tears. But it had not. The hurt would always be deep inside her, but she was able to contain it now.

'Harry said I should ask Gorran to take me home to Cornwall.'

'Will you?'

'I don't know what I'm going to do. Somehow, I don't think I'll be able to go home to Mevagissey to live. Too much has happened to me.'

Lady Fraser sighed. 'The army does that to a person. When I return to England I'm appalled at the frivolous lives most women seem to lead. I actually heard one young lady describe the war in the Peninsula as 'a bit of a bore'! It seems it has reduced the number of eligible young men available for parties and dances. If I had my way I'd send every young girl out here to follow the army for six months. Can you imagine some of them trying to pick their dainty way through the mud of an autumn retreat?'

Cassie gave Lady Fraser a wan smile. 'I think you're being a little hard on them.'

'Perhaps I am, but too many girls will grow up never knowing there's a real world beyond the bounds of their own narrow little lives. It really is time they realised that a woman's place is no longer at a spinning wheel in the tower of some castle, occasionally giving an excited wave of a kerchief when a handsome knight passes by at a discreet distance.'

'The women who work in the fish cellars in Mevagissey have never followed the army through a campaign but they're aware of what life is all about.' Cassie gave a gentle reminder that her companion had enjoyed a fair share of cosseting.

Lady Fraser gave Cassie a sharp, almost haughty look and then laughed. 'You're quite right, Cassie. My husband is always telling me I'm far too dogmatic when I'm airing my views – but I do hate to see women frittering their lives away. We have quite as much to offer the world as do men.'

Suddenly and quite unexpectedly, Lady Fraser gave Cassie a brief hug. 'It's nice to have someone around I can talk to, Cassie. Someone who won't allow me to get away with any outrageous or ridiculous statements. Now, tomorrow morning I've arranged for us to meet James MacGrigor. You'll like him. He's a very highly regarded surgeon and between us we're hoping we might persuade some of the divisional commanders to detail certain men to help the wounded. Drummers, cooks . . . all the men you mentioned to me before. James MacGrigor thinks he might even be able to obtain the services of some Portuguese infantrymen to act as stretcher bearers. They'll be very useful for removing the worst wounded to field hospitals – although I think it will probably take another company of British soldiers to watch *them*. I daren't tell MacGrigor that it's been tried before. The Portuguese spent their time gathering booty instead of men and more than half of them deserted. But it's the best we can do and perhaps we can put them to a better use this time.'

James MacGrigor was a vigorous man in his mid-forties with fair, curly hair and an energy that gathered up others and drew them along in his wake. He greeted Cassie and in the same breath praised her grasp of the needs of men wounded in battle. He confirmed much of what Lady Fraser had already said. The French commander-in-chief was preparing his army for a battle at Toulouse, believing that the fate of south and west France depended upon the outcome – possibly the fate of the French nation too. It would be a hard-fought and savage conflict. James MacGrigor's medical department would be concentrating all its most able surgeons and hospital facilities in the vicinity of Toulouse.

Later that day the energetic inspector of hospitals was to address the wives of men belonging to those regiments likely to be engaged in the battle. Medical packs similar to those used by Cassie would be issued to wives and they would be urged to take to the battlefield as soon as the conflict allowed.

At Cassie's suggestion, James MacGrigor agreed to emphasise that should the husband of any of the wives be among the wounded the wife would be on hand with a medical pack. She would also forgo her duties in order to give all her attention to him.

When James MacGrigor left the house the two women knew that at the battle of Toulouse those who fell would have the support of more medical facilities than had ever been gathered for a British army fighting anywhere in the world. What they could not know was the tragic extent to which they would be required.

Cassie was in Emma Fraser's nursery helping the little girl's Spanish nanny to pack toys away for the move on Toulouse which the headquarters was soon to commence. She had her back to the door when it opened, but believing it to be Lady Fraser entering the room, she called, 'We won't be more than another ten minutes, then everything will be packed ready to load on the wagon.'

When she received no reply she turned – and saw Gorran Fox standing in the doorway. Travel-weary and looking somehow frail, he said simply, 'Hello, Cassie.'

Behaving in a manner she could never afterwards explain, Cassie ran across the room and flung herself at him. When the surprised captain took her in his arms, she burst into tears. Cassie had no idea how long she cried, but she was vaguely aware of Gorran murmuring words of comfort to her as she gradually gained control of herself and pushed away from him.

'I'm sorry, Gorran . . . I don't know what came over me.'

'Please don't apologise, Cassie. If you do I shall need to do the same – and I don't want to.'

Still confused, Cassie looked around the nursery and saw she and Gorran were alone.

'I fear we might have shocked Lady Fraser's nurse-maid,' explained Gorran. 'She took young Emma off somewhere rather quickly.'

'Oh!' Cassie found meeting his eyes embarrassing. 'How did you know where to find me?'

'Lady Fraser sent me up. She seemed to think you'd be pleased to see me. I'm more sorry than I can say about Harry, Cassie. He was a splendid soldier and a good man. I really did want to come to you earlier, but it just wasn't possible.'

'I've come to terms with Harry's death now, Gorran . . . at least, I thought I had, until just now.'

'I shouldn't have arrived without sending word first. It was unthinking of me . . .'

'No, it's wonderful to see you again, Gorran. But what are you doing here? Are you on your way to rejoin the Thirty-second for the battle . . . for Toulouse?'

'No such luck, Cassie. Would you believe that with a great battle in the offing, possibly the last one of the campaign, the Thirty-second is being sent to the coast – to be issued with new uniforms! It's absolutely ridiculous!'

'It's not before time,' declared Cassie, feeling as though a great weight had been lifted from her. 'Their clothes are in a dreadful state. As for their boots! They've been begging cowhide from the regimental butchers to bind about their feet. They're paying the penalty for being part of the "Marching Division".'

Gorran's smile lit up his tired face. 'No one could accuse you of not being partisan, Cassie, or be in any doubt to which regiment you belong.'

'*Did* belong,' Cassie corrected him. 'I'm not part of any regiment now.'

'That's partly why I'm here to see you, Cassie.

Everyone in the Thirty-second still thinks of you as belonging to us, so if you'd like to travel with the regiment until you decide to return to England I'm sure it can be arranged. Then when you're ready to go home I'll see you're put safely on board a ship. It would give me a great deal of pleasure to have you stay with the regiment.'

'I won't be returning to England for a while, at least. Lady Fraser thinks there'll be work for us both to do soon.'

'At Toulouse?' Gorran Fox frowned. 'There's going to be some fierce fighting before the town is taken, I know. The Light Companies chased the French almost to the city gates and I've seen the defences they have prepared. You don't have to go there, Cassie. I'm sure Lady Fraser will understand.'

'I know you're only thinking of my safety, Gorran, but I want to be there, just as you do. I want to be there because I believe I'll be useful. Do you understand?'

'I wish I didn't. I'd rather you were in a place where I knew you were safe, but perhaps if I speak to the colonel he'll allow me to go to Toulouse with another regiment.'

'I'd rather you didn't, Gorran. Anyway, I wouldn't be any safer with you there. It would just give me an extra thing to worry about. Your place is with the Thirty-second – and I'm pleased to know the regiment won't be involved in the battle.'

For a few moments Cassie and Gorran stood looking at each other uncertainly, then they heard someone mounting the stairs to the nursery. It was Lady Fraser.

'Hello, you two. Have you sorted out what you're both going to do?'

Gorran smiled resignedly. 'We can't agree on the matter, but yes, we both know what we'll be doing. It seems I must go to the coast with my regiment while Cassie remains with you.'

'I'm relieved. Cassie's help is important, you know. One day all the things we are fighting so hard for will be taken for granted – but only if we can prove the need for them now.'

'Perhaps I might find it easier to accept if I were taking part in the battle, instead of going off to pick up new uniforms.' Gorran's face expressed his exasperation.

'Why are all men so bloodthirsty? Sir William is exactly the same. Be grateful to miss this battle, Captain Fox. If it's the last one of the war, as many believe it to be, you'll have survived the campaign with enough experience to warrant future promotion. If my arguments fail to convince you I'd like you to join us for dinner tonight. Lord Wellington will be there and you may have an opportunity to plead your case to him in person – but I offer you a word of caution. Whatever his decision, accept it without argument. Lord Wellington is impatient with those who disagree with him.'

Gorran knew he should return to his regiment, but an opportunity to dine with the commander-in-chief could not be turned down. The colonel of the 32nd would agree, especially if he was able to persuade Lord Wellington to allow the regiment to fight at Toulouse.

*　　*　　*

Dinner was a convivial affair. Lady Fraser was a superb hostess and Lord Wellington a charming guest. Cassie had been concerned that her ignorance of the social graces would expose her to ridicule, but during the last few days Lady Harriet Fraser had been cleverly teaching by example and she was satisfied Cassie would not disgrace either of them.

Lady Fraser had always believed her protégée possessed sufficient self-confidence to carry herself through such an occasion, and when she saw Cassie wearing a dress she had loaned to her, she knew she would be a great success. She realised, with a twinge of envy, that Cassie possessed a youthful beauty that would make her the focus of every man's attention at dinner.

The evening went exactly as Harriet Fraser believed it would. Lord Wellington was as attracted to a beautiful woman as any other man. He paid Cassie a great deal of attention, as did almost every other man in the room.

Before the dinner party, Lady Fraser had informed her guests that Cassie had very recently been widowed and asked them to make no mention of her late husband lest it upset her. Consequently, only Lady Fraser and Gorran knew that Cassie had been married to a sergeant in the 32nd Regiment.

Gorran was less successful in his attempt to have the 32nd's issue of new uniforms put back until the battle for Toulouse had been fought. Fixing him with a decidedly frosty look, the great general said, 'Your wish to have your regiment take part in a major battle is admirable, Captain Fox. However, if I am to lead a victorious army through France it will need to *look* like a victorious army. One or two regiments might almost be mistaken for Spanish partisans. The Thirty-second is one. If you're so keen to have your regiment do battle it might be better if you were with them now, and not enjoying yourself at a party. You might be able to hurry them along a little.'

The commander-in-chief's reply stung Gorran, but before he could make a reply, Lady Fraser was at his side and had a firm grip on his arm. Smiling at Wellington, she said, 'You don't mind if I take Captain Fox off for a while, my lord? He rode in only today after chasing the French army all the way to Toulouse with the Light Companies. I'd like him to talk with Cassie for a while.'

Leading Gorran firmly away, Harriet Fraser smiled at him to disguise her words. 'Lose that angry expression if you value your career – and quickly! Not even generals are allowed to look at Lord Wellington in such a way.'

'I thank you for your concern, Lady Fraser, but Lord Wellington shows no gratitude for the onerous duties performed by the Thirty-second Regiment – which is the reason they are "as ragged as Spanish partisans".'

'There are officers more generous with their praise than my Lord Wellington, but if he believes he has been unfair, either to you or your regiment, he will make amends in his own fashion. Do not expect an apology. You must also realise he has a great deal on his mind at the moment. You've heard of the antics of the Duc d'Angoulême, Pretender to the throne of France?'

Gathering Cassie on her other arm, Harriet Fraser put the question to both Cassie and Gorran as she led them towards the marble fireplace at the far end of the room. Both her companions confessed their ignorance of the deeds of the Pretender to the throne of France.

'Let me explain, then perhaps you might at least understand our commander-in-chief's irascibility. Lord Beresford was sent with the Fourth and Seventh Divisions to occupy Bordeaux. This he did without opposition. The Duc d'Angoulême, following close behind, entered the city and had himself proclaimed King Louis the Eighteenth. He then issued a statement that he was in France to destroy Napoleon and bring back the monarchy!

'When Lord Beresford withdrew his cavalry and the Fourth Division from Bordeaux the peasants began burning the houses of those gentlemen who had rallied to the banner of the Duc. He became alarmed and demanded that Lord Wellington supply troops and money to protect him and his followers.

'Lord Wellington replied by pointing out that the Duc d'Angoulême must look for money from the men who proclaimed him king. He had no troops to spare to protect either the Duc's supporters, or their property. Furthermore, if the "King" did not repudiate the more objectionable sections of the Royal Proclamation, Lord Wellington would be obliged to do so himself and, by so doing, publicly announce that the Duc d'Angoulême does not have his support.'

Releasing the arms of her two guests and beaming at both of them, Lady Fraser said, 'So, you see, Lord Wellington is not only fighting a war, he is obliged to chasten "Kings" and tread the narrow and precarious

503

line of diplomacy. It is demanding a great deal from a man who wishes only to fight and win battles. Now, you two have a nice chat together, and please, do not judge Lord Wellington too harshly.'

As Lady Fraser made her way along the room, pausing to talk to another group of guests, Gorran rubbed his jaw ruefully. 'I think I've just been admonished – but very charmingly.'

'Do I understand from what's been said that Lord Wellington has refused permission for the Thirty-second to take part in the battle for Toulouse?'

'Not only that but he told me I should be with the regiment now and not enjoying myself at a party.'

'That's hardly fair! Although, I must admit, I'm relieved the Thirty-second won't be involved in the fighting. But if you want to leave the party I don't mind leaving too. Lady Fraser is a wonderful person, but I feel out of place among her guests.'

'Nonsense, Cassie! You wouldn't be out of place in any company in that dress. I'm the envy of every man here because you're talking to me. I'm the one who doesn't belong. I'm the only officer of junior rank here. The next lowest is a colonel – and rumour has it that he'll be a brigadier-general before the battle begins.'

'That's probably because he hasn't shown any particular eagerness to take part in Lord Wellington's battles.'

'Possibly – but you're just as keen as I am to be at Toulouse.'

'I don't want to be there. I'd be far happier if there was no battle. Unfortunately, if there is we're going to have a great many wounded and they'll need help. I know that if I were in England and had a husband, son or father fighting out here, I'd like to know there was someone to care for him if he was wounded. It's as though I'm doing it for Harry. He had no one to care for him for so many years . . .'

'I see.' Gorran knew better than to try to dissuade Cassie from carrying out her intentions, but he was unhappy at the thought of her being so close to the fighting, especially as he would not be there. 'Don't do anything foolish, Cassie. I want you to promise me you'll not take any unnecessary risks.'

Cassie smiled at him, but she made no promises.

At that moment a red-faced major-general approached them and said loudly, 'Come now, captain. You mustn't keep such a beautiful young lady to yourself. We cavalrymen don't have many opportunities to chat with young ladies, you know. Not like you infantrymen.'

Cassie looked at Gorran, silently pleading with him not to leave her, but he was speaking to the major-general. 'I relinquish her company with great reluctance, sir, but as Lord Wellington has reminded me, it's time I returned to my regiment.'

Gorran bowed low to Cassie. 'Remember, Cassie, take care. I'll be looking for you when I return.'

Cassie hardly listened to the major-general as she watched Gorran walking the length of the room. She wished there had been an opportunity to say something more personal to him. To tell *him* to take care.

Gorran paused to thank Sir William and Lady Fraser before leaving. He had almost reached the door when the voice of Lord Wellington halted him and silenced the room.

'Captain Fox!'

Gorran spun around and looked towards the commander-in-chief, believing he had unwittingly offended him, such was the tone of Lord Wellington's voice.

'Where are you off to, sir?'

'Returning to my regiment, my lord.'

'To take them to collect new uniforms?' The commander-in-chief's tone was only mocking for a moment. 'My adjutant-general informs me your Light Infantry Company recently took the brunt of an attack by a large French force and drove them back to their own lines in no uncertain manner.'

'My company had that honour, my lord.'

'I can't afford to have such men parading like popinjays when there's a battle to be fought. Return to the Thirty-second and tell your colonel I have need of your company. You will join up with the Light Division and remain with them until Toulouse is taken.'

Before Gorran could recover from his surprise, Wellington was walking away and calling for Sir William Fraser.

Looking down the long room, Gorran's smile threatened to split his face as he raised a hand in a triumphant farewell to Cassie before turning and hurrying from the house.

41

※

The city of Toulouse was a defending general's dream. Behind the fortified town a wide and impassable river curved around the city walls. In front was a range of low but steep-sided hills, on the crest of which had been constructed a series of defences calculated to deter the most reckless attacker. Even the roads criss-crossing the heights were sunk beneath the ground, deep enough to be used as trenches and so wide that cavalry would be useless. At the same time, cannon had been cleverly positioned so as to command the sunken roads should an enemy try to take advantage of the cover they promised.

For two whole days Lord Wellington observed the French defences while planning his attack. All the time his cavalry and light infantry were probing and observing, mapping and reporting to him.

During these two days Cassie assisted Lady Fraser.

They discussed the best way to use their meagre resources during the forthcoming battle, but realised from the outset that providing any form of organised aid was not going to be an easy task. No wife wanted to be treating wounded men in one place while her husband was fighting in another. It was a similar story with the Portuguese and Spanish camp followers. Although they had no official status, most of the women cared a great deal for the men some had followed across half a continent. They had little interest in any others. Those women who cared less would be following close behind the army anyway, but for more sinister reasons.

On the eve of battle, while Lord Wellington was spelling out his plans to his generals, help was offered to Lady Fraser from two unexpected sources. The first was Father Michael.

The Dominican friar found Cassie and Lady Fraser checking medical packs in the wagon from which they would be distributed before the fighting began. The news he brought overjoyed them both. A company of Portuguese troops had just arrived from their homeland to join the army fighting in France. None of the new arrivals had any experience of war – few had even received any training. In view of the importance of the forthcoming engagement the British commander of the Portuguese troops refused to send them into battle. He readily agreed to Father Michael's suggestion that they be used to assist the wounded. Such a role would give them useful experience of battlefield conditions.

The Portuguese troops knew no more about the treatment of wounded men than they did of warfare, but at least they could gather the wounded and save them from the attentions of the battlefield predators.

Cassie was pleased to see the Dominican friar once more and when Harriet Fraser left for a meeting with James MacGrigor the two spoke together for a couple of hours as Father Michael helped Cassie with her work. He promised that when the battle began he would be on hand to deal with any problems of language that might arise, even though Lady Fraser knew sufficient Spanish to make her orders understood.

The second offer of help was on a much smaller scale and arrived as Father Michael was leaving.

'Well, well! It looks as though you're to be visited by another old friend, Cassie. Aren't you the most popular one today? Or would the young lady have someone else on her mind?'

Turning to follow the direction of Father Michael's glance, Cassie saw Sarah Coombe leading a small donkey towards them. When Sarah saw Cassie she waved cheerily.

'I'll leave you to speak with your friend,' said the Irish friar hurriedly. 'There's something about that little lady that causes me to remember the man I once was. It bothers me.'

'Sarah has that effect on most men, Father, but she has a kind heart.'

'I must remember that when I next think unkindly of her.' Nodding to Sarah as he passed her by, the black-robed friar mounted his horse and rode away.

'He seemed in a hurry to be off,' commented Sarah to Cassie. 'Was it something he thought I might say?'

'Father Michael finds men easier to understand than he does women – but what are you doing here, so far from the Thirty-second?'

Cassie looked to where a long line of horses was picketed along the bank of a nearby stream. 'I suppose it has nothing to do with the presence of a certain regiment of dragoons?'

'That's hardly a charitable remark to make, Cassie, and you so friendly with men of the Christian Church. As it happens I did recognise a certain dragoon lieutenant as I passed by the camp, but the main reason I'm not with the Thirty-second is because Damian is here with Captain Fox and his Light Company.'

'But the Light Companies don't take their wives with them.'

'Exactly. That's why I'm here with you, Cassie. I heard you and Lady Fraser were hard put to find women to bring comfort to wounded soldiers. Sarah, I thought, it sounds just the job for you. Chances are I'll also be able to keep an eye on that husband of mine at the same time, and, believe me, this one needs more looking after than most of the others put together.'

'Well, we can certainly use your help. Have you seen the French defences on the hills over there? A lot of lives are going to be lost when we try to take them.'

'Why is it necessary to try to take them?' Sarah suddenly sounded bitter. 'Rumour has it that things are going so badly for Napoleon, he'll be forced to end the war soon. If Lord Wellington waits for a few days the war will probably be over.'

'Where did you hear such a rumour?'

510

Sarah shrugged. 'It's all around the army. It seems a captured French officer has said everyone in the French army expects the fighting to cease in days rather than weeks.'

'It can't be true. Lord Wellington would never fight such a terrible battle as this promises to be if he didn't have to.'

Sarah shrugged again. 'I'm not saying he would – but I'm not saying he wouldn't, neither. All I know is that a general needs to fight battles if he's to get honours from a grateful country.'

'I wouldn't let Lady Fraser hear you talk about Lord Wellington in such a way – and here she comes now.'

Lady Fraser was delighted to welcome Sarah to the ranks of her helpers. 'That's splendid. *Splendid!* Do you have somewhere to stay tonight? I expect I can find somewhere for you.'

'There's no need to bother. I've an old friend in one of the regiments over there.' Carefully avoiding Cassie's eyes, Sarah flapped her hand in a vague, meaningless gesture.

'Well, if you're quite certain. Cassie, dear, I need to go to headquarters. I want to ask Lord Wellington where we're most likely to be needed tomorrow. Will you see that the girl puts Emma to bed on time? I want her to have a good night's sleep. We none of us know what tomorrow will bring.'

When Lady Fraser had gone, Cassie asked, 'Where was it you said you were spending the night, Sarah?'

'I didn't say. Does it matter to anyone but me?'

'It shouldn't, I suppose, but I thought you had a very

511

low opinion of Mr Dalhousie and never wanted to see him again.'

'Did I ever say that? Well, he doesn't give a damn for me, that's for sure, but he does have a certain charm. It probably has something to do with the fact that he's an officer – and a gentleman.'

'I wouldn't know.'

'Is that the truth? Then Captain Fox must be coming this way to see someone else.'

As Cassie swung around to see Gorran riding towards them, Sarah added, 'If you allow Captain Fox to get away from you then you need shooting, Cassie Clymo. He's a man, same as a corporal, a private, or a sergeant – and he's had a thing going for you since before you were married. All you need do is hold out your arms and take him. If you don't, you're a fool.' With this advice, Sarah walked away and left Cassie to greet the 32nd Regiment's captain.

When Gorran reached Cassie, he said, 'Wasn't that Sarah, Damian Coombe's wife, I saw just leaving? What's she doing here? She should know wives aren't allowed to travel with light infantry companies.'

'Sarah knows regulations better than most soldiers. She came to offer her services to Lady Fraser, for tomorrow.'

'I see. Did Sarah say anything to upset you? You seem a little flustered.'

'I've known Sarah far too long to be upset by anything she says. But what are you doing here? I thought you'd be preparing for tomorrow.'

'It's tonight for the Light Company, Cassie, and all is

512

in readiness. The general sent me here to see if Lord Wellington has any last-minute orders for us.'

'So there is to be a battle?' After what Sarah had said, Cassie had half hoped there would be no more fighting.

'Oh yes, there is to be a battle – and a major one at that. You will take care, Cassie? I wish you were some-where safe, with the other Thirty-second Regiment women.'

'I no longer belong to the Thirty-second, Gorran. You know that.'

'I'll always think of you as part of the regiment, Cassie. Take care tomorrow.'

'I'll be the one doing all the worrying. Don't take any foolish chances, Gorran.'

They were standing very close together and when Cassie saw the way Gorran was looking at her she caught her breath.

'Cassie! Did I leave my shawl here? William wants to take me—Oh! Hello, Captain Fox. I didn't realise you were here.'

Lady Fraser realised she had arrived at a most inop-portune moment and could have kicked herself. She believed Cassie and Gorran were ideally suited to each other. The problem was to make them both see it for themselves.

'Ah, here it is.' She picked up the shawl and draped it around her shoulders. 'I'm sorry to have disturbed you.'

'There's no need to apologise. I'm just leaving. I need to rejoin my company.'

'A few minutes more will make no difference to anyone. Stay with Cassie for a while.'

'I've been away far too long already. Goodbye, Lady Fraser, Cassie.'

'Take care, Gorran.' Her thoughts in a turmoil, Cassie desperately wanted him to stay, but he had already reached his horse. Swinging into the saddle he paused to wave once, and then he was gone.

Lady Fraser had been watching Cassie's face and now she took her hands in both her own. 'I am terribly sorry, Cassie. Had I realised Captain Fox was with you I would never have come looking for such a silly thing as a shawl.'

'It was kind of him to come at all. He wished us luck for tomorrow. Said he'd be thinking of . . . us.'

Cassie was still confused. Watching Gorran Fox ride away had been like seeing a part of herself leave. She felt incomplete in a way she never had before.

Still watching Cassie's face, Harriet Fraser squeezed her hands. 'He'll be back, my dear, and perhaps tomorrow won't be as bad as we all fear.'

42

❧

The tenth of April in the year 1814 was a day that would be remembered by tens of thousands of soldiers who fought in Wellington's army. The day began early for everyone – and ended equally early for a great many.

It was 2 a.m. when the Light Company passed through the British lines and crossed a bridge over the River Garonne, many miles from Toulouse. They then set out on a rapid march that would bring them close to the French positions in time to clear a path for the advance of the main British army.

At 6 a.m., in the dawn light, the first shots were fired and the first men died as the Light Company drove the French pickets back to their own lines. At the same time the various divisions of the British army moved forward to take up the positions assigned to them by the commander-in-chief.

To Cassie, Sarah and Lady Fraser, waiting with the

soldiers' wives on the slopes of a hill at the rear of the army, it was as though they were watching some gigantic and colourful pageant unfolding before their eyes.

As befitting such a spectacle there was a vast audience. They lined the fortified walls of Toulouse and gathered on the surrounding hills, from where Lord Wellington had taken careful notes of the enemy's defences. Many more were gathered around Cassie and the other women. Wagon drivers and drovers, sutlers and commissaries, pedlars and prostitutes, children and sick soldiers – some genuine, others with pre-battle illnesses. All watched the drama beginning to unfold before them.

Almost sixty thousand allied troops were involved in the attack and they moved over the country on their predetermined routes, all converging on differing sections of the French-held heights. Here and there a squadron of British or German horsemen was chasing French cavalry back to their lines in almost leisurely fashion. It all seemed so unreal that when Sarah spoke to Cassie it was in a whisper.

'It's almost as though they're rehearsing for something.' Then, in her normal voice, she said, 'I wish they'd hurry up and get on with whatever they intend doing. I didn't have any breakfast this morning and my belly thinks my throat's been cut.'

Sarah had not remained in the headquarters' camp the previous night. At dawn she had arrived from the direction of the dragoon quarters.

Hardly had her complaint been uttered when the artillery of both armies commenced a noisy, long-range battle overture. Much of the French firing was aimed at the 4th and 6th Divisions who were moving from right to left along the front of the heavily fortified French-held hills. The country they were traversing was marshy and criss-crossed with numerous streams, making the advancing soldiers slow-moving targets. Unable to get out of range because of a river on their left, the unfortunate infantry had no alternative but to flounder on, heading for the designated position from which they would launch their attack.

There were already a number of casualties among the men of the two British divisions and Lady Fraser called on Cassie and some of the wives to come with her to aid them. The women were intercepted by a sergeant of the provost marshal's department before they could reach a small bridge that spanned the river separating the women from the battleground.

Putting his horse in front of them, the sergeant said, 'Sorry, ladies. I have orders to stop you going any further.'

'Orders? *Whose* orders?' Lady Fraser bristled with indignation.

'They came from Lord Wellington himself, ma'am. There's an attack developing and you might find yourself caught up in the fighting . . .'

A shell landed nearby and the explosion caused the sergeant's horse to dance in a full circle. When he had the animal under control, the sergeant leaned from his saddle and said, 'Between you and me, ma'am, it's the Spanish who are going in. Chances are they'll come running back again so fast you're all likely to be trampled into the ground by 'em.'

'Very well. We'll remain on this side of the river for the moment but you may remind Lord Wellington that we're not here as spectators. Men are being wounded and need attention. I intend they shall have it – so he'd better drive the French from their positions as quickly as possible.'

'Yes, ma'am, I'll make sure his lordship is told of your wishes.' Highly amused at the thought of passing such a message to the illustrious commander-in-chief of the British army at the height of such a crucial battle, the sergeant rode away.

'Shall we go back to where we were?' The querulous question came from one of the wives as another shell exploded about a hundred paces from them, seemingly aimed at the narrow bridge across the river.

'We'll remain here . . .'

'There go the Spanish infantrymen.' Cassie passed on the news as she saw two long lines of Spanish soldiers fan out to assault one of the strongpoints on the crest of a hill to the right of the watching women.

'God help 'em!' commented Sarah as the Spanish troops extended their line to sweep around the side and front of the hill.

There must have been three thousand soldiers in each of the two lines, with another three thousand held in reserve. Heavy cannon fire from the French stronghold was already creating great gaps in the two advancing ranks.

As the Spanish soldiers drew closer to the hilltop fortifications, musket fire from the defenders added to the destruction in their ranks. Before long it seemed there were almost as many blue-uniformed soldiers lying on the ground as were advancing.

Suddenly the second line wavered – and broke. Soldiers turned and fled headlong down the hill. Deserted by so many of their companions, many men of the leading line also fled, but hundreds more, in advance of the others, rushed for the sanctuary of a road that ran through a shallow ravine just ahead of them.

It proved to be a ghastly error. A battery of French guns on their flank was trained along this road and it immediately laid down a devastating barrage. At the same time the French defenders on the hilltop left their own trenches. Lining the top of the shallow ravine they poured volley after volley of musket shots into the dead and wounded soldiers lying in a bloody tangle on the roadway twenty-five feet below them. It was not a battle but slaughter.

Meanwhile, at the foot of the hill Spanish officers rallied their troops and with the added strength of their reserves rushed back up the hill. This time the momentum of their charge carried them all the way to the edge of the sunken road where their countrymen lay in mangled masses. One look at the horrific carnage was enough. The Spanish soldiers turned tail and fled once more.

This time French soldiers poured down the hill after them until British artillery ranged on them, and men of the Light Company ran to head them off.

The British army was in motion now, attacking in a number of places but with mixed success. At a canal bridge close to the Spanish débâcle, General Picton with some of the most experienced soldiers in the British army was repulsed, leaving four hundred men of the 3rd Division on the ground behind him.

Meanwhile the 4th and 6th Divisions, their passage across the front of the French positions marked by a trail of dead and wounded men, turned to face their attackers. When the order to attack came they fixed bayonets and, with a cheer, charged up the slope, eager for revenge. At the same time, British cavalry swept around the hills to the rear of the defences, intent upon cutting off the enemy's line of retreat.

Surveying the extensive area of battle, littered with casualties, Lady Fraser reached a decision.

'If we wait any longer there won't be enough hours in the day to help those who have been wounded already – and I fear the fighting has hardly begun. Come along.'

With many of the women leading donkeys, the panniers of which were stuffed with medical packs, Lady Fraser led the way across the bridge to where the battle raged along a front of almost a mile. All semblance of organisation ceased immediately. There were wounded men everywhere they looked – British, Spanish, Portuguese, even a few French.

Cassie and Sarah found themselves working among the Spanish soldiers, many of whom were suffering from shock in addition to their wounds. They understood nothing of what the two women said to them but there was no need for talk when wounds were being dressed.

As she worked, Cassie became aware that the battle was not slackening off as might have been expected had the assault been successful.

At one point Father Michael came up the slope and Cassie asked him to speak to a seriously wounded Spanish soldier who had been fingering a crucifix during the whole of the time she was binding a serious chest wound. When the friar returned a few minutes later he was carrying the crucifix.

'He's dead?' It was more a statement than a question.

'Yes, but before he died he asked me to give you this,' said Father Michael, handing Cassie the crucifix. 'Take care of it, Cassie. It's gold, probably ancient and quite valuable, I should think. It came with the gratitude of a dying man.'

'There will be many dying men today, I fear.'

Father Michael nodded. 'The Spanish have lost fifteen hundred, Picton's attack on the bridge cost four hundred lives and they say the slaughter on the hill where the Fourth and Sixth Divisions are fighting is indescribable. The Black Watch have lost all but a handful of men and some regiments have scarcely any officers left alive.'

'What of the Light Company?'

'They seem to have had a comparatively easy day so far. They've been holding the canal against any surprise crossing, but I believe they're being used to support the Spanish now. They want to have another attempt at this hill . . .'

Cassie's heart sank. 'Haven't enough men been killed and wounded on one stupid hill?'

Resting a hand on her head for a moment, Father Michael said, 'This is a day for making sacrifices on insignificant hills, Cassie, or have you forgotten it's Easter Sunday?'

'Cassie!' Sarah's call interrupted the conversation between Father Michael and Cassie. 'Do you have any more bandages there? I'm running short.'

'There are plenty in the panniers on my donkey. Bring another pack up for me too, will you?'

Cassie's donkey was tethered at the foot of the hill, in the shade of the single remaining wall of a derelict cottage. As Sarah picked her way down the slope a troop of Light Dragoons came past the cottage at the trot. Sarah waved furiously in their direction and Cassie recognised the officer in charge as Lieutenant Dalhousie.

The dragoon officer raised his hand to return her wave when suddenly Sarah pitched to the ground. Cassie's first thought was that Sarah had tripped and would rise quickly, feeling extremely foolish to have fallen on her face in Lieutenant Dalhousie's sight. Then the dragoon turned his horse away from his troop and Cassie realised Sarah was not going to rise to her feet.

She began running down the hill and Father Michael led his horse after her. Lieutenant Dalhousie reached the prone figure first and was off his horse and crouching by Sarah's side when Cassie reached the spot.

There was no need to ask what had happened. A rapidly spreading patch of blood stained the back of Sarah's dress and there was a small round hole in the material, just beneath Sarah's right shoulder blade.

As Cassie threw her medical pack down beside her friend and dropped to her knees beside it, Lieutenant Dalhousie looked up at her angrily. 'There was no need for anyone to shoot her. The French could see plainly she is a woman. There was no need.'

Cassie ripped the dress away from the wound and could see frothy blood bubbling from the blue-tinged hole. She had treated enough wounds to realise nothing could be done for Sarah. When she turned her over she was doubly sure. Blood was spilling from a hole high in Sarah's stomach. Fired from the heights behind them, the musket ball had passed right through Sarah's slim body.

Cassie had thought Sarah was unconscious, but as she tore the front of the dress away and applied a pad of lint to the wound, Sarah said breathlessly, 'I'm glad you came back to see me.'

When Cassie looked up from her hopeless task she saw Sarah was gazing up at Lieutenant Dalhousie.

'Sarah, you know very well I'd ride to the ends of the earth if I thought it would give you pleasure.'

The exaggerated claim came off Lieutenant Dalhousie's tongue so glibly it had to be a lie, but it pleased Sarah. There was triumph as well as despair in the look she gave to Cassie.

Suddenly Sarah's body stiffened in pain beneath Cassie's hands and her head fell back. Closing her eyes, she whispered, 'This is silly . . . So damned silly,' and with these words on her lips, Sarah died.

Standing up and blinking through her tears, Cassie looked at Lieutenant Dalhousie. 'That was a very kind thing you did for Sarah.'

Lieutenant Dalhousie pulled on his white leather gloves that had become smeared with Sarah's blood. 'It cost me nothing. I'd do the same for any girl. Now I suggest you take cover. There's a French sharpshooter up there who isn't fussy about shooting women. I know there are many more women in this world, but Captain Fox might not be so easily consoled. Goodbye, Cassie.'

When Cassie turned back to Sarah, Father Michael was kneeling beside her murmuring a prayer and Cassie thrust the crucifix at him. 'Here . . . I'd like this to be buried with her.'

As Cassie turned away to make her way towards the donkey, Father Michael said softly, 'I'm sure she'll have a very special place in heaven, Cassie. Our Lord always had a soft spot in his heart for sinners.'

Cassie dressed many more wounds that day but remembered the details of very few of them. When the 6th Division took the heights and began sweeping the enemy before them the French called it a day and withdrew into the fortified town of Toulouse. It was still only 5 p.m., but the battle of Toulouse was over.

Now the battle-weary troops retraced their footsteps to help gather their wounded and bury their dead – and there were a great many of each. Even so, the medical attention given to more than 4200 allied casualties achieved a standard never before attained during the whole of the Peninsular campaign.

Lady Fraser gave this information to Cassie two days after the battle when they were helping to fit out a convent in Toulouse as a hospital. There had been no fighting on the day following the battle and some time during the night of 11 April the French army stole away from the town. Behind them they left an additional 1800 French wounded for the British surgeons to attend to.

The two women were making up beds when they

heard the murmur of nun's voices raised in protest moments before Gorran Fox strode through the door. Unshaven and muddy, he saw Cassie with Lady Fraser and his face broke into an expression of relief. Cassie felt an overwhelming sense of joy and it seemed the most natural thing in the world to run to him and hug him.

As he held her, Gorran exclaimed, 'Thank God! I rode into Toulouse to be told one of Lady Fraser's helpers had been shot dead. The man who told me thought it was you. I was looking for Lady Fraser, expecting to hear the worst.'

'It was Sarah who was shot.' As Cassie broke from Gorran's clasp sadness clouded her happiness. 'If you don't know, then her husband will probably need to be told.'

'Damian Coombe? He'll never know, Cassie. He was one of the first men killed when we went to the aid of the Spanish on the day of the battle.'

'So Sarah outlived him, too.' Cassie managed a sad smile. 'She would like to have known that.'

Looking up into Gorran's face Cassie saw a deep weariness there. 'Come and sit down and tell me where you've been. I was worried about you, even though I knew your name wasn't on any of the casualty lists.'

'We were sent to watch the road to Villefranche. The French army made its way there during the night and we followed them.'

Cassie's spirits sank. 'Does that mean we'll now have a battle for Villefranche and more casualties?'

'There will be no more battles, Cassie. Two colonels,

one French, the other English, rode in from Paris today. Napoleon Bonaparte abdicated on 7 April. The war is over. It has been over for five days.'

'So Sarah was right! The battle for Toulouse should never have been fought. All the men who were killed and maimed ... Sarah ... They died in vain. None of it need have happened.'

'No one could have known, Cassie. Least of all the soldiers who fought and died.' Lady Fraser entered the conversation. 'It's one of the great tragedies of war that such things happen.'

Cassie looked at Gorran's drawn and tired face and tried not to allow her bitterness to show.

'No doubt you're right. Gorran, you look exhausted. Where is your company now?'

'The men are settled in comfortable billets. I'll seek new orders for them tomorrow.'

'You look as though you need a good night's sleep.' Cassie looked questioningly at Lady Fraser.

'He must stay in our house. The room at the end of the corridor. You take him – and arrange a meal for him while you're there. I've never yet met a soldier returning from war who didn't have a ravenous appetite.'

The room Lady Fraser had put at Gorran's disposal was large and comfortable. Too comfortable. Looking at the large bed and all the trappings of an ordered household, suddenly all the proprieties that were forgotten on a campaign were remembered.

'I'll go and find something for you to eat. If you're cold you can put a light to the fire laid in the grate.'

'Cassie, before you go I need to talk to you.'

526

'You look so tired I doubt if you can even think straight.'

'I did all the thinking that was needed before I came here. Now I need to discuss those thoughts with you.'

'Later, Gorran. I'll go and find you some food.'

Before he could argue again, Cassie was out of the room and hurrying along the corridor. Her thoughts and emotions were in turmoil. She believed she knew what Gorran wanted to say to her. She believed he would ask her to marry him ... and she did not know what her reply would be. She loved him, she knew that for certain now. Loved him in a way she never had poor Harry. That had been a young girl's love. An adventure into adult life, with a result no sixteen-year-old girl could have anticipated.

Now there was Gorran. Looking back it seemed there had always been Gorran, even though she had not needed to face up to it before. Now she had to, and she was confused.

Pushing open the door to his room with a tray of food in her hands, Cassie steeled herself to give him the reply she felt was the only one possible, but Gorran was asleep. Lying on the bed, half clothed, exhaustion had beaten him. Pulling the bedclothes over him carefully, Cassie's resolve weakened momentarily as she gazed down at the sleeping man, but he would never know ...

When Lady Fraser returned to the house, Cassie told her that Gorran had fallen asleep without having anything to eat.

'The poor man must be quite exhausted,' said Lady

Fraser sympathetically. 'Yet he came looking for you instead of going straight to bed. You must marry him quickly, Cassie. He absolutely adores you, it's clear to everyone. He's also a very eligible young man. When the regiment returns to England there will be any number of young women after him.'

'I can't marry him. His father has money and land. Mine is a fisherman. Our backgrounds are totally different.'

'What utter nonsense! There might possibly be problems if Captain Fox belonged to one of the so-called great families of the land – although there are plenty of precedents for such a marriage here too – but he's from good, sound, solid stock – and so are you. What's more, you're an intelligent and attractive girl. Any father would be delighted to welcome you into his family. Marry him, Cassie – before someone else does.'

43

Gorran slept through the remainder of that day and the night that followed. He came to the breakfast table next morning cleaner and newly shaved, but his eyes were puffy as a result of an excess of unaccustomed sleep.

Lady Fraser cut short his apologies. 'After the trials and exertions of the past few weeks I'm surprised you didn't sleep for a week. William went to headquarters only half an hour ago, feeling as guilty as you. After rising before dawn every morning for almost five years it will take everyone a long time to become accustomed to civilised ways once more. I can't wait for the day when the sun beats Lord Wellington to his doorway. By dawn his lordship has usually spent two hours writing reports, having issued detailed orders for each of his divisional commanders. We're a peacetime army now, and I for one am not sorry. I will soon need to give some thought to educating Emma. What are your immediate plans, Gorran?'

'My regiment is on its way here and is expected to arrive in about a week's time. There's little sense in marching my company to meet them. The men are in need of a good rest. We'll wait for the regiment to arrive.'

'Splendid!' Lady Fraser had already thought of a few ways in which Cassie and Gorran might be thrown together. 'You'll stay on in your room, of course, and you can escort Cassie and me to all the balls and parties the mayor and everyone else in Toulouse seem determined to throw in our honour. If I know Sir William he'll think up a hundred and one reasons why he can't attend.'

With her customary perceptiveness, Lady Fraser saw the fleeting expression of concern that crossed Cassie's face and correctly diagnosed its cause. Cassie would have had little opportunity to learn to dance.

'You and I must find someone to teach us the steps of the dances they enjoy here, Cassie. I'll do something about it right away.'

That afternoon, after Gorran had checked that the men of his company had no problems, he borrowed a horse for Cassie and they went riding to the north of the town. It was fairy-tale country containing great houses with rounded, high-roofed turrets, some perched on the edge of river-edge cliffs, others surrounded by flowering trees and bushes. Most also had a field or two of grapes.

At one such house, Cassie and Gorran were admiring the garden through an open gateway when a horseman came along the road behind them, riding towards the house. They pulled their horses to one side, but the man reined in when he reached them. Looking at Gorran's uniform he asked in French to which regiment he belonged.

When Gorran began to explain in indifferent French, the man interrupted him in amazement. 'You are English? But what are you doing here – and with your lady? Are you not afraid of the soldiers of Napoleon Bonaparte?'

'Not any longer.' Gorran explained about the cease-fire and Napoleon's abdication.

'Are you quite certain of this?' The man's disbelief was almost comical.

'The news was brought from Paris by French and English officers. The allies are in Paris. Louis the Eighteenth is expected to reach there any day now.'

'This is wonderful news. We have been living in fear of Napoleon's soldiers coming through the countryside again and robbing us as they have every year since Spain was conquered. Please, come to the house and tell your news to my wife. She lived in England during the darkest years of the Revolution and will be delighted to meet you.'

It was the beginning of a wonderful day. The château produced its own wine, a superb red that the proprietor and his wife assured them was the finest they would taste in France. In the late afternoon Gorran protested that he and Cassie must leave in order to find their way back to Toulouse before darkness fell. The proprietor would not hear of such a thing. He promised he would send men to guide them back to Toulouse when it was time – but the party was only just beginning.

Not until dawn was showing grey above the distant hills did Gorran and Cassie, with an escort of twenty estate workers, arrive at the gates of Toulouse. With them they brought cases of wine for the 'Great Lord Wellington'. It had been a wonderful party and Lady Fraser rejoiced to see the young couple animatedly recalling the experiences they had shared at the river's-edge château.

Cassie and Gorran shared many other pleasures during the ensuing week as they rode through the French countryside around Toulouse. At the end of it Cassie knew beyond all doubt that she loved him. She was also more determined than ever that she would not be responsible for holding back his career.

On the day before the 32nd Regiment reached Toulouse, Gorran received promotion to the rank of major. Delighted, he jokingly told Cassie it was entirely due to the excellence of the wine they had brought for Lord Wellington. Later, Sir William Fraser informed Cassie it was a reward for his bravery when leading the Light Company.

Gorran Fox's company reluctantly left the comfort of their town billets and moved to the less comfortable tents, pitched beyond the walls of the town. Gorran, now he was a major, was able to choose to remain in the house of Major-General Sir William Fraser and his energetic wife.

Early in May, news was received that Lord Wellington, who was *en route* to Paris, had been created Duke of Wellington. To celebrate the event, Lady Fraser decided that her husband, as the senior officer remaining in Toulouse, should throw a grand ball. Her suggestion was received with great enthusiasm by the army and the citizens of Toulouse.

The ball took place in the Toulouse Capitol and was attended by all the civic dignitaries and by the senior officers of every one of the regiments stationed in and about the town. It was the most glittering occasion seen for many years in Toulouse. On a raised platform on two ornate, throne-like chairs, receiving guests, sat the mayor of Toulouse and Major-General Sir William Fraser, flanked by their ladies.

The festivities had been going on for some hours and a very fine claret had been flowing freely when, in a break between dances, Cassie suddenly found herself face to face with a Captain Anstey of the 32nd Regiment, who had once been a lieutenant in Gorran's company. He had been drinking heavily and he peered drunkenly at Cassie before pushing his face up close to hers, saying, 'What are you doing here?'

A young ensign in the same company was on the spot in an instant. 'It's all right, sir. The lady is here with Major Fox.'

'I don't care who she's with. This "lady" is the wife of a man serving in the ranks of the Thirty-second. She has no right to be here at all. What's she doing here, I say?'

'Mrs Clymo is a widow, captain, and she's the guest of Major Fox. Come along, sir. I believe you are with a party over here. Let me guide you across the floor, it's becoming very crowded.'

Captain Anstey allowed himself to be led away by the quick-thinking and diplomatic young ensign, but he went on his way muttering about wives of soldiers knowing their place.

Absolutely devastated, Cassie stood in the centre of the dance floor, certain that everyone in the room had heard the cruel and unthinking words of the 32nd Regiment captain. In fact, the incident had been over-heard by a mere handful of people, most of whom were French and who understood very little of what had been said. One of the few English women to overhear was Lady Harriet Fraser and she spoke urgently to her husband.

Cassie had still not recovered from the shock of the captain's verbal attack when Major-General Sir William Fraser was standing before her. Bowing to Cassie, he said, 'My dear, the orchestra is about to play one of these new-fangled dances the French are so keen on. Will you do me the honour of dancing it with me – and I ask your forgiveness in advance for my clumsiness.'

It was the first time Sir William Fraser had danced that evening. That he had chosen Cassie as his partner not only restored any status Cassie might have lost as a result of the drunken captain's words, but it made her the focus of interest at the grand ball. Gorran, told of what had happened by the alert young ensign, had to push his way through a crowd of men and women to reach Cassie's side when the dance was over.

The prompt attention given to her by Major-General Sir William Fraser had restored much of Cassie's confidence, but when she saw Gorran she broke off a rather difficult conversation she was having with a French official who spoke very little English and, clutching Gorran's arm, said, 'Gorran, I think I'd like to leave now.'

'You mustn't take the remarks of one drunken man to heart, Cassie. From what the ensign tells me he's drunk so much his tongue has lost touch with his brain.'

'He only said what a lot of people are thinking. Please, Gorran, take me back to the house.'

'All right, but only if you're certain it's what you want.'

'It is.'

Lady Fraser saw Cassie and Gorran leave the ballroom. Angry with the 32nd Regiment captain, she was filled with sympathy for Cassie. On the other hand, it might have helped to bring Cassie and Gorran closer together. Sir William also saw the young couple leaving and offered to go and bring them back.

'No, William, we must leave them.' She squeezed his arm affectionately. 'This is something that needed to be brought out into the open. That drunken captain might even have done them both a favour.'

Somewhat mystified, Sir William shook his head. 'I'm damned if I understand any of your matchmaking, my dear, but she's a fine girl. Dancing with her has reawakened my interest in dancing. Shall we?'

Cassie and Gorran walked in silence through the near-empty streets to the house commandeered for the Fraser household. Once inside, at the foot of the wide staircase that dominated the hall, Cassie said, 'Goodnight, Gorran. I'm sorry to drag you from the ball, but I really didn't want to stay there any longer.'

'I'm not unhappy to have left. I've always known that dancing is one of my less successful accomplishments. But you're not going to bed yet. I want to talk to you.'

'If you're going to try to explain away what Captain Anstey said to me, you needn't bother. Sooner or later I knew someone was bound to say the same thing. It just happened that tonight was the time and place. It could have happened anywhere, at any time.'

'The words of a drunken man mean nothing to me – and they shouldn't matter to you, either. What I want to say to you is far more important.'

'If it's what I think it is, it might be better left unsaid.'

'Dammit, Cassie! I beg your pardon, but at least hear me out. Come along to the library and have a drink. I could do with one.'

Reluctantly, Cassie followed Gorran to the small, comfortable library but she declined a drink and remained standing while he poured himself a large cognac.

'Cassie, please don't stand there looking as though you're awaiting an opportunity to run off to your room. Sit down and listen to what I have to say.'

Cassie perched herself on the edge of a hard, leather-seated chair while Gorran paced the room for a full minute. When he stopped he drank half the contents of his glass before saying, 'Cassie, I want you to marry me. I want it more than anything else in this world.'

Gorran's obvious sincerity almost made Cassie weaken but her expression gave nothing away when she said, 'You're being ridiculous, Gorran. What happened tonight should have proved to you that marriage to me is out of the question for you. It would be disastrous for your career.'

'Why? Because of something a drunken man said? If we are to bring my career into this, then it's far more significant that a major-general on the commander-in-chief's staff chose you to accompany him in his first dance of the evening.'

'We both know why he did that,' Cassie retorted. 'It doesn't alter the facts. I was married to a man in the ranks. Such women don't marry officers.'

'Then we'll prove them all wrong, Cassie, or, if it really bothers you, then I'll leave the army.'

'I couldn't allow you to do that. You love the army – and sooner or later you'd hate me if I were your reason for leaving. No. Face facts, Gorran. You and I come from different backgrounds. Marriage wouldn't work for us.'

'Are you saying you don't – or *couldn't* love me?'

'No. If I didn't care so much for you I'd marry you.'

'That's a damned tortuous argument, Cassie.'

Cassie looked at Gorran for a long time, gathering the courage for what she said next. 'Gorran, if you want me to come to bed with you, I will, but I won't marry you.'

Now she had said it Cassie wondered what she would do if Gorran agreed to the sort of proposition that might have come from poor Sarah.

'Sharing a bed with you is something I've dreamed of for a thousand uncomfortable nights on this campaign, Cassie – but I want it to be a matrimonial bed.'

Unsure whether her feelings were of relief or disappointment, Cassie shook her head. 'Marriage would be wonderful for both of us, but only for a while. What would your family say? Your father?'

'My father would be absolutely delighted. If you don't believe me perhaps you'll read this.' Reaching into a pocket, Gorran pulled out a crumpled letter and handed it to her, saying, 'It's a letter from him.'

'You've told him about me?' Cassie looked at him in disbelief.

'About you and your family. He's been to meet them. Read what he has to say about them.'

Opening the letter, Cassie read with increasing incredulity. Gorran's father had been to see her family, had stayed for most of one day and her family had

537

returned his visit! It was apparent the two men had got along well together. So well that Gorran's father wanted to combine his money with the expertise of Cassie's father in a joint fishing venture. A large fish cellar ... New and larger boats ... !

When Cassie looked up again Gorran was smiling indulgently. 'I have some more surprising information for you. My great-grandfather on my mother's side was a fisherman – when he wasn't smuggling full-time. It was his money that helped rescue the fortunes of my father's family. They had never recovered from the turmoil of the Civil War in Cornwall. If it hadn't been for him I too would probably have joined the army as a private soldier.'

'But you're not a private soldier, you are Major Gorran Fox.' Cassie handed the letter back. She was more impressed than she would say with all that Gorran had done, but it changed nothing. 'You're a promising officer who will one day be a general – if you don't do anything silly such as marrying the widow of one of your sergeants.'

'Cassie.' Gorran spoke in desperation now. He had played his ace card – and still he had lost. 'Won't you even think about all I've said?'

'Yes, Gorran.' Cassie rose from her seat to go to her room. 'I doubt if I'll think of anything else for a very long time to come ... but I won't change my mind.'

44

❀

A few days after the celebration ball in Toulouse, the 32nd Regiment marched away from the town, heading for the French sea port of Bordeaux. Cassie went with them, and so too did Lady Fraser and Emma.

Lady Fraser was deeply disappointed that all her efforts at matchmaking had proved in vain. It was perfectly obvious to her that Gorran Fox and Cassie were head over heels in love with each other but they were no closer to marriage than before. Yet she had not given up hope.

The Duke of Wellington had sent for Sir William Fraser to join him in Paris. The allied powers were meeting to discuss treaties and the division of the empire built up by Napoleon Bonaparte. Afterwards Wellington would be discussing defence requirements. Sir William Fraser's knowledge and administration skills would be needed. Lady Fraser declined to accompany him. Instead she intended taking Emma back to England where she would await her husband.

The regiment marched to Bordeaux by easy stages, passing through some of France's most beautiful countryside and sampling the country's finest wines.

Cassie's plans went no farther than Bordeaux. The 32nd Regiment had been ordered to Cork, in Ireland. She would not be going with them and leaving the regiment would be like losing a part of herself. She put the thought behind her for most of the day and spent the evenings in Gorran's company, but as they drew nearer to the French port she found sleep ever more elusive during the dark, lonely night hours.

She hoped it might be possible for her and Gorran to have a few weeks together at Bordeaux but a British ship was due to sail in four days' time from a port along the Garonne and Lady Fraser had booked them both a passage on the vessel.

Cassie did have one pleasant surprise at Bordeaux. Father Michael was here. The Portuguese army had returned to its homeland for disbandment and had no further use for a Dominican friar. As a result, Father Michael decided to visit his homeland once more before setting off to do God's bidding elsewhere.

Bordeaux and the surrounding area were crowded with British troops – and their women. Every day there were harrowing scenes on the riverside quays as the women were forced to bid farewell to the men they had followed and loved, some for as long as five years. There were children here, too, many old enough to feel the hurt and confusion of watching a father walk away from them for ever.

It was among these unfortunate women and children that Father Michael found much to occupy his time. The departing regiments collected as much money as was available to them to help the women and children, and the Dominican friar was given the unenviable task of sharing it among Portuguese, Spanish and even French women who were left behind.

It was a cause which Lady Fraser also took up with her usual enthusiasm. She badgered senior officers to release payment to the troops under their command so that more money might be passed on to the unfortunate abandoned women.

Late on the final evening in Bordeaux, Cassie was waiting for Gorran to come to the house where she and Lady Fraser were staying. It would be the last night she and Gorran would have together and she had hoped he might arrive early but it was well past his usual time for visiting. He had asked Cassie again the previous evening if she would marry him. Once more she had refused, although her resolve was by no means as strong as it had been. Every minute that brought their parting closer made her increasingly uncertain.

Gorran had still not arrived by ten o'clock when Lady Fraser returned to the house accompanied by Father Michael. By now Cassie had almost convinced herself that Gorran was staying away deliberately, perhaps because of her latest refusal to marry him.

Lady Fraser dismissed the thought out of hand. 'Major Fox isn't like that, as well you know, Cassie. He'd move heaven and earth to be here with you on your last night.'

'Perhaps he had to go down to the quayside,' volunteered Father Michael. 'I understand one of his officers has been arrested for killing a brother officer in a duel.'

'One of the Thirty-second's officers arrested? Who?'

'A captain. Captain Anstey.'

'Anstey!' Cassie and Lady Fraser spoke the name together, their thoughts on the man who had insulted Cassie at the ball in Toulouse. If he and Gorran had met, perhaps with Anstey drunk again . . . !

'Where did this duel take place?'

'You surely don't think Major Fox was involved in any way?'

'Where? I want you to take me there.'

'You go on, Cassie. I'll remain here in case Gorran arrives after you've left.' Lady Fraser sounded unhopeful. She did not believe he would return.

There were many drunken men in the vicinity of the riverside quays but Cassie hardly noticed them and pushed them out of the way with far more energy than the burly friar.

By the time they reached the riverside inn where the duel had taken place, Cassie had convinced herself that Gorran had been killed. She was telling herself that if she had agreed to marry him he would not have been out tonight.

'Here we are . . . out of the way, you drunken oafs!'

Two men blocking the doorway had their heads banged together for their drunken torpitude. As they staggered off into the night, each clutching his ringing

542

head, Father Michael ploughed a furrow through the crowded room, ensuring Cassie was close behind him.

Father Michael seemed to know his way around the inn. Passing out through another door, he entered a room where half a dozen young British officers sat carousing with the same number of young – and not-so-young – town girls. The unexpected arrival of the black-robed friar and an English woman startled the officers. They jumped to their feet so hastily that one French girl was dumped heavily on her backside on the flagstone floor.

'There was a duel fought here tonight. Do you know who was involved?'

'It was the Thirty-second Regiment, I believe.' The reply came from a young ensign.

'We know a Thirty-second captain was arrested. What of the man who was killed?'

The ensign repeated the question in fluent, educated French to the girl who had so unceremoniously fallen to the floor.

She shrugged and made a short reply – and Cassie caught the gist of her words before the ensign interpreted them. *The dead man was a major.*

Cassie could not remember leaving the crowded inn, or walking through the busy streets with Father Michael's arm about her shoulders.

As they approached the house where she and Lady Fraser were staying, his arm tightened. 'I'll take you inside, then I'll go off and find where they've taken him.'

Cassie could only nod, holding back her anguish.

Lady Fraser could be heard talking as they approached the closed door of the drawing room and Cassie tried to pull away from Father Michael. She felt she could not face strangers tonight – but the Dominican friar maintained his grip on her. Pushing open the door, the first person Cassie saw was Lady Fraser, relaxing in a large armchair. Standing across the room from her, talking easily, was . . . Gorran!

Cassie's cry of sheer joy was lost as she ran across the room and flung herself at him.

'Gorran . . . Oh, Gorran! I thought you were dead . . . I felt I'd died inside, too.' Of a sudden, Cassie felt too choked up to talk.

'I'm sorry to have caused you so much concern . . . My regiment received orders to embark today on a transport anchored downriver. I've spent the day there.'

'But . . . Captain Anstey? They said he'd fought a duel and killed someone . . . a major. We . . . Father Michael and I, believed it was you.'

'Captain Anstey shot and killed a *French* major who refused to accept that the war is over. I needed to spend some time sorting that out, too. Anstey is now on board the transport, as officer in charge of the men taking passage to Cork. I have a few more days here before I and the colonel sail for Ireland in another vessel. Cassie, I'm asking you one more time. Please marry me. Come to Ireland with me as my wife.'

Cassie suddenly realised that she and Gorran were alone. Lady Fraser had discreetly ushered the Irish friar from the room.

'Are you really sure it's what you want, Gorran?'

'Am I sure? Cassie, does that mean you will marry me?'

544

Cassie nodded. 'I don't ever want to feel the way I did tonight, when I thought I'd lost you for ever.'

Later that evening, after celebrating with Lady Fraser and Father Michael, Cassie and Gorran stood alone on a balcony at the rear of the house. Moonlight cast a gentle mantle over the countryside and downriver they could see the gently swaying lights of a line of transports.

'Are those the ships taking the men to Ireland?'

'That's right, Cassie. Our regiment. Yours and mine. Major and Cassie Fox . . . of the Thirty-second.'

Epilogue

Cassie and Gorran were married by Father Michael on the day before they set sail for Ireland. Lady Fraser attended Cassie, the colonel of the 32nd Regiment performed the duty of the best man and the friendship of all endured for the whole of Cassie's and Gorran's colourful lives.

Eight months after the 32nd arrived in Ireland, Napoleon Bonaparte escaped from his island exile on Elba and landed in France where he quickly gathered another great army about him. The 32nd was one of the first British regiments to land in Europe to join the army being assembled by the Duke of Wellington to oppose his old adversary.

The two armies met in bloody and desperate conflict within the hearing of the residents of Brussels. In spite of their long rivalry, it was the first occasion on which either of the great commanders had pitted his personal generalship against the other – and it was a close-fought action.

The Duke of Wellington emerged the victor, but at a tragically high cost. British casualties amounted to 15,000, their German allies lost half that number, and the French army lost more than both.

Among the regiments with the highest casualties was the 32nd, suffering more losses than any other regiment in the army. From a strength of 674, the regiment lost 545 officers and men in the twin battles of Quatre Bras and Waterloo.

Major Gorran Fox was one of those who fell wounded at Waterloo and Cassie risked cannon fire and a bayonet charge in order to drag him from the battlefield. He recovered his health, but was forced to leave the army two years later, holding the rank of lieutenant-colonel.

He and Cassie put their joint energies into the family lands near Lostwithiel in Cornwall and raised seven children, two of the sons entering the army as surgeons. One of the daughters continued the work begun by Cassie and Lady Fraser when she joined Florence Nightingale's brave band of nurses, working to improve the lot of the wounded soldier during the Crimean War.

For the whole of their lives, Cassie and Gorran maintained their links with the 32nd (Cornwall) Regiment, every officer being assured of a warm welcome at their home, and every ex-soldier down on his luck given a generous hand-out and, wherever possible, work on the Fox lands.

Occasionally they were visited by Richard and Josefa Kennelly and their constantly expanding family. Among the children were sprinkled the names of Gorran, Cassie, Estefanía, Elijah, Rose and Harry.

Cassie and Gorran lived to see the coveted title of 'Light Infantry' bestowed on the regiment in 1858, in recognition of its heroic defence of Lucknow during the Indian mutiny when four Victoria Crosses were won by its soldiers.

Richmal Crompton was born in Lancashire in 1890.
The first story about William Brown appeared in
Home magazine in 1919, and the first collection
of William stories was published in book form
three years later. In all, thirty-eight William books
were published, the last one in 1970, after Richmal
Crompton's death.

'Probably the funniest, toughest children's books
ever written'
Sunday Times on the Just William series

'Richmal Crompton's creation [has] been famed for
his cavalier attitude to life and those who would
seek to circumscribe his enjoyment of it ever since
he first appeared'
Guardian

30131 05608063 0

LONDON BOROUGH OF BARNET

More William

RICHMAL CROMPTON

Foreword by Martin Jarvis

Illustrated by Thomas Henry

MACMILLAN CHILDREN'S BOOKS

First published in 1922
This selection first published 1995 by Macmillan Children's Books

This edition published 2015 by Macmillan Children's Books
an imprint of Pan Macmillan
20 New Wharf Road, London N1 9RR
Associated companies throughout the world
www.panmacmillan.com

ISBN 978-1-4472-8559-5

All stories copyright © Edward Ashbee and Catherine Massey
This selection copyright © Edward Ashbee and Catherine Massey 2005
Foreword copyright © Martin Jarvis 2009
Illustrations copyright © Thomas Henry Fisher Estate

All rights reserved. No part of this publication may be
reproduced, stored in a retrieval system, or transmitted, in any form or by
any means (electronic, mechanical, photocopying, recording or otherwise),
without the prior written permission of the publisher.

1 3 5 7 9 8 6 4 2

A CIP catalogue record for this book is available from the British Library.

Typeset by Nigel Hazle
Printed and bound by CPI Group (UK) Ltd, Croydon CR0 4YY

This book is sold subject to the condition that it shall not, by way of trade
or otherwise, be lent, resold, hired out, or otherwise circulated without
the publisher's prior consent in any form of binding or cover other than
that in which it is published and without a similar condition including this
condition being imposed on the subsequent purchaser.

The text of this book remains true to the original in every way. Some stories may appear out of
date to modern-day readers, but are reflective of the language and period in which they were
originally written. Macmillan believes changing the content to reflect today's world would
undermine the authenticity of the original, so have chosen to leave the text in its entirety. This
does not, however, constitute an endorsement of the characterization and content.

CONTENTS

FOREWORD

More William? Yes, please.

This is one of the funniest books I've ever read. When I was recording it for BBC Audio a few years ago there were times when I could hardly keep going, simply because of the situations in which William gets embroiled and the brilliant hilarity of Richmal Crompton's writing. I'd be hooting with laughter and have to start a paragraph all over again. Then, just when I thought I'd regained some semblance of professional control, I'd glance up from the microphone, only to see the studio engineer and my co-producer doubled up with mirth on the other side of the glass . . . which would set me off once more. Exquisite agony!

Richmal Crompton was a hugely popular author: her timeless brainchild, eleven-year-old William Brown, was certainly the Harry Potter of the 1920s. Children, and parents, would wait anxiously for William's latest adventures before pouncing on them and racing away to devour more exploits of their lateral-thinking hero.

William's magic lies in his own personality, uniquely endowed by the generous genius of his creator. It's true that some of the starchier folk in William's village consider him mischievous, naughty, probably mendacious. His long-suffering family can think of even less flattering words to describe him. But we know that William pretty well always sets out with good intentions. It's just that, being him, things often go wrong; though, as in 'The May King' or 'William and the Smuggler', they can go surprisingly, gloriously right.

His motto invariably is 'Doin good, ritin' rongs and persuin' happiness for all'. Not a bad motive for life in any generation, let alone a world recovering from the staggering tragedies of World War I. 'Let me show you a good time,' William seems to say. 'It's jus' over there.' He's keen to bring justice (as he sees it) to an often unjust world, to prick the bubble of pomposity and, as the dance bands of the 1920s were already expressing in musical terms, to paint the clouds with sunshine.

Here, in this joyous book, William is at his imaginative best. Whether he's conjuring up a ghost to give a batty aunt a spiritual thrill, attempting (with unexpected results) to assist a team of removal men or airily offering the hospitality of his home to a tramp with no ears, it's all approached with an utmost seriousness of purpose that can only result in laugh-out-loud comedy.

Crompton's world is still real, still recognizable, reflecting both the absurdity and blessedness of British life. William, though of his time, is for all time. Throughout Richmal Crompton's long writing career, until her death in 1969, William, always aged eleven, celebrated many birthdays and Christmases, righted numerous wrongs and brought much happiness to generations of fans. He still does.

William Brown's voice resonates down the years. Surely he's telling us, even now: 'Seems to me those people who keep sayin' I'm scruffy or a scamp, or worse – an' want to see and hear *less* of me – well, they'd better read this book, that's all I can say. S'jolly funny, an' it's all about me. S'called *More William*, not less, an' – ackshully – that's the way I like it.'

Martin Jarvis OBE

CHAPTER 1

A BUSY DAY

William awoke and rubbed his eyes. It was Christmas Day – the day to which he had looked forward with mingled feelings for twelve months. It was a jolly day, of course – presents and turkey and crackers and staying up late. On the other hand, there were generally too many relations about, too much was often expected of one, the curious taste displayed by people who gave one presents often marred one's pleasure.

He looked round his bedroom expectantly. On the wall, just opposite his bed, was a large illuminated card hanging by a string from a nail – 'A Busy Day is a Happy Day'. That had not been there the day before. Brightly coloured roses and forget-me-nots and honeysuckle twined round all the words. William hastily thought over the three aunts staying in the house, and put it down to Aunt Lucy. He looked at it with a doubtful frown. He distrusted the sentiment.

A copy of *Portraits of our Kings and Queens* he put aside as beneath contempt. *Things a Boy Can Do* was more promising. *Much* more promising. After inspecting a penknife, a pocket compass, and a pencil box (which shared the fate of *Portraits of our Kings and Queens*), William returned to *Things a Boy Can Do*. As he turned the pages, his face lit up.

He leapt lightly out of bed and dressed. Then he began to arrange his own gifts to his family. For his father he had bought a bottle of highly coloured sweets, for his elder brother Robert (aged nineteen) he had expended a vast sum of money on a copy of *The Pirates of the Bloody Hand*. These gifts had cost him much thought. The knowledge that his father never touched sweets, and that Robert professed scorn of pirate stories, had led him to hope that the recipients of his gifts would make no objection to the unobtrusive theft of them by their recent donor in the course of the next few days. For his grown-up sister Ethel he had bought a box of coloured chalks. That also might come in useful later. Funds now had been running low, but for his mother he had bought a small cream jug which, after fierce bargaining, the man had let him have at half price because it was cracked.

Singing 'Christians, Awake!' at the top of his lusty young voice, he went along the landing, putting his gifts outside the doors of his family, and pausing to yell 'Happy

Christmas' as he did so. From within he was greeted in each case by muffled groans.

He went downstairs into the hall, still singing. It was earlier than he thought – just five o'clock. The maids were not down yet. He switched on lights recklessly, and discovered that he was not the only person in the hall. His four-year-old cousin Jimmy was sitting on the bottom step in an attitude of despondency, holding an empty tin.

Jimmy's mother had influenza at home, and Jimmy and his small sister Barbara were in the happy position of spending Christmas with relations, but immune from parental or maternal interference.

'They've gotten out,' said Jimmy, sadly. 'I got 'em for presents yesterday, an' they've gotten out. I've been feeling for 'em in the dark, but I can't find 'em.'

'What?' said William.

'Snails. Great big suge ones wiv great big suge shells. I put 'em in a tin for presents an' they've gotten out an' I've gotten no presents for nobody.'

He relapsed into despondency.

William surveyed the hall.

'They've got out right enough!' he said, sternly. 'They've got out right *enough*. Jus' look at our hall! Jus' look at our clothes! They've got out *right* enough.'

Innumerable slimy iridescent trails shone over hats, and coats, and umbrellas, and wallpaper.

'Huh!' grunted William, who was apt to overwork his phrases. 'They got *out* right enough.'

He looked at the tracks again and brightened. Jimmy was frankly delighted.

'Oo! Look!' he cried. 'Oo *funny*!'

William's thought flew back to his bedroom wall – 'A Busy Day is a Happy Day'.

'Let's clean it up!' he said. 'Let's have it all nice an' clean for when they come down. We'll be busy. You tell me if you feel happy when we've done. It might be true wot it says, but I don't like the flowers messin' all over it.'

Investigation in the kitchen provided them with a large pail of water and scrubbing brush each.

For a long time they worked in silence. They used plenty of water. When they had finished the trails were all gone. Each soaked garment on the hatstand was sending a steady drip on to the already flooded floor. The wallpaper was sodden. With a feeling of blankness they realised that there was nothing else to clean.

It was Jimmy who conceived the exquisite idea of dipping his brush in the bucket and sprinkling William with water. A scrubbing brush is in many ways almost as good as a hose. Each had a pail of ammunition. Each had a good-sized brush. During the next few minutes they experienced purest joy. Then William heard threatening movements above, and decided hastily that the battle must cease.

'Backstairs,' he said shortly. 'Come on.'

Marking their track by a running stream of water, they crept up the backstairs.

But two small boys soaked to the skin could not disclaim all knowledge of a flooded hall.

William was calm and collected when confronted with a distracted mother.

'We was tryin' to clean up,' he said. 'We found all snail marks an' we was tryin' to clean up. We was tryin' to help. You said so last night, you know, when you was talkin' to me. You said to *help*. Well, I thought it was helpin' to try an' clean up. You can't clean up with water an' not get wet – not if you do it prop'ly. You said to try an' make Christmas Day happy for other folks and then I'd be happy. Well, I don't know as I'm very happy,' he said, bitterly, 'but I've been workin' hard enough since early this mornin'. I've been workin',' he went on pathetically. His eye wandered to the notice on his wall. 'I've been *busy* all right, but it doesn't make me *happy* – not jus' now,' he added, with memories of the rapture of the fight.

That certainly must be repeated some time. Buckets of water and scrubbing brushes. He wondered he'd never thought of that before.

William's mother looked down at his dripping form.

'Did you get all that water with just cleaning up the snail marks?' she said.

William coughed and cleared his throat. 'Well,' he said, deprecatingly, 'most of it. I think I got most of it.'

'If it wasn't Christmas Day . . .' she went on darkly.

William's spirits rose. There was certainly something to be said for Christmas Day.

It was decided to hide the traces of the crime as far as possible from William's father. It was felt – and not without reason – that William's father's feelings of respect for the sanctity of Christmas Day might be overcome by his feelings of paternal ire.

Half an hour later William, dried, dressed, brushed, and chastened, descended the stairs as the gong sounded in a hall which was bare of hats and coats, and whose floor shone with cleanliness.

'And jus to think,' said William, despondently, 'that it's only jus' got to brekfust time.'

William's father was at the bottom of the stairs. William's father frankly disliked Christmas Day.

'Good morning, William,' he said, 'and a happy

Christmas, and I hope it's not too much to ask of you that on this relation-infested day one's feelings may be harrowed by you as little as possible. And why the deu— dickens they think it necessary to wash the hall floor before breakfast, heaven only knows!'

William coughed, a cough meant to be a polite mixture of greeting and deference. William's face was a study in holy innocence. His father glanced at him suspiciously. There were certain expressions of William's that he distrusted.

William entered the dining-room morosely. Jimmy's sister Barbara – a small bundle of curls and white frills – was already beginning her porridge.

'Goo' mornin',' she said, politely, 'did you hear me cleanin' my teef?'

He crushed her with a glance.

He sat eating in silence till everyone had come down, and Aunts Jane, Evangeline, and Lucy were consuming porridge with that mixture of festivity and solemnity that they felt the occasion demanded.

Then Jimmy entered, radiant, with a tin in his hand.

'Got presents,' he said, proudly. 'Got presents, lots of presents.'

He deposited on Barbara's plate a worm which Barbara promptly threw at his face. Jimmy looked at her reproachfully and proceeded to Aunt Evangeline. Aunt Evangeline's gift was a centipede – a live centipede that ran gaily off the tablecloth on to Aunt Evangeline's lap before anyone could stop it. With a yell that sent William's father to the library with his hands to his ears, Aunt Evangeline leapt to her chair and stood with her skirts held to her knees.

'Help! Help!' she cried. 'The horrible boy! Catch it! Kill it!'

Jimmy gazed at her in amazement, and Barbara looked with interest at Aunt Evangeline's long expanse of shin.

'*My* legs isn't like *your* legs,' she said pleasantly and conversationally. 'My legs is knees.'

It was some time before order was restored, the centipede killed, and Jimmy's remaining gifts thrown out of the window. William looked across the table at Jimmy with respect in his eye. Jimmy, in spite of his youth, was an acquaintance worth cultivating. Jimmy was eating porridge unconcernedly.

Aunt Evangeline had rushed from the room when the slaughter of the centipede had left the coast clear, and refused to return. She carried on a conversation from the top of the stairs.

'When that horrible child has gone, I'll come in. He

may have insects concealed on his person. And someone's been dropping water all over these stairs. They're *damp*!'

'Dear, dear!' murmured Aunt Jane, sadly.

Jimmy looked up from his porridge.

'How was I to know she didn't like insecks?' he said, aggrievedly. '*I* like 'em.'

William's mother's despair was only tempered by the fact that this time William was not the culprit. To William also it was a novel sensation. He realised the advantages of a fellow criminal.

After breakfast peace reigned. William's father went out for a walk with Robert. The aunts sat round the drawing-room fire talking and doing crochet work. In this consists the whole art and duty of aunthood. *All* aunts do crochet work.

They had made careful inquiries about the time of the service.

'You needn't worry,' had said William's mother. 'It's at ten thirty, and if you go to get ready when the clock in the library strikes ten it will give you heaps of time.'

Peace . . . calm . . . quiet. Mrs Brown and Ethel in the kitchen supervising the arrangements for the day. The aunts in the drawing-room discussing over their crochet work the terrible way in which their sisters had brought up their children. That, also, is a necessary part of aunt-hood.

Time slipped by happily and peacefully. Then William's mother came into the drawing-room.

'I thought you were going to church,' she said.

'We are. The clock hasn't struck.'

'But – it's eleven o'clock!'

There was a gasp of dismay.

'The clock never struck!'

Indignantly they set off to the library. Peace and quiet reigned also in the library. On the floor sat William and Jimmy gazing with frowns of concentration at an open page of *Things a Boy Can Do*. Around them lay most indecently exposed the internal arrangements of the library clock.

'William! You *wicked* boy!'

William raised a frowning face.

'It's not put together right,' he said; 'it's not been put together right all this time. We're makin' it right now. It must have wanted mendin' for ever so long. *I* dunno how it's been goin' at all. It's lucky we found it out. It's put together wrong. I guess it's *made* wrong. It's goin' to be a lot of trouble to us to put it right, an' we can't do much when you're all standin' in the light. We're very busy – workin' at tryin' to mend this ole clock for you all.'

AROUND THEM LAY MOST INDECENTLY EXPOSED THE
INTERNAL ARRANGEMENTS OF THE LIBRARY CLOCK.

'Clever,' said Jimmy, admiringly. 'Mendin' the clock. *Clever!*'

'William!' groaned his mother. 'You've ruined the clock. What *will* your father say?'

'Well, the cog wheels was wrong,' said William doggedly. 'See? An' this ratchet-wheel isn't on the pawl prop'ly – not like what this book says it ought to be. Seems we've got to take it all to pieces to get it right. Seems to me the person wot made this clock didn't know much about clock-making. Seems to me—'

'Be *quiet*, William!'

'We was be quietin' 'fore you came in,' said Jimmy severely. 'You 'sturbed us.'

'Leave it just as it is, William,' said his mother.

'You don't *unnerstand*,' said William with the excitement of the fanatic. 'The cog wheel an' the ratchet ought to be put on the arbor different. See, this is the cog wheel. Well, it oughtn't to be like wot it was. It was put on all *wrong*. Well, we was mendin' it. An' we was doin' it for *you*,' he ended, bitterly, 'jus' to help an' – to – to make other folks happy. It makes folks happy havin' clocks goin' right, anyone would *think*. But if you *want* your clocks put together wrong, *I* don't care.'

He picked up his book and walked proudly from the room followed by the admiring Jimmy.

'William,' said Aunt Lucy patiently, as he passed, 'I don't want to say anything unkind, and I hope you won't remember all your life that you have completely spoilt this Christmas Day for me.'

'Oh, dear!' murmured Aunt Jane, sadly.

William, with a look before which she should have sunk into the earth, answered shortly that he didn't think he would.

During the midday dinner the grown-ups, as is the foolish fashion of grown-ups, wasted much valuable time in the discussion of such futilities as the weather and the political state of the nation. Aunt Lucy was still suffering and aggrieved.

'I can go this evening, of course,' she said, 'but it's not quite the same. The morning service is different. Yes, please, dear – *and* stuffing. Yes, I'll have a little more turkey, too. And, of course, the Vicar may not preach tonight. That makes such a difference. The gravy on the potatoes, please. It's almost the first Christmas I've not been in the morning. It seems quite to have spoilt the day for me.'

She bent on William a glance of gentle reproach. William was quite capable of meeting adequately that or any other glance, but at present he was too busy for minor hostilities. He was *extremely* busy. He was doing his utmost to do full justice to a meal that only happens once a year.

'William,' said Barbara pleasantly, 'I can *dweam*. Can you?'

He made no answer.

'Answer your cousin, William,' said his mother.

He swallowed, then spoke plaintively. 'You always say not to talk with my mouth full,' he said.

'You could speak when you've finished the mouthful.'

'Dear, *dear*!' murmured Aunt Jane.

This was Aunt Jane's usual contribution to any conversation.

He looked coldly at the three pairs of horrified aunts' eyes around him, then placidly continued his meal.

Mrs Brown hastily changed the subject of conversation. The art of combining the duties of mother and hostess is sometimes a difficult one.

Christmas afternoon is a time of rest. The three aunts withdrew from public life. Aunt Lucy found a book of sermons in the library and retired to her bedroom with it.

'It's the next best thing, I think,' she said with a sad glance at William.

William was beginning definitely to dislike Aunt Lucy.

'Please'm,' said the cook an hour later, 'the mincing machine's disappeared.'

'Disappeared?' said William's mother, raising her hand to her head.

'Clean gone'm. 'Ow'm I to get the supper'm? You said as 'ow I could get it done this afternoon so as to go to church this evening. I can't do nuffink with the mincing machine gone.'

'I'll come and look.'

They searched every corner of the kitchen, then William's mother had an idea. William's mother had not been William's mother for eleven years without learning many things. She went wearily up to William's bedroom.

William was sitting on the floor. Open beside him was *Things a Boy Can Do*. Around him lay various parts of the mincing machine. His face was set and strained in mental and physical effort. He looked up as she entered.

'It's a funny kind of mincing machine,' he said, crushingly. 'It's not got enough parts. It's *made* wrong—'

'Do you know,' she said, slowly, 'that we've all been

15

looking for that mincing machine for the last half-hour?'

'No,' he said without much interest, 'I di'n't. I'd have told you I was mendin' it if you'd told me you was lookin' for it. It's *wrong*,' he went on aggrievedly. 'I can't make anything with it. Look! It says in my book "How to make a model railway signal with parts of a mincing machine". Listen! It says, "Borrow a mincing machine from your mother—"'

'Did you borrow it?' said Mrs Brown.

'Yes. Well, I've got it, haven't I? I went all the way down to the kitchen for it.'

'Who lent it to you?'

'No one *lent* it to me. I *borrowed* it. I thought you'd like to see a model railway signal. I thought you'd be interested. Anyone would think anyone would be interested in seein' a railway signal made out of a mincin' machine.'

His tone implied that the dullness of people in general was simply beyond him. 'An' you haven't got a right sort of mincin' machine. It's wrong. Its parts are the wrong shape. I've been hammerin' them, tryin' to make them right, but they're *made* wrong.'

Mrs Brown was past expostulating. 'Take them all down to the kitchen to Cook,' she said. 'She's waiting for them.'

On the stairs William met Aunt Lucy carrying her volume of sermons.

'It's not quite the same as the spoken word, William dear,' she said. 'It hasn't the *force*. The written word doesn't reach the *heart* as the spoken word does, but I don't want you to worry about it.'

William walked on as if he had not heard her.

It was Aunt Jane who insisted on the little entertainment after tea.

'I *love* to hear the dear children recite,' she said. 'I'm sure they all have some little recitation they can say.'

Barbara arose with shy delight to say her piece.

Lickle bwown seed, lickle bwown bwother,
And what, pway, are you goin' to be?
I'll be a poppy as white as my mother,
Oh, DO be a poppy like me!
What, you'll be a sunflower? Oh, how I shall miss you
When you are golden and high!
But I'll send all the bees up to tiss you.
Lickle bwown bwother, goodbye!

She sat down blushing, amid rapturous applause.

Next Jimmy was dragged from his corner. He stood up

as one prepared for the worst, shut his eyes, and –

> *Licklaxokindness lickledeedsolove –*
> *make – thisearfanedenliketheeav'nabovethasalliknow.*

He gasped it all in one breath, and sat down panting.

This was greeted with slightly milder applause.

'Now, William!'

'I don't know any,' he said.

'Oh, you *do*,' said his mother. 'Say the one you learnt at school last term. Stand up, dear, and speak clearly.'

Slowly William rose to his feet.

> *'It was the schooner Hesperus that sailed the wintry sea,'*

he began.

Here he stopped, coughed, cleared his throat, and began again.

> *It was the schooner Hesperus that sailed the wintry sea.*

'Oh, get *on*!' muttered his brother, irritably.

'I can't get on if you keep talkin' to me,' said William

18

sternly. 'How can I get on if you keep takin' all the time up, *sayin'* get on? I can't get on if you're talkin', can I?'

'It was the Hesper Schoonerus that sailed the wintry sea an' I'm not goin' on if Ethel's goin' to keep gigglin'. It's not a funny piece, an' if she's goin' on gigglin' like that I'm not sayin' any more of it.'

'Ethel, dear!' murmured Mrs Brown, reproachfully.

'IT WAS THE HESPER SCHOONERUS THAT SAILED THE
WINTRY SEA AN' I'M NOT GOIN' ON IF ETHEL'S GOIN'
TO KEEP GIGGLIN'.'

Ethel turned her chair completely round and left only her back exposed to William's view. He glared at it suspiciously.

'Now, William, dear,' continued his mother, 'begin again and no one shall interrupt you.'

William again went through the preliminaries of coughing and clearing his throat.

It was the schooner Hesperus that sailed the wintry seas.

He stopped again, and slowly and carefully straightened his collar and smoothed back the lock of hair which was dangling over his brow.

'*The skipper had brought*—' prompted Aunt Jane, kindly.

William turned on her.

'I was *goin'* to say that if you'd left me alone,' he said. 'I was jus' thinkin'. I've got to think sometimes. I can't say off a great long pome like that without stoppin' to think sometimes, can I? I'll – I'll do a conjuring trick for you instead,' he burst out, desperately. 'I've learnt one from my book. I'll go an' get it ready.'

He went out of the room. Mr Brown took out his handkerchief and mopped his brow.

'May I ask,' he said patiently, 'how long this exhibition is to be allowed to continue?'

Here William returned, his pockets bulging. He held a large handkerchief in his hand.

'This is a handkerchief,' he announced. 'If anyone'd like to feel it to see if it's a real one, they can. Now I want a shilling.' He looked round expectantly, but no one moved. 'Or a penny would do,' he said, with a slightly disgusted air. Robert threw one across the room. 'Well, I put the penny into the handkerchief. You can see me do it, can't you? If anyone wants to come an' feel the penny is in the handkerchief, they can. Well,' he turned his back on them and took something out of his pocket. After a few contortions he turned round again, holding the handkerchief tightly. 'Now, you look close' – he went over to them – 'an' you'll see the shil— I mean, penny,' he looked scornfully at Robert, 'has changed to an egg. It's a real egg. If anyone thinks it isn't a real egg—'

But it *was* a real egg. It confirmed his statement by giving a resounding crack and sending a shining stream partly on to the carpet and partly on to Aunt Evangeline's black silk knee. A storm of reproaches burst out.

'First that horrible insect,' almost wept Aunt Evangeline, 'and then this messy stuff all over me. It's a good thing I don't live here. One day a year is enough . . . My nerves! . . .'

'Dear, dear!' said Aunt Jane.

'Fancy taking a new-laid *egg* for that,' said Ethel severely.

William was pale and indignant.

'Well, I did jus' what the book said to do. Look at it. It says: "Take an egg. Conceal it in the pocket." Well, I took an egg an' I concealed it in the pocket. Seems to me,' he said bitterly, 'seems to me this book isn't *Things a Boy Can Do*. It's *Things a Boy Can't Do*.'

Mr Brown rose slowly from his chair.

'You're just about right there, my son. Thank *you*,' he said with elaborate politeness, as he took the book from William's reluctant hands and went over with it to a small cupboard in the wall. In this cupboard reposed an airgun, a bugle, a catapult, and a mouth organ. As he unlocked it to put the book inside, the fleeting glimpse of his confiscated treasures added to the bitterness of William's soul.

'On Christmas Day, too!'

While he was still afire with silent indignation Aunt Lucy returned from church.

'The Vicar *didn't* preach,' she said. 'They say that this morning's sermon was beautiful. As I say, I don't want William to reproach himself, but I feel that he has deprived me of a very great treat.'

'*Nice* William!' murmured Jimmy sleepily from his corner.

As William undressed that night his gaze fell upon the flower-bedecked motto: 'A Busy Day is a Happy Day'.

'It's a story,' he said, indignantly. 'It's jus' a wicked ole story.'

CHAPTER 2

RICE-MOULD

'Rice-mould,' said the little girl next door bitterly. 'Rice-mould! Rice-mould! Every single day. I *hate* it, don't you?'

She turned gloomy blue eyes upon William, who was perched perilously on the ivy-covered wall. William considered thoughtfully.

'Dunno,' he said. 'I just eat it; I never thought about it.'

'It's *hateful*, just *hateful*. Ugh! I've had it at dinner and I'll have it at supper – bet you anything. I say, you are going to have a party tonight, aren't you?'

William nodded carelessly.

'Are you going to be there?'

'Me!' ejaculated William in a tone of amused surprise. 'I should think so! You don't think they could have it without *me*, do you? Huh! Not much!'

She gazed at him enviously.

'You *are* lucky! I expect you'll have a lovely supper – not rice-mould,' she said bitterly.

'Rather!' said William with an air of superiority.

'What are you going to have to eat at your party?'

'Oh – everything,' said William vaguely.

'Cream blancmange?'

'Heaps of it – *buckets* of it.'

The little girl next door clasped her hands.

'Oh, just think of it! Your eating cream blancmange and me eating – *rice-mould*!' (It is impossible to convey in print the intense scorn and hatred which the little girl next door could compress into the two syllables.)

Here an idea struck William.

'What time do you have supper?'

'Seven.'

'Well, now,' magnanimously, 'if you'll be in your summer house at half past, I'll bring you some cream blancmange. Truly I will!'

The little girl's face beamed with pleasure.

'Will you? Will you *really*? You won't forget?'

'Not me! I'll be there. I'll slip away from our show on the quiet with it.'

'Oh, how *lovely*! I'll be thinking of it every minute. Don't forget. Goodbye.'

She blew him a kiss and flitted daintily into the house.

William blushed furiously at the blown kiss and descended from his precarious perch.

He went to the library where his grown-up sister Ethel and his elder brother Robert were standing on ladders at opposite ends of the room, engaged in hanging up festoons of ivy and holly across the wall. There was to be dancing in the library after supper. William's mother watched them from a safe position on the floor.

'Look here, mother,' began William. 'Am I or am I not coming to the party tonight?'

William's Mother sighed.

'For goodness sake, William, don't open that discussion again. For the tenth time today, you are *not*!'

'But *why* not?' he persisted. 'I only want to know why not. That's all I want to know. It looks a bit funny, doesn't it, to give a party and leave out your only son, at least' – with a glance at Robert, and a slight concession to accuracy – 'to leave out one of your only two sons? It looks a bit queer surely. That's all I'm thinking of – how it will look.'

'A bit higher your end,' said Ethel.

'Yes, that's better,' said William's mother.

'It's a *young* folks' party,' went on William, warming to his subject. 'I heard you tell Aunt Jane it was a *young* folks' party. Well, I'm young, aren't I? I'm eleven. Do you want me any younger? You aren't ashamed of folks seeing me, are you? I'm not deformed or anything.'

'IF YOU'LL BE IN YOUR SUMMER HOUSE AT HALF PAST, I'LL
BRING YOU SOME CREAM BLANCMANGE. TRULY I WILL!'
SAID WILLIAM

'That's right! Put the nail in there, Ethel.'

'Just a bit higher. That's right!'

'P'raps you're afraid of what I'll *eat*,' went on William bitterly. 'Well, everyone eats, don't they? They've got to – to live. And you've got things for us – them – to eat tonight. You don't grudge me just a bit of supper, do you? You'd think it was less trouble for me to have my bit of supper with you all, than in a separate room. That's all I'm thinking of – the trouble—'

William's sister turned round on her ladder and faced the room.

'Can't *anyone*,' she said desperately, 'stop that child talking?'

William's brother began to descend the ladder. 'I think I can,' he said grimly.

But William had thrown dignity to the winds, and fled.

He went down the hall to the kitchen, where Cook hastily interposed herself between him and the table that was laden with cakes and jellies and other delicacies.

'Now, Master William,' she said sharply, 'you clear out of here!'

'I don't want any of your things, Cook,' said William, magnificently but untruthfully. 'I only came to see how you were getting on. That's all I came for.'

'We're getting on very well indeed, thank you, Master

William,' she said with sarcastic politeness, 'but nothing for you till tomorrow, when we can see how much they've left.'

She returned to her task of cutting sandwiches. William, from a respectful distance, surveyed the table with its enticing burden.

'Huh!' he ejaculated bitterly. 'Think of them sitting and stuffing, and stuffing, and stuffing away at *our* food all night! I don't suppose they'll leave much – not if I know the set that lives round here!'

'Don't judge them all by yourself, Master William,' said Cook unkindly, keeping a watchful eye upon him. 'Here, Emma, put that rice-mould away in the pantry. It's for tomorrow's lunch.'

Rice-mould! That reminded him.

'Cook,' he said ingratiatingly, 'are you going to make cream blancmange?'

'I am *not*, Master William,' she said firmly.

'Well,' he said, with a short laugh, 'it'll be a queer party without cream blancmange! I've never heard of a party without cream blancmange! They'll think it's a bit funny. No one ever gives a party round here without cream blancmange!'

'Don't they indeed, Master William,' said Cook, with ironic interest.

29

'No. You'll be making one, p'raps, later on – just a little one, won't you?'

'And why should I?'

'Well, I'd like to think they had a cream blancmange. I think they'd enjoy it. That's all I'm thinking of.'

'Oh, is it? Well, it's your ma that tells me what to make and pays me for it, not you.'

This was a novel idea to William.

He thought deeply.

'Look here!' he said at last. 'If I gave you' – he paused for effect, then brought out the startling offer – 'sixpence, would you make a cream blancmange?'

'I'd want to see your sixpence first,' said Cook, with a wink at Emma.

William retired upstairs to his bedroom and counted out his money – twopence was all he possessed. He had expended the enormous sum of a shilling the day before on a grass snake. It had died in the night. He *must* get a cream blancmange somehow. His reputation for omnipotence in the eyes of the little girl next door – a reputation very dear to him – depended on it. And if Cook would do it for sixpence, he must find sixpence. By fair means or foul it must be done. He'd tried fair means, and there only remained foul. He went softly downstairs to the dining-room, where, upon the mantelpiece, reposed the missionary box. He'd tell someone next day, or put it back, or something. Anyway, people did worse things than that in the pictures. With a knife from the table he extracted the contents – three halfpence! He glared at it balefully.

'Three halfpence!' he said aloud in righteous indignation. 'This is supposed to be a Christian house, and three halfpence is all they can give to the poor heathen. They can spend pounds and pounds on' – he glanced round the room and saw a pyramid of pears on the sideboard – 'tons of pears an' – an' green stuff to put on the walls, and they give three halfpence to the poor heathen! Huh!'

He opened the door and heard his sister's voice from the library. 'He's probably in mischief somewhere. He'll be a perfect nuisance all the evening. Mother, couldn't you make him go to bed an hour earlier?'

William had no doubt as to the subject of the conversation. *Make him go to bed early!* He'd like to see them! He'd just like to see them! And he'd show them, anyway. Yes, he would show them. Exactly what he would show them and how he would show them, he was not as yet very clear. He looked round the room again. There were no eatables in it so far except the piled-up plate of huge pears on the sideboard.

He looked at it longingly. They'd probably counted them and knew just how many there ought to be. Mean sort of thing they would do. And they'd be in counting them every other minute just to see if he'd taken one. Well, he was going to score off somebody, somehow. Make him go to bed early indeed! He stood with knit brows, deep in thought, then his face cleared and he smiled. He'd got it! For the next five minutes he munched the delicious pears, but, at the end, the piled-up pyramid was apparently exactly as he found it, not a pear gone, only – on the inner side of each pear, the side that didn't show, was a huge semicircular bite. William wiped his mouth with his coat sleeve. They were jolly good pears. And a blissful vision came to him of the faces of the guests as they took the pears, of the faces of his father and mother and Robert and Ethel. Oh, crumbs! He chuckled to himself as he went down to the kitchen again.

'I say, Cook, could you make a small one – quite a small one – for threepence-halfpenny?'

Cook laughed.

'I was only pulling your leg, Master William. I've got one made and locked up in the larder.'

'That's all right,' said William. 'I – wanted them to have a cream blancmange, that's all.'

'Oh, *they'll* have it all right; they won't leave much for you. I only made *one*!'

'Did you say locked in the larder?' said William carelessly. 'It must be a bother for you to *lock* the larder door each time you go in?'

'Oh, no trouble, Master William, thank you,' said Cook sarcastically; 'there's more than the cream blancmange there; there's pasties and cakes and other things. I'm thinking of the last party your ma gave!'

William had the grace to blush. On that occasion William and a friend had spent the hour before supper in the larder, and supper had to be postponed while fresh provisions were beaten up from any and every quarter. William had passed a troubled night and spent the next day in bed.

'Oh, *then*! That was a long time ago. I was only a kid then.'

'Umph!' grunted the cook. Then, relenting, 'Well, if there's any cream blancmange left I'll bring it up to you in bed. Now that's a promise. Here, Emma, put these sandwiches in the larder. Here's the key! Now mind you *lock it* after you!'

'Cook! Just come here for a minute.'

It was the voice of William's mother from the library. William's heart rose. With Cook away from the scene of action great things might happen. Emma took the dish of sandwiches, unlocked the pantry door, and entered. There was a crash of crockery from the back kitchen. Emma fled out, leaving the door unlocked. After she had picked up several broken plates, which had unaccountably slipped from the shelves, she returned and locked the pantry door.

William, in the darkness within, heaved a sigh of relief. He was in, anyway; how he was going to get out he wasn't quite sure. He stood for a few minutes in rapt admiration of his own cleverness. He'd scored off Cook! Crumbs! He'd scored off Cook! So far, at any rate. The first thing to do was to find the cream blancmange. He found it at last and sat down with it on the bread pan to consider his next step.

Suddenly he became aware of two green eyes staring at him in the darkness. The cat was in too! Crumbs! The cat was in too! The cat, recognising its inveterate enemy, set up a vindictive wail. William grew cold with fright. The rotten old cat was going to give the show away!

'Here, Pussy! Good ole Pussy!' he whispered hoarsely. 'Nice ole Pussy! Good ole Pussy!'

The cat gazed at him in surprise. This form of address from William was unusual.

'Good ole Pussy!' went on William feverishly. 'Shut up,

then. Here's some nice blancmange. Just have a bit. Go on, have a bit an shut up.'

He put the dish down on the larder floor before the cat, and the cat, after a few preliminary licks, decided that it was good. William sat watching for a bit. Then he came to the conclusion that it was no use wasting time, and began to sample the plates around him. He ate a whole jelly, and then took four sandwiches off each plate, and four cakes and pasties off each plate. He had learnt wisdom since the last party. Meanwhile, the cat licked away at the cream blancmange with every evidence of satisfaction. It even began to purr, and as its satisfaction increased so did the purr. It possessed a peculiar penetrating purr.

'Cook!' called out Emma from the kitchen.

Cook came out of the library where she was assisting with the festoon hanging. 'What's the matter?'

'There's a funny buzzing noise in the larder.'

'Well, go in and see what it is. It's probably a wasp, that's all.'

Emma approached with the key, and William, clasping the blancmange to his bosom, withdrew behind the door, slipping off his shoes in readiness for action.

'Poor Puss!' said Emma, opening the door and meeting the cat's green, unabashed gaze. 'Did it get shut up in the nasty dark larder, then? Who did it then?'

She was bending down with her back to William, stroking the cat in the doorway. William seized his chance. He dashed past her and up the stairs in stockinged feet like a flash of lightning. But Emma, leaning over the cat, had espied a dark flying figure out of the corner of her eye. She set up a scream. Out of the library came William's mother, William's sister, William's brother and Cook.

'A burglar in the larder!' gasped Emma. 'I seed 'im, I did! Out of the corner of my eye, like, and when I looked up 'e wasn't there no more. Flittin' up the 'all like a shadder, 'e was. Oh, lor! It's fairly turned me inside! Oh, lor!'

'What rubbish!' said William's mother. 'Emma, you must control yourself.'

'I went into the larder myself, 'm,' said Cook indignantly, 'just before I came in to 'elp with the greenery ornaments, and it was hempty as – hair. It's all that silly Emma! Always 'avin' the jumps she is—'

'Where's William?' said William's mother with sudden suspicion. 'William!'

William came out of his bedroom and looked over the balusters.

'Yes, Mother,' he said, with that wondering innocence of voice and look which he had brought to a fine art, and which proved one of his greatest assets in times of stress and strain.

'What are you doing?'

'Jus' readin' quietly in my room, Mother.'

'Oh, for heaven's sake don't disturb him, then,' said William's sister.

'It's those silly books you read, Emma. You're always imagining things. If you'd read the ones I recommend instead of the foolish ones you will get hold of—'

William's mother was safely mounted on one of her favourite hobby horses. William withdrew to his room and carefully concealed the cream blancmange beneath his bed. He then waited till he heard the guests arrive and exchange greetings in the hall. William, listening with his door open, carefully committed to memory the voice and manner of his sister's greeting to her friends. That would come in useful later on, probably. No weapon of offence against the world in general and his own family in particular, was to be despised. He held a rehearsal in his room when the guests were all safely assembled in the drawing-room.

'Oh, *how* are you, Mrs Green?' he said in a high falsetto, meant to represent the feminine voice. 'And how's the *darling* baby? *Such* a duck! I'm dying to see him again! Oh, Delia, darling! There you are! *So* glad you could come! What a perfect darling of a dress, my dear. I know whose heart you'll break in that! Oh, Mr

Thompson!' – here William languished, bridled and ogled in a fashion seen nowhere on earth except in his imitations of his sister when engaged in conversation with one of the male sex. If reproduced at the right moment, it was guaranteed to drive her to a frenzy: 'I'm *so* glad to see you. Yes, of course I really am! I wouldn't say it if I wasn't!'

The drawing-room door opened and a chatter of conversation and a rustling of dresses arose from the hall. Oh, crumbs! They were going in to supper. Yes, the dining-room door closed; the coast was clear. William took out the rather battered-looking delicacy from under the bed and considered it thoughtfully. The dish was big and awkwardly shaped. He must find something that would go under his coat better than that. He couldn't march through the hall and out of the front door, bearing a cream blancmange, naked and unashamed. And the back door through the kitchen was impossible. With infinite care but little success as far as the shape of the blancmange was concerned, he removed it from its dish on to his soap dish. He forgot, in the excitement of the moment, to remove the soap, but, after all, it was only a small piece. The soap dish was decidedly too small for it, but, clasped to William's bosom inside his coat, it could be partly supported by his arm outside. He descended the stairs cautiously. He tiptoed lightly past the dining-room door (which was slightly ajar), from which came the shrill, noisy, meaningless, conversation of the grown-ups. He was just about to open the front door when there came the sound of a key turning in the lock.

William's heart sank. He had forgotten the fact that his father generally returned from his office about this time.

William's father came into the hall and glanced at his youngest offspring suspiciously.

'Hello!' he said. 'Where are you going?'

William cleared his throat nervously.

'Me?' he questioned lightly. 'Oh, I was jus' – jus' goin' for a little walk up the road before I went to bed. That's all I was going to do, Father.'

Flop! A large segment of the cream blancmange had disintegrated itself from the fast-melting mass, and, evading William's encircling arm, had fallen on to the floor at his feet. With praiseworthy presence of mind William promptly stepped on to it and covered it with his feet. William's father turned round quickly from the stand where he was replacing his walking stick.

'What was that?'

William looked round the hall absently. 'What, Father?'

William's father now fastened his eyes upon William's person.

'What have you got under your coat?'

'Where?' said William with apparent surprise.

Then, looking down at the damp excrescence of his coat, as if he noticed it for the first time, 'Oh, that!' with a mirthless smile. 'Do you mean *that*? Oh, that's jus' – jus' somethin' I'm takin' out with me, that's all.'

Again William's father grunted.

'Well,' he said, 'if you're going for this walk up the road why on earth don't you go, instead of standing as if you'd lost the use of your feet?'

William's father was hanging up his overcoat with his back to William, and the front door was open. William wanted no second bidding. He darted out of the door and down the drive, but he was just in time to hear the thud of a falling body and to hear a muttered curse as the Head of the House entered the dining-room feet first on a long slide of some white, glutinous substance.

'Oh, crumbs!' gasped William as he ran.

The little girl next door was sitting in the summer house, armed with a spoon, when William arrived. His precious burden had now saturated his shirt and was striking cold and damp on his chest. He drew it from his coat and displayed it proudly. It had certainly lost its pristine, white, rounded appearance. The marks of the cat's licks were very evident; grime from William's coat adhered to its surface; it wobbled limply over the soap dish, but the little girl's eyes sparkled as she saw it.

'Oh, William, I never thought you really would! Oh, you are wonderful! And I had it!'

'What?'

'Rice-mould for supper, but I didn't mind, because I thought – I hoped, you'd come with it. Oh, William, you *are a nice* boy!'

William glowed with pride.

'William!' bellowed an irate voice from William's front door.

William knew that voice. It was the voice of the male parent who has stood all he's jolly well going to stand from that kid, and is out for vengeance. They'd got to the pears! Oh, crumbs! They'd got to the pears! And even the thought of Nemesis to come could not dull for William the bliss of that vision.

'Oh, William,' said the little girl next door sadly, 'they're calling you. Will you have to go?'

'Not me,' said William earnestly. 'I'm not going – not till they fetch me. Here! You begin. I don't want any. I've had lots of things. You eat it all.'

Her face radiant with anticipation, the little girl took up her spoon.

William leant back in a superior, benevolent manner

and watched the smile freeze upon her face and her look of ecstasy change to one of fury. With a horrible suspicion at his heart he seized the spoon she had dropped and took a mouthful himself.

He had brought the rice-mould by mistake!

WILLIAM LEANT BACK IN A SUPERIOR, BENEVOLENT MANNER
AND WATCHED THE SMILE FREEZE UPON HER FACE AND HER
LOOK OF ECSTASY CHANGE TO ONE OF FURY.

CHAPTER 3

WILLIAM'S BURGLAR

When William first saw him he was leaning against the wall of the White Lion, gazing at the passers-by with a moody smile upon his villainous-looking countenance.

It was evident to any careful observer that he had not confined his attentions to the exterior of the White Lion.

William, at whose heels trotted his beloved mongrel (rightly named Jumble), was passing him with a casual glance, when something attracted his attention. He stopped and looked back, then, turning round, stood in front of the tall, untidy figure, gazing up at him with frank and unabashed curiosity.

'Who cut 'em off?' he said at last in an awed whisper.

The figure raised his hands and stroked the long hair down the side of his face.

'Now yer arskin',' he said with a grin.

'Well, who *did*?' persisted William.

'That 'ud be tellin',' answered his new friend, moving unsteadily from one foot to the other. 'See?'

'You got 'em cut off in the war,' said William firmly.

'I didn't. I bin in the wor orl right. Stroike me pink, I bin in the wor and *that's* the truth. But I didn't get 'em cut orf in the wor. Well, I'll stop kiddin' yer. I'll tell yer strite. I never 'ad none. *Nar!*'

William stood on tiptoe to peer under the untidy hair at the small apertures that in his strange new friend took the place of ears. Admiration shone in William's eyes.

'Was you born without 'em?' he said enviously.

His friend nodded.

'Nar don't yer go torkin' about it,' he went on modestly, though seeming to bask in the sun of William's evident awe and respect. 'I don't want all folks knowin' 'bout it. See? It kinder *marks* a man, this 'ere sort of thing. See? Makes 'im too easy to *track*, loike. That's why I grown me hair long. See? 'Ere, 'ave a drink?'

He put his head inside the window of the White Lion and roared out, 'Bottle o' lemonide fer the young gent.'

William followed him to a small table in the little sunny porch, and his heart swelled with pride as he sat and quaffed his beverage with a manly air. His friend, who said his name was Mr Blank, showed a most flattering interest in him. He elicited from him the whereabouts of his house and the number of his family, a description

44

of the door and window fastenings, of the dining-room silver and his mother's jewellery.

William, his eyes fixed with a fascinated stare upon Mr Blank's ears, gave the required information readily, glad to be able in any way to interest this intriguing and mysterious being.

'Tell me about the war,' said William at last.

'It were orl right while it larsted,' said Mr Blank with a sigh. 'It were orl right, but I s'pose, like mos' things in this 'ere world, it couldn't larst fer ever. See?'

William set down the empty glass of lemonade and leant across the table, almost dizzy with the romance of the moment. Had Douglas, had Henry, had Ginger, had any of those boys who sat next him at school and joined in the feeble relaxations provided by the authorities out of school, ever done *this* – ever sat at a real table outside a real public-house drinking lemonade and talking to a man with no ears who'd fought in the war and who looked as if he might have done *anything?*

Jumble, meanwhile, sat and snapped at flies, frankly bored.

'Did you' – said William in a loud whisper – 'did you ever *kill* anyone?'

Mr Blank laughed a laugh that made William's blood curdle.

'DID YOU' – SAID WILLIAM IN A LOUD WHISPER – 'DID YOU
EVER *KILL* ANYONE?'

'Me kill anyone? Me kill anyone? *'Ondreds!*'

William breathed a sigh of satisfaction. Here was
romance and adventure incarnate.

'What do you do now the war's over?'

Mr Blank closed one eye.

'That 'ud be tellin', wudn't it?'

'I'll keep it awfully secret,' pleaded William. 'I'll never
tell anyone.'

Mr Blank shook his head.

'What yer want ter know fer, anyway?' he said.

William answered eagerly, his eyes alight.

''Cause I'd like to do jus' the same when I grow up.'

Mr Blank flung back his head and emitted guffaw after guffaw of unaffected mirth.

'Oh 'ell,' he said, wiping his eyes. 'Oh, stroike me pink! That's good, that is. You wait, young gent, you wait till you've growed up and see what yer pa says to it. Oh 'ell!'

He rose and pulled his cap down over his eyes.

'Well, I'll say good day to yer, young gent.'

William looked at him wistfully.

'I'd like to see you again, Mr Blank, I would, honest. Will you be here this afternoon?'

'Wot d'yer want to see me agine fer?' said Mr Blank suspiciously.

'I *like* you,' said William fervently. 'I like the way you talk, and I like the things you say, and I want to know about what you do!'

Mr Blank was obviously flattered.

'I may be round 'ere agine this arter, though I mike no promise. See? I've gotter be careful, I 'ave. I've gotter be careful 'oo sees me an' 'oo 'ears me, and where I go. That's the worst of 'aving no ears. See?'

47

William did not see, but he was thrilled to the soul by the mystery.

'An' you don't tell no one you seen me nor nothing abart me,' went on Mr Blank.

Pulling his cap still farther over his head, Mr Blank set off unsteadily down the road, leaving William to pay for his lemonade with his last penny.

He walked home, his heart set firmly on a lawless career of crime. Opposition he expected from his father and mother and Robert and Ethel, but his determination was fixed. He wondered if it would be very painful to have his ears cut off.

He entered the dining-room with an air of intense mystery, pulling his cap over his eyes, and looking round in a threatening manner.

'William, what *do* you mean by coming into the house in your cap? Take it off at once.'

William sighed. He wondered if Mr Blank had a mother.

When he returned he sat down and began quietly to remodel his life. He would not be an explorer, after all, nor an engine driver nor chimney sweep. He would be a man of mystery, a murderer, fighter, forger. He fingered his ears tentatively. They seemed fixed on jolly fast. He glanced with utter contempt at his father who had just come in.

His father's life of blameless respectability seemed to him at that minute utterly despicable.

'The Wilkinsons over at Todfoot have had their house broken into now,' Mrs Brown was saying. '*All* her jewellery gone. They think it's a gang. It's just the villages round here. There seems to be one every day!'

William expressed his surprise.

'Oh, 'ell!' he ejaculated, with a slightly self-conscious air.

Mr Brown turned round and looked at his son.

'May I ask,' he said politely, 'where you picked up that expression?'

'I got it off one of my fren's,' said William with quiet pride.

'Then I'd take it as a personal favour,' went on Mr Brown, 'if you'd kindly refrain from airing your friends' vocabularies in this house.'

'He means you're never to say it again, William,' translated Mrs Brown sternly. '*Never.*'

'All right,' said William. 'I won't. See? I da— jolly well won't. Strike me pink. See?'

He departed with an air of scowling mystery and dignity combined, leaving his parents speechless with amazement.

That afternoon he returned to the White Lion. Mr

Blank was standing unobtrusively in the shadow of the wall.

''Ello, young gent,' he greeted William, 'nice dorg you've got.'

William looked proudly down at Jumble.

'You won't find,' he said proudly and with some truth, 'you won't find another dog like this – not for *miles*!'

'Will 'e be much good as a watchdog, now?' asked Mr Blank carelessly.

'Good?' said William, almost indignant at the question. 'There isn't any sort of dog he isn't good at!'

'Umph,' said Mr Blank, looking at him thoughtfully.

'Tell me about things you've *done*,' said William earnestly.

'Yus, I will, too,' said Mr Blank. 'But jus' you tell me first 'oo lives at all these 'ere nice 'ouses an' all about 'em. See?'

William readily complied, and the strange couple gradually wended their way along the road towards William's house. William stopped at the gate and considered deeply. He was torn between instincts of hospitality and a dim suspicion that his family would not afford to Mr Blank the courtesy which is a guest's due. He looked at Mr Blank's old green-black cap, long, untidy hair, dirty, lined, sly old face, muddy clothes and gaping boots, and decided quite finally that his mother would not allow him in her drawing-room.

'Will you,' he said tentatively, 'will you come roun' an' see our back garden? If we go behind these ole bushes and keep close along the wall, no one'll see us.'

To William's relief Mr Blank did not seem to resent

HE DEPARTED WITH AN AIR OF SCOWLING MYSTERY,
LEAVING HIS PARENTS SPEECHLESS WITH AMAZEMENT.

the suggestion of secrecy. They crept along the wall in silence except for Jumble, who loudly worried Mr Blank's trailing boot strings as he walked. They reached a part of the back garden that was not visible from the house and sat down together under a shady tree.

'P'raps,' began Mr Blank politely, 'you could bring a bit o' tea out to me on the quiet like.'

'I'll ask Mother—' began William.

'Oh no,' said Mr Blank modestly. 'I don't want ter give no one no trouble. Just a slice o' bread, if you can find it, without troublin' no one. See?'

William had a brilliant idea.

'Let's go 'cross to that window an' get in,' he said eagerly. 'That's the lib'ry and no one uses it 'cept Father, and he's not in till later.'

Mr Blank insisted on tying Jumble up, then he swung himself dexterously through the window. William gave a gasp of admiration.

'You did that fine,' he said.

Again Mr Blank closed one eye.

'Not the first time I've got in at a winder, young gent, nor the larst, I bet. Not by a long way. See?'

William followed more slowly. His eyes gleamed with pride. This hero of romance and adventure was now his guest, under his roof.

'Make yourself quite at home, Mr Blank,' he said with an air of intense politeness.

Mr Blank did. He emptied Mr Brown's cigar box into his pocket. He drank three glasses of Mr Brown's whiskey

MR BLANK MADE HIMSELF QUITE AT HOME.

and soda. While William's back was turned he filled his pockets with the silver ornaments from the mantelpiece. He began to inspect the drawers in Mr Brown's desk. Then:

'William! Come to tea!'

'You stay here,' whispered William. 'I'll bring you some.'

But luck was against him. It was a visitor's tea in the drawing-room, and Mrs de Vere Carter, a neighbour, there, in all her glory. She rose from her seat with an ecstatic murmur.

'Willie! *Dear* child! *Sweet* little soul!'

With one arm she crushed the infuriated William against her belt, with the other she caressed his hair. Then William in moody silence sat down in a corner and began to eat bread and butter. Every time he prepared to slip a piece into his pocket, he found his mother's or Mrs de Vere Carter's eyes fixed upon him and hastily began to eat it himself. He sat, miserable and hot, seeing only the heroic figure starving in the next room, and planned a raid on the larder as soon as he could reasonably depart. Every now and then he scowled across at Mrs de Vere Carter and made a movement with his hands as though pulling a cap over his eyes. He invested even his eating with an air of dark mystery.

Then Robert, his elder brother, came in, followed by a thin, pale man with eyeglasses and long hair.

'This is Mr Lewes, Mother,' said Robert with an air of pride and triumph. 'He's editor of *Fiddle Strings*.'

There was an immediate stir and sensation. Robert had often talked of his famous friend. In fact Robert's family was weary of the sound of his name, but this was the first time Robert had induced him to leave the haunts of his genius to visit the Brown household.

Mr Lewes bowed with a set, stern, self-conscious expression, as though to convey to all that his celebrity was more of a weight than a pleasure to him. Mrs de Vere Carter bridled and fluttered, for *Fiddle Strings* had a society column and a page of scrappy 'News of the Town', and Mrs de Vere Carter's greatest ambition was to see her name in print.

Mr Lewes sat back in his chair, took his teacup as though it were a fresh addition to his responsibilities, and began to talk. He talked apparently without even breathing. He began on the weather, drifted on to art and music, and was just beginning a monologue on The Novel, when William rose and crept from the room like a guilty spirit. He found Mr Blank under the library table, having heard a noise in the kitchen and fearing a visitor. A cigar and a silver snuffer had fallen from his pocket to the floor. He hastily replaced them. William went up and took another look at the wonderful ears and heaved a sigh of relief. While parted from his strange friend he had a horrible suspicion that the whole thing was a dream.

'I'll go to the larder and get you sumthin',' he said. 'You jus' stay there.'

'I think, young gent,' said Mr Blank, 'I think I'll just go an' look round upstairs on the quiet like, an' you needn't mention it to no one. See?'

Again he performed the fascinating wink.

They crept on tiptoe into the hall, but – the drawing-room door was ajar.

'William!'

William's heart stood still. He could hear his mother coming across the room, then – she stood in the doorway. Her face filled with horror as her eyes fell upon Mr Blank.

'*William!*' she said.

William's feelings were beyond description. Desperately he sought for an explanation for his friend's presence. With what pride and sangfroid had Robert announced his uninvited guest! William determined to try it, at any rate. He advanced boldly into the drawing-room.

'This is Mr Blank, Mother,' he announced jauntily. 'He hasn't got no ears.'

Mr Blank stood in the background, awaiting developments. Flight was now impossible.

The announcement fell flat. There was nothing but horror upon the five silent faces that confronted William. He made a last desperate effort.

'He's bin in the war,' he pleaded. 'He's – killed folks.'

Then the unexpected happened.

Mrs de Vere Carter rose with a smile of welcome. In her mind's eye she saw the touching story already in print – tattered hero – the gracious lady – the age of Democracy. The stage was laid and that dark, pale young man had only to watch and listen.

'Ah, one of our dear heroes! My poor, brave man! A cup of tea, my dear,' turning to William's thunderstruck mother. 'And he may sit down, may he not?' She kept her face well turned towards the sardonic-looking Mr Lewes. He must not miss a word or gesture. 'How *proud* we are to do anything for our dear heroes! Wounded, perhaps? Ah, poor man!' She floated across to him with a cup of tea and plied him with bread and butter and cake. William sat down meekly on a chair, looking rather pale. Mr Blank, whose philosophy was to take the goods the gods gave and not look to the future, began to make a hearty meal. 'Are you looking for work, my poor man?' asked Mrs de Vere Carter, leaning forward in her chair.

Her poor man replied with simple, manly directness that he 'was dam'd if he was. See?' Mr Lewes began to discuss The Drama with Robert. Mrs de Vere Carter raised her voice.

'*How* you must have suffered! Yes, there is suffering ingrained in your face. A piece of shrapnel? Ten inches square? Right in at one hip and out at the other? Oh, my poor man! *How* I feel for you. How all class distinctions vanish at such a time. How—'

She stopped while Mr Blank drank his tea. In fact, all conversation ceased while Mr Blank drank his tea, just as conversation on a station ceases while a train passes through.

Mrs Brown looked helplessly around her. When Mr Blank had eaten a plate of sandwiches, a plate of bread and butter, and half a cake, he rose slowly, keeping one hand over the pocket in which reposed the silver ornaments.

'Well 'm,' he said, touching his cap. 'Thank you kindly. I've 'ad a fine tea. I 'ave. A dam' fine tea. An' I'll not forget yer kindness to a pore ole soldier.' Here he winked brazenly at William. 'An' good day ter you orl.'

Mrs de Vere Carter floated out to the front door with him, and William followed as in a dream.

Mrs Brown found her voice.

'We'd better have the chair disinfected,' she murmured to Ethel.

Then Mrs de Vere Carter returned smiling to herself and eyeing the young editor surmisingly.

'I witnessed a pretty scene the other day in a suburban drawing-room . . .' It might begin like that.

'ARE YOU LOOKING FOR WORK, MY POOR MAN?' ASKED
MRS DE VERE CARTER.

William followed the amazing figure round the house again to the library window. Here it turned to him with a friendly grin.

'I'm just goin' to 'ave that look round upstairs now. See?' he said. 'An' once more, yer don't need ter say nothin' to no one. See?'

With the familiar, beloved gesture he drew his old cap down over his eyes, and was gone.

William wandered upstairs a few minutes later to find his visitor standing at the landing window, his pockets bulging.

'I'm goin' to try this 'ere window, young gent,' he said in a quick, business-like voice. 'I see yer pa coming in at the front gate. Give me a shove. Quick, nar.'

Mr Brown entered the drawing-room.

'Mulroyd's had his house burgled now,' he said. 'Every bit of his wife's jewellery gone. They've got some clues, though. It's a gang all right, and one of them is a chap without ears. Grows his hair long to hide it. But it's a clue. The police are hunting for him.'

He looked in amazement at the horror-stricken faces before him. Mrs Brown sat down weakly.

'Ethel, my smelling salts! They're on the mantelpiece.'

Robert grew pale.

'Good Lord – my silver cricket cup,' he gasped, racing upstairs.

The landing window had been too small, and Mr Blank too big, though William did his best.

There came to the astounded listeners the sound of a fierce scuffle, then Robert descended, his hair rumpled and his tie awry, holding William by the arm. William looked pale and apprehensive. 'He was there,' panted Robert, 'just getting out of the window. He chucked the things out of his pockets and got away. I couldn't stop him. And – and William was there—'

William's face assumed the expression of one who is prepared for the worst.

'The plucky little chap! Struggling with him! Trying to pull him back from the window! All by himself!'

'I *wasn't*,' cried William excitedly. 'I was *helping* him. He's my *friend*. I—'

But they heard not a word. They crowded round him, praised him, shook hands with him, asked if he was hurt. Mrs de Vere Carter kept up one perpetual scream of delight and congratulation.

'The *dear* boy! The little *pet*! How *brave*! What *courage*! What an *example* to us all! And the horrid, wretched man! Posing as a *hero*. Wangling himself into the sweet child's confidence. Are you hurt, my precious? Did the nasty man hurt you? You *darling* boy!'

When the babel had somewhat subsided, Mr Brown

came forward and laid a hand on William's shoulder.

'I'm very pleased with you, my boy' he said. 'You can buy anything you like tomorrow up to five shillings.'

William's bewildered countenance cleared.

'Thank you, Father,' he said meekly.

CHAPTER 4

THE KNIGHT AT ARMS

'A knight,' said Miss Drew, who was struggling to in-spire her class with enthusiasm for Tennyson's 'Idylls of the King', 'a knight was a person who spent his time going round succouring the oppressed.'

'Suckin' wot?' said William, bewildered.

'Succour means to help. He spent his time helping anyone who was in trouble.'

'How much did he get for it?' asked William.

'Nothing, of course,' said Miss Drew, appalled by the base commercialism of the twentieth century. 'He helped the poor because he *loved* them, William. He had a lot of adventures and fighting and he helped beautiful, persecuted damsels.'

William's respect for the knight rose.

'Of course,' said Miss Drew hastily, 'they needn't necessarily be beautiful, but, in most of the stories we have, they were beautiful.'

There followed some stories of fighting and adventure and the rescuing of beautiful damsels. The idea of the thing began to take hold of William's imagination.

'I say,' he said to his chum Ginger after school, 'that knight thing sounds all right. Suckin' – I mean helpin' people an' fightin' an' all that. I wun't mind doin' it an' you could be my squire.'

'Yes,' said Ginger slowly, 'I'd thought of doin' it, but I'd thought of *you* bein' the squire.'

'Well,' said William after a pause, 'let's be squires in turn. You first,' he added hastily.

'Wot'll you give me if I'm first?' said Ginger, displaying again the base commercialism of the age.

William considered.

'I'll give you first drink out of a bottle of ginger ale wot I'm goin' to get with my next money. It'll be three weeks off 'cause they're takin' the next two weeks to pay for an ole window wot my ball slipped into by mistake.'

He spoke with the bitterness that always characterised his statements of the injustice of the grown-up world.

'All right,' said Ginger.

'I won't forget about the drink of ginger ale.'

'No, you won't,' said Ginger simply. 'I'll remind you all right. Well, let's set off.'

''Course,' said William, 'it would be *nicer* with armour an' horses an' trumpets, but I 'spect folks 'ud think anyone a bit soft wot went about in the streets in armour now, 'cause these times is different. She said so. Anyway, she said we could still be knights an' help people, di'n't she? Anyway, I'll get my bugle. That'll be *something*.'

William's bugle had just returned to public life after one of its periodic terms of retirement into his father's keeping.

William took his bugle proudly in one hand and his pistol (the glorious result of a dip in the bran tub at a school party) in the other, and, sternly denying themselves the pleasures of afternoon school, off the two set upon the road of romance and adventure.

'I'll carry the bugle,' said Ginger, ''cause I'm squire.'

William was loath to give up his treasure.

'Well, I'll carry it now,' he said, 'but when I begin fightin' folks, I'll give it you to hold.'

They walked along for about a mile without meeting anyone. William began to be aware of a sinking feeling in the region of his waist.

'I wonder wot they *eat*,' he said at last. 'I'm gettin' so's I wouldn't mind sumthin' to eat.'

'We di'n't ought to have set off before dinner,' said the squire with after-the-event wisdom. 'We ought to have waited till *after* dinner.'

'You ought to have *brought* sumthin',' said William severely. 'You're the squire. You're not much of a squire not to have brought sumthin' for me to eat.'

'An' me,' put in Ginger. 'If I'd brought any I'd have brought it for me more'n for you.'

William fingered his minute pistol.

'If we meet any wild animals . . .' he said darkly.

A cow gazed at them mournfully over a hedge.

'You might go an' milk that,' suggested William. 'Milk 'ud be better'n nothing.'

'*You* go an' milk it.'

'No, I'm not squire. I bet squires did the milkin'. Knights wun't of done the milkin'.'

'I'll remember,' said Ginger bitterly, 'when you're squire, all the things wot you said a squire ought to do when I was squire.'

They entered the field and gazed at the cow from a respectful distance. She turned her eyes upon them sadly.

'Go on!' said the knight to his reluctant squire.

'I'm not good at cows,' objected that gentleman.

'Well, I will, then!' said William with reckless bravado, and advanced boldly upon the animal. The animal very slightly lowered its horns (perhaps in sign of greeting) and emitted a sonorous mo-o-o-o. Like lightning the gallant pair made for the road.

'Anyway,' said William gloomily, 'we'd got nothin' to put it in, so we'd only of got tossed for nothin', p'raps, if we'd gone on.'

They walked on down the road till they came to a pair of iron gates and a drive that led up to a big house. William's spirits rose. His hunger was forgotten.

'Come on!' he said. 'We might find someone to rescue here. It looks like a place where there might be someone to rescue.'

There was no one in the garden to question the right of entry of two small boys armed with a bugle and a toy pistol. Unchallenged they went up to the house. While the knight was wondering whether to blow his bugle at the front door or by the open window, they caught sight suddenly of a vision inside the window. It was a girl as fair and slim and beautiful as any wandering knight could desire. And she was speaking fast and passionately.

William, ready for all contingencies, marshalled his forces.

'Follow me!' he whispered and crept on all fours nearer the window. They could see a man now, an elderly man with white hair and a white beard.

'And how long will you keep me in this vile prison,' she was saying in a voice that trembled with anger, 'base wretch that you are?'

'Crumbs!' ejaculated William.

'Ha! Ha!' sneered the man. 'I have you in my power. I will keep you here a prisoner till you sign the paper which will make me master of all your wealth, and beware, girl, if you do not sign, you may answer for it with your life!'

'Golly!' murmured William.

Then he crawled away into the bushes, followed by his attendant squire.

'Well,' said William, his face purple with excitement, 'we've found someone to rescue all *right*. He's a base wretch, wot she said, all *right*.'

'Will you kill him?' said the awed squire.

'How big was he? Could you see?' said William the discreet.

'He was ever so big. Great big face he had, too, with a beard.'

'Then I won't try killin' him – not straight off. I'll think of some plan – somethin' cunnin'.'

He sat with his chin on his hands, gazing into space, till they were surprised by the opening of the front door and the appearance of a tall, thick-set, elderly man. William quivered with excitement. The man went along a path through the bushes. William and Ginger followed on all fours with elaborate caution. At every almost inaudible sound from Ginger, William turned his red, frowning face on to him with a resounding 'Shh!' The path ended at a small shed with a locked door. The man opened the door – the key stood in the lock – and entered.

Promptly William, with a snarl expressive of cunning and triumph, hurled himself at the door and turned the key in the lock.

'Here!' came an angry shout from inside. 'Who's that? What the devil—'

'You low ole caitiff!' said William through the keyhole.

'Who the deuce—' exploded the voice.

'You base wretch, like wot she said you was,' bawled William, his mouth still applied closely to the keyhole.

WILLIAM AND GINGER FOLLOWED ON ALL FOURS WITH
ELABORATE CAUTION.

'Let me out at once, or I'll—'

'You mean ole oppressor!'

'Who the deuce are you? What's the tomfool trick? Let me *out*! Do you hear?'

A resounding kick shook the door.

'I've gotter pistol,' said William sternly. 'I'll shoot you dead if you kick the door down, you mangy ole beast!'

The sound of kicking ceased and a scrambling and scraping, accompanied by oaths, proceeded from the interior.

'I'll stay on guard,' said William with the tense expression of the soldier at his post, 'an' you go an' set her free. Go an' blow the bugle at the front door, then they'll know something's happened,' he added simply.

Miss Priscilla Greene was pouring out tea in the drawing-room. Two young men and a maiden were the recipients of her hospitality.

'Dad will be here in a minute,' she said. 'He's just gone to the darkroom to see to some photos he'd left in toning or fixing, or something. We'll get on with the rehearsal as soon as he comes. We'd just rehearsed the scene he and I have together, so we're ready for the ones where we all come in.'

'How did it go off?'

'Oh, quite well. We knew our parts, anyway.'

'I think the village will enjoy it.'

'Anyway, it's never very critical, is it? And it loves a melodrama.'

'Yes. I wonder if Father knows you're here. He said he'd come straight back. Perhaps I'd better go and find him.'

'Oh, let me go, Miss Greene,' said one of the youths ardently.

'Well, I don't know whether you'd find the place. It's a shed in the garden that he uses. We use it half as a darkroom and half as a coal-cellar.'

'I'll go—'

He stopped. A nightmare sound, as discordant as it was ear-splitting, filled the room. Miss Greene sank back into her chair, suddenly white. One of the young men let a cup of tea fall neatly from his fingers on to the floor and there crash into fragments. The young lady visitor emitted a scream that would have done credit to a factory siren. Then at the open French window appeared a small boy holding a bugle, purple-faced with the effort of his performance.

One of the young men was the first to recover speech. He stepped away from the broken crockery on the floor as if to disclaim all responsibility for it and said sternly:

'Did you make that horrible noise?'

Miss Greene began to laugh hysterically.

'Do have some tea now you've come,' she said to Ginger.

Ginger remembered the pangs of hunger, of which excitement had momentarily rendered him oblivious, and, deciding that there was no time like the present, took a cake from the stand and began to consume it in silence.

'You'd better be careful,' said the young lady to her hostess; 'he might have escaped from the asylum. He looks mad. He had a very mad look, I thought, when he was standing at the window.'

'He's evidently hungry, anyway. I can't think why Father doesn't come.'

Here Ginger, fortified by a walnut bun, remembered his mission.

'It's all right now,' he said. 'You can go home. He's shut up. Me an' William shut him up.'

'You see!' said the young lady, with a meaning glance around. 'I *said* he was from the asylum. He looked mad. We'd better humour him and ring up the asylum. Have another cake, darling boy,' she said in a tone of honeyed sweetness.

Nothing loath, Ginger selected an ornate pyramid of icing.

At this point there came a bellowing and crashing and tramping outside and Miss Priscilla's father, roaring fury and threats of vengeance, hurled himself into the room. Miss Priscilla's father had made his escape by a small window at the other end of the shed. To do this he had had to climb over the coals in the dark. His face and hands and clothes and once-white beard were covered with coal. His eyes gleamed whitely.

'An abominable attack . . . utterly unprovoked . . . dastardly ruffians!'

Here he stopped to splutter because his mouth was full of coal dust. While he was spluttering, William, who had just discovered that his bird had flown, appeared at the window.

'He's got out,' he said reproachfully. 'Look at him. He's got out. An' all our trouble for nothing. Why di'n't someone *stop* him gettin' out?'

William and Ginger sat on the railing that separated their houses.

'It's not really much *fun* bein' a knight,' said William slowly.

'No,' agreed Ginger. 'You never know when folks *is* oppressed. An' anyway, wot's one afternoon away from school to make such a fuss about?'

'HE'S GOT OUT,' HE SAID REPROACHFULLY.
'WHY DI'N'T SOMEONE STOP HIM GETTIN' OUT?'

'Seems to me from wot Father said,' went on William gloomily, 'you'll have to wait a jolly long time for that drink of ginger ale.'

An expression of dejection came over Ginger's face.

'An' you wasn't even ever squire,' he said. Then he brightened.

'They were jolly good cakes, wasn't they?' he said.

William's lips curved into a smile of blissful reminiscence.

'*Jolly* good!' he agreed.

CHAPTER 5

WILLIAM'S HOBBY

Uncle George was William's godfather, and he was intensely interested in William's upbringing. It was an interest with which William would gladly have dispensed. Uncle George's annual visit was to William a purgatory only to be endured by a resolutely philosophic attitude of mind and the knowledge that sooner or later it must come to an end. Uncle George had an ideal of what a boy should be, and it was a continual grief to him that William fell so short of this ideal. But he never relinquished his efforts to make William conform to it.

His ideal was a gentle boy of exquisite courtesy and of intellectual pursuits. Such a boy he could have loved. It was hard that fate had endowed him with a godson like William. William was neither quiet nor gentle, nor courteous nor intellectual – but William was intensely human.

The length of Uncle George's visit this year was beginning to reach the limits of William's patience. He was beginning to feel that sooner or later something must happen. For five weeks now he had (reluctantly) accompanied Uncle George upon his morning walk, he had (generally unsuccessfully) tried to maintain that state of absolute quiet that Uncle George's afternoon rest required, he had in the evening listened wearily to Uncle George's stories of his youth. His usual feeling of mild contempt for Uncle George was beginning to give way to one which was much stronger.

'Now, William,' said Uncle George at breakfast, 'I'm afraid it's going to rain today, so we'll do a little work together this morning, shall we? Nothing like work, is there? Your Arithmetic's a bit shaky, isn't it? We'll rub that up. We *love* our work, don't we?'

William eyed him coldly.

'I don't think I'd better get muddlin' up my school work,' he said. 'I shouldn't like to be more on than the other boys next term. It wouldn't be fair to them.'

Uncle George rubbed his hands.

'That feeling does you credit, my boy,' he said, 'but if we go over some of the old work, no harm can be done. History, now. There's nothing like History, is there?'

William agreed quite heartily that there wasn't.

'We'll do some History, then,' said Uncle George briskly. 'The lives of the great. Most inspiring. Better than those terrible things you used to waste your time on, eh?'

The 'terrible things' had included a trumpet, a beloved motor hooter, and an ingenious instrument very dear to William's soul that reproduced most realistically the sound of two cats fighting. These, at Uncle George's request, had been confiscated by William's father. Uncle George had not considered them educational. They also disturbed his afternoon rest.

Uncle George settled himself and William down for a nice quiet morning in the library. William, looking round for escape, found none. The outside world was wholly uninviting. The rain came down in torrents. Moreover, the five preceding weeks had broken William's spirits. He realised the impossibility of evading Uncle George. His own family were not sympathetic. They suffered from him considerably during the rest of the year and were not sorry to see him absorbed completely by Uncle George's conscientious zeal.

So Uncle George seated himself slowly and ponderously in an armchair by the fire.

'When I was a boy, William,' he began, leaning back and joining the tips of his fingers together, 'I loved my studies. I'm sure you love your studies, don't you? Which do you love most?'

'Me?' said William. 'I like shootin' and playin' Red Injuns.'

'Yes, yes,' said Uncle George impatiently, 'but those aren't *studies*, William. You must aim at being *gentle*.'

'It's not much good bein' *gentle* when you're playin' Red Injuns,' said William stoutly. 'A *gentle* Red Injun wun't get much done.'

'Ah, but why play Red Indians?' said Uncle George. 'A nasty rough game. No, we'll talk about History. You must mould your character upon that of the great heroes, William. You must be a Clive, a Napoleon, a Wolfe.'

'I've often been a wolf,' said William. 'That game's nearly as good as Red Injuns. An' Bears is a good game too. We might have Bears here,' he went on brightening. 'Jus' you an' me. Would you sooner be bear or hunter? I'd sooner be hunter,' he hinted gently.

'You misunderstand,' said Uncle George. 'I mean Wolfe the man, Wolfe the hero.'

William, who had little patience with heroes who came within the school curriculum, relapsed into gloom.

'What lessons do we learn from such names, my boy?' went on Uncle George.

William was on the floor behind Uncle George's chair endeavouring to turn a somersault in a very restricted space.

'History lessons an' dates an' things,' he said shortly.

'An' the things they 'spect you to remember—' he added
with disgust.

'No, no,' said Uncle George, but the fire was hot and
his chair was comfortable and his educational zeal was
dying away, 'to endure the buffets of fate with equanimity,

WILLIAM WAS ON THE FLOOR BEHIND UNCLE GEORGE'S
CHAIR ENDEAVOURING TO TURN A SOMERSAULT IN A VERY
RESTRICTED SPACE.

to smile at misfortune, to endure whatever comes, and so on—'

He stopped suddenly.

William had managed the somersault, but it had somehow brought his feet into collision with Uncle George's neck. Uncle George sleepily shifted his position.

'Boisterous! Boisterous!' he murmured disapprovingly. 'You should combine the gentleness of a Moore with the courage of a Wellington, William.'

William now perceived that Uncle George's eyelids were drooping slowly and William's sudden statuesque calm would have surprised many of his instructors.

The silence and the warmth of the room had their effect. In less than three minutes Uncle George was dead to the world around him.

William's form relaxed, then he crept up to look closely at the face of his enemy. He decided that he disliked it intensely. Something must be done at once. He looked round the room. There were not many weapons handy. Only his mother's workbox stood on a chair by the window, and on it a pile of socks belonging to Robert, William's elder brother. Beneath either arm of his chair one of Uncle George's coat-tails protruded. William soon departed on his way rejoicing, while on to one of Uncle George's coat-tails was firmly stitched a bright blue sock and on to the other a brilliant orange one. Robert's taste in socks was decidedly loud. William felt almost happy. The rain had stopped and he spent the morning with some of his friends whom he met in the road. They went bear-hunting in the wood; and though no bears were found, still their disappointment was considerably allayed by the fact that one of them saw a mouse and another one distinctly smelt a rabbit. William returned to lunch whistling to himself and had the intense satisfaction of seeing Uncle George enter the dining-room, obviously roused from his slumbers by the luncheon bell, and obviously quite unaware of the blue and orange socks that still adorned his person.

'Curious!' he ejaculated, as Ethel, William's grown-up sister, pointed out the blue sock to him. 'Most curious!'

William departed discreetly, muttering something about 'better tidy up a bit', which drew from his sister expressions of surprise and solicitous questions as to his state of health.

'Most curious!' said Uncle George again, who had now discovered the orange sock.

When William returned, all excitement was over and Uncle George was consuming roast beef with energy.

'Ah, William,' he said, 'we must complete the History

lesson soon. Nothing like History. Nothing like History. Nothing like History. Teaches us to endure the buffets of fate with equanimity and to smile at misfortune. Then we must do some Geography.' William groaned. 'Most fascinating study. Rivers, mountains, cities, etc. Most improving. The morning should be devoted to intellectual work at your age, William, and the afternoon to the quiet pursuit of – some improving hobby. You would then find the true joy of life.'

To judge from William's countenance he did not wholly agree, but he made no objection. He had learnt that objection was useless, and against Uncle George's eloquence silence was his only weapon.

After lunch Uncle George followed his usual custom and retired to rest. William went to the shed in the back garden and continued the erection of a rabbit hutch that he had begun a few days before. He hoped that if he made a hutch, Providence would supply a rabbit. He whistled blithely as he knocked nails in at random.

'William, you mustn't do that now.'

He turned a stern gaze upon his mother.

'Why not?' he said.

'Uncle George is resting.'

With a crushing glance at her he strolled away from the shed. Someone had left the lawn mower in the middle of the lawn. With one of his rare impulses of pure virtue he determined to be useful. Also, he rather liked mowing the grass.

'William, don't do that now,' called his sister from the window. 'Uncle George is resting.'

He deliberately drove the mowing machine into the middle of the garden bed and left it there. He was beginning to feel desperate. Then:

'What *can* I do?' he said bitterly to Ethel, who was still at the window.

'You'd better find some quiet, improving hobby,' she said unkindly as she went away.

It is a proof of the utterly broken state of William's spirit that he did actually begin to think of hobbies, but none of those that occurred to him interested him. Stamp-collecting, pressed flowers, crest-collecting – Ugh!

He set off down the road, his hands in his pockets and his brows drawn into a stern frown. He amused himself by imagining Uncle George in various predicaments, lost on a desert island, captured by pirates, or carried off by an eagle. Then something in the window of a house he passed caught his eye and he stopped suddenly. It was a stuffed bird under a glass case. Now that was something *like* a hobby, stuffing dead animals! He wouldn't mind having that for a hobby. And it was quite quiet. He could do it while Uncle George was resting. And it must be quite easy. The first thing to do of course was to find a dead animal. Any old thing would do to begin on. A dead cat or dog. He would do bigger ones like bears and lions later on. He spent nearly an hour in a fruitless search for a dead cat or dog. He searched the ditches on both sides of the road and several gardens. He began to have a distinct sense of grievance against the race of cats and dogs in general for not dying in his vicinity. At the end of the hour he found a small dead frog. It was very dry and shrivelled, but it was certainly a *dead* frog and would do to begin on. He took it home in his pocket. He wondered what they did first in stuffing dead animals. He'd heard something about 'tannin'' them. But what was 'tannin'', and how did one get it? Then he remembered suddenly having heard Ethel talk about the 'tannin'' in tea. So *that* was all right. The first thing to do was to get some tea. He went to the drawing-room. It was empty, but upon the table near the fire was a tea tray and two cups. Evidently his mother and sister had just had tea there. He put the frog at the bottom of a cup and carefully filled the cup with tea from the teapot. Then he left it to soak and went out into the garden.

A few minutes later William's mother entered the drawing-room.

Uncle George had finished resting and was standing by the mantelpiece with a cup in his hand.

'I see you poured out my tea for me,' he said. 'But rather a curious taste. Doubtless you boil the milk now. Safer, of course. Much safer. But it imparts a curious flavour.'

He took another sip.

'But – I didn't pour out your tea—' began Mrs Brown.

Here William entered. He looked quickly at the table.

'Who's meddlin' with my frog?' he said angrily. 'It's my hobby, an' I'm stuffin' frogs an' someone's been an' took my frog. I left it on the table.'

'On the table?' said his mother.

'Yes. In a cup of tea. Gettin' tannin'. You know. For stuffin'. I was puttin' him in tannin' first. I—'

Uncle George grew pale. In frozen silence he put a spoon into his cup and investigated the contents. In still more frozen silence Mrs Brown and William watched. That moment held all the cumulative horror of a Greek tragedy. Then Uncle George put down his cup and went silently from the room. On his face was the expression of

IN FROZEN SILENCE HE PUT A SPOON INTO HIS CUP AND
INVESTIGATED THE CONTENTS. IN STILL MORE FROZEN
SILENCE MRS BROWN AND WILLIAM WATCHED.

one who is going to look up the first train home. Fate had
sent him a buffet he could not endure with equanimity,
a misfortune at which he could not smile, and Fate had
avenged William for much.

CHAPTER 6

THE RIVALS

William was aware of a vague feeling of apprehension when he heard that Joan Clive, the little girl who lived next door, was having a strange cousin to stay for three weeks. All his life, William had accepted Joan's adoration and homage with condescending indifference, but he did not like to imagine a possible rival.

'What's he *coming* for?' he demanded with an ungracious scowl, perched uncomfortably and dangerously on the high wall that separated the two gardens and glaring down at Joan. 'What's he comin' *for*, anyway?'

''Cause mother's invited him,' explained Joan simply, with a shake of her dark curls. 'He's called Cuthbert. She says he's a sweet little boy.'

'*Sweet!*' echoed William in a tone of exaggerated horror. 'Ugh!'

'Well,' said Joan, with the smallest note of indignation in her voice, 'you needn't play with him if you don't like.'

'*Me?* Play? With *him?*' scowled William as if he could not believe his ears. 'I'm not likely to go playin' with a kid like wot *he'll* be!'

Joan raised aggrieved blue eyes.

'You're a *horrid* boy sometimes, William!' she said. 'Anyway, I shall have him to play with soon.'

It was the first time he had received anything but admiration from her.

He scowled speechlessly.

Cuthbert arrived the next morning.

William was restless and ill at ease, and several times climbed the ladder for a glimpse of the guest, but all he could see was the garden inhabited only by a cat and a gardener. He amused himself by throwing stones at the cat till he hit the gardener by mistake and then fled precipitately before a storm of abuse. William and the gardener were enemies of very long standing. After dinner he went out again into the garden and stood gazing through a chink in the wall.

Cuthbert was in the garden.

Though as old and as tall as William, he was dressed in an embroidered tunic, very short knickers, and white socks. Over his blue eyes his curls were brushed up into a golden halo.

He was a picturesque child.

'What shall we do?' Joan was saying. 'Would you like to play hide and seek?'

'No; leth not play at rough gameth,' said Cuthbert.

With a wild spasm of joy William realised that his enemy lisped. It is always well to have a handle against one's enemies.

'What shall we do, then?' said Joan, somewhat wearily.

'Leth thit down an' I'll tell you fairy thorieth,' said Cuthbert.

A loud snort from inside the wall just by his ear startled him, and he clutched Joan's arm.

'What'th that?' he said.

There were sounds of clambering feet on the other side of the wall, then William's grimy countenance appeared.

'Hello, Joan!' he said, ignoring the stranger.

Joan's eyes brightened.

'Come and play with us, William,' she begged.

'We don't want dirty little boyth,' murmured Cuthbert fastidiously. William could not, with justice, have objected to the epithet. He had spent the last half-hour climbing on to the rafters of the disused coach house, and dust and cobwebs adorned his face and hair.

'He's *always* like that,' explained Joan carelessly.

By this time William had thought of a suitable rejoinder.

'All right,' he jeered, 'don't look at me then. Go on tellin' fairy *thorieth*.'

Cuthbert flushed angrily.

'You're a nathty rude little boy,' he said. 'I'll tell my mother.'

Thus war was declared.

He came to tea the next day. Not all William's pleading could persuade his mother to cancel the invitation.

'Well,' said William darkly, 'wait till you've *seen* him, that's all. Wait till you've heard him *speakin*'. He can't talk even. He can't *play*. He tells fairy stories. He don't like *dirt*. He's got long hair an' a funny long coat. He's *awful*, I tell you. I don't *want* to have him to tea. I don't want to be washed an' all just because *he's* comin' to tea.'

But as usual William's eloquence availed nothing.

Several people came to tea that afternoon, and there was a sudden silence when Mrs Clive, Joan and Cuthbert entered. Cuthbert was in a white silk tunic embroidered with blue, he wore white shoes and white silk socks. His golden curls shone. He looked angelic.

'Oh, the darling!'

'Isn't he adorable?'

'What a *picture*!'

'Come here, sweetheart.'

Cuthbert was quite used to this sort of thing.

They were more delighted than ever with him when they discovered his lisp.

His manners were perfect. He raised his face, with a charming smile, to be kissed, then sat down on the sofa between Joan and Mrs Clive, swinging long bare legs.

William, sitting, an unwilling victim, on a small chair in a corner of the room, brushed and washed till he shone again, was conscious of a feeling of fury quite apart from the usual sense of outrage that he always felt upon such an occasion. It was bad enough to be washed till the soap went into his eyes and down his ears despite all his protests. It was bad enough to have had his hair brushed till his head smarted. It was bad enough to be hustled out of his comfortable jersey into his Eton suit which he loathed. But to see Joan, *his* Joan, sitting next to the strange, dressed-up, lisping boy, smiling and talking to him, that was almost more than he could bear with calmness. Previously, as has been said, he had received Joan's adoration with coldness, but previously there had been no rival.

'William,' said his mother, 'take Joan and Cuthbert and show them your engine and books and things. Remember you're the *host*, dear,' she murmured as he passed. 'Try to make them happy.'

He turned upon her a glance that would have made a stronger woman quail.

Silently he led them up to his play room.

'There's my engine, an' my books. You can play with them,' he said coldly to Cuthbert. 'Let's go and play in the garden, you and me, Joan.'

But Joan shook her head.

'I don't thuppoth the'd care to go out without me,' said Cuthbert airily. '*I'll* go with you. Thith boy can play here if he liketh.'

And William, artist in vituperation as he was, could think of no response.

He followed them into the garden, and there came upon him a wild determination to show his superiority.

'You can't climb that tree,' he began.

'I can,' said Cuthbert sweetly.

'Well, *climb* it then,' he said grimly.

'No, I don't want to get my thingth all methed. I *can* climb, but you can't. He can't climb it, Joan, he'th trying to pretend he can climb it when he can't. He knowth I can climb it, but I don't want to get my thingth methed.'

Joan smiled admiringly at Cuthbert.

'I'll *show* you,' said William desperately. 'I'll just *show* you.'

He showed them.

He climbed till the treetop swayed with his weight, then descended, hot and triumphant. The tree was covered with green lichen, a great part of which had deposited itself upon William's suit. His efforts had also twisted his collar round till its stud was beneath his ear. His heated countenance beamed with pride.

For a moment Cuthbert was nonplussed. Then he said scornfully:

'Don't he look a *fright*, Joan?'

Joan giggled.

But William was wholly engrossed in his self-imposed task of 'showing them'. He led them to the bottom of the garden, where a small stream (now almost dry) disappeared into a narrow tunnel to flow under the road and reappear in the field at the other side.

'You can't crawl through that,' challenged William, 'you can't *do* it. I've *done* it, done it often. I bet *you* can't. I bet you can't get halfway. I—'

'Well, *do* it, then!' jeered Cuthbert.

William, on all fours, disappeared into the mud and slime of the small round aperture. Joan clasped her hands, and even Cuthbert was secretly impressed. They stood in silence. At intervals William's muffled voice came from the tunnel.

'It's jolly muddy, too, I can *tell* you.'

'I've caught a frog! I say, I've caught a frog!'

'Crumbs! It's got away!'

'It's nearly quicksands here.'

'If I tried I could nearly *drown* here!'

At last, through the hedge, they saw him emerge in the field across the road. He swaggered across to them aglow with his own heroism. As he entered the gate he was rewarded by the old light of adoration in Joan's blue eyes, but on full sight of him it quickly turned to consternation. His appearance was beyond description. There was a malicious smile on Cuthbert's face.

'Do thumthing elth,' he urged him. 'Go on, do thumthing elth.'

'Oh, William,' said Joan anxiously, 'you'd better not.'

But the gods had sent madness to William. He was drunk with the sense of his own prowess. He was regardless of consequences.

He pointed to a little window high up in the coal-house.

'I can climb up that an' slide down the coal inside. That's what I can do. There's *nothin'* I can't do. I—'

'All right,' urged Cuthbert, 'if you can do that, do it, and I'll believe you can do anything.'

For Cuthbert, with unholy glee, foresaw William's undoing.

'Oh, William,' pleaded Joan, 'I *know* you're brave, but don't—'

'I CAN CLIMB UP THAT AN' SLIDE DOWN THE COAL INSIDE.
THAT'S WHAT I CAN DO. THERE'S *NOTHIN'* I CAN'T DO!'
SAID WILLIAM.

But William was already doing it. They saw his disappearance into the little window, they heard plainly his descent down the coal heap inside, and in less than a minute he appeared in the doorway. He was almost unrecognisable. Coal dust adhered freely to the moist consistency of the mud and lichen already clinging to his suit, as well as to his hair and face. His collar had been almost torn away from its stud. William himself was smiling proudly, utterly unconscious of his appearance. Joan was plainly wavering between horror and admiration. Then the moment for which Cuthbert had longed arrived.

'Children! Come in now!'

Cuthbert, clean and dainty, entered the drawing-room first and pointed an accusing finger at the strange figure which followed.

'He'th been climbing treeth an' crawling in the mud, an' rolling down the coalth. He'th a nathty rough boy.'

A wild babel arose as William entered.

'*William!*'

'You *dreadful* boy!'

'Joan, come right away from him. Come over here.'

'What *will* your father say?'

'William, my *carpet*!'

For the greater part of the stream's bed still clung to William's boots.

Doggedly William defended himself.

'I was showin' 'em how to do things. I was bein' a host. I was tryin' to make 'em *happy*! I—'

'William, don't stand there talking. Go straight upstairs to the bathroom.'

It was the end of the first battle, and undoubtedly William had lost. Yet William had caught sight of the smile on Cuthbert's face and William had decided that the smile was something to be avenged.

But fate did not favour him. Indeed, fate seemed to do the reverse.

The idea of a children's play did not emanate from William's mother, or Joan's. They were both free from guilt in that respect. It emanated from Mrs de Vere Carter. Mrs de Vere Carter was a neighbour with a genius for organisation. There were few things she did not organise till their every other aspect or aim was lost but that of 'organisation'. She also had what amounted practically to a disease for 'getting up' things. She 'got up' plays, and bazaars, and pageants, and concerts. There were, in fact, few things she did not 'get up'. It was the sight of Joan and Cuthbert walking together down the road, the sun shining on their golden curls, that had inspired her with the idea of 'getting up' a children's play. And Joan must be the Princess and little Cuthbert the Prince.

Mrs de Vere Carter was to write the play herself. At first she decided on Cinderella. Unfortunately there was a dearth of little girls in the neighbourhood, and therefore it was decided at a meeting composed of Mrs de Vere Carter, Mrs Clive, Mrs Brown (William's mother), and Ethel (William's sister), that William could easily be dressed up to represent one of the ugly sisters. It was, however, decided at a later meeting, consisting of William and his mother and sister, that William could not take the part. It was William who came to this decision. He was adamant against both threats and entreaties. Without cherishing any delusions about his personal appearance, he firmly declined to play the part of the ugly sister. They took the news with deep apologies to Mrs de Vere Carter, who was already in the middle of the first act. Her already low opinion of William sank to zero. Their next choice was Little Red Riding Hood, and William was lured, by glowing pictures of a realistic costume, into consenting to take the part of the Wolf. Every day he had to be dragged by some elder and responsible member of his family to a rehearsal. His hatred of Cuthbert was only equalled by his hatred of Mrs de Vere Carter.

'He acts so *unnaturally*,' moaned Mrs de Vere Carter. 'Try really to *think* you're a wolf, darling. Put some spirit into it. Be – *animated*.'

William scowled at her and once more muttered monotonously his opening lines:

A wolf am I – a wolf on mischief bent,
To eat this little maid is my intent.

'Take a breath after "bent", darling. Now say it again.'

William complied, introducing this time a loud and audible gasp to represent the breath. Mrs de Vere Carter sighed.

'Now, Cuthbert, darling, draw your little sword and put your arm round Joan. That's right.'

Cuthbert obeyed, and his clear voice rose in a high chanting monotone:

Avaunt! Begone! You wicked wolf, away!
This gentle maid shall never be your prey.

'That's beautiful, darling. Now, William, slink away. *Slink* away, darling. Don't stand staring at Cuthbert like that. Slink away. I'll show you. Watch me slink away.'

Mrs de Vere Carter slunk away realistically, and the sight of it brought momentary delight to William's weary soul. Otherwise the rehearsals were not far removed from torture to him. The thought of being a wolf had at first attracted him, but actually a wolf character who had to repeat Mrs de Vere Carter's meaningless couplets and be worsted at every turn by the smiling Cuthbert, who was forced to watch from behind the scenes the fond embraces of Cuthbert and Joan, galled his proud spirit unspeakably. Moreover, Cuthbert monopolised her both before and after the rehearsals.

'Come away, Joan, he'th prob'bly all over coal dutht and all of a meth.'

The continued presence of unsympathetic elders prevented his proper avenging of such insults.

The day of the performance approached, and there arose some little trouble about William's costume. If the wearing of the dining-room hearthrug had been forbidden by Authority it would have at once become the dearest wish of William's heart and a thing to be accomplished at all costs. But, because Authority decreed that that should be William's official costume as the Wolf, William at once began to find insuperable difficulties.

'It's a dirty ole thing, all dust and bits of black hair come off it on me. I don't think it *looks* like a wolf. Well, if I've gotter be a wolf folks might just as well *know* what I am. This looks like as if it came off a black sheep or sumthin'. You don't want folks to think I'm a *sheep* 'stead of a *wolf*, do you? You don't want me to be made look ridiclus before all these folks, do you?'

He was slightly mollified by their promise to hire a wolf's head for him. He practised wolf's howlings (though these had no part in Mrs de Vere Carter's play) at night in his room till he drove his family almost beyond the bounds of sanity.

Mrs de Vere Carter had hired the Village Hall for the performance, and the proceeds were to go to a local charity.

On the night of the play the Hall was packed, and Mrs de Vere Carter was in a flutter of excitement and importance.

'Yes, the dear children are splendid, and they look *beautiful*! We've all worked so *hard*. Yes, entirely my own composition. I only hope that William Brown won't *murder* my poetry as he does at rehearsals.'

The curtain went up.

The scene was a wood, as was evident from a few small branches of trees placed here and there at intervals on the stage.

Joan, in a white dress and red cloak, entered and began to speak, quickly and breathlessly, stressing every word with impartial regularity.

A little maid am I – Red Riding Hood,
My journey lies along this dark, thick wood.
Within my basket is a little jar
Of jam – a present for my grandmamma.

Then Cuthbert entered – a prince in white satin with a blue sash. There was a rapt murmur of admiration in the audience as he made his appearance.

William waited impatiently and uneasily behind the scenes. His wolf's head was very hot. One of the eyeholes was beyond his range of vision, through the other he had a somewhat prescribed view of what went on around him. He had been pinned tightly into the dining-room hearthrug, his arms pinioned down by his side. He was distinctly uncomfortable.

At last his cue came.

Red Riding Hood and the Prince parted after a short conversation in which their acquaintance made rapid strides, and at the end of which the Prince said casually as he turned to go:

So sweet a maid have I never seen,
Ere long I hope to make her my wife and queen.
Red Riding Hood gazed after him, remarking (all in the same breath and tone):

How kind he is, how gentle and how good!
But, see what evil beast comes through the wood!

Here William entered amid wild applause. On the stage he found that his one eyehole gave him an excellent view of the audience. His mother and father were in the second row. Turning his head round slowly he discovered his sister Ethel sitting with a friend near the back.

'William,' hissed the prompter, 'go on! "A wolf am I—"'

But William was engrossed in the audience. There was Mrs Clive about the middle of the room.

'"A wolf am I" – go *on*, William!'

William had now found the cook and housemaid in the last row of all and was turning his eyehole round in search of fresh discoveries.

The prompter grew desperate.

'"A wolf am I – a wolf on mischief bent." *Say* it, William.'

William turned his wolf's head towards the wings. 'Well, I was *goin'* to say it,' he said irritably, 'if you'd lef' me alone.'

The audience tittered.

'Well, say it,' said the voice of the invisible prompter.

'Well, I'm going to,' said William. 'I'm not goin' to say

that again wot you said 'cause they all heard it. I'll go on from there.'

The audience rocked in wild delight. Behind the scenes Mrs de Vere Carter wrung her hands and sniffed strong smelling salts. 'That boy!' she moaned.

Then William, sinking his voice from the indignant clearness with which it had addressed the prompter, to a muffled inaudibility, continued:

To eat this little maid is my intent.

But there leapt on the stage again the radiant white and blue figure of the Prince brandishing his wooden sword.

Avaunt! Begone! You wicked wolf, away!
This gentle maid shall never be your prey.

At this point William should have slunk away. But the vision revealed by his one available eyehole of the Prince standing in a threatening attitude with one arm round Joan filled him with a sudden and unaccountable annoyance. He advanced slowly and pugnaciously towards the Prince; and the Prince, who had never before acted with William in his head (which was hired for one evening only) fled from the stage with a wild yell of fear. The curtain was lowered hastily.

There was consternation behind the scenes. William, glaring from out of his eyehole and refusing to remove his head, defended himself in his best manner.

'Well, I di'n't tell him to run away, did I? I di'n't *mean* him to run away. I only *looked* at him. Well, I was goin' to slink in a minit. I only wanted to look at him. I was *goin'* to slink.'

'Oh, never mind! Get on with the play!' moaned Mrs de Vere Carter. 'But you've quite destroyed the *atmosphere*, William. You've spoilt the beautiful story. But hurry up, it's time for the grandmother's cottage scene now.'

Not a word of William's speeches was audible in the next scene, but his attack on and consumption of the aged grandmother was one of the most realistic parts of the play, especially considering the fact that his arms were imprisoned.

'Not so roughly, William!' said the prompter in a sibilant whisper. 'Don't make so much noise. They can't hear a word anyone's saying.'

At last William was clothed in the nightgown and nightcap and lying in the bed ready for little Red Riding Hood's entrance. The combined effect of the rug and the head and the thought of Cuthbert had made him hotter and crosser than he ever remembered having felt before. He was conscious of a wild and unreasoning indignation against the world in general. Then Joan entered and began to pipe monotonously:

Dear grandmamma, I've come with all quickness
To comfort you and soothe your bed of sickness.
Here are some little dainties I have brought
To show you how we cherish you in our thought.

Here William wearily rose from his bed and made an unconvincing spring in her direction.

But on the stage leapt Cuthbert once more, the vision in blue and white with golden curls shining and sword again drawn.

'Ha! Evil beast—'

It was too much for William. The heat and discomfort of his attire, the sight of the hated Cuthbert already about to embrace *his* Joan, goaded him to temporary madness. With a furious gesture he burst the pins which attached the dining-room hearthrug to his person and freed his arms. He tore off the white nightgown. He sprang at the petrified Cuthbert – a small wild figure in a jersey suit and a wolf's head.

Mrs de Vere Carter had filled Red Riding Hood's basket with packages of simple groceries, which included, among other things, a paper bag of flour and a jar of jam.

William seized these wildly and hurled handfuls of

flour at the prostrate, screaming Cuthbert. The stage was suddenly pandemonium. The other small actors promptly joined the battle. The prompter was too panic stricken to lower the curtain. The air was white with clouds of flour. The victim scrambled to his feet and fled, a ghost-like figure, round the table.

'Take him off me,' he yelled. 'Take him *off* me. Take William off me.' His wailing was deafening.

The next second he was on the floor, with William on top of him. William now varied the proceedings by emptying the jar of jam on to Cuthbert's face and hair.

They were separated at last by the prompter and stage manager, while the audience rose and cheered hysterically. But louder than the cheering rose the sound of Cuthbert's lamentation.

'He'th a nathty rough boy! He puthed me down. He'th methed my nith clotheth. Boo-hoo!'

Mrs de Vere Carter was inarticulate.

'That boy . . . that *boy* . . . *that boy*!' was all she could say.

William was hurried away by his family before she could regain speech.

'You've disgraced us publicly,' said Mrs Brown plaintively. 'I thought you must have gone *mad*. People will never forget it. I might have known . . .'

THE SIGHT OF THE HATED CUTHBERT ABOUT TO EMBRACE HIS
JOAN, GOADED WILLIAM TO TEMPORARY MADNESS.

When pressed for an explanation, William would only say:

'Well, I felt hot. I felt awful hot, an' I di'n't like Cuthbert.'

He appeared to think this sufficient explanation, though he was fully prepared for the want of sympathy displayed by his family.

'Well,' he said firmly, 'I'd just like to see you do it, I'd just like to see you be in the head and that ole rug an' have to say stupid things an' – an' see folks you don't like, an' I bet you'd *do* something.'

But he felt that public feeling was against him, and relapsed sadly into silence. From the darkness in front of them came the sound of Cuthbert's wailing as Mrs Clive led her two charges home.

'*Poor* little Cuthbert!' said Mrs Brown. 'If I were Joan, I don't think I'd ever speak to you again.'

'Huh!' ejaculated William scornfully.

But at William's gate a small figure slipped out from the darkness and two little arms crept round William's neck.

'Oh, *William*,' she whispered, 'he's going tomorrow, and I'm glad. Isn't he a softie? Oh, William, I do *love* you, you do such *'citing* things!'

CHAPTER 7

THE GHOST

William lay on the floor of the barn, engrossed in a book. This was a rare thing with William. His bottle of lemonade lay untouched by his side, and he even forgot the half-eaten apple which reposed in his hand. His jaws were arrested midway in the act of munching.

'Our hero,' he read, 'was awakened about midnight by the sound of the rattling of chains. Raising himself on his arm he gazed into the darkness. About a foot from his bed he could discern a tall, white, faintly gleaming figure and a ghostly arm which beckoned him.'

William's hair stood on end.

'Crumbs!' he ejaculated.

'Nothing perturbed,' he continued to read, 'our hero rose and followed the spectre through the long winding passages of the old castle. Whenever he hesitated, a white, luminous arm, hung around with ghostly chains, beckoned him on.'

'Gosh!' murmured the enthralled William. 'I'd have bin scared!'

'At the panel in the wall the ghost stopped, and silently the panel slid aside, revealing a flight of stone steps. Down this went the apparition followed by our intrepid hero. There was a small stone chamber at the bottom, and into this the rays of moonlight poured, revealing a skeleton in a sitting attitude beside a chest of golden sovereigns. The gold gleamed in the moonlight.'

'Golly!' gasped William, red with excitement.

'William!'

The cry came from somewhere in the sunny garden outside. William frowned sternly, took another bite of apple, and continued to read.

'Our hero gave a cry of astonishment.'

'Yes, I'd have done that all right,' agreed William.

'*William!*'

'Oh, shut *up*!' called William, irritably, thereby revealing his hiding place.

His grown-up sister, Ethel, appeared in the doorway.

'Mother wants you,' she announced.

'Well, I can't come. I'm busy,' said William, coldly, taking a draught of lemonade and returning to his book.

'Cousin Mildred's come,' continued his sister.

William raised his freckled face from his book.

'Well, I can't help that, can I?' he said, with the air of one arguing patiently with a lunatic.

Ethel shrugged her shoulders and departed.

'He's reading some old book in the barn,' he heard her announce, 'and he says—'

Here he foresaw the complications and hastily followed her.

'Well, I'm *comin'*, aren't I?' he said. 'As fast as I can.'

Cousin Mildred was sitting on the lawn. She was elderly and very thin and very tall, and she wore a curious, long, shapeless garment of green silk with a golden girdle.

'Dear child!' she murmured, taking the grimy hand that William held out to her in dignified silence.

He was cheered by the sight of tea and hot cakes.

Cousin Mildred ate little but talked much.

'I'm living in *hopes* of a psychic revelation, dear,' she said to William's mother. '*In hopes!* I've heard of wonderful experiences, but so far none – alas! – have befallen me. Automatic writing I have tried, but any communication the spirits may have sent me that way remained illegible – quite illegible.'

She sighed.

William eyed her with scorn while he consumed reckless quantities of hot cakes.

'I would *love* to have a psychic revelation,' she sighed again.

'Yes, dear,' murmured Mrs Brown, mystified. 'William, you've had enough.'

'*Enough?*' said William in surprise. 'Why I've only had—' He decided hastily against exact statistics and in favour of vague generalities.

ETHEL APPEARED IN THE DOORWAY. 'MOTHER WANTS YOU,' SHE ANNOUNCED.

'I've only had hardly any,' he said aggrievedly.

'You've had *enough*, anyway,' said Mrs Brown firmly.

The martyr rose, pale but proud.

'Well, can I go then, if I can't have any more tea?'

'There's plenty of bread and butter.'

'I don't want bread and butter,' he said, scornfully.

'Dear child!' murmured Cousin Mildred, vaguely, as he departed.

He returned to the story and lemonade and apple, and stretched himself happily at full length in the shady barn.

'But the ghostly visitant seemed to be fading away, and with a soft sigh was gone. Our hero, with a start of surprise, realised that he was alone with the gold and the skeleton. For the first time he experienced a thrill of cold fear and slowly retreated up the stairs before the hollow and, as it seemed, vindictive stare of the grinning skeleton.'

'I wonder wot he was grinnin' at?' said William.

'But to his horror the door was shut, the panel had slid back. He had no means of opening it. He was imprisoned on a remote part of the castle, where even the servants came but rarely, and at intervals of weeks. Would his fate be that of the man whose bones gleamed white in the moonlight?'

'Crumbs!' said William, earnestly.

Then a shadow fell upon the floor of the barn, and Cousin Mildred's voice greeted him.

'So you're here, dear? I'm just exploring your garden and thinking. I like to be alone. I see that you are the same, dear child!'

'I'm readin',' said William, with icy dignity.

'Dear boy! Won't you come and show me the garden and your favourite nooks and corners?'

William looked at her thin, vague, amiable face, and shut his book with a resigned sigh.

'All right,' he said, laconically.

He conducted her in patient silence round the kitchen garden and the shrubbery. She looked sadly at the house, with its red brick, uncompromisingly modern appearance.

'William, I wish your house was *old*,' she said sadly.

William resented any aspersions on his house from outsiders. Personally he considered newness in a house an attraction, but, if anyone wished for age, then old his house should be.

'*Old!*' he ejaculated. 'Huh! I guess it's *old* enough.'

'Oh, is it?' she said, delighted. 'Restored recently, I suppose?'

'Umph,' agreed William, nodding.

'Oh, I'm so glad. I may have some psychic revelation here, then?'

'Oh yes,' said William, judicially. 'I shouldn't wonder.'

'William, have you ever had one?'

'Well,' said William, guardedly, 'I dunno.'

His mysterious manner threw her into a transport.

'Of course not to anyone. But to *me* – I'm one of the sympathetic! To me you may speak freely, William.'

William, feeling that his ignorance could no longer be hidden by words, maintained a discreet silence.

'To me it shall be sacred, William. I will tell no one – not even your parents. I believe that children see – clouds of glory and all that,' she said vaguely. 'With your unstained childish vision—'

'I'm eleven,' put in William indignantly.

'You see things that to the wise are sealed. Some manifestation, some spirit, some ghostly visitant—'

'Oh,' said William, suddenly enlightened, 'you talkin' about *ghosts*?'

'Yes, ghosts, William.'

Her air of deference flattered him. She evidently expected great things of him. Great things she should have. At the best of times with William imagination was stronger than cold facts.

He gave a short laugh.

'Oh, *ghosts*! Yes, I've seen some of 'em. I guess I *have*!'
Her face lit up.

'Will you tell me some of your experiences, William?'
she said, humbly.

'Well,' said William, loftily, 'you won't go *talkin'* about
it, will you?'

'Oh, *no*.'

'Well, I've seem 'em, you know. Chains an' all. And
skeletons. And ghostly arms beckonin' an' all that.'

William was enjoying himself. He walked with a
swagger. He almost believed what he said. She gasped.

'Oh, go on!' she said. 'Tell me all.'

He went on. He soared aloft on the wings of imagination, his hands in his pockets, his freckled face puckered
up in frowning mental effort. He certainly enjoyed
himself.

'If only some of it could happen to *me*,' breathed his
confidante. 'Does it come to you at *nights*, William?'

'Yes,' nodded William. 'Nights mostly.'

'I shall – watch tonight,' said Cousin Mildred. 'And
you say the house is old?'

'Awful old,' said William, reassuringly.

Her attitude to William was a relief to the rest of the
family. Visitors sometimes objected to William.

'She seems to have almost taken to William,' said his

mother, with a note of unflattering incredulity in her voice.

William was pleased yet embarrassed by her attentions. It was a strange experience to him to be accepted by a grown-up as a fellow being. She talked to him with interest and a certain humility, she bought him sweets and seemed pleased that he accepted them, she went for walks with him, and evidently took his constrained silence for the silence of depth and wisdom.

Beneath his embarrassment he was certainly pleased and flattered. She seemed to prefer his company to that of Ethel. That was one in the eye for Ethel. But he felt that something was expected from him in return for all this kindness and attention. William was a sportsman. He decided to supply it. He took a book of ghost stories from the juvenile library at school, and read them in the privacy of his room at night. Many were the thrilling adventures which he had to tell Cousin Mildred in the morning. Cousin Mildred's bump of credulity was a large one. She supplied him with sweets on a generous scale. She listened to him with awe and wonder.

'William . . . you are one of the elect, the chosen,' she said, 'one of those whose spirits can break down the barrier between the unseen world and ours with ease.' And always she sighed and stroked back her thin locks, sadly.

'Oh, how I wish that some experience would happen to *me*!'

One morning, after the gift of an exceptionally large tin of toffee, William's noblest feelings were aroused. Manfully he decided that something *should* happen to her.

Cousin Mildred slept in the bedroom above William's. Descent from one window to the other was easy, but ascent was difficult. That night Cousin Mildred awoke suddenly as the clock struck twelve. There was no moon, and only dimly did she discern the white figure that stood in the light of the window. She sat up, quivering with eagerness. Her short, thin little pigtail stuck out horizontally from her head. Her mouth was wide open.

'Oh!' she gasped.

The white figure moved a step forward and coughed nervously.

Cousin Mildred clasped her hands.

'Speak!' she said, in a tense whisper. 'Oh, speak! Some message! Some revelation!'

William was nonplussed. None of the ghosts he had read of had spoken. They had rattled and groaned and beckoned, but they had not spoken. He tried groaning and emitted a sound faintly reminiscent of a seasick voyager.

'Oh, *speak*!' pleaded Cousin Mildred.

Evidently speech was a necessary part of this performance. William wondered whether ghosts spoke English or a language of their own. He inclined to the latter view and nobly took the plunge.

'Honk. Yonk. Ponk,' he said, firmly.

Cousin Mildred gasped in wonder.

'Oh, explain,' she pleaded, ardently. 'Explain in our poor human speech. Some message—'

William took fright. It was all turning out to be much more complicated than he had expected. He hastily passed through the room and out of the door, closing it noisily behind him. As he ran along the passage came sound came like a crash of thunder. Outside in the passage were Cousin Mildred's boots, William's father's boots, and William's brother's boots, and into these charged William in his headlong retreat. They slid noisily along the polished wooden surface of the floor, ricocheting into each other as they went. Doors opened suddenly and William's father collided with William's brother in the dark passage, where they wrestled fiercely before they discovered each other's identity.

'I heard that confounded noise and I came out—'

'So did I.'

'Well, then, who *made* it?'

SHE SAT UP, QUIVERING WITH EAGERNESS. HER SHORT, THIN
LITTLE PIGTAIL STUCK OUT HORIZONTALLY FROM HER HEAD.
HER MOUTH WAS WIDE OPEN.

'Who did?'

'If it's that wretched boy up to any tricks again—'

William's father left the sentence unfinished, but went with determined tread towards his younger son's room. William was discovered, carefully spreading a sheet over his bed and smoothing it down.

Mr Brown, roused from his placid slumbers, was a sight to make a brave man quail, but the glance that William turned upon him was guileless and sweet.

'Did you make that confounded row kicking boots about the passage?' spluttered the man of wrath.

'No, Father,' said William, gently. 'I've not bin kickin' no boots about.'

'Were you down on the lower landing just now?' said Mr Brown, with compressed fury.

William considered this question silently for a few seconds, then spoke up brightly and innocently.

'I dunno, Father. You see, some folks walk in their sleep, and when they wake up they dunno where they've bin. Why, I've heard of a man walkin' down a fire escape in his sleep, and then he woke up and couldn't think how he'd got to be there where he was. You see, he didn't know he'd walked down all them steps sound asleep, and—'

'Be *quiet*,' thundered his father. 'What in the name

of— What on earth are you doing making your bed in the middle of the night? Are you insane?'

William, perfectly composed, tucked in one end of his sheet.

'No, Father, I'm not insane. My sheet just fell off me in the night and I got out to pick it up. I must of bin a bit restless, I suppose. Sheets come off easy when folks is restless in bed, and they don't know anythin' about it till they wake up jus' same as sleepwalkin'. Why, I've heard of folks—'

'Be *quiet*—'

At that moment William's mother arrived, placid as ever, in her dressing gown, carrying a candle.

'Look at him,' said Mr Brown, pointing at the meek-looking William.

'He plays rugger up and down the passage with the boots all night and then he begins to make his bed. He's mad. He's—'

William turned his calm gaze upon him.

'*I* wasn't playin' rugger with the boots, Father,' he said, patiently.

Mrs Brown laid her hand soothingly upon her husband's arm.

'You know, dear,' she said, gently, 'a house is always full of noises at night. Basket chairs creaking—'

Mr Brown's face grew purple.

'*Basket chairs*—' he exploded, violently, but allowed himself to be led unresisting from the room.

William finished his bed-making with his usual frown of concentration, then, lying down, fell at once into the deep sleep of childish innocence.

But Cousin Mildred was lying awake, a blissful smile upon her lips. She, too, was now one of the elect, the chosen. Her rather deaf ears had caught the sound of supernatural thunder as her ghostly visitant departed, and she had beamed with ecstatic joy.

'Honk,' she murmured dreamily. 'Honk. Yonk. Ponk.'

William felt rather tired the next evening. Cousin Mildred had departed leaving him a handsome present of a large box of chocolates. William had consumed these with undue haste in view of possible maternal interference. His broken night was telling upon his spirits. He felt distinctly depressed and saw the world through jaundiced eyes. He sat in the shrubbery, his chin in his hand, staring moodily at his adoring mongrel, Jumble.

'It's a rotten world,' he said, gloomily. 'I've took a lot of trouble over her and she goes and makes me feel sick with chocolates.'

Jumbled wagged his tail, sympathetically.

CHAPTER 8

THE MAY KING

William was frankly bored. School always bored him. He disliked facts, and he disliked being tied down to detail, and he disliked answering questions. As a politician a great future would have lain before him. William attended a mixed school because his parents hoped that feminine influence might have a mellowing effect upon his character. As yet the mellowing was not apparent. He was roused from his daydreams by a change in the voice of Miss Dewhurst, his form mistress. It was evident that she was not talking about the exports of England (a subject in which William took little interest) any longer.

'Children,' she said brightly. 'I want you to have a little May Queen for the first of May. The rest of you must be her courtiers. I want you all to vote tomorrow. Put down on a piece of paper the name of the little girl you think would make the sweetest little Queen, and the rest of you shall be her swains and maidens.'

'We're goin' to have a May Queen,' remarked William to his family at dinner, 'an' I'm goin' to be a swain.'

His interested died down considerably when he discovered the meaning of the word swain.

'Isn't it no sort of animal at all?' he asked indignantly.

'Well, I'm not going to be in it, then,' he said when he heard that it was not.

The next morning Evangeline Fish began to canvass for votes methodically. Evangeline Fish was very fair, and was dressed always in that shade of blue that shrieks aloud to the heavens and puts the skies to shame. She was considered the beauty of the form.

'I'll give you two bull's eyes if you'll vote for me,' she said to William.

'*Two!*' said William with scorn.

'Six,' she bargained.

'All right,' he said, 'you can give me six bull's eyes if you want. There's nothing to stop you givin' me six bull's eyes if you want, is there? Not that I know of.'

'But you'll have to promise to put down my name on the paper if I give you six bull's eyes,' she said suspiciously.

'All right,' said William. 'I can easy promise that.'

Whereupon she handed over the six bull's eyes. William returned one as being under regulation size, and waited frowning till she replaced it by a larger one.

'Now, you've promised,' said Evangeline Fish. 'They'll make you ill an' die if you break your promise on them.'

The May King

William kept his promise with true political address. He wrote 'E. Fish – I *don't* think!' on his voting paper and his vote was disqualified. But Evangeline Fish was elected May Queen by an overwhelming majority. She was, after all, the beauty of the form and she always wore blue. And now she was to be May Queen. Her prestige was established for ever. 'Little angel,' murmured the elder girls. The small boys fought for her favours. William began to dislike her intensely. Her voice, and her smile, and her ringlets, and her blue dress began to jar upon his nerves. And when anything began to jar on William's nerves something always happened.

It was not till about a week later that he noticed Bettine Franklin. Bettine was small and dark. There was nothing 'angelic' about her. William had noticed her vaguely in school before and had hardly looked upon her as a distinct personality. But one recreation in the playground he stood leaning against the wall by himself, scowling at Evangeline Fish. She was surrounded by a crowd of admirers, and was prattling to them artlessly in her angelic voice.

'I'm going to be dressed in white muslin with a blue sash. Blue suits me, you know. I'm so fair.' She tossed back a ringlet. 'One of you will have to hold my train and the rest must dance round me. I'm going to have a crown

127

and—' She turned round in order to avoid the scowling gaze of William in the distance. William had discovered that his scowl annoyed her, and since then had given it little rest. But there was no satisfaction in scowling at the back of her well-curled head, so he relaxed his scowl and let his gaze wander round the playground. And it fell upon Bettine. Bettine was also standing by herself and gazing at Evangeline Fish. But she was not scowling. She was looking at Evangeline Fish with wistful envy. For Evangeline Fish was 'angelic' and a May Queen, and she was neither of these things. William strolled over and lolled against the wall next to her.

''Ullo!' he said, without looking at her, for this change of position had brought him again within range of Evangeline Fish's eye, and he was once more simply one concentrated scowl.

''Ullo,' murmured Bettine shyly and politely.

'You like pink rock?' was William's next effort.

'Um,' said Bettine, nodding emphatically.

'I'll give you some next time I buy some,' said William munificently, 'but I shan't be buying any for a long time,' he added bitterly, ''cause an ole ball slipped out my hands on to our dining-room window before I noticed it yesterday.'

She nodded understandingly.

'I don't mind!' she said sweetly. 'I'll like you jus' as much if you don't give me any rock.'

William blushed.

'I di'n't know you liked me,' he said.

'I do,' she said fervently. 'I like your face an' I like the things you say.'

William had forgotten to scowl. He was one flaming mixture of embarrassment and delight. He plunged his hands into his pockets and brought out two marbles, a piece of clay, and a broken toy gun.

'You can have 'em all,' he said in reckless generosity.

'You keep 'em for me,' said Bettine sweetly. 'I hope you dance next to me at the maypole when Evangeline's Queen. Won't it be lovely?' and she sighed.

'Lovely?' exploded William. 'Huh!'

'Won't you like it?' said Bettine wonderingly.

'Me!' exploded William again. 'Dancin' round a pole! Round that ole girl?'

'But she's so pretty.'

'No, she isn't,' said William firmly, 'she jus' isn't. Not *much*! I don' like her narsy shiny hair an' I don't like her narsy blue clothes, an' I don' like her narsy face, an' I don't like her narsy white shoes, nor her narsy necklaces, nor her narsy squeaky voice—'

He paused.

Bettine drew a deep breath.

'Go on some more,' she said. 'I *like* listening to you.'

'Do *you* like her?' said William.

'No. She's awful *greedy*. Did you know she was awful *greedy*?'

'I can *b'lieve* it,' said William. 'I can b'lieve *anything* of anyone wot talks in that squeaky voice.'

'Jus' watch her when she's eatin' cakes – she goes on eatin' and eatin' and eatin'.'

'She'll bust an' die one day then,' prophesied William solemnly, 'an' *I* shan't be sorry.'

'But she'll look ever so beautiful when she's a May Queen.'

'You'd look nicer,' said William.

Bettine's small pale face flamed.

'Oh, *no*,' she said.

'Would you like to be a May Queen?'

'Oh, *yes*,' she said.

'Um,' said William, and returned to the discomfiture of Evangeline Fish by his steady concentrated scowl.

The next day he had the opportunity of watching her eating cakes. They met at the birthday party of a mutual classmate, and Evangeline Fish took her stand by the table and consumed cakes with a perseverance and determination worthy of a nobler cause. William accorded her a certain grudging admiration. Not once did she falter or faint. Iced cakes, cream cakes, pastries melted away before her and never did she lose her ethereal angelic appearance. Tight golden ringlets, blue eyes, faintly flushed cheeks, vivid pale blue dress remained immaculate and unruffled, and still she ate cakes. William watched her in amazement, forgetting even to scowl at her. Her

WILLIAM ACCORDED HER A CERTAIN GRUDGING ADMIRATION. ICED CAKES, CREAM CAKES, PASTRIES MELTED AWAY BEFORE HER.

capacity for cakes exceeded even William's, and his was no mean one.

They had a rehearsal of the maypole dance and crowning the next day.

'I want William Brown to hold the Queen's train,' said Miss Dewhurst.

'*Me?*' ejaculated William in horror. 'D'you mean *me?*'

'Yes, dear. It's a great honour to be asked to hold little Queen Evangeline's train. I'm sure you feel very proud. You must be her little courtier.'

'Huh!' said William, transferring his scowl to Miss Dewhurst.

Evangeline beamed. She wanted William's admiration. William was the only boy in the form who was not her slave. She smiled at William sweetly.

'I'm not *good* at holdin' trains,' said William. 'I don't *like* holdin' trains. I've never bin *taught* 'bout holdin' trains. I might do it wrong on the day an' spoil it all. I shan't like to spoil it all,' he added virtuously.

'Oh, we'll have heaps of practices,' said Miss Dewhurst brightly.

As he was going Bettine pressed a small apple into his hand.

'A present for you,' she murmured. 'I saved it from my dinner.'

He was touched.

'I'll give you somethin' tomorrow,' he said, adding hastily, 'if I can find anythin'.'

They stood in silence till he had finished his apple.

'I've left a lot on the core,' he said in a tone of unusual politeness, handing it to her, 'would you like to finish it?'

'No, thank you. William, you'll look so nice holding her train.'

'I don't want to, an' I bet I *won't*!' You don't *know* the things I can do,' he said darkly.

'Oh, William!' she gasped in awe and admiration.

'I'd hold your train if you was goin' to be queen,' he volunteered.

'I wouldn't want you to hold my train,' she said earnestly. 'I'd – I'd – I'd want you to be May King with me.'

'Yes. Why don't they have May Kings?' said William, stung by this insult to his sex.

'Why shouldn't there be a May King?'

'I speck they *do*, really, only p'raps Miss Dewhurst doesn't know about it.'

'Well, it doesn't seem sense not having May Kings, does it? I wun't mind bein' May King if you was May Queen.'

*

The rehearsal was, on the whole, a failure.

'William Brown, don't hold the train so high. No, not quite so low. Don't stand so near the Queen, William Brown. No, not so far away – you'll pull the train off. Walk when the Queen walks, William Brown, don't stand still. Sing up, please, train-bearer. No, not quite so loud. That's deafening and not melodious.'

In the end he was degraded from the position of train-bearer to that of ordinary 'swain'. The 'swains' were to be dressed in smocks and the 'maidens' in print dresses, and the maypole dance was to be performed round Evangeline Fish, who was to stand in queenly attire by the pole in the middle. All the village was to be invited.

At the end of the rehearsal William came upon Bettine, once more gazing wistfully at Evangeline Fish, who was coquetting (with many tosses of the fair ringlets) before a crowd of admirers.

'Isn't it lovely for her to be May Queen?' said Bettine.

'She's a rotten one,' said William. 'I'm jolly glad *I've* not to hold up her rotten ole train an' listen to her narsy squeaky voice singin' close to, an' I'll give you a present tomorrow.'

He did. He found a centipede in the garden and pressed it into her hand on the way to school.

'They're jolly int'restin',' he said. 'Put it in a matchbox

and make holes for its breath and it'll live ever so long. It won't bite you if you hold it the right way.'

And because she loved William she took it without even a shudder.

Evangeline Fish began to pursue William. She grudged him bitterly to Bettine. She pirouetted near him in her sky-blue garments, she tossed her ringlets about him. She ogled him with her pale blue eyes.

And in the long school hours during which he dreamed at his desk, or played games with his friends, while highly paid instructors poured forth their wisdom for his benefit, William evolved a plan. Unfortunately, like most plans, it required capital, and William had no capital. Occasionally William's elder brother Robert would supply a few shillings without inconvenient questions, but it happened that Robert was ignoring William's existence at that time. For Robert had (not for the first time) discovered his Ideal, and the Ideal had been asked to lunch the previous week. For days before Robert had made William's life miserable. He had objected to William's unbrushed hair and unmanicured hands, and untidy person, and noisy habits. He had bitterly demanded what She would think on being asked to a house where She might meet such an individual as William; he had insisted that William should be taught habits of cleanliness and silence before

She came; he had hinted darkly that a man who had William for a brother was hampered considerably in his love affairs because She would think it was a queer kind of family where anyone like William was allowed to grow up. He had reserved some of his fervour for the cook. She must have a proper lunch – not stews and stuff they often had – there must be three vegetables and there must be cheese straws. Cook must learn to make better cheese straws. And William, having swallowed insults for three whole days, planned vengeance. It was a vengeance which only William could have planned or carried out. For only William could have seized a moment just before lunch when the meal was dished up and Cook happened to be out of the kitchen to carry the principal dishes down to the coal cellar and conceal them beneath the best nuts.

It is well to draw a veil over the next half-hour. Both William and the meal had vanished. Robert tore his hair and appealed vainly to the heavens. He hinted darkly at suicide. For what is cold tongue and coffee to offer to an Ideal? The meal was discovered during the afternoon in its resting place and given to William's mongrel, Jumble, who crept about during the next few days in agonies of indigestion. Robert had bitterly demanded of William why he went about the world spoiling people's lives and ruining their happiness. He had implied that when William met with the One and Only Love of his Life he need look for no help or assistance from him (Robert), because he (William) had dashed to the ground his (Robert's) cup of happiness, because he'd never in his life met anyone before like Miss Laing, and never would again, and he (William) had simply condemned him to a lonely and miserable old age, because who'd want to marry anyone that asked them to lunch and then gave them coffee and cold tongue, and he'd never want to marry anyone else, because it was the One and Only Love of his Life, and he hoped he (William) would realise, when he was old enough to realise, what it meant to have your life spoilt and your happiness ruined all through coffee and tongue, because someone you'd never speak to again had hidden the lunch. Whence it came that William, optimist though he was, felt that any appeal to Robert for funds would be inopportune, to say the least of it.

But Providence was on William's side for once. An old uncle came to tea and gave William five shillings.

'Going to dance at a maypole, I hear?' he chuckled.

'P'raps,' was all William said.

His family were relieved by his meekness with regard to the May Day festival. Sometimes William made such a foolish fuss about being dressed up and performing in public.

'You know, dear,' said his mother, 'it's a dear old festival, and quite an honour to take part in it, and a smock is quite a nice manly garment.'

'Yes, Mother,' said William.

The day was fine – a real May Day. The maypole was fixed up in the field near the school, and the little performers were to change in the schoolroom.

William went out with his brown paper parcel of stage properties under his arm and stood gazing up the road by which Evangeline Fish must come to the school. For Evangeline Fish would have to pass his gate. Soon he saw her, her pale blue dress radiant in the sun.

''Ullo!' he greeted her.

She simpered. She had won him at last.

'Waitin' to walk to the school with me, William?' she said.

He still loitered.

'You're awful early.'

'Am I? I thought I was late. I meant to be late. I don't want to be too early. I'm the most 'portant person, and I want to walk in after the others, then they'll all look at me.'

She tossed her tightly wrought curls.

'Come into our ole shed a minute,' said William. 'I've got a present for you.'

She blushed and ogled.

'Oh, *William*!' she said, and followed him into the woodshed.

'Look!' he said.

His uncle's five shillings had been well expended. Rows of cakes lay round the shed; pastries, and sugar cakes, and iced cakes, and currant cakes.

'Have a lot,' said William. 'They're all for you. Go on! Eat 'em all. You can eat an' eat an' eat. There's lots an' lots of time and they can't begin without you, can they?'

'Oh, *William*!' she said.

She gloated over them.

'Oh, may I?'

'There's heaps of time,' said William. 'Go on! Eat them all!'

Her greedy little eyes seemed to stand out of her head.

'Oo!' she said in rapture.

She sat down on the floor and began to eat, lost to everything but icing and currants and pastry. William made for the door, then he paused, gazed wistfully at the feast, stepped back, and, grabbing a cream bun in each hand, crept quietly away.

Bettine in her print frock was at the door of the school.

'Hurry up!' she said anxiously. 'You're going to be late. The others are all out. They're waiting to begin. Miss

'HAVE A LOT,' SAID WILLIAM. 'THEY'RE ALL FOR YOU. GO ON!
EAT 'EM ALL. YOU CAN EAT AN' EAT AN' EAT.'

Dewhurst's out there. They're all come but you an' the
Queen. I stayed 'cause you asked me to stay to help you.'

He came in and shut the door.

'You're goin' to be May Queen,' he announced firmly.

'*Me?*' she said in amazement.

'Yes. An' I'm goin' to be King.'

He unwrapped his parcel.

'Look!' he said.

He had ransacked his sister's bedroom. Once Ethel had been to a fancy-dress dance as a fairy. Over Bettine's print frock he drew a crumpled gauze slip with wings, torn in several places. On her brow he placed a tinsel crown at a rakish angle. And she quivered with happiness.

'Oh, how lovely!' she said. 'How lovely! How lovely!'

His own preparations were simpler. He tied a red sash that he had taken off his sister's hat over his right shoulder and under his left arm on the top of his smock. Someone had once given him a small bus conductor's cap with a toy set of tickets and clippers. He placed the cap upon his head with its peak over one eye. It was the only official headgear he had been able to procure. Then he took a piece of burnt cork from his parcel and solemnly drew a fierce and military moustache upon his cheek and lip. To William no kind of theatricals was complete without a corked moustache.

Then he took Bettine by the hand and led her out to the maypole.

The dancers were all waiting holding the ribbons. The audience was assembled and a murmur of conversation was rising from it. It ceased abruptly as William and

Bettine appeared. William's father, mother and sister were in the front row. Robert was not there. Robert had declined to come to anything in which that little wretch was to perform. He'd jolly well had enough of that little wretch to last his lifetime, thank you very much.

William and Bettine stepped solemnly hand in hand upon the little platform which had been provided for the May Queen.

Miss Dewhurst, who was chatting amicably to the parents till the last of her small performers should appear, seemed suddenly turned to stone, with mouth gaping and eyes wide. The old fiddler, who was rather short-sighted, struck up the strains, and the dancers began to dance. The audience relaxed, leaning back in their chairs to enjoy the scene. Miss Dewhurst was still frozen. There were murmured comments. 'How curious to have that boy there! A sort of attendant, I suppose.'

'Yes, perhaps he's something allegorical. A sort of pageant. Good Luck or something. It's not quite the sort of thing I expected, I must admit.'

'What do you think of the Queen's dress? I always thought Miss Dewhurst had better taste. Rather tawdry, I call it.'

'I think the moustache is a mistake. It gives quite a

common look to the whole thing. I wonder who he's meant to be? Pan, do you think?' uncertainly.

'Oh, no, nothing so *pagan*, I hope,' said an elderly matron, horrified. 'He's that Brown boy, you know. There always seems to be something queer about anything he's in. I've noticed it often. But I *hope* he's meant to be

WILLIAM AND BETTINE STEPPED SOLEMNLY HAND IN HAND
UPON THE LITTLE PLATFORM WHICH HAD BEEN PROVIDED
FOR THE MAY QUEEN.

something more Christian than Pan, though one never knows these days,' she added darkly.

William's sister had recognised her possessions, and was gasping in anger.

William's father, who knew William, was smiling sardonically.

William's mother was smiling proudly.

'You're always running William down,' she said to the world in general, 'but look at him now. He's got a very important part, and he said nothing about it at home. I call it very nice and modest of him. And what a dear little girl.'

Bettine, standing on the platform with William's hand holding hers and the maypole dancers dancing round her, was radiant with pride and happiness.

And Evangeline Fish in the woodshed was just beginning the last currant cake.

CHAPTER 9

THE REVENGE

William was a scout. The fact was well known. There was no one within a five-mile radius of William's home who did not know it. Sensitive old ladies had fled shuddering from their front windows when William marched down the street singing (the word is a euphemism) his scout songs in his strong young voice. Curious smells emanated from the depth of the garden where William performed mysterious culinary operations. One old lady whose cat had disappeared looked at William with dour suspicion in her eyes whenever he passed. Even the return of her cat a few weeks later did not remove the hostility from her gaze whenever it happened to rest upon William.

William's family had welcomed the suggestion of William's becoming a scout.

'It will keep him out of mischief,' they had said.

They were notoriously optimistic where William was concerned.

William's elder brother only was doubtful.

'You know what William is,' he said, and in that dark saying much was contained.

Things went fairly smoothly for some time. He took the scout's law of a daily deed of kindness in its most literal sense. He was to do one (and one only) deed of kindness a day. There were times when he forced complete strangers, much to their embarrassment, to be the unwilling recipients of his deed of kindness. There were times when he answered any demand for help with a cold: 'No, I've done it today.'

He received with saint-like patience the eloquence of his elder sister when she found her silk scarf tied into innumerable knots.

'Well, they're jolly good knots,' was all he said.

He had been looking forward to the holidays for a long time. He was to 'go under canvas' at the end of the first week.

The first day of the holidays began badly. William's father had been disturbed by William, whose room was just above and who had spent most of the night performing gymnastics as instructed by his scoutmaster.

'No, he didn't *say* do it at nights, but he said do it. He said it would make us grow up strong men. Don't you *want* me to grow up a strong man? He's ever so strong an' *he* did 'em. Why shun't I?'

His mother found a pan with the bottom burnt out and at once accused William of the crime. William could not deny it.

'Well, I was makin' sumthin', sumthin' he'd told us an' I forgot it. Well, I've *got* to make things if I'm a scout. I didn't *mean* to forget it. I won't forget it next time. It's a rotten pan, anyway, to burn itself into a hole jus' for that.'

At this point William's father received a note from a neighbour whose garden adjoined William's and whose life had been rendered intolerable by William's efforts upon his bugle.

The bugle was confiscated.

Darkness descended upon William's soul.

'Well,' he muttered, 'I'm goin' under canvas next week an' I'm jolly *glad* I'm goin'. P'r'aps you'll be sorry when I'm gone.'

He went out into the garden and stood gazing moodily into space, his hands in the pocket of his short scout trousers, for William dressed on any and every occasion in his official costume.

'Can't even have the bugle,' he complained to the land-scape. 'Can't even use their rotten ole pans. Can't tie knots in any of their ole things. Wot's the good of *bein'* a scout?'

His indignation grew and with it a desire to be avenged upon his family.

'I'd like to *do* somethin',' he confided to a rose bush
with a ferocious scowl. 'Somethin' jus' to show 'em.'

Then his face brightened. He had an idea.

He'd get lost. He'd get really lost. They'd be sorry then
all right. They'd p'r'aps think he was dead and they'd be
sorry then all right. He imagined their relief, their tearful
apologies when at last he returned to the bosom of his
family. It was worth trying, anyway.

He set off cheerfully down the drive. He decided to
stay away for lunch and supper, and to return at dusk to
a penitent, conscience-stricken family.

He first made his way to a neighbouring wood, where
he arranged a pile of twigs for a fire, but they refused to
light, even with the aid of the match that William found
adhering to a piece of putty in the recess of one of his
pockets.

Slightly dispirited, he turned his attention to his
handkerchief and tied knots in it till it gave way under
the strain. William's handkerchiefs, being regularly used
to perform the functions of blotting paper among other
duties not generally entrusted to handkerchiefs, were
always in the last stages of decrepitude.

He felt rather bored and began to wonder whether it
was lunchtime or not.

He then 'scouted' the wood and by his woodlore traced

three distinct savage tribes' passage through the wood and found the tracks of several elephants. He engaged in deadly warfare with about half a dozen lions, then tired of the sport. It must be about lunchtime. He could imagine Ethel, his sister, hunting for him wildly high and low with growing pangs of remorse. She'd wish she'd made less fuss over that old scarf. His mother would recall the scene over the pan and her heart would fail her. His father would think with shame of his conduct in the matter of the bugle.

'Poor William! How cruel we were! How different we shall be if only he comes home . . . !'

He could almost hear the words. Perhaps his mother was weeping now. His father – wild-eyed and white-lipped – was pacing his study, waiting for news, eager to atone for his unkindness to his missing son. Perhaps he had the bugle on the table ready to give back to him. Perhaps he'd even bought him a new one.

He imagined the scene of his return. He would be nobly forgiving. He would accept the gift of the new bugle without a word of reproach. His heart thrilled at the thought of it.

He was getting jolly hungry. It must be after lunchtime. But it would spoil it all to go home too early.

Here he caught sight of a minute figure regarding

him with a steady gaze and holding a paper bag in one hand.

William stared down at him.

'Wot you dressed up like that for?' said the apparition, with a touch of scorn in his voice.

William looked down at his sacred uniform and scowled. 'I'm a scout,' he said loftily.

''Cout?' repeated the apparition, with an air of polite boredom. 'Wot's your name?'

'William.'

'Mine's Thomas. Will you catch me a wopse? Look at my wopses!'

He opened the bag slightly and William caught sight of a crowd of wasps buzzing about inside the bag.

'Want more,' demanded the infant. 'Want lots more. Look. Snells!'

He brought out a handful of snails from a miniature pocket, and put them on the ground.

'Watch 'em put their horns out! Watch 'em walk. Look! *They're walkin'*. They're *walkin'*.'

His voice was a scream of ecstasy. He took them up and returned them to their pocket. From another he drew out a wriggling mass.

'Woodlice!' he explained, casually 'Got worms in 'nother pocket.'

The Revenge

He returned the woodlice to his pocket except one, which he held between a finger and thumb laid thoughtfully against his lip. 'Want wopses now. You get 'em for me.'

William roused himself from his bewilderment.

'How – how do you catch 'em?' he said.

'Wings,' replied Thomas. 'Get hold of their wings an' they don't sting. Sometimes they do, though,' he added casually. 'Then your hands go big.'

A wasp settled near him, and very neatly the young naturalist picked him up and put him in his paper prison.

'Now you get one,' he ordered William.

William determined not to be outshone by this minute but dauntless stranger. As a wasp obligingly settled on a flower near him, he put out his hand, only to withdraw it with a yell of pain and apply it to his mouth.

'Oo – ou!' he said. 'Crumbs!'

Thomas emitted a peal of laughter.

'You stung?' he said. 'Did it sting you? *Funny!*'

William's expression of rage and pain was exquisite to him.

'Come on, boy!' he ordered at last. 'Let's go somewhere else.'

William's bewildered dignity made a last stand.

'*You* can go,' he said. 'I'm playin' by myself.'

151

'All right!' agreed Thomas. 'You play by you'self an' me play by myself, an' we'll be together – playin' by ourselves.'

He set off down a path, and meekly William followed.

It must be jolly late – almost teatime.

'I'm hungry' said Thomas suddenly. 'Give me some brekfust.'

'I haven't got any,' said William irritably.

'Well, find some,' persisted the infant.

'I can't. There isn't any to find.'

'Well, buy some!'

'I haven't any money.'

'Well, buy some money.'

Goaded, William turned on him.

'Go away!' he bellowed.

Thomas's blue eyes, beneath a mop of curls, met his coldly.

'Don't talk so loud,' he said sternly. 'There's some blackberries there. You can get me some blackberries.'

William began to walk away, but Thomas trotted by his side.

'There!' he persisted. 'Jus where I'm pointing. Lovely great big suge ones. Get 'em for my brekfust.'

Reluctantly the scout turned to perform his deed of kindness.

Thomas consumed blackberries faster than William could gather them.

'Up there,' he commanded. 'No, the one right up there I want. I want it *kick*. I've etten all the others.'

William was scratched and breathless, and his shirt was torn when at last the rapacious Thomas was satisfied. Then he partook of a little refreshment himself, while Thomas turned out his pockets.

'I'll let 'em go now,' he said.

One of his woodlice, however, stayed motionless where he put it.

'Wot's the matter with it?' said William, curiously.

'I 'speck me's the matter wif it,' said Thomas succinctly. 'Now, get me some lickle fishes, an' tadpoles an' water sings,' he went on cheerfully.

William turned round from his blackberry bush.

'Well, I won't,' he said decidedly. 'I've had enough!'

'You've had 'nuff brekfust,' said Thomas sternly. 'I've found a lickle tin for the sings, so be *kick*. Oo, here's a fly! A green fly! It's sittin' on my finger. Does it like me 'cause it's sittin' on my finger?'

'No,' said William, turning a purple-stained countenance round scornfully.

It must be nearly night. He didn't want to be too hard on them, to make his mother ill or anything. He wanted to be as kind as possible. He'd forgive them at once when he got home. He'd ask for one or two things he wanted, as well as the new bugle. A new penknife, and an engine with a real boiler.

'Waffor does it not like me?' persisted Thomas.

William was silent. Question and questioner were beneath contempt.

'Waffor does it not like me?' he shouted stridently.

'Flies don't like people, silly.'

'Waffor not?' retorted Thomas.

'They don't know anything about them.'

'Well, I'll *tell* it about me. My name's Thomas,' he said to the fly politely. 'Now does it like me?'

William groaned. But the fly had now vanished, and Thomas once more grew impatient.

'Come *on*!' he said. 'Come on an' find sings for me.'

William's manly spirit was by this time so far broken that he followed his new acquaintance to a neighbouring pond, growling threateningly but impotently.

'Now,' commanded his small tyrant, 'take off your boots an' stockings an' go an' find things for me.'

'Take off yours,' growled William, 'an' find things for yourself.'

'No,' said Thomas, 'crockerdiles might be there an'

bite my toes. An pittanopotamuses might be there. If you don't go in, I'll scream an' scream an' *scream*!'

William went in.

He walked gingerly about the muddy pond. Thomas watched him critically from the bank.

'I don't like your *hair*,' he said confidingly.

William growled.

He caught various small swimming objects in the tin, and brought them to the bank for inspection.

'I want more'n that,' said Thomas calmly.

'Well, you won't *get* it,' retorted William.

He began to put on his boots and stockings, wondering desperately how to rid himself of his unwanted companion. But Fate solved the problem. With a loud cry a woman came running down the path.

'Tommy' she said. 'My little darling Tommy. I thought you were lost!' She turned furiously to William. 'You ought to be ashamed of yourself,' she said. 'A great boy of your age leading a little child like this into mischief! If his father was here, he'd show you. You ought to know better! And you a scout.'

William gasped.

'Well!' he said. 'An' I've bin doin' deeds of kindness on him all morning. I've—'

She turned away indignantly, holding Thomas's hand.

'You're never to go with that nasty rough boy again, darling,' she said.

'Got lots of wopses an' some fishes,' murmured Thomas contentedly.

They disappeared down the path. With a feeling of depression and disillusionment William turned to go home.

SHE TURNED FURIOUSLY TO WILLIAM. 'YOU OUGHT TO BE ASHAMED OF YOURSELF,' SHE SAID.

Then his spirits rose. After all, he'd got rid of Thomas, and he was going home to a contrite family. It must be about supper time. It would be getting dark soon. But it still stayed light a long time now. It wouldn't matter if he just got in for supper. It would have given them time to think things over. He could see his father speaking unsteadily and holding out his hand.

'My boy . . . let bygones be bygones . . . if there is anything you want . . .'

His father had never said anything of this sort to him yet, but, by a violent stretch of imagination, he could just conceive it.

His mother, of course, would cry over him, and so would Ethel.

'Dear William . . . do forgive us . . . we have been so miserable since you went away . . . we will never treat you so again.'

This again was unlike the Ethel he knew, but sorrow has a refining effect on all characters.

He entered the gate self-consciously. Ethel was at the front door. She looked at his torn shirt and mud-caked knees.

'You'd better hurry if you're going to be ready for lunch,' she said coldly.

'Lunch?' faltered William. 'What time is it?'

'Ten to one. Father's in, so I warn you,' she added unpleasantly.

He entered the house in a dazed fashion. His mother was in the hall.

'*William!*' she said impatiently. 'Another shirt torn! You really are careless. You'll have to stop being a scout if that's the way you treat your clothes. And *look* at your knees!'

Pale and speechless, he went towards the stairs. His father was coming out of the library smoking a pipe. He looked at his son grimly.

'If you aren't downstairs *cleaned* by the time the lunch bell goes, my son,' he said, 'you won't see that bugle of yours this side of Christmas.'

William swallowed.

'Yes, Father,' he said meekly.

He went slowly upstairs to the bathroom.

Life was a rotten show.

CHAPTER 10

THE HELPER

The excitement began at breakfast. William descended slightly late, and, after receiving his parents' reproaches with an air of weary boredom, ate his porridge listlessly. He had come to the conclusion that morning that there was a certain monotonous sameness about life. One got up, and had one's breakfast, and went to school, and had one's dinner, and went to school, and had one's tea, and played, and had one's supper, and went to bed. Even the fact that today was a half-term holiday did not dispel his depression. *One* day's holiday! What good was *one* day? We all have experienced such feelings.

Half-abstractedly he began to listen to his elders' conversation.

'They promised to be here by *nine*,' his mother was saying. 'I do hope they won't be late!'

'Well, it's not much good their coming if the other house isn't ready, is it?' said William's grown-up sister Ethel. 'I don't believe they've even finished *painting*!'

'I'm so sorry it's William's half-term holiday,' sighed

Mrs Brown. 'He'll be frightfully in the way.'

'They comin' removin' this *morning*?' he inquired cheerfully.

'Yes, DO try not to hinder them, William.'

'*Me?*' he said indignantly. 'I'm goin' to *help*!'

'If William's going to help,' remarked his father, 'thank heaven *I* shan't be here. Your assistance, William, always seems to be even more devastating in its results than your opposition!'

William smiled politely. Sarcasm was always wasted on William.

'Well,' he said, rising from the table, 'I'd better go an' be gettin' ready to help.'

Ten minutes later Mrs Brown, coming out of the kitchen from her interview with the cook, found to her amazement that the steps of the front door were covered with small ornaments. As she stood staring William appeared from the drawing-room staggering under the weight of a priceless little statuette that had been the property of Mr Brown's great-grandfather.

'WILLIAM!' she gasped.

'I'm gettin' all the little things read for 'em jus' to carry straight down. If I put everything on the steps they don't need come into the house at all. You *said* you didn't want 'em trampin' in dirty boots!'

It took a quarter of an hour to replace them. Over the fragments of a blue Delft bowl Mrs Brown sighed deeply.

'I wish you'd broken *anything* but this, William.'

'Well,' he excused himself, 'you said things *do* get broken removin'. You said so *yourself*! I didn't break it on purpose. It jus' got broken removin'.'

At this point the removers arrived.

There were three of them. One was very fat and jovial, and one was thin and harassed-looking, and a third wore a sheepish smile and walked with a slightly unsteady gait. They made profuse apologies for their lateness.

'You'd better begin with the dining-room,' said Mrs Brown. 'Will you pack the china first? William, get out of the *way*!'

She left them packing, assisted by William. William carried the things to them from the sideboard cupboards.

'What's your names?' he asked, as he stumbled over a glass bowl that he had inadvertently left on the hearthrug. His progress was further delayed while he conscientiously picked up the fragments. 'Things *do* get broken removin',' he murmured.

'Mine is Mister Blake and 'is is Mister Johnson, and 'is is Mister Jones.'

'Which is Mr Jones? The one that walks funny?'

They shook with Herculean laughter, so much so that

a china cream jug slipped from Mr Blake's fingers and lay in innumerable pieces round his boots. He kicked them carelessly aside.

'Yus,' he said, bending anew to his task, ''im wot walks funny.'

'Why's he walk funny?' persisted William. 'Has he hurt his legs?'

'Yus,' said Blake with a wink. ''E 'urt 'em at the Blue Cow comin' 'ere.'

Mr Jones's sheepish smile broadened into a guffaw.

'Well, you rest,' said William sympathetically. 'You lie down on the sofa an' rest. *I'll* help, so's you needn't do *anything*!'

Mr Jones grew hilarious.

'Come on!' he said. 'My eye! This young gent's all *roight*, 'e is. You lie down an' rest, 'e says! Well, 'ere goes!'

To the huge delight of his companions, he stretched himself at length upon the Chesterfield and closed his eyes. William surveyed him with pleasure.

'That's right,' he said. 'I'll – I'll show you my dog when your legs are better. I've gotter *fine* dog!'

'What sort of a dog?' said Mr Blake, resting from his labours to ask the question.

'He's no *partic'lar* sort of a dog,' said William honestly, 'but he's a jolly fine dog. You should see him do tricks!'

WILLIAM SURVEYED HIM WITH PLEASURE. 'I'LL SHOW YOU
MY DOG WHEN YOUR LEGS ARE BETTER,' HE SAID.

'Well, let's 'ave a look at 'im. Fetch 'im art.'

William, highly delighted, complied, and Jumble showed off his best tricks to an appreciative audience of two (Mr Jones had already succumbed to the drowsiness that had long been creeping over him and was lying dead to the world on the Chesterfield).

Jumble begged for a biscuit, he walked (perforce, for William's hand firmly imprisoned his front ones) on his hind legs, he leapt over William's arm. He leapt into the very centre of an old Venetian glass that was on the floor by the packing case and cut his foot slightly on a piece of it, but fortunately suffered no ill effects.

William saw consternation on Mr Johnson's face and hastened to gather the pieces and fling them lightly into the waste-paper basket.

'It's all right,' he said soothingly. 'She *said* things get broken removin'.'

When Mrs Brown entered the room ten minutes later, Mr Jones was still asleep, Jumble was still performing, and Messrs Blake and Johnson were standing in negligent attitudes against the wall appraising the eager Jumble with sportsmanlike eyes.

''E's no breed,' Mr Blake was saying, 'but 'e's orl *roight*. I'd loik to see 'im arfter a rat. I bet 'e'd—'

Seeing Mrs Brown, he hastily seized a vase from the

mantelpiece and carried it over to the packing case, where he appeared suddenly to be working against time. Mr Johnson followed his example.

Mrs Brown's eyes fell upon Mr Jones and she gasped.

'Whatever—' she began.

''E's not very well 'm,' explained Mr Blake obsequiously. ''E'll be orl roight when 'e's slep' it orf. 'E's always orl roight when 'e's slep' it orf.'

'He's hurt his legs,' explained William. 'He hurt his legs at the Blue Cow. He's jus' *restin*'!'

Mrs Brown swallowed and counted twenty to herself. It was a practice she had acquired in her youth for use in times when words crowded upon her too thick and fast for utterance.

At last she spoke with unusual bitterness.

'Need he rest with his muddy boots on my Chesterfield?'

At this point Mr Jones awoke from sleep, hypnotised out of it by her cold eyes.

He was profuse in his apologies. He believed he had fainted. He had had a bad headache, brought on probably by exposure to the early morning sun. He felt much better after his faint. He regretted having fainted on to the lady's sofa. He partially brushed off the traces of his dirty boots with an equally dirty hand.

'You've done *nothing* in this room,' said Mrs Brown.

'We shall *never* get finished. William, come away! I'm sure you're hindering them.'

'Me?' said William in righteous indignation. '*Me?* I'm *helpin'*!'

After what seemed to Mrs Brown to be several hours they began on the heavy furniture. They staggered out with the dining-room sideboard, carrying away part of the staircase with it in transit. Mrs Brown, with a paling face, saw her beloved antique cabinet dismembered against the doorpost, and watched her favourite collapsible card table perform a thorough and permanent collapse. Even the hatstand from the hall was devoid of some pegs when it finally reached the van.

'This is simply breaking my heart,' moaned Mrs Brown.

'Where's William?' said Ethel, gloomily, looking round.

'Shh! I don't know. He disappeared a few minutes ago. I don't know *where* he is. I only hope he'll stay there!'

The removers now proceeded to the drawing-room and prepared to take out the piano. They tried it every way. The first way took a piece out of the doorpost, the second made a dint two inches deep in the piano, the third knocked over the grandfather clock, which fell with a resounding crash, breaking its glass, and incidentally a tall china plant stand that happened to be in its line of descent.

Mrs Brown sat down and covered her face with her hands.

'It's like some dreadful *nightmare*!' she groaned.

Messrs Blake, Johnson and Jones paused to wipe the sweat of honest toil from their brows.

'I dunno *'ow* it's to be got out,' said Mr Blake despairingly.

'It got in!' persisted Mrs Brown. 'If it got in it can get out.'

'We'll 'ave another try' said Mr Blake with the air of a hero leading a forlorn hope. 'Come on, mites.'

This time was successful and the piano passed safely into the hall, leaving in its wake only a dislocated door handle and a torn chair cover. It then passed slowly and devastatingly down the hall and drive.

The next difficulty was to get it into the van. Messrs Blake, Johnson and Jones tried alone and failed. For ten minutes they tried alone and failed. Between each attempt they paused to mop their brows and throw longing glances towards the Blue Cow, whose signboard was visible down the road.

The gardener, the cook, the housemaid, and Ethel all gave their assistance, and at last, with a superhuman effort, they raised it to the van.

They then all rested weakly against the nearest

support and gasped for breath.

'Well,' said Mr Jones, looking reproachfully at the mistress of the house, 'I've never 'andled a pianner—'

At this moment a well-known voice was heard in the recesses of the van, behind the piano and sideboard and hatstand.

'Hey! Let me out! What you've gone blockin' up the van for? I can't get out!'

There was a horror-stricken silence. Then Ethel said sharply:

'What did you go *in* for?'

The mysterious voice came again with a note of irritability.

'Well, I was *restin'*. I mus' have some rest, mustn't I? I've been helpin' all mornin'.'

'Well, couldn't you *see* we were putting things in?'

The unseen presence spoke again.

'No, I can't. I wasn't lookin'!'

'You can't get out, William,' said Mrs Brown desperately. 'We can't move everything again. You must just stop there till it's unpacked. We'll try to push your lunch in to you.'

There was determination in the voice that answered:

'I want to get out! I'm *going* to get out!'

There came tumultuous sounds – the sound of the

ripping of some material, of the smashing of glass and of William's voice softly ejaculating 'Crumbs! that ole lookin'-glass gettin' in the way!'

'You'd better take out the piano again,' said Mrs Brown wanly. 'It's the only thing to do.'

With straining, and efforts, and groans, and a certain amount of destruction, the piano was eventually lowered again to the ground. Then the sideboard and hatstand were moved to one side, and finally there emerged from the struggle – William and Jumble. Jumble's coat was covered with little pieces of horsehair, as though from the interior of a chair. William's jersey was torn from shoulder to hem. He looked stern and indignant.

'A nice thing to do!' he began bitterly. 'Shuttin' me up in that ole van. How d'you expect me to breathe, shut in with ole bits of furniture. Folks can't live without air, can they? A nice thing if you'd found me *dead*!'

Emotion had deprived his audience of speech for the time being.

With a certain amount of dignity he walked past them into the house followed by Jumble.

It took another quarter of an hour to replace the piano. As they were making the final effort William came out of the house.

'Here, *I'll* help!' he said, and laid a finger on the side. His presence rather hindered their efforts, but they succeeded in spite of it. William, however, was under the impression that his strength alone had wrought the miracle. He put on an outrageous swagger.

'I'm jolly strong,' he confided to Mr Blake. 'I'm stronger than most folk.'

Here the removers decided that it was time for their midday repast and retired to consume it in the shady back garden. All except Mr Jones, who said he would go down the road for a drink of lemonade. William said that there was lemonade in the larder and offered to fetch it, but Mr Jones said hastily that he wanted a special sort. He had to be very particular what sort of lemonade he drank.

Mrs Brown and Ethel sat down to a scratch meal in the library. William followed his two new friends wistfully into the garden.

'William! Come to lunch!' called Mrs Brown.

'Oh, leave him alone, Mother,' pleaded Ethel. 'Let us have a little peace.'

But William did not absent himself for long.

'I want a red handkerchief,' he demanded loudly from the hall.

There was no response.

He appeared in the doorway.

WILLIAM'S JERSEY WAS TORN FROM SHOULDER TO HEM.
HE LOOKED STERN AND INDIGNANT.

'I say, I want a red handkerchief. Have you gotter red
handkerchief, Mother?'
'No, dear.'

171

'Have you, Ethel?'

'NO!'

'All right,' said William aggrievedly. 'You needn't get mad, need you? I'm only askin' for a red handkerchief. I don't want a red handkerchief off you if you haven't *got* it, do I?'

'William, go *away* and shut the door.'

William obeyed. Peace reigned throughout the house and garden for the next half-hour. Then Mrs Brown's conscience began to prick her.

'William must have something to eat, dear. Do go and find him.'

Ethel went out to the back garden. A scene of happy restfulness met her gaze. Mr Blake reclined against one tree consuming bread and cheese, while a red handkerchief covered his knees. Mr Johnson reclined against another tree, also consuming bread and cheese, while a red handkerchief covered his knees. William leant against a third tree consuming a little heap of scraps collected from the larder, while on his knees also reposed what was apparently a red handkerchief. Jumble sat in the middle catching with nimble, snapping jaws dainties flung to him from time to time by his circle of admirers.

Ethel advanced nearer and inspected William's red handkerchief with dawning horror in her face. Then she gave a scream.

'*William*, that's my silk scarf! It was for a hat. I've only just bought it. Oh, Mother, do *do* something to William! He's taken my new silk scarf – the one I'd got to trim my leghorn. He's the most *awful* boy. I don't think—'

Mrs Brown came out hastily to pacify her. William handed the silk scarf back to its rightful owner.

'Well, I'm *sorry*. I *thought* it was a red handkerchief. It *looked* like a red handkerchief. Well, how could I *know* it wasn't a red handkerchief? I've given it her back. It's all right, Jumble's only bit one end of it. And that's only jam what dropped on it. Well, it'll *wash*, won't it? Well, I've said I'm sorry.

'I don't get much *thanks*,' William continued bitterly. 'Me givin' up my half holiday to helpin' you removin', an' I don't get much *thanks*!'

'Well, William,' said Mrs Brown, 'you can go to the new house with the first van. He'll be less in the way there,' she confided distractedly to the world in general.

William was delighted with this proposal. At the new house there was a fresh set of men to unload the van, and there was the thrill of making their acquaintance.

Then the front gate was only just painted and bore a notice 'Wet Paint'. It was, of course, incumbent upon William to test personally the wetness of the paint. His trousers bore testimony to the testing to their last day, in spite of many applications of turpentine. Jumble also tested it, and had in fact to be disconnected from the front gate by means of a pair of scissors. For many weeks the first thing that visitors to the Brown household saw was a little tuft of Jumble's hair adorning the front gate.

William then proceeded to 'help' to the utmost of his power. He stumbled up from the van to the house staggering under the weight of a medicine cupboard, and leaving a trail of broken bottles and little pools of medicine behind. Jumble sampled many of the latter and became somewhat thoughtful.

It was found that the door of a small bedroom at the top of the stairs was locked, and this fact (added to Mr Jones's failure to return from his lemonade) rather impeded the progress of the unpackers.

'Brike it open,' suggested one.

'Better not.'

'Per'aps the key's insoide,' suggested another brightly.

William had one of his brilliant ideas.

'Tell you what I'll do,' he said eagerly and importantly. 'I'll climb up to the roof an' get down the chimney an' open it from the inside.'

They greeted the proposal with guffaws.

They did not know William.

It was growing dusk when Mrs Brown and Ethel and

the second van load appeared.

'What is that on the gate?' said Ethel, stooping to examine the part of Jumble's coat that brightened up the dullness of the black paint.

'It's that *dog*!' said Mrs Brown.

Then came a ghostlike cry, apparently from the heavens.

'Mother!'

Mrs Brown raised a startled countenance to the skies. There seemed to be nothing in the skies that could have addressed her.

Then she suddenly saw a small face peering down over the coping of the roof. It was a face that was very frightened, under a superficial covering of soot. It was William's face.

'I can't get down,' it said hoarsely.

Mrs Brown's heart stood still.

'Stay where you are, William,' she said faintly. 'Don't *move*.'

The entire staff of removers was summoned. A ladder was borrowed from a neighbouring garden and found to be too short. Another was fetched and fastened to it. William, at his dizzy height, was growing irritable.

'I can't stay up here for *ever*,' he said severely.

At last he was rescued by his friend Mr Blake and

brought down to safety. His account was confused.

'I wanted to *help*. I wanted to open that door for 'em, so I climbed up by the scullery roof, an' the ivy, an' the drainpipe, an' I tried to get down the chimney. I didn't know which one it was, but I tried 'em all an' they were all too little, an' I tried to get down by the ivy again but I couldn't, so I waited till you came an' hollered out. I wasn't scared,' he said, fixing them with a stern eye. 'I wasn't scared a bit. I jus' wanted to get down. An' this ole black chimney stuff tastes beastly. No, I'm all right,' he ended, in answer to tender inquiries. 'I'll go on helpin'.'

He was with difficulty persuaded to retire to bed at a slightly earlier hour than usual.

'Well,' he confessed, 'I'm a bit tired with helpin' all day.'

Soon after he had gone Mr Brown and Robert arrived.

'And how have things gone today?' said Mr Brown cheerfully.

'Thank heaven William goes to school tomorrow,' said Ethel devoutly.

Upstairs in his room William was studying himself in the glass – torn jersey, paint-stained trousers, blackened face.

'Well,' he said with a deep sigh of satisfaction, 'I guess I've jolly well HELPED today!'

CHAPTER 11

WILLIAM AND THE SMUGGLER

William's family were going to the seaside for February. It was not an ideal month for the seaside, but William's father's doctor had ordered him a complete rest and change.

'We shall have to take William with us, you know,' his wife had said as they discussed plans.

'Good heavens!' groaned Mr Brown. 'I thought it was to be a *rest* cure.'

'Yes, but you know what he is,' his wife urged. 'I daren't leave him with anyone. Certainly not with Ethel. We shall have to take them both. Ethel will help with him.'

Ethel was William's grown-up sister.

'All right,' agreed her husband finally. 'You can take all responsibility I formally disown him from now till we get back. I don't care *what* trouble he lands you in. You know what he is and you deliberately take him away with me on a rest cure!'

'It can't be helped, dear,' said his wife mildly.

William was thrilled by the news. It was several years since he had been at the seaside.

'Will I be able to go swimmin'?'

'It *won't* be too cold! Well, if I wrap up warm, will I be able to go swimmin'?'

'Can I catch fishes?'

'Are there lots of smugglers smugglin' there?'

'Well, I'm only *askin'*, you needn't get mad!'

One afternoon Mrs Brown missed her best silver tray and searched the house high and low for it wildly, while dark suspicions of each servant in turn arose in her usually unsuspicious breast.

It was finally discovered in the garden. William had dug a large hole in one of the garden beds. Into the bottom of this he had fitted the tray and had lined the sides with bricks. He had then filled it with water and taking off his shoes and stockings stepped up and down his narrow pool. He was distinctly aggrieved by Mrs Brown's reproaches.

'Well, I was practisin' paddlin', ready for goin' to the seaside. I didn't *mean* to rune your tray. You talk as if I *meant* to rune your tray. I was only practisin' paddlin'.'

At last the day of departure arrived. William was instructed to put his things ready on his bed, and his mother would then come and pack for him. He summoned her proudly over the balusters after about twenty minutes.

'I've got everythin' ready, Mother.'

Mrs Brown ascended to his room.

Upon his bed was a large popgun, a football, a dormouse in a cage, a punchball on a stand, a large box of 'curios', and a buckskin which was his dearest possession and had been presented to him by an uncle from South Africa.

Mrs Brown sat down weakly on a chair.

'You can't possibly take any of these things,' she said faintly but firmly.

'Well, you *said* put my things on the bed for you to pack an' I've put them on the bed, an' now you say—'

'I meant clothes.'

'Oh, *clothes*!' he said scornfully. 'I never thought of *clothes*.'

'Well, you can't take any of these things, anyway.'

William hastily began to defend his collection of treasures.

'I *mus'* have the popgun 'cause you never know. There may be pirates an' smugglers down there, an' you can *kill* a man with a popgun if you get near enough and know the right place, an' I might need it. An' I *must* have the football to play on the sands with, an' the punchball to practise boxin' on, an' I *must* have the dormouse, 'cause – 'cause to feed him, an' I *must* have this box of things and this skin to show to folks I meet down at the seaside 'cause they're int'restin'.'

But Mrs Brown was firm, and William reluctantly yielded.

In a moment of weakness, finding that his trunk was only three quarters filled by his things, she slipped in his beloved buckskin, while William himself put the popgun inside when no one was looking.

They had been unable to obtain a furnished house, so had to be content with a boarding house. Mr Brown was eloquent on the subject.

'If you're deliberately turning that child loose into a boarding house full, presumably of quiet, inoffensive people, you deserve all you get. It's nothing to do with me. I'm going to have a rest cure. I've disowned him. He can do as he likes.'

'It can't be helped, dear,' said Mrs Brown mildly.

Mr Brown had engaged one of the huts on the beach chiefly for William's use, and William proudly furnished its floor with the buckskin.

'It was killed by my uncle,' he announced to the small crowd of children at the door who had watched with interest his painstaking measuring on the floor in order to place his treasure in the exact centre. 'He killed it dead – jus' like this.'

William had never heard the story of the death of the buck, and therefore had invented one in which he had gradually come to confuse himself with his uncle in the role of hero.

'It was walkin' about an' I – he – met it. I hadn't got no gun, and it sprung at me an' I caught hold of its neck with one hand an' I broke off its horns with the other, an' I knocked it over. An' it got up an' ran at me – him – again, an' I jus' tripped it up with my foot an' it fell over again, an' then I jus' give it one big hit with my fist right on its head, an' it killed it an' it died!'

There was an incredulous gasp.

Then there came a clear, high voice from behind the crowd.

'Little boy, you are not telling the truth.'

William looked up into a thin, spectacled face.

'I wasn't tellin' it to you,' he remarked, wholly unabashed.

A little girl with dark curls took up the cudgels quite needlessly in William's defence.

'He's a very *brave* boy to do all that,' she said indignantly. 'So don't you go *saying* things to him.'

'Well,' said William, flattered but modest, 'I didn't say I did, did I? I said my uncle – well, partly my uncle.'

Mr Percival Jones looked down at him in righteous wrath.

'You're a very wicked little boy. I'll tell your father – er – I'll tell your sister.'

For Ethel was approaching in the distance and Mr Percival Jones was in no way loath to converse with her.

Mr Percival Jones was a thin, pale, aesthetic would-be poet who lived and thrived on the admiration of the elderly ladies of his boarding house, and had done so for the past ten years. Once he had published a volume of poems at his own expense. He lived at the same boarding house as the Browns, and had seen Ethel in the distance at meals. He had admired the red lights in her dark hair and the blue of her eyes, and had even gone so far as to wonder whether she possessed the solid and enduring qualities which he would require of one whom in his mind he referred to as his 'future spouse'.

He began to walk down the beach with her.

'I should like to speak to you – er – about your brother, Miss Brown,' he began, 'if you can spare me the time, of course. I trust I do not er – intrude or presume. He is a charming little man but – er – I fear – not veracious. May I accompany you a little on your way? I am – er – much

182

attracted to your – er – family. I – er – should like to know you all better. I am – er – deeply attached to your – er – little brother, but grieved to find that he does not – er – adhere to the truth in his statements. I – er—'

Miss Brown's blue eyes were dancing with merriment.

'Oh, don't worry about William,' she said. 'He's *awful*. It's much better just to leave him alone. Isn't the sea gorgeous today?'

They walked along the sands.

Meanwhile William had invited his small defender into his hut.

'You can look round,' he said graciously. 'You've seen my skin what I – he – killed, haven't you? This is my gun. You put a cork in there and it comes out hard when you shoot it. It would kill anyone,' he said impressively, 'if you did it near enough to them and at the right place. An' I've got a dormouse, an' a punchball, an' a box of things, an' a football, but they wouldn't let me bring them,' bitterly.

'It's a *lovely* skin,' said the little girl. 'What's your name?'

'William. What's yours?'

'Peggy.'

'Well, let's be on a desert island, shall we? An' nothin' to eat nor anything, shall we? Come on.'

She nodded eagerly.

'How *lovely*!'

They wandered out on to the promenade, and among a large crowd of passers-by bemoaned the lonely emptiness of the island and scanned the horizon for a sail. In the far distance on the cliffs could be seen the figures of

'YOU'RE A VERY WICKED LITTLE BOY!' SAID
MR PERCIVAL JONES.

Mr Percival Jones and William's sister, walking slowly away from the town.

At last they turned towards the hut.

'We must find somethin' to eat,' said William firmly. 'We can't let ourselves starve to death.'

'Shrimps?' suggested Peggy cheerfully.

'We haven't got nets,' said William. 'We couldn't save them from the wreck.'

'Periwinkles?'

'There aren't any on this island. I know! Seaweed! An' we'll cook it.'

'Oh, how *lovely*!'

He gathered up a handful of seaweed and they entered the hut, leaving a white handkerchief tied on to the door to attract the attention of any passing ship. The hut was provided with a gas ring and William, disregarding his family's express injunction, lit this and put on a saucepan filled with water and seaweed.

'We'll pretend it's a wood fire,' he said. 'We couldn't make a real wood fire out on the prom. They'd stop us. So we'll pretend this is. An' we'll pretend we saved a saucepan from the wreck.'

After a few minutes he took off the pan and drew out a long green strand.

'You eat it first,' he said politely.

The smell of it was not pleasant. Peggy drew back.

'Oh, no, you first!'

'No, you,' said William nobly. 'You look hungrier than me.'

She bit off a piece, chewed it, shut her eyes and swallowed.

'Now you,' she said with a shade of vindictiveness in her voice. 'You're not going to not have any.'

William took a mouthful and shivered.

'I think it's gone bad,' he said critically.

Peggy's rosy face had paled.

'I'm going home,' she said suddenly.

'You can't go home on a desert island,' said William severely.

'Well, I'm going to be rescued then,' she said.

'I think I am, too,' said William.

It was lunchtime when William arrived at the boarding house. Mr Percival Jones had moved his place so as to be nearer Ethel. He was now convinced that she was possessed of every virtue his future 'spouse' could need. He conversed brightly and incessantly during the meal. Mr Brown grew restive.

'The man will drive me mad,' he said afterwards. 'Bleating away! What's he bleating about anyway? Can't you stop him bleating, Ethel? You seem to have influence.

Bleat! Bleat! Bleat! Good Lord! And me here for a *rest* cure.'

At this point he was summoned to the telephone and returned distraught.

'It's an unknown female,' he said. 'She says that a boy of the name of William from this boarding house has made her little girl sick by forcing her to eat seaweed. She says it's brutal. Does anyone *know* I'm here for a rest cure? Where is the boy? Good heavens! Where is the boy?'

But William, like Peggy, had retired from the world for a space. He returned later on in the afternoon, looking pale and chastened. He bore the reproaches of his family in stately silence.

Mr Percival Jones was in great evidence in the drawing-room.

'And soon – er – soon the – er – spring will be with us once more,' he was saying in his high-pitched voice as he leant back in his chair and joined the tips of his fingers together. 'The spring – ah – the spring! I have a – er – little effort I – er – composed on – er – the Coming of Spring – I – er – will read to you sometime if you will – ah – be kind enough to – er – criticise – ah – impartially.'

'*Criticise!*' they chorused. 'It will be above criticism. Oh, do read it to us, Mr Jones.'

'I will – er – this evening.' His eyes wandered to the

door, hoping and longing for his beloved's entrance. But Ethel was with her father at a matinee at the Winter Gardens and he looked and longed in vain. In spite of this, however, the springs of his eloquence did not run dry, and he held forth ceaselessly to his little circle of admirers.

'The simple – ah – pleasures of nature. How few of us – alas! – have the – er – gift of appreciating them rightly. This – er – little seaside hamlet with its – er – sea, its – er – promenade, its – er – Winter Gardens! How beautiful it is! How few appreciate it rightly!'

Here William entered and Mr Percival Jones broke off abruptly. He disliked William.

'Ah! Here comes our little friend. He looks pale. Remorse, my young friend? Ah, beware of untruthfulness. Beware of the beginnings of a life of lies and deception.' He laid a hand on William's head and cold shivers ran down William's spine. '"Be good, sweet child, and let who will be clever," as the poet says.' There was murder in William's heart.

At that minute Ethel entered.

'No,' she snapped. 'I sat next to a man who smelt of bad tobacco. I hate men who smoke bad tobacco.'

Mr Jones assumed an expression of intense piety.

'I may boast,' he said sanctimoniously, 'that I have never thus soiled my lips with drink or smoke . . .'

There was an approving murmur from the occupants of the drawing-room.

William had met his father in the passage outside the drawing-room. Mr Brown was wearing a hunted expression.

'Can I go into the drawing-room,' he said bitterly, 'or is he bleating away in there?'

They listened. From the drawing-room came the sound of a high-pitched voice.

Mr Brown groaned.

'Good Lord!' he moaned. 'And I'm here for a *rest* cure and he comes bleating into every room in the house. Is the smoking-room safe? Does he smoke?'

Mr Percival Jones was feeling slightly troubled in his usually peaceful conscience. He could honestly say that he had never smoked. He could honestly say that he had never drunk. But in his bedroom reposed two bottles of brandy purchased at the advice of an aunt 'in case of emergencies'. In his bedroom also was a box of cigars that he had bought for a cousin's birthday gift, but which his conscience had finally forbidden to present. He decided to consign these two emblems of vice to the waves that very evening.

Meanwhile William had returned to the hut and was composing a tale of smugglers by the light of a candle. He was much intrigued by his subject. He wrote fast in an illegible hand in great sloping lines, his brows frowning, his tongue protruding from his mouth as it always did in moments of mental strain.

His sympathies wavered between the smugglers and the representatives of law and order. His orthography was the despair of his teachers.

'"*Ho!*" *sez Dick Savage,*' he wrote. '"*Ho! Gadzooks! Rol in the bottles of beer up the beach. Fill your pockets with the baccy from the bote. Quick, now! Gadzooks! Methinks we are observed!*" *He glared round in the darkness. In less time than wot it takes to rite this he was srounded by pleesemen and stood, proud and defiant, in the light of there electrick torches wot they had wiped quick as litening from their busums.*

'"*Surrender!*" *cried one, holding a gun at his brain and a drorn sord at his hart, "Surrender or die!*"

'"*Never,*" *said Dick Savage, throwing back his head, proud and defiant. "Never. Do to me wot you will I die.*"

'*One crule brute hit him a blo on the lips and he sprang back, snarling with rage. In less time than wot it takes to rite this he had sprang at his torturer's throte and his teeth met in one mighty bite. His torturer dropped ded and lifless at his feet.*

'"*Ho!*" *cried Dick Savage, throwing back his head,*

190

proud and defiant again. "So dies any of you wot insults my proud manhood. I will meet my teeth in your throtes."

'*For a minit they stood trembling, then one, bolder than the rest, lept forward and tide Dick Savage's hands with rope behind his back. Another took from his pockets bottles of beer and tobacco in large quantities.*

'*"Ho!" they cried exulting. "Ho! Dick Savage the smugler caught at last!"*

'*Dick Savage gave one proud and defiant laugh, and, bringing his tide hands over his hed he bit the rope with one mighty bite.*

'*"Ho! Ho!" he cried, throwing back his proud hed. "Ho, ho! You dirty dogs!"*

'*Then, draining to the dregs a large bottle of poison he had concealed in his busum he fell ded and lifless at there feet.*'

There was a timid knock at the door and William, scowling impatiently, rose to open it.

'What d'you want?' he said curtly.

A little voice answered from the dusk.

'It's me – Peggy. I've come to see how you are, William. They don't know I've come. I was awful sick after that seaweed this morning, William.'

William looked at her with a superior frown.

'Go away,' he said. 'I'm busy.'

'What are you doing?' she said, poking her little curly head into the doorway.

'I'm writin' a tale.'

She clasped her hands.

'Oh, how lovely! Oh, William, do read it to me. I'd *love* it!'

Mollified, he opened the door and she took her seat on his buckskin on the floor, and William sat by the candle, clearing his throat for a minute before he began. During the reading she never took her eyes off him. At the end she drew a deep breath.

'Oh, William, it's beautiful. William, are there smugglers now?'

'Oh, yes. Millions,' he said carelessly.

'*Here?*'

'Of course there are!'

She went to the door and looked out at the dusk.

'I'd love to see one. What do they smuggle, William?'

He came and joined her at the door, walking with a slight swagger as became a man of literary fame.

'Oh, beer an' cigars an' things. *Millions* of them.'

A furtive figure was passing the door, casting suspicious glances to left and right. He held his coat tightly round him, clasping something inside it.

'I expect that's one,' said William casually.

They watched the figure out of sight.

Suddenly William's eyes shone.

'Let's stalk him an' catch him,' he said excitedly. 'Come on. Let's take some weapons.' He seized his popgun from a corner. 'You take' – he looked round the room – 'you take the waste-paper basket to put over his head an' – an' pin down his arms an' somethin' to tie him up! – I know – the skin I – he – shot in Africa. You can tie its paws in front of him. Come on! Let's catch him smugglin'.'

He stepped out boldly into the dusk with his popgun, followed by the blindly obedient Peggy carrying the waste-paper basket in one hand and the skin in the other.

Mr Percival Jones was making quite a little ceremony of consigning his brandy and cigars to the waves. He had composed 'a little effort' upon it which began,

O deeps, receive these objects vile
Which nevermore mine eyes shall soil.

He went down to the edge of the sea and, taking a bottle in hand, held them out at arms' length, while he began in his high-pitched voice,

O deeps, receive these—

193

He stopped. A small boy stood beside him holding out at him the point of what in the semi-darkness Mr Jones took to be a loaded rifle. William mistook his action in holding out the bottles.

'It's no good tryin' to drink it up,' he said severely. 'We've caught you smugglin'.'

Mr Percival Jones laughed nervously.

'My little man!' he said. 'That's a very dangerous – er –

'WE'VE CAUGHT YOU SMUGGLIN'!'
WILLIAM SAID SEVERELY.

thing for you to have! Suppose you hand it over to me, now, like a good little chap.'

William recognised his voice.

'Fancy you bein' a smuggler all the time!' he said with righteous indignation in his voice.

'Take away that – er – nasty gun, little boy,' pleaded his captive plaintively. 'You – ah – don't understand it. It – er – might go off.'

William was not a boy to indulge in half measures. He meant to carry the matter off with a high hand.

'I'll shoot you dead,' he said dramatically, 'if you don't do jus' what I tell you.'

Mr Percival Jones wiped the perspiration from his brow.

'Where did you get that rifle, little boy?' he asked in a voice he strove to make playful. 'Is it – ah – is it loaded? It's – ah – unwise, little boy. Most unwise. Er – give it to me to – er – take care of. It – er – might go off, you know.'

William moved the muzzle of his weapon, and Mr Percival Jones shuddered from head to foot. William was a brave boy, but he had experienced a moment of cold terror when first he had approached his captive. The first note of the quavering high-pitched voice had, however, reassured him. He instantly knew himself to be the better man. His captive's obvious terror of his popgun almost persuaded him that he held in his hand some formidable death-dealing instrument. As a matter of fact Mr Percival Jones was temperamentally an abject coward.

'You walk up to the seats,' commanded William. 'I've took you prisoner for smugglin' an' – an' – jus' walk up to the seats.'

Mr Percival Jones obeyed with alacrity.

'Don't – er – *press* anything, little boy,' he pleaded as he went. 'It – ah – might go off by accident. You might do – ah – untold damage.'

Peggy, armed with the waste-paper basket and the skin, followed open-mouthed.

At the seat William paused.

'Peggy, you put the basket over his head an' pin his arms down – case he struggles, an' tie the skin wot I shot round him, case he struggles.'

Peggy stood upon the seat and obeyed. Their victim made no protest. He seemed to himself to be in some horrible dream. The only thing of which he was conscious was the dimly descried weapon that William held out at him in the darkness. He was hardly aware of the waste-paper basket thrust over his head. He watched William anxiously through the basketwork.

'Be careful,' he murmured. 'Be careful, boy!'

He hardly felt the skin which was fastened tightly round

his unresisting form by Peggy the tail tied to one front paw. Unconsciously he still clasped a bottle of brandy in each arm.

Then came the irate summons of Peggy's nurse through the dusk.

'Oh, William,' she said panting with excitement, 'I don't want to leave you. Oh, William, he might *kill* you!'

'You go on. I'm all right,' he said with conscious valour. 'He can't do nothin' 'cause I've got a gun an' I can shoot him dead' – Mr Percival Jones shuddered afresh – 'an' he's all tied up an' I've took him prisoner an' I'm goin' to take him home.'

'Oh, William, you *are* brave!' she whispered in the darkness as she flitted away to her nurse.

William blushed with pride and embarrassment.

Mr Percival Jones was convinced that he had to deal with a youthful lunatic, armed with a dangerous weapon, and was anxious only to humour him till the time of danger was over and he could be placed under proper restraint.

Unconscious of his peculiar appearance, he walked before his captor, casting propitiatory glances behind him.

'It's all right, little boy,' he said soothingly, 'quite all right. I'm – er – your friend. Don't – ah – get annoyed, little boy. Don't – ah – get annoyed. Won't you put your –

gun down, little man? Won't you let me carry it for you?'

William walked behind still pointing his popgun.

'I've took you prisoner for smugglin',' he repeated doggedly. 'I'm takin' you home. You're my prisoner. I've took you.'

They met no one on the road, though Mr Percival Jones threw longing glances around, ready to appeal to any passer-by for rescue. He was afraid to raise his voice in case it should rouse his youthful captor to murder. He saw with joy the gate of his boarding house and hastened up the walk and up the stairs. The drawing-room door was open. There was help and assistance, there was protection against this strange persecution. He entered, followed closely by William. It was about the time he had promised to read his 'little effort' on the Coming of Spring to his circle of admirers. A group of elderly ladies sat round the fire awaiting him. Ethel was writing. They turned as he entered and a gasp of horror and incredulous dismay went up. It was that gasp that called him to a realisation of the fact that he was wearing a waste-paper basket over his head and shoulders, and that a mangy fur was tied round his arms.

'Mr *Jones*!' they gasped.

He gave a wrench to his shoulders and the rug fell to

the floor, revealing a bottle of brandy clasped in either arm.

'Mr *Jones*!' they repeated.

'I caught him smugglin',' said William proudly. 'I caught him smugglin' beer by the sea an' he was drinking those two bottles he'd smuggled an' he had thousands an' *thousands* of cigars all over him, an' I caught him, an' he's a smuggler, an' I brought him up here with my gun. He's a smuggler an' I took him prisoner.'

Mr Jones, red and angry, his hair awry, glared through the wickerwork of the basket. He moistened his lips. 'This is an outrage,' he spluttered.

Horrified elderly eyes stared at the incriminating bottles.

'He was drinkin' 'em by the sea,' said William.

'Mr *Jones*!' they chorused again.

He flung off his waste-paper basket and turned upon the proprietress of the establishment who stood by the door.

'I will not brook such treatment,' he stammered in fury. 'I leave your roof tonight. I am outraged – humiliated. I – I disdain to explain. I – leave your roof tonight.'

'Mr *Jones*!' they said once more.

Mr Jones, still clasping his bottles, withdrew, pausing to glare at William on his way.

'You *wicked* boy! You *wicked* little, *untruthful* boy,' he said.

William looked after him. 'He's my prisoner an' they've let him go,' he said aggrievedly.

Ten minutes later he wandered into the smoking-room. Mr Brown sat miserably in a chair by a dying fire beneath a poor light.

'Is he still bleating there?' he said. 'Is this still the only

'I CAUGHT HIM SMUGGLIN',' WILLIAM EXPLAINED
PROUDLY. 'HE HAD THOUSANDS AN' THOUSANDS
OF CIGARS AND THAT BEER!'

corner where I can be sure of keeping my sanity? Is he reading his beastly poetry upstairs? Is he—'

'He's goin',' said William moodily. 'He's goin' before dinner. They've sent for his cab. He's mad 'cause I said he was a smuggler. He was a smuggler 'cause I saw him doin' it, an' I took him prisoner an' he got mad an' he's goin'. An' they're mad at me 'cause I took him prisoner. You'd think they'd be glad at me catchin' smugglers, but they're not,' bitterly. 'An' Mother says she'll tell you an' you'll be mad too an'—'

Mr Brown raised his hand.

'One minute, my son,' he said. 'Your story is confused. Do I understand that Mr Jones is going and that you are the cause of his departure?'

'Yes, 'cause he got mad 'cause I said he was a smuggler an' he was a smuggler an' they're mad at me now, an'—'

Mr Brown laid a hand on his son's shoulder.

'There are moments, William,' he said, 'when I feel almost affectionate towards you.'

CHAPTER 12

THE REFORM OF WILLIAM

To William the idea of reform was new and startling and not wholly unattractive. It originated with the housemaid whose brother was a reformed burglar now employed in a grocer's shop.

''E's got conversion,' she said to William. ''E got it quite sudden, like, an' 'e give up all 'is bad ways straight off. 'E's bin like a heavenly saint ever since.'

William was deeply interested. The point was all innocently driven in later by the Sunday-school mistress. William's family had no real faith in the Sunday school as a corrective to William's inherent wickedness, but they knew that no Sabbath peace or calm was humanly possible while William was in the house. So they brushed and cleaned and tidied him at 2.45 and sent him, pained and protesting, down the road every Sunday afternoon. Their only regret was that Sunday school did not begin earlier and end later.

Fortunately for William, most of his friends' parents were inspired by the same zeal, so that he met his old cronies of the weekdays – Henry, Ginger, Douglas and all the rest – and together they beguiled the monotony of the Sabbath.

But this Sunday the tall, pale lady who, for her sins, essayed to lead William and his friends along the straight and narrow path of virtue, was almost inspired. She was like some prophetess of old. She was so emphatic that the red cherries that hung coquettishly over the edge of her hat rattled against it as though in applause.

'We must all *start afresh*,' she said. 'We must all be *turned* — that's what *conversion* means.'

William's fascinated eye wandered from the cherries to the distant view out of the window. He thought suddenly of the noble burglar who had turned his back upon the mysterious, nefarious tools of his trade and now dispensed margarine to his former victims.

Opposite him sat a small girl in a pink and white checked frock. He often whiled away the dullest hours of Sunday school by putting out his tongue at her or throwing paper pellets at her (manufactured previously for the purpose). But today, meeting her serious eye, he looked away hastily.

'And we must all *help someone*,' went on the urgent voice. 'If we have *turned* ourselves, we must help someone else to *turn* . . .'

Determined and eager was the eye that the small girl turned upon William, and William realised that his time had come. He was to be converted. He felt almost thrilled by the prospect. He was so enthralled that he received absent-mindedly, and without gratitude, the mountainous bull's eye passed to him from Ginger, and only gave a halfhearted smile when a well-aimed pellet from Henry's hand sent one of the prophetess's cherries swinging high in the air.

After the class the pink-checked girl (whose name most appropriately was Deborah) stalked William for several yards and finally cornered him.

'William,' she said, 'are you going to *turn*?'

'I'm goin' to think about it,' said William guardedly.

'William, I think you ought to turn. I'll help you,' she added sweetly.

William drew a deep breath. 'All right, I will,' he said.

She heaved a sigh of relief.

'You'll begin *now*, won't you?' she said earnestly.

William considered. There were several things that he had wanted to do for some time, but hadn't managed to do yet. He had not tried turning off the water at the main, and hiding the key and seeing what would happen; he hadn't tried shutting up the cat in the hen house; he hadn't tried painting his long-suffering mongrel Jumble with the pot of green paint that was in the tool shed; he hadn't tried pouring water into the receiver of the telephone; he hadn't tried locking the cook into the larder. There were, in short, whole fields of crime entirely unexplored. All these things – and others – must be done before the reformation.

'I can't begin *jus'* yet,' said William. 'Say day after tomorrow.'

She considered this for a minute.

'Very well,' she said at last reluctantly, 'day after tomorrow.'

The next day dawned bright and fair. William arose with a distinct sense that something important had happened. Then he thought of the reformation. He saw himself leading a quiet and blameless life, walking sedately to school, working at high pressure in school, doing his homework conscientiously in the evening, being exquisitely polite to his family, his instructors, and the various foolish people who visited his home for the sole purpose (apparently) of making inane remarks to him. He saw all this, and the picture was far from unattractive – in the distance. In the immediate future, however, there were various quite important things to be done. There was a whole normal lifetime of crime to be crowded into one day. Looking out of his window he espied the gardener bending over one of the beds. The gardener had a perfectly bald head. William had sometimes idly imagined the impact of a pea sent violently from a pea-shooter at the gardener's bald head. Before there had been a lifetime of experiment before him, and he had put off this one idly in favour of something more pressing. Now there was only one day. He took up his pea-shooter and aimed carefully. The pea did not embed itself deeply into the gardener's skull as William had sometimes thought it would. It bounced back. It bounced back quite hard. The gardener also bounced back with a yell of anger, shaking his fist at William's window. But William had discreetly retired. He hid the pea-shooter, assumed his famous expression of innocence, and felt distinctly cheered. The question as to what exactly would happen when the pea met the baldness was now for ever solved. The gardener retired grumbling to the potting shed, so, for the present, all was well. Later in the day the gardener might lay his formal complaint before authority, but later in the day was later in the day. It did not trouble William. He dressed briskly and went down to breakfast with a frown of concentration upon his face. It was the last day of his old life.

No one else was in the dining-room. It was the work of a few minutes to remove the bacon from beneath the

THE PEA DID NOT EMBED ITSELF INTO THE GARDENER'S
SKULL AS WILLIAM HAD SOMETIMES THOUGHT IT WOULD. IT
BOUNCED BACK. THE GARDENER ALSO BOUNCED BACK.

big pewter cover and substitute the kitten, to put a table-
spoonful of salt into the coffee, and to put a two-days-old
paper in place of that morning's. They were all things that

he had at one time or another vaguely thought of doing, but for which he had never yet seemed to have time or opportunity. Warming to his subject he removed the egg from under the egg cosy on his sister's plate and placed in its stead a worm which had just appeared in the window box in readiness for the early bird.

He surveyed the scene with a deep sigh of satisfaction. The only drawback was that he felt that he could not safely stay to watch results. William possessed a true strategic instinct for the right moment for a retreat. Hearing, therefore, a heavy step on the stairs, he seized several pieces of toast and fled. As he fled he heard through the open window violent sounds proceeding from the enraged kitten beneath the cover, and then the still more violent sounds proceeding from the unknown person who removed the cover. The kitten, a mass of fury and lust for revenge, came flying through the window. William hid behind a laurel bush till it had passed, then set off down the road. School, of course, was impossible. The precious hours of such a day as this could not be wasted in school. He went down the road full of his whole purpose. The wickedness of a lifetime was somehow or other to be crowded into this day. Tomorrow it would all be impossible. Tomorrow began the blameless life. It must all be worked off today. He skirted the school by a field path in case any of those narrow souls paid to employ so aimlessly the precious hours of his youth might be there. They would certainly be tactless enough to question him as he passed the door. Then he joined the main road. The main road was empty except for a caravan – a caravan gaily painted in red and yellow. It had little lace curtains at the window. It was altogether a most fascinating caravan. No one seemed to be near it. William looked through the window. There was a kind of dresser with crockery hanging from it, a small table and a little oil stove. The further part was curtained off but no sound came from it, so that it was presumably empty too. William wandered round to inspect the quadruped in front. It appeared to be a mule – a mule with a jaundiced view of life. It rolled a sad eye towards William, then with a deep sigh returned to its contemplation of the landscape. William gazed upon caravan and steed fascinated. Never, in his future life of noble merit, would he be able to annex a caravan. It was his last chance. No one was about. He could pretend that he had mistaken it for his own caravan or had got on to it by mistake or – or anything. Conscience stirred faintly in his breast, but he silenced it sternly. Conscience was to rule him for the rest of his life and it could jolly well let him alone *this* day. With some difficulty he climbed on to the driver's seat, took the reins, said 'Gee up' to the melancholy mule, and the whole equipage with a jolt and faint rattle set out along the road. William did not know how to drive, but it did not seem to matter. The mule ambled along and William, high up on the driver's seat, the reins held with ostentatious carelessness in one hand, the whip poised lightly in the other, was in the seventh heaven of bliss. He was driving a caravan. He was driving a caravan. He was driving a caravan. The very telegraph posts seemed to gape with envy and admiration as he passed. What ultimately he was going to do with his caravan he neither knew nor cared. All that mattered was, it was a bright sunny morning, and all the others were in school, and he was driving a red and yellow caravan along the high road. The birds seemed to be singing a paeon of praise to him. He was intoxicated with pride. It was *his* caravan, *his* road, *his* world. Carelessly he flicked the mule with the whip. There are several explanations of what happened then. The mule may not have been used to the whip; a wasp may have just stung him at that particular minute; a wandering demon may have entered into him. Mules are notoriously accessible to wandering demons. Whatever the explanation, the mule suddenly started forward and galloped at full speed down the hill. The reins dropped from William's hands; he clung for dear life on to his seat, as the caravan, swaying and jolting along the uneven road, seemed to be doing its utmost to fling him off. There came a rattle of crockery from within. Then suddenly there came another sound from within – a loud, agonised scream. It was a female scream. Someone who had been asleep behind the curtain had just awakened.

William's hair stood on end. He almost forgot to cling to the seat. For not one scream came but many. They rent the still summer air, mingled with the sound of breaking glass and crockery. The mule continued his mad career down the hill, his reins trailing in the dust. In the distance was a little gipsy's donkey cart full of pots and pans. William found his voice suddenly and began to warn the mule.

'Look out, you ole softie,' he yelled. 'Look out for the donk, you ole ass.'

But the mule refused to be warned. He neatly escaped the donkey cart himself, but he crashed the caravan into it with such force that the caravan broke a shaft and overturned completely on to the donkey cart, scattering pots and pans far and wide. From within the caravan came inhuman female yells of fear and anger. William had fallen on to a soft bank of grass. He was discovering, to his amazement, that he was still alive and practically unhurt. The mule was standing meekly by and smiling to himself. Then out of the window of the caravan climbed a woman – a fat, angry woman, shaking her fist at the world in general. Her hair and face were covered with sugar and a fork was embedded in the front of her dress. Otherwise she, too, had escaped undamaged.

The owner of the donkey cart arose from the melee of pots and pans and turned upon her fiercely. She screamed at him furiously in reply. Then along the road could be seen the figure of a fat man carrying a fishing rod. He began to run wildly towards the caravan.

'*Ach! Gott im Himmel!*' he cried as he ran. 'My beautiful caravan! Who has this to it done?'

He joined the frenzied altercation that was going on between the donkey man and the fat woman. The air was rent by their angry shouts. A group of highly appreciative villagers collected round them. Then one of them pointed to William, who sat, feeling still slightly shaken, upon the bank.

'It was 'im wot done it,' he said, 'it was 'im that was a-drivin' of it down the 'ill.'

With one wild glance at the scene of devastation and anger, William turned and fled through the wood.

'*Ach! Gott im Himmel!*' screamed the fat man, beginning to pursue him. The fat woman and the donkey man joined the pursuit. To William it was like some ghastly nightmare after an evening's entertainment at the cinema.

Meanwhile the donkey and the mule fraternised over the

debris and the villagers helped themselves to all they could find. But the fat man was very fat, and the fat woman was very fat, and the donkey man was very old, and William was young and very fleet, so in less than ten minutes they gave up the pursuit and returned panting and quarrelling to the road. William sat on the further outskirts of the wood and panted. He felt on the whole exhilarated by the adventure. It was quite a suitable adventure for his last day of unregeneration. But he felt also in need of

WILLIAM'S HAIR STOOD ON END. HE ALMOST FORGOT
TO CLING TO THE SEAT. FOR NOT ONE SCREAM
CAME BUT MANY, MINGLED WITH THE SOUND OF
BREAKING GLASS AND CROCKERY.

bodily sustenance, so he purchased a bun and a bottle of lemonade at a neighbouring shop and sat by the roadside to recover. There were no signs of his pursuers.

He felt reluctant to return home. It is always well to follow a morning's absence from school by an afternoon's absence from school. A return in the afternoon is ignominious and humiliating. William wandered round the neighbourhood experiencing all the thrill of the outlaw. Certainly by this time the gardener would have complained to his father, probably the schoolmistress would have sent a note. Also – someone had been scratched by the cat.

William decided that all things considered it was best to make a day of it.

He spent part of the afternoon in throwing stones at a scarecrow. His aim was fairly good, and he succeeded in knocking off the hat and finally prostrating the wooden framework. There followed an exciting chase by an angry farmer.

It was after teatime when he returned home, walking with careless bravado as of a criminal who has drunk of crime to its very depth and flaunts it before the world. His spirits sank a little as he approached the gate. He could see through the trees the fat caravan-owner gesticulating at the door. Helped by the villagers, he had tracked William.

Phrases floated to him through the summer air.

'Mine beautiful caravan . . . *Ach* . . . *Gott im Himmel!*'

He could see the gardener smiling in the distance. There was a small blue bruise on his shining head. William judged from the smile that he had laid his formal complaint before authority. William noticed that his father looked pale and harassed. He noticed, also, with a thrill of horror, that his hand was bound up, and that

WILLIAM'S SPIRITS SANK A LITTLE AS HE APPROACHED THE GATE. HE COULD SEE THROUGH THE TREES THE FAT CARAVAN-OWNER GESTICULATING AT THE DOOR.

there was a long scratch down his cheek. He knew the cat had scratched *somebody*, but . . . Crumbs!

A small boy came down the road and saw William hesitating at the open gateway.

'*You'll* catch it!' he said cheerfully. 'They've wrote to say you wasn't in school.'

William crept round to the back of the house beneath the bushes. He felt that the time had come to give himself up to justice, but he wanted, as the popular saying is, to be sure of 'getting his money's worth'. There was the tin half full of green paint in the tool shed. He'd had his eye on it for some time. He went quietly round to the tool shed. Soon he was contemplating with a satisfied smile a green and enraged cat and a green and enraged hen. Then, bracing himself for the effort, he delivered himself up to justice. When all was said and done no punishment could be really adequate to a day like that.

Dusk was falling. William gazed pensively from his bedroom window. He was reviewing his day. He had almost forgotten the stormy and decidedly unpleasant scene with his father. Mr Brown's rhetoric had been rather lost on William, because its pearls of sarcasm had been so far above his head. And William had not been really loath to retire at once to bed. After all, it had been a very tiring day.

Now his thoughts were going over some of its most exquisite moments – the moments when the pea and the gardener's head met and rebounded with such satisfactory force; the moment when he swung along the high road, monarch of a caravan and a mule and the whole wide world; the moment when the scarecrow hunched up and collapsed so realistically; the cat covered with green paint . . . After all it was his last day. He saw himself from tomorrow onward leading a quiet and blameless life, walking sedately to school, working at high pressure in school, doing his homework conscientiously in the evening, being exquisitely polite to his family and instructors – and the vision failed utterly to attract. Moreover, he hadn't yet tried turning off the water at the main, or locking the cook into the larder, or – or hundreds of things.

There came a gentle voice from the garden.

'William, where are you?'

William looked down and met the earnest gaze of Deborah.

'Hello,' he said.

'William,' she said. 'You won't forget that you're going to start tomorrow, will you?'

William looked at her firmly.

'I can't jus' tomorrow,' he said. 'I'm puttin' it off. I'm puttin' it off for a year or two.'

CHAPTER 13

WILLIAM AND THE ANCIENT SOULS

The house next to William's had been unoccupied for several months, and William made full use of its garden. Its garden was in turns a jungle, a desert, an ocean, and an enchanted island. William invited select parties of his friends to it. He had come to look upon it as his own property. He hunted wild animals in it with Jumble, his trusty hound; he tracked Red Indians in it, again with Jumble, his trusty hound; and he attacked and sank ships in it, making his victims walk the plank, again with the help and assistance of Jumble, his trusty hound. Sometimes, to vary the monotony, he made Jumble, his trusty hound, walk the plank into the rain tub. This was one of the many unpleasant things that William brought into Jumble's life. It was only his intense love for William that reconciled him to his existence. Jumble was one of the very few beings who appreciated William.

The house on the other side was a much smaller one, and was occupied by Mr Gregorius Lambkin. Mr Gregorius Lambkin was a very shy and rather elderly bachelor. He issued from his front door every morning at half past eight holding a neat little attaché case in a neatly gloved hand. He spent the day in an insurance office and returned, still unruffled and immaculate, at about half past six. Most people considered him quite dull and negligible, but he possessed the supreme virtue in William's eyes of not objecting to William. William had suffered much from unsympathetic neighbours who had taken upon themselves to object to such innocent and artistic objects as catapults and pea-shooters, and cricket balls. William had a very soft spot in his heart for Mr Gregorius Lambkin. William spent a good deal of his time in Mr Lambkin's garden during his absence, and Mr Lambkin seemed to have no objection. Other people's gardens always seemed to William to be more attractive than his own – especially when he had no right of entry into them.

There was quite an excitement in the neighbourhood when the empty house was let. It was rumoured that the newcomer was a Personage. She was the President of the Society of Ancient Souls. The Society of Ancient Souls was a society of people who remembered their previous existence. The memory usually came in a flash. For instance, you might remember in a flash when you were looking at a box of matches that you had been Guy Fawkes. Or you might look at a cow and remember in a flash that you had been Nebuchadnezzar. Then you joined the Society of Ancient Souls, and paid a large subscription, and attended meetings at the house of its President in costume. And the President was coming to live next door to William. By a curious coincidence her name was Gregoria – Miss Gregoria Mush. William awaited her coming with anxiety. He had discovered that one's next-door neighbours make a great difference to one's life. They may be agreeable and not object to mouth organs and whistling and occasional stone-throwing, or they may not. They sometimes – the worst kind – go to the length of writing notes to one's father about one, and then, of course, the only course left to one is one of Revenge. But William hoped great things from Miss Gregoria Mush. There was a friendly sound about the name. On the evening of her arrival he climbed up on the roller and gazed wistfully over the fence at the territory that had once been his, but from which he was now debarred. He felt like Moses surveying the Promised Land.

Miss Gregoria Mush was walking in the garden. William watched her with bated breath. She was very long, and very thin, and very angular, and she was reading poetry out loud to herself as she trailed about in her long draperies.

'"Oh, moon of my delight . . ."' she declaimed, then

her eyes met William's. The eyes beneath her pince-nez were like little gimlets.

'How dare you stare at me, you rude boy?' she said.

William gasped.

'I shall write to your father,' she said fiercely, and then proceeded still ferociously, '". . . that knows no wane".'

'Crumbs!' murmured William, descending slowly from his perch.

She did write to his father, and that note was the first of many. She objected to his singing, she objected to his shouting, she objected to his watching her over the wall, and she objected to his throwing sticks at her cat. She objected both verbally and in writing. This persecution was only partly compensated for by occasional glimpses of meetings of the Ancient Souls. For the Ancient Souls met in costume, and sometimes William could squeeze through the hole in the fence and watch the Ancient Souls meeting in the dining-room. Miss Gregoria Mush arrayed as Mary, Queen of Scots (one of her many previous existences) was worth watching. And always there was the garden on the other side. Mr Gregorius Lambkin made no objections and wrote no notes. But clouds of Fate were gathering round Mr Gregorius Lambkin. William first heard of it one day at lunch.

'I saw the old luny talking to poor little Lambkin today,' said Robert, William's elder brother.

'HOW DARE YOU STARE AT ME, YOU RUDE BOY?' SHE SAID.

In these terms did Robert refer to the august President of the Society of Ancient Souls.

And the next news Robert brought home was that 'poor little Lambkin' had joined the Society of Ancient Souls, but didn't seem to want to talk about it. He seemed very vague as to his previous existence, but he said that Miss Gregoria Mush was sure that he had been Julius Caesar. The knowledge had come to her in a flash when he raised his hat and she saw his bald head.

There was a meeting of the Ancient Souls that evening, and William crept through the hole and up to the dining-room window to watch. A gorgeous scene met his eye. Noah conversed agreeably with Cleopatra in the window seat, and by the piano Napoleon discussed the Irish question with Lobengula. As William watched, his small nose flattened against a corner of the window, Nero and Dante arrived, having shared a taxi from the station. Miss Gregoria Mush, tall and gaunt and angular, presided in the robes of Mary, Queen of Scots, which was her favourite previous existence. Then Mr Gregorius Lambkin arrived. He looked as unhappy as it is possible for man to look. He was dressed in a toga and a laurel wreath. Heat and nervousness had caused his small waxed moustache to droop. His toga was too long and his laurel wreath was crooked. Miss Gregoria Mush received him effusively.

She carried him off to a corner seat near the window, and there they conversed, or, to be more accurate, she talked and he listened. The window was open and William could hear some of the things she said.

'Now you are a member you must come here often . . . you and I, the only Ancient Souls in this vicinity . . . we will work together and live only in the Past. . . . Have you remembered any other previous existence? . . . No? Ah, try, it will come in a flash any time . . . I must come and see your garden . . . I feel that we have much in common, you and I . . . We have much to talk about . . . I have all my past life to tell you of . . . What train do you come home by? . . . We must be friends – real friends . . . I'm sure I can help you much in your life as an Ancient Soul . . . Our names are almost the same . . . Fate in some way unites us . . .'

And Mr Lambkin sat, miserable and dejected and yet with a certain pathetic resignation. For what can one do against Fate? Then the President caught sight of William and approached the window.

'Go away, boy!' she called. 'You wicked, rude, prying boy, go away!'

Mr Lambkin shot a wretched and apologetic glance at William, but William pressed his mouth to the open slit of the window.

'All right, Mrs Jarley!' he called, then turned and fled.

William met Mr Lambkin on his way to the station the next morning. Mr Lambkin looked thinner and there were lines of worry on his face.

'I'm sorry she sent you away, William,' he said. 'It must have been interesting to watch – most interesting to watch. I'd much rather have watched than – but there, it's very kind of her to take such an interest in me. *Most* kind. But I – however, she's very kind, *very* kind. She very kindly presented me with the costume. Hardly suitable, perhaps, but *very* kind of her. And, of course, there *may* be something in it. One never knows. I *may* have been Julius Caesar, but I hardly think – however, one must keep an open mind. Do you know any Latin, William?'

'Jus' a bit,' said William, guardedly. 'I've *learnt* a lot, but I don't *know* much.'

'Say some to me. It might convey something to me. One never knows. She seems so sure. Talk Latin to me, William.'

'Hic, haec, hoc,' said William obligingly.

Julius Caesar's reincarnation shook his head.

'No,' he said, 'I'm afraid it doesn't seem to mean anything to me.'

'Hunc, hanc, hoc,' went on William monotonously.

'I'm afraid it's no good,' said Mr Lambkin. 'I'm afraid it

proves that I'm not – still one may not retain a knowledge of one's former tongue. One must keep an open mind. Of course, I'd prefer not to – but one must be fair. And she's kind, very kind.'

MR LAMBKIN SAT, MISERABLE AND DEJECTED, AND YET WITH A CERTAIN PATHETIC RESIGNATION.

Shaking his head sadly, the little man entered the station.

That evening William heard his father say to his mother:

'She came down to meet him at the station tonight. I'm afraid his doom is sealed. He's no power of resistance, and she's got her eye on him.'

'Who's got her eye on him?' said William with interest.

'Be quiet!' said his father with the brusqueness of the male parent.

But William began to see how things stood. And William liked Mr Lambkin.

One evening he saw from his window Mr Gregorius Lambkin walking with Miss Gregoria Mush in Miss Gregoria Mush's garden. Mr Gregorius Lambkin did not look happy.

William crept down to the hole in the fence and applied his ear to it.

They were sitting on a seat quite close to his hole.

'Gregorius,' the President of the Society of Ancient Souls was saying, 'when I found that our names were the same I knew that our destinies were interwoven.'

'Yes,' murmured Mr Lambkin. 'It's so kind of you, so kind. But – I'm afraid I'm overstaying my welcome. I must—'

'No. I must say what is in my heart, Gregorius. You live in the Past, I live in the Past. We have a common mission – the mission of bring to the thoughtless and uninitiated the memory of their former lives. Gregorius, our work would be more valuable if we could do it together, if the common destiny that has united our nomenclatures could unite also our lives.'

'It's so *kind* of you,' murmured the writhing victim, 'so kind. I am so unfit, I—'

'No, friend,' she said kindly. 'I have power enough for both. The human speech is so poor an agent, is it not?'

A doorbell clanged in the house.

'Ah, the Committee of the Ancient Souls. They were coming from town tonight. Come here tomorrow night at the same time, Gregorius, and I will tell you what is in my heart. Meet me here – at this time – tomorrow evening.'

William here caught sight of a stray cat at the other end of the garden. In the character of a cannibal chief he hunted the white man (otherwise the cat) with bloodcurdling war-whoops, but felt no real interest in the chase. He bound up his scratches mechanically with an ink-stained handkerchief. Then he went indoors. Robert was conversing with his friend in the library.

'Well,' said the friend, 'it's nearly next month. Has she landed him yet?'

'By Jove!' said Robert. 'First of April tomorrow!' He looked at William suspiciously. 'And if you try any fool's tricks on me you'll jolly well hear about it.'

'I'm not thinkin' of you,' said William crushingly. 'I'm not goin' to trouble with you!'

'Has she landed him?' said the friend.

'Not yet, and I heard him saying on the train that he was leaving town on the second and going abroad for a holiday.'

'Well, she'll probably do it yet. She's got all the first.'

'It's bedtime, William,' called his mother.

'Thank heaven!' said Robert.

William sat gazing into the distance, not seeing or hearing.

'*William!*' called his mother.

'All right,' said William irritably. 'I'm jus' thinkin' something out.'

William's family went about their ways cautiously the next morning. They watched William carefully. Robert even refused an egg at breakfast because you never knew with that little wretch. But nothing happened.

'Fancy your going on April Fool's day without making a fool of anyone,' said Robert at lunch.

'It's not over, is it? Not yet,' said William with the air of a sphinx.

'But it doesn't count after twelve,' said Robert.

William considered deeply before he spoke, then he said slowly:

'The thing what I'm going to do counts whatever time it is.'

Reluctantly, but as if drawn by a magnet, Mr Lambkin set off to the President's house. William was in the road.

'She told me to tell you,' said William unblushingly 'that she was busy tonight, an' would you mind not coming.'

The tense lines of Mr Lambkin's face relaxed.

'Oh, William,' he said, 'it's a great relief. I'm going away early tomorrow, but I was afraid that tonight—' he was almost hysterical with relief. 'She's so kind, but I was afraid that – well, well, I can't say I'm sorry – I'd promised to come, and I couldn't break it. But I was afraid – and I hear she's sold her house and is leaving in a month, so – but she's kind – *very* kind.'

He turned back with alacrity.

'Thanks for letting me have the clothes,' said William.

'Oh, you're quite welcome, William. They're nice things for a boy to dress up in, no doubt. I can't say I –

but she's *very* kind. Don't let her see you playing with them, William.'

William grunted and returned to his back garden.

For some time silence reigned over the three back gardens. Then Miss Gregoria Mush emerged and came towards the seat by the fence. A figure was already seated there in the half dusk; a figure swathed in a toga with the toga drawn also over its drooping head.

'Gregorius!' said the President. 'How dear of you to come in costume!'

The figure made no movement.

'You know what I have in my heart, Gregorius?'

Still no answer.

'Your heart is too full for words,' she said kindly. 'The thought of having your destiny linked with mine takes speech from you. But have courage, dear Gregorius. You shall work for me. We will do great things together. We will be married at the little church.'

Still no answer.

'Gregorius!' she murmured tenderly.

She leant against him suddenly, and he yielded beneath the pressure with a sudden sound of dissolution. Two cushions slid to the ground, the toga fell back, revealing a broomstick with a turnip fixed firmly to the top. It bore the legend:

APRIL FOOL

And from the other side of the fence came a deep sigh of satisfaction from the artist behind the scenes.

'GREGORIUS!' SAID THE PRESIDENT. 'HOW DEAR OF YOU TO COME IN COSTUME!' THE FIGURE MADE NO MOVEMENT.

CHAPTER 14

WILLIAM'S CHRISTMAS EVE

It was Christmas. The air was full of excitement and se-crecy. William, whose old-time faith in notes to Father Christmas sent up the chimney had died a natural death as the result of bitter experience, had thoughtfully presented each of his friends and relations with a list of his immediate requirements.

He had a vague and not unfounded misgiving that his family would begin at the bottom of the list instead of the top. He was not surprised, therefore, when he saw his father come home rather later than usual carrying a parcel of books under his arm. A few days afterwards he announced casually at breakfast.

'Well, I only hope no one gives me *The Great Chief*, or *The Pirate Ship*, or *The Land of Danger* for Christmas.'

His father started.

'Why?' he said sharply.

'Jus' 'cause I've read them, that's all,' explained William with a bland look of innocence.

The glance that Mr Brown threw at his offspring was

not altogether devoid of suspicion, but he said nothing. He set off after breakfast with the same parcel of books under his arm and returned with another. This time, however, he did not put them in the library cupboard, and William searched in vain.

Things I want for
Crismus

1. A Bicycle.
2. A grammerfone.
3. A pony.
4. A snake.
5. A monkey
6. A Bugal.
7. A trumpit
8. A red Injun Uniform
9. A ~~sl~~ lot of sweets
10. A lot of books.

The question of Christmas festivities loomed large upon the social horizon.

'Robert and Ethel can have their party on the day before Christmas Eve,' decided Mrs Brown, 'and then William can have his on Christmas Eve.'

William surveyed his elder brother and sister gloomily.

'Yes, an' us eat up jus' what they've left,' he said with bitterness. '*I* know!'

Mrs Brown changed the subject hastily.

'Now let's see whom we'll have for your party, William,' she said, taking out pencil and paper. 'You say whom you'd like and I'll make you a list.'

'Ginger an' Douglas an' Henry and Joan,' said William promptly.

'Yes? Who else?'

'I'd like the milkman.'

'You can't have the milkman, William. Don't be so foolish.'

'Well, I'd like to have Fisty Green. He can whistle with his fingers in his mouth.'

'He's a butcher's boy, William! You *can't* have him.'

'Well, who *can* I have?'

'Johnnie Brent?'

'I don't like him.'

'But you must invite him. He asked you to his.'

'Well, I didn't want to go,' he said irritably, 'you made me.'

'But if he asks you to his you must ask him back.'

'You don't want me to invite folks I don't *want*?' William said in the voice of one goaded against his will into exasperation.

'You must invite people who invite you,' said Mrs Brown firmly; 'that's what we always do at parties.'

'Then they've got to invite you again and it goes on and on and on,' argued William. 'Where's the *sense* of it? I don't like Johnnie Brent an' he don't like me an' if we go on inviting each other an' our mothers go on making us go, it'll go on and on and *on*. Where's the *sense* of it? I only jus' want to know where's the *sense* of it?'

His logic was unanswerable.

'Well, anyway, William, I'll draw up the list. You can go and play.'

William walked away, frowning, with his hands in his pockets.

'Where's the *sense* of it?' he muttered as he went.

He began to wend his way towards the spot where he, and Douglas, and Ginger, and Henry met daily in order to while away the hours of the Christmas holidays. At present they lived and moved and had their being in the characters of Indian Chiefs.

As William walked down the back street, which led by a short cut to their meeting place, he unconsciously assumed an arrogant strut, suggestive of some warrior prince surrounded by his gallant braves.

'Garn! *Swank!*'

He turned with a dark scowl.

On the doorstep sat a little girl, gazing up at him with blue eyes beneath a tousled mop of auburn hair.

William's eyes travelled sternly from her Titian curls to her bare feet. He assumed a threatening attitude and scowled fiercely.

'You better not say *that* again,' he said darkly.

'Why not?' she said with a jeering laugh.

'Well, you'd just better *not*,' he said with a still more ferocious scowl.

'What'd you do?' she persisted.

He considered for a moment in silence. Then: 'You'd see what I'd do!' he said ominously.

'Garn! *Swank!*' she repeated. 'Now do it! Go on, do it!'

'I'll – let you off *this* time,' he said judicially.

'Garn! *Softie*. You can't do anything, you can't! You're a softie!'

'I could cut your head off an' scalp you an' leave you hanging on a tree, I could,' he said fiercely, 'an' I will, too, if you go on calling me names.'

'*Softie! Swank!* Now cut it off! Go on!'

He looked down at her mocking blue eyes.

'You're jolly lucky I don't start on you,' he said threateningly. 'Folks I do start on soon get sorry, I can tell you.'

'What do you do to them?'

He changed the subject abruptly.

'What's your name?' he said.

'Sheila. What's yours?'

'Red Hand – I mean, William.'

'I'll tell you sumpthin' if you'll come an' sit down by me.'

'What'll you tell me?'

'Sumpthin' I bet you don't know.'

'I bet I *do*.'

'Well, come here an' I'll tell you.'

He advanced towards her suspiciously. Through the open door he could see a bed in a corner of the dark, dirty room and a woman's white face upon the pillow.

'Oh, come *on*!' said the little girl impatiently.

He came and sat down beside her.

'Well?' he said condescendingly. 'I bet I knew all the time.'

'No, you didn't! D'you know,' she sank her voice in a confidential whisper, 'there's a chap called Father

Christmas wot comes down chimneys Christmas Eve and leaves presents in people's houses?'

He gave a scornful laugh.

'Oh, that *rot*! You don't believe *that* rot, do you?'

'Rot?' she repeated indignantly. 'Why it's *true* – *true* as *true*! A boy told me wot had hanged his stocking up by the chimney an' in the morning it was full of things an' they was jus' the things wot he'd wrote on a bit of paper an' thrown up the chimney to this 'ere Christmas chap.'

'Only *kids* believe that rot,' persisted William. 'I left off believin' it years and *years* ago!'

Her face grew pink with the effort of convincing him.

'But the boy *told* me, the boy wot got things from this 'ere chap wot comes down chimneys. An' I've wrote wot I want an' sent it up the chimney. Don't you think I'll get it?'

William looked down at her. Her blue eyes, big with apprehension, were fixed on him, her little rosy lips were parted. William's heart softened.

'I dunno,' he said doubtfully. 'You might, I s'pose. What d'you want for Christmas?'

'You won't tell if I tell you?'

'No.'

'Not to no one?'

'No.'

'Say, "Cross me throat".'

239

'GARN! *SWANK!*' WILLIAM TURNED
WITH A DARK SCOWL.

William complied with much interest and stored up the phrase for future use.

'Well,' she sank her voice very low and spoke into his ear.

'Dad's comin' out Christmas Eve!'

She leant back and watched him, anxious to see the effect of this stupendous piece of news. Her face expressed pride and delight. William's merely bewilderment.

'Comin' out?' he repeated. 'Comin' out of where?'

Her expression changed to one of scorn.

'*Prison*, of course! *Silly!*'

William was half offended, half thrilled.

'Well, I couldn't *know* it was prison, could I? How could I *know* it was prison without bein' told? It might of been out of anything. What' – in hushed curiosity and awe – 'what was he in prison for?'

'Stealin'.'

Her pride was unmistakable. William looked at her in disapproval.

'Stealin's wicked,' he said virtuously.

'Huh,' she jeered, 'you *can't* steal! You're too soft! *Softie!* You *can't* steal without bein' copped fust go, you can't.'

'I *could*!' he said indignantly. 'And, anyway, he got copped, di'n't he? Or he'd not of been in prison, *so there!*'

'He di'n't get copped fust go. It was jus' a sorter mistake, he said. He said it wun't happen again. He's a jolly good stealer. The cops said he was and *they* oughter know.'

'Well,' said William changing the conversation, 'what d'you want for Christmas?'

'I wrote it on a bit of paper an' sent it up the chimney,' she said confidingly. 'I said I di'n't want no toys nor sweeties nor nuffin'. I said I only wanted a nice supper for Dad when he comes out Christmas Eve. We ain't got much money, me an' Mother, an' we carn't get 'im much of a spread, but – if this 'ere Christmas chap sends one fer 'im, it'll be – *fine*!'

Her eyes were dreamy with ecstasy. William stirred uneasily on his seat.

'I tol' you it was *rot*,' he said. 'There isn't any Father Christmas. It's jus' an' ole tale folks tell you when you're a kid, an' you find out it's not true. He won't send no supper jus' 'cause he isn't anythin'. He's jus' nothin' – jus' an ole tale—'

'Oh, shut *up*!' William turned sharply at the sound of the shrill voice from the bed within the room. 'Let the kid 'ave a bit of pleasure lookin' forward to it, can't yer? It's little enough she 'as, anyway.'

William arose with dignity.

'All right,' he said. 'Go'bye.'

He strolled away down the street.

'*Softie!*'

It was a malicious sweet little voice.

'*Swank!*'

William flushed but forbore to turn round.

That evening he met the little girl from next door in the road outside her house.

'Hello, Joan!'

'Hello, William!'

In these blue eyes there was no malice or mockery. To Joan William was a godlike hero. His very wickedness partook of the divine.

'Would you – would you like to come an' make a snowman in our garden, William?' she said tentatively.

William knit his brows.

'I dunno,' he said ungraciously. 'I was jus' kinder thinkin'.'

She looked at him silently, hoping that he would deign to tell her his thoughts, but not daring to ask. Joan held no modern views on the subject of the equality of the sexes.

'Do you remember that ole tale 'bout Father Christmas, Joan?' he said at last.

She nodded.

'Well, s'pose you wanted somethin' very bad, an' you believed that ole tale and sent a bit of paper up the chimney 'bout what you wanted very bad and then you never got it, you'd feel kind of rotten, wouldn't you?'

She nodded again.

'I did one time,' she said. 'I sent a lovely list up the chimney and I never told anyone about it and I got lots of things for Christmas and not *one* of the things I'd written for!'

'Did you feel awful rotten?'

'Yes, I did. Awful.'

'I say, Joan,' he said importantly, 'I've gotter secret.'

'*Do* tell me, William!' she pleaded.

'Can't. It's a crorse-me-throat secret!'

She was mystified and impressed.

'How *lovely*, William! Is it something you're going to do?'

He considered.

'It might be,' he said.

'I'd love to help.' She fixed adoring blue eyes upon him.

'Well, I'll see,' said the lord of creation. 'I say, Joan, you comin' to my party?'

'Oh, *yes*!'

'Well, there's an awful lot comin'. Johnnie Brent an' all

that lot. I'm jolly well not lookin' forward to it, I can *tell* you.'

'Oh, I'm so sorry! Why did you ask them, William?'

William laughed bitterly.

'Why did I invite them?' he said. '*I* don't invite people to my parties. *They* do that.'

In William's vocabulary 'they' always signified his immediate family circle.

William had a strong imagination. When an idea took hold upon his mind, it was almost impossible for him to let it go. He was quite accustomed to Joan's adoring homage. The scornful mockery of his auburn-haired friend was something quite new, and in some strange fashion it intrigued and fascinated him. Mentally he recalled her excited little face, flushed with eagerness as she described the expected spread. Mentally also he conceived a vivid picture of the long waiting on Christmas Eve, the slowly fading hope, the final bitter disappointment. While engaging in furious snowball fights with Ginger, Douglas, and Henry, while annoying peaceful passers-by with well-aimed snow missiles, while bruising himself and most of his family black and blue on long and glassy slides along the garden paths, while purloining his family's clothes to adorn various unshapely snowmen, while walking across all the ice (preferably cracked) in the neighbourhood and being several times narrowly rescued from a watery grave – while following all these light holiday pursuits, the picture of the little auburn-haired girl's disappointment was ever vividly present in his mind.

The day of his party drew near.

'*My* party,' he would echo bitterly when anyone of his family mentioned. 'I don't *want* it. I don't *want* ole Johnnie Brent an' all that lot. I'd just like to uninvite 'em all.'

'But you want Ginger and Douglas and Henry,' coaxed his mother.

'I can have them any time an' I don't like 'em at parties. They're not the same. I don't like *anyone* at parties. I don't *want* a party!'

'But you *must* have a party, William, to ask back people who ask you.'

William took up his previous attitude.

'Well, where's the *sense* of it?' he groaned.

As usual he had the last word, but left his audience unconvinced. They began on him a full hour before his guests were due. He was brushed and scrubbed and scoured and cleaned. He was compressed into an Eton suit and patent leather pumps and finally deposited in the drawing-room, cowed and despondent, his noble spirit all but broken.

The guests began to arrive. William shook hands

politely with three strangers shining with soap, brushed to excess, and clothed in ceremonial Eton suits – who in ordinary life were Ginger, Douglas, and Henry. They then sat down and gazed at each other in strained and unnatural silence. They could find nothing to say to each other. Ordinary topics seemed to be precluded by their festive appearance and the formal nature of the occasion. Their informal meetings were usually celebrated by impromptu wrestling matches. This being debarred, a stiff, unnatural atmosphere descended upon them. William was a 'host', they were 'guests'; they had all listened to final maternal admonitions in which the word 'manners' and 'politeness' recurred at frequent intervals. They were, in fact, for the time being, complete strangers.

Then Joan arrived and broke the constrained silence.

'Hullo, William! Oh, William, you do look *nice*!'

William smiled with distant politeness, but his heart warmed to her. It is always some comfort to learn that one has not suffered in vain.

'How d'you do?' he said with a stiff bow.

Then Johnnie Brent came and after him a host of small boys and girls.

William greeted friends and foes alike with the same icy courtesy.

Then the conjurer arrived.

Mrs Brown had planned the arrangement most carefully. The supper was laid on the big dining-room table. There was to be conjuring for an hour before supper to 'break the ice'. In the meantime, while the conjuring was going on, the grown-ups who were officiating at the party were to have their meal in peace in the library.

William had met the conjurer at various parties and despised him utterly. He despised his futile jokes and high-pitched laugh and he knew his tricks by heart. They sat in rows in front of him – shining-faced, well-brushed little boys in dark Eton suits and gleaming collars, and dainty white-dressed little girls with gay hair ribbons. William sat in the back row near the window, and next to him sat Joan. She gazed at his set, expressionless face in mute sympathy. He listened to the monotonous voice of the conjurer.

'Now, ladies and gentlemen, I will proceed to swallow these three needles and these three strands of cotton and shortly to bring out each needle threaded with a strand of cotton. Will any lady step forward and examine the needles? Ladies ought to know all about needles, oughtn't they? You young gentlemen don't learn to sew at school, do you? Ha! Ha! Perhaps some of you young gentlemen don't know what a needle is! Ha! Ha!'

William scowled, and his thoughts flew off to the

little house in the dirty back street. It was Christmas Eve. Her father was 'comin' out'. She would be waiting, watching with bright, expectant eyes for the 'spread' she had demanded from Father Christmas to welcome her returning parent. It was a beastly shame. She was a silly little ass, anyway, not to believe him. He'd told her there wasn't any Father Christmas.

'Now, ladies and gentlemen, I will bring out the three needles threaded with the three strands of cotton. Watch carefully, ladies and gentlemen. There! One! Two! Three! Now, I don't advise you young ladies and gentlemen to try this trick. Needles are very indigestible to some people. Ha! Ha! Not to me, of course! I can digest anything – needles, or marbles, or matches, or glass bowls – as you will soon see. Ha! Ha! Now to proceed, ladies and gentlemen.'

William looked at the clock and sighed. Anyway, there'd be supper soon, and that was a jolly good one, 'cause he'd had a look at it.

Suddenly the inscrutable look left his countenance. He gave a sudden gasp and his whole face lit up. Joan turned to him.

'Come on!' he whispered, rising stealthily from his seat.

The room was in half darkness and the conjurer was

just producing a white rabbit from his left toe, so that few noticed William's quiet exit by the window followed by that of the blindly obedient Joan.

'You wait!' he whispered in the darkness of the garden. She waited, shivering in her little white muslin dress, till he

FEW NOTICED WILLIAM'S QUIET EXIT BY THE WINDOW,
FOLLOWED BY BLINDLY OBEDIENT JOAN.

returned from the stable wheeling a handcart, consisting of a large packing case on wheels and finished with a handle. He wheeled it round to the open French window that led into the dining-room. 'Come on!' he whispered again.

Following his example, she began to carry the plates of sandwiches, sausage rolls, meat pies, bread and butter, cakes and biscuits of every variety from the table to the handcart. On the top they balanced carefully the plates of jelly and blancmange and dishes of trifle, and round the sides they packed armfuls of crackers.

At the end she whispered softly, 'What's it for, William?'

'It's the secret,' he said. 'The crorse-me-throat secret I told you.'

'Am I going to help?' she said in delight.

He nodded.

'Jus' wait a minute,' he added, and crept from the dining-room to the hall and upstairs.

He returned with a bundle of clothing which he proceeded to arrange in the garden. He first donned his own red dressing gown and then wound a white scarf round his head, tying it under his chin so that the ends hung down.

'I'm makin' believe I'm Father Christmas,' he deigned to explain. 'An' I'm makin' believe this white stuff is hair an' beard. An' this is for you to wear so's you won't get cold.'

He held out a little white satin cloak edged with swansdown.

'Oh, how *lovely*, William! But it's not my cloak! It's Sadie Murford's!'

'Never mind! You can wear it,' said William generously. Then, taking the handle of the cart, he set off down the drive. From the drawing-room came the sound of a chorus of delight as the conjurer produced a goldfish in a glass bowl from his head. From the kitchen came the sound of the hilarious laughter of the maids. Only in the dining-room, with its horrible expanse of empty table, was silence.

They walked down the road without speaking till Joan gave a little excited laugh.

'This is *fun*, William! I do wonder what we're going to do.'

'You'll see,' said William. 'I'd better not tell you yet. I promised a crorse-me-throat promise I wouldn't tell anyone.'

'All right, William,' she said sweetly. 'I don't mind a bit.'

The evening was dark and rather foggy, so that the strange couple attracted little attention, except when passing beneath the street lamps. Then certainly people stood still and looked at William and his cart in open-mouthed amazement.

At last they turned down a back street towards a door that stood open to the dark, foggy night. Inside the room was a bare table at which sat a little girl, her blue, anxious eyes fixed on the open door.

'I hope he gets here before Dad,' she said. 'I wouldn't like Dad to come and find it not ready!'

The woman on the bed closed her eyes wearily.

'I don't think he'll come now, dearie. We must just get on without it.'

The little girl sprang up, her pale cheek suddenly flushed.

'Oh, *listen*,' she cried; '*something's* coming!'

They listened in breathless silence, while the sound of wheels came down the street towards the empty door. Then – an old handcart appeared in the doorway and behind it William in his strange attire, and Joan in her fairy-like white – white cloak, white dress, white socks and shoes – her dark curls clustered with gleaming fog jewels.

The little girl clasped her hands. Her face broke into a rapt smile. Her blue eyes were like stars.

'Oh, oh!' she cried. 'It's Father Christmas and a fairy!'

Without a word William pushed the cart through the

doorway into the room and began to remove its contents and place them on the table. First the jellies and trifles and blancmanges, then the meat pies, pastries, sausage rolls, sandwiches, biscuits, and cakes – sugar-coated, cream-interlayered, full of plums and nuts and fruit. William's mother had had wide experience and knew well what

FIRST THE JELLIES AND BLANCMANGES – THEN THE
MEAT PIES AND TRIFLES.

food most appealed to small boys and girls. Moreover, she had provided plentifully for her twenty guests.

The little girl was past speech. The woman looked at them in dumb wonder. Then:

'Why you're the boy she was talkin' to,' she said at last. 'It's real kind of you. She was gettin' that upset. It 'ud have broke her heart if nothin' had come an' I couldn't do nothin'. It's real kind of yer, sir!' Her eyes were misty.

Joan placed the last cake on the table, and William, who was rather warm after his exertions, removed his scarf.

The child gave a little sobbing laugh.

'Oh, isn't it *lovely*? I'm so happy! You're the funny boy, aren't you, dressed up as Father Christmas? Or did Father Christmas send you? Or were you Father Christmas all the time? May I kiss the fairy? Would she mind? She's so beautiful!'

Joan came forward and kissed her shyly, and the woman on the bed smiled unsteadily.

'It's real kind of you both,' she murmured again.

Then the door opened, and the lord and master of the house entered after his six months' absence. He came in no sheepish hangdog fashion. He entered cheerily and boisterously as any parent might on returning from a hard-earned holiday.

''Ello, Missus! 'Ello, Kid! 'Ello! Wot's all this 'ere?' His eyes fell upon William. ''Ello, young gent!'

'Happy Christmas,' William murmured politely.

'Sime to you an' many of them. 'Ow are you, Missus? Kid looked arter you all right? That's *right*. Oh, I *sye*! Where's the grub come from? Fair mikes me mouth water. I 'aven't seen nuffin' like *this* – not fer *some* time!'

There was a torrent of explanations, everyone talking at once. He gave a loud guffaw at the end.

'Well, we're much obliged to this young gent and this little lady, and now we'll 'ave a good ole supper. This is all *right*, this is! Now, Missus, you 'ave a good feed. Now, 'fore we begin, I sye three cheers fer the young gent and little lady. Come on, now, 'Ip, 'ip, 'ip, *'ooray*! Now, little lady, you come 'ere. That's fine, that is! Now 'oo'll 'ave a meat pie? 'Oo's fer a meat pie? Come on, Missus! That's right. We'll *all* 'ave meat pie! This 'ere's sumfin *like* Christmas, eh? We've not 'ad a Christmas like this – not for many a long year. Now, 'urry up, Kid. Don't spend all yer time larfin. Now, ladies an' gents, 'oo's fer a sausage roll? All of us? Come on, then! I mustn't eat too 'eavy or I won't be able to sing to yer arterwards, will I? I've got some fine songs, young gent. And Kid 'ere'll dance fer yer. She's a fine little dancer, she is! Now, come on, ladies an' gents, sandwiches? More pies? Come on!'

They laughed and chattered merrily. The woman sat up in bed, her eyes bright and her cheeks flushed. To William and Joan it was like some strange and wonderful dream.

And at that precise moment Mrs Brown had sunk down upon the nearest dining-room chair on the verge of tears, and twenty pairs of hungry horrified eyes in twenty clean, staring, open-mouthed little faces surveyed the bare expanse of the dining-room table. And the cry that went up all round was:

'*Where's William?*'

And then:

'*Where's Joan?*'

They searched the house and garden and stable for them in vain. They sent the twenty enraged guests home supperless and aggrieved.

'Has William eaten *all* our suppers?' they said.

'Where *is* he? Is he dead?'

'People will never forget,' wailed Mrs Brown. 'It's simply dreadful. And where *is* William?'

They rang up police stations for miles around.

'If they've eaten all that food – the two of them,' said Mrs Brown almost distraught, '– they'll *die*! They may be dying in some hospital now! And I do wish Mrs Murford would stop ringing up about Sadie's cloak. I've told her it's not here!'

Meantime there was dancing, and singing, and games, and cracker-pulling in a small house in a back street not very far away.

'I've never had such a *lovely* time in my life,' gasped the Kid breathlessly at the end of one of the many games into which William had initiated them. 'I've never, never, *never*—'

'We won't ferget you in a 'urry, young man,' her father added, 'nor the little lady neither. We'll 'ave many talks about this 'ere!'

Joan was sitting on the bed, laughing and panting, her curls all disordered.

'I wish,' said William wistfully, 'I wish you'd let me come with you when you go stealin' some day!'

'I'm not goin' stealin' *no* more, young gent,' said his friend solemnly. 'I got a job – a real steady job – bricklaying, an' I'm goin' to stick to it.'

All good things must come to an end, and soon William donned his red dressing gown again and Joan her borrowed cloak, and they helped to store the remnants of the feast in the larder – the remnants of the feast would provide the ex-burglar and his family with food for many days to come. Then they took the empty handcart and, after many fond farewells, set off homeward through the dark.

Mr Brown had come home and assumed charge of operations.

Ethel was weeping on the sofa in the library.

'Oh, dear little William!' she sobbed. 'I do *wish* I'd always been kind to him!'

Mrs Brown was reclining, pale and haggard, in the armchair.

'There's the Roughborough Canal, John!' she was saying weakly. 'And Joan's mother will always say it was our fault. Oh, *poor* little William!'

'It's a good ten miles away,' said her husband drily. 'I don't think even William—' He rang up fiercely. 'Confound these brainless police! Hello! Any news? A boy and girl and supper for twenty can't disappear off the face of the earth. No, there had been *no* trouble at home. There probably *will* be when he turns up, but there was none before! If he wanted to run away, why would he burden himself with a supper for twenty? Why – one minute!'

The front door opened and Mrs Brown ran into the hall.

A well-known voice was heard speaking quickly and irritably.

'I jus' went away, that's all! I jus' thought of something I wanted to do, that's all! Yes, I *did* take the supper. I jus' wanted it for something. It's a secret what I wanted it for, I—'

'*William!*' said Mr Brown.

Through the scenes that followed William preserved a dignified silence, even to the point of refusing any explanation. Such explanation as there was filtered through from Joan's mother by means of the telephone.

'It was all William's idea,' Joan's mother said plaintively. 'Joan would never have done *anything* if William hadn't practically *made* her. I expect she's caught her death of cold. She's in bed now—'

'Yes, so is William. I can't *think* what they wanted to take *all* the food for. And he was just a common man straight from prison. It's dreadful. I do hope they haven't picked up any awful language. Have you given Joan some quinine? Oh, Mrs Murford's just rung up to see if Sadie's cloak has turned up. Will you send it round? I feel so *upset* by it all. If it wasn't Christmas Eve—'

The house occupied by William's and Joan's

'WASN'T SHE A JOLLY LITTLE KID?'
WILLIAM SAID EAGERLY.

families respectively were semi-detached, but William's and Joan's bedroom windows faced each other, and there was only about five yards between them.

There came to William's ears as he lay drowsily in bed the sound of a gentle rattle at the window. He got up and opened it. At the opposite window a little white-robed figure leant out, whose dark curls shone in the starlight.

'William,' she whispered, 'I threw some beads to see if you were awake. Were your folks mad?'

'Awful,' said William laconically.

'Mine were too. I di'n't care, did you?'

'No, I di'n't. Not a bit!'

'William, wasn't it *fun*? I wish it was just beginning again, don't you?'

'Yes, I jus' do. I say, Joan, wasn't she a jolly little kid and di'n't she dance fine?'

'Yes,' – a pause – then, 'William, you don't like her better'n me, do you?'

William considered.

'No, I don't,' he said at last.

'YES,' – A PAUSE – THEN, 'WILLIAM, YOU DON'T LIKE HER BETTER'N ME, DO YOU?'

A soft sigh of relief came through the darkness.

'I'm so *glad*! Go'night, William.'

'Go'night,' said William sleepily, drawing down his window as he spoke.

THE END